MISSING WINGS: CHRONICLES OF THE ARANYSARGAS

Andrea Luhman

By Andrea Luhman

The Aranysargas Series
Missing Wings
Wings Prophecy

ISBN: 978-17322817-1-4
ISBN: 978-1-7322817-5-2
ISBN-13: 978-1-7322817-4-5

Cover design by: Ryan Alexander Lee
Library of Congress Control Number: 2018675309
Printed in the United States of America

To my husband Chris, I love you.

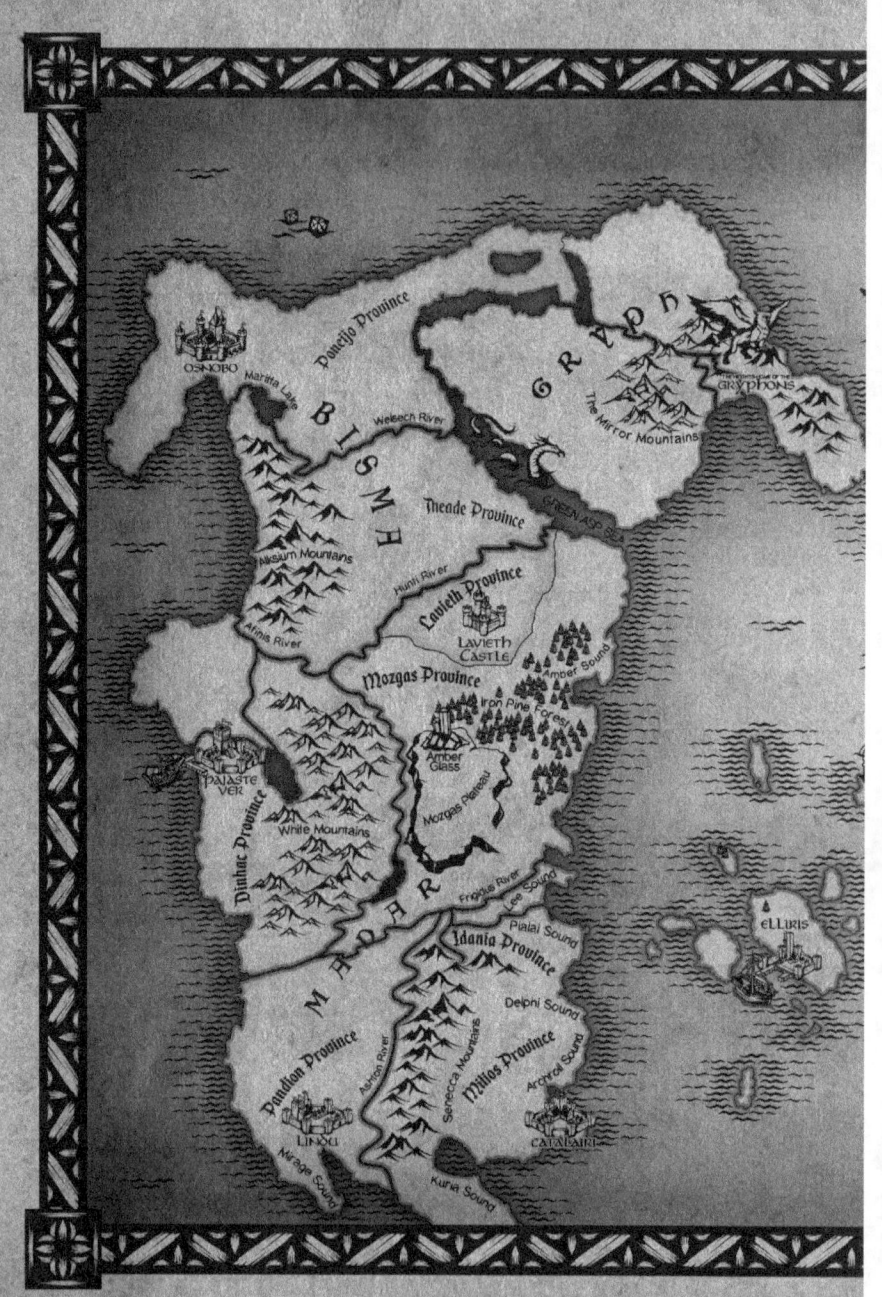

Forms Of Veilede

1) Airetti – Known as "the first" because they were the first to be blessed by God. The rarest form of Veilede. Airetti have visions that the Veilede consider divine in nature. In shifted form they have feathered wings and are able to fly.

2) Mahigan – The warrior class of shifter. In shifted form they have black scaled armor plates, sharp weapon appendages, and wings that look like gnarled skin and bone. They possess preternatural speed. Mahigans can shift into a full or partial warrior form.

3) Alvara – Have the ability to shift another person's mind. Most Alvara become guardians, scholars, or leaders of the faith. They are incapable of telling a lie and can sense when someone is being dishonest.

4) Fayette – People shifters, and the most common Veilede form. Fayette are known to either work very hard at mastering their ability or not use it at all.

5) Regiek – They were the people who begged God to take them, and he almost did. They stepped so close to God time for them became stretched. They can live twice the average lifespan of other Veilede, and possess amazing powers including the ability to harness light and imbed objects with special qualities. They had abilities so unusual they were hunted, captured, and brought to extinction long before the Airetti genocide.

6) Delphi – Known as the "the last" because they were blessed as "the last who can see all," and given the ability to look at any Veilede and know their form. Their shifted form can resemble dolphins or seals.

Madar, home of the Veilede. Madar consists of six provinces: Mozgas, Milios, Idania, Pandion, Dinhac, and the Delphi. Each regency has a Regent and Airetti Guide. The Airetti Guide's visions are used to determine God's will within each province. The provincial regencies work together on the Madar Council and elect a member to head the council and mediate any disputes between the provinces.

The Regency of Mozgas:

Regent Pavaldon Aranysarga of the Mozgas Province
Pavaldon's first wife Lady Tellydia of Mozgas, Fayette
Their children: Prince Valgustatuile Aranysarga, Mahigan, eldest son of Pavaldon
Pavaldon's second wife, Lady Oshana of Mozgas, Fayette
Their children: Prince Solyom Aranysarga, Mahigan, second son of Pavaldon
Pavaldon's third wife, Lady Lena of the Lavieth province in Bisma, human
Their children: Princess Katrina Aranysarga, Airetti, eldest daughter of Pavaldon
Pavaldon's fourth wife, Regina Delany of the Lavieth province in Bisma, Airetti
Their children: Prince Massie Aranysarga, Fayette, third son of Pavaldon; Princess Owl Aranysarga, Airetti, second daughter of Pavaldon
Pavaldon's fifth wife, Lady Juniper of Pandion, Fayette

Their children: Princess Nuala Aranysarga, third daughter of Pavaldon, Fayette; Princess Ilona Aranysarga, fourth daughter of Pavaldon, Alvara Pavaldon's sixth wife, Lady Miandes, from a Skrieni village in Mozgas, Fayette

Their children: Aaron, Lady Miandes son by a dead Skrieni villager, Airetti. At the age of four Aaron was brought to the Mozgas Palace and raised among Pavaldon's children. Prince Dermot Aranysarga, fourth son of Pavaldon, Mahigan

1

The Legacy of Pavaldon

Katrina stared at her mother's empty chair. The vacancy made her heart race. Her mother never missed meals. She might hate every adult at the table, but her mother attended her duties.

The Aranysarga family carried on with breakfast. Searching for her voice, Katrina watched her father, Pavaldon Aranysarga, the Regent of Mozgas.

"My Regent," she said.

Her father, and every other person in the room, turned. Her face grew hot.

Across the table, her brother Sol's eyes widened. She and Sol began taking meals in the adult dining room when they turned ten. A privilege with certain restrictions: any improper behavior or unnecessary talk meant banishment back to the nursery.

"Yes, Katrina," her father said, setting down his glass.

"Where is my mother?"

His golden eyes hardened.

"I was told Lady Lena went to visit Lord and Lady Larksbur in Lavieth," he said. "While I encourage visits to family, it's curious for her to fail in providing the rest of us with more forewarning."

She bowed her head.

Her father retrieved his glass as his first wife, Lady Tellydia, diverted his attention to new conversation.

With her plate full of food, Katrina gripped the napkin in her lap. Wringing the napkin she stared at her mother's chair again. Her fingers became entwined and her thumb swept the snakebite scar beneath her left thumb.

Massie, her younger brother, once found a snake. Small and slight, the creature's odd unblinking stare frightened her. Massie placed it on her arm and in half a breath it slipped down, coiled around her wrist, and sank fangs below her thumb. She screamed before her oldest brother Valgu had grabbed it by the head, ripped it off, and flung it away.

She rubbed the healed bite mark. That stupid snake. Its bite was what her mother's absence felt like: cold, sharp, unexpected.

A hand rested on her shoulder as Valgu kneeled beside her. He looked the most like their father, with straight blonde hair down to his shoulders and bright gold eyes. Her hair was the same shade, but her eyes were tainted. They were blue like her human mother's.

"I'm done eating," he said. "Want to take a walk?"

She glanced at the adults. They were all too involved in their conversation, or pretended not to notice the children. She nodded.

Valgu pulled her seat out. She gripped his hand and together they escaped into the hallway.

"I don't understand," she said as Valgu guided her to a padded bench.

"She's always taken me to see my grandparents. What did I do wrong?"

"Nothing," he said pulling her into a hug. "You did nothing wrong."

"She didn't say goodbye." She shut her eyes tight.

"Your right," Valgu said. "That's very unlike her. I'm sure there's a good reason. She dotes on you, you know that."

Katrina opened her eyes and glared up at him.

"Honest," Valgu said. "You're the only person in all of Madar that Lady Lena enjoys."

His words mollified her some.

"I wouldn't have let her take you anyway," he said. "I'm going into the Mahigan compound soon - I need you here for my farewell."

She cracked a smile. Valgu needed nothing of the sort. Resting her head on his shoulder she squeezed him tighter.

"I'm going to miss you."

"You all right?" Sol said, as he exited the dining room and walked over to them.

She released Valgu and gave Sol a weak nod.

"Come on," Valgu said. "Let's go outside before the family leaves breakfast."

They stood and she walked sandwiched between her two older brothers. Valgu was five years her senior, but just a little over a month separated her and Sol.

She felt the conservatory before she saw it: humidity dampened her skin and warmth leached into the hall, fogging the etched glass entrance.

"You're not going to be sad all day, are you?" Sol asked.

"No," she said.

"Good," Sol said. "You promised we'd race this morning. Anyway, it's going to be nice with her gone a few days."

Katrina shoved him. "Don't say that."

"Make me don't say it," Sol said. He grinned and avoided her swipe before running at the conservatory door. She chased him. They dodged around massive decorative containers and the dais where their father sat during court. Sol burst through the double doors exiting into the garden. Katrina slipped on the mosaic floor and caught herself on a door before running outside after him.

He laughed over his shoulder. Somehow the running managed to ease her pain. She gained ground and shot out ahead of him. He fell an arms length behind, and she grinned. His laughter continued. She whipped around and faced his charge. He stopped short, smiling. They stood poised with arms outstretched. Each waited for the other to make a move. A gust of wind danced across the garden, yanked at her skirts, and tossed sunlight through their golden hair.

"I won," she said.

Sol tilted his head in consent and lowered his arms. Despite his taunt, Sol was usually the most agreeable of her brothers. Valgu would have demanded a rematch, while Massie would have shouted endless complaints before wrestling her to the ground. Win or lose, Sol stayed happy. His easy going nature made him her favorite companion.

"Race you to the foyer?" He said.

Her blue eyes sparkled as her smile tightened. She nodded once.

"No-flying!" He yelled, but his amend came too late.

She reached for her wings, pulling them with an instinctual desire to fly. They rose from her body. Branching from the base of her shoulders, her wings flowed out in a smooth extension. Her cream colored covert feathers blended with her fair complexion. Speckles of light brown primary and secondary feathers added contrast.

In a burst of motion she stretched her wings. Like a ships sail, they captured the air and manipulated it with ease. One stroke lifted her from the ground and with the second she escaped Sol's grasp.

"Katrina," Sol said through clenched teeth.

"Come on Sol, you're not giving up now, are you?"

"When I graduate the compound, I'll fly, and you'll lose."

She giggled. "I'm not losing now."

Diving forward, she outpaced him. She rounded a corner and flew along the eastern wall of the Mozgas Palace. The lush garden plants swayed beneath her until the grass of the manicured front lawn replaced them. Slowing her descent, she landed on tiptoes at the front steps.

Before her feet touched the stones, Sol's arms grasped her about the waist. She shrieked a laugh as he swung her up and behind him. He sped ahead into the palace.

She chased him across the vast foyer and into a corridor. With a huffing breath Katrina slowed and walked to where Sol stopped. He lay flush with the edge of a doorway. He beckoned her closer. She stepped to the opposite side of the doorway and peeked into the room.

They're talking about you, he said in a wander, his words heard only in her mind.

They are?

Laughter drifted into the hallway. Pavaldon stood with his back to them, his long blonde hair contrasting against the black on black brocade fabric of his tunic.

Delany Aranysarga, the Regina of Mozgas, and Pavaldon's fourth wife, sat facing the doorway with her attention trained on her husband. Delany's layers of caramel colored hair hung in large curls. Her Aranysarga diadem hidden under a tier of curls, only showing itself across her forehead.

Katrina admired Regina Delany's Bisma accent, so like her mother's. They were sisters, after all.

"I think we should be honored by the request," Delany said. "It's from the Tiarnas of Dinhac."

"No," Pavaldon said with a laugh in his voice. "Selig should be irate such a request left his household."

Delany looked down at a letter she held in her lap.

"I'm sorry, I still view these kinds of things through human eyes."

"Yes, it's human monarchs who deal in children this way," Pavaldon said.

"Union's made through betrothal are still honored in Madar," Delany said.

In slow backward steps, Pavaldon moved closer to the doorway where Katrina and Sol hid.

"They are," he said. "But it's a disgrace to the Veilede male bound to it. Betrothals go against our tradition, and paint us as weak. A male bound to betrothal is viewed as someone unable to claim or defend what should be earned."

Katrina and Sol ducked their heads back and hugged the wall on their side of the door.

"I would never dishonor one of my sons by putting forth such a request." Pavaldon's voice became clear as he came closer. Her father grinned as he appeared in front of her. She caught her breath as he scooped her up, flung her over his shoulder, and hauled her into the room.

"Father!" she protested as Pavaldon began spinning in a circle.

"I would never, ever, dream of dishonoring one of my children with the likes of that," Pavaldon said, pointing to the letter in Delany's lap.

He stopped spinning and gathered Katrina into his arms. His gold eyes smiled at her.

"No, a betrothal isn't good enough for my beautiful blue-eyed baby girl."

She loved it when he called her that. The endearment also a reassurance of his acceptance of her half human ancestry.

"My Katrina will be a blessing for the Mahigan who wins her rally."

The strong conviction in his voice left her with no doubts. Her father never tossed around lies, even casual ones. He urged honesty among his children saying, "The most painful truth is better than bearing the weight of easy lies. Lies are pack animals and where there's one, there's a dozen."

Pavaldon carried her to the couch and sat down beside Delany.

"You shall only ever be the bride of the Mahigan who wins you." His tone light despite his serious look.

"What if Katrina likes Tiarna's princes?" Delany said with a chide.

Katrina frowned at the thought of the three Princes from Dinhac. She met them during the birth celebration for her sister Owl. The Tiarna's princes said nothing to her and only wanted to play games with her brothers.

"Dinhac?" Katrina said.

"A nervous mother wants me to promise you to the next Dinhac Regent," Pavaldon said.

She pushed hair behind one ear as she considered her best response.

The Dinhac Mountains were the namesake for Madar's Dinhac province. Sitting on the western border to Mozgas, Dinhac took three days riding to reach, with the capitol city of Pajiste Ver another full days travel from there.

"I might like sledding in Dinhac," she said. The only nice thing she could think of as she considered marriage to a Tiarna's Prince.

"Me too, I want to go sledding there too," Sol said as he came to stand next to them.

"I still think it's a great honor they should think of us," Delany said.

"If one of those Tiarna's boys wants my Katrina, he will have to win her himself," Pavaldon said.

"You won all the rallies you were in," Sol said.

"Yes," he said. "I rallied for all of my wives, except the one given to me. It's rude to refuse a gift, especially when the gift is a beautiful woman. I was very grateful to receive Lady Lena."

Katrina tried to hold her smile, but the mention of her mother's name made it slide away. From what she knew, her mother held none of the same affection for her father that she heard in his voice as he spoke of her.

"Bisma royals don't take multiple wives," her mother had told her. "Only monsters like your father marry several women, and make them live under the same roof to try and share the same role."

A cry sounded from the hall. Her younger sister Owl ran into the room.

"Mama," Owl said, running into her mother, Regina Delany's arms. Pha, an Alvara guardian trailed in. Her deep brown eyes set with concern.

"What is it, love?" Delany said, folding Owl into her embrace.

Owl gave no answer but scrunched up her eyes and tucked her caramel curl laden head into her mother's shoulder.

"My Princess has not been herself," Pha said. "I can't get her to say what the trouble is."

"Is my darling one feeling sick?" Delany said, gently stroking Owl's head.

Owl shook her head. Katrina eased from her father's lap, extending her hands out to Owl. As she rested one hand on Owls back, a trace of dread crept up her arm. An image of Regina Delaney lying dead at Lady Lena's feet flashed through her mind. Katrina caught her breath as she yanked her hand back. Katrina shot a glance to Pha, and searched her face for an explanation. Pha's worried expression remained unchanged as she met her glance.

Owl's frightened manner contrasted with her usual light hearted sweetness. A girl who bounced, sang, and danced through each day. The easiest of her siblings to love.

"Want to go outside and play?" Sol asked.

Owl shook her head no.

"Are you sure," Katrina said, still rattled by Owl's wander. "We could go see the baby swallows."

They had discovered the swallow's nest under the eve where the conservatory connected to the stone bricks of the main palace. Its occupants became one of Owl's favorite things to spy on when she practiced flying. She believed the fluff and beak baby swallows enjoyed her visits and were soothed to sleep with her lullabies.

Owl pulled away from her mother and spied Katrina from the corner of her eye. A raw fear shined in Owl's green eyes.

"We could read?" Katrina asked.

5

Owl blinked a few times as the fear in her eyes tapered. With a little nod of her head she extended her hand. Katrina hesitated before she took it. She inhaled, relieved Owl's disturbing wander made no reoccurrence.

Owl lead her away, their pace increasing to a jog as they passed Pha, and entered the hallway. Katrina liked reading alone in the ornate chair beside her bed. Owl fidgeted too much for sitting. They climbed into her bed, crawled under the blankets, and propped themselves up on pillows. Owl pressed a book into Katrina's hands.

They were two pages in when their father stood at the foot of her bed. He folded his arms across his chest, but grinned. His posture, a favorite cue, sent both girls squealing with delight as they wormed under the covers.

"Huh," he said in fake bewilderment. "I could have sworn my daughters ran in here. I saw them, but they disappeared."

Owl giggled from beneath the blankets.

"Where could they be?" he said.

His hands tickled them through blankets. They laughed and kicked. Pavaldon pulled back the blankets to see their faces.

"Oh look, here you are, I was looking for you," he said.

Owl continued laughing. A full laugh with long floating shouts, sighing dips, and a few giggling bumps. Others quieted at the sound, enjoying the uninhibited joy in her laughter. No one had a better laugh than Owl.

Pavaldon dropped between them and turned onto his back. Katrina and Owl tucked themselves under his arms as Katrina handed him the book.

They loved to nestle this close to him. His voice amplified as they pressed their heads closer to his chest. Between the turn of a page, his hand found the time to stroke their hair.

Sol joined them, hopping up to tuck in beside Katrina. Massie frowned when he discovered them. He stood in the door with both hands on his hips. Five years old, Massie had the same blonde hair as their father, but it curled like his mother, Regina Delany's. Massie endeavored to be Katrina and Sol's peer, but on occasion maintained his small boy manner. Preferring a cuddle in his mother's arms to time spent romping with them.

"It's not bedtime," Massie said, crossing his arms.

"Come here, Massie," Owl said, sitting up and beckoning him with both hands.

"Why didn't you tell me?" Massie grumbled. With a hurried step he uncrossed his arms and made his way to the bed. His scowl broke into a thin smile as he claimed a place under the same arm draping Owl.

The spontaneous moment with their father was a treat. Katrina relaxed, surrounded by her family. The children enjoyed their father's reading for a good two hours before it ended and all were summoned to dinner.

Lady Lena remained absent. Everyone offered reassurances when Katrina asked about her. A full month passed without a letter or formal report on her mother's travels.

Owl grew more withdrawn in the passing days, and ignored the distractions of play. She preferred sleep, and took naps outside her routine. She hid when Pha or the other Alvara guardians thought she went off to play. Later they would find her asleep under a couch or a table.

Owl's laughter vanished, and she ate very little. Whenever Delany left Owl's side, she sobbed. The healers found nothing wrong with her, and had no treatment to revive her spirits.

Owl lay beside Katrina, limp and withdrawn. The book she read offered no distraction from the mystery of her mother's long absence. She closed the book and lay it on her chest. Repeated gusts of wind knocked tree branches against her windows and pressed the songbirds into silence. Owl's small hand grabbed hers. Katrina startled at the touch, which sent the book sliding off her to the bed. Dread raced up her arm. Owl squeezed her hand as her eyes welled with tears.

"Will you come back?"

"From where?" Katrina said. She squeezed Owl's hand and gently prodded her grip loose. "I'm not going anywhere, silly."

"Promise, you'll come back."

"I'm not going anywhere," Katrina said, swiping away a tear from Owl's face.

"What if Lady Lena comes back? What if she takes you?"

A chill ran over Katrina's body.

"What do you mean?"

Owl blinked, sending long tears down her cheeks. She rolled away from her. Owl's face twisted in fear even as she closed her eyes. Owl's haunted expression faded as she relaxed into sleep. Katrina's thoughts tossed between Owl's odd behavior and the confusion and hurt from her mother's absence.

"Katrina?" Sol said from the hallway.

In here, she wandered.

The door opened and Sol peeked around it.

She motioned with her head to Owl. *She's asleep again.*

Owl breathed slow, her face peaceful now, with her caramel colored curls covering half her face.

Sol stepped close to the bed inspecting her. "She didn't make it through the *Bears in the Valley of Bells.* That's her favorite. They sent me in to get both of you."

"Who did?"

"My mother. It's Valgu, he's going in to the Mahigan compound today."

The adults had discussed the afternoons festivities at dinner every night that week. As a Mahigan, Valgu would live and train for a time in isolation from females and other forms of Veilede. A Mahigan's coming of age made their base mating instincts overwhelming and dangerous. The compound protected the local population and functioned as a place where young Mahigans learned to govern themselves and use their mature form.

Katrina sighed and rolled off the bed. With a gentle hand she stroked Owl's forearm.

"Owl love, wake up. Wake up, we have to go see Valgu."

Owl rustled and adjusted her position. Katrina shook her arm again. Owl took a deep breath and let out a slow sigh.

"Everything always has to take forever," Massie said from the hall.

"Are you not leaving today?" Sol spoke to Valgu as they entered the room. Massie and Pha trailed in behind them.

"I'm leaving," Valgu said. He grinned seeing Katrina, and she smiled back. She admired him in the new auburn tunic he wore. She liked its gold stitching and brown suede accents. In her opinion all her brothers were handsome, but perhaps because he was older, Valgu stood out.

"The Regent is held up," Pha said. "There's no hurry."

"We're waiting on Father and Lady Lena," Valgu said.

"My mother?" Katrina said.

"Yes," Pha said. She smoothed the side of Katrina's hair. "Owl fell asleep again?"

Katrina nodded and looked from Pha to Valgu, and then back at Pha saying, "My mother is back? Have you seen her?"

Valgu gave a shrug and Pha shook her head.

It was no surprise to see their indifference at her mother's return. Before she left, Lady Lena's demeanor ranged from distant and cross to hostile. Massie especially disliked her mother, and Katrina knew the feeling was mutual. When Katrina tried to defend her mother, Massie would cut her off by talking over her.

"She's mean. She's mean because she's human, and everybody knows, humans don't like us."

Katrina said nothing, unable to deny what her mother often said. When her mother told the story of her arrival to Mozgas, it was more a list of offenses. She even swore an oath that her own father, Lord Larksbur, would never be forgiven for giving her to a "Mahigan monster."

There was one occasion however, where the story of how her parents met changed. After consuming more than one glass of wine, her mother had dipped her head to side and smiled.

"I fell in love with a monster," she said. "The most handsome man I've ever beheld. He consumed every part of my being before I had a chance to think twice."

Katrina leaned into Pha, who patted her shoulder and said, "It's good news, my Princess. Your mother's home again."

Massie approached Owl who still lay asleep on the bed. He brushed her curls back and spoke in the tender tone he only used with Owl.

"You need to get up, sleepy. Valgu's going, and I know you want to say goodbye."

Owl yawned and blinked. Her green eyes opened. She focused on Massie and said, "I'm hungry."

"Come on," Massie said.

Owl rolled and slid her small body to the floor. Seeing Valgu, she smiled and rushed to hug him around one leg.

"Carry me," she said.

Valgu obliged leaning over and heaving her into his arms. She wrapped her small arms around his shoulders and buried her face in his neck. He kissed her hair and said, "Should we go find everyone else?" Owl nodded and Valgu turned, leading everyone from the room.

Lady Tellydia, Pavaldon's first wife and Valgu's mother, stood outside a door near the end of the corridor. Her mouth was drawn and her hands were on her hips. She was a tall and elegant woman, but her perpetual scowl gave many the false impression she was foul tempered.

"Where is my Regent?" Lady Tellydia said.

"Still in his meeting," Valgu said.

Lady Tellydia shook her head and marched past Lady Oshana, Pavaldon's second wife.

Lady Oshana stood in the doorway to Lady Tellydia's sitting room. Her flat brown eyes scanned the corridor. The widow's peak in her wavy brown hair pointed to a round pleasant face. Of all of her father's wives, Katrina liked the quiet manners of Lady Oshana best. She often doted on her as much as she did her own son, Sol. She also had the most remarkable way of providing a sunny opinion on just about anything.

Lady Tellydia waved them into the room before crossing her arms and marching over to where Delany sat.

Even though Delany was Pavaldon's fourth wife, she was his only Airetti wife. Of the various Veilede forms, the Airetti were known as 'the first' since they were the first to be blessed by God. According to religious edict, an Airetti was needed to co-rule in each Madar province. The Airetti ruler, referred to as the guide, was deemed essential to the continued prosperity of the Veilede. The Airetti were blessed with prophetic visions, and helped ensure actions within a province were sanctioned by God. Most Airetti were born female, which meant the majority of Madar's provincial guides were Reginas.

Airetti herself, Katrina was eager to learn more about the specific tasks of guides. When did God impart sacred information? Did God appear, or just wander the answers to questions? Having a human mother, Katrina posed these kind of questions to Pha.

"You'll know more about all that sooner than later," Pha said. "Until then, just be what God wants you to be, a child."

Regina Delany smiled when she saw Valgu enter carrying Owl.

"Oh, Tellydia, what are we going to do without Valgu?"

Lady Tellydia's scowl softened into a grin as she gazed with pride at her son. Regina Delany rose and went to Valgu. Owl allowed Valgu to pass her off to her mother.

"Now, if only we knew where his father was," Lady Tellydia said, moving to stand beside Delany. She placed a hand on Valgu's shoulder and turned him to face her. She inspected his attire and smoothed the shoulders of his tunic.

Valgu grinned at her. "Is it that bad?"

"My son walks next to his father to the Mahigan Compound today." Her posture exuded pride, as her voice ran high with the tightness of tears.

Valgu grabbed her hands and pulled her to him. The motion surprised her and she smiled while trying to resist him.

"Valgustatuile! Stop that," she grumbled, and then gave in to him sweeping her up in his embrace. His size dwarfed the slender frame of his mother.

"You are just like your father," she said.

Regina Delany exchanged a look with Pha. With a small tilt of her head, Pha turned and left the room. Hopefully in search of her father and mother. Sol edged close to Katrina and gave her a thin smile. Without a word, Sol managed to allay her fears about Valgu's departure and her mother's sudden return.

"Dear God, what's happened to you?" Delany said.

Lady Lena stood in the doorway panting. Her mother's gaze locked with hers before she rushed across the room. Katrina stepped back as her mother moved in. Her mother's braid hung limp and disheveled. A giant slash ran along her dress hem, allowing fabric and lace to drag along the floor.

Katrina shrunk from her mother, who snatched her upper arm and began to pull her to the door. Delany stepped in the way.

"What's happened?" Delany asked.

"You can have him, all of him," her mother said, and tried moving around Delany.

Her mother's nails dug into her arm.

"Stop it, that hurts," Katrina cried, and pushed against her mother's hand. She dug her heels in, threw her weight back, and tried to wrench free.

"What kind of nonsense? Lena stop," Lady Tellydia ordered.

"My sister, my very own sister," Lady Lena said, reinforcing her hold on Katrina and pulling her in close. "You couldn't stand to see me happy. You went and found the perfect way to take him from me."

"Not this fight, not today," Delany said, throwing a hand up in annoyance.

"Move, I'm done with him, I'm done with all of you," her mother said.

"He prizes you. More than me, more than any of us," Delany said. "We're the ones who should be jealous of you."

"I'm the human wife. Remember?" her mother said. Her voice strangled with resentment.

"Lena —" Delany said.

"I'm leaving," her mother said, yanking Katrina's arm .

Lady Tellydia blocked her. "Not with the Princess Katrina."

"Katrina stays with me," her mother said.

"She's the daughter of My Regent," Lady Tellydia said. "She remains here, in the protection of this household."

An ear piercing scream stilled everyone in the room. Katrina caught her breath. Every eye in the room widened.

"Father," Valgu said.

"Daddy," Owl said. Her small form went limp in Regina Delany's arms.

Delany cradled Owl and dropped to her knees before laying Owl on the floor.

"Owl, honey? Owl, my sweet, wake up darling, wake up."

Lady Tellydia grabbed Lady Lena by the shoulders and shook her.

"What have you done?"

Lady Lena's grasp went lax. Katrina jerked free and fled to the back of the room. Massie took her hand and glared at Lady Lena. Sol placed an arm around her. They huddled close together as Lady Oshana placed herself in a protective stance in front of them.

Another scream tore down the corridor. It was so loud Katrina felt it in her chest. The whole room recognized the distinct scream of a Mahigan.

Katrina reached out with her wander sense, searching for her father. Normally, the moment she reached for him, she found him. Now she found no trace of him. Alarmed, her concentration broke. She took a deep breath and refocused. She wander sensed for him again, pressing the search as far as she could. She found no trace of him.

Few things caused someone to lose their wandering ability. The primary cause was death.

"White Fire," her mother said, jutting out her chin with pride.

"Poison," Lady Tellydia said. "You poisoned him? How could you? How dare you!"

Her mother faced Lady Tellydia's rage, and dropped her voice to a harsh whisper.

"I should have saved some for all of you."

The next Mahigan scream had everyone except Valgu and Sol doubled over clutching their ears. Katrina pressed her hands to her ears so hard they hurt. Massie burrowed between her and Sol. She relaxed as the screaming stopped. She looked up at Sol as he wrapped his arms around she and Massie. She hoped he had some an idea of what was going on. Sol gazed back at her, bewildered.

Strong hands clamped on her shoulders and yanked her away from Sol and Massie. Thrown off balance, she stumbled and tried to regain her footing. Her mother dragged her to the door.

"Mother," Katrina said in a desperate croak. "Mother stop, stop."

Lady Lena sped up her pace, forcing her to scramble to stay on her feet. Her mother's speed made it impossible to pull away or stay upright. Her heartbeat pounded in her ears as they jerked to a stop. Released from her mother's grip, the sudden stop sent her stumbling back. She lost her footing and fell to her knees.

Everyone in the room stared at the door. She turned and saw her father in Mahigan form standing in the doorway.

Thick dented plates covered his body. Black and grey, they ranged in size from as small as the palm of her hand to large lengths that spanned his forearms and broad leg muscles. In joints the plates overlapped and allowed movement.

One continuous scale composed his face shield, wrapping from ear to ear. His head seemed enlarged under the ridged dome on the back of his head. His right hand gripped a long weapon, which resembled a long black sword. Mahigan weapons were harder than metal and organically as much a part of them as teeth or eyes.

Her father advanced in slow deliberate steps, his weapon leveled at her mother.

Katrina wanted to run, to scream, to wake up from this dreadful nightmare. It took all her concentration to sit upright. Her mother held her ground, straightened her shoulders, and raised her face to her father as he stepped within striking distance.

"Do it," her mother said.

Regina Delany shouted, "No!" She rushed in front of Lady Lena and gripped her shoulders. She attempted to push her back.

Her father lunged before realizing who blocked his intended target. Delany gasped in pain, and crumbled into Lady Lena's arms.

Katrina breathed hard, her lungs straining for air as her eyes blurred. A Mahigan screamed. Massie wailed and kicked in Lady Oshana's hold. All the noise Katrina heard through the ruffled echo of her own breathing. Light headed, she gasped for breath, but with each exhale the room spun.

What she witnessed mixed with her internal thoughts. Both came together so fast none of it made sense. All of it faded as her vision narrowed. Blinking hard, she tried to right her senses.

Lady Tellydia fell to the floor. Her dress destroyed by a growing stain of crimson blood. Both Regina Delany and Lady Tellydia lay motionless on the floor.

Katrina fell sideways. Her limbs heavy and unresponsive as her vision went black.

2

Wings Broken

Katrina awoke to a cool draft of air. It stroked her face and neck. Her hands ached with cold. A thick blanket barred cold air from finding the rest of her. She opened her eyes and searched the darkness. A rock wall moved past, as dim light made shadows bounce and bob along the narrow ceiling overhead. She lay on a stretcher. Her body bumped and swayed in rhythm with the steps of those hauling her. Where was she?

Exhaustion held her in place despite the urge to roll onto her back. She recalled in sickening clarity the way Regina Delany fell against her mother. The blood around Lady Tellydia on the floor. Her breath picked up, and like vanished fog, she remembered what happened.

Tears pricked her eyes. She bit her lower lip and tried to swallow the pain constricting her throat. Where was everyone? Was her mother dead too? What happened to her father?

She glanced about, trying to see who carried her. A cloaked figure held the handles near her feet.

"What's going on?" she asked.

Frantic hisses erupted from all around. The stretcher jolted to a stop. Her mother's face lowered over hers from the top of the stretcher. Seeing her mother, she relaxed. Her mother spoke in a sharp whisper.

"Don't talk."

"Where are we going?"

"Be quiet," her mother said with more urgency.

Katrina closed her mouth and obeyed. She breathed the cold air and it chilled her from the inside out. Pulling the blankets over her hands, she sunk into them. She balled her body, and shrunk away from her mother's glare.

Silent tears fell. She remembered Massie's scream and her insides rang with the same wail. She wanted her bed, and an explanation for everything that happened.

The air warmed and the ceiling began to rise. The walls gave way to a chamber with a gate leading to the outside. Lowered to the floor, she turned over and crawled to a stand. The air still cold, she grabbed the blanket from the stretcher. Pulling it around her shoulders, she clung to it as she glanced about trying to piece together where they were.

The room was filled with at least a dozen cloaked figures and many were picking up packs and hoisting them onto their backs. Katrina's mother stood over her.

"The Regent is dead," her mother said.

Katrina swallowed as more tears fell. Dead, her father was dead? Massie's wail became her own, and Lady Lena took her by the shoulders and shook her.

"Stop this, you can cry for him later. It's not safe here, we need to leave."

"We can't, what about Sol?" She wiped the side of her face with the back of her hand. "Where's Valgu? Massie and Owl, who's with them?"

"It's not our concern."

"We can't leave them," she said, her voice a high pitched plea.

"They will be fine."

"How?"

Her mother's tight hands grabbed her by the shoulders and shook. Her head bobbed and she closed her eyes in preparation for something worse.

"If I go back they'll kill me!"

The shaking stopped, but her mother maintained her firm grip.

"We can't leave without them," she said. "I'll go back —"

"I risk my life to keep you safe and you want to go back. Do you want your mother to die? Slaughtered, like Delany, and Tellydia?"

"No," she said. Her thoughts tumbled. Logic eluded her. The tears clouded everything.

"We're going," Her mother said.

"I don't want to," she said.

"Come," her mother said. She released her.

Katrina's first instinct was to scream, "No!" and run back into the tunnel. Guilt held her hostage.

Cloaked figures opened the gate, and one by one entered the sunlight of late afternoon. Her mother followed them. Katrina remained behind. She considered the cloaked figures in front of her and the tunnel at her back. This was her chance to go back. Uncertain, she peeked over her shoulder into the darkness. Could she make that walk alone, in the dark? It would take hours. What if the tunnel split somewhere? Even with a light source, walking the tunnel alone daunted her. She pulled the blanket tighter around her shoulders. Using its coarse edge, she swiped at her tears with it.

She squinted at the daylight beyond the door. A sniffled inhale caught a whiff of the Iron Pine forest looming in front of her.

The enormous rock wall of the Mozgas Plateau rose above her, its top lost somewhere high against the sky. Home lay somewhere up that wall. She considered throwing off her blanket and shifting into her wings, but her body recoiled with fatigue. She would never even clear five branches of the closest Iron Pine. She leaned on the doors gate as the chance to turn back slipped further away.

Studying the forest ahead, she considered where they were headed. Who were these men in cloaks? If her mother was in danger, was she in danger too? Could she go home? She needed to go home.

Her mother stopped walking. Hands on her hips, her mother turned around and faced her. Jaw set, her mother squinted back at her with impatience.

Fear and anguish pulled and pushed Katrina in both directions. Her mother sighed and her annoyed posture shifted into exhausted resignation. Her look of defeat drove a thorn of guilt into Katrina. Gripping the blanket, she took a step forward.

The dense forest air felt heavy. Darkness lurked in her mind. Images of Regina Delany and Lady Tellydia played over and over. She squelched one before another arrived to trip her into fresh pain. Raw and unwelcome, the memories bit hard. Her mother reacted to her plight with more annoyance than sympathy. Her mother's face twisted in exasperation everytime she stopped to look back at her.

Grappling with her situation, Katrina pushed her thoughts to her surroundings. She tried to differentiate one cloaked figure from another. Her stride shortened with fatigue and she straggled behind them in this endless walk. The urge to revolt goaded her to stop and lie down where she stood. She could curl into a ball and fall asleep on the long soft pine needles covering the ground.

The hours wore on under a blank blue sky. The Iron Pines stood vigil. Unlike regular trees, Iron Pines grew into giants, the tallest trees in existence. They were powerful with lifespans exceeding centuries. A dozen men standing shoulder to shoulder would not be seen from the other side.

Katrina's blanket hung loose and her fingers quaked.

"I'm hungry."

"Me too," Lady Lena said. "I'm sure they'll have something when we get there."

"When we get where?"

New faces appeared around them. Men sprang up from the ground and walked out of trees. Their clothing performed the magic of disguise; made of fabrics that imitated the forest. They transformed into the bark of tree trunks or a bed of pine needles on the ground.

Intrigued, Katrina stared at their magic clothing. Greetings were being made in a language similar to the common one used in Madar. They changed pronunciations and twisted up normal phrases. She caught words she recognized from Bisma, and formal phrases no longer used outside religious circles.

She studied the men, and guessed they were Mahigan. Their size and posture marked them as Mahigan, but they carried swords and knives. While her eyes identified them as Mahigan, her wandering sense confirmed they were not Veilede. None of them triggered her senses as a wanderer would.

The closest Veilede she felt sat far away. At this distance, her ability to communicate in a wander to them would be near impossible. She lacked the experience and concentration needed. If she even tried the effort would sap her energy dry. She would wander though. Tonight, on the edge of sleep, she would enter neutral. There she would summon other wanderers from a distance. The greater the distance, the harder it was to focus and find a person. Wandering neutral would cut into her rest, but leave her with some energy for the next day.

A tall man in a pine needle patterned cloak approached her mother. He wore a heavy chain of gold and silver loops around his neck. Pushing back his hood, he revealed a head of ruddy brown hair that receded at his temples. His face was long with lean cheeks and a hard chin. A scar traced one side of his jaw and stood out against his stubble. His face looked placid but his dark brown eyes gazed with a heated intensity. He stood in front of Lady Lena.

"You were to do it and get out."

"And I did," Lady Lena said. She stepped towards him and ducked her head. Using slow hands, she slid her arms beneath his cloak and clasped one of his hands. His eyes still burned, but his voice stayed low.

"What possessed you to bring her here?"

"She's my daughter."

"She must go back," he said.

"No."

"She must."

"If she goes back then I do too," her mother said.

The man took her mother's hands in both of his and pulled her close.

"I know you're tired," he said. "But I'm offering no options. She must leave."

Her mother resisted him and straightened her shoulders.

"I am tired, but if you send her back, I'll go with her. Before they execute me, I'll be forced to tell them everything."

"You'd bring death to us all," he said and raised a hand to push a lock of disheveled hair behind her mother's ear.

"Give her the tea," her mother said. "Please, she's only a child."

"It's too great a risk."

Her mother blinked fast, and nodded as she swallowed hard. The man released her hands and stepped away from her, hanging his head. A long silence hung between them.

"Alright," he said. "For tonight. When I find a suitable situation, she must leave."

Her mother beckoned her over. Obeying, she tried to pick up her feet as she walked over. Her mother wrapped an arm around her shoulders.

"Lord Dacamera may I present my daughter, Katrina."

Katrina peeked up at her mother confused. Why did she use his formal title, but omit hers?

"Greetings, Lord Dacamera," she said.

"Greetings."

She gave a small nod and turned away from her mother's odd smile. Who was this man, this Lord? Lord of what? They walked a great distance to get here, but she knew they remained within the borders of Mozgas. They had traveled northeast towards Bisma. By road it took two days to reach the northern border by carriage. It would take over a week walking through forest. Even then, her grandfather, Lord Larksbur ruled Bisma's border province Lavieth.

Lord Dacamera and his cloaked men led them to a larger clearing where a camp was set up. The camp provided some dismal clues about their destination. Based on the quick shelters and lack of carts or animals, wherever they were going, would likely take days of walking dense forest to reach.

They received bowls of a stew with a weak mushroom broth and what looked like carrots or turnips. The earthy mushroom taste did not improve as she ate. She sipped and nibbled it, trying to deaden her hunger.

Only later, when she sat alone in a tent with her mother, did she unleash her many questions. Her mother claimed the men were human and from some Kingdom called Shakendal.

"There's no place called Shakendal in Bisma," Katrina said.

"Yes, I know," Her mother chided, speaking Bisma. Since she was a baby, her mother taught her native Bisma language to Katrina by speaking it to her when they were alone.

"Where is Shakendal then?" Katrina said.

"It borders Mozgas."

Katrina furrowed her brow and groaned as she shook her head. "No such place exists." She listed off the places that did on her fingers. "Mozgas is bordered by the Delphi's ocean province in the east, Dinhac in the west, Idania in the south, and Bisma in the North."

"Yes, thank you for the geography lesson, dear."

"So where is this Shakendal?"

"Your Regent would say it's in Mozgas, but the Skrieni occupied the area before the Veilede took the Mozgas Plateau."

"The Skrieni," she said. "That's who you want us to live with, the Skrieni?"

"Yes, now please let's sleep."

Valgu told her about the Skrieni. They were a group of Veilede separatists, Madar born, that liked to declare themselves human. An outrageous claim. If you were born in Madar, you were born a form of Veilede, no exceptions. Even the bordering human region birthed the occasional Veilede, like Regina Delany. Choosing not to shift was one thing, but claiming to be human when you're not, was madness.

Lady Lena rolled away from her, pulling a blanket over her shoulder. Katrina's questions multiplied, but she settled in her bedroll. Her mother would say no more tonight.

Skrieni had brought them from the palace. She never knew a Skrieni, but her initial impression that the cloaked men were Mahigan had to be correct. They were pretending to be human. How ridiculous, the only real human out here was her mother. If Katrina felt more like herself, she would have laughed.

It took her a great deal of effort to remain awake enough to enter neutral. She needed sleep badly, but she had to do this. The further she traveled with the Skrieni, the harder summoning her brothers would become. She focused on Sol.

Her mind constructed a replica of her favorite part of the Mozgas Palace, the conservatory. Large pains of etched glass comprised the ceiling and the upper third of the conservatory's walls. They trapped the sunlights warmth and kept the building an even temperature year round. The conservatory rivaled an oversized ballroom, with a perimeter of lush plants and exotic looking trees. Elaborate chairs with carvings of vines and flowers were tucked between large plant containers and trees. The expansive mosaic tile floor entertained the eye with strong shades of yellow, blue and green, woven in symmetrical patterns of exotic flowers.

A subtle vibration moved through the conservatory as Sol appeared. He gripped her into a tight hug and held on. They breathed in relief and exchanged weak smiles. She felt grateful they needed no words to express their mutual grief.

"Lady Lena poisoned father," Sol said. "It's why he did what he did."

"I can't believe he's dead," she said, her voice waffling on the edge of collapse.

"Dead?"

"My mother said he died."

Sol shook his head.

She gripped his arms. "He's alive? He's okay?"

"Not really," he said.

"But, he's alive?"

"Yes, but he's changed, he…" Sol fumbled for words, and wore an unfamiliar expression of concern.

"He's sick?"

"He's scary. He says things that don't make sense. He seemed fine, then he started screaming again. My mother said they have to keep him away from us, for a while. They don't want him to hurt us."

"Katrina?" Pavaldon said.

She and Sol looked up to see their father standing a few feet away.

"Daddy?" Katrina said turning and reaching a hand out to him.

"Where has she taken you?" Pavaldon asked. He walked towards them but within a few steps vanished.

Staring where her father stood a moment ago, she dropped her hand and faced Sol.

"The poison," she said.

Sol nodded and ran one hand through the side of his hair.

"Lord Dacamera did this," she said.

"Lord Dacamera?" he said, not hiding doubt from his voice.

"He's in charge of the Skrieni we're with. Tell Pha that's who has us."

"Pha already left," he said. "She went to find you when they discovered Lady Lena gone."

"Then tell your mother, tell everyone, we're with Lord Dacamera."

"I've never heard of a Lord Dacamera?"

"I know, he's Skrieni."

"Your mother's in a lot of trouble for this."

Swallowing hard she nodded. "Is Pha the only one out searching?"

"Everyone's searching," Sol said. "Just find a way to run. Someone will find you and bring you home."

"I will, but there's a lot of Skrieni," she said.

"Your mother has a better chance if father's army finds you first. They care more about finding you than the hunt for her."

"Maybe," she said with a grimace. "If there's that many looking, they can easily do both."

He pulled her into a hug. "I'll go tell everyone who has you."

"I'm scared."

"I bet Pha finds you first," he said. "Watch her find you tonight. You'll be home by tomorrow."

She sat huddled under blankets as the Skrieni broke camp the next morning. She debated the best opportunity to flee. The memory of her mother's lie about her father's death wore at the thin composure she managed to muster.

Her mother sat up and Katrina faced her. Even waking from a night spent sleeping on the hard ground, her mother looked beautiful. Her blue eyes, the shade of a perfect summer sky, searched Katrina's face. Her mother knew the signs to look for in someone who wandered neutral during the night. Even at home, wandering neutral left her weary looking.

"Who did you see last night?" her mother asked.

"Sol," she said.

Her mother pursed her lips in thought and made a small nod.

"You lied. Father's not dead. He's sick."

"Is he?" Her mother stood up and smoothed the front of her dress.

"I need to go home."

"I know this is all very different for you, but we can't. Things will get better for us soon."

"Why are we out here?"

"Brush out your hair before coming out. It's a mess," her mother said.

"Everyone's looking for us," she said.

"All the more reason we need to get going." Her mother waved her hand in a dismissive gesture and turned to go.

Katrina rose from her bedroll with her hands balled in fists. "The whole Mahigan Army is looking for us. I'm going back."

Her mother glanced over her shoulder and said, "We're in this together."

"I need to go. You'll have to hide. I'll tell them I don't know where you are—"

"No."

Her mother spoke in a steady firm voice that brokered no argument. "Where I go, you go."

Her mother tilted her head up in the way she did to communicate all pleading or arguments were useless. With an irritated sigh Katrina bowed her head. Her mother wanted compliance, nothing more. A powerless child she may be, but even she knew outrunning a Mahigan Army was impossible. The longer Katrina waited to run, the more jeopardy her mother was in.

Their breakfast came as a dense round bread. Chewing it took effort and the dry coarseness of it demanded water . Hunger over rode the displeasure of eating it, and she gnawed her way through it over the morning. Her face screwed up in disgust when they handed her more of the same bread for lunch.

She waited for the chance to sneak away. Fumbling near the back, the cloaked Skrieni men stalked her. They waited besides her mother for her to catch up, or fell back to walk beside her.

That night she plotted as the days failure weighed on her. She lacked something. The cleverness to puzzle out the best escape. The courage to take a bold risk, and walk away as they watched. The audacity to sit down and make them carry her.

She fell asleep. The usual restorative benefits of sleep eluded her. Muscles protested movement and her mind resumed the puzzle of the night before.

Her legs shook with fatigue as another day of walking ended. In the darkness her mother guided her by the hand to a small clearing. A Skrieni man hoisted her onto a wooden disk suspended from a rope. The Skrieni called the device a lift entrance. As they harnessed her to the disk, she watched as Skrieni men sat on more of the disks nearby. When they leaned back, the rope jerked, and the lift sent them up into the darkness of the tree canopy above. Someone pulled down on the rope she sat suspended from. This action activated a lever and pulley system. With amazing speed she rose straight up. Tree limbs passed her in a blur of pine boughs and shadow. The lift stopped at a landing near a conglomeration of suspended platforms and small buildings.

There were no permanent residents here, just empty rooms forming a temporary camp of some sort. Everyone filed off into a separate shack, each lined up along one narrow path made of wood planks. Everything rocked underfoot as wind moved the tree tops and made the wood supports groan. She followed her mother into a room the size of a large horse stall. Someone followed behind them to dump a pile of blankets before retreating and closing the door. Her mother arranged the blankets on the floor and covered her as she lay down. Huddling under her blanket her body was more content to rest than protest the awful hardness of her makeshift bed. Nagging questions kept her awake. Only sketches of shadows were visible in the deep darkness of the room. Loud gusts of wind crashed like waves against the pine trees outside and her insides rolled with the perpetual swaying of the trees.

"I don't like it here," she said.

"Go to sleep," her mother said.

"What if the wind knocks us out of the trees? What if we can't fly out of here before we hit the ground?"

Her mother sighed, "You forget I can't fly. Please go to sleep. We have more walking tomorrow."

"Why do we have to keep walking? The Army will catch up with us."

"I'm very tired, and I know you are too."

"When are you going to tell me why we're out here? Why did you hurt father? He loves us."

"I'm not discussing it with you. Don't ask, you're too young to understand."

"No, I'm not."

"It's not time for talking, it's time for bed. Stop talking and go to sleep."

Katrina's throat constricted in anger and resentment. Being treated like she was a child Owl's age insulted her. Tears began coursing down her face and tickled at the edge of her ears.

"You left without saying goodbye or telling me where you were going. No one would tell me anything. They didn't know when you'd be back, and most of them didn't care." She sniffed and turned away from her mother mumbling, "You shouldn't have come back."

She cried and her mother offered no comfort. Punishment for what she said. There would be more hostility in the morning. Her mother never let her speak her mind without retribution.

A cold trace of guilt snaked through her stomach and coiled with the horrible rolling. The fear of her mother's wrath was minor compared to the fear of her mother's fate when the Army found them. She had to get away. Her mother's opportunity for survival was slipping away. Tomorrow she would gather her strength and escape.

She awoke with a start the next morning. The unfamiliar surroundings a cold reminder that all the comforts of home and family were gone. Sitting up, she closed her eyes and tried reaching out with her wandering sense. She sensed nothing. Impossible, she could feel her father's army yesterday. A numb horror hit her. Trembling, she stood, opened the door and stepped outside to survey the Skrieni sending gear down on the lifts. It was them, they had done something to her wandering talent. She needed to leave, now.

She walked to the edge of walkway. She felt her face tighten into a mask of hate as she yanked at the ties to her dress. Pulling her dress down she exposed her back while restricting her shoulders. Her mother came at her in a rush, grabbed her by the arm as she yanked her dress up and flipped her around like she weighed nothing.

"Get away from me! How could you let them do this?" Katrina shouted.

"Stop it, don't you dare shift here!" her mother said as she shook her so hard she lost her footing.

"They're poisoning me! I won't stay here, let go-let go!"

Jerking back against her mother's strength she fell to the ground. Her mother toppled with her. They landed with her mother holding her down under her weight. Katrina stared up into her mother's blue eyes that twitched with rage.

"You're staying with me," her mother said. "You're coming with me, and from now on we're human. We don't wander, and we never shift. That's the rules and you'll follow them or there will be consequences."

"That's crazy!"

Screaming, Katrina wrestled and tried to worm out of her mother's hold.

"Stop it, Katrina!"

"What's this now?" Lord Dacamera said standing over them. Katrina stopped fighting and glowered up at his imposing form. Her mother eased off of her as Lord Dacamera bent down, grasped her behind the neck, and hauled her up onto tiptoes. Thrusting his face into hers, his breath wafted the pungent reek of garlic against her face. She shrunk back, placing her hands against where he gripped her about the neck, but he held her in place.

"You will show your mother respect, and you'll do what she tells you. We don't treat disobedience with kindness. You follow the rules, and I won't catch you crossing her again." He released her with a shake and she regained her feet.

Lord Dacamera assisted her mother to her feet and she dusted off.

It took effort to hold back the curses her mind flung at them. The theft of her wandering ability emboldened her. There would also be new opportunities in her mother's punishing silence.

Today one of two things would happen. She would get away, or they were going to have to tie her up and carry her. Let her mother and Lord Dacamera make good on their threats. A Mahigan army was coming. No punishment from her mother could rival the pain of her death.

Unharnessed from the lift, Katrina collected her morning ration of bread, stole a flask of water, and walked south in the direction they had come. She walked alone, but expected someone to snatch her up at any moment. Her stomach rejected the idea of food. She willed herself to remain calm but she sucked in each breath as if she were running. Her heartbeat a fluttering chant of, "go-back, go-back, go-back!" Time passed and when she dared consider the possibility of success, she started to hear the shouts of many people calling her name.

"Katrina! Katrina!"

Her heart raced faster and she moved her feet into a jog and then a run.

"Katrina!"

She stumbled and fell. Her palms burned as she slid accross beds of thick pine needles. Picking herself up she ran. The sound of tromping boots came from close behind her.

Arms encircled her, lifting her from the ground. She yelped and kicked as the man who held her swung her around.

"Put me down! Let go of me. Let me go!"

Skrieni men surrounded her again, saying nothing as she was heaved over a man's shoulder and hauled back to the group. She beat on his back as he immobilized her legs with his arms. She scratched and hit until she was tossed to the ground with a force so great it knocked the wind from her lungs and left her stunned and gasping.

Her mother stood over her with crossed arms and motioned for her to stand.

Katrina blinked and answered with a small head shake. Tears welled in her eyes as fear mixed with anger. Wild emotions took over in a rush so strong she hardly understood her own screaming protests.

"No!" With fists she pounded the ground then scooped up and flung needles and debris in every direction. "No, I won't. I'm going home!"

"You're coming with us," her mother said grabbing her by the hair and thrusting her face close to hers.

"No! I'm not!"

The back of her mother's hand connected with the left side of her face in a slap that knocked her sideways. Her scalp burned and her eyes blurred. Slumping forward, she blinked to right her vision. She touched the biting heat on her cheek. Her mother gripped her by the shoulders and yanked her up in an effort to haul her onto her feet. Katrina let her head loll as she hung limp in her grasp.

"We don't have time for this. Stop humiliating me and get up."

"No."

"I am your mother, and you will obey me. Get up this instant."

Katrina's fury melted into a sobbing plea. "Let me go. They'll kill you. You can't die—"

A hand descended over her nose and mouth. A wet cloth hindered her breathing. Laboring for breath, Katrina pulled at the arms trapping her from behind, against the arms locking her against the offenders chest. After three desperate attempts for air, every reason to fight vanished. Her mother's eyes were the last thing she saw as her mind slipped away. A deceptively happy sky blue hue.

She awoke in darkness with a throbbing headache. Moving to touch her head, she found both of her hands tied to a litter. Her mother walked beside her and explained how the Skrieni used a medical treatment to put her to sleep. A treatment strong enough to make adults sleep for the better part of a day.

"I slept an entire day?" Katrina asked.

"No, you've been asleep for two," her mother said.

"And the Army's not found us yet?"

Her mother sighed and gave her a curt, "No."

"They should have found us already."

"We'll be welcome to enter their village, but only if you promise not to carry on like before. You broke my heart behaving so poorly. I haven't raised you to act in such a way."

"I'm thirsty," Katrina said.

Her mother rested her hand on her restraints. "Are you going to behave yourself, carry yourself in the manner I taught you?"

Gritting her teeth Katrina nodded.

"Say it, promise me you will."

She paused and stared at her mother.

"I'll behave."

She had never uttered a blatant lie before.

Her mother released the restraints. When she sat up, muscles all over her body ached. She sat still and sipped at a cup of water. The last attempt she made to flee, cost two whole days. Her pulse quickened as she thought about the Army coming for them. She swore she sensed them. That at any moment a Mahigan scream would sound and armored figures would step clear of the trees. Maybe she hadn't lied? What was the point of running now? Dread trickled a shiver up her spine. Escape and the chance to save her mother was gone.

Birds chattered overhead as Katrina followed her mother and their Skrieni escort to the lift entrances. Lord Dacamera's Skrieni kingdom looked little more than a series of small villages. Built high in the canopy of the Iron Pines, the buildings were similar to the elevated encampment they overnighted in. The buildings here were larger. Wide wooden platforms spanned the lengths between these and the trees. The supports to the structures seemed sturdier, and wind rocked the village less.

Lord Dacamera greeted them at the top of the lift entrance and led them to his house. It looked like a paupers lodgings and smelled like stale bread and campfire. Nothing about it appeared fit for a powerful leader or noble.

A brown haired boy sat at a table in the main room. He lounged in his chair with both feet propped on the table. He was lean with long limbs and a narrow chest. His face held youth's softness but budded with the angled features of a man. Lord Dacamera took one look at him before shrugging off his pack and throwing it across the room. The boy sat up straight in his chair but smirked at Lord Dacamera.

"Is Lady Lena home for good, My Lord?"

The boys amber gold eyes met her gaze and his face lit up with mischief. He made a clucking sound and tilted his head.

"You brought the Regent's daughter home? Should we start evacuating everyone now?"

"Get out of here," Lord Dacamera said, watching him from the corner of his eyes.

"Yes, my Lord," the boy said, but rose from his chair with a lazy pace. "I don't like the idea of being sliced up by Pavaldon's Mahigan Army. Most people here don't."

"You don't come in here without my consent, understand? If I feel the need to speak with you, I'll summon you."

"As you command," the boy said with dramatic sarcasm. The boy made a fist, and took a deep breath even as his posture stiffened. His face clouded in conflict and he barred his teeth as he spoke. "I saw this."

Lord Dacamera's eyes widened in anger.

"I hoped it was something I dreamed up," the boy said. "But now I see it for the warning it was. You've brought us more than the curse of a Dark Reminder, you brought us a death sentence."

Lord Dacamera continued to glare at the boy. Shaking his head, the boy frowned at the floor. He turned in haste and left.

Katrina hated to see him go. His audacity thrilled her. Who was he, and how did he get away with his behavior? Maybe he went unpunished because he was right. A serious danger was coming to their village. While the boy cared for this village and its strange occupants, she felt nothing for them. They helped poison her father. They used their poisons on her. They deserved what was coming.

"You." Lord Dacamera said in a voice near shouting. He startled her from her thoughts. When he knew he had her attention he pointed to the floor in a gesture better suited for trained dogs.

"Don't leave this house," he said.

While she said nothing, she did her best to school her face to keep it from betraying her defiant thoughts.

"You leave my house, and there isn't a person up here who'll welcome you. Nobody's going to bow down and thank God for creating you. For your mother's sake, I'll look out for you. But if you leave this house without escort, I won't be able to help you."

"I can understand if they aren't welcoming," her mother said. "Surely we're not in any danger here."

"I don't say things I don't mean. If I say she needs to stay in this house, you should make sure she stays in the house."

"Yes, I understand. There's no need to scare Katrina. Your people wouldn't treat her poorly."

"They will, little girl or no. She's a Dark Reminder. She's dangerous."

Her mother sighed and made a dismissive chuckle, "Dark Reminder? Dangerous, honestly. Obstinate perhaps, but she's a girl whose bloom to womanhood is years away."

"Her kind is God's warning to us, reminding us of what we lost."

"From the days your ancestors thought it a good idea to try and wipe out her kind, yes I'm aware of the archaic superstition." Her mother waved a dismissive hand. "She wasn't born here."

"That doesn't matter. She's a Dark Reminder and the apothecaries won't tolerate anything that impedes our ability to stay human. They can't stop a Dark Reminders visions, but first chance they get, they'll put her through transformation. It's bad, most don't survive."

Her mother straightened and her features turned fierce. "No. No one up here will lay a finger on my daughter."

"Then she better not set foot outside this house." Lord Dacamera shifted his gaze to Katrina. Fear outlined his frown. He really was trying to protect her. For a long moment the three of them sat in silence.

Lord Dacamera cleared his throat and scratched behind his ear. "Come on Katrina, I need to clear a space for you."

Out of the main room and down a narrow hall, Lord Dacamera opened a door to what looked like an all-purpose storage room. Shelves were built into the walls at either end. An odd assortment of seasonal clothing, hunting paraphernalia, and ceramic jars of preserved food lined the shelves.

"I'll fetch a mattress for you and set it in here, and you can have this shelf here."

Holding her disgust in check she nodded as he proceeded to clear the bottom shelf. A kind gesture, but a waste of time.

Lord Dacamera left to find a mattress and Katrina rejoined her mother in the main all purpose room of the house. Her mother still sat at the table with her arms folded.

"Why are we here?" Katrina asked.

Her mother looked at her and away again. Katrina walked to the table and gripped the back of a chair.

"Why did you help them poison my father?"

"You have no idea what I've been through," Lady Lena said. "All, to keep you safe."

"Safe from what?" Katrina asked as she moved to her mother.

Her mother's expression turned wild. Her eyes darted about seeking escape. Standing up, she stretched out her arms and backed away.

"You're so ungrateful," Her mother said. She turned and rushed down the narrow hallway. Throwing open the door to Lord Dacamera's room, she ducked inside, and slammed the door.

Confused and tired Katrina sat down at the table. She deserved an explanation. She also knew pursuing her mother now would get her nothing. Nagging her mother for answers would be as useful as banging her head on the floor.

If she persisted her mother would do one of two things. Smack her accross the face or talk over her in a hedge about unrelated nonsense. Her mind drifted to Lord Dacamera and the mattress he promised. The physical desire for sleep conflicted with her resolution to escape. She should sleep. It would be easier to leave in the middle of the night. She might still be able to put some distance between her and her mother before Pha or the Army came.

Lord Dacamera returned with a mattress and a Skrieni woman carrying a tray of food. Her mother emerged from the bedroom with puffy eyes and an odd red tint to her cheeks.

The Skrieni woman conversed with Lord Dacamera in their odd language. She doled out stew from a covered crock, and stole several long glances at Katrina.

Katrina stared back at the woman, unafraid of showing her irritation.

"Send her out," her mother said. "Tell her, she's to never look at Katrina or myself again."

"Lena—"

"Get her out of here." Her mother stood abruptly, her posture fixed like she would charge the woman. The Skrieni woman barked a few words and dropped the crock with a thud onto the table. Lord Dacamera waved Lena back and spoke rapid strange words to the woman, motioning to the door.

The woman brushed her hands down her skirt, muttered what might be a curse, and with a fluid about face walked out.

Katrina picked at her food. When would one of the adults seated at the table like to answer her questions? They avoided her eyes, giving their food rapt attention. She wanted to ask her questions, but years of ingrained table etiquette held her silent.

When her mother finished eating she said, "Katrina, why don't you go lay down. You look very tired."

Katrina stood and moved to obey her mother. This was too unfair. She deserved the truth about what had happened and why.

"My Lord," Katrina said, using the formal tone every child of a Regent masters early in life. "May I have use of one of your lamps?"

Lord Dacamera nodded and motioned to the one sitting on a small table near the main door. She retrieved it and walked to the storage room. She set the lamp on the empty shelf before flopping down on the mattress. Thoughts buzzed in her mind before jolting to a halt as she caught the first scraps of conversation in the other room. Her mother and Lord Dacamera spoke in soft tones.

"You weren't supposed to bring her," Lord Dacamera said.

"I'm her mother, I'm not leaving her to be raised by monsters."

"What kind of insane logic are you using?"

"Excuse me, what?"

"When you breed with a monster, the progeny's always a monster. And the monster, who's progeny you bore, happens to still be alive. Why is that Lena?"

"I don't know."

"How can he still be alive?"

"I did what I was supposed to."

"You botched it. Then you grabbed his daughter and made it worse."

"My daughter."

"She goes back. I'm sending her tomorrow."

"She's not going back."

"If you came alone, as planned, I could've protected you indefinitely. Bringing her here's changed everything. Her staying here isn't an option."

"And where are we supposed to go?"

"It doesn't matter. Get her away from here."

"I can't be rushed. I need a few days to sort things out."

"No," Lord Dacamera said. He dropped the quiet tone, and his words were heard with full clarity. "You've risked our lives. The apothecaries won't stand for it. They'll come in here, and they'll do what they will to mitigate the risk."

"What?"

"I can fend them off for a day or two, but that's it. They'll take her and force her through transition."

"No, she's not to undergo any such thing."

"If she lives, it'll be weeks-months before she's healed. Can you handle watching her suffer or die?"

"You're in charge. You tell them not to touch her. Or don't they follow your orders?"

"You're the only one here who disobeyed me."

"I told you-"

"No, you don't get to tell me anything. You have one choice. Leave with her, or send her back."

"I - I need time to plan."

"In the morning I'll give you one chance. If you don't have an answer, then I decide what happens."

"No, that's-"

"Understand me Lena, not making a decision, is a decision."

Tears stung Katrina's eyes. Clamping her eyes shut, she rolled over putting her back to the door. Why were they here? Why did her mother keep insisting they stay? She poisoned her father, why? The questions pressed down on her with suffocating weight. Crying released some of the pain, but even as her tears ran out, the questions lingered. The dim lamp stood vigil in the darkness. Sleep tugged at her and she closed her eyes to the nightmare of being awake.

Moans startled her awake. She listened, hoping she heard wrong. More moans, and not the kind made when someone fell sick. Coupling, those were coupling moans. A distinct and unforgettable type.

The first time she heard it, she was with Sol. Together they followed the noise to a hidden corridor behind the nursery. They found a stable hand propping up a kitchen maid in a stairwell corner. At first it looked like the stable hand was attacking the poor girl. The way he pinned her and pressed his body urgently against hers. Katrina stood ready to order him off the maid, but then saw the maids face. She smiled, pulled him closer, and wrapped her legs around his bare behind. The maid kissed him in a way that displayed nothing but approval. After telling Valgu what they witnessed, he provided a brief explanation of sex. A physical marriage act necessary for producing children, but one often enjoyed between lovers. Her mother and Lord Dacamera were lovers? She knew what she heard, but it still surprised her. Her mother was father's favorite wife. What did she see in Lord Dacamera to make him her lover? Katrina cringed with disgust.

She sat up and took a visual inventory of the closet contents. The lamp glowed dim in the dismal closet. She pulled a leather bag down from a higher shelf. It held a small knife, a wooden cup, and a heavy coil of rope. She rolled up the blanket she had slept under and stuffed it into the bag. Sifting through the food stores, she grabbed a ceramic container of pine nuts. She nestled it into the blanket and fastened the bag.

Wrapping the bag's thick strap accross her body, she grabbed the lamp and pushed open the storage room door. Minus the bedroom noise, the rest of Lord Dacamera's house stood quiet. A cold chill prickled her skin as she crept to the main room. What happened if her mother caught her? What was worse than bringing her here? She remembered Lord Dacamera's cautions about the Skrieni apothecaries.

She pushed away the worry crowding her train of thought and inspected the dinner tray left out on the table. There were no good scraps to take with her. She drank the remains of the water pitcher and scanned the room for any other objects to nab for her journey. The many unknowns of what lay ahead ate away at her resolve to leave. As a privileged Regents daughter, she was taught many things beyond the years of other children her age. All that schooling, and no one taught her about traveling the woods alone. Worry returned, and the dangers multiplied as she considered them. They made her stomach clench and her hands clammy. Still, these were nothing compared to the threat against her mother's life. Hefting the bag and lantern, she exited Lord Dacamera's house.

Recalling the walk here, she turned in the direction of the closest lift. A man's figure stepped from the shadows of a house accross the walkway. She yelped, and hesitated before running past him. Heart hammering, she caught her breath as the man called after her in Skrieni. His words meant nothing, but the cautionary tone increased her alarm. The man shouted, calling to someone. A distant voice answered from the darkness. Within three paces someone else echoed the call. They were repeating a warning call. She heard footfalls coming up behind her.

Walking fast she stumbled up a staircase, and climbed to a forked platform. She had to get away. Turning right she ran, then slowed. The lift entrance was back the other way. Fear clouded her mind. She made a mistake. There was no time to double back to the lift entrance. They had better clearance for descending in the dark, but she would have to make the most of launching off the nearest side.

Jerking to a halt, she pulled at her bodice laces. Growling under her breath, she set the lantern down and yanked the bag off. With one fluid movement she hauled her dress over her head and off. Throwing the bag over one shoulder, she lay her dress over it and grabbed the lantern. The number of footsteps pursing her increased. She picked an open space between two trees and ran to the railing. Climbing up, she perched on the top rung.

Wind greeted her as she shifted into her wings. It flew around her, whispering a roar through the trees. It chilled her naked torso, and ran an invisible hand accross the arches of her wings.

A shout in Skrieni came from behind her. A small crowd of four women were gathered on the nearest platform. They shrieked, chattering gibberish and motioning for her to come down. One of their phrases stood out, 'Dark Reminder.'

"No, Dark Reminder, no-no."

Glaring at them, Katrina steadied her footing on the top of the rail.

The door to a house further down clattered shut. A short woman moved through the crowd of Skrieni, surveying the situation with a lantern hefted over her head. The light deepened the short woman's withered features. The grey braid slung over her shoulder glinted silver in the lamp light. Her plain garments contrasted with her elaborate looping necklace of bone and amber beads. She approached with a raised hand, and waved for Katrina to step down.

Katrina shook her head, faced the forest, and stretched her wings. Gripping the bag and lantern, she took one step, and dropped off the railing in a free fall.

The women behind her erupted in shouts.

Extending her wings, she began a slow descent. The press of air a familiar and good thing among so much unknown.

Her momentum ended with a jerking halt. A net folded around her. Screaming in frustration she kicked and cried. The thin metal strands of a finely woven Mahigan net swallowed her whole. The threads were all but cutting into her skin. They constricted her arms and legs and pinned her knees to her chest. The netting tugged and shifted around the feathers of her wings. She shifted out of them and the thin fibers clung at her naked back. Helpless, she swung into the the side of a tree. The impact stole her breath. Her scalp and back burned where bark pulled her hair and rent scratched accross her back. A lurching bounce pulled her away from the tree.

A wild chatter erupted above. The grey haired woman barked orders. The Skrieni worked above to unfasten the net from its station's before hauling her net constricted body up onto the platform. Many hands lifted her and she was carried behind the grey haired woman into a building.

The door clunk shut behind them. Set on the floor, Katrina tried to stretch and pull free of the net. A useless effort. Mahigan nets were designed to collapse and leech strength. Any movement triggered these abilities. Curled in a tight ball, Katrina knew none of the right Skrieni words.

"No, stop, please."

They ignored her. Each one busy following orders from the grey haired woman. She sat and extended an open a hand as she barked at them to fetch her items. Hot coals glowed on a rock hearth. The grey haired woman set a pan over the coals and dumped a container of what appeared to be grey sand. The grey haired woman stirred the grey sand until a pungent smoke filled the air, smelling of burnt hair and dirt. Katrina gagged as the grey haired woman took the smoking pan off the hearth and set it down by her face.

The grey haired woman received another ceramic jar containing a bundle of long thin sticks, each stripped clean of any bark. She gave an order, and the women loosened the Mahigan net. They pulled Katrina's limbs from the nets confines before rolling her over to lay face down. The Mahigan net stayed wrapped around her waist and thighs and continued to do its job, draining strength from her muscles. Her body remained immobile from the waist down.

"What are you doing? Let me go, let me go!"

The grey haired woman ran a damp cloth back and forth accross her back. She fumbled in the pocket of her apron before pulling out a knife. Katrina stared in horror at the unsheathing of what looked thin like a dagger but short like a table knife. With a scream she yanked hard against the women holding her down. Their fingers dug into her bare arms and shoulders, pressing her harder against the floor. The grey haired woman took a stick from the container and sunk it into the pans mixture. The smoke rose as she stirred the mixture with the stick's tip. When she pulled it out, a black substance balled at the tip.

"Please, no!" Katrina said, her body trembling. She eyed the knife blade until it disappeared from view.

The blade pierced her skin. A bright pain sunk into the muscles of her right shoulder. Shrieking, she lurched against the hands holding her down. Tears flooded her eyes. The knife retreated, and a stick with the smelly substance replaced it. Fingers pressed down on her wound, trapping the stick in place.

Her screams brought no one to her aid. Over and over the grey haired woman pierced her back and inserted a goo coated stick. Each stab brought fresh pain, but the sticks inflicted something more. A half breath of rest came as her blood pooled around each new knife wound. Her next breath stalled as they thrust a fresh stick there. The sticks ignited an intense burning sensation. Every breath moved the sticks against her knife wounds. It flared the burning to a level so intense her thoughts scrambled. Nothing existed but pain and her need to escape it.

Restrained and panting, she watched the grey haired woman set the knife aside. She counted each breath. By her fourth exhale, she prayed this marked the end of her torture.

The grey haired woman griped one of the sticks embedded in her back. The stick snapped. Katrina's body convulsed. A new pain waved through her and she whimpered. The clipped portion of the stick fell away. The grey haired woman shoved the severed end deeper into Katrina's back. Her breath came in small pants and the room spun. Another stick snapped. Gasping for breath, she closed her eyes to the blurring room. Her stomach heaved as the motion increased. Everything came to an abrupt halt as she tipped into swift darkness.

The angry shouts of her mother woke her. She opened her eyes and closed them. They hurt, and her mouth tasted dry. Blinking hard, she squinted against the sting in her eyes and tried to see. She wanted to sleep more. Asleep she escaped this pain.

Shrill words melted to devastated sobs when she met her mother's gaze. Falling to her knees, her mother smoothed hair back from her face and wept.

"What kind of depravity, who did this? What did they do? How did this happen?"

Katrina said nothing as her mother cried. The warm daylight of mid afternoon filled the room. She lay facedown on a cot. Tight bandages bound her torso. A dull burning ache emanated from the wounds riddling her back.

Lord Dacamera entered the grey haired woman's home. He attempted to collect her mother in his arms. Enraged, her mother flung her arms about and shoved him away.

"How could you let this happen?"

He held his hands up in surrender and stepped back. "You caused this."

With a nasal sequel her mother launched herself at him. She swiped at him with awkward aim. Lord Dacamera blocked the attack, catching her arms and holding on. He flipped her around, and they both faced her. Leaning over her mother's shoulder he looked at her as he spoke into her mother's ear.

"If she dies, it's your doing."

Her mother's knees buckled and he let her go to collapse on the floor. Lord Dacamera gazed at her with pity. The worthless man pitied her. Anger woke her up. Her heartbeat hitched and pain increased as her body tensed. He walked to the door. Good, he needed to leave. She hated him. Lord Dacamera, she hated him and every other Skrieni here. He shoved the door open. It flew wide, banging against the house exterior. He disappeared as the door slammed shut.

Skrieni women carried Katrina back to Lord Dacamera's house. She lay curled on the mattress in the closet. Holding her body still, she controlled each breath to avoid more pain.

Her mother tucked a blanket around her and sat at the edge of the mattress.

"What happened?" her mother asked. Her voice timid with grief.

Katrina moved only her eyes to peer at her mother, and said nothing.

"Tell me," her mother said. "Please."

Ready for a blast of pain, Katrina's words came slow and quiet through shallow breaths. "Why are we here?"

"Did they come in here? Take you by force?"

"No," Katrina said. "I had to go. You'll die."

She should have answered the question with another question. Her mother looked weary. Weariness might weaken her mother's talent at dodging questions.

Katrina had to muster strength and use this opportunity. Grimacing, she shut her eyes. Forming even a basic question took effort. It was too hard. Too hard to breath, or hold still, or blink her eyes. This must be what dying felt like. Would she pass without knowing why any of this happened?

Her mother brought food. Tears flowed unchecked when her mother pulled her into a sitting position to eat. She sat limp, to drained to eat or brush away tears. Stunned silent by the deep burning in her back.

Her mother hid behind a face of indifference. A silly tactic to try on her daughter. Katrina recognized the panic behind her mother's fluttering staccato blinks and sharp set jaw.

Every bite of food came back up. The wrenching of her guts hurt more than sitting up. She refused her next meal after water proved too challenging to keep down.

Pain migrated from her back to her joints. A fever set in the next day. It proved to be her mother's breaking point. Katrina had no memory of her mother shedding real tears. Sometime during the night her mother stopped pacing, fell to her knees, and openly wept.

Katrina idly wondered which of them would die first? The Army was overdue. As her fever grew she sensed deaths approach. That distant event she never spared a moment on, now loomed close. Part of her, overwhelmed by the scorching waves of pain, begged to be deaths willing recipient. She stared with unfocused eyes at the storage room contents.

A conversation between her mother and Lord Dacamera began. Their voices too close to be ignored.

"She needs a healer, someone to treat the damage," her mother said.

"There's no one," Lord Dacamera said.

"Your village must have at least one healer."

"There's several here, but the apothecaries won't undo what they've done."

"They carved her back to shreds. Slain animals are treated with less cruelty. She has a fever, an infection."

"I'll ask if they can give her something for the pain."

Footsteps drifted in and out of the hallway. Doors opened and shut. The storage room door opened. Katrina squinted her eyes open. The audacious brown haired boy stood in the doorway. Tall and lean, he crossed long limbs over a narrow chest as he surveyed her.

A small face with a mop of raven dark hair poked around his thigh, a little boy. He looked the same age as Owl. He crept around the brown haired boy and bent down to stare at her on the mattress.

"Don't be rude, Aaron," the brown haired boy said. "I'm sure our new Dark Reminder isn't in the mood for company."

"Who?" She asked, her voice hoarse and cracked. She swallowed and tried to clear her throat.

"This is Aaron, he's a Dark Reminder too," said the brown haired boy.

Aaron, glared up in annoyance and shoved him. The older boy barely budged.

"Why the, stupid title," she said.

The brown haired boy's smirk became a smile as he nodded in concession to the boy. "Yes. I'm a Dark Reminder too."

"Your name?" she asked.

The brown haired boy looked down at Aaron and his eyes softened and he ruffled his hair.

"Cyphias, but Aaron here calls me Cye."

"Cyphias," she said.

"Just call me Cye," he said, and sat down on the floor beside her bed.

Aaron shadowed Cye, nestling in as close as he could to him. He reminded her so much of Owl.

Her heart ached as she tried to shut out the mental image of Owl laughing. A lump grew in her throat as she thought of home. Owl, Sol, Valgu, Massie, she missed them all. In her weakened state tears came quicker. Holding them back took all her concentration. Succumbing to crying caused only more pain.

"I have a salve to put on your back," Cye said, holding up a small pot. "This should help numb the pain. May I?"

Starting the slow roll from her side onto her stomach, she answered through clenched teeth, "Yes."

Cye cut the bindings of her dressing. Using care he removed her bandages with gentle hands. Opening the salve pot, he began the slow process of dabbing the contents around each wound on her back.

"Dark Reminder, why are we called that?" she asked.

"Because names have power," Cye said.

Cye added more salve to her back as Katrina considered his answer.

"This," she said and sucked in her breath. Cringing she paused and exhaled slow. "Did they do this to you too?"

"Of course."

"Why?"

"Because, there's really no other way for us to be human."

"I'm not human."

"They think this works, and they decide what's best for us." There was a long pause before he said, "I think they want us to be as inconsequential as them."

"I want to go home," she said.

"You don't like my Lord's hospitality?" Cye said in a gentle mock.

"No."

With a hushed laugh Cye dabbed salve to the wounds on her mid back. "Aaron and I live on the village edge. Aaron with his mother, Miandes."

"And you?"

"Me? Nobody."

"No," she said.

"It's true," he said,

"Hmm-mm," she said.

Cye grinned and shrugged. "Maybe. How old do you think I am?"

She sucked in her breath and braced against a shockwave of pain. Relaxing, she wondered what the most unoffensive answer might be. "Fifteen?"

Unsurprised, Cye said, "I'm older than Lord Dacamera."

"What?" She reflexively raised her head to gape at Cye. The gesture released a jolt of pain up her back. Whimpering, she dropped her head to the mattress sucking air in and out fast.

"I've long surpassed that age of living in my father's house."

Relaxing back to the mattress she studied his face. His claim baffled her. There might be wrinkles at the corner of his eyes, but youth overrode any trace of the age he claimed.

"No one knows why I'm stuck this way. I've been no more than fifteen for over twenty years."

"Why stay?"

"Why not?"

"Because," she scrunched her face in pain, exasperated that he even questioned the obvious.

"I know," he said reassuring. "They took my wings, same as you."

Why did he have to say it. She fought against another swell of tears. She glanced at Aaron and her eyes opened wide in horror.

"Will they?"

Cye lowered his voice. "He's a boy. It'll be several years before that."

"Why stay?"

"It's our home."

"That's stupid," she said and fought the urge to shake her head.

"Don't get pretentious," Cye said. "You can't assume your way of life is better than everyone else's."

"It is better. You'd be an advisor," she said.

"I'm already an advisor," Cye said.

"A guide," she said.

"A Dark Reminder," Cye said.

"Respected," she said.

Cye gave no indication he heard her as he said, "That's the last one."

He wiped the excess salve from his fingers into the jar. Placing the lid on it, he set it on a shelf.

"One of the first," he mumbled.

"Yes," she said.

"A guide. Is that your life's ambition? Too bad you're here where there's no such thing as a first or a last."

His words shocked her into silence.

She wanted to be a guide. She never heard anyone disregard a guide before. Was her aspiration silly? An unrealistic notion common to every young Airetti girl? Her father talked about her future as a guide like it was promised to her. His enthusiasm had made his vision her own. A belief so ingrained, she never imagined herself in any other occupation. At sixteen she could begin studies at a University. Afterward she would most likely apprentice under a Regina in another Madar provincial court. At some point her father would announce her rally, and the winner would be her consort. That was the plan.

"What's wrong with it?"

"Ah, little guide, you are such a sweet thing," he said. "I shouldn't be so hard on you. Your struggle, it reminds me of my own. I want to help you."

He sat facing the door with his back to her. She glared at him, as her confusion simmered to resentment.

He sighed and glanced over his shoulder at her. "When I laid like this, I realized what God's real interest in me was."

Her resentment vanished as she considered the way Cye had suffered too. His taunts were his warning to her. A clumsy attempt to prepare her for a similar loss. Her mind whirled with a repeating chant of "No." She refused to think about such blaspheme. She didn't need his warnings. If she lived through this, she would blame those rightfully responsible.

Aaron tucked his little body against Cye in a comforting gesture. Cye pet Aaron's hair and then placed an arm around him.

"Do you think you could eat anything?" Cye asked. "We can go get some soup. How about some water?"

"No."

"You can kick us out when you're tired. Aaron and I won't go far. Lord Dacamera wants us to help watch over you. To try and help you with the pain."

They had helped her. The salve eased her discomfort. The burning pain had dulled. Closing her eyes, she willed her headache to dull too. A clear image of her mother filled her mind. With lifted skirts and debris marred hair, her mother ran. She hurried through dense forest from an opponent impossible to outrun.

Katrina blinked her eyes open and looked at Cye's back. Cye and Aaron sat relaxed on the floor leaning against the side of her bed.

"The Army," she said.

Cye glanced over his shoulder at her. He knew something. Cye stood, stepped to the door, and leaned out just enough to see down the hallway. He returned and sat back down.

He spoke in a low voice, "Tomorrow, or the day after at the latest. Another village sent us a message this morning."

"They're here?"

"Yes. Some of our village left right away, but too many have stayed. The message didn't convince everyone that there's danger. They have too much faith in their methods of hiding."

"You should go," she said.

Cye nodded in agreement. "I know. I know what's going to happen. I've seen what will happen."

Katrina's eyes widened as she realized what he meant. "A vision." He had an Airetti's guided vision about the Army's arrival.

"Twice, that's how I know for sure it's going to happen." Cye angled his body, leaned closer, and held her gaze. "They can take our wings little guide, but there's nothing they can do to prevent the visions."

"Why don't you run?"

Cye made a small laugh. "Why? Me and Aaron aren't in any danger. We're one of your sacred Airetti, remember? The worst your Army will do is protect and take us home with them. Drag us off to live on some plateau in the south."

Narrowing her eyes at his chide, she relaxed and enjoyed his humor. "You'll like it," she said.

"I might." His eyes smiled past the restrained grin on his lips. "There's worse   places   we   could   end   up."

3

Life Will Never Be Normal

Katrina fell asleep with Cye and Aaron sitting watchful at her bedside. She was roused later by her mother's pleading. Katrina tried to wake and shake off her mother's insistent prodding. She opened her eyes for a brief moment. Mortal fear marred the beauty of her mother's features. Katrina lay helpless. Sleep overpowered her, tugging her back into mired restlessness. Conversations went on around her with no way of telling if they were part of her dreams or real.

"What are we to do?" Her mother said.

"I've answered that question, several times now," Cye said. "Pack her up and go. She needs a real healer or she's going to die."

"That's impossible, she's in no state for travel," her mother said. "She must be treated here."

"He's right," Lord Dacamera said.

"I am. I know this fever," Cye said. "She's not going to make it through the night."

Their words faded into a quiet chatter as the heavy beat of drums sounded.

With every drum beat light flashed over the Skrieni village. A thick smoke danced and swirled as a chant in an unknown language began. Strange music tore into the village. Buildings collapsed and fell to the forest floor below. The drums rhythm clashed with the stilted conversation.

"I can pay the wine trader to take you both in his wagon," Lord Dacamera said. "His first stop is Lavieth."

"That's a six hour journey," her mother said.

"What better place to seek refuge and a healer, than your father's house," Lord Dacamera said.

"There really is no other option," her mother said.

"No," Lord Dacamera said. "Not unless you return to Mozgas."

Hands grabbed hold of Katrina's arms and legs and lifted her. A jolt of pain roused her. She whimpered and shifted awkwardly against the device carrying her. The stale smell of Lord Dacamera's house disappeared. A gust of cold air announced her exit outside. Despite the chill, sleep claimed her again.

More drumming, but instead of seeing the Skrieni village, she saw the walls and ceiling of the Mozgas tunnels. Dim light cast narrow moving shadows. They clung and climbed the walls around her before taking on dark solid forms. The drumming emanated from the forms as they pounded and tore at the walls. Large stone bricks pulled away and shattered in clouds of dust. Delicate carved reliefs appeared on the tunnel walls.

Her whole body dropped as her stomach fluttered. The plummeting sensation of descent washed her in familiar comfort. She fought to open her eyes, eager to take in the sight of Iron Pine limbs passing her on all sides.

Sleep stayed back for a small moment. Her eyes closed as the odd drumming returned.

She stood alone on a beach watching the surf.

The drum sounded again and she stood alone in a strange forest.

More drum pounding. She stood alone in an ancient arena beside a massive Gryphon statue.

Confused by this strange dream and drumming, she began walking. Each slow pound of the drum she found herself in one of three different places. The first, a beach, with dark water and a grey sky. A storm edged closer to the shore as wind pressed painfully against her. The second, a forest, with trees expanding wide overhead as sunlight winked through leaves that spanned two lengths of her hand. The third, an arena, with walls made of dim glass and stairs constructed in a grey stone with the most vivid veins of blue running through it.

The beach, something watched her, but she stood alone. The drum beat.

The forest, something hidden in the trees was hunting her. The drum beat.

The arena, the urge to run flooded her senses but she had no idea why.

The drum beat continued on, cycling her through beach, forest, arena.

A storm broke out over the ocean. The drum beat.

The forest canopy rustled overhead as something moved in the corner of her vision. The drum beat.

A ghost like image appeared on the nearby wall of the arena. The drum beat.

She turned away from the storm and ran up the beach away from the surf. The higher dunes loomed far away from the narrow sandbar beneath her. The route ahead rinsed away with each pounding wave. The drum beat.

The forest grew hot and the bark on the tree beside her moved. A growling low hiss sent a chill through her. The drum beat.

She approached the dim figure in the nearby wall, and recognized Sol. Over and over he struck the wall that separated them. She ran to him, afraid he was trapped, then realized his banging was to get her attention. The drum beat again.

Her feet were underwater, the sand bar ahead gone. Lightning flared accross the sky above her. The drum beat.

Tree bark sheared away and flung itself to the ground. It coast in a fluid sliding motion in her direction. The drum beat.

Sol yelled inaudible words through the translucent wall. He splayed his hands against the rock, and she lifted her hands to the wall, mirroring the gesture. Sol shout, and his muffled words came through. "Katrina, come home."

Her whole body lurched. The pressure of landing flat on her back sent a searing sharp pain through her body. Her eyes flew open as she cried out. Her mother gripped her hand and helped roll her onto her side as she spoke in a soothing voice.

"I know, I know. We're going to find a healer."

Her mother was speaking, but her words were drowned out by the clattering noise from the crates of cargo being stacked about them. She and her mother were in the back of a large wagon.

"The driver's doing his best. I know this ride must be cruel."

"The drumming," Katrina mumbled.

"What?"

"I can still hear it," Katrina said.

"Hear what?"

"Drumming, won't stop. Sol's trapped."

Her mother lay a cool cloth against her forehead and then another against her neck.

"Don't fade on me," her mother said. "Where's Sol trapped?"

A headache pulsed from the base of her neck to the front of her skull. The wounds on her back throbbed and burned so hot she expected her clothes to catch fire. Her damp garments tortured her. Pressing heavy where they clung, or chaffing her skin enough to form cutting abrasions where they moved. Sleep pulled hard again, but she fought to stay awake this time it took less effort. Shifting, she rolled to lay facedown. The position lessening the pain from the wagon's jarring, but despite her relaxed posture, muscles in her arms and legs twitched with cramps.

Her mouth was so dry her lips stuck to her teeth. Her mind took up a new cry for water. It joined the never ending plea to make the pain stop. The demands refused to let her think about anything else besides how she could answer them. She debated taking a drink, and weighed relief against the pain of heaving it back up.

"Katrina, are you still awake?"

"Yes," she said.

"Please, tell me something, anything. Just talk to me."

Unwavering love and devotion should have made her obey. Her mother wanted talk. Talking used to be easy. An everyday activity she thought nothing about. Now words took effort. Talking meant pain.

She let the racket of the wagon fill the silence. Her disobedience causing her no feelings of guilt or remorse. Emptiness existed where her love and devotion for her mother once reigned. If she searched for more she found numb distrust and a current of scorn.

Her mother closed her eyes in tired frustration. A tear edged out from beneath her lashes.

Contempt flared in Katrina. Her mother had no right to cry. She did this, she brought them here. How dare she tell her to talk. She needed to talk. She could talk just fine, and explain all the things she refused to discuss.

"We're going to Lavieth," her mother said with forced levity. "We'll see your grandparents, Lord and Lady Larksbur. It's been too long. I'm sure they'll be thrilled to see us. What do you think, are you excited to see them?"

Katrina tried concentrating on her mother's chatter. Excited to see her grandparents? Pain cut off the mental pictures of extended family. No, they only mattered if they could stop the pain.

Her mother shifted a blanket around her shoulders. "Are you thirsty? You must be thirsty, you haven't had a drink in hours."

Her mother rifled around and brought over a jug and a cup. The wagon's jostling splashed water over her hands as she filled the cup. Katrina turned her head away as her mother leaned forward offering the cup.

"Please, don't do that. You need to drink this."

Katrina's words came slow, each one cracked and quiet. "Why did you poison father?"

Wagon noise muffled her words.

"What?" her mother asked leaning over in earnest to hear.

Katrina swallowed, and took a deep breath. This time she enunciated each word, pausing between them, and speaking louder. "Why did you poison father?"

Her mother sucked in a breath. She sat back fast and her gaze darted away. Looking down at the cup of water, she raised it and drank it down. Drying the inside of the cup with an edge of blanket, she set it aside. Her mother stared daggers in a long glance then huddled into the opposite corner of the wagon.

Katrina had learned a lot of new and unusual things in the short time since her mother's treachery. The most useful discovery was her mother's reaction to certain questions. Direct questions about her father's poisoning compelled her mother to do one of two things: stop all conversation, or flee the room. An almost mute on command response, which so far remained consistent. If she tired of her mother's harassment, the question worked every time.

It would be wonderful if her mother shocked her, and actually answered her question. That was a conversation worth holding focus for. Staying awake to hear anything else wasted her strength. She released herself to the pull of sleep and closed her eyes. Her mind drifted as far from the tether of pain as she could. The drumming returned and she let the beat lure her away.

She stood alone in the last room she remembered being in at the Mozgas Palace. The floor where Regina Delany died showed no trace of blood. She turned to inspect where Lady Tellydia fell, and it too was free from any stains. The awful memories from that day surrounded her. For the first time her father had frightened her. Thinking of him now, she missed him.

Her surroundings vibrated. Astonished, she watched the phenomenon with rising hope. This shifting of surroundings indicated the entrance or exit of someone from neutral. What she saw now was no fever dream. She was in neutral.

"Katrina?" Her father said.

She turned around. The sight of her father made her heart jump. Relief coursed through her as she stared at him.

"Daddy," she cried, and stumbled as she tried walking to him.

"My Katrina," he said closing the gap between them in a few quick strides. He stooped down and gathered her in his arms. "My beautiful, blue eyed baby girl. Where have you been?"

She clung to him, terrified this would melt away. He touched her face and examined her. One hand smoothed across the middle of her back. The gentle touch felt like a knife being dragged across her skin. She yelped and fell away from him.

"What's this?"

She sat hunched on the floor breathing hard.

"Tell me, tell me what's happened."

Her muscles were contracting beyond her control and her whole body shook.

"Let me see your wings," he said, his voice straining to hide his concern. He knelt, grabbed her by the shoulders, and lifted her up. He held her at arms length. "Katrina, show me your wings."

Chin dimpling, her lips quivered as tears filled her eyes.

"I can't," she said. "They took them."

Her father brought her into a soft embrace, tucking her into his shoulder as he smoothed her hair.

"Shhh, it's all right. It's going to be all right. We'll fix this. I'll get every healer in Madar if I have to. We'll fix this. I promise. Tell me where you are, where did she take you?"

"Lord Dacamera's village. My fever's worse, so we're going to Lavieth."

"Fever?"

She nodded.

Her father's regal poise cracked into a stricken look. He paused and regained his composure.

"You're my daughter, and you're strong. I need you to be as strong as you can and fight this fever. I will find you. Promise me, you'll hold on and be strong for me."

Katrina nodded as tears dripped from her eyes. "I promise."

"You shouldn't be here sick. The stress is too much. "

Katrina nodded in quiet understanding, already feeling sleeps hold.

"You can wake up or sleep, but you must avoid coming here until you're better."

He held her gently about the shoulders and kissed the top of her head. She absorbed the familiar cedar and spice smell of him. She wanted to meld herself into his assuring touch. Her father was here. He would find her. Order would be restored. His presence somehow guaranteed her release from hurt and chaos.

"I love you," he said. "Keep your promise to me, and I'll see you soon."

Their surroundings vibrated and the form of her father slipped from her grasp. Rather than her normal peaceful exit from neutral, it came as a fast jolt. Her head bounced and struck the hard wagon bed. The wagon bounced her body once more, but this time she tilted her head back and avoided the second impact. She waited for more before nestling against the blanket and settling into the erratic rhythm of the road. Obeying her father, she went to sleep.

The sensation of cool water pressed to her mouth made her stir. It dripped down her chin while some of it wet her tongue. She sucked in, her parched mouth pulling in what moisture she could. Her eyes fluttered open to find her mother holding a wet cloth to her mouth. They were still in the wagon, but it had stopped. The noise of many people and horses could be heard outside the confines of the wagon.

"Katrina?" her mother asked.

She worked to focus on her mother's hazy form.

"Let me help you up, to take a drink."

Hands guided her and propped her up against the side of a crate. Ignoring her fear of retching, Katrina allowed her mother to place the cup to her lips. She drank small sips of water, welcoming the effect as it wet her throat.

"I sent a message to my father," her mother said. "Someone from the household should be out to collect us."

While her mother's voice projected confidence, the small shift in her shoulders shouted unease. Her mother took the cup, refilled it with water, and handed it back to her.

Katrina drank larger gulps of water, and waited to see if her stomach allowed it to remain.

A man made an inquiry to their wagon driver. Her mother sucked in a breath and smiled.

"Jerard." Her mother set the cup down and stooped in a crouch, working her way out of the wagon.

Katrina met her Uncle Jerard a few times. His blue eyes and brown hair matched her mother's. During the visits to Lavieth, Uncle Jerard took very little time becoming acquainted with his sisters children.

Squinting, she tried to see outside the wagon. She recognized the main gate of Lavieth Castle. Bisma's Lavieth province sat along the northern border of Madar. Her grandfather, Lord Jasper Larksbur controlled Lavieth and had raised his family here at the castle.

"The gate guards barred me from passing," her mother said.

Jerard sighed and her mother's voice grew in angry agitation.

"They insisted the daughter of their Lord would not be traveling in the company of a Skrieni tradesman."

"Father's banned entrance to all Skrieni."

"When?"

"A few days ago. He's showing good faith to his son-in-law, the Regent of Mozgas."

"Katrina needs a healer," her mother said.

"He's desperately looking for her, you too apparently. Wants you back."

"Is Master Dessie still at the Castle?" her mother asked.

"Yes," Jerard said.

"If we can't go in, then bring him out."

"Dessie knows nothing about treating the Veilede," Jerard said.

"She's ill, with a fever. He can treat that."

"He can't," Jerard said.

"Well, he's going to have to try," her mother said.

"No, Father doesn't want either one of you anywhere on the castle grounds. You need to go."

"He's barring me? Denying me help?"

"I'm sorry," Jerard said.

"He got me into this. What's he afraid of? Pavaldon? All he has to do is deny our presence."

Her mother looked stricken. She crossed her arms.

Jerard looked about before stepping closer to her mother. He placed a hand on her shoulder and lowered his voice.

"Father sent me out to give you this," he pulled out a small purse and a rolled parchment. He pried one of her hands free and forced them into it.

Her mother unrolled the parchment, read it, and gaped.

"His legacy," she said. "I'm his daughter, one of his children. What other legacy does he have?" She rolled the parchment up.

Jerard shook his head. "I can't explain his motives anymore than I can yours."

"Please Jerard, I'm desperate. I'm not exaggerating Katrina's sickness. She needs immediate help."

"Then you should turn around and take her home," Jerard said. "Go home, and beg for your husbands mercy."

"No," her mother said. The anger left her voice in a way to indicate it was something she already considered. Her voice floated with a soft but mournful sincerity. "It's too late. Even if he forgives me, I'll be put to death for the others."

"You can run to the coast, but Qurashi's in Benmar."

"I don't care. I'm trying to save her life."

There was a long silence before her Uncle spoke again.

"Pay the wagon driver and go to Benmar. Have Katrina treated by the port healer. Maybe you should find Qurashi."

"There's a port healer?"

"Two actually, but don't see the traveling one. He's worthless."

"Thank you," her mother said.

"Go," he said. "The longer you stay, the more people here might remember you."

Her mother nodded, tucked the letter and purse between her skirts, and walked off. Jerard stepped near the back of the wagon. Peeking in, he inspected her. His brow furrowed before he turned on his heel and walked back to the castle.

Katrina chewed at a crack in her lower lip. Slumping onto her stomach, she gazed out the back of the wagon at the castle. Her vision swam. The drumming sound returned. Her Uncle passed through the main gate. He was almost out of sight, when the walls to the gate exploded in a hailstorm of rock and debris. Jerking with surprise, Katrina blinked several times trying to refocus her eyes. Was that real or part of another fever dream?

"The castle," she said as her mother lay a cool cloth on the back of her neck.

"I know," her mother said. "I'm so sorry."

A massive boulder dropped from the sky. It hit a different section of castle wall. Another boulder fell beside it crumbling a long section. The drums pounded in her ears. The beat hit a crescendo with each boulder strike. Their tremor matched the frenzied rhythm.

"The boulders," She said.

Her mother looked up at the castle and then back to her. "What's that?"

"Hitting the castle."

Her mother glanced back for a moment. Using one hand she smoothed her hair back.

"I must have missed it. Try and rest."

The wagon lurched into motion. In a lumbering turn it moved onto the road. Katrina continued to stare at the castle as the drum beat on. More boulders pounded the castle. The fortification collapsed on itself. The teeth chattering hits felled the great towers. She lay mesmerized watching the castle turn to ruin. When it disappeared behind the cover of trees, she closed her eyes.

She stood on the wooden planks of Lord Dacamera's village. Another fever dream, but her surroundings were vivid. Morning sun sat on the horizon as she walked behind a Veilede soldier in full Mahigan form. His armored plates shined like polished onyx and the bony structure of his wings lay folded against his back. She hurried to match his stride as they entered a large gathering hall.

In the doorway she froze. Before her knelt Lord Dacamera with hands restrained and a battered face. Blood oozed from a cut above his left eye and a trail of bruises lead down to swollen lips and more cuts. Lord Dacamera's men knelt beside him.

"We're done here." Her father said.

She jerked around to see him standing tall and partially shifted into the armor plates of his Mahigan form.

A current of anger rose beneath his calm words. "I've been tolerant, generous even. I've allowed you this."

He gestured to the surroundings and said, "I've given you and your misfits leave to carry on pretending you're something you're not. You've mistaken my kindness as weakness."

One of the men kneeling sobbed.

"It's possible," her father said, "that I would have looked past you taking my unhappy and jealous wife. It's possible."

In a blur of movement her father crossed the room and took hold of Lord Dacamera by the collar.

"But never one of my children. You took my daughter. You dared to touch my child. You hurt her and damaged what is sacred. Everyone in this stick village you call kingdom, will pay for what was done to her. You will die knowing what was here will be destroyed. I will break you and see this village fall away to ash."

"It was the apothecary," Lord Dacamera said. "I can fix it, don't do this. I'll make them fix her."

With the ease of snapping a twig, her father lifted Lord Dacamera's body and brought him down on his knee. A short pop and crack sounded as Lord Dacamera's back broke. Her father cast the limp body to the floor and stood over him. With shoulders drawn up tight, he balled each of his hands into fists before snatching the closest kneeling man.

One by one her father executed Lord Dacamera's men. Reality or a dream, she witnessed their death. She felt nothing. No shock, or fear, happiness or sorrow. With rapt attention she watched the brutal display, absorbing the methods her father used as he extracted life from the Skrieni men. Without flinching or shrinking away, she saw them die with fast snaps and crunching yelps. She envied the power and strength of her father. If she possessed his strength no one would have dared touch her.

When every Skrieni man lay dead, her father circled them, inspecting his work. She stepped in his path. If this were real, or some odd summoning in neutral, he would see her. His eyes looked through her before he brushed by her.

"The remaining males here have a choice," he said to his soldiers in the room. "Die or return with us to the plateau. Every apothecary returns with us, no exceptions." Her father stopped beside an officer Katrina recognized, Major Vygranth Luca.

Her father addressed Major Luca. "The rest I leave in your hands Vy. This village needs to be burned to the ground by nightfall."

"Yes My Regent," Major Luca said. "I'd like a brief moment with you, to report a unique situation."

"Go on."

"We found two of the first here. Boys, both of them."

Her father's eyebrows twisted. "Two male Airetti here?"

"I thought you'd want to know. It's such an odd circumstance knowing the few male Airetti counted in the last census? All of Madar has less than twenty, but we find two Airetti boys up here?"

"I believe the count was seventeen," her father said. "Did they maim them?"

"One, yes pretty bad. They didn't touch the other one, but he's barely weened."

"Two of the first here," her father said. "Made to live as orphans I suspect."

"The older one, yes. The younger one's with his mother."

Her father walked another circle around the dead on the floor. "The mother and both boys will be housed as guests in my household."

"Yes, My Regent." Major Luca said.

Her father scanned the faces of the other soldiers in the room and said, "Remind everyone about the apothecaries. We don't need any poison injuries holding us up."

"Yes, My Regent," Major Luca said. He rubbed a discolored area on the lower part of his forearm. "I'll ensure we take the right precautions. With their behavior so far, it'd be easier if we just killed them."

Her father nodded, "If they're too much trouble, you may. For Princess Katrina's sake, I prefer them as prisoners."

"We'll handle them for travel," Major Luca said. His expression became a concerned question as he waited for her father's reply. "I'll personally see they make the journey back."

"Very Good," her father said. He walked towards her and she expected his eyes to meet hers, but again they passed over her. His footsteps slowed and life's normal pace stalled. Everything around them dragged in long drawn out movements. With each of her father's steps, the drum beat sounded. He shifted into his full Mahigan form. Black armored plates rose over his skin. They formed over his clothes, wrapping around his torso, and neck. One wide scale eclipsed his face as a long weapon extended from his arm.

The drum beat sounded and a Mahigan screamed.

Covering her ears, she doubled over from the painful sound. The floor at her feet moved. The coarse wood planks of the Skrieni village swirled. It churned, mixed, and flowed beneath her. It settled into the intricate wooden parquet floors of the Mozgas Palace. She took in the rich sight of her home. Hands gripped her from behind. Her mother held her shoulders.

"Do it!" Her mother shouted.

Katrina stared up at the Mahigan form of her father. She extended her arms and screamed, "No!"

The drum beat and her father lifted his weapon.

"No! Mother, no! No!"

A shockwave of pain shot up her back. Something pressed there, the intense pressure made her gasp for breath.

"Katrina," her mother pleaded. "Katrina wake up, wake up. I'm right here. Wake up, it's only a dream."

The drum beat in a frenzy or maybe she was hearing her own heart beat. Thrashing, she tried to pull away from the force on her back. When she regained herself she lay cradled against her mother.

"It's just a dream, everything's fine," her mother said and ran a damp cloth accross her forehead and then down the sides of her neck.

"Take deep breaths, good, good. There see, it's fine. Everything's going to be all right. We're close, we're almost there."

Pain held her attention and refused to let her sleep. It strangled her awareness, scattering her concentration. She knew when they took her from the wagon. All the touching, pulling, and movement. She screamed in protest, but her voice sounded in a weak cry.

"This won't take long Katrina," said a man's voice. He called to her, over and over, ordering her to look at him. "I need you to open your eyes and follow my instructions."

She panted each breath, but managed to force her eyes open. The face of a young man blurred in her vision. His features held a Delphi cast. A high forehead, dark amber eyes, and a tight ponytail of long dark hair.

"I need you to drink this," he held a cup to her lips. "This will help fight the infection."

Hands raised her up and the Delphi man held her head steady as she sipped the medicine down. Honey sweetened its strong herbal flavor. When she finished, hands guided her onto her stomach. Her muscles clenched and shook, but now they pressed against the soft give of a mattress. Steam emanated from an oversized ceramic tea pot. It's spout spread a warming floral vapor across her face.

"This will take care of the pain and you're going to fall into a deep sleep."

He promised to take away the pain. No more pain, no more fever dreams. The strength of her gratitude overwhelmed her. Tears filled her eyes. Then in one massive wave the pain stopped. Sleep rushed up, set her pain adrift, and yanked her beneath its swell. She slipped down pulled by a current of pain free oblivion.

Repeated lurches moved Katrina's whole body in a jarring sway. The air was thick with a heavy smell of mold and damp. For a moment she wondered who took the shelves out of Lord Dacamera's storage room and packed everything in tight piles to the ceiling. Why would anyone take the shelves out? She remembered the sound Lord Dacamera's back made before her father killed him. Her father, where was he? And the Army? The wagon with its awful clambering? She remembered her Uncle and Lavieth Castle. She had lay in the wagon, until the healer helped her. She could picture him and his Delphi features. The healing house and how it smelled of herbs.

She sat up. Stabbing pain riddled her back. With a deep wince she held her breath and waited for the pain to deaden. Exhaling, she clutched at her blankets hoping the muffled ache in her head would clear. She worked her body out from underneath blankets and inspected her surroundings more. Goods were stacked floor to ceiling. They formed walls and left a narrow floor path to a stairwell. She had to be in the belly of a ship.

A row of round glass housings hung from the ceiling lighting the floor path. Each glowed with light from small binti light stones. A binti light gave off a constant shine and made it the most valuable stone in the world. The ones overhead were small and round with no carvings. The absence of decoration seemed odd. The Delphi who harvested the special florescent rock took great pride in the carving and crafting of each binti light. The ones overhead were raw. A sad and sterile comparison to the intricate binti lights in the Mozgas Palace.

The throbbing in her head picked up as the floor dropped and she stumbled sideways into a stack of crates. Boots pounded across the deck overhead. She clung to the wall of crates and regained her footing. With small steps she reached the stairwell and grabbed hold of the railing. She hitched her skirt and ascended what was more a ladder than stairs. Gripping the door latch, she fumbled with the lever until the whole door jerked free of her hand. Daylight blinded her and a gust of fresh air threw her against the railing.

"Katrina?" Her mother said.

She squinted until her eyes adjusted and her mother's image became clear. Her beautiful mother, with a balanced face, slender neck, and clear blue eyes. Her dark brown hair glistened with sunlight.

"I was about to come check on you," her mother said. "Here hold onto me."

Taking hold of her shoulders, her mother guided her on to the ships deck. In numb silence Katrina watched as her mother gave orders.

"You," she said pointing at the nearest sailor. "Secure the door." She pointed another finger at the man beside him. "Fetch some food and drink, keep it simple, nothing heavy."

Each man gave a quick, "Yes, Ma'am." Before doing as they were told.

Katrina's focus trained on the horizon. Her eyes searched, strained for a glimpse of an iron pine shoreline. In every direction the ocean met a white overcast sky.

Her mother ran a hand through errant strands of Katrina's hair and felt her cheeks with the palm of her hand.

"Your fever broke. I'm so happy to see you up, but how you managed those stairs I'll never know. You need more rest."

Katrina wanted to run. If she could shift she would fly. Grief gutted her. Each of her limbs felt heavy and numb. She would collapse without her mother propping her up. Gazing at deep green water, she wished she could swim. She was trapped in a cage disguised as a ship. Her mother won. Each of her attempts to run home were ruined. Somehow her mother managed to best every obstacle. Outrunning her father and an entire Mahigan Army. The defeat exhausted her. It drained away her fight. She considered her one remaining choice. Live and take the loss with dignity, like Sol, or throw herself overboard and die.

Her voice came rasped and vacant, "Where are we?"

"Plenty of time to talk about it later," her mother said. She guided Katrina over to the closest side rail. Katrina clutched it, relieving her mother from the burden of holding her up.

"You need to eat and drink something," her mother said. "Then you must rest. It's the only way you'll recover."

Light reflected off the countless waves. Dancing dots of white on an endless expanse of dark water. She was buoyed above it, the grace of the ships hull the only thing keeping her safe from the water below. How did sailors do this each day? All the ways they could get lost, or sunk, where cold water replaced air. She needed to accept the miracle the ship provided or the nightmare scenarios creeping at the edge of her mind would paralyze her.

A large splash produced a wave of water that hit the hull and crept up the side. It faded to a dusting of droplets as it reached her at the side rail. Water masked the identity of the creature responsible. Only a side or back of its smooth body was visible. More creatures appeared, their bodies rolled in arches as they breached the water. Each one too big to be a fish. Large fins broke the water in a rhythm. The creatures swam keeping pace with the ship. Curious, she leaned over the rail and tried to get a better look.

Hello, a voice called in a wander to her.

Hello there, wandered another voice.

Then a series of unfamiliar voices were wandering greetings to her.

A large animal jumped out of the water straight up in a spin to land in a large splash. The display was followed by another. She received another wave of chipper greetings, before the water erupted with a series of wild acrobatic leaps all around them.

Hello!

Katrina wandered back. *Hello.*

The ocean on all sides of the ship began to move with fins, faces, and squeaks. The sight of so many dolphins was new, but these were not dolphins. These were Delphi, the most common Veilede form. To feel the presence of this many wanderers reminded her of home. She closed her eyes, enjoying the familiar wanderer vibrations resonating around her. The Delphi, who shifted into aquatic animals, occupied the mostly ocean Delphi Province. An expansive territory that surpassed in size all of Madar's land provinces combined.

Katrina opened her eyes. She extended a hand and waved to them.

Her mother stepped beside her, eyes wide with fear. She seized Katrina's shoulders, causing a jolt of pain to radiate up her spine. Katrina gasped and her knees weakened. She would have fallen except she was pinned between her mother and the side rail.

"Mother," she said, her voice a thin cry.

Her mother's frightened eyes met hers. The intense blue inspected Katrina. Her mother was worried. Fascinating, when had she ever seen her mother like this? Now and then during her fever, but sorrow had dominated her features. This brand of worry was new.

"What did you say to them?" Her mother said.

"What?"

"Don't pretend with me," her mother said.

"I said hello." She shrunk from her mother. "Please, that hurts."

Her mother loosened her grip, but pulled her from the railing, steering her back to the stairwell.

"Lena," a deep male voice called from behind them.

Her mother stopped and looked over her shoulder at the man. She cleared her throat, but her answer came out strained.

"They saw her Devon. I didn't think. It's my fault. She was up on deck and wandering to them before I realized."

Devon approached with relaxed confidence. He stood before them with sweat glistening on his bald head. Freckled skin dominated every space vacant of his indigo ringed tattoos. His pants billowed like the sails overhead. They contrasted with the short fitted vest he wore laced over a long tunic shirt. Years of working outdoors had cemented deep wrinkles around his eyes and mouth. She caught her breath as she realized what looped through a series of holes in his ears. Large silver snake earrings, the duo fit to the top of each ear. They sat poised for a strike, and were adorned in garish detail, their jeweled eyes winked above gapping mouths of fangs.

"Everything's fine," Devon said, "let her take in some fresh air."

"But we're surrounded," her mother said. "Look, they're everywhere."

Devon glanced over the side and shrugged.

"Sure, they always are," he said narrowing his eyes in amusement. "A ship can't leave the way we've come without em'."

"They've seen Katrina." Her mother pushed her forward to emphasize her point. "She spoke to them."

"And?"

Devon stared in confusion at her mother's panic. Katrina understood it, but recognized how Devon, a human, would be oblivious. While humans knew the common phrase, "the last" referenced the Delphi, they failed to know full meaning behind it. All the Veilede forms had nicknames. Most of these were tied to when God blessed their kind with their shifting ability. The book known as The Covenant of the Blessed describes how God blessed the Delphi as, "the last who can see all." The Delphi were the last to receive their form, but more they could recognize the form of any unshifted Veilede on sight.

Perhaps twenty or thirty Delphi had just greeted her. She knew all of them identified her as Veilede, and that her form was Airetti.

"They're Veilede," her mother said, her voice trembling in exasperation at Devon's nonchalance. "Pavaldon's allies."

Devon shook his head, stepped closer and laid a comforting hand on her mother's shoulder. Katrina looked back at her mother and saw tears welling in her eyes.

"My dear, calm yourself. I've never seen you like this before."

"After everything," her mother said. "All the planning and the setbacks. How could we've overlooked something so obvious?"

"We didn't," Devon said.

"We have no options out here. We're completely boxed in."

"There's nothing to be afraid of," Devon said. "The Delphi know me. They know who's aboard. We'd have never left the sound if they cared about Pavaldon's interests."

"There's no way for us to know that."

"Have some faith in me, eh?"

"Swear to me then. Swear we're not risking our lives out here."

"I swear it. Just watch, Katrina can go and mind chit chat with them all she likes. It's not going to change our course."

Katrina watched the figures swimming a little further off. She swayed and staggered against the steady rise and fall of the large ship beneath her. Her mother had let go of her. Devon tucked her mother in his embrace. He soothed her with quiet words and comforting hands. Judging by her mother's frown, he failed to convince her of their safety.

A new spark of hope flared in Katrina. Devon might be right about the Delphi. However, her mother had lived over a decade as a Regents wife. She knew who her father's allies were. Of course her father had Delphi allies, she remembered them. Now she just needed to find them.

The man her mother ordered to get food appeared with a the requested food and water. Her mother slid away from Devon. She ordered the hold door open, and Katrina was herded back to the bunk below.

Katrina sat on her bunk drinking water, as she eyed the soup and bread on the tray beside her. A plain broth and roll of dark bread. Her hunger transformed them into a marvelous feast. Prolonging her hunger took effort, but she elected to sip the water first.

Her mother paced the narrow passage. With one arm held accross her middle, she tugged at her lower lip.

"You're not to wander with any Delphi," her mother said.

Katrina inspected the water remaining in her cup. Her mother stepped close to where she sat and looked down.

"Did you hear me? Do you understand? No wandering, with any Delphi."

Katrina made herself look at her before nodding. A few more lies like that and she might get good at them. Her mother sighed in irritation and resumed her pacing. Or not. Why did she bother? Her mother already knew, she predicted the first thing she would try. Did it matter?

Her mother could lock her in this hold for the rest of the journey, but she would never know who Katrina wandered with. The only things hindering her now were headache and fatigue. She needed her focus and strength back.

"You'll stay here the rest of the voyage. Go up those steps and a crew member appointed door guard will greet you."

Katrina drained the remaining water in her glass. She snatched the bread from the tray and bit into it. The crust was tough and the flavor dull. She barely chewed her first bite before she took another.

"Understand?" Her mother asked.

Katrina spoke with a full mouth of bread. "Can I have more water please?"

For the time being she had to obey her mother. When her strength returned, a guarded door would be a minor inconvenience. She would wander with every Delphi she could find. She would deprive herself of sleep and enter neutral every night until she found her father. Her mother glared at her as she took the glass. Katrina lifted the bowl of broth. Chicken flavored water filled her mouth. She gulped it before tasting it, and set the bowl down empty.

"May I have more?" She asked.

Days passed and Katrina spent the majority of her time in the ships hold asleep. When she did wake her mind raced with over alert and hyper thoughts. An excess of energy trapped inside a body plagued by fatigue. One more miserable experience to add to the growing collection of misery crowding her thoughts. She tried to decipher them. To find an explanation or some greater meaning.

Evil runs the world.

That made sense. It made a pattern. Fulfilled a logical motivation. It had to be true, because her God was good. The lessons supporting her beliefs never contradicted this.

Evil ruled here.

Her body would be whole in a world run by good. She would be where she belonged, home with her family. Her father would be fine and her mother content. Regina Delany and Lady Tellydia would be alive.

Evil continued to have its way with her unchecked. It sat beside her, chuckling with pleasure at the twisted state of her life. She needed her life back.

The door opened. A wave of cold guilt jolted her mind silent. Her mother descended the stairs feet first. Her mother knew. Her mother knew her thoughts, and she was coming to berate her for them. Her mother lingered at the stairs caught up in a conversation with the guard above. Katrina's paranoid tension faded.

Why the shock of guilt? Who had betrayed who anyway? The unconditional ties of love to her mother loosened a little more each day. They frayed and gave way to her growing resentment. The more she acknowledged this truth, the more her stomach roiled with misery. Someone needed to explain how this was part of a good God's plan.

Pha had told her, "God takes an active interest in the daily life of his creations."

If Pha was right, then where was God now? She shut her eyes and pleaded a silent prayer.

God please help me!

An immediate response came.

"Wait."

Katrina's eyes flew open, as she inhaled a sharp breath. A shocking sensation stood up the hair on her neck and arms. She looked around for the person who had spoken aloud, in a wander, or both. Her mother's conversation carried on uninterrupted.

"Wait for what?" she whispered.

No other response came. What was she to do with that answer?

The door to the staircase clattered shut. She heard her mother's footsteps down the narrow aisle to her.

Did God really answer her? With a single word. Had it really happened? The questions bread doubt. Logic made dismissing the exchange easy. How did anyone follow a plan for their life without knowing the plan? If God refused to share his plans, then maybe her mother's ambivalence about God had merit. The more she considered the exchange, the more confusing it became. Her instincts were less certain the more she tried to reason what occurred. She pressed the situation against her logic, until the answer, "Wait," became, "No, and I don't care."

Her mother stopped beside the bed with her arms crossed and a relaxed smile. She sat down beside Katrina and rifled through a bag at the edge of the bed. Her mother removed a hairbrush, and tugged the fastener to Katrina's braid free. Katrina's hair lifted off her back as her mother brushed it with slow even strokes. Katrina relaxed and closed her eyes, relieved by the benign activity. Her mind quieted and she felt the tug of sleep.

Her mother lay down and tucked herself in close beside her. Her mother wrapped her arms around Katrina and brushed fingers across her forehead. The touch reminded her of being small. Of a time when her mother liked to laugh. When her mother still reigned as the most perfect woman in her world.

"I don't want you to die," Katrina said.

"I know, love," her mother said. "Go to sleep."

"You're taking a bath, first thing," her mother said. "No exceptions, no tours or introductions before it. I've been craving a real bath and change of clothes for days."

She had come into the hold and spent over an hour rustling their few belongings into a bag, all while talking non stop. Her mother paused, then smiled as she took a deep breath.

"Aren't you excited, even just a little bit?"

Katrina would have shrugged, but substituted the gesture with a less painful tilting of her head.

Her mother's smile faded and she sighed. "Sulking really doesn't suit you." She motioned to the door. "Come on now, let's go up and get a look at our new home."

The bright clear sky stung her eyes as she navigated the last few steps from the stairs to deck. The sun sat at midmorning, but already the decking pressed heat through the soles of her shoes. A breeze played with the rigging overhead and chilled her sweat soiled dress.

The normal pace of activity slowed. The whole crew seemed intent on watching the ship coast into port. Her mother walked them to bridge. Devon acknowledged them with a nod. He stood alert, his expertise at work interpreting the ships activity. Here and there he gave an order to one of the two men beside him. Her mother took a seat on the stairs leading up to the bridge. With one arm her mother pulled Katrina to sit down beside her. They huddled there in the small staircase sanctuary that buffered the wind.

"This is the Island of Etrasa," her mother said.

The city surrounding the port they approached had no building over two stories tall. Their construction had a consistent look even though the stucco exteriors were painted in different bright pastels. In the distance, orchard hills and bluffs rolled and grew into an expansive wilderness that surrounded a pair of mountains. Each peak sat draped in green vegetation. The only exposed rock seemed to lay on the mountain summits or near the shoreline.

Her mother pointed, "Do you see the two mountain peaks there?"

Katrina nodded.

"The bigger one is Etta, and the other is Rasa. The people here believe they represent God separating one being into two. The one mountain of Etrasa became Etta and Rasa, the same way God pulled the first woman from the first man."

"When did you learn that?" Katrina said.

Her mother chuckled and sighed. "A long time ago. I desperately wanted to come here for school."

"You never told me that. You said a respectable Bisma royal attends school in the Bisma capitol."

"Right, because it's true. But I had my heart set on going to school here."

Katrina eyed the island with a dubious glare. "Why?"

"There's more opportunities for a Lady at the House of Etrasa. There's also a raw beauty here. Something the capitol of Bisma and all its opulence can't replicate."

"Mother," she said in rebuke.

"What?" Her mother said. "I like nature."

Katrina squinted at her ridiculous claim. "Viewed from afar."

Her mother laughed and looked back at the ever increasing island. "Lord Larksbur had other plans for me. I couldn't come here. You however, will have the very best of the human world."

The clear sky and lush mountain view were wasted on Katrina. Arriving in the dark of night would have suited her mood better. Going from ship to shore. No, this was terrible. They were just transferring her from one cage to another.

They waited through the ships long docking and unloading process before debarking. Devon walked with them to the pier where he assigned two crewmen as their escort.

"Don't throttle me later," Devon said as he pulled her mother into an intimate embrace. "The way they'll take you is the safest route this time of day."

"When will I see you next?"

"Dinner."

Katrina diverted her gaze from their goodbye and wandered away. The streets were made of glossy cobalt stones. Even worn and debris laden, the long spans of blue gave the modest town a rich look. Her slow pace clashed with the milling pace of the people around her. She stopped in the shade of a building. Pivoting back to the docks, she stepped back in surprise at the sight of a tall man. He kneeled down in front of her. Long black hair spilled over his shoulders and his smile reached his deep amber eyes. She recognized him as Delphi. He spoke in Madar's ancient dialect as he made a formal greeting.

"I bow before one of the first to be blessed by God, may the Airetti forever help us."

Katrina swallowed, unsure what to say. The traditional Veilede greeting for an Airetti had never been offered to her. She knew it, but adults used it on other adults. She never learned a proper reply.

"Take this," The Delphi man said as he held out his hand.

"Katrina?" Her mother called from accross the pier.

"You're being summoned," the Delphi man said. He smiled and took her hand, pressing a small figure into her palm. "I'm Linbodo. The crew of the Swift Sound is docked here. You should come and visit us."

"Katrina?" Her mother called. Her name echoed in more shouts from their two assigned crewmen.

Katrina stood torn between taking the risk of leaving with this stranger, and a fear of what her mother would do if she found her talking to him.

"Good day," Linbodo said. He stood and gave her a wink before disappearing into the crowd.

Katrina looked down at the figure in her hand, a carved dolphin. Even in daylight the white binti light stone glowed.

"Honestly Katrina," Her mother said.

Katrina closed her hand and let her arm fall to her side.

"One step off the ship and you run off."

"I was looking for a place to sit down," she said.

"No, no time for sitting," her mother said. "Come on."

The crewmen led them off the pier and into the city. The taller of the two crewmen hesitated at the entrance to a vast market stretch. He looked over his shoulder at Katrina.

"What's the hold up?" Her mother asked.

"Sorry Ma'am," he said. "It's just, you might not like what the young lady sees down this way."

"So I've been warned," her mother said. "Please proceed."

The crewmen nodded and brought them onto the right side of the thoroughfare. With so few people about, the wide stretch seemed excessive. An ill looking sailor passed by with a weaving trudge. A woman sat on a balcony dressed only in bright colored undergarments. Another woman rushed by with a basket of fruit and another basket stuffed with long loaves of bread.

The street broadened to accommodate long manicured medians. The two story statues on the medians helped her understand the crewman's hesitation earlier. Raised flowerbeds surrounded the towering statues of naked couples arranged in different intimate poses. She looked from the statues to her mother, who walked with her eyes fixed ahead trying to pass them as if they were ordinary.

Katrina diverted her eyes to the buildings. Those were usually safe. Her eyes widened. All the buildings had carved columns that featured more naked couples. The stucco of one building was painted with an elaborate scene of a naked man who kissed a woman's naked breasts. More naked women surrounded him, with one kissing his exposed penis. The shock of the prominent statues and building decor shifted into curiosity.

"Mother," Katrina said.

"This market," Lady Lena said quietly, "it's where men come to buy sex. I'm sorry you had to see it, but you are not too young to learn about these things. Soldiering is the oldest occupation for a man, as prostitution is for a woman. The demand for experts in both fields will always exist, but only one is considered honorable."

They passed the last statue. Even after the statues were out of sight, her mind replayed the images from the market. She wondered about their unusual facial expressions and the ways their bodies intertwined. The thoroughfare dead ended at a paved fountain surround. The shops around the fountain sold more austere items. Signs hung over doors advertising hats, custom garments, shoes, and specialty soap. The crewmen led them onto one of the single lane residential streets.

"This is it here Ma'am," the short crewman said. He gestured to a house with pale green stucco and white window shutters. The front door stood open. A tall man stood over a short woman in a dark green jacket and tailored pants. Her grey hair was pulled back. The style exposed the ringed tattoos stretching up her neck and ending at the edge of her jaw. She dismissed the taller man in front of her and settled steel colored eyes on them.

"My lady, I hope your journey was pleasant."

"Yes, thank you Camille," Her mother said, entering the house. "Is the bath ready yet?"

"It's being prepared now," Camille said, "For your daughter as well. Will you be shopping today or tomorrow?"

"Tomorrow," Her mother said as she entered the stairs. She sighed and turned back to Camille. "But there's a few things I do need today."

"I'll wait for your list."

"I've missed you Camille," her mother said, resuming her walk up the stairs.

"Yes, Ma'am, you as well."

At the top of the stairs Katrina paused, and opened her mouth to speak. Her mother cut her off without turning around.

"A long time ago, and it's not a story I'm in the mood to discuss. Don't dawdle dear, I really want to bathe while the waters still warm."

Katrina's bath was still hot when she stepped in. She sat on the edge of the tub dangling her feet in the water. She waited for the water to cool. She needed to avoid submerging her back, and opted to stand and bathe as best she could.

Her thoughts spun in several directions as she submerged her legs into the tub and stood. What should she do first? Gather her strength to wander to her father or brothers. A safe choice, something she could do in secret. But how long would Linbodo and the Swift Sound remain at the pier? There were many things that could happen to her if she sneaked back to the pier. It seemed daunting. If she ignored the opportunity would she get another like it? She wanted to be certain of her choices, but lacked information. Her mind trailed off with thoughts of all the things that could go wrong. Her last big risk did not boost her confidence. She failed, injuring herself and putting more distance between her and home.

She sat in a strange house, on a strange island, surrounded by strangers. Her mother was the only person she really knew. Then again after observing her mother this morning, Katrina wondered. When did her mother and Devon form an attachment? Was that normal, to leave a husband for another man, then take up with an entirely different man? All in less than a month. Her mother once wanted to go to school here. What's so great about the school here, and why had her mother never told Katrina about it? And how could her mother possibly know Camille before today?

Tilting her head forward she wet her hair. Katrina managed to wet all her hair without submerging her head. Leaning forward she worked a cake of soap against her hair and then her scalp.

Something thud against the outside of the tub. Katrina raised her head. Camille stood by the tub.

"I've been instructed to ensure your hair is well washed," Camille said.

"I could do that for you, if your back is making it a difficulty."

Katrina began working the cake of soap in her hair again and shook her head no. Camille walked over to lean against the wall next to the door.

"I had a nasty scratch once," Camille said. "It ran all the way up this thigh." She ran her hand in a long gestured up the thigh of her right leg. "I couldn't stand for it to get touched. Even as it started to heal, soap and water made it burn. I imagine your back doesn't feel much better."

"It doesn't hurt to breathe like it used to," Katrina said. "You've worked for my mother, in the past?"

Camille nodded her head.

"When?" Katrina asked.

"A long time ago."

"Where?"

Camille answered in heavily accented Bisma, "You're full of questions." Camille arched an eyebrow at her, and switched back to the common tongue. "The answer doesn't matter, I'm a servant. I once had the pleasure of working for your mother in the past."

Trying to hide her annoyance, Katrina rubbed the bar of soap hard against her hair. When soap coated every inch of her hair, she dropped the bar. It bobbed to the surface and floated away.

"Could you help me rinse my hair, please?" Katrina asked.

Camille obliged, picking up a small bucket from beside the tub. She scooped water into the bucket and slowly poured it over Katrina's lowered head. Katrina worked clean water through her hair. Camille scooped and poured water, and then assisted her out of the tub. Katrina dried off and got dressed in a light blue dress Camille provided her with. Camille brushed Katrina's hair and worked it into a fast braid.

Camille led Katrina down to the kitchen and left her with a kitchen maid. The maid sat her at one of the work tables where a large pile of peelings sat beside a bowl of separated oranges.

"Don't mind those, I'm saving them," the maid said as she pushed them aside and set a meal of bread and soft cheese before her.

The maid crossed the kitchen to tend the cooking fire. Katrina eyed the back door a few feet away. It stood open to coax heat from the kitchen. While still facing the kitchen maids back, Katrina grabbed one of the orange portions and her bread. Popping the orange into her mouth she stood and walked out the door.

The orange overpowered her with flavor. She paused in the kitchen garden, fighting the sudden urge to rush back and swipe the entire bowl of oranges. The orange was the most delightfully sweet thing she had eaten since leaving home. She gave up another attempt at orange theft and continued walking. She passed a large outbuilding beside the only exit, an alleyway. The rotting stink of garbage accompanied her down the alley. Coming here, they walked uphill. She proceeded downhill out of the alley and onto the nearest street. One narrow street led to another, and then another intersection. She tore off and ate pieces of bread as she walked. She hoped eating would help her blend in more, but she devoured it too fast. The street ended at another intersection. She was lost, but continued going downhill.

The sound of people singing a lively tune caught her attention. She followed it and sighed with relief to see the naked statues. More people walked the thoroughfare now. The music came from a group seated in front of a cafe. Women dressed in bright colored undergarments led patrons in a lively song. Their chorus of, "lift your glass and give us a smile, we aren't going anywhere for quite awhile," followed Katrina.

She passed the last statue and the thoroughfare narrowed. Searching for the street to the pier frustrated her. Every intersection looked the same. A hand grabbed her wrist and a man spoke into her ear.

"Aren't you a fresh one, where are you going?"

Katrina jerked her arm from his grasp.

"The new ones, always so cute and shy," he said.

Katrina ran, glancing back once. The man crossed his arms, staying in place. He had dark hair and wore a deep orange and yellow uniform. Still running, she turned left at the next intersection. She passed a dozen doorways before falling against the side of a building and doubling over. Pressing one hand against the pain in her side, she stood up. When did running become hard? Breathing heavy, she walked on. Massie could have run farther than that, and his gloating would be the worst. She still felt the man's grip. Placing a hand over her wrist she shuddered. Shaking her head she exhaled and willed her disgust and heart rate to subside.

People shouting orders, crates banging, and a chorus of shuddering carts greeted her arrival to the pier. Unsure where to start, she watched the activity around the vast array of ships. Her plan seemed simple. Walk to the pier, find Linbodo. Plans and then what actually happened following one were two totally different things. She moved through the crowd and walked onto the pier, searching for Linbodo or the ship named Swift Sound. Her feet ached and she wanted to sit down. The walk here took longer than she planned. By now the green house staff knew of her absence. She needed to find Linbodo before Claire sent one of the servants here for her.

She caught a glimpse of Linbodo. Shouting his name, she dodged though the crowd.

"Linbodo! Linbodo I'm here."

Linbodo turned, saw her and hesitated. Pivoting fast, he walked away from her.

Katrina shoved past a man who stepped in her path, and ran after Linbodo. She extended her hand, reaching for him. Grabbing hold of the back of his shirt she pulled and he stopped. She fell against him and he turned back, yanking his shirt from her grip.

"What do you think you're doing?" he said in a whispering hiss.

"Why did you walk away?" she said.

"I don't know what you want," he said. "I'm not interested to find out. Good day." He looked about and walked away again.

She sped up, matching his pace, and searching his face for some clue about why he refused to speak to her.

"You told me to come find you, and I did."

Not here, not with you dressed like that, he said in a wander.

"What?"

He stopped short, leaned forward, and wandered to her. *Talking to a candidate to the House of Etrasa is a death sentence.*

"But, I'm not." she said.

"That," he said, pointing to the light blue dress she wore. He stepped back and looked around as he continued in a wander, *is a candidates dress.*

He turned and resumed walking away from her.

"NO!" she shouted after him.

Everyone in the immediate vicinity paused their activity to gawk at her.

"No," she said. Her face growing hot with frustration and the threatening tears. "I came all the way back here, to talk to you. I came at your request."

Linbodo turned slow and faced her. He inspected the many people watching them and swallowed. Katrina stepped in close, invading his space, and making it impossible for him to ignore her.

"Please," she said. "I need help. I need to get home. I'm not supposed to be here."

Linbodo shook his head.

"Will you pass a message for me? A letter?"

He stood silent, and scanned the crowd. Here and there his gaze darted back to hers. Like a cornered animal, he looked ready to bolt.

A heavy hand clapped down on Linbodo's shoulder. He flinched and shifted away. Another man grabbed his other shoulder and hauled him back.

Katrina kicked as someone circled their arms around her and lifted her up.

"Please," Linbodo begged. "She chased me down, she has me confused with someone else. Just ask her, I have no idea who she is."

"Put me down!" she screamed.

The man who grabbed her wrist earlier stood beside her. "I don't recognize this one," he said to the man restraining her. "Do you?"

"No," said the man holding her.

"Take her up to the house." The dark haired man made a gesture with one hand to the two men restraining Linbodo. "Don't waste time. Rules are rules."

One of the men proffered a knife. He placed it at Linbodo's neck and drew it across in one efficient swipe. Linbodo tried lunging away, but the momentum only dug the blade deeper into his neck.

A spray of blood coated the hem of Katrina's dress as Linbodo fell face down on the pier.

Katrina tried to scream, but it came out as a small yelp. She stilled, her breath caught in her throat. She blinked and tried to see Linbodo as she was carried off the pier.

The big man carried her uphill through the narrow streets. They passed an elaborate iron and stone gate. Traveling on a wide road, they approached what had to be a mansion. She had seen drawings of the mansion lined streets near the castle of Bisma. This one stood three stories, and looked more castle than house. Entering a side door, they passed several people. All wore similar attire of deep orange and yellow.

"What do you got there Bonner?" called one woman after him.

"Not sure. Tell Gan when he gets in that I put her in room four."

"Room four, will do."

"She needs a fresh uniform too."

The woman groaned and yelled after him, "You know I've got sixty other things I'm to be doing."

"You're welcome," Bonner said. Katrina watched the old scar accross Bonner's lips as he talked. He grinned, and the scar stretched. Bonner hauled her up a flight of stairs, taking the steps two at a time.

Room four had a window on the far wall, a small bed, and nothing else. Bonner closed the door and set her on the bed. He stood back, crossed his arms, and inspected her with interest. She stared back, unafraid even if the large man's head did rise above the door frame.

"I'm good with remembering people," he said. "I haven't seen you, but you look familiar. How long have you been at the house?"

Katrina made no answer. She stared at the scar on his lips. Whatever caused the old injury had nicked one side of his nostril too.

Bonner grunted and ran a hand through the tight crop of light hair. They continued to eye one another. Someone knocked on the door, before opening it, and hitting Bonner's back. He stepped aside and the woman he gave orders to earlier, peeked around the door.

"Here," she said, thrusting a hand out. It clutched several light blue dresses. "One of these should fit."

Bonner took the dresses then looked stricken as the woman disappeared.

"Wait, where are you going?" he shouted after her.

"Sixty things, remember?"

"No way woman, I can't dress the girl."

"Fine," she said with a huff. She came around the door and snatched the dresses back. "Get out, and go find Ollie for me."

"Ollie from the kitchen?"

"No, Ollie your brother," the woman said, shoving Bonner out the door. "Of course Ollie from the kitchen. Is there another Ollie in Etrasa?"

She shut the door and mumbled something to herself. She motioned for Katrina to stand.

"Up-up dearie, I don't have all day."

Katrina slid to her feet and stood. The woman frowned at the hem of her skirt. She turned Katrina around and unlaced the back of her dress. She worked fast, but as she jerked the dress up, she pulled at Katrina's still healing wounds. At least one of her scars was rent open and she cried out from the sudden pain.

"What's the matter?" the woman asked, stopping her activity. Katrina took a few deep breaths, with the fabric of the dress bunched around her shoulders. With more care, the woman resumed and pulled the dress off.

"Oh Etta and Rasa! What happened to you?"

Katrina stood still. The woman grabbed her arms and turned her around to face her. She bent down and looked her in the eye. Her concern was genuine, but Katrina said nothing.

"I see," the woman said. "We need to bandage that and get you dressed before Gan gets here."

The woman left and returned with clean dressing and a jar of ointment.

"I'm so sorry," the woman said as she cleaned and dressed Katrina's reopened wound. "I'll be gentle this time dressing you, I promise."

Katrina turned and lifted her arms in acknowledgement. The woman lifted the clean blue dress over her head. She finished lacing it when they heard footsteps and the echo of a conversation in the hall. Katrina recognized Bonner's voice.

"Naw, she said nothing."

The door opened and the man who grabbed her by the wrist entered the room. Bonner trailed behind him. The woman scooped up her blood soiled dress, and made a respectful nod saying, "Gan."

"Thank you," Gan said.

Gan tilted his head as he considered Katrina. He smiled and then chuckled quietly.

"I know who this one is."

"Yeah?" Bonner said.

"Look at the eyes," Gan said. "You'll see it."

Bonner stepped closer to Katrina.

"Eyes up here girl," Bonner said gesturing to his face.

Katrina raised her face. She intended to meet his eyes, but got lost staring at his scar again.

"She's Lena's," Gan said.

Bonner let out hoot of laughter. "How'd I miss that?"

"Because she's short, and stick thin," Gan said.

"Little Lena of Lavieth's girl, of course she is. She's got the same pretty eyes," Bonner said.

"Where's your mother?" Gan asked.

Katrina tilted her head in an odd shrug.

"I know you can talk," Gan said. "Where's your mother?"

"I don't know," she said. "A green house."

"A green house," Bonner said. He smiled and laughed. "Leave her be Gan. She doesn't know. Her mum will show."

Gan smiled and nodded his head in agreement. "Keep an eye on her. I'll let Rudolph know." He moved to the door and Bonner followed him. Gan opened the door and turned around blocking Bonner's exit.

"When I said keep and eye on her, I meant stay here."

"Rasa's ball's," Bonner said.

"We found her roaming the docks," Gan said. "We need to make sure we have her when Rudolph sends for her."

"I get it," Bonner said. He stepped back and ran a hand over his scalp. He looked back at Katrina and sighed. "I'll stay here and watch her."

Someone brought him a chair. He placed it in front of the door, sat down, and proceeded to fall asleep in it. Acclimated to many recent days in solitude, Katrina stretched out on the bed. She hated waiting.

The view from the window overlooked a large stable, with a pasture and the strange forest behind it. A procession of fine looking women on horseback emerged from the stable. They rode into the forest on a well manicured trail. The sky remained cloud free, and the sun cast long shadows when the procession of women on horseback returned.

Dinner arrived on a tray. Bonner served up plates with some small roast bird, some kind of cooked root vegetable, and thick slices of bread. The dessert consisted of a fruit Bonner called shaddock. A sweet syrup coated the fruit to help make its tartness more palatable. Katrina ate her fill, enjoying the first meal in days to consist of more than just bread or soup

Bonner refrained from talking, limiting his questions to those addressing her immediate care.

When the sun went down Bonner had someone bring in a lamp. The leaf etched into the lamps glass panes cast shadows on the floor. The flower shaped binti stone at the lamp's center glowed orange. Bonner resumed his post, seated in the chair in front of the door. Climbing under the bedcovers, Katrina faced away from Bonner. She closed her eyes and reached for neutral.

She succeeded entering neutral, and stood surrounded by her home, the Mozgas Palace. A jolt of longing rang through her. She made it into her bedroom.

Reaching for her father, she waited. Minutes passed and she grew impatient. She tried to summon Sol. Where were they? Did she mess this up? Did she fall asleep and dream she made it to neutral? After waiting a long time, she decided to try one more time and reached for Valgu. He appeared, arms crossed and a look of confused shock on his face. He stared at her a moment, opened his mouth to speak, but instead closed his eyes and shook his head. When he opened his eyes he stepped towards her and folded her in an embrace.

"Dear God, you are alive," he said. "This is some kind of miracle. God knows we need one right now. Are you well?"

"No," she said.

"You're still sick with fever?"

"No. My back still hurts. Three of the cuts came open. Where's father, and Sol? Why didn't they come?"

Valgu closed his eyes and took both lips into his mouth and held them there a moment. With a small shake of his head he opened his eyes with a look of anguish.

"They can't come right now," he said.

"Why not?"

"Father," he said, and paused searching for his words.

"Just say it, tell me," she said, bracing herself for the worst.

"Did you and Sol see Father when you were in neutral?" he asked.

She nodded, "We did, he appeared for only a second and then he was gone."

"The poison hasn't killed father, but he's suffering its effects. He can't wander, or control his wandering ability. His moods are odd."

"What do you mean odd?"

"I mean he changes for no reason, and he's dangerous."

"I saw him kill Lord Dacamera and the other Skrieni men," Katrina said.

Valgu's eyes widened with surprise. "He did. Then he burned that entire village. How did you see it?"

"I think I saw it, when it happened. But I wasn't there, I dreamt it. I saw a lot of things when I had the fever."

"He told me about finding you in neutral," Valgu hesitated, and his voice softened. "He told us about your fever, and what the Skrieni did."

Katrina gave a small nod and looked away.

"He ran the Army all the way to Lavieth, then to the coast. You'd already been gone a day. They took you, but everyone said you boarded a ship in a coffin. We thought you died of the fever."

Katrina left Valgu's embrace and sat on the edge of her bed. She traced her fingers along the gold stitching of feathers embroidered on her blanket.

"Why can't Sol come here now?"

"Father accused him of hiding you. We knew it was the poison, but father...he attacked Sol."

"No," She said.

Valgu sat beside her. "Lady Oshana tried to help. When she intervened, she was killed."

Katrina fell against Valgu, hitting his arm with clenched fists.

"Tell me, where's Sol?"

"He hasn't woken up." Valgu grabbed her wrists. "The healers say he's either going to wake up, or sleep until he dies."

"No, no," she said, her voice whimpering. She quit struggling and Valgu pulled her into a hug.

"Are you safe where you are?" he said.

"I don't know."

"Has Lady Lena put you into more or less danger?"

She hesitated, wanting to defend her mother, but recognized the sincere concern in Valgu's words.

"Etrasa, it's an island."

Valgu nodded in recognition.

"There's this human school my mother wants me to attend. But I can get away. I've already worked out a way to get home."

"No, if you're not in any immediate danger, I want you to stay where you are. Go to school, stay out of trouble, and don't wander neutral with anyone."

"I need to go home."

"Do this, do it for me? It's easier for me to keep you safe if you stay where you are. We don't know how to help father right now. Please, I need you to wait until I'm out of the Mahigan compound."

"Father won't hurt me," she said.

"You didn't see him attack Sol."

"He's going to find me, he promised."

"Yes, maybe he will, but we need time. We can't risk you wandering neutral with anyone."

"No wandering," she said. "You don't want me to come home, and I can't wander neutral."

"I want you home, I do. Finding you alive—it's a miracle. I'll bring you home when I know I can keep you safe."

"What if I'm not safe here?"

"I'll send Pha."

"But I did figure out a way to get home."

"And I applaud your cleverness. But my kid sister, crossing an ocean to get home, all by herself. It's not safe."

"I could wait until Pha gets here. All I need to do is find father's Delphi allies. There's Delphi trader ships at the port here. Pha and I can pay for them to take us home."

Valgu took both of her shoulders in his hands and lowered his head to look her in the eye. He spoke quiet but with an urgency that frightened her. "You shouldn't go anywhere near the Delphi. They'll take you home, to their home—not yours. Do all you can to stay away from them."

His words crushed the plan she had nurtured. The information stung more as she remembered the innocent man killed at the docks that morning.

"Do you understand?" he asked.

She nodded and he released her.

He closed his eyes and took a deep breath.

"This is hard, I know. What I'm asking you to do is not easy, and I know it's not what you want."

Valgu wrapped an arm around her shoulders. She leaned into his side and rested her head on his shoulder.

"There is some good news," he said. "The healers at the University believe what happened to your wings can be fixed. Father's been bringing in healers. They've been summoned from all over Madar. He's charged them all with the task of restoring your wings."

"Why did he summon them if he believes I'm dead?"

"He's the only one who's convinced you're still alive. He said you promised him you'd live."

Valgu's words were a mild comfort. Like the salve Cye used to dull the sharp pain in her back, Valgu gave her something to take the edge off a deep aching despair.

"How long will I have to stay here?"

"It could be awhile, I don't know how long I'll take in the Mahigan compound. I'll send Pha, and keep meeting with you here. Between Pha and I, we'll make sure you're taken care of. Will you do it? Will you wait?"

"Yes."

"Good."

"I have to know if Sol's okay."

"I promise, when he wakes up, I'll make sure you get to see him for yourself."

"Bonner!" a female voice shouted from behind the door. Katrina turned over at the sound. The door handle jiggled. It opened, knocking against the back of Bonner's head, and sending him forward. The door slammed against his chair again.

"Give me an eye blink to stand up, will you," Bonner said. He stood, and the door swept the chair aside. The woman who helped change her dress the day before, walked in with a tray of food.

"Take this, it's heavy," she said, passing off the tray to Bonner. "Gan said to bring her down to the theatre after she's eaten."

The woman crossed the room and motioned to Katrina. "Up-up sweet girl, I'll work on your hair while you eat."

Katrina obliged and got out of bed. The woman groaned, "You slept all night in your dress." She turned to Bonner, "Why did you let her do that for?"

Bonner set the food tray beside Katrina on the bed and served up two plates of food. "That's a stupid question Marjorie."

"It is not. You could have fetched me."

"Miss sixty things. No."

"We can't send her to the theatre in a rumpled dress."

"Then change her. I don't really care," Bonner said before stuffing a slice of bread smothered with jam into his mouth.

"We only have so many clean and pressed candidate dresses for a girl her size. They don't poof-grow in the forest."

"Then poof," Bonner said, flaring the finger of one hand at her. "Go and get her one."

Marjorie huffed, put both hands on her hips, and glared at Bonner. Katrina smiled at their antics. A welcome distraction from the depressing news from last night. Marjorie left the room and Katrina took the plate of food Bonner offered her.

They ate in silence. Marjorie returned with a fresh dress. She styled Katrina's hair and after sending Bonner from the room, changed her into the fresh dress.

Once dressed, Bonner led her from the mansion. Side by side they walked past the large stone and iron gate and into the city.

"That's where we're going," Bonner said, pointing a finger at a large building sitting where the street they were on ended. Hundreds of orange flowers adorned the steps leading into the Parade Theatre. Stairs of large brick slabs shined with the same blue enameled glaze as the small brinks on the street. The flowers pressed into these were enhanced by the added orange glaze. A larger orange flower adorned the relief over the main doors.

"What's the orange flower called?" Katrina asked.

"The Etrasa Waterlily, they're out in the swampy part of the forest. They're pretty, but hard to find."

Bonner spoke to a woman in a maroon dress guarding the door. She directed them to wait in a vestibule of the main lobby. They waited what had to be the entire morning. A large door to the theatre opened and Gan peeked around it.

"Did you tell her what to do?" Gan asked.

"No. I don't know none of that." Bonner said.

Gan sighed and came around the door letting it close. He bent down and spoke to her.

"You're going to follow me up on stage. Stay where I place you. Rudolph's going to ask you questions, and you just answer him honestly. Understand?"

"Yes," she said.

"Come on then," Gan said motioning for her to follow.

They passed the audience seats and climbed a flight of stairs to the stage. Gan pointed to a place on the floor rimmed with light shining down from special lamps above. She stepped into the pool of light. It dimmed the visibility of the audience. Rudolph addressed her, his husky voice coming from one of the darkened rows further back in the audience.

"I'm addressing the candidate and only the candidate. If I wish to hear from you, Lena, I will address you. Is that understood?"

"Yes," Lady Lena said.

Startled by the sound of her mother's voice, Katrina found the dim outline of her mother standing in an unlit area opposite her on stage. She expected to see her at some point today, but not here standing on this stage with her.

"What is your name?" Rudolph asked.

"Katrina."

"Why are you here?"

"To attend school, Sir."

"And who is to be your husband?"

Her eyes widened as she looked over to where her mother stood.

"I don't want your mother's answer," Rudolph said. "I want yours. Who will be your husband?"

For Princess Katrina Aranysarga, the answer to his question was simple. Her husband would be her rally winner. If she lived in the human world, she blanched at the idea.

"I don't know, Sir."

"Do you want to attend school here?" he asked. "Be honest."

"Honestly Sir," she hesitated and glanced at her mother again. "It's not my first choice."

"What school would you prefer?"

"A university."

Rudolph made a rasping chuckle, "A girl your age wants to attend university. Ambitious, are you smart enough for it?"

"Yes, Sir."

"We'll see then won't we. You're not the first of my girls with a desire for more of the traditional academics. We have a nice agreement with the university here."

Her mother cried out with a small strangled protest. Rudolph paused and then continued.

"Learn everything we require you to learn, and we'll see."

Rudolph sat as a motionless shadow in the back.

"I'm a bit concerned about you candidate." Rudolph stood and took his time walking to the aisle. She got a good look at him as he approached the edge of the stage. A man of thin stature, he had close cut black hair, and dark eyes. She never would have guessed this plain looking man was the one in charge.

"I'm aware of what transpired yesterday. There's no reason for my school to deal with disobedience." He climbed the stairs, inspecting Katrina up close. "Should I gamble on you?"

Katrina held his gaze, unsure of her answer. Valgu needed her to remain here at least a year, but this school would require several years to complete. She weighed lying to him against the days spent alone with her mother if she told the truth. Stuck who knows where, listening to her mother rant about her rejection from this human school.

"Yes," she said. "You should."

"Lena, I agreed to your daughter's candidacy, based on the favor I owe you. I agreed, despite the risk it placed on the reputation of The House of

Etrasa. After yesterday, I need more if you expect me to take on more risk."

"We were guaranteed candidacy," her mother said.

"And I was guaranteed nothing from her background would interfere," he said.

"She recently recovered from fever. She went out for some fresh air and got lost."

"She's here less than a day, and I'm dealing with Delphi non compliance on the docks."

"My father can advance you more money."

Rudolph paced to where her mother stood, pivoted, and walked back to Katrina.

"What more are you asking for?" her mother asked.

Rudolph gave a hoarse laugh. He crossed his arms and Katrina watched his dark eyes move over her features.

"I thought your daughter would have a more exotic look to her. Except for the blue eyes she inherited from you, she's ordinary. What kind of Veilede is she anyway?"

"She's not, she can't shift," her mother said.

The man laughed again.

"I mean, she can't shift anymore. She sustained an injury."

"I don't like marketing a false commodity."

"Truly, she can only live as a human now," her mother said, standing rigid with her arms held tight at her sides.

Katrina swallowed and tried to let her mother's words roll past her.

"As for her appearance, she's young. Isn't it better for her to be a simple girl who'll grow into a beautiful woman, than a pretty girl who sours with age?"

"In my experience, simple girls become simple women," he said. "I'll only agree to her candidacy, if she goes under contract."

"Contract? Her tuition's prepaid."

"She's too big a gamble, and half a bid price isn't worth the elbow grease it'll take to get a man to look at her."

Rudolph stood relaxed, waiting for a reply. Katrina waited for her mother to rebuff him. She expected a flash of the angry dramatics her mother used in arguments with Lady Tellydia.

"What are the contract terms?" her mother asked, her voice calm.

"The usual," he said. "She belongs to The House. We take over responsibility for all her basic needs. She attends school, is housed, and will do whatever we assign her. After her selection at parade, her full bid price is remitted to The House."

"The usual contract," her mother said.

"Yes, except any disciplinary issue terminates her candidacy. She'll work off her debt in the market, and you'll join her."

Her mother's lips drew together tight as her eyebrows bowed in worry. The look told Katrina which market Rudolph meant. One mistake, and colossal naked statues would be part of her everyday life.

"My time is valuable," Rudolph said. "Yes or no."

Lady Lena gave a small nod as she said, "Yes."

"Then it's my pleasure to welcome Katrina to the House of Etrasa." Rudolph faced the audience and yelled. "Where's Gan?"

"Here, I'm right here," Gan said, standing up from a seat in the back.

"Take Katrina over to the row houses, and make sure she has what she needs."

"Rudolph," her mother said. "She can stay with me—"

He cut her off with a quick, "No."

"She's too young to be on her own," her mother said.

"Katrina's going to the row houses," Rudolph said. "You may live with her, but you're in charge of your own boarding and expenses."

Rudolph stepped down from the stage, giving her mother a backwards wave of his refusal to hear more.

"This way," Gan said to Katrina.

She followed, and the stomping footsteps of her mother echoed behind her as they left.

The House of Etrasa candidates lived in row houses set along a wide street beneath the road leading to the House of Etrasa Mansion.

"Candidates are well protected here," Gan said. "The dormitories for The House staff and guards surround the row houses. Helps keep our candidates away from those they don't need to associate with."

Her mother pushed past Gan and entered the assigned house first. Hands on hips she frowned at the white washed walls, and wooden furnishings.

"Isn't this marvelous? Well done. Devon provides us with the best accommodations on the island, and your little walk lands us here."

Katrina ignored her. The more her mother complained, the more Katrina wanted to like it. The main floor of the house had a modest dining room, kitchen and servants room. One long hall lead to a kitchen garden, and the only staircase in the house. Upstairs was a washroom, and two bedrooms.

"I hope you like it," her mother said.

Katrina was on the back stairs when she replied, "No one's making you stay."

4

The Goals of a Lady

The following morning Gan came for Katrina. She walked with him and noticed they were trailing behind a crowd of girls, all wearing a dress like hers, and ranging in age from a few years younger than herself to full grown women. To the left and right of the group walked men and women in deep orange and yellow attire like Gan's. They walked uphill to The House of Etrasa mansion. For some reason the mansion and school were referred to with one interchangeable name, "The House."

Gan left her in a classroom of girls her own age. The girls talked and moved about the room as they waited for the first class of the day. Katrina watched them in awe and sat at a seat near the door. Pangs of loss and loneliness troubled her. She lacked experience making friends. She wanted to join the girls, but sat watching them instead. It occurred to her then what an isolated life she lived in Mozgas. She had friends, they all just happened to be her siblings.

A girl with hazel eyes sat down beside her. Her eyes were exquisite, a burst of celery green through a russet brown. Their depth of color was gem like and complemented the curves of her dark tan face.

"I'm Mahogany, from the South Trident Province."

"Katrina, nice to meet you. I'm from, well um, Lavieth."

"Lavieth. Hm, never heard of it."

"It's a province, in Bisma."

"Oh," Mahogany said frowning. "Well, that's days from here."

"Yes, it is."

"You've probably never heard of the South Trident Province."

"Actually, the ship I came here on, the whole crew was from there. You're the first person I've met from there, who doesn't have half a head full of ringed tattoos."

Mahogany laughed, "you're wondering where mine are?"

Katrina shrugged.

"Come on," Mahogany said standing up and offering her hand, "Let's go meet the girls from Encartha everyone's excited about."

Dazzled by the offer, she took her hand. They remained a pair for the rest of the day. Mahogany seemed to know and enjoy everyone indiscriminately. Gifted with a knack for simple chatter, Mahogany's alluring charm effected everyone. It was pure delight when Mahogany sought her out the next day. Sliding up beside her, Mahogany tucked her arm under hers, like they had been walking together as friends their whole lives. Within a week they were inseparable.

Katrina sat alone in her room on her bed flipping through a book of human history. There was a knock at the front door. She peeked out her window, but her mother already let them in. Setting the book aside, she went out to the stairs and listened.

"I should have expected you," her mother said. "Of course you're here. You'd have nursed her as baby if I'd let you."

"Lady Lena," Pha said.

Katrina's stomach jumped. She wanted to run down the stairs to her, but inched down the stairs until she could see them.

"I'll allow you to stay," her mother said.

Pha brushed past her entering the house. "You have no say in the matter."

"Or what, you'll send back information about me?"

"I'd love to," Pha said, dropping her bag with a thud. "But I'm not here for you."

"How did you find us? The Delphi?"

"The real question is why did you do it?"

"I'm a little surprised they didn't force you to stay in Madar," her mother said. "Who else do they trust enough to guard over the monsters perfect prodigy."

Pha handled the ties to the wraps covering her hands, speaking through clenched teeth, "Don't slander Prince Valgu."

"Put your scarred hands away," her mother said, walking to the kitchen. "Your witchcraft is entirely unnecessary."

"Where's my Princess?" Pha asked.

"Don't," her mother said turning back from the kitchen in a rush. "You cannot refer to her that way. Not here."

Katrina ducked out of sight, inching back up the stairs, and into her room.

"My Katrina then," Pha said.

"She's upstairs."

A few minutes later her door opened and Pha stepped in.

Brushing happy tears from her eyes, Katrina threw her arms around Pha.

"Praise God," Pha said smoothing Katrina's hair. "My dear girl, I knew we'd find you."

Pha moved into the servants room off the kitchen. She became Katrina's touchstone, the one thing from home her mother was powerless to take away or alter. Pha helped her adapt to what she often called, "This miserable human place."

There were twenty-three other girls in Katrina's year group at The House. Candidates spent their days in specialized classes meant to teach the skills prized in human women born to more illustrious noble families. Once properly trained, candidates graduated and were called ladies. The ladies of The House met and entertained suitors who traveled to Etrasa for a biannual season of events, known as parade. During the culminating finale event, suitors announced and arranged payment for the lady they chose to take home as their future bride.

When Pha learned of this, she ranted and screamed at Lena. Katrina listened with envy as Pha banged about the kitchen. She wanted to lift her voice and rage at her mother too. If only some berating were all it took to rattle the obstinate conviction responsible for trapping them here.

Every night Katrina refrained from falling asleep right away. She lingered at the outer edge of neutral. Far enough away to remain hidden, but close enough to enter if summoned.

A familiar vibration pulled her into neutral. She smiled as the shifting image of her bedroom settled. Valgu stood by the bedroom door with Sol beside him. Katrina ran to them hugging first Sol and then Valgu.

"I promised you'd see him when he woke up," Valgu said.

"I'm so happy you're okay," Katrina said.

Sol shook his head saying, "N-nn-no, I-I-I I am."

Katrina tried hiding her shock at the way Sol struggled through the simple sentence.

Sol wandered to her then, "I'm happy you're alive. The healers tell me to talk more. That practice will help me, but I don't believe them."

Her heart hurt. Her kind and good natured brother survived their father's attack, but now struggled with a permanent speech impediment.

Sol touched her shoulder and nodded like he heard her thoughts and wandered, "I never did talk much."

"I met with Pha," Valgu said. "She wandered neutral with me the night she found you."

"Yes, she's here," Katrina said.

"And, things are going well?" Valgu asked.

Katrina bit back a harsh no, giving him a more polite "I'm glad she's here."

Valgu waited for her to expand and Katrina said, "How's father?" She cringed at her unconscious mistake.

Valgu and Sol's demeanor stiffened. Sol looked grief stricken and shook his head.

"We'll have to go," Valgu said.

"I'm sorry," she said. Her thoughts of their father, as well as saying his name could summon him.

Wrapping one arm around each brother, she pulled them in a hug. Her carelessness cut their time together short. The weight of their arms came around her as everything shifted. The room vibrated and her brothers disappeared. If she opened her eyes she would cry. The strain of holding onto neutral exhausted her. Burying her frustration she let go. Sleep fell on her then, with the speed of a weighted gate.

The first year went by slow. Valgu entered the Mahigan compound, and his visits were short and infrequent. Katrina immersed herself in her education, and avoided thoughts of home. She still found herself counting each day. Her anticipation remained. The strong desire for home too embedded to shake. Pha recommended she spend less time focused on the future and more time in the present.

"Be grateful," Pha said. She stood on a stool next to the kitchen table. She used the stool's height to access the table top where she kneaded bread dough. Katrina sat accross the table from her watching her work.

"Today's a gift, enjoy it," Pha said. "There are good things happening right now. Don't miss out by dwelling about what you don't have."

"I'm trying," Katrina said. "But at the end of the day, I still want to go home."

Pha sliced the dough and formed it into round balls. Each ball she placed on a pan.

"Going home's a good plan. But sometimes our plan, and what we want, isn't the plan God has for us."

Katrina groaned, squeezing her cheeks between both hands. "That's too much. I'm still stuck at the being grateful part."

Pha laughed, "Oh my girl, you'll figure it out. Practice gratitude, I promise it will help ease your frustration."

Her mother occupied the bedroom accross the hall from Katrina's. Most nights her mother slept there. Other nights her mother stayed at the green house with Devon. Katrina expected her mother to furnish the row house with the finer furnishings she liked in the green house. However, the only piece of furniture her mother brought in was a massive custom ordered tapestry rack. Her mother had taught her to thread a needle the same year she learned to pen her name. Katrina welcomed its presence in the back hallway. The only place in the row house where the ceiling accommodated it's towering frame.

Katrina liked when her mother worked on her tapestries. Once in awhile, Katrina caught her mother smiling there as she composed beautiful images with a needle and thread. Katrina would sit near her dawdling over her smaller projects and they talked about the mundane.

"You should use this next," her mother said.

"And make a full tapestry?" Katrina said.

"Yes."

Astonished, but unsure of her answer Katrina focused on her next stitch. The idea of starting such a large project. It excited her.

"You should sketch some ideas, and I'll place an order for new thread."

"Maybe," she said. She wanted to say yes, but thoughts of home held her back. Any day Valgu would call her home, and she hated to leave projects unfinished.

"What are you afraid of?" her mother said.

"Oh, I don't have any good ideas."

"Yet," her mother said. "You don't have any good ideas yet. You'll come up with something."

Katrina tucked her embroidery away in the sewing basket. Stashing it next to the stool she stood to go when her mother reached out, took her by the hand, and held her back.

"You can design your own tapestry."

Katrina looked from her mother's hand to her eyes. They transformed into a more beautiful shade of blue when she cried.

"I know you can," her mother said. "If you were meant to leave me, Pha would have taken you by now."

Why had she ever doubted her mother's awareness?

"I've never stopped wanting to go," Katrina said.

"I know," her mother said. "You know what will happen to me."

A sick feeling of guilt washed over her. She wanted to yank her hand back and run.

"Why did you poison father?"

Her mother released her hand and turned away. Katrina hurled herself up the stairs, refusing to think about why she remained in Etrasa. Her stomach churned. She never wanted her mother to die. Her mother would be alive when she left Etrasa, but could she accept her mother's fate?

She lay in bed, waiting for her sick stomach to ease. Logic battled her heart. One by one, she listed all the reasons her mother owned her own fate. Yet, her heart rejected it. Somehow her mother's plight deadened her eagerness to return home.

Before tonight, she planned to summon Valgu and demand he tell her when she could come home. Acknowledging her mother's plight made her urgent desire vanish. Valgu would call her home, but the unbearable wait became tolerable. Living here, she was procrastinating, but it was easier than abandoning her mother.

Valgu's time in the Mahigan Compound came and went. Katrina learned Etrasa's seasons. The constant rain in winter. The migration of sea birds, and colorful exotic flowers of spring. The dreadful humid heat of summer, that drove every island occupant indoors mid day. The dense fog during autumn's cool mornings. It drifted down streets and draped over the forest like a gauze blanket.

Katrina sought out Pha in the evening. She retold her days lessons as Pha went about her work and listened. Perched on the edge of a garden box, rays of the summers evening sun made the parchment on her lap board glow with warm light.

"If I ask you a question, about home, will you answer it?" Katrina asked. "Will you tell me the honest truth?"

Pha stopped digging and met Katrina's eyes. She set down the spade in her grip and brushed dirt from her hand wraps.

"My darling girl, I'm Alvara. I couldn't tell a lie to you if I tried."

"I know," Katrina said. "But you can choose to not say anything. It's what my mother does."

"I'm not your mother."

"I know, and it's worse when you do it. Usually you answer me."

Pha frowned and considered Katrina.

"Ask me what you want, I'll give you an answer."

"Has Valgu told you when we're going home?"

"Yes," Pha said, her eyes softened as she hesitated.

Katrina braced herself for the burning sting of disappointment.

"We're to stay here," Pha said. "Longer than we expected."

Katrina sucked in her breath, but felt nothing. She took one breath and then another, and realized she anticipated this answer.

"Because of father?"

"Yes," Pha said.

"Valgu wants me here, until father dies."

"Not necessarily," Pha's voice pitched with uncertainty. "If you were in jeopardy, you would be brought home. Prince Valgu must be made ready to take over the Regency."

Katrina stared at the distant mountains of Eta and Rassa. The sky around them grew pink in the fading sunlight. She gripped her ink and stylus and hugged her lapboard as she stood up. She moved to go and stopped at the hushed tone Pha used.

"Prince Valgu's at university, and as long as your father's well enough, he remains Regent. Your brother needs to focus on his studies. It's easier for him if we're here. We also need to secure a way to get you home. It's been harder to acquire than we expected."

Katrina held Pha's gaze and waited for anger to rise or bring to tears to her eyes, but nothing came. When she saw Valgu, he never discussed her return.

"It's not the answer you wanted to hear," Pha said.

"It's the truth," Katrina said stepping onto the walk leading to the back door. "The truth's better than hearing nothing."

She entered the house. Her mother sat in the back hallway working on her tapestry. Katrina slumped down on the stool beside it and watched her mother work. Her mother drew a stitch and glanced up at her.

"You came to sit with me? I'm honored."

Katrina let her lapboard drop forward revealing the drawing on her parchment.

"I've sketched this out," Katrina said. "I want to know what you think about it."

Her mother's eyebrows arched as she sat back. She let her needle drop and reached for the sketch. Katrina gave it to her.

"You've included color annotation too."

"I did it the way you taught me."

Her mother grinned and ran a finger down the list of colors.

"So?" Katrina said.

"So," her mother said.

"What do you think?" Katrina asked.

"It's good," her mother said. "I'll place an order for thread and fresh muslin tomorrow."

As a candidate in the House of Etrasa, Katrina learned basic human history.

Her ability to read and write were refined. All candidates learned enough mathematics to run a household. The simple math they were taught provided little challenge. Most of it she knew before she arrived here, but the instructors praised her mastery of it. She hoped it would help get her closer to acceptance at the university on Etrasa.

When Katrina's body began to morph and take on a woman's shape, the House of Etrasa sat her to learning languages. She expected her coursework to advance into more complicated lessons. Instead it stagnated. Older candidates spent time practicing various dance steps, or learning how to determine menus for seasonal gatherings. They walked without slumping, knew how to sit in any garment, and could recite every rule of appropriate conversation. They were given handheld mirrors and taught the art of smiling. Katrina liked holding the mirror up because it blocked Instructor Able's view when she talked to Mahogany.

"Did you know we would have a several week course on smiling?" Katrina asked. "Why don't they just bring play actors in and have them teach us everything?"

"They are teaching us everything. They can't have one of their ladies sent to a court in Encartha or the Palace Islands who can't read facial expressions. She'd be eaten alive."

"Why am I even complaining to you?"

"It's what friends do."

"You shouldn't even have to do this. You knew all of this before you came here."

"I do know it. Now I get to perfect it," Mahogany said. "Don't scowl at me. We're supposed to be smiling with ours eyes."

Katrina's frown eased into a smile.

"I know your mother can do it," Mahogany said. "I've seen her. She could teach this class, she's amazing."

Katrina nodded and let the mirror drop to her lap. Thinking about her mother's various smiles and voice inflections made her stir in her seat. Children knew the sincerity of their parents words better than anyone. She knew her mother's sincerity, didn't she?

"I don't see why all this is necessary," Katrina said. "How is learning to pay the right compliment going to further the career of a man who is incapable of gaining a wife with his own faculties?"

Mahogany laughed, and continued to laugh long enough for Katrina to grow anxious about what she found so funny.

"Honestly Katrina, you're such a pessimist," Mahogany said. "It's not just third sons and rich merchants seeking rank who come here. Some are normal men from respectable houses. Coming here is a very simple and practical way to meet a variety of equals without the expense of traveling everywhere."

Katrina scowled but Mahogany's argument was too practical and obvious to dismiss. She disliked it when her own bias blinded her to arguments with as much merit as her own.

She caught sight of Instructor Able walking the room in their direction. A former Lady of Etrasa, Able accepted a position as an instructor. One rumor said she had failed twenty Parade seasons and had no other choice. The other rumor contended she was selected as the wife of a Renao Lords son. Civil war broke out in Renao, her husband died, and Able returned to Etrasa to escape. Katrina guessed Able was around the same age as her mother. Ever poised and soft spoken, Able's waif appearance had turned hard with age.

Katrina pitched her voice into the eager conversational tone they were expected to practice.

"If you could pick your suitor, where would he be from?" Katrina asked.

"Very good," Mahogany cheered. "Let see if I have some sort of answer." She tilted the mirror higher and made a flirtatious expression with her eyes, raising a single eyebrow in a bowing arch.

Instructor able stopped in front of them, and Katrina and Mahogany set their mirrors in their lap.

"Good afternoon, candidates."

Katrina and Mahogany replied in tandem, "Good afternoon, Instructor."

"Mahogany," Instructor Able said. "Pretend I am a rival, give me a triumphant smile, one that tells me you've already won."

The look started in Mahogany's eyes. They roamed down instructor Able as the corners creased with a grin. She tilted her head and lifting her chin. Her lips parted and hinted at a smile before her eyes came up to lock with Able's.

"Well done," Instructor Able said.

"Katrina, I saw your mother marked with a neck tattoo this morning. When did she become the property of a trader?"

Instructor Able meant to throw her off with the question, and it worked. Katrina paused too long and tried to recover with a short a laugh.

"I suppose she got the tattoo the same day she went down to the beach to chat with a bunch of Delphi. I assure you, my mother has done neither."

"You hesitated too long, and your laugh was from nerves not sarcasm," Instructor Able said.

"Yes, instructor," Katrina said.

"Stupid questions always get what?"

"Stupid answers," Katrina said.

"At least you remembered that, carry on." Instructor Able walked on and Katrina looked over to see Mahogany smiling in her mirror.

"I would marry a man from my country," Mahogany said.

"What?" Katrina said.

"You asked if I if I could pick my own suitor, where would he be from. I would pick a man from home."

"I thought you wanted to go somewhere far away and exotic."

"You mean like where your from."

"Bisma's not exotic."

"For me it is. Don't be offended when I say this, but Bisma's come into too many problems. Breaking peace with Madar was a bad move. Now Gryph has too much say in what they do with their own country."

"So no suitor from Bisma for you, but yes to one from Gryph?" Katrina teased.

Mahogany's eyes went wide as she shook her head. "No, no, no. They're far too political."

"You like political," Katrina said.

"Yes, when there's something to be gained. Politics are pointless in Gryph. There's no real way to influence an outcome there."

"I'm confused, if you can't influence politics, then how is it political?"

"Because of the Gryphons. They decide which humans are in charge. The ones to woo for power in Gyph are the Gryphons, and they can't be wooed."

"But the people there still try?" Katrina asked.

"Of course," Mahogany said as she laughed. "Can you imagine?"

"No," Katrina said.

"It's not like anyone from Gryph ever comes here. Their families all prefer to intermarry."

"I thought there was a lord from Gryph at Parade last year?"

"Was there?" Mahogany made an exaggerated frown into her mirror. "I don't remember. Now you must tell me, where would your perfect suitor be from?"

"I think I feel the same way you do. I'd prefer a man who will bring me home."

Mahogany sat back and clutched her mirror to her chest. "It's never going to happen for you or I, but I'll keep praying."

"You pray?" Katrina asked with genuine shock.

Mahogany looked at her in reproach. "Of course I do."

Instructor able rang a small bell and the candidates all stood from their seats.

"Dinner service," Instructor Able said. "Fetch your aprons and I'll see you in the dining room."

Before the candidates ate dinner they served dinner to the full ladies of the House. Instructor Able said the best way candidates learned about a dinner service was by serving it themselves. Katrina thought this was just a way to gain cheap labor. Then she discovered no two dinners were the same. Proving the House of Etrasa spared no expense training its ladies how to dress, dance, talk, and even eat according to customs from every corner of the human world.

Katrina stood filling a water glass when Lady Genevieve of the Encartha Peninsula entered the dining room. Everyone called her 'Lady Ginny'. Her dark hair lay tied in a tight braid that matched the severe cut of her a navy military cadet uniform. She pulled the bag slung over her shoulder off and dropped it to the floor. She sat down in a vacant chair and lifted her water glass and met Katrina's eyes, making a silent plea for water. Katrina moved around the table and filled Lady Ginny's glass.

Lady Ginny's family paid her tuition to the House. After she became a lady, she achieved a perfect score on her University of Etrasa exam. The University trained cadets into military officers. As a guest cadet, Lady Ginny forfeit any future as a commissioned officer. She and the handful of other guest cadet ladies attended strictly for the academic opportunity.

"Still good enough to dine with us," Lady Terra said from accross the table. Lady Terra's thin brown hair never lay quite right, and her brown eyes were small. Mahogany claimed the instructors made Lady Terra wear bright colored bodices to draw eyes down to her best feature, enormous breasts.

Lady Ginny eyed her counterpart and Katrina marveled. Lady Ginny was using the exact expression Mahogany demonstrated for Instructor Able earlier.

A candidate whispered nearby, "Did you see the boots she's wearing?"

Lady Ginny locked Lady Terra in a look of triumph and said, "I'd hate missing the pleasure of dinner among my peers."

A tense silence followed the exchange. The child like voice of Lady Paige Wendt broke it. "Ginny's my hero," she said, projecting in her odd singsong.

Katrina wondered when she had ever shared an identical opinion with the odd Lady Paige.

"Honestly Terra," Lady Paige said. She pointed her knife at a few of the candidates. "The candidates in here could have delivered a better line than that."

"Please stop talking, Paige," Lady Terra said. "No one here wants to hear to you speak. Someday you should learn to open your mouth and sound like a grown up."

"Ginny's a Lady of the best kind," Lady Paige said. "And jealousy doesn't suit you."

Katrina caught Mahogany's glance and they shared a look of amusement.

"Thank you, Paige," Lady Ginny said.

"Do well, Ginny," Lady Paige said. "Most of us here are not steeped in envy. We're very proud of you."

Katrina wanted to shout her agreement with Lady Paige's sentiment, but settled for refilling her water glass. Katrina wanted to go with Lady Ginny and the other guest cadet ladies as they trekked up to the University everyday. If she was going to be stranded in a human life, she wanted to live it as brazen as Lady Ginny did.

Katrina graduated to the status of Lady during her seventh year on Etrasa. Her days were a mix of freedom and captivity. She became a prisoner to the next parade, but enjoyed the freedom to pursue her own studies. She developed a routine of leaving the House in the afternoon under the guise of working on her tapestry. She walked the road from the mansion down to the village, and when no one could see her, ducked into the island forest. Two hours of tapestry work in the evening was enough to cover for the time she stole for hiking.

Pha said little about her hikes.

"You should remain close to the Mansion," Pha said. "Stick to clearings, and stay away from fruit and nut trees."

"I should worry about the fruit trees?" Katrina asked in an amused tone.

"Leave them and the fruit eating creatures alone."

"I should worry about the noisy fruit eating birds?"

"Not them, worry about the beasts that'll eat them. Don't get within twenty paces of fruit tree."

Katrina blanched, "Don't worry, I've always avoided them."

Despite Pha's awareness, and the wear and tear to Katrina's shoes, her mother remained oblivious to her forest walks. If she had known, it would become one of the many things she liked to nag about. Lady Lena's idea of having a conversation with her daughter consisted of her nagging and Katrina listening. Katrina developed a mental callus to cope with it, but the less her mother had to nag about, the better.

The forest on Etrasa was fascinating. Flowers grew in abundance, many an ever-blooming variety who never fell out of season. Their unique beauty, mixed with the amazing number of new plants, made routine hikes forever interesting. Even the strange trees bloomed spicy fragrant flowers. The trunks of trees bared smooth bark and grew slender. They reached up together into tall expansive canopies. Their branches flowed from one tree to the other, a wide thick net of green with only the slender stakes of trunks to prop it up. She found trees with leaves twice the width of her hand, and others hung billowing strands of delicate fringe that drifted in the breeze. A few plants climbed free of the shaded ground cover, sending long narrow spindles up to the branches high above.

Her favorite hike overlooked the training areas used by the University of Etrasa. She liked to spy the cadets engaged in mock combat. Sometimes they passed her, burdened with packs and equipment, making the long hike around the perimeter of the university training areas. Their activities appeared difficult, but she rarely saw them disgruntled. They might look tired, or pensive, but most of the time they carried themselves with a determined contentment.

Hiking her preferred route, she encountered a thick hazy steam wafting accross the trail. Curious, she followed it off the path. The steam rose from under the base of a large cliff overhang. She found it most concentrated at a short opening near the cliff base. She pulled a small binti light lantern from her bag, and crawled into the opening. The walls were slick with damp. Dripping water pattered and a faint slosh echoed over and over somewhere nearby.

Overhead the ceiling twinkled from small jagged crystals encrusting every space her small lamp illuminated. The crystals were a muddy beige color, like the walls and floor. She wanted to fly up and inspect them closer. A spasm of muscle pain knotted the muscles in her mid back and shoulders. Her body stiffened and she doubled over as she closed her eyes against the pain. The years since her wings were taken did little to stall her instinctual urges to shift and fly. Her body obeyed, and the attempts always brought pain. Moments like this revived her frustrations. Her back pain connected her to memories of home, her family, her wings, and how everything was taken away. Grimacing she breathed. Pressing her shoulder forward she stretched the aching muscles and rotated her head.

The floor slanted, she crept down the gentle incline. The air felt warmer at the bottom. She heard a louder sloshing noise of rushing water. The lamplight illuminated a large body of water. Small round wells dotting the edge of a massive underground lake. Water rose and fell in each well, spraying water and producing an odd blubbering. Steam rose from the waters surface, which turned slow under the power of a distant churning current.

Kneeling down, she peered into the lake. It's bottom glowed. Raw binti stone in cheerful colors of yellow and orange covered the lake bottom. She held her hand over the water, the steam wafted through her fingers and kissed damp to the skin of her palm. Afraid of burns, she tested the water by dipping the pad of her little finger into the water. A tolerable heat, she sunk her fingertips into the water before immersing her whole hand. Her skin flushed pink as she closed her eyes and enjoyed the warm water enveloping her hand.

A large splash erupted. Her eyes flew open as she jerked her hand back. Looking around, she scanned the dark corners of the cave. Steadying her breath she sat stiff and listened.

Another slosh and slap, but her eyes caught nothing from the direction it came. Straining to hear more, she raised her lamp, trying to cast its light farther. She fought to keep her thoughts logical. Trying to calm the growing fear she sat in the dwelling of some dangerous island creature.

A bright white binti light moved through the water towards her. She shrieked and gapped at the large figure behind it. A mass obscured by odd streams of light and dark shadow.

Fumbling as she backed away, she lost hold of her lantern. She screamed but what emerged sounded little more than a whimpering croak. Wide eyed with panic, she stood immobilized as the dark mass emerged from the water.

The white binti light shined brighter as it broached the water. It illuminated pockets of the cave untouched by the light from the lake bottom and her lamp. The binti light hung from a lanyard and was carved into a simple disk. It sat nestled against the bare chest of a tall young man. He had long black hair and deep amber colored eyes. Pushing wet hair from his face he gave her a wide confident smile. He held out her lantern in one hand. He had caught it mid fall.

"I didn't mean to scare you, I'm sorry."

Shifting her stance, Katrina rubbed sweat from her hands onto the sides of her dress.

He shrugged and walked out of the pool, sloshing water in large torrents. His wide forehead balanced well with his jaw, and his only clothes were a loin cloth. Holding the lamp out to her, he knelt in front of her, and proceeded to recite the Veilede honorary greeting for an Airetti.

"I bow before one of the first to be blessed by God. May the airetti forever help us."

Clutching the fabric of her skirt she stared at him in disbelief. He continued to kneel. After a long pause, he opened his eyes and peeked up at her.

"Well?" he said.

"Well what?"

"Aren't you going to give me a reply? Maybe tell me to get up?" He sounded amused.

She snatched the lamp from him and worked her lips into a hard line.

"May I get up?" he said.

"Please, yes get up," she said in a fluster.

Her eyes traveled his form as he stood. His muscles were long with subtle definition. He lacked the bulk of a Mahigan, but she liked the way water slid across his bare torso. He rivaled a Mahigan in height, and stood with the posture of a warrior. He was Delphi, and handsome.

"Did I stump you or just make you upset?" he said settling into a relaxed stance.

"I haven't heard that in a really long time," she said.

He tilted his head and narrowed his eyes at her. "You haven't? What kind of people do you spend time with?"

"Excuse me?"

He stepped closer, grinning as he gazed down at her.

"I heard about you. The Airetti Princess, born with blue eyes like her mother's, but shaped just like her father's. It's nice to meet you Princess."

"Who are you?" she asked.

"My name is Puternic Jenke," he said in a jovial tone, grinning as if he just answered a question she already knew the answer to.

"Jenke?" she said. "You're the Delphi's Prince."

He gave no confirmation, but continued to grin at her. Katrina knew she was right. She remembered meeting his father, Raynes Jenke the Regent of the Delphi. Puternic and his father had a remarkable family resemblance.

"What's the Delphi Prince doing here? Shouldn't you be at a university in one of the mainland provinces?"

Puternic grinned as he leaned to the side and squeezed water from his hair. "There's more than one of us you know."

"More than one what?"

"My little brother Bryant. He's a Delphi Prince, and the cleverest three year old you'll ever meet."

Katrina fiddled with the handle on her lamp, gently flipping it back and forth. Owl was three when she was taken. She sobered under her quick calculation of Owl's current age, and the number of years that had passed since she had seen her.

"I didn't know about Prince Bryant. The last Delphi I spoke to, died the same day we met."

"They claim you died of a fever."

"Clearly, I'm not dead."

"I know. Your mother brought you here."

"Yes, we're both still here, pretending to be dead."

"Because Regent Pavaldon's mad."

Katrina resisted the urge to gnaw on her lower lip.

"Do your brothers know you live in a cave?" He said, gesturing to their surroundings.

Katrina gave him a weak smile.

"There's better caves to play dead in. The nearest is on another island not far from here."

Katrina's smile grew slightly as she stifled a quiet laugh.

"You must miss your family," he said.

"I do."

"Even your father?"

Katrina narrowed her eyes at him.

"Regent Pavaldon," Puternic looked to the side and his face grew serious. "He's called mad, but I've never witnessed it."

"You see My Regent often?" she asked.

He dipped his head to the scorn in her voice, and made no reply.

"My father used to tell me the Delphi were unreliable," she said.

"And my father told me the world is unreliable." His gaze met hers. The pity in his eyes repulsed her. "We must do our best to exist in it."

They stood in silence for a time.

"That sounds like a very elegant way of saying deal with it," she said.

She intended for her words to rebuff him, but he gave her a cheerful smile. Chuckling, he shook his head and put both hands on his hips.

"I like you," he said before letting his head fall forward into more laughter. With a sigh he lifted his hand, wagging a finger, and said, "I really like you."

His unexpected reaction left her unsure and wondering how to explain the change in her reaction. A moment ago she loathed him for pitying her and insinuating he knew about her father's madness. Now her agitation was gone. She wanted to laugh with him, and declare her own fondness for him.

How had he disarmed her? Was it because he was Veilede? Was it his big smile and heavy Delphi accent? Maybe it was the way he looked at her, like nothing about her was hidden from his dark amber eyes. The encounter was potent, unexpected, and somewhere a part of her knew this was more. She entered a moment that already held meaning.

Puternic turned and walked back to the waters edge.

"Where are you going?"

He stopped and looked over his shoulder sending her a sideways grin.

"I'm going to go sit back in the water. Is that okay?"

Puternic's smile mocked her but he waited for her response as if he really did need her permission. She nodded her consent and he proceeded to wade back into the lake. Moving to his knees, he eased down to lay on his stomach, and propped his torso under his elbows. Katrina inched closer to the water and sat down facing him.

Searching his eyes, she wondered if he really could see through her. What could the Delphi see in her that was invisible to everyone else?

"You should come in here," he said, gesturing to the water. "It feels wonderful."

"I can't," she said.

"Why not?"

"I have to go to dinner. My instructors would have endless questions if I arrived with wet hair."

"Tomorrow then," he said.

His bold demand to see her again, made her smile.

"We'll see," she said.

"I need to know if you can swim."

"I can't," she said.

"I guess we can't be friends then," he said sinking far enough in the water to cover his shoulders.

"That's ridiculous," she said.

"No it isn't," he said. "You're going to have to promise me you'll fix this. You must learn how to swim, or you and I can't be friends."

"Since when is friendship based on someone's swimming ability? What if I made you promise to learn how to fly."

"That's not the same Princess," he said, "I don't have wings to fly, but you possess everything you need to swim."

"My name is Katrina."

"Then tomorrow we swim, Katrina."

"It's very presumptuous of you, assuming I'll even come back here tomorrow."

"Why wouldn't you? I'm the most exciting thing you've found in this forest."

She faltered, just like when Instructor Able asked her a stupid question. Only Puternic's question wasn't stupid.

"Exciting, yes. You did scare me."

"But I don't scare you now," he said reaching a hand forward and taking one of hers.

His touch, the strength of his hand around hers made her heart pick up. Her stomach fluttered the same way it did flying, when she dove into her favorite free fall. The effect of his hand mesmerized her. She wanted him to pull her into the lake, take both her hands, touch her, and tell her how to chase this new sensation.

"Why are you really here?" she asked.

Puternic lowered their joined hands, submerging them in the water. He held her gaze as a flash of excited joy rang through her, tumbling and colliding with her new free fall sensation.

"To meet a dead Airetti Princess."

Too much, the feeling passing between them was too intense. How was this possible? It took every ounce of her self control to let go of his hand. The sensation between them lulled and then stopped as a she pulled her hand from the water.

"It was nice meeting you Prince Puternic."

Puternic shadowed her, rising from the water with amazing speed. He stood close and water drops collided on the flushed skin of his torso. She looked up and found him grinning down at her. Her cheeks warmed and she cleared her throat.

"I have to go."

"I'll see you tomorrow," he said.

Katrina regret picking up her bag and lantern. Each step out of the cave troubled her as a part of her pleaded to go back and sit with Puternic, her hand in his. The humidity of the cave left her hair and dress damp and she shivered from a passing breeze. It swayed the trees and scattered the steam about. The chill eased her troubled thoughts as she regained her senses.

Walking back to the House mansion, her stomach growled with hunger. Meeting Puternic, she needed to keep it to herself if she wanted to see him again. She exited the forest, stepped onto the Mansion road, and stopped. She did, she wanted to see him again. She shook her head and continued walking. No, she needed to swear off seeing him again. Reporting this would be bad enough. Pha trusted her, but Valgu would forbid future hikes. But why even bother him? Valgu checked on her what, six, seven months ago? He was busy. There was no need to trouble him or ruin her favorite past time over one harmless meeting.

Katrina startled as someone fell into step beside her.

"Lady Katrina," Bonner said.

Her throat constricted and dread pooled in her gut. Where had Bonner come from? Her words came out with a breathy pitch. "Guard Bonner, good evening."

"Slow down a tick. You and me need a chat."

She halted, and heard her heartbeat in her ears. She looked around to see who else she failed to notice.

"I don't mind trailing you accross the island, but I'm not going in no caves. Understand?"

"What?"

"No caves. Watch the Cadets, hike the cliffs, take a nap-I don't care. We know your walks are harmless."

"Harmless," she said too fast, "Yes, they are."

"It's why Gan don't mind. I've never seen you do nothing, but you can't be going in those caves."

"Oh," she said. "Alright. I didn't, well I-"

"No caves," he said.

"No caves," she said, nodding her head.

Bonner escorted her to House mansion and opened the door for her.

"I almost forgot," he said rubbing his eyes. "There's no walk tomorrow.

Gan says you're to meet him at the stables dressed in the orange."

House Ladies dressed in deep orange colored dresses when they traveled outside the boundaries patrolled by the House Guards. Katrina nodded and searched Bonner's face for an explanation.

"I'll be there," she said. "As instructed."

"Have a good dinner, Lady Katrina."

Her heart continued to race as she sat down to dinner. Mahogany sent her a quizzical look from accross the table. Katrina shook her head and took a long drink of water. She thought of all the afternoons she spent hiking the forests, never once suspecting Bonner or one of the other House guards trailed her. A mix of humiliation and fear held her appetite hostage. What if Bonner had followed her into the cave? Where would she and her mother be tonight if a House Guard witnessed her meeting Puternic in that cave? Such real consequences should have destroyed the temptation to see him again. But a part of her continued to glory in what happened. She wanted to gloat over the handsome man who sought her out and wanted to see her again. Pure foolishness, but she sat ready to walk back to that cave and do it all over again.

The following afternoon Katrina went to the stables. Four other Ladies dressed in their deep orange attire, stood at the stable entrance.

Guard Master Gan exited the stables on horseback. A procession of groomsmen and horses followed him out.

"Ladies," Gan said in greeting. "Good to see you, good to see you." He pointed at Katrina and smiled. "How are you even old enough to be wearing the orange."

"Good afternoon, Guard Master," she said.

"Saddle up Ladies," Gan said. "I know some of you have the stamina to walk where we're going, but why walk if we don't have to?"

The women ascended into saddles, some smiling and giggling like they were still candidates. The Ladies took hold of their reigns, and one by one followed Gan down to the city.

They followed the main street, passing the row houses, and onto a road with the sole destination of the University of Etrasa. They crossed the last intersection and Lady Elana let out a hiccuping sob. She reigned in her horse and the Ladies behind her rode by. Katrina stopped beside her and watched as Gan and the other Ladies continued on.

Lady Elana had a strong sturdy figure, but she looked frail hunched forward in the saddle crying.

"I can't do it, I can't be a Cadet," she said shaking her head as large tears fell from her big brown eyes.

"Elana," Katrina soothed, "This is an honor. You should be happy."

Lady Elana glared at her, "Honor? To train at arms like a common man."

"To be educated, as an officer."

"I am educated!"

"I know, I'm sorry," Katrina said. "What I mean is, this is an opportunity."

"Yes, an opportunity to make Rudolph more money."

Katrina nodded and sighed. "That's why we're here, isn't it? We learn more, and somehow it increases our value."

Lady Elana pressed the palms of her hands to her swollen eyes. "Rudolph will teach us anything if human noblemen say it makes us better brides."

"If you didn't want to attend the university, why didn't you deliberately fail the exam? It's what many of the others did."

Lady Elana shook her head, "The House might have believed it if I failed, but not my father. He knows me. He would've made Rudolph test me again and again until I passed. He worries, fears I'll be passed over to often at Parade."

"He's right to," Katrina said. Lady Elana shot her a hurt glance, which softened when she saw her sarcasm. "After this, we'll know all the things that will make a noblemen want us. How to set a table for a Jintari ambassador, the five steps to the spring festival dance in Houg, and how to hack apart our enemies with a sword."

Lady Elana huffed a laugh and took a deep breath and played along. "You're right, I don't know why my father's concerned."

They urged their horses on again, following in a slow pace after Master Guard Gan. Katrina gave Lady Elana a conspiratorial grin.

"There's another perk they don't talk about when they test us for the University."

"What's that?" Lady Elana asked.

Katrina lowered her voice and watched Guard Master Gan to be sure he remained ahead and out of earshot. "We'll be surrounded. Everyday. By men in uniform."

"Oh, well," Lady Elana said. She sniffed and her normal posture returned. "Well, that is something to consider."

"We'll have to see, very athletic men, everyday."

"Yes," Lady Elana said. "The cadets are rather athletic aren't they. That's much more," she smiled and faint flush filled her cheeks. "Well it's much more convincing than telling me about taking classes in calculus."

Katrina laughed and urged her mare into a short gallop. Laughing, Lady Elana came beside her and together they closed the gap between them and the others up ahead.

They traveled uphill on the journey to the university. The road leveled off at a large manicured field. A series of buildings sat alined on the far side of it. They were larger than she expected. The entire campus seemed invisible from down in town. The buildings looked Encarthean, made of wide grey stones and plain windows. They had little in common with the islands local architecture. They had a more formal appearance that matched the inhabitants nearby dressed in uniforms of dark blue.

The ladies followed by Gan, dismounted. A stable hand took the reins from her. Gan stood beside an officer who waited for them. When the ladies all gathered at the step, the officer led them into a building. It contained rooms full of vacant dining tables and chairs. They passed through a foyer and into a large formal dining room where Rudolph sat beside an older man in uniform. They stood as the Ladies approached the table.

"Please, join us," Rudolph said, and motioned to the vacant seats at the table. He introduced the ladies to their host, General Taylor, the Commander of Cadets.

"Ladies, you have all been accepted as guest cadets here at the University of Etrasa. There are two ways you many be enrolled. The first is partial enrollment, where you only attend the academic classes offered here. Those partially enrolled can't complete a degree. To attain a degree, you must choose the second option and be a fully enrolled cadet. You must complete all the tasks and coursework of a regular cadet. You may choose what's most suitable for you, however I encourage full enrollment. As an added incentive, those selecting full enrollment have extended curfew, are allowed to take their meals here with their cadet class, and will be awarded an unlimited Parade wardrobe stipend."

One of the Ladies made an excited squeak, and Katrina grinned. The wardrobe stipend was a great incentive. It might be the only thing capable of saving her from a nagging marathon with her mother, because she had every intention of taking the full enrollment option. Her mother would do more than nag over this. She would rage.

As predicted, her new cadet status triggered one of her mother's more colorful lectures.

"Don't let those women touting swords fool you," she said. "Soldiering is a man's occupation. Why would you ever want to learn a man's trade? You've always had too much of your father's arrogance."

Her mother's words stung, and she fought the urge to scream. She inhaled and let the sting fade. It sunk into the hollow where she stored the rest of her animosity for her mother. Exhaling, she held her lips tight and formed her best passive expression.

Pha looked neither pleased nor displeased with the news. She adjusted the wraps on her hands and spoke with a calm sincerity.

"Some weapons are harder than others to wield. I think it's a good idea to understand how lethal such things are. It decreases your chances of using one carelessly."

She went to bed early, hiding in the small sanctuary of her bedroom. One by one she peeled the layers of doubt her mother had thrown over her decision. She sat at the edge of neutral knowing her brother would forget about her again tonight. She sat there anyway, unsure if she sat there out of loyalty or habit.

A hand gripped her shoulder, pulling her into a flurry of vibration. She sat up and found herself on the floor of the cave where she met Puternic. His hand kept hold of her shoulder and his deep amber eyes inspected her with a look of pure panic.

"Where have you been?" he said.

"What?"

"I waited for you, all day."

He looked different, he had more clothes on. A sleeveless tan tunic and grey lightweight pants. She looked at his hand on her shoulder and back at him. He loosened his grip, but his frown increased.

"I'm not allowed in the sea caves."

Puternic released her and stood crossing his arms.

"Finc, where can we meet?"

Katrina sat forward and wrapped her arms around her knees.

"We can't."

"Why, because of your family?"

"No, I'm guarded. I didn't know they were escorting me on my hikes. I found that out when I was scolded for coming in here."

Puternic dropped to the floor. His scowl remained as he stretched out on the floor beside her, leaning on one elbow.

"The House," Puternic said. "You fear the people there."

"Yes," she said.

"I thought it was me," he said. His frown softened.

Holding his gaze became difficult, especially as she confessed the truth.

"No," she said. "I wanted to come back. I really did."

His face lit up with a big smile and he took one of her hands. Her heart leapt at his touch. His hand felt smooth and warm, but the contact lacked the overwhelming intensity of their first meeting.

"Why is this different now?" she asked, looking at their joined hands.

He considered her question and brightened. "Because, we were in the water before."

She looked over at the lake. "What if we were in the water now?"

He huffed a laugh, "No, water in neutrals not the same."

"But if we were in real water, it could happen again?"

"It's very likely."

"I don't understand," she said.

"It's second nature for us. It's something the Delphi do to communicate underwater. In the ocean it can be hard to read a face. We can't always see or hear what we need to, and it can be faster to pass our feelings than wander."

"All the Delphi do that, all the time second nature. And you don't get overwhelmed?"

"No," he said and squeezed her hand. "Did I overwhelm you?"

"Yes, you most certainly did."

He looked pleased by her confession and she wanted to yank her hand back and shove him. He pet her hand as if it were a prize and it distressed her how much she enjoyed it.

"You came all the way to Etrasa to meet me," she said.

He traced each finger on her hand with his index finger.

"I did. It's my obligation as the future Regent to find the next Regina of the

Delphi. I'm proud to say, I've met every living Airetti in Madar. That is to say, all of them, except for you."

"Then you know my sister Owl?"

He nodded and met her eyes. "Not well. I don't think anyone outside your family knows her well."

Katrina folded her fingers over the edge of his hand and squeezed, "Tell me about her, please. I never get to see her or Massie."

"The last time I saw Owl was at the celebration for Princess Nuala's birth."

"Princess Nuala, of what province?"

He frowned and stared at her in confusion. "Of Mozgas, Princess Nuala Aranysarga of Mozgas, born to Regent Pavaldon and Lady Juniper."

"My father married again?"

He nodded, "I believe she's the fifth wife and Lady Miandes is the sixth? But she's been in his household longer. I don't know, I could have them reversed."

"What?"

"He rallied for Lady Juniper, but shortly after, married his sixth wife Lady Miandes. She came back with his Army when they returned from the search for you. She was living in the palace before Lady Juniper's rally."

"Two more wives. I have another sister."

Puternic hesitated, "Another sister, and brother. Lady Miandes gave birth to Prince Dermot seven summers ago. You were never told?"

"He's been," she said and her words fell away. "I'm sorry, this is just. I don't know."

He sat up, leaning in close as gentle fingers intertwined with hers.

"I apologize," he said. "I assumed you were kept informed."

"No don't, I'm glad you told me. It's a shock, a really big shock." A gross understatement. The news stabbed her heart. She heaved a breath and looked to the ceiling.

"Part of playing dead must mean you don't get to see them very often."

"No, I don't."

She widened her eyes and fought back the tears blurring her vision.

"I really messed up, didn't I," he said.

She met his dark amber eyes and he brushed away the first tear from her cheek.

"I never meant to make you cry."

Her heart hitched at the comfort of his close proximity. Why did he need to come here? She should dislike him. Instead an opposite emotion pulled her to him. Like a change in tides he pulled in a direction that widened the gap even further between her and her family.

"You were supposed to come to the cave today," he said. "We were going to go swimming. I was going to declare myself your suitor."

"My suitor?" she said, and gave a short laugh at the ridiculous idea of it. "What, are you going to claim me at Parade?"

He frowned and shook his head. "We're Veilede."

"It's too bad we're here, and I have no clue what to do with a Veilede suitor."

He eased away from her. "I knew you'd be a challenge."

"You did not," she said with a huff.

"I did too," he said, stretching onto his back but keeping a possessive hold on her hand.

"Why's that?"

"Because, you're an Aranysarga."

She shook her head. "I'm tired. I should go."

"I can't let you leave," he said. "Not until you tell me when I'll see you again."

"I don't know," she said. "I don't know how much freedom I'll have as a cadet."

"That's not an answer," he said.

"I'll figure it out, and see you in neutral."

"Tomorrow night, summon me tomorrow night."

"You're pushing," she said.

"Tomorrow night, promise me."

"Fine, tomorrow. Good night."

"Katrina."

"What?"

"I'm your suitor."

"Oh really," she tried and failed to contain the smile spreading on her face. "And what does that make me?"

"The next Regina of the Delphi."

He let go of neutral then. The cave, the binti bottomed lake, and the grip of his hand vibrated and disappeared.

She awoke early. A keen awareness of her new secret, Puternic lingered. She dressed alone in the darkness. She needed to clear her thoughts. Keep the elation and devastation from her meeting with Puternic at bay. Greeting her mother on the stairs, Katrina met her eyes without trouble. Her secret seemed trivial compared to the things her mother kept concealed.

Hearing Pha in the kitchen, Katrina darted past the kitchen door. Pha would notice her absence this morning. Katrina feared the time she spent loitering each morning with Pha. A pain pierced her heart and she fought back tears again. Pha knew about her father's wives. About her sister and brother's birth. Why did she keep their existence a secret? The shock of all the changes at home rushed up again to swamp her. She collected her bag and fled the row house. She walked fast up the main street and took the curve onto the road leading to the university.

She got lost at the university in a frenzy of the new. New clothes, people, expectations, classrooms, schedules, books, and instructors. She jumped in, eager for the diversion. Embracing it, she did her best to forget last night and keep pace with the day.

A runner was sent to pull her from her first afternoon lecture. He escorted her to the office of Assistant Dean, Colonel Hackler. The office contained plain wooden furniture, the well groomed figure of Colonel Hackler, and based on his uniform what appeared to be a first year cadet.

The cadet stood over seven feet tall, not including his horns. Brown fur covered his bull face and faded into dark tanned skin of his man's body. He was a sight, something she had never seen outside of few drawings in textbooks. The cadet was a Minotaur, and his size alone made the office feel small and cramped.

Colonel Hackler looked from a piece of paper in his hand, to Katrina.

"What's your name cadet?"

She pulled her body to attention, a position she had learned that morning.

"Cadet Katrina Larksbur."

"This is Cadet Thedmir," Colonel Hackler said. "He wrote here that you possess the ability to wander. Is that correct?"

"Yes, Sir," she said.

"Well good, that fixes that. Cadet Larksbur, meet your new best friend. You and Cadet Thedmir here are going to be assigned together for the duration of your time here."

Katrina looked from Colonel Hackler to Cadet Thedmir and wondered how else she should greet her classmate.

"Cadet Thedmir, you should still keep paper and something to write with handy," Colonel Hackler said. "We can't rely on Cadet Larksbur's presence all the time. I'll make sure your schedule is built around hers. Other than that, dismissed."

Unsure what to do, Katrina gave the one reply she had mastered that morning. "Yes, Sir."

When they were free of the Colonel's office, Thedmir wandered to her.

What is one of the Veilede doing here?

Katrina craned her neck to try and meet his gaze as she wandered. *I'm trapped here pretending I'm a human. What's your excuse?*

A rumbling deep chuckle echoed in her mind. *Someone hates me.*

Thedmir offered her one of his big hands. She took it and marveled at its balanced proportions. His hands held the same rustic strength of his bull features, but were elegant and contrasted against his more obvious features.

Is Thedmir your full name?

In Tvarchus, we have names based off our tribe locations. I'm Thedmir of the lowlands by the Green Mountains. Colonel Hackler said here I'm to go by Cadet Thedmir.

Katrina knew little about Tvarchus other than it was the Minotaur homelands, and it sat an equal distance from Etrasa as Madar only in the opposite direction.

Katrina looked up and down the hallway and guessed the way back to the afternoon lecture hall.

"What if I wasn't here?" she said. "Would you have spent your entire time here communicating with a pencil and paper?"

I think so. Usually we're sent here with an interpreter, a human who can speak for us.

"But they sent you here without one? Someone really must hate you."

It's fortunate I found a Veilede woman outside.

"You didn't refer to me as that, did you?"

No.

Thedmir offered her the paper he had used to communicate with Colonel Hackler. She frowned as she read near the top, *The small female cadet in my Battalion, she can wander.*

You are small. The other females in the Battalion are all taller than you.

"Not by that much. How did you notice my height? Everyone here must look small to you?"

The description is accurate.

Her mother stood in the threshold of the back door. The sun sunk further into the horizon and the binti lamps glowed overhead. Katrina tried her best to work on her tapestry, but her mother distracted her. The tension of her mother's presence, pulled at Katrina's focus. Her mother made slow steps to her, drinking as she walked. She carried a plain goblet, and her lips were stained with more than one pour of red wine.

"Don't ever let them fool you into believing they see you as an equal. No man does."

Katrina halted her progress and looked up at her mother.

"Don't get caught making a man look bad. It's an offense they'll begrudge other men, but never a woman. That kind of slight the average male ego can't withstand. Conceal your actions or deflect the blame on someone else."

"I get it, mother. I'm a female and I should accept my place in the hierarchy of the sexes. I should find Rudolph tonight and quit the university before I've started."

"No darling, you're not listening. That's not what I said."

She faced her mother who stood looking up at the ceiling in frustration.

"I know, I'm your mother. I shouldn't say anything. You're only going to ignore me." Her mother took a sip of wine and cleared her throat. "But I wish you'd listen to me more. Pha isn't the only woman in this house worth listening to. I do know a few things. I've lived in the Bisma court. I was the favorite wife of, well arguably the most powerful Regent in Mozgas."

"What are you trying to tell me?"

"Darling," the lamplight flashed in her mother's blue eyes. "It's important you be ready."

"Ready for what?"

"The headiness of it," her mother grinned and her eyes drifted off as she remembered something. "It's heady to see a man's face when he realizes he's underestimated you."

"And I need to be ready for that," Katrina said.

"Oh yes, absolutely. Once they figure it out, they'll either adore you, or want to kill you."

"I see," Katrina said.

"Good, because knowing a man's character won't help you predict their reaction." Her mother walked to the back staircase and climbed each step one at a time. "I'm just trying to prepare you. You're going to be around lots of boys pretending to be men. All of them armed. Try to not get anyone killed."

Exhausted, Katrina regretted agreeing to see Puternic tonight. She still reeled from the revelation about her family the night before. The drain to her body from their time in neutral made the day when she really needed focus, difficult. The start time tomorrow was earlier than her accustomed routine, which meant less sleep. She thought of Puternic's easy smile and how close he sat to her. The way his proximity seemed to bend her will to his. She had to make this visit fast or suffer more tomorrow. Hovering outside of neutral, she hesitated going in. She spent so much time on the edge of neutral waiting for a summon. Did she remember how to summon someone on her own?

Entering neutral, she envisioned the cave, the lake, and the way Puternic held her hand. A whispering pulse of vibration tapped her chest. Opening her eyes, Puternic vibrated into focus. He squeezed her hand and smiled.

"I can't stay long," she said.

She meant what she said, but now he was here, holding her hand again. Did she have to go anywhere?

He laughed, "Of course you can."

"No, I can't. I want to, but I honestly can't. I have to start waking earlier than I'm used to. I'm already going to be short sleep. I don't want to sit through each of my lectures tomorrow fighting sleep."

"You have lectures tomorrow?"

"At the university."

Puternic laughed.

"Why is that funny?"

"A human university."

"I guess it is a little odd."

Puternic snickered again.

"It's not like I have other options here."

"I can give you other options," he said, caressing her upper arm with his free hand. "Better options. I declared myself to you. I can get you away from the House."

"What?"

"You can leave here with me. We could go away tonight."

"You're serious," she said, and shook her head. "What about my mother, and Pha?"

"What about them?"

"I don't think they'll want to go anywhere with you. I know Pha won't let me go anywhere with you."

"Who's Pha?"

"My guardian."

"Your guardian," he said, as his free hand found its way to her waist. "You're a grown woman, not a helpless child."

"Perhaps, but if I leave, and my contract with the House is unfulfilled, my mother will be made a slave on the sex market. I can't abandon her to that."

"Do you really intend to stay in Etrasa and fulfill that contract?"

She went still. He searched her eyes, waiting for an answer she had ignored for years. Then she moved. Releasing his hand, she shied away from his touch.

"No," she said, and stepped away from him.

He pursued her, following, remaining in her space.

"That's her fate then. You can't save her from that."

His hands extended to her, begging her to return to him.

"No," she said. "I know I can't save her, but my brothers will figure something out."

"Really?" he asked dropping his arms. His jaw clenched. "They're going to ensure the safety of the woman who poisoned their father? The one responsible for the death of their mothers?"

"She's my mother."

"If she's smart, she'll find her own way out of the contract."

"I'm not leaving here until Valgu brings me home."

"And when was the last time you saw him?"

"That doesn't matter."

Puternic gestured to his chest and threw his other arm out in frustration as he raised his voice.

"I'm the one who told you about the existence of your father's fifth and sixth wife. I'm the one who watched you cry after learning you have a brother and sister you've never known."

Katrina shook her head at him and took another step back. "You don't understand."

He dropped his arms and inched his way back to her. "No, I do. They abandoned you here."

"I need to stay here."

"You're one of the first," he said, stopping in front of her. If he were any closer his body would press against hers.

"You don't belong here. Let me bring you home."

"Not tonight," she said.

He let out a growl of frustration and grabbed his forehead, pulling the hair at his scalp as he paced away. He walked a small circle before coming to stop, where he glowered and crossed his arms. She stared back, her will to fight drained. They held each others gaze and she did what she could to brace herself for the next verbal blow. He had uncovered every fear she kept hidden. Prying them out with the honest force of his words, and now she stood raw and exposed.

"In five days, I'll have a free afternoon," she said. "We can meet in the cave."

His eyebrow arched with interest as he realized she meant they would meet in person. "In the cave you've been banned from."

"It's up to you. We don't have to meet if you don't want to risk a run in with the House guards."

"I'll see you in five days," he said uncrossing his arms and walking to her.

"Five days," Katrina said. She released neutral before he could reach her or give a response.

Pha hummed a quiet tune as she rubbed her arm.

"Come on," Pha said, prodding her with a gentle push. "I promised I'd have you out the door on time this morning."

Katrina opened her eyes and blinked a few times.

"Are you awake my Katrina?"

"I'm awake." Katrina stayed prone, but focused on Pha who busied with the buttons on her cadet uniform jacket.

Pha turned and motioned for her to get up. "Sit up so you don't nod off."

Katrina obeyed, maneuvering her legs over the side of the bed. Her muscles protested and she pushed away every thought of how her tired body would endure more punishment today.

Being a cadet consumed almost every hour of her day. In the classroom she thrived. On the field during physical pursuits she floundered. Her body struggled to gain the endurance and strength many of her classmates already possessed.

"I washed this one out as soon as you got back," Pha said as she reached up and smoothed her jackets shoulders. "It feels dry."

Katrina nodded.

"I set a few of the biscuits you like by your bag downstairs. You can eat them on your way, or maybe later if you get hungry."

"I'm always hungry," she said.

"Running hard will do that," Pha said.

"I thought I liked running," she said. "The university's changed my mind. I hate it."

Pha motioned for Katrina to sit down in her chair. She sat and Pha proceeded to brush out and braid her hair.

"At the House, the men come, meet a woman they like. Then they'll declare themselves a Lady's suitor, and pay the House for the right to marry her."

"Yes," Pha said.

"How does it work, back home? Does a man see a woman he likes, tell her he's her suitor, and then go off to win her rally?"

Pha chuckled, "Maybe, if the woman has no father, or brothers, to watch over her interests. Veilede men usually spend a little time getting to know the woman they're attracted to. Most consider it impolite to attend a rally for a total stranger."

"So he meets her, tells her he's her suitor, then declares rally?"

"Close, but first her family needs to announce she's ready to entertain suitors. Word gets out, and depending on her popularity, she'll receive requests to spend time with interested men. It's the right of a woman's family, or if she is without the care of a male relation, her Regency may declare her rally. Rallies are only to occur during the regulated times dictated by the Madar Council. The rally takes place, her suitors fight, and she marries the winner."

"In my case, father or Valgu will make the announcement?"

"Yes."

"Men will show up, meet me, and then maybe declare themselves my suitor?"

"No, that's unlikely for you. Mahigans won't show up at your door."

"I'll only have Mahigan suitors?"

"My girl, you're one of the first," Pha chuckled. "Any man pursuing you who's not Mahigan, has a death wish and you should ignore them. A Mahigan will send a request to meet you through your father or brothers. Or they'll write you a letter."

"Why?"

"It's a hardship for a Mahigan to be near an eligible Airetti. The stress for them to maintain control of their instincts, it's something they shouldn't need to endure if the Airetti woman's not interested."

"So how did the Regent of Idania marry his Regina? He isn't Mahigan."

"A rare exception, acceptable under the laws of a Regent's first rights. You'll probably never have to worry about that. Mozgas is the only Regency that might have a new Regent anytime soon. And your brother is perfectly capable of rallying for his own Airetti wife. No, I predict when yours is announced, you'll have more Mahigan suitors than you can count."

Pha tied off her work. Katrina stood and faced Pha who gave her an odd grin as she stared up at her.

Katrina looked down self consciously and then back at Pha. "What? What's wrong?"

"It's so nice, to talk with you again. You haven't said more than a handful of words to me in days. I've thought about nothing but what I must have done to upset you."

"Oh," Katrina said.

"You can tell me what I did. You can say whatever. I've always listened and let you say what you needed to say, haven't I?"

"Yes, always."

"I did do something then, didn't I?"

Katrina struggled to find the right words. "It's me. I've been overwhelmed. Adjusting, to things I've learned. It's been a long week."

"Oh my girl," Pha said cupping her cheeks between her hands. "I sense you're speaking the truth, but there's something you're not telling me."

"When have you ever done anything against me?" Katrina asked, reaching up and holding Pha's hands to her face.

Pha shook her head.

"I know you would do everything in your power to never say or do anything if you thought it would hurt me."

"I do what I can." Pha pulled Katrina to her and wrapped her in a hug.

"I have to go," Katrina said. "Thank you for the biscuits. I'll see you this evening."

"I'll see you this evening."

Katrina sat in the last lecture before lunch twirling her writing stylus with one hand. After this, her classmates would eat and return to the dormitory for common area maintenance, and two hours of free time. Since she still lived in the row house, her free time started after lunch. She could even skip lunch.

May I ask you something? Thedmir wandered.

Katrina switched her stylus to her other hand and tried to hold it still.

Yes, she wandered back.

Who is this?

Thedmir wandered a clear image of Puternic.

Katrina's mouth went dry and she coughed. She held her chest as her breathing settled, then glanced at him out of the corner of her eye.

A friend, she wandered.

You think of him often, he distracts you.

Thedmir, Katrina asked in a cautious tone, *Are you able read my thoughts when I'm not deliberately passing them to you?*

Many of them, yes. The images mostly.

My friend, you can't tell anyone about him, okay? He and I are a secret.

You can't share affection, and remain a secret. It's not what friends do.

It's complicated.

If he cared about you, he wouldn't hide his affection for you.

He's not the one hiding anything, I am. I'm the bad friend.

Your planning says otherwise.

Please, promise me, you'll refrain from discussing anything about it with anyone.

I don't need to promise. I wouldn't waste time writing all that down. Dear cadet class leader, my assigned classmate left lunch early this afternoon. She plans to go swimming in a forbidden sea cave with a man who plans to mate her.

Katrina shrunk down in her seat, holding her breath, and trying not to laugh.

"Stop," she whispered, then wandered, *We don't mate. He doesn't plan to mate with me, he want's to make me his wife.*

The meaning is equal, Thedmir wandered. *A mate and a wife produce children.*

Both have sex, both have children, but they aren't the same.

I viewed the statues in the sex market. It's the same. They're all mating.

"No, Thedmir," Katrina said as she massaged her eyebrows. "How did I ever get assigned to you?"

Should I come with you to this cave? I could keep watch for the men in the orange uniforms.

"No, thank you. That's very generous, but I'll be fine."

Katrina saw none of the House guards during her first week as a guest cadet. She often looked over her shoulder for Guard Bonner. She never saw him. When she did spot him, he was out on his usual rounds escorting the Ladies to and from the House mansion.

She and the other guest cadet ladies walked unescorted, to and from the University, at all sorts of random times throughout each day. A guard came around at eight to mark them in for curfew, unless they were scheduled to sleep outdoors during training.

She accepted the risks of getting caught. They worried her as she hiked through the forest to the cave. She did her best to stay alert. Hoping with every step no one followed or found her. Fear, and the anticipation of seeing Puternic made her heart pound. A jolt of excitement mixed with assurance raced through her when she saw him sitting crossed legged beside the lake. She started navigating the steep incline near the entrance. He stood and hurried over to her.

"I'm so glad to see you," he said.

He extended his hand and she took it. Letting him help her down the rest of the slope to where the floor leveled out.

"Me too." She let him keep hold of her hand. He pulled her after him as he walked backwards, leading them back the warm rock at the lakes edge.

"It's been a really long five days," he said. "I've thought of you constantly. Worried you were done with me."

"I thought about it. I thought a lot, since we talked."

"I wanted too much too fast."

"You made me consider the truth of things."

"I overstepped, and I'm sorry."

"I thought about how you said you're my suitor."

"Yes," he said.

"But we know neither my father or my brothers have announced me as ready to entertain suitors."

"Yes," he said sitting down. He pulled at her hand, and she sat down accross from him.

"You proclaimed yourself to me, and said you would make me the next Regina of the Delphi."

"Yes, I did."

"How?"

"How?" He blinked in confusion.

"Yes, how, because you can't take me back to Mozgas, or anywhere in the mainland and claim I'm your wife. The Mahigan population won't allow it, and neither will my family."

"That bothers you?"

"Yes."

"Yet, you're here."

"Yes."

"I'll take you back to Madar. We'll live with the Delphi. Most of Madar believes you're dead, and unless your family denies it, we'll let that remain. Someday, when my father passes, we'll reveal the truth. I'll make you the Regina of the Delphi according to a Regents first rights."

"Why me?"

"You know why."

"No, I don't. We've had three conversations."

"Are you denying what you felt when I first held your hand? What you feel right now? Why you're holding it now, or the pull to be together?"

"No. I still worry."

"There's no need."

"There's plenty. There's also something you must consider, before you take me anywhere. And I won't be angry if it changes your mind."

"What is it?"

Katrina unbuttoned her uniform top, removed it and set it aside. She began pulling up her undershirt when Puternic reached out and stopped her.

"What are you doing?"

"I'm showing you."

He released her and she rose to her knees. Turning her back to him, she removed her undershirt. She untied the lacing to her undergarments and pulled it free to fully expose her back. She held the clothes in her lap as she waited for him to speak.

"What happened to you?"

"My mother took me to a Skrieni village after she poisoned my father. The apothecaries there got ahold of me. They took my wings."

She heard him move and tensed as his arms came around her. He kissed her shoulder and pleasure bloomed on her skin. He guided her into his lap, and urged her to rest her back against his torso.

"What they did, that's why people believe you're dead." He twined their fingers together and rested his face on her shoulder. "You thought I'd reject you, because you can't shift."

"You've made it your mission to meet every living airetti. Maybe the one you pick as wife and make the Delphi Regina, should be normal."

"You're plenty normal."

"Taking me from here is a big risk, one you shouldn't if I'm not qualified to fulfill the roll."

"Of course you can fulfill the roll. You're still airetti. I knew it the moment I saw you. Every Delphi who sees you knows what you are. You'll never have to worry about proving your form by shifting among us."

She leaned to the side so she could look over his shoulder and meet his gaze.

"I don't think you should settle on me because the circumstances are convenient."

He laughed, "Settle? Are you kidding me? The woman of my dreams is in my arms half naked right now."

Katrina's heart beat faster as Puternic scanned her expression and his face inched closer to hers. Their eyes were open when his lips touched hers for the first time. Thoughts and questions flooded her mind. Her blood rushed through her body in such a frenzy she wondered if she might faint.

His lips pressed firmer to hers, coaxing them apart. When his tongue sought hers, they collided in a fumbling and unsophisticated dance. The intensity of it so foreign, her favorite part was being released from it. His hand softly cupped her cheek and he trailed kisses on her forehead and across her cheekbone to the base of her ear. He eased her down and she lay on her back beneath him.

"Was that okay?"

She made a shy nod as she smiled at him. She took a long strand of his black hair in-between her fingers. The texture was thick and smooth, and it slid like silk against her touch.

"Did you like it?" she said.

Puternic's deep gold eyes shied away for a moment, as he tasted his lips.

"Of course," he said smiling when his gaze met hers again. "But of course I've never done this before."

Katrina fell into a fit of giggles. "You liar," she said. Closing her eyes she huddled into his shoulder and tried to hide her face. "You have too," she said. "Don't pretend."

He made a deep chuckle, "Maybe once or twice before."

"I've never even kissed anyone before," she said.

"Well, come back here. Let me do it again."

Beaming with excitement, Puternic prodded her out of his shoulder and pressed his lips to hers with his eyes closed this time. His body shifted over her and he rested some of his weight against her. She followed his lead, letting her eyes drift shut as she focused on his kiss. Relaxing, she became more comfortable. Unhurried, his lips brushed against hers and their tongues fell into a soft rhythm. It sent a warm excitement through her body.

His hips rolled in a slow press against the seam between her thighs. Her body seemed to unfold of its own accord under his prodding rhythm.

He pushed up and rocked back on his knees. He raised one of her legs, hooked it in the crook of his arm, and proceeded to unlace and remove her boot. He grabbed her other leg and removed her other boot. When he reached to unfasten her pants, she covered them with one hand and pointed to his shirt.

"Take yours off first."

He smiled and yanked on the tie to his tan shirt. He pulled it loose and then over his head. He stood and pulled his pants down in one swift motion. She marveled at the sight of him. Lithe and graceful, from head to toe his body was all lean muscle. Such a breathtaking man, with a smile she yearned to see everyday since they first met. He stood proud before her with a full erection. The first man she witnessed naked like this. How did she get this lucky? To have him be the first man to kiss and touch her. The first man she wanted inside her.

He unfastened her pants and pulled her remaining undergarments off.

"You still want to claim me," she said.

"I am claiming you."

His declaration warmed her in unexpected places and she grinned, happy to feel none of the tense worry she always expected to feel in this moment. Leaning down he placed a chaste kiss against the pink tip of her breast. Her nipples pebbled in response and a gasp caught in her throat. His mouth covered her nipple and the kiss made a flush of pleasure bloom inside her. Releasing her breast he paused for a moment, and his dilated eyes stared into hers.

"I'd be stupid not to."

He grabbed her other breast and lapped at her nipple. He left a trail of kisses along her collarbone and she welcomed the heat of his bare torso and the bump and press of his erection against her thigh. She relaxed as his hands drifted down and took their time exploring her body.

Her mother lectured her about this. Repeating over and over how a man should never be allowed to touch her because, "Every man becomes a relentless animal when in pursuit of what women sell at the sex market."

She lay naked, pinned beneath a man, but was it wrong when her own body matched his relentless pursuit. Something in her grew frantic for him. A sensation called from her insides, screaming for his every touch. She enjoyed this too much. Her mother's lecture became a dull echo compared to the shouting chant of her body as it demanded he hurry up and claim her as his.

He spread her legs and ran a gentle finger between her thighs. She shuddered under the shock of sensation as he slipped a finger between her folds and inside. His finger swirled the slick moisture there and he made a low groan. He dipped his finger into her again and again, causing the new sensation to grow. Her hips bucked in response. He removed his finger and replaced it with the head of his erection. Her body trembled with excitement. Ready for him to enter the part of her never seen, let alone touched by a man. With a slow effort he pressed in. She tensed and he stopped part way inside. He held still and placed soft kisses on her mouth. She relaxed, welcoming his kisses. He pushed further. The intrusion burned and her whole body went rigid. He halted in place again, and kissed the edge of her ear. His words were quiet as he soothed her.

"Every second, of every day, since I met you, I've wanted to be this close to you."

He pushed his full length into her and she gasped. He held himself there, as she gripped his shoulders, absorbing the burn and new overfull sensation. He held still, only bending his head to take her mouth in a deep kiss. The burn faded and she relaxed to the feel of him inside her. He pulled back and fully entered her again. Repeating the motion, he moved in a slow rhythm. His eyes burned with excitement. She marveled at the expressions of him lost in pleasure.

The lack in her body's response confused her. She expected the desire that carried her to this point, to usher her forward unsuspended. Something was off. Maybe it was the initial burn? Maybe the way his thrusting made her acutely aware of the uneven floor? The heat must be effecting her, it was too warm in here. Were there special instructions for this? Ones you only get before your rally. She waited, watching Puternic, hoping he would know how to help her.

His pace picked up and the rhythm jostled her. He looked overcome with ecstasy, and she envied him. Leaning her head up, she kissed his lips. Puternic's eyes met hers and he stopped moving.

"Are you okay?"

"I don't know," she said. "I don't know what to do."

He gave her a reassuring smile and pressed a soft kiss to her lips.

"You feel so amazing I got lost. Here,"

He pressed his hips adding pressure to where they were joined, a spark of pleasure rang through her body. Relaxing back, he repeated the movement. She caught her breath from an even stronger spark. Her desire flared up. She needed him to do it again. When he stopped she looked at him with a curious frown.

"Why did you stop?"

"You move," he said. "I'll follow you. There's no question I'm enjoying this."

She pushed her hips up, replicated his movement, and found her need for more. Now each press of his length inside her became a long surge of pleasure. Her confidence grew with her renewed desire. Their movement became more fluid and a cry of bliss broke from her throat. Their breath increased, mingling as they continued the climb.

"Katrina wait, Katrina-" Puternic gasped. He took firm hold of her hips and lodged himself deep inside her. He moaned, and his face strained as his body turned rigid with his release. His breathing slowed and he relaxed against her.

"I'm so sorry. I held out as long as I could, but you feel so good."

"Oh." She swallowed and worked to steady her breath. "That's it then?"

"I'm so-so sorry," he said. His erection made a slow retreat from her and he pulled out.

She wanted to screech in frustration.

"I'll make it up to you I swear," he peppered kisses to her forehead before nestling his face against her neck. "Give me a little time and we'll do it again."

"Oh," she said.

Wound tight with need, she refrained from cursing. Agitation rippled her body. Taking a deep breath, she waited for the angry roar of her body to die down.

Puternic continued to kiss and caress her face.

"When will we go?"

"Soon," he said.

"When?"

He gave her a thin smile and touched a finger to her lips. He studied her face and moved to kiss her again. She resisted his advance.

"When Puternic?"

"Katrina," his tone accused her of already knowing the answer. The determination in her eyes increased.

"I'll take you home, when we know you're with child."

Her face paled, and she diverted her gaze to study the curve of his shoulder. Gnashing her teeth she wanted to push him off. As if she startled awake, the enormity of what they did hit her. She cleared her throat and took a deep breath. "That could take awhile."

"Or not."

"What happened to you taking me home right away?"

"Five days ago I had Delphi soldiers surrounding us. I could have stolen you from the island without causing a disruption to the Delphi whose livelihood depends on the trade here. I would have hidden you on an island, the way most Delphi hide their new brides. Now Etrasa will have to be where I hide you while we wait."

"Is this a Delphi tradition?"

"My Delphi ancestors were a little crazy about fending off competition. You can't fight over what you can't find. Mahigan's rally for their brides, we hide ours. Once you're pregnant my claim won't be challenged."

Why did she lay with a man who needed to manipulate tradition to be with her? He was Delphi, incapable of winning her rally or the honor of claiming her. He would die if he tried. He admitted the only place they could go was the Delphi province, but it seemed even that would not be enough to protect his claim.

A cold guilt spun through her as she doubted her decision. If she were home today, her family, especially her father, would prevent any situation like this until she was released for rally. She shut her eyes, shamed by the blame Pha would receive. Why did her new affection for one person have to hurt so many others? Her emotions took sides and stood divided. She disliked Puternic's lack of merit, but his reckless devotion enamored her.

"Are you okay?"

"I don't know," she said.

"What is it?"

"My family will be upset. My father has strong views about rallying and marriage."

He traced fingers along her collarbone. "He's Mahigan, that's what every Mahigan thinks."

"They'll say you can't defend me."

"You're too young to be such a skeptic. Do you think I can't defend you? That I won't defend you?"

"It's what they'll say," she said.

"And it won't matter."

"And what about my father.?"

"The 'Mad Regent'," he said. "What about him?"

She scowled at him, but his confident expression did not change.

"He'll kill you for claiming me. My brothers will search you out. They'll kill you."

"Do I look scared?"

She shook her head. His cockiness annoyed and pleased her at the same time.

"They'll say you're unworthy," she said.

"Am I?" he said. "I don't care what they think. I care what you think. Do you find me unworthy?"

"No," she said. Unsure she spoke the truth.

"You'll see my Princess," he bent his head and kissed along her neck. "I have you, and I'm not letting you go."

His hands cupped her breasts and the smooth pads of his thumbs passed over her nipples. The sensation flew a jolt of pleasure through her. The sudden yearning to be joined with him again surprised her.

"Will you let me take care of you?" He asked, his mouth above hers. He touched a light kiss to her lips prodding for a reply. He nestled between her thighs as she realized he asked two questions. The press of his hard erection made her body clamor with anticipation, and demand what he offered.

"Yes," she said.

He thrust into her, and she cooed in approval. A haze of desire lifted her body back into its climb. She moved with new aptitude, eager to reclaim what he left unfinished.

"Trust me," he said. "Let go of everything else, and trust me."

"Yes," she replied.

He stared at her, watching every shift in her expression.

She tightened around him, as pleasure from each thrust grew more and more intense.

"You're close," he said. "So close."

Panting, her response came out a pleading, "Yes."

He squeezed her hips as she moved faster. He matched her pace and she clung to his shoulders. The muscles in her legs grew taught where they laced around his. Her body peaked and she cried out. Waves of ecstasy held him deep inside her with the most wonderful pulsing grip. She relaxed against the heat of the floor, floating in a daze.

"That, was beautiful," he said, grinning with satisfaction. He leaned down and placed soft kisses to her lips. "I need to see you do that again."

"Is that even possible?" she mumbled, regaining her breath.

"I thought you just said you were going to trust me?"

They spent the afternoon as new lovers, indulging in a passion of tangled limbs and discovery. She hated parting with him and promised to return between dinner and her curfew in two nights. She walked home sore in new places, and with a clear understanding of the expressions on every giant statue in the sex market thoroughfare.

"When are you going to tell me the real reason you're smiling all the time?" Mahogany said, her lean casual as she whispered.

Katrina stiffened in her seat. They were in the audience of the Parade Theatre, rehearsing for the Parade season opener, set to begin that week.

"You've been happy recently," Mahogany said. "More happy than I've seen you in a long time? And don't even try to tell me it's from the time you spend everyday at the university."

Katrina held her breath and grappled for an answer. Puternic, she had been thinking about him again. He was the cause of her unconscious smile, and she wanted to confess all her thoughts about him to her dear friend. This was the first secret she kept hidden from Mahogany, who knew almost everything else about her. Where she grew up, her true identity, even the origins of her disfigured back. Katrina wanted to tell her about Puternic. It pained her to shrug her shoulders and channel her thoughts into finding a lie.

Waiting for an answer, Mahogany eyed her with suspicion.

"I'll have a visit with my brother soon," Katrina said. "That's all."

"Huh," Mahogany said, twisting her lips into a glower. With one hand she covered her mouth and whispered into Katrina's ear, "Don't do anything stupid."

Color drained from Katrina's face. She made a sheepish attempt to look dumbfounded. Mahogany smirked, which transitioned into a smile as she looked over to ask Lady Elena if the blue ribbon in her hair was new. Was it possible to see someone's attachment without firm knowledge it existed?

Puternic's attention had grown in importance to her. Most of her thoughts revolved around him and any sign of pregnancy. A result they failed at three times.

Guarding her expressions better, Katrina willed the morning to move faster.

She made it to the cave an hour after lunch, claiming she needed a few hours study in the university library. She entered the cave and began to strip off her uniform. Each garment fell to one of the blankets Puternic stashed in the cave. He spent so many days here. Days marked by a small pile of books, scraps of leftover food, towels, and random articles of his clothing.

Arms circled her torso and lifted her off her feet. Startled, she shrieked before relaxing into Puternic's hold. She fell into a fit of laughter as he spun her around in circles.

"Put me down."

"You took forever, I need to punish you," he said. He stopped his twirl, and lifted her into a carry.

"I came right away, I swear," she said, trying not to laugh.

Puternic waded into the pool and tossed her into the water, causing her to shriek again.

The waters familiar warmth enveloped her. The pressure from Puternic's dive pressed against her. A poor swimmer, she remained an enthusiastic pupil. He claimed she knew the essentials, enough to stay alive in an emergency. Kicking her way to the surface, he hovered next to her beaming with pride.

"Let's work on floating on your back."

She grinned her compliance and took a deep breath. Arching her back she floated her body into a stiff line parallel with the waters surface. His hands beneath her skimmed fingers in soft contact with her back. She concentrated on breathing, flowing the right amount of air in and out of her lungs to maintain buoyancy. She was light, relaxed, and flushed from the heat of the water and him.

"What did you do this morning?" she asked.

"The usual, waited here for you. Kept myself from carrying out my plans to kill every human male who spends more time with you than me."

"You need a better hobby."

"I have to stay focused on my priorities. It's important work getting you pregnant."

She closed her eyes and signed. The exhale lowered her body out of position.

"I want to go," she said.

His hand pressed the small of her back, coaching her back up into position.

"You just got here," he said.

"No, you know what I mean," she said.

She rotated onto her stomach, rolling her body into an awkward dunk, which sent her head underwater. Kicking her legs she surfaced and wiped water from her eyes. His hands found her waist where he held on to support her. He brought her close and she relaxed letting him do the work of treading water.

"We need to go. I can't keep going to class, or the House and pretending I care about any of it."

"I want to too, but we've talked about this."

"No, we haven't. You say this is what's best, but I don't understand what difference it makes. You and I leave in a boat and go to the Delphi Province or you and I leave in a boat and go live in some human territory until I'm pregnant."

"You and I are not leaving in a boat, and taking you from here requires help."

"No, it doesn't, not really. We get a boat, and I sneak away. Then we go. It's that simple."

"It'll take more than that."

"Why? It'll be easy, and I should know, I'm the one who has to do all the sneaking away."

"No, we've discussed this."

"Not true."

"My father gave an order." His words silenced her. This was the first time he mentioned the Delphi Regent knowing anything about them. "I'll have Delphi soldiers, and we'll leave here on a ship. That's how we're going, after my claim on you is secure."

She moved to swim away, but he pulled her back, rotating her around to face him again.

"You've had no troubles coming here. What's changed?"

She huffed, wormed from his grasp, and kicked her legs to propel herself to the shallows. With one smooth arm stroke he caught up to her. Her feet found the smooth bottom and she walked. Moving faster on her feet than she could swimming.

"Come on, Katrina. What's changed?"

Water coursed around her ankles when she stopped and turned around. She stood for a moment, torn between leaving and letting him get closer so she could strangle him. She sat down at the waters edge, and stretched her feet to the water. Leaning back on her arms she frowned at him as he swam closer. He reached the shallows and crawled on all fours until he rested in her lap.

"Katrina," he said, wrapping his arms around her thighs. He held her butt and placed his chin on her torso. He looked up at her with pleading eyes.

"Parade," she said. "The parade season starts next week."

"So?"

"I'll be watched, I'm expected to work for a suitors attention. If I don't, they'll suspect something. I think I can fake my way through it, but what happens if I'm selected?"

"I'll kill him."

"I'm being serious."

"So am I," he said bringing his head level with hers. He pulled her legs around him and leaned into her, coaxing her onto her back. "No one's coming between you and me."

"Do you promise?"

"I promise."

She lay caged in his body's warmth and the fan of his dark hair. He kissed her, and she kissed him back. Her anger turning into a searing need for him. The brightness of her time spent with him, made the risks bearable. She no longer cared what happened yesterday or what would happen tomorrow. Her life became a bland stretch of hours until she was with him. The only thing that mattered was Puternic and the child they needed.

Katrina leaned on the front door frame as she waited. The orange clad House Guard taking the night's attendance was new. Katrina waved to him as he strolled by, checking and rechecking the list of the Ladies enrolled at the University. He bowed his head and gave a formal, " Lady Katrina."

Katrina nodded, then shut the door. Crossing the living space, she entered the back hallway. Pha exited the kitchen and followed Katrina as she ascended the stairs.

"It's good they saw you tonight," Pha said. "The guard yesterday was real cross when you weren't standing at the door."

"Please don't worry about that," Katrina said. "I won't let it happen again."

Katrina began pulling off her uniform before she entered her room.

"Did you re-braid this?" Pha said, touching her hair. "Why's your hair damp again?"

"I went for a swim, so I needed to re-braid it." Katrina shrugged off her uniform jacket and handed it to Pha.

Pha took the jacket and stood for a moment watching her with narrowed eyes. "When did you learn to swim?"

"It's a skill every officer should have," Katrina said as she yanked her shirt over her head.

"Uh-huh," Pha said, setting the jacket in the wardrobe and retrieving a nightgown.

Katrina wrestled out of her damp undergarment and reached for the nightgown.

Pha's eyes went wide as she focused on Katrina's breasts. Bending her head in curiosity, Pha leaned in to get a closer look. Katrina backed away and looked down to see what Pha was staring at. On the left side of her right breast was a round purple mark. Puternic had made it. A wave of cold dread hit her, as she tried to think of some rational explanation for it. Grabbing the nightgown, she shrugged her shoulders and pulled it on. Pha grabbed her wrist and looked into her eyes as she wandered.

"You've been with a boy."

Grasping for an explanation, Katrina made a sheepish grin. She let out a shaky breath and was about to shake her head no.

"Don't lie to me darling," Pha said. "I should have known it was more than the forest keeping you out. You're lucky it was I who talked to the House guard yesterday and not your mother. Who is he?"

Katrina shook her head as she looked down where Pha held her wrist.

"What would happen to you if a house worker spied that?" Pha said.

Katrina closed her eyes tight, cringing at the answer.

"Really, Katrina you're smarter than this. Is it that apprentice boy from the bakery who likes you?"

"No."

"There isn't a boy on this island worthy enough to touch you," Pha said. "Did you ever stop and think what will happen to him?"

"No, they'd never catch him," Katrina said. She held her breath and wandered, He's not from the island, he's one of the last.

Pha's eyes went wide with surprise.

"How?" She whispered.

"An underground cave that leads out to the ocean."

"You shouldn't darling, you can't," Pha said.

With a meek grin, Katrina said, "I don't know, you might not think that when I tell you who he is."

"I don't care who he is," Pha said, her shrill tone cutting the quiet.

"Puternic Jenke," Katrina said, hoping his identity would mollify Pha's anger and slow her own growing shame.

Hearing Puternic's name, Pha closed her eyes and lolled her head back. Pha squeezed Katrina's wrist before opening her eyes. Releasing her, Pha turned away with a look of determination that sent a spike of fear through Katrina.

"Don't tell Valgu, please," Katrina begged, grabbing Pha's shoulder and turning her around.

"You stop seeing him," Pha said.

Katrina shook her head.

Pha fixed her with a sharp tone she rarely used. "No more."

Katrina straightened and rubbed her wrist. "No. He's taking me home."

Pha shook her head.

"We're going home," Katrina repeated. "Go ahead, tell Valgu. What does he care? Tell my mother, what will she do — turn me into Rudolph? Land us both on the sex market? Twice a year I'm already for sale. How many Parades will I suffer before some strange man buys me?"

"You know better," Pha said. Pha looked at her with resigned disappointment. Taking a deep breath, Pha let it out with a long sigh.

They stared at one another until Pha bent down to retrieve Katrina's discarded clothes. She spun them together in a haphazard mess, grabbing them up with none of the care she often gave to the task. Heaving the clothes up, she moved to the door. Katrina rushed to pull her back.

"Please don't tell any of this to Valgu."

Pha turned to Katrina and shook her head, "This saddens me, my Princess. You're still so young. I don't believe you have a clue about what you've done."

Katrina blinked tears from her eyes that made long trails down her face, each halting to remain poised at the edge of her jaw.

Pha shook her head and eased through the doorway saying, "Valgu's going to kill that boy."

Sobbing, Katrina closed her eyes, listening as Pha walked down the stairs. Pha would take the first opportunity to enter neutral and notify Valgu. He would know her disobedience, her foolishness. Her head fell forward as she sunk down onto the bed. Tonight Valgu would learn what she planned.

Pha's words were true. Valgu would kill Puternic. Her family posed a real threat to Puternic, especially if he remained unaware of their discovery. She needed to go, she had to find Puternic — warn him. She needed to convince him to take her away tonight. She stood and opened the chest at the foot of her bed, and pulled out a clean uniform. Throwing on her clothing, she yanked her boots on and grabbed her bag. Pha would have to use her powers if she wanted to stop her. Katrina made it down the stairs, through the back hall, and out into the kitchen garden without pause.

The quiet song of tree frogs filled the night air. The night sky was overcast, and the little light available came from the binti lamps hung from row house porches. A strong wind brought the smell of late winter rain and sent a damp chill under her loose coat. She buttoned it as she turned onto the unlit path leading up the hill towards the University. The rain started as Katrina stepped onto the small path to the cave. The forest canopy sheltered her from the dense rain, but she still arrived at the cave drenched.

"Puternic," she called. Crouched down she entered the cave and slid down the sloped floor. She stood where the floor leveled off. The brightest light in the cave came from a white binti lamp set on a blanket. Beside it stood Pha with her arms crossed.

"Where is he?" Katrina demanded.

"I told him Prince Valgu's been informed of his ploy to seduce you," Pha said.

A swell of panic rose from Katrina's stomach. She charged past Pha to the edge of the binti bottom lake.

"Maybe I wanted to be seduced," Katrina said.

"He's gone," Pha said.

"No, he wouldn't leave me here."

"You don't have the luxury of forgetting who you are," Pha said. "I trained you better, and you know better."

A strangling tightness knotted in Katrina's chest; it stretched up and tried to close her throat. Tears grew in her eyes.

Pha gave her a withering look. "I know with every piece of my soul that — you meeting that Delphi Prince was no accident. You should've told me the day you met him. Why didn't you tell me? My Katrina's a smart girl, why didn't you suspect his motivations?"

Katrina knelt down beside the lake and placed both hands inside the water. She wanted to feel the light brush of joyful emotion she grew accustomed to him passing her in the water. Her hands only sensed the waters heat.

"I know what you're saying," Katrina said. "I knew why he came here. But he offered what I wanted, the chance to go home."

The lake glowed, its water moving in a slow ebb, but there was no sign of Puternic. She reached with her wandering sense for him. The distance between them was farther than she expected. He was traveling north, away from Etrasa, even as she reached for him.

Puternic.

He made no reply.

Puternic, please. His silence and the ever growing reach she had to extend brought a fresh swell of tears to her eyes. *Answer me, please. Take me with you. Come back, and take me with you.*

"If you care about him," Pha said. "You best pray for him. He's going to need it."

Katrina sunk to the cave floor at the waters edge. Tears flowed unchecked while her mind became congested in grief and regrets. She believed he would return for her, even while she sensed the growing distance between them. Puternic had to return for her. All her plans, her future life, was tied to Puternic. She became paralyzed by the prospective loss of him and the happy day dream of their future together.

Katrina fell asleep on the cave floor. When she later roused, she had dreamt nothing. She remained on the cave floor, even as the desire for a drink of water grew. She would wait here for Puternic. Her body ached from sleeping on stone, and then from waves of chills. She felt cold, even as she lay against the warmth of the cave floor. She coughed and turned to see who lay a hand on her shoulder. She opened her eyes but her vision swam too much to make out a face.

"Puternic," she said.

"Come on Cadet, let's get you out of here," an unidentified male voice said. Hands lifted her and the cold humid air outside hit and sent another wave of chills through her body.

"No," she protested, "No, I can't—" A fit of coughing cut her off as what she recognized as a University medical team placed her on a stretcher.

The medical team hauled her down the hill to her row house. They carried her to bed where a medic assisted Pha in removing her muddy boots and damp uniform. Dressed in a clean nightgown, she was tucked into bed.

The sickness ran its course. Her mother and the House staff believed she took shelter from the rain coming home, and the cold rain had made her ill. No one questioned her sullenness, even when she returned to her normal routine.

Once recovered, Katrina expected Valgu to summon her in neutral. The vibration of him when he called her to the glen, still came as a shock. Fighting the urge to bolt, Katrina entered the private outdoor area, located just beyond the Mozgas Palace gardens. An outdoor patio sat in the center of the glen. Nestled between forest, large boulders, and a pond. Flush fieldstone covered the ground beneath a table and chairs made of iron and wood.

Valgu stood in a formal posture by his chair. He waited until she sat before taking his seat.

"Pha told me," he said with calm authority.

Swamped in misery, Katrina leaned back in her chair. Unconcerned about her casual manners, she rested her head on one hand. Her chest ached with an emptiness. She tried to feign dignity, hold her head up, and face her brother's disappointment.

"This is serious," he said. "You can never be the wife of a Delphi."

For a brief moment his words gave her hope. Her shoulders straightened, but her head dropped. Silly foolish hope. Even now her heart pleaded for Puternic to return and claim her as his. She clipped her words with bitterness.

"If only I'd known all it took to grab your attention was a man claiming me."

"You have no idea what you've done," he said. His composure began to crumble as his eyes glistened with anger. "He's a coward. Who has left you right where he found you, because he's a deadman. He's already forfeit any claim he's made of you. I tried summoning him and he won't face me. I will find him, and then I will kill him. That is, unless Massie beats me to him first."

She closed her eyes in fear for Puternic. "Why did you tell Massie?"

"They were classmates. He might know an easy way to find him. I don't know what kind of promises he made you, but Puternic was sent to Etrasa to claim you. His sole intent was to gain the Delphi an Airetti Regina."

"Yes, he said he'd take me home, once I was pregnant."

Valgu sucked an audible breath and spoke in a measured tone. "Even if you have his child, Puternic's claim will never be endorsed, it will be considered a fraud."

"Even if I care about him? I agreed to it."

"There's nothing I can do," he said, the rigidness in his face softening. "I can't endorse his claim in good faith, and Father never will. If he knew about this, he'd start a war. Accuse Regent Raynes of betraying him."

"Regent Raynes didn't know," she said.

"There's nothing Raynes can say or do to prove he was unaware of your location all these years," he said. "There's more evidence to the contrary. I have no doubt he knew exactly where you were, and sent Puternic on a mission to seduce you."

"Puternic told me his father advised him to leave me alone," she said.

"You're thinking like a child if you believe that's true." His words stung and she shrank under his glare.

"You've known my whereabouts all this time," she said, and her words drifted into a low mutter. "What happens when Father figures that out?"

"If I endorse Puternic's claim on you, every Mahigan in Madar will demand the union made void. They'll start killing Delphi with or without my approval. They'll remedy Puternic's illegal claim, by killing him and rallying for you. And if the Delphi try and hide you away, they'll ignite a war until you're returned."

"As you say, brother," she said, sliding down in her seat and leaning against one armrest.

"Don't see Puternic," he said. She stared at him without giving an answer. Somehow his insistence made it seem possible Puternic would return for her. Her insides raged between wanting to be reunited with Puternic and embracing Valgu's cold logic.

"Be done with him, promise me," he said. "The potential for war is real, I've seen it started over pettier things."

"I can only make that promise, under one condition."

"You dare to make a demand of me?"

"You're my brother, not my Regent, and I have every right. He never forced me. If you want me to openly renounce his claim, then you should be a little more willing to bargain."

"Fine," he said.

"Promise not to kill him, or send anyone else to kill him for you."

"My sister," he said. "Such charity, for a coward. A man, whose mission it was to find you and take advantage of you." Shaking his head, Valgu eased back in his chair with a sigh.

"If you leave Puternic unharmed, I'll deny his claim if he makes any. I'll do what I should have in the beginning. I'll tell you if he comes to see me."

"When was the last time you saw or spoke with him?"

Katrina bowed her head. "The same evening Pha discovered."

Valgu's posture stiffened and he frowned. "That was weeks ago."

"I know."

"You've tried to wander to him."

"Yes, I've tried wandering and summoning him in neutral. He hasn't responded."

"Takes advantage of you, abandons you, and you still want to protect him?"

"Yes, please Valgu. If he's truly abandoned me, then you have nothing worry about."

Valgu worked his jaw. When she made no other remark he made a low sigh. His lips tightened as he consented with a short nod. "Fine, but someday when your fancy for him wears off, you'll wish I had."

In the silence she admired the man her eldest brother had become. Still handsome like their father, Valgu's youthful gaze was hardened. He possessed knowledge beyond his years, and it rimmed his eyes with sadness. The responsibility of running Mozgas was more important than doting on her. She regretted her perceived slights and childish reactions to his lack of visits. They were a silly way to cope with her missing his company and affection.

"How long do you really think I'll be able to put off the inevitable?" she asked. "The longer I'm stuck here, the greater my chances are of being stolen or bought and made someone's wife."

"Unless you allow it, that's not going to happen," he said.

"You're being unreasonable. Think about why you summoned me here."

He said nothing and she let her head fall to one side where she massaged her forehead. Her selfish impulses created the situation with Puternic. However there was only so much she could do to keep patrons to the House of Etrasa disinterested.

"I can't stop someone from bidding on me," she said.

"You can, and you will."

She hid her face in her hands and closed her eyes. "And what if I can't?"

"Then it'll be time to bring you home," he said, his voice soothing and coming from beside her. Valgu knelt at her elbow. The kind and generous brother she knew and loved wore a look of regret. A hitch formed in her throat. Valgu placed a hand on her shoulder, as he looked her in the eye.

"I promise you."

"I'm so sorry," she said with tears welling in her eyes. "I should have told you. I knew I should have, and I didn't. I didn't think it mattered, and when I knew it did, I was excited to go. I care about him, and he, well I believe he cares about me. I-I should've known better. I never meant to create such a mess."

Valgu pulled her into a hug and held her. "We're both going to do better from now on. Nothing's happened that can't be fixed. Some of this is my fault. I'm supposed to look after you, and I didn't do it right. I hope you can forgive me."

Katrina wiped her eyes and nodded her head.

"I'll do better. I won't do it again." She relaxed as she spoke her promise, one she knew she would keep.

Many days later she found herself sitting outside the cave entrance. Heavy air rolled under the forest canopy, disturbing the trees with occasional bursts of wind. Its smell promised rain. The birds squawked in protest. Fussing about as they searched for the best perch to ride out another pending winter storm. A crumbling crack of rocks falling came from above on the cliff wall. She startled at the sight of Thedmir standing high up on its edge. He moved back and out of view. A few minutes later he approached where she sat.

I thought we were done coming here, he wandered.

"I'm following the rules."

Are you?

"He's not here, and I'm not in the cave."

You'd prefer to be breaking the rules.

Katrina tried to ignore what he meant, and cleared her mind of the intimate memories of being wrapped in Puternic's arms. She picked at the bits of rock on the ground beside her. Palming one of the larger pebbles, she aimed at nothing and tossed it across the trail.

"What do you mean by, we're done coming here?"

Where you go I go. You're my assigned classmate.

She gaped at him, "Not everywhere — that's when we're training. You followed me out here? Every time?"

You put yourself at risk.

"I can't believe you did that."

I read. Kept an eye out for the guards in orange uniforms.

"Did you ever see any of them?"

No. But if you were caught, my presence would've erased suspicions.

Unsure of his logic she nodded. His unhindered access to her thoughts often left her feeling exposed. The revelation of his guarding her eased her discomfort. Solidifying a new level of trust between them. One she never expected.

Why are we here?

She focused on the ground. Sifting through the pebbles, she searched for some with tiny traces of binti stone.

"To sit here and sulk," she said. "Fantasize that he'll come back. I have this vacant hole. He made me see it. Now I do, but now he's gone and I don't know what to do with it. I don't know when it will stop reminding me of how I much I miss him. Or how it's my fault that I hurt. I'm the one who got careless, and got caught. I'm the one who picked the wrong man."

She spotted a yellow binti pebble.

"Ha! Look at that," she said, picking it up. Brushing dirt away, she raised it between her thumb and forefinger. Thedmir extended an open hand and she set it there.

"I think that one might be worth something," she said.

I like yellow binti stone, he offered it back to her. *Good find.*

"You keep it," she said, moving to her feet. She stretched and sighed. "Let's go."

He gestured for her to take the lead. Together they walked in companionable silence. A light rain started. It filtered through the trees, leaving their hair and clothes damp. A low growl of thunder echoed in the distance as they exited the forest. With synchronized steps they crossed the parade field.

"Have you ever felt lost?" she asked.

I'm a Minotaur, living on an island, populated by humans.

"I don't mean that kind of lost. I mean, have you ever lost yourself? Like you knew who you were, and then somehow that person went away. Or maybe that person's still there, but you don't recognize them anymore."

That isn't being lost. What you described is how it feels to grow. Some parts never change, while others will never be the same.

5

The Life of a Cadet

Stopping, Katrina shifted the weight of her pack. With a yank at her right shoulder strap her load shifted. She resumed her pace among her cadet classmates. Ahead of her stretched an efficient line. A stream of bulging packs bobbing down the road from the university campus to the forested training areas. This was it. Their final field test. When the mock battles and exercises ended, they would carry back the most physical of the certifications needed to graduate. A training instructor waved them onto the gated path leading to the restricted training area. Terrain used for the final field test.

Used only a year, the forest reclaimed whatever campsites and trails the former class created here. This was one of many factors that made this the most difficult training area. The cadets faced six weeks spent in steep terrain, dense forest, hazardous obstacles, and off limits pockets. The winter rains were over, but spring storms occurred often this high in the mountain foothills.

The restricted terrain maps were a mess to study. Bunched up terrain marks, water indicated with blue; black ovals marked caves; blue green orbs for sinkholes; and the brown dots mud pots. Each class studied the maps, and tried to memorize the red X'd out off-limits pockets. Entering one cost a cadet certification points, and put them in territory occupied by the more dangerous animals on the island.

Excited apprehension shadowed the Cadets. Former training exercises taught them the fatigue of working from before the sun broke the horizon to whenever the instructors sent them to bed. They spent the past year learning the tactics they would be tested on. They remembered the stories graduates told about the final test. They knew this would not be fun.

"No pots for me!" a cadet said. A chant repeated a moment later by another cadet.

The cadets ahead stopped to retrieve pebbles from the ground. Katrina joined them. After scanning the gravel she scooped up a grey pebble. She glanced over at Thedmir who loitered beside her. He tossed his ears in agitation.

"Where's your pebble?" she asked.

His large brown eyes narrowed, but he said nothing.

"It's tradition, Thedmir. Get a pebble. Hurry up, it's almost our turn."

She inched closer in the line formed in front of the mud pot named Muir's Gurgle. Cadet superstition claimed if Muir's Gurgle held onto your pebble you would not fall into a mud pot during the test.

How hard can it be to avoid a mud pot? Thedmir wandered.

"I don't know." She stepped up and took aim at Muir's Gurgle.

You believe in this superstition?

"Of course not." She tossed her pebble. Muir's Gurgle flubbed and steam whispered off the liquid grey mud. Her pebble landed off center before sinking into Muir's bubbling mud. "No pots for me!"

A second pebble landed behind hers. Thedmir acknowledged his achievement with raised hands and splayed fingers.

She laughed at his feigned enthusiasm.

Wind pushed them to the forest. The press eased under the tree's sanctuary. Branches rocked overhead, swaying in battle against the gales. The bright song of tree frogs greeted them with birds chortling in a lower chorus. The cadets gathered where the class halted beneath the trees.

Cadet Mickle, a member of their squad, approached. A wiry man of average height, his appearance made his true physical strength deceptive. His sharp wit and insight made up for any lack of brawn. Meticulous about his appearance, he shaved his brown hair close to his scalp. Katrina considered the common soldier haircut ugly, but Mickle had the right head shape for it.

"Your frog friends are excited to see you, Thedmir," Cadet Mickle said.

Thedmir huffed and made a hand gesture. A Minotaur hand signal, it translated as a desire to kill an opponent in hand-to-hand combat.

Mickle chuckled and stopped beside them.

Katrina grinned, she found the tree frog noise pleasant. Her many years in Etrasa left her deaf to it. Thedmir's aversion to the grey and purple frogs came from their similarity to frogs in Tvarchus. For him, the Etrasa frogs sang an off-key version of the Tvarchus frog's song. The Etrasa frogs irritated Thedmir, and this amused their classmates who rarely saw him upset about anything. Thedmir never hurt an Etrasa frog, but she often caught him gesturing threats or wandering curses at them.

They hiked most of the day to one of the few clearings on the course. They set up camp. When the instructors gave the order to bed down, the class obeyed. Everyone eager for as much sleep as possible.

Katrina woke the following morning, certain she had just closed her eyes. Cold water dropped on her eyelid. Another drop followed, landing on her forehead. It trickled down the bridge of her nose. She shrunk under her wool blanket and scrubbed more rain from her face. Her sleep ended, she saw the night sky retreating. Sitting up she noticed her breath fogged into the cold rain. She cast a jealous eye at Thedmir who slept on.

Instructor Wells walked across the clearing towards the huddle of waking cadets. A few younger cadets accompanied him. She recognized two and knew they competed on the University's weapon team. They all carried swords and protective equipment. Her stomach flipped into a knot. She woke up to rain and an examination in one of her worst proficiencies, weapons.

Instructor Wells had Katrina slated to go first. A position that could be considered a curse or a mercy. Instructor Wells sectioned off an area in the clearing for the exam. He called for her and Sophomore Cadet Trax to take position. She gripped at her training weapon in reflex. Cadet Trax earned his position on the weapons team. His moves were clean and executed with an effortless grace uncommon in men his age. She never wanted to spar against him, least of all during this exam.

Instructor Wells controlled the exam by giving Cadet Trax a series of hand gestures for the moves he would complete. Katrina earned a point for each correct response, and two for successful attacks or exploitations. The skill level started out basic, and moved up in increments. They moved through the first two sets fast.

She failed a block. Her torso took the hit and punched the breath from her lungs. Trax kicked her hip, and knocked her to the ground sideways.

"End." Instructor Wells said.

Cold bore into Katrina's exposed hands as rain dripped from her lashes. A fresh downpour of rain transformed the soft ground into mud.

Instructor Wells cued the next set. Cadet Trax ran at her, lifting his sword over his head, in an assault capable of taking her head off. A brilliant display of intimidation. Something the average person flinched away from on reflex. Years of practice trained the flinch out of her. She concentrated on pressing into the fight, and muffled the screaming instinct telling her to run and hide. Holding her ground, she plotted a reply.

Dodging left, she raised her sword in a two-hand grip, and aimed all her strength into the parry she needed. Deflected, his sword came up to stoke her side. Never very quick with transitions, she deflected just in time. Cadet Trax followed the strike by carrying his momentum into another hip kick.

She flew to the ground. A slight pain throbbed where she landed, but her pride hurt more.

"End," Instructor Wells said.

Panic crept in. She needed to pass this. They got up and assumed start positions again. She could do this. She knew enough, had practiced plenty, to pass this and graduate. Instructor Wells gave the next hand signal. Cadet Trax's eyes flashed to hers through the narrow slits in their visors. He came at her with a classic forward assault. His sword trained front as he ran. With seconds to decide her move she held on, waiting to determine the side he wanted to hit. Her smaller size provided a minor advantage, he needed to move more to reach her. His body lilted just enough to give away his plan of attack. Cadet Trax lifted his sword and she shifted her stance. She grunted as their blades made contact. Pushing up, she held on. He pressed in, determined to land his blow. Her arms burned, outmatched by his strength, she was a breath away from caving.

Thedmir wandered to her an image with a recommendation, *The blade is not the only part of a sword.*

"Right," she said.

Tilting her blade, she held Cadet Trax off. She eased back, and pulled his momentum forward. Sliding his blade left, she created a narrow window of time for her move. One she succeeded with when she used it on Thedmir. With a deep breath and all her strength, she pushed Cadet Trax off and drove the pommel of her sword back against Cadet Trax's chin. It left him searching for his breath. Returning the favor, she hit his right torso with the broad side of her sword, and made a swiping kick that landed Trax on the ground.

"End," Instructor Wells said.

She took a deep breath and for a moment her worry faded. A surge of hope made her glance at Thedmir.

Thanks for the reminder, she wandered.

Cadet Trax got to his feet and moved around stretching and shifting his weight. She needed to complete an attack, but so far Cadet Trax rebuffed her every attempt. She had one reliable move. A very basic move, but it got the job done. It worked best on those with a weak parry and were right hand dominant. Given Cadet Trax's skill, it might be worthless. Instructor Wells cued their set. She stood still, holding a false attack position. If he underestimated her ability to conduct a feint, she could trick him and make her real assault work.

He underestimated her. She moved in, slashed his right side and in quick succession placed another blow to his left torso. She finished with a kick. Mud slogged around him as he hit the ground.

"End." Instructor Wells said.

"That was good," Cadet Mickle called out.

The Cadets from her squad were watching her test from the side of the field. A small wave of relief passed over her. One good assault done. She waited, hoping this was enough to hear Wells declare her test completed. Assuming nothing she got into the ready stance. If Cadet Trax had underestimated her, he no longer did. His next series of assaults hit her hard, and he kicked her into the mud at every opportunity. He never let up, and she persevered. Landing hits and deflecting blows until her muscles burned from the exertion.

"Finished, good work," Instructor Wells said.

She studied Instructor Wells unsure who he praised.

"Thank you Cadet Trax, go rest," Instructor Wells said. He looked at her and made a motion with his head.

"You passed, Cadet. Get off my course."

Light-headed, she joined Cadet Trax in organizing their safety gear for the next test. Removing his protective gloves, Cadet Trax extended his hand.

"Good job. My side still hurts, I shouldn't have underestimated you."

"I'm pretty sure my bruises are going to be uglier than yours," she said.

He smiled as they shook hands and parted ways.

Joining her squad, she eased down to lay against her pack.

"How'd it go?" Cadet Staley asked.

"I passed," she said, feeling her grin transform into a wide smile. "I passed, and I will never have to do that again."

"Barely," Cadet Voss said from where he sat with his squad behind them.

She ignored him, and watched the faces of the Cadets in her squad. They each straightened and turned to find who made the remark.

"You got something you want to say?" Cadet Vacek said, as he stood up.

"Please tell me Voss didn't just say that?" Mickle said.

"Sorry, didn't mean to offend the princess," Voss said.

"Let's see you spar against Trax," Mickle said.

"Who cares," she said, "he's right." She angled her body enough to see Cadet Voss. An attractive man, he relied on his charm whenever possible. Getting by in his academic classes by grasping the bare minimum. His greatest proficiency was getting others to do his work, which made her forever grateful for his assignment to a different squad.

"It's just Voss," she said. "I think he still blames me for his screw-up last week."

The week before the final test, Cadet Voss briefed an order he developed off of the wrong material. Their entire class witnessed his failure, but she had been called on to explain his mistake.

"You ratted me out!" Voss said.

"How is that even possible?" she said. "Ratting implies I knew you intended to mess up."

"Your brief was broken, Voss," Vacek said. "Everyone in the room knew except you. Instructor Jults told her to name what was wrong. What was she going to do, lie about it?"

"Ratted me out," Voss said.

"Go ahead," Katrina said. "Be mad at me for saying you used the wrong course of action. I don't care."

Voss jumped up and walked out of the clearing and their encampment.

Cadet Mickle shouted after him. "Don't forget to tell us what fool's army buys your commission, Voss. I want to be sure I take mine somewhere else."

Katrina looked over at Thedmir. His eyes were soft with amusement, and a smile returned to her face.

I passed.

She sat relaxed in the company of her squad as they each went up to complete the weapons test. A panicked scream came from somewhere uphill of the encampment and halted the exam activities. Thedmir moved to his feet and Katrina followed. They walked in the direction of the noise. At the edge of the clearing they heard scuffling and something colliding with underbrush.

"Help! I need help!"

More cadets gathered. Katrina and Thedmir moved through the forest in the direction of the distress call. They filtered into a narrow clearing between the steep hill and a massive overturned tree. Exposed roots hung above a sinkhole. Tangled in the roots clung a frantic Cadet Voss. He thrashed about, buried up to his chest in the sinkhole. He pulled at the roots trying to free himself.

"Voss," Instructor Wells barked. He prodded the edge of the sinkhole with his boot. "Quit kicking. Hang on, and we'll get something to pull you out of there."

The gathered cadets shared looks of disbelief. A few snickered and some stepped away trying to hide their laughter.

"Leave it to Voss," one said.

"How did you not see this?" another asked.

"Quiet," Instructor Wells barked. "If you're not willing to help, go find someone who is."

Katrina touched Thedmir's forearm.

"You can get him out of there the quickest," she said.

With a low groan Thedmir joined Instructor Wells at the edge of the sinkhole. With one hand Thedmir reached out and grabbed Voss by the back of his uniform collar.

"Lay on your back," Instructor Wells said.

Voss tried to comply as Thedmir dragged him to the sinkhole edge. More cadets reached down and assisted Instructor Wells in pulling Voss out. Between gasps Voss uttered his thanks.

"How did that even happen, Cadet? Were you sleepwalking?" Instructor Wells said.

Cadet Voss shook his head and pointed in the direction of his fall. "No, Instructor. I was up there, past those bushes, when these Delphi grabbed me. They held me down, and one hit me."

"Delphi?" Instructor Wells asked in a tone of disbelief.

Cadet Voss pressed the only clean part of his uniform sleeve to a bleeding cut on his lower lip.

"They tossed me down here," Voss said.

"Delphi," Instructor Wells said. "randomly attacked you, in the restricted area."

"Yes, Instructor. I swear."

Instructor Wells squinted as he watched Cadet Voss stand up.

"Did they say anything to you?"

"No," Cadet Voss said. He held his left arm with his right and stood favoring his left side. He groaned as he looked down at the mud dripping from his uniform.

Thedmir turned in a slow circle, scanning the forest. Katrina inspected the hill and disturbed brush beaten down when Cadet Voss fell. They found no sign of Cadet Voss's attackers. She met Thedmir's gaze, and without a word or sign, followed him as they walked back to the weapons exam area.

In the evening the cadets bedded down in the base camp, and swapped stories of their day. Word of Cadet Voss's mishap spread, and cadets teased him with playful reenactments. Cadet Voss took it well. Laughing, as he scoured sinkhole mud from his boots.

I don't think the instructors believe Voss's story, Thedmir wandered.

"They didn't do any real searching," she said. "His story sounds made up. It's more likely another cadet attacked him, or he tripped, and got banged up on his fall down the hillside. It's too hard to believe an outsider came into this training area to attack a cadet. When have you ever seen one?"

During our first year, he said and wandered the image of Puternic to her. *Voss has an argument with you, and then gets attacked by Delphi. I know you've thought about this.*

Katrina nodded.

It's a strange coincidence.

"I know," she said. "But it seems unlikely."

Voss's telling the truth, Thedmir wandered. *Delphi attacked him, and I think they're connected to you.*

"I hope you're wrong."

An unexplained instinct told her he was right.

She wasted no time crawling into her bedroll. The occasional pang of soreness in her sword arm promised a bigger ache in the morning. Ready for her crossover to sleep, she startled at the vibration of entering neutral. She stood in the cave by the lake. A nervous dread circled in her stomach. Puternic stepped into view.

"Katrina," he said, standing in an expectant pose, like he was ready for her to run into his embrace. "What's the matter?"

When she remained in place he dropped his arms.

"You must be a little pleased to see me? I'm so happy to see you."

She stared at him, searching for a hint of sarcasm.

"No," she said. "What are you doing summoning me?"

He looked away unable to hide the hurt.

"Oh God," she said. "You really are out here."

"I'm keeping watch on what's mine."

"You did it, you attacked Voss."

"He insulted you."

"He made a stupid remark. I don't need you defending me. You shouldn't even be here."

"Neither should you."

"Don't hurt my classmates, or do anything to mess with my test. Do you understand?"

He crossed his arms and held her gaze.

"Please," she said.

"I have good news."

"I don't care. I need to go."

"Katrina-"

"I haven't seen you in over three years."

"I know."

"You left me without a word," she said. "No farewell. No note, letter, nothing. Three years, and now, of all times, you come back."

"You got caught."

"I did, but you broke your promise."

He ducked his head, hiding his eyes.

"I need to go," she said. "I've worked too hard to fail out because you want to talk."

"What, this test, it's more important than what I have say?"

"I need sleep."

"We need to talk."

"I disagree. Don't summon me here again."

"I understand you're mad, but please listen to me."

"No, I have to go disrupt Valgu," she paused letting the full meaning of her words sink in. "Then I need to sleep during the little time I'll have left."

She let go of neutral, and woke, sitting up with a start. Thedmir dozed beside her. She yanked at her bedroll blankets as she lay back down. She kicked and turned over as furious frantic thoughts made it difficult to focus. She took a series of deep breaths and cleared her mind as she focused on Valgu, and how she intended to keep her promise. When she calmed enough to enter neutral, she reached for Valgu and entered the glen.

Valgu arrived, with a look of astonished concern.

"What's happened?" he said.

"He's back," she said. "Puternic's on Etrasa."

"You saw him?"

"No, but he attacked my classmate today, and he summoned me."

"What did he say?"

"I don't know. I'm sorry, I refused to talk to him. He said he has good news."

"What else?"

"That's it really, I didn't give him time to tell me anything else."

"Katrina."

"I'm sorry. I got upset. I can't believe he's back."

"He's probably come to take you to the Delphi Province."

"What do I do?"

"Kill him, stall him, do whatever you need to do to stay where you are. I will come collect you. Convince him to put off whatever he has planned, for as long as you can."

"Okay," Katrina said, covering her eyes with both hands. They shook and a headache began throbbing above her brow.

Strong arms wrapped her in a hug and she felt Valgu breath a chuckle.

"Why are you laughing?"

"Because, I'm intervening." He waited until she dropped her hands before continuing. "It's time for you to come home."

"Really?"

Valgu nodded and she jumped up, throwing her arms around him.

"Don't let him take you," he said, squeezing her to him. "My plan does take a bit of time to get in motion."

"I won't. Besides, I'll need to kill him if he tries to take me before graduation."

"Do whatever's necessary. You have my enthusiastic consent to use some of your more lethal officer training on him."

She grinned up at his full smile before a neutral vibration rocked her from his grasp.

A jolt of cold air woke her. Squinting, she found Thedmir beside her holding the top layer of her bedroll.

"Was that necessary?" she said.

"Yes," he said. "You didn't wake to anything else."

She sat up slow and pressed both hands to her headache.

"I'm sorry, I was in neutral most of the night."

"I was right about the Delphi," he said.

Katrina looked up and nodded.

"Get your gear on, Cadets," Wells said. "We're moving to range four in fifteen minutes."

In silence, cadets secured wet gear and pulled on packs. They shifted and shrugged, as cold fingers grappled with slick straps. One by one they straightened and walked after Instructor Wells. Ready for a day of training missions, endless hiking, and more rain.

Days passed and the rain continued. Katrina's eyes were sore from the number of times she wiped rain from them. She guessed the next time they saw clear skies and sunshine would be on the day the final test ended. She no longer put words to her misery of being cold and wet. Puddles she tried avoiding during the first few days of rain, she now plowed through without a second thought. With sore feet, she envied Thedmir's leisurely stride. He adjusted it to keep pace with her.

"I've always felt bad," she said. "You having to pace yourself off me and my little human stride."

It took time, he said. I'm used to it now.

Thedmir moved fast when he walked at his normal pace. She imagined the terror of facing a Minotaur army, with each soldier possessing such speed. Mowing down a line of humans would take little effort.

Yes, but you'll never be on the receiving end of that, he said. He wandered peaceful images of his home. Of Minotaurs working trades, studying, and farming. *Quiet strength is stronger and more sustainable than brute force, but God will put you in situations to build your strength and keep you strong.*

She frowned some. She felt ignorant of the God Thedmir talked about.

"Is that why I'm here?" she said. "Did God put me in this situation? How can He love the way you describe, while everyday people in places all over suffer and die?"

Suffering is not what God wants for us. He never places illness or death in your life. On the ship that brought you here, you knew that. You recognized the enemy of your soul. How evil controls this world. It pushes pain, suffering, and death on us. Our God is the master of turning such work on end. Our God repurposes what evil has marred. He overturns the bad, and like a slingshot flies what is His out of evil's pursuit. Someday you will land back home, where he intended you to be, and you'll be repurposed. You'll be even better equipped for the fight ahead.

"If I've been repurposed," she said, "Then my preparation must be for a really dark future."

Or repurposed to guide others away from the darkness you've witnessed.

"Sounds dismal either way," she said.

Are you afraid of it?
"No."

Reaching out, she wandered into his thoughts. He had accessed her mind this way often, and without shame. It bothered her at first, but she learned to accept it as Minotaur behavior. It's what they did among friends in Tvarchus, and he showed her how to wander his thoughts. Her ease at doing this now surprised her. She followed his path of logic. Looking at the images of her own memories through his perspective. His point of view stripped away the confusion and desperation from the moment. It rendered the event into something focused and clear.

"You believe God heard me then? God really did tell me to wait?"

Thedmir laughed into her mind and he made his hand gesture for yes. *That's what he told you, my most impatient friend.*

"You always like to make me look back on things I've already made up my mind about."

You as a child had, but now you're an adult. I think you should spend time considering these old events from your new perspective.

"And return to a God I've ignored for so long."

God understands.

"Then He's much more forgiving than me."

Always.

Routine mock battles became hard under extreme fatigue. Something the instructors wanted for the final test. The instructors claimed this the most accurate testing method for leadership and character. Wet uniforms allowed cold nights to leech warmth from their bodies. Cadets suffered the effects of hypothermia and sleep deprivation. They were irritable and exhaustion hampered their physical and mental reaction speed.

The intensity of the final test tried their nerves, but the cadets rarely complained. They suffered in silence. If a regular soldier complained, their gripes would be tolerated. If an officer joined in, griping in unison, it would be a grievous event. As future officers, the cadets endured in silence. One of their leadership burdens, categorized as leading by example. Even after four years, Katrina hated this, and struggled with the way her face liked to say what she meant to keep quiet. Thedmir let her wander her complaints to him, and she wondered what she would have done without him.

Puternic remained in the restricted training area. Close enough to watch her, but far enough away to hide. She caught a glimpse of his profile once, but when she moved in for a closer look, he vanished. He never wandered to her, but if she reached out with her wander sense she felt him. His presence distracted her. She worried about his plans. She wanted to summon him and put an end to his stalking, but decided against initiating a conversation, which might give him the wrong idea.

Her worries eased when Pha came out to watch over her. The instructors and her other classmates ignored Pha. She stayed out of the way, and followed from a ways off, keeping pace with her short even stride. Even when Pha hummed, no one mentioned it. Rain dripped off Katrina's jacket hood as she pulled it forward. Pha stopped ahead of her dressed in a traditional Alvara robe. A garment too thin for the rain. Pha looked over her shoulder and winked at her before walking on. Katrina gave a quiet laugh. Thedmir angled his gaze with a questioning look.

"I'm bundled in a coat and Pha's out here wearing that," Katrina said.

She's not. Pha's not really out here.

Katrina looked from Thedmir back to where Pha walked ahead. Her guardian vanished.

"Then is Puternic is really not out here either?"

No, he's still out here.

"But I'm hallucinating Pha."

Correct, it's common when you have very little sleep, over many days.

It was a late afternoon when Cadet Vacek assumed control of the squad, and his mission evaluation began. He chose Katrina and Thedmir to stay behind as guards in an observation point. The cadets prized the assignment for the opportunity to rest. The squad removed their packs and left as she and Thedmir fashioned a rain cover for the gear. When the cover was secured, Katrina crawled under it and settled among the packs. Thedmir sprawled out in the drizzling rain, dozing against a tree.

Puternic emerged from the cover of trees. Katrina's blood went cold even as her heart began to race. She watched him walk through a curtain of slow rain. His long black hair lay wet against his naked torso. Rain coursed across his face and body. A body she remembered too well. If she was hallucinating him, then her mind indulged in all her favorite details. She feared the old lust. It held no reservations about being lost in his possession again. She could never let herself touch him. No touching, but she let herself admire him. He stopped in front of her.

"Who's that?" Puternic asked.

"Thedmir. You ever fought anyone that big?"

"No."

"Then you should hope he's really asleep. He doesn't like you."

"Can we talk?" he said, crouching down. He dropped back, sitting with his arms hugged around his legs in a posture that mirrored hers.

"Do I have a choice?"

"Please," he said. "I'm here to take you home. My father approved the use of a Delphi Regiment."

She huffed a tired laugh. "I'm not going anywhere with you."

"I understand you're mad at me. Give me an opportunity to make things right, to make things up to you."

"I'm a little busy right now," she said, tilting her head. "I have a lot going on before graduation."

"This graduation's that important?"

"Yes." She said brokering no argument. "So go and tell your Regent you won't need his Regiment. I'm staying for graduation."

"From your human university."

"I know, you like to disparage it. It's human, and that somehow makes it inferior to all things Veilede."

"You're not human."

"Look at me." She said throwing her hands in the air. "Do you think I'd be out here doing this if it wasn't important to me?"

"What about going home?"

"What about it? You can't take me there, at least not anytime soon. You have to ensure your claim. Remember?"

"I can take you home."

"Yeah, I already fell for that lie once."

"It's the honest truth."

"I begged you to take me home. But, no it wasn't safe. I had to be carrying your child."

"I found a way; my father's willing to help support my claim."

"Your claim, and what happens if I don't feel like honoring that? Are you going to force me?"

"Can you give me another chance?"

"I took every chance on you. I risked everything to be with you. You're the one who left me."

Puternic clenched his hands into claws as he screamed, "I've come back for you!"

Thedmir stirred, and the echo of Puternic's shout faded into the pattering sound of rain. Certain her squad and instructors heard the outburst, she scanned for any sign of them.

Puternic flexed his feet, and pressed his heels into the ground. Grabbing his knees with both hands, his head slumped forward between his arms. He took a few deep breaths before speaking more temperately.

"Please."

She considered him, letting the sounds of tree frogs and rain fill the silence.

"Not unless you let me finish this," she said. "I don't want to see you again before graduation."

Puternic kept his gaze guarded as he stood up. He brushed debris away and gave her one head nod. Turning around he walked into the woods and out of sight.

When her squad returned, the instructors questioned her about the outburst. She claimed doing it when she tripped over something. She lost a point for improper noise discipline during a mission.

The squad huddled into jackets as Cadet Nellmon briefed the next mission. His plan lay drawn out in sticks and mud on the ground. With aching cold fingertips, Katrina pulled her map from her pocket. She chewed at her bottom lip as she compared the route on the ground to the landmarks on her map. Nellmon's route skirted a steep ravine beside one of the largest off limits areas. If they shifted west the climb would be harder. She liked this better than the risk of crossing into an off limits area and getting a points penalty.

A nervous energy hit her. Altering their course west went from an idea to a sudden urgent need. She shifted on her feet as she waited for Nellmon to finish. Clearing her throat, she raised her hand. He nodded for her to speak.

She crouched over the dirt drawn map, and pointed to the route, and the change she recommended.

Nellmon crossed his arms and titled his head. "I see what you're saying, but we'll stick with the current route. Mostly for safety. It's raining and we'll hit less of an incline."

Katrina looked over at Mickle pleading for his support, but he looked distracted. She dropped her gaze and nodded as she stood up.

Her nervous urgent need morphed into a feeling of dread. Cold rain dripped under her collar and trailed down her back, sending a chill across her body. She watched the reaction of instructors Leems and Hutter. They maintained neutral expressions. She tried using their lack of reaction as reassurance. As the cadets moved to get ready to go, she caught a shared look between the instructors. They were concerned. About what was unknown, but in her opinion, the route was the only flaw in Nellmon's plan. She tried to think of how she could change Nellmon's mind without looking like a frantic lunatic. Nothing came to mind.

Entering elevation above the tree line, their path transitioned from mud to loose rock. The mountain foothills channeled them into an unexpected single file. They climbed until they reached an uneven path cut right into the side of a bluff. To the left rose a vertical wall of rock. To the right, a drop off into the deep forested ravine of the off limits area.

An image of Nellmon dropping from the path flashed through her mind. Alarmed, she stopped walking. Craning her neck, she tried to find Nellmon. As the acting leader, he walked all the way in the front and out of view. Her dread grew. She fought the urge to run up and beg Nellmon to turn them around. If she broke ranks like a first year cadet the instructors would dock her more points.

This route's dangerous, Thedmir wandered. *And a one point penalty is nothing to ten points if we fall into that restricted area. Go stop him.*

"Nellmon," she shouted, arching up on her toes. The squad's file came to a halt. The cadets turned and looked back at her. She edged around Mickle. Vacek stepped aside and let her pass. Staley faced forward and began walking again before she passed him. The nervous constriction in her stomach sent a taste of bile to her mouth. She swallowed it back as she skirted around Staley. Instructor Leems let her pass him, watching with interest as she progressed forward.

She caught sight of the back of Nellmon's bobbing head.

"Nellmon!"

He never paused or turned around. The sound of skidding gravel came, followed by the crack and thud of falling rock. Further up the path rocks rolled down from the bluffs wall to the ravine. A voice shouted and there was a prolonged scream. The cadets behind Nellmon backed up and fell against the bluff wall covering their heads. When the noise stopped, Nellmon was gone.

Instructor Leems ran to the edge where Nellmon disappeared. Wrenching off his pack, Leems sat at the edge of the bluff and slid down the pile of fallen rocks.

"Get back, everyone get back!" Instructor Hutter shouted as he moved up to where Nellmon fell.

Katrina followed in his wake. The recent rain caused the entire path to collapse beneath Nellmon. Painful screams echoed up from the ravine.

Instructor Hutter turned back to the squad.

"Larksbur, Thedmir, Vacek, drop your packs and grab your weapons. You're following me. Staley, take Mickle and hike to the emergency out post near Range Four. Tell them we need a medical team to extract Nellmon. The rest of you stay here and get some ropes ready to help us climb out."

Instructor Hutter dropped to his rear and scooted into the ravine. She, Thedmir and Vacek followed him as ordered.

Nellmon cried out between short rapid breaths. He writhed on the ground, color draining from his face. His right leg hung limp, bent to the side at an odd angle. Instructor Leems talked to Nellmon in a calm voice, explaining everything he did as he evaluated the injury.

"Weapons ready, Cadets," Instructor Hutter said. "I need you three to form a perimeter. Guard us while we get Nellmon ready to move."

Katrina, Thedmir, and Vacek drew their weapons and spread out, facing the forest around Nellmon and their instructors. The ground crunched underfoot and she looked down. Rotting cashew apples and broken hulls lay scattered around the ground. She swallowed and gripped her sword as she took up a ready stance. She scanned the cashew trees, they were everywhere. The enormity of the danger they faced sunk in. She knew the creature responsible for making this ravine off limits, a snake. The locals called them island monster snakes. A fitting name for something so large and grotesque. They liked to camouflage their massive brown bodies in coils around the trunks of fruit and nut trees. They grew to a length that averaged twenty feet, and had a lethal venomous bite. Monster snakes ate a staple diet of monkeys and birds, but were known to eat dogs, and small farm animals. Nocturnal creatures, if they were disturbed during the day they often attacked.

Why did Leems have to pick her to guard against those things?

Katrina caught the motion of something in the corner of her eye. She felt Thedmir panic before she could process his thoughts. Thedmir stared down a monster snake. Its head poised mid-air in front of his torso, as its body uncoiled from a nearby tree. She stood too far away to be any help. A deep hissing sound came from the left. Her skin crawled as she faced the sound. An even bigger monster snake stared her down as it began to uncoil from a tree. The snake's low hiss sounded more like a rumbled growl.

There was no time to think or wait for the snake to finish uncoiling. She lunged and buried her sword in the top of its head. She jabbed down, staking the beast to the ground. The snake's body lurched and rolled. Throwing her weight down, Katrina straddled its neck to prevent it from rearing back into a strike. Cadet Vacek jumped onto its back behind her, helping keep the snake pinned. They held on as it shook and screeched before going limp with a grunt. The monster snake relaxed into its demise, but she kept it pinned as she looked around for Thedmir.

He assessed how to best kill the monster snake he faced. It bared its fangs and lunged at him. Thedmir struck behind the creature's head. The blow sent the snake off course and left it partially decapitated. With a bloody twitch it slumped to the ground. Thedmir struck again, severing its head off.

Huffing Thedmir walked over to evaluate the snake beneath her and Vacek. Grabbing the pommel of her sword, he decapitated it in one strike. Thedmir exhaled with a huff. He looked at her with wide dilated eyes.

I do not like snakes, he said. This island has the most horrific breed.

"I agree," she said, standing up and inspecting the blood on her jacket. "I swear this one growled."

"It was growling," Vacek said. He stood and reached down to press a hand to one of the snake's wide brown scales. "You ever eat snake?"

"No," Katrina said.

"The locals say these things don't taste any good," Vacek said. "I wonder if I should try it?"

"I can't believe looking at this thing, you want to eat it," she said.

"Of course I'm thinking about eating it," Vacek said. "I'm hungry. We haven't had a hot meal or fresh meat in weeks."

She put a hand up in protest and shook her head as she walked to take up her guard position again.

"Please, don't get everyone talking about food again," she said. "It's torture."

The instructors made Nellmon drink a fast-acting medicine for the pain. Then they all carried him to the edge of the ravine. A medical team arrived. Using a stretcher, they lifted Nellmon out of the restricted area. Ropes were lowered to the rest of them, and they climbed back up the ravine wall. The squad and instructors escorted the medical team to the main road. They watched in silence as the medical team left, carrying Nellmon back to the University campus. The instructors led them to the clearing they slept in the first night. There they were allowed to build a fire, ordered to eat, and given the liberty to rest for the remainder of the evening.

I hate those snakes, Thedmir wandered. Did you know those things were back there?

"No," she said. "I only figured it out when I saw all the cashew trees."

You were the one being guided.

"What are you talking about?"

You were given the vision of Nellmon falling.

She watched him clean his sword. Still rattled by the incident, she hesitated agreeing with his claim.

"I saw him fall. I didn't see snakes," she said.

Thedmir sheathed his sword and offered her the cleaning rag. Katrina took it. She worked it along her simple blade, sweeping away what remained of the monster snake blood. She returned his rag and glanced at his sword. She passed him the memory of the one and only time she tried to move his sword. The size and weight of it were too awkward for her to control, and she fell over backwards. Thedmir laughed into her thoughts.

I told you not to do that.

"I listened to what my mind and body were telling me, but it still happened," she said.

You need to trust what you're given, he gestured to his head. You have a gift, a connection meant to help others. You need to believe in it. That's the only way that kind of knowledge can become wisdom.

6

The Guest Instructor

Ignoring the chatter of her classmates, Katrina searched the sky. Every class of cadets stood assembled on the parade field ready to greet their expected guests. Thedmir stood next to her. Leaning over he bumped her and sent her off balance.

They're not here yet.

Katrina smiled up at him shaking her head.

"It's a good thing it's me you tease like that. Do that to a first year and they might piss themselves."

I have to use physical force for that. You only need to smile at them.

"That's not true," she said.

I will tell Mickle and we will make wagers. Thedmir gestured over her head to Mickle.

"No, you will not," she said, reaching up and trying to push his hand back.

"Wagers?" Mickle asked. "What do you want to wager, friend?"

"Nothing," she said. "He's not wagering anything."

Yes, we are. Thedmir made a series of gestures to Mickle. *We are quite the pair. Every new cadet class stares at us for months. I, a Minotaur, and you, being you. They enjoy looking at us.*

"Right," she said. "It's a shame our novelty for the current first years has already worn off. I'm so disappointed we missed our chance."

"Alright, Cadets, listen up," Instructor Wells said. His voice barked over the chattering fourth year class and silenced them. "You're fourth years, act like it. If any of you embarrass me you'll be doing first year chores until graduation."

He fished a piece of paper from his pocket.

"This evening the top five seniors will dine in Professor's hall with our guest. That means, Bronson, Chadwick, Siers, Monten, and Larksbur, you need to be to the receiving line before third bell."

Katrina stiffened as she second guessed what Wells said.

The perks of your endless studies. Thedmir said.

"I thought I only made the top ten, not the top five? I've never eaten in the Professor's mess hall."

Wells looked over at Cadet Voss in the front rank. "Voss, none of your stupid questions today. I don't want to hear a single question out of you."

Cadet Voss smiled and quipped back. "Aw, Sir, this is a place of higher learning. How can you ban me from asking questions?"

The class broke out into snickering quiet laughter.

"Voss, I forbid you from embarrassing us," Wells said. As serious as he sounded, the lightness in his features hinted at a smile. "If you're too lazy to read up on Gryph then you're not asking any questions today. Your mid semester marks demonstrate you haven't been reading much of anything."

"We were supposed to read something?" Voss said.

Wells grinned and more of the class laughed. Wells straightened up, putting his notes away. He gave a command, bringing everyone in the class to attention.

The entire field became quiet as the murmuring of Cadets and the echo of instructor commands faded. The University's cadets stood at attention for the headmaster, General Gerros Taylor, as he walked to the front of the formation and spoke.

"Cadets, today's an exciting day. We are greeting an officer of Gryph, Captain Jance Willmont. He's here to offer commissions to some of our new graduates and will be our honored guest at graduation."

Katrina envisioned what it must be like to battle while flying. Delivering a death blow with both feet on the ground seemed hard enough. She chewed at the edge of her lip, and recalled statues of Mahigans battling in flight. She melded the images with what she knew about Gryphons and their riders. The Mahigan would win.

I think you're right. Thedmir wandered.

A faint screeching grabbed the attention of everyone assembled. Her eyes fixed on a dot at the horizon. The dot grew and a large animal, a massive animal, an actual Gryphon flew onto the parade field. A magnificent sight in real life. Better than all the paintings and illustrations Katrina had ever seen.

The Gryphon set down on the ground with lithe grace despite its size. Its tawny colored feathers had flecks of white and a dark brown. Gold colored eyes peered over a dark yellow beak. Black talons bigger than a human head emerged from yellow feet, which poked out from legs thickly wrapped in feathers.

The Gryphon blinked and reared its head inspecting the gathering as the human officer dismounted. His feet found the bottom rung of a specialized saddle before his Gryphon lowered its body to the ground. He stepped off as he removed his helmet, revealing a pleasant strong face and a head piled with a mass of tousled dark hair. An intimidating man without his relaxed smile. He looked too young for his rank. He rendered a confident salute to General Taylor, who returned the gesture and walked forward to greet him.

They wander, Thulane and Captain Willmont, Thedmir wandered.

Thulane's, the Gryphon?

Yes. It's a courtesy with any humans, as a wanderer you identify yourself to those who wander. It's rude not to. Similar to eavesdropping.

She whispered back, "Why is that important?"

I'm reminding you.

What for? I'm a guest cadet, he has no reason to speak to me.

You'll be at dinner with him tonight.

She sighed. *Do human wanderers always walk around sensing for others who wander?*

You get close enough you can tell, he wandered.

How was I supposed to know? He's all the way over there.
He flew here on a Gryphon. It would be odd if he didn't.
"Yes, yes, you're right," she said.

Hello fellow wanderer, came a female voice in a wander. *I am Thulane of Gryph. I am grateful to be among friends.*

Katrina stared in disbelief at Thulane who even from across the parade field looked focused on her.

"What do I say?"

Reply back, with the same greeting she gave. Just be sure you say who you really are.

"Huh?"

Gryphons can see you for who you are, he wandered. *Don't lie to them.*

Her heart pounded. After years of being Katrina Larksbur, she found it a little odd to state her real name.

Greetings Thulane I'm Katrina Aranysarga, Princess of the Mozgas Province. I am grateful to be among friends.

Thulane blinked at her in confirmation.

Katrina had enjoyed the reading assigned to her class on Gryph. A land famous for dominating the sky, with people who lived among the only known colony of Gryphons. Wealthy and prestigious, Gryph was by far the most coveted place for one of her classmates to be commissioned as an officer.

Captain Willmont's presentation finished and the cadets were dismissed to their normal routines.

"Did you see that guy?" Cadet Flint said, "I bet he blinks and ladies are lifting their skirt for him."

"You have no class." Cadet Mickle said, pointing with his gaze to Katrina who walked behind him.

Cadet Flint jerked around. His smile withered. "Oh, hey Larksbur."

"You're right," she said. "It's a good thing I'm wearing pants."

A chuckle of laughter erupted around them.

It's a good thing you will be wearing pants later. You have the best opportunity to wander with him tonight in the Professors hall.

"You're still nagging me about their stupid ritual," she said. "What if I don't want to, or I forget?"

Then he will confirm what he already knows. You grew up isolated on an island with no culture.

"You're baiting me, with a challenge."

Am I?

"I think this ritual's excessive."

It's great practice for you.

"Why do I have to do a wanderer greeting, after I just said a greeting out loud?"

Thedmir steadied his gaze at her. It's a human courtesy, and he's an officer, so you need to do it. I also know you would not risk offending the royal house of Willmont.

"Stop it,"she said. "Don't do the thing where you sound like my mother. I know who Jance Willmont is."

Yes, I bet Lena does too. He huffed at her frown. *It's just a greeting.*

In Etrasa everyone assumed if you were a visiting unwed male of royal lineage, you were there to participate in Parade. A common assumption, because it was so often correct. With the next Parade season starting, it would be a mistake to conclude Captain Willmont only traveled to Etrasa for graduation.

Her mother waited at the front door with an excited fervor in her eyes. Katrina gritted her teeth. Her mother's cunning network of associates loved to drop by with bits and pieces of gossip. Most of their chatter did nothing but waste time, but Katrina admired their speed.

"Did you see the Willmont Prince?" her mother said.

"Oh mother please, yes," she said, avoiding her eyes as she eased by her into the house. "Me, and the entire university."

"Did you talk to him? Did he see you?"

"You do realize I stood with an assembly of about six hundred people, all of them wearing what I'm wearing."

"So?"

Her eyebrows lifted in a moment of exasperated shock. She sighed and then chuckled as she shook her head. "I'm sorry mother," she grabbed the railing to the back stairs. "No, I didn't say hello to Captain Willmont, but I might see him tonight at the Professor's mess."

Her mother trilled in approval and Katrina cringed. In a rush her mother shuffled around her and up the stairs.

Pha helped Katrina change into her formal uniform and worked a fresh braid into her hair.

"I don't know what she expects from me at a formal officer's dinner," Katrina said.

"Yes, you do," Pha said.

"I'm not going to flirt with the graduation guest of honor, like I'm at the House during Parade season."

Pha chuckled and leaned in to speak in her ear.

"Darling you'll never need to flirt to grab a man's attention."

Katrina smiled, "Thank you."

There were times she caught her reflection and glanced back, wondering who the lady was. Recognizing herself she walked on, caught off guard by her mistake. Even after she adjusted to the body of a woman, the look of her own face befuddled her. She often forgot how much attention her appearance could garner. Becoming an attractive woman was like being dressed in a flashy costume she could never take off. It drew attention she neither sought nor wanted. External beauty really was a gift and a curse. If she had grown up attractive, she might have gained the skill to leverage her appearance as an asset. Instead fate cheated her out of the time needed to learn such games, and it was all she could do now to address its curses.

Pha finished her braid. Patting Katrina's back, Pha gestured to the door. "That's my Katrina. Tell me all about the food when you get back."

The Professor's Mess sat in the same building as the Cadet's mess. She entered the formal greeting line, following her classmates as one by one they greeted the senior officers.

"Cadet Larksbur," General Taylor said. He took Katrina's hand in a brief handshake. He turned to the officer beside him. "Captain Willmont, this is Cadet Katrina Larksbur."

Katrina held her breath as she met Captain Willmont's gaze. The man had the presence of someone twice his rank, and it reminded her of Valgu. Did his confidence come from his abilities as an officer, or his royal upbringing?

"Sir, it's nice to meet you," she said.

"You as well."

She marveled at the dark navy blue color of his eyes. Stunned by Captain Willmont's presence, Katrina forced herself to look away, afraid she had already stared at him. Her mother would be disappointed. A man like Captain Willmont needing to buy his wife, unlikely.

She was eager to be released, yet he kept hold of her hand.

Wait, Katrina? Hello fellow wanderer, I'm Jance of the house of Willmont. I am grateful to be among friends.

Katrina paused and remembered the human courtesy Thedmir had gone on and on about that morning.

"Sir I'm sorry," she said. "Thedmir told me I needed to be ready when I saw you."

But you're Veilede. Your people don't have such formalities.

Katrina took a breath at his bold declaration. Desperate to be free from his attention she focused on his eyes and composed her words. Even as she said her true name it felt foreign. Something no longer hers, but that of a dead Airetti girl.

Hello fellow wanderer, I'm Katrina Aranysarga, Princess of the Mozgas Province. I am grateful to be among friends.

Captain Willmont smiled and released her hand.

"Perfect, you can tell Thedmir you were successful."

Katrina fought to hold his gaze, not stare, appear confident, and keep her eyes off the safety of the floor. A strange excitement bubbled up. A frightening sensation since the last man to cause it was Puternic.

"Thank you, Sir."

The awkwardness of walking away pained her. What if he saw her response to him, or the pathetic way she kept replaying their introduction?

Everyone stood by their assigned seat.

General Taylor walked to his chair and announced, "Good evening everyone, please take seats."

She was just seated when Captain Willmont addressed her.

"Cadet Larksbur, where's your family from?"

Guarded, she wondered at his motives.

"Sir, my mother was born in a small province of Bisma called Lavieth."

General Taylor's even voice injected, "Captain, I heard your brother recently married a Bisma Princess."

"Yes," Captain Wilmont said. "My sister by marriage, Princess Armina. I meant to inquire about it earlier Sir, the high number of female cadets enrolled here, it's remarkable. Does someone travel around to specifically recruit women?"

"Surely you know Willmont, this is Etrasa. Our island has the highest concentration of eligible Ladies in the region, well … probably anywhere." General Taylor said.

She watched Captain Willmont's reaction with interest.

"Does it?" Captain Willmont said, with a light tone in his voice. His gaze shifted to hers, grinning the faintest of smiles, as if they shared a private joke.

General Taylor began bragging about Cadet Chadwick, the top academic in Katrina's class. Cadet Bronson's achievement came next. He earned a scholarship for his exemplary performance as a soldier in the Bisma Army. Cadet Siers straightened in his seat when General Taylor mentioned his second sparring competition win within the same year. Cadet Monten's accolades came from his maintaining the highest academic test scores, and possessing the fastest run time during the cross-country season. Katrina waited to see what General Taylor might say about her, but apparently being a female was interesting enough.

Captain Willmont's eyes were on Katrina again. When she noticed he gave a small smile. He engaged in conversation with the table, but his focus seemed to always find its way back to her.

"Sir, what do you think about the rumors of conflict in Bisma?" Cadet Bronson asked.

"I'd say there's more truth than rumor of a conflict," Captain Willmont said. "It's not a surprise, hostilities have been brewing at their border for a long time."

"Will Gryph take sides?" Cadet Chadwick said, his eagerness betraying his youth.

"I don't know," Captain Willmont said.

"My dad always said, a man with a brain doesn't fight the Veilede," Cadet Bronson said. "Those that try, are those who die." His Bisma lilt more enhanced as he repeated his father's words.

Trying to refrain from nodding in agreement, she took a drink of water.

"The Veilede would be a formidable opponent," Captain Willmont said.

"I heard killing a Mahigan's like trying to kill a dragon, impossible," Cadet Chadwick said.

She grinned at the comparison, and looked forward to telling Valgu about it.

"I disagree," Captain Willmont said. "It's possible to kill a Mahigan, even though I hope I never need to."

"How?" Katrina said. The word escaped her lips before she could think twice.

Captain Willmont's gaze settled on her before he answered. She stared back, daring him to spout nonsense to a group whose true knowledge of a Mahigan was rudimentary and bordered on folklore.

"The Veilede look human, how would someone know who is one and who's not?" Cadet Bronson said.

"A Gryphon can see what's hidden inside anyone," Captain Willmont said. "Sometimes they see things people don't know about themselves."

"How do you kill a Mahigan?" Cadet Siers said.

"If you net one, however you like," Captain Willmont said. "Otherwise, a knife to the throat here works." He gestured with two fingers to the part of his neck directly under the side of his jaw. "In a sudden attack, preferably while they still hold a human form, but you can slide a knife under their armor plates here as well."

"The Gryph soldier with the notoriety of killing a Mahigan without a net must have died a long time ago," Katrina said. "Who is he? I'd be fascinated to read about him."

"You're certain he died long ago," Captain Willmont said.

"He must have," she said. "Gryph hasn't participated in any open combat with the Veilede for over two hundred years. The soldier you speak of must be dead."

"Someone has been doing her assigned reading," Captain Willmont said. "Well done."

"Cadet Larksbur has me intrigued, tell us who this Gryph soldier is," General Taylor said.

"I'm sorry to say this, but I don't know the man's name," Captain Willmont said.

"Then you must cite your source," Colonel Hankler said.

"I'm also sorry for crediting the act to someone fighting on behalf of Gryph. The Mahigan was killed while Gryph fought alongside the Veilede."

"Was it during the battles in the lost desert?" Katrina asked. She took keen interest in studying any battle where Skrieni were defeated.

"Right again cadet, that's when Thulane witnessed a Mahigan die by taking a knife to the throat."

The novelty of a human killing a Mahigan vanished for her. The Skrieni in question was most likely a Mahigan before rejecting his Veilede heritage. Making the fight evenly matched and insignificant.

"From the hidden people," she said, taking petty enjoyment calling the Skrieni by an alternate and less preferred name.

"Or as they like to be called, the Skrieni," Captain Willmont said.

"Thulane saw this but you didn't Sir?" Cadet Siers said.

Katrina shot Siers a condemning look. The battles in the lost desert were covered in their assigned reading.

"No, this happened over one hundred years ago," Captain Willmont said.

"How old is Thulane, or will she get upset by my asking?" Colonel Hankler asked.

"The Gryphons don't remember, or more likely just won't say how old they are," Captain Willmont said. "Gryph keeps detailed accounts and records on all of them. According to these, Thulane is two hundred and ninety-seven years old, but she can play that memory for me like it happened yesterday."

Captain Willmont spent the rest of dinner focusing on the cadets and asking questions about their career aspirations.

Katrina gaped at the multi layer chocolate cake with dark chocolate icing served for dessert. Her first bite of cake sat forked when Captain Willmont turned his attention to her.

"And you Cadet Larksbur, where do you hope to gain your commission?"

She longed for her forked bite of cake, but forced a small grin to her face. Following proper etiquette, she set her fork down before answering his question.

"Sir, I'm a guest Cadet. I'll not be seeking a commission."

She reached for her fork.

"Have you had your fill of soldiering?" Captain Willmont asked.

Cake, she wanted a bite of cake. Instead she endured Captain Willmont's torture as he asked meaningless questions he could probably guess the answer to.

"I've enjoyed my time here very much Sir," she said.

She quickly took hold of her fork, and jealously spied the rest of the table who were half way through their dessert.

"What have you enjoyed during your time here?" Captain Willmont asked.

She grit her teeth. His questions were easy. She just wished he had singled her out during the asparagus course.

"I like planning and staff work," she said.

With a quick grab she slipped the first bite of cake into her mouth. Rich and moist, the creamy frosting had the right balance of sweet and flavor. All the layers combined created a superb mix of bittersweet chocolate.

"Then you would be ahead of the curve as an officer. Most of my time is spent planning." Captain Willmont said.

Rational thought reinforced the likelihood Captain Willmont was either already married or surrounded by eligible court women ready for the job. However, his constant questions were allowing doubt to snake in. The glint in his eyes coiled around her conviction and killed her certainty.

General Taylor cleared his throat to speak, and she relaxed. Grateful to relinquish Captain Willmont's attention, she forked another bite of cake.

"Too much of my whole career has been behind a desk," General Taylor said. The other commissioned officers at the table laughed, each nodding their heads in agreement. The cadets sat with blank stares, trying to decipher their laughter.

She eased back in her chair, and worked to restrain her adoration as she ate another bite of cake. Did chocolate always evoke this simmering pleasure?

Bringing up memories of a particular sea cave. She cleared every morsel of the cake from her plate, and wondered who needed to be bribed to get another slice.

The social hour started as the dessert plates cleared. Protocol required her to remain until the most senior ranking officer present retired for the evening. Katrina remained at the table as everyone else stood, stretched, and mingled about the room. The other cadets, who all sought Gryph commissions, gathered around Captain Willmont like hungry chickens. Crowding him, they asked questions about officer training in Gryph. General Taylor bid the room goodnight, and she perked up. Exiting her seat, she left the dining room behind him, and went straight home.

The Cadet dining hall buzzed with the usual afternoon activity. Katrina turned a page in the open book set in front of her on the table. She took a bite of dark bread, and lifted her eyes from the book as Thedmir sat down across from her.

"You don't have to read my thoughts on last night, I'm happy to tell you about it."

Thedmir narrowed his eyes and she glared at him.

"He said I should tell you I did well. Does that settle your concerns about me and human wandering rituals? Are you done fretting over our new wandering friends, or are you going to spring some other new ritual on me?"

Thedmir did a throat chortle that mimicked a human laugh. An odd and eerie sound coming from someone without audible speech. He did the laugh to tease her, knowing how much she hated the sound.

"Don't do your creepy throat chortle at me. Throat chortle at me again and I won't talk to you for the rest of the day."

Turning her eyes to her book she felt Thedmir's continued gaze. Katrina looked up again.

"What?"

He could talk to you about the human traditions. The human wandering things I don't know to teach you.

Thedmir was right. It would be nice to pick a human wanderer's brain.

"Yes, but that's not a good idea. It would be an odd request too."

He began laughing into her thoughts. *You like him.* With his words Thedmir mirrored back a series of images and her initial impressions of Captain Willmont.

"I would deny that if you couldn't see my thoughts," she said. "Of course I like him."

I haven't seen thoughts like these from you in a long time.

"You know the restrictions I'm under."

Thedmir began to eat. *We'll see.*

"What do you want to know about my thoughts? Is he handsome? Yes, he's attractive. Smart? Certainly. Attached? Absolutely. There's something wrong with a man like that if he's not." Katrina closed her book and hefted it into her bag.

You like him.

"No, now don't go getting confused over this. I admire him for his accomplishments, and for being from a very interesting place, but I don't know him well enough to like him."

That's not where your thoughts have been loitering.

"Oh please, don't get my infatuation with the chocolate cake confused with my impressions of Captain Willmont."

I think you'd mate both if you had the opportunity.

She laughed and shook her head. "I'm going to grab some tea before lecture, do you want anything?"

Thedmir waved her off with his no hand gesture. Collecting her bag, she walked over to the drink table.

Thedmir teased her with the truth about where her mind went when she thought about Captain Willmont. She did admire him. A part of her hoped he came to Etrasa for more than graduation. A surprising and ridiculous idea, that made her realize she regretted having greater obligations than the House of Etrasa. A troubling realization. She would go home soon, as Valgu had promised. Her only goal since childhood would soon be realized. Yet the pending change now daunted her, as the appeal of being only a Lady from the House grew.

She looked across the room to where Captain Willmont sat talking with an instructor. Captain Willmont kept his jet-black hair short on the sides. It transitioned into a well-groomed mass of curls at the top of his head. An acceptable style, male officers rarely wore it, claiming it too close to a breach of uniform standards. She liked his risky choice. Maybe his dark hair reminded her of Puternic's, but Captain Willmont's appeal was more in the way he carried himself. A no-nonsense swagger mixed with the confidence of a trained royal like her brother Valgu.

Looking down she prepared her tea, and glanced up to take one more peek at him. He looked in her direction. She made a subtle glance around to see who had his attention. Looking back, he smiled and gave a small two finger wave. She gave him a polite closed mouth smile, nodded her head once, and did a swift about face. Walking away, she gripped her cup like it would keep her from falling over. Sliding next to Thedmir they exited the dining hall.

"Throat chortle at me and not only will I not talk to you today, I will hurt you," she said. "I mean it."

7

Friends and The Future

The image of pine trees and a stone path came into view as Katrina stepped into the glen in neutral.

Seeing Sol approach, her steps picked up. In a flash she became wrapped in Sol's embrace as he danced her in a circle.

I've missed you.

"I've missed you too," she said.

Despite the softer angles of Sol's face, his gold eyes looked just like their father's. A bright reminder of his Aranysarga heritage that contrasted with his quiet demeanor.

Valgu stood close with his arms crossed and his usual stoic expression. Seeming to change his mind, he dropped the brooding stance, reached over, and pulled her into a hug. The gesture made her laugh.

"I get to see both of you tonight," she said. "I'm guessing by this, you have good news for me."

Valgu steered her towards the table and gestured for her to sit down. An unknown man sat across from her seat with boots propped on the table. His build reminded her of Cadet Vacek or Captain Willmont, a descent size for a human man, but small beside her Mahigan brothers Valgu and Sol. His close cut blonde hair and style of clothing made him appear human, but the shape and flash in his green eyes told her he was something else.

"Is this my sister who killed, what was it called again?" he asked, looking to Valgu for the words, "A beast snake? Is this really my big sister?" Dropping his feet to the floor he sat forward and narrowed his eyes at her. "I tried to tell the adults how rough you were with me, but you never got in trouble. Not once. Valgu told me a crazy story about you almost getting eaten by a snake?"

Realizing who he was forced Katrina to face her new fear of awkward reunions and fake pleasantries. The fear passed as soon as it arrived and she smiled. If she met Massie anywhere but here he would have been a stranger. Here where her siblings gathered in neutral, she felt him and recognized his Aranysarga eyes. She knew their familiar but dormant tie, an old childhood connection.

"The only snake that's ever tried to eat me, was the one you handed me," she said, getting comfortable in her seat. "What's happened to that little tormenting brother of mine? And where are all the blond curls? Why would you ever chop those off?"

Massie frowned as he ran a hand through the top of his closely shorn hair, as if checking for the absent curls. "You don't look anything like the Katrina I remember. You're far too beautiful to be my big sister." Massie lifted his eyebrows and looked over at Sol. "Maybe it was a bad choice to send Jance to fetch her?"

Tilting her head forward she narrowed her eyes.

"You sent who to fetch me?"

"Captain Jance Willmont has agreed to assist us in bringing you home," Valgu said.

Sitting back, Katrina laughed to herself. "That explains it."

"Has Puternic contacted you?" Valgu said.

"Not since I saw him during the Final Test," she said. "Has something happened?"

"There have been private discussions between the Delphi and a few Madar council members," Massie said. "Regent Raynes is seeking support to sanction Puternic's claim on you."

"I'm guessing it's not just talk," she said.

"Correct," Massie said. "We know they've already developed a plan to overrun the island and take you."

"When?"

"We aren't sure, but we can't afford to wait," Massie said. "Jance and Thulane, they're our best chance at extracting you."

"When will we leave?"

Massie grinned, "After Jance selects you at Parade of course."

Her mouth hung open.

"You're to graduate, complete the Parade season, and then travel with Captain Willmont to Gryph," Valgu said.

"Why aren't I leaving tomorrow? Why risk staying?"

"He agreed to be the honorary guest at your graduation," Massie said. "And needs to present commissioning offers to some of your classmates."

"It also releases you from your House contract," Valgu said.

"Graduation I understand, but parade and my contract, who cares about that?"

"Selection at Parade also releases your mother," Massie said. "Some of us want to know where she'll go when her daughter is safely married off."

"If you want to apprehend her, why let her even leave the island?"

Valgu looked at Massie and spoke in a tone that brokered no objection.

"We're not apprehending Lady Lena."

Massie lowered his face and shifted in his seat.

"She doesn't know about any of this, does she?" she asked.

"No," Valgu said. "We think it's better if she believes you're actually being selected at Parade. We will meet you in Gryph, and the Willmonts will be paid the reward Father's sending for your safe return."

She noticed another man enter the glen. Valgu stopped his slow pace as he waved the man over to the table. The man stopped beside Valgu and they shared commiserating looks over a formal handshake. Valgu grasped the man's shoulder. The man wore his sandy blonde hair tapered at the sides, but long on top. It hung low enough to just graze his ears. His height matched Valgu's, and based on his build, he was most likely Mahigan.

"What did I step into?" the man said in collusion to Valgu.

Valgu glowered and shook his head.

"Tegija, pull up a chair friend, join the party!" Massie said.

She recognized the name Tegija. He was Valgu's closest friend, and a professor at the University of Mozgas. Valgu and Tegija's friendship formed during their time in the Mahigan compound.

Tegija crossed his arms and glowered at Massie.

"Any good news?" Valgu asked Tegija.

"Yes," Tegija said. His washed out gold eyes scanned the table stopping as they landed on her. A strange pulse of interest ran through her as she held his gaze.

"If we need to, we can get her home over water," Tegija said.

"Yes!" Massie cheered, "The professor saves the day."

She tried not to snicker at Massie's antics, while Sol caved to a quiet laugh. Tegija eyed Massie with patient amusement.

"We have the right formula of a drug to mask a wandering ability," Tegija said. "It's temporary, but it'll hide a wanderer from other wanderers. If the Delphi lose sight of her, they won't be able to locate her using that."

"That's the best news I've had all week," Valgu said.

"I'll accompany whoever might need to use it," Tegija said. "It's a powerful drug. We still need to determine the side effects."

"Of course," Valgu said, nodding.

"My team will want to start the restoration of her shifting ability as soon as possible. They need to be notified the day before she's brought back to the palace complex."

Tegija's direct manner as he spoke to Valgu held an audacity outside his rank. He handled himself a little too well beside her brothers. While his expression remained formal, it was more collegial than subordinate.

Usually, she considered Valgu a solid judge of character. She found it easy to concede trust to those he would call friend. But this man, and his brazen claim that he had the ability to restore her wings. Tegija seemed task oriented, and had an air of self-important pride, common traits among attractive men. Tegija was in all things the exact opposite of her private nightmare. The one where her brothers failed to retrieve her, and the House sold her off to some nervous indecisive man child.

No one had even bothered to introduce them.

I'll meet you in Gryph, Sol wandered.

"I'll arrive in Etrasa at some point," Massie said.

"Well," she said. "I guess I have one last question. Who do I introduce myself as?" She held Tegija's gaze as she said it, but Valgu missed her prod.

"Gryph is a short stop in your journey home," he said. "You will use the title you were born with as soon as it's appropriate to do so."

Tegija gave her a small knowing grin, as if they shared a private joke. Of course he knew her identity. Still, Valgu had no reason to ignore basic courtesy.

Looking at Valgu in irritation, she said, "Of course."

He stared at her, puzzled by her tone. She shook her head and sighed. Even perfect older brothers had blind spots.

Pha had to wake Katrina the next day. Her time in neutral leeched her strength and left her desperate for more sleep. She climbed out of bed with the tortured desire to climb back in. She dragged herself over to sit on the stool at her dressing table. Pha came up behind her, and began brushing her hair.

Katrina grinned at Pha through the mirror, and whispered. "I saw Sol, and Massie."

Pha froze and looked up. Her astonished eyes met Katrina's.

"We were together too long. I'm a tired wreck, but it was worth it."

Pha gripped her shoulder with her free hand and squeezed. She replied in an excited whisper. "I'm so glad for you."

"Valgu told me to say he would wander with you tonight, to explain more details."

"Are we still to go by boat?"

"Massie's worked out something new." She turned around, facing Pha as she wandered. *Captain Willmont is taking me home.*

"Interesting," Pha said.

We're to leave my mother be. Let her believe his interest in me during the Parade season is genuine.

Pha nodded and Katrina stood with new found energy. She removed her nightclothes as Pha retrieved her uniform. She adjusted her undergarments as Pha extended her a clean shirt. Pha's eyes focused on something far off. Katrina took the shirt and ran each arm into the sleeves. Pha's motions retrieving her pants and uniform jacket were mindless.

"You don't look happy," Katrina said.

"I am, I am," Pha said, giving her head a small shake, blinking to bring her focus back to the present. "Don't fret about my thinking. It's what I do. It's what I have to do to make sure my Katrina's taken care of properly."

Katrina buttoned her jacket and Pha's hand gripped her forearms. The gesture halted Katrina's work. Pha swatted her hands aside and finished the remaining buttons herself.

"Did you see all your brothers?" Pha asked. She tried masking the mix of fear and regret clouding her voice.

Katrina's lips twitched into a small grin. She loved Pha, and wanted to laugh at the way she put this conversation off for so long.

"No," she said. "I still haven't met Dermot."

"You know then," Pha said. "When did Valgu tell you?"

Katrina shrugged, "He didn't. I learned about them from Puternic. A long time ago."

"I see," Pha said.

"It bothered me, that he told me, instead of you or Valgu. But, you've never hoarded truths from me out of self interest like my mother."

"I'm sorry," Pha said.

"No, don't be. I forgave you long before I'd forgiven Valgu. I knew he must have ordered you, or you were trying to protect me."

"It was both."

"It was a shock to learn, but I put it from my mind. Thinking about home, its never done me any good."

"Well," Pha said. "It's time you start again. You'll be thinking a lot about it from now on."

She did allow herself to think about home, and even the amazing prospect of getting her wings back. She thought about it all the way to the University campus. With a relaxed step, she entered the University library. Crossing the main floor, she walked up a circular stairwell. The stone steps shone from so many years of wear. She climbed to the fifth floor and exited into the ancient art section.

The number of stairs to this section kept other cadets from contending for her favorite study spot. A yellow carpet depicting birds in flight over water framed a simple wood table and chairs. A comfortable high backed chair rested by the single large window. Across the room stood an impractical ornamental fireplace. Aside from the window, it offered the only break in the floor to ceiling bookshelves rimming the room.

Putting her bag by the high backed chair, Katrina picked a book off the table. She liked how the completion of her studies meant she had more time to read what she wanted. The only duties she and Thedmir needed to complete today were a uniform fitting and a graduation ceremony rehearsal. She had a whole hour to study before breakfast. She flopped down in the chair and lost herself in the books pages.

She paused at the sound of someone on the stairs. When the footsteps continued to her level, she looked over at the door. Captain Willmont strode in.

Her heart seemed to stop and jolt her awake at the same time. She rose from her seat and stood at attention.

"Good Morning, Sir."

"Good Morning," he said, and waved one hand in dismissal. "Please, sit, and do call me Jance."

With a random look around the room she tried to process why he was here at this hour. Sitting down, she reached for her bag and pulled it into her lap.

He glanced around the room and walked over to the fireplace. He ran a hand along the mantle before looking back over his shoulder to her. "You don't mind if I join you?"

"Sir, please feel free."

He grabbed a wooden chair from beside the table, and placed it in front of her. Then dropped down into it.

"I came looking for you, I was hoping we could talk. Get to know each other some."

"Get to know me?"

"I'm not used to this much free time. I decided you were the most interesting thing on the island to occupy my time."

With a short laugh, she shook her head. "Me? That's an odd comparison. What does that say about the island?"

"That I'll see everything it has to offer in the span of one day if I don't pace myself."

"Potentially," she said. "It would depend on what you find amusing."

"Exactly," he said. "Besides, isn't it customary for you to entertain the various suitors who attend parade?"

"I do as the House instructs, but I like to avoid conversations with suitors."

"Avoid them, how have you managed to avoid them?"

"It's not too difficult," she said.

"You insult them all, don't you?"

"Maybe a few. But the plan to get me home has never involved me being selected at Parade as the wife of a human."

"I see," he said. "You're too good for me."

"No Sir, that's not what I meant."

"I think it's exactly what you meant," he said. "Which makes it good that this Parade thing for you and me is all pretend. Am I really that bad?"

"No Sir, not at all. I'll be shocked if nobody questions why you're here in the first place."

"You have to do something for me," he said. "You have to stop calling me Sir. I can't stand it, I'm trying to get to know you and this will not work if you keep calling me Sir. Call me Jance."

She hesitated, wondering about his request.

"I don't think you need to worry about formalities," he said. "I trust we can remain professional in uniform. Here, when we're alone, or when we wander, please call me Jance."

"It sounds like you plan on us spending a lot of time together," she said.

"Of course I am," he said as his grin became an excited smile.

She was troubled by the part of her enjoying his flirtation. It was irrational and needed to be stopped before temptation let it go further.

"Jance," she said trying out his name, "I'm curious, how did you get brought into the plan to bring me home?"

"I'll just say, it's something I've been assigned to do."

"You were given it as an assignment?"

"Yes, and when my mother, Queen LaBell, asks you to do something, you usually do it."

"That's an unusual assignment," she said

"Massie got us involved. He and I are good friends, so I have no problem with it. What about your mother? Is she excited about Parade, and your prospective human marriage?"

"Yes," she said. "My mother will be ecstatic. However, if this were real, my father, and the rest of my family would strongly object."

"What about you, would you object?"

"Whom I marry has nothing to do with what I want," she said.

"But you know what you want?"

Katrina narrowed her eyes, "I know what I like, but I won't have a say."

"Is it easier to tell me what you don't like?"

"Yes," she said. "I really don't like the idea of being bought the same way some purchase a horse."

He sat quiet for a moment, reflecting on her statement before saying, "Purchased like a horse."

"What about you, will your real wife be an assignment too?"

Jance laughed and nodded his head. "There's a strong possibility she will."

"What would your family think if this were real, and you brought a Veilede woman home as your bride? You can speak truthfully. I'm well-versed in the prejudice humans have. I promise, you won't offend me."

"You're the one who doesn't want to marry a human," he said.

"For good reason, I don't like innocent people being killed."

"I'm from Gryph, we basically invented most of the human prejudice that exists," he said.

"But here you are, on an assignment from the Queen, helping my Veilede family."

"I am," he said. "My assignments usually have nothing to do with what I want."

"But you know your own prejudices."

"I do, and I respect your kind. It's my belief there's more opportunity when people are united. I willingly accepted this assignment."

"I see."

"Good, because as my soon-to-be-Lady, I'd appreciate your help navigating this Parade business. What can I expect now that I'm your suitor?"

Katrina frowned and shook her head. "I am not your Lady. I can advise you as a friend here at the University, but you'll need to ignore me whenever you see me at the House."

"What for?"

"If a man like you takes an interest in me, it will attract the attention of every suitor attending activities this season. You'll have to ignore me until the very end."

"Then what am I supposed to do between now and then?"

"It's customary you spend time meeting each one of the Ladies from the House."

"All of them? I didn't agree to that," he said. "Now I for sure need your help."

"No, I don't think the likes of Captain Jance Willmont needs my help meeting a Lady. I suspect you've had practice winning the affection of many women."

"Ah well, thank you very much, my Lady," he said. "However you have inside information that's useful. As my friend, you must help me."

His playful declaration made her smile. "It's easy, Jance, all you have to do is meet them, and talk to them. It's what you do before you pick one."

"Before I pick you," he said.

Jance leaned towards her. "I say you and I meet in neutral. It'll give us a chance to talk, very informal, no stress."

"I don't know," she said, shifting her bag to ease the strap over one shoulder.

"What's the harm, at least one time?" He held up his index finger emphasizing one. "I'll find you tonight."

"One time."

She backed into the staircase and began her descent. Proceeding down, she looked back once. With crossed arms and a grin, he watched her go from the top of the stairs. Mild air greeted her outside as she walked to the dining hall. A small breeze passed her, cooling the flush of sweat on her back. Closing her eyes she lowered her head and tried to shake away the internal groan resonating in her mind. She had to endure his extra attention, and part of her spun and rejoiced at the prospect.

Her mother smiled over her wine glass, and Katrina regretted agreeing to join her for dinner. A meal spent with her mother could never be just a meal.

"We received a letter from the house of Etrasa today. It announced Captain Willmont of Gryph as one of the suitors. Tell me, did you succeed in capturing his interest?"

Pha's activity at the table came to a halt, and she shifted her gaze to Katrina.

"It's hard to tell," Katrina said. She grabbed her own glass and took a long swig of wine.

"I should fetch some water," Pha said leaving the room.

"Gryph, such a surprise," Katrina said. "When I met him, I thought for sure he was married."

A smile of pleasure played on Lady Lena's face as she crooned over her food. "I knew once he laid eyes on you he would want you. I bet his requests to see you will arrive within the day." She raised her glass. "To a successful Parade."

Katrina raised her glass. "To a successful Parade."

They drank and Katrina sat back cradling her wine glass. She fingered the rim lightly as she spoke. "Do you know the Willmonts'?"

"Yes, that arrogant little dynasty. Perfectly suited to rule an arrogant nation. So superior because they fly around on overgrown birds."

"You visited Gryph, did you like it?"

"Of course, it's very grand. My family were guests at Queen LaBell's wedding. You'll see, the Willmonts' are nothing if not extravagant."

"If that's true, why would they prefer his marriage to a woman from Etrasa?"

"Hmm, it's a good question. I heard he and his brother, Chane, the crown prince, haven't spoken to one another since Chane married. But my friend who travels to Gryph often said the brothers have never gotten along. Twin's, not identical, they've fought one another since infancy. I've heard several say they'd even fought over the same girl once."

"That doesn't explain why one of them would come here to choose a wife."

"It doesn't, but everyone I've talked to mentions his brother as his motive for coming here. However, the explanation might be much simpler than that. He could have a preference for men. If that were well known, a Lady from the House would be far less expensive than negotiating for a suitable bride in Gryph."

"Did one of your gossips say that?" Katrina said.

Her mother's eyebrow arched and she took a sip of wine. "No, but it's something everyone wonders when a prize like him appears. I've always believed it was that sort of man who helped the House get its start. If Prince Jance Willmont is more partial to men, but pays your bidding price, we're not in a position to protest."

Katrina set her wine glass down and sat back. "Why? Why are you so eager for me to marry a man you know nothing about?"

"Do you think it's better in Madar? That you'll have any say there in deciding the man who'll rally for you and claim you as his wife?" Her mother kept her eyes trained on her while she leveled a finger at Pha who stood clearing an empty platter. "I promise you, whatever courtship nonsense she's told you about rallying, it's a lie."

Pha glared at her mother, and dropped the empty platter to the table. It clattered and bounced, sending two utensils flying to the floor. Pha met Katrina's gaze and shook her head. Adjusting the wraps on her hands, Pha balled her hands into fists, turned and left the room.

The rest of the evening Katrina spent in front of her tapestry. Tree frogs sang in the dark beyond the open back door. Night chilled the spring air, and she considered standing up to close the back door. Her mother entered the hallway with her slow heavy stomp. She carried her wine glass, and took a long sip as she eyed Katrina's tapestry.

"See, it's almost done. Aren't you glad you'll get to use this one instead of your old one?"

"Yes." Katrina said keeping her tone measured. She had no desire for nagging lectures about her tapestry's completion or a successful Parade.

"There was this one tapestry I made — it was perfect." Lady Lena said.

Katrina paused and slowly peeked over her shoulder at her mother.

"Which one?"

Lady Lena's lips formed a thin smile. "I don't think you'd remember. It doesn't matter, I was entirely wrong about it. It wasn't very good."

Katrina turned back to her tapestry and schooled the surprise from her face. Composed, she looked over her shoulder again and inspected her mother's glass. How much wine had her mother indulged in tonight?

"Have I seen it?" she asked.

Lady Lena answered with a small shake of her head. "You know how you start something, and it comes together better than you imagined it would?" Katrina turned her body and sat intently listening. "You get excited, the colors go together better than you thought. The subjects are all proportioned right, and you rarely need to run out and rematch a thread."

She nodded, intrigued by her mother's rare spontaneity.

"That was what it was like working on it. All of these happy things occurred like magic, and it was so perfect. I just wanted to stare at it. I loved it more than anything I made before it. Then it was put to use. Hung on a wall, set into a collection. Looking at it beside the others, my mistakes were glaringly obvious. I don't know what I was thinking, it was barely ordinary."

"Where is it now?"

"I don't know. I couldn't bear looking at it. It had more flaws than I could keep track of and I wanted it cut apart, and burned. I did such a terrible job, and took pride in this terrible piece. I never wanted anyone to lay eyes on it and know I'd made it."

"I can't picture it," Katrina said, "Everything you've ever made is impeccable. Even the beginner things you showed me, the things you made as a girl."

"No, this one was bad. I was so lost in it I didn't see my own mistakes. I'd used too many greens, and there was a section on the right side where a whole series of stitches were uneven."

"What did you do with it? Did you actually cut it up?"

"No, no, I had it taken down and set aside. I don't know where it is now."

Katrina was at a loss for what to say; it was rare for her mother to make conversation without some agenda, and this was a story her mother had never shared about a work she'd never seen.

"Are you trying to tell me you don't like this?" Katrina said motioning to her tapestry and giving her mother a playful smile.

Her mother let out a quick laugh. "No, not at all my love, this is stunning. I'm sure what happened to me will never happen to you. You're not one to get distracted. You're able to see what works, what doesn't, even when something barely has shape. I can't see you getting caught up and losing focus like I did."

Stunned, Katrina waited for words to undercut the nicest thing her mother had ever said to her. Her mother rested a hand gently on her shoulder and took a long drink from her cup. Katrina tried placing her own hand over her mother's, but it was gone. Her mother already gripped the handrail and plodded up the staircase.

"Good night darling," her mother called back. "It's cold back here, you should close the door."

When Katrina heard her mother's door shut, she straightened the small work area, closed the back door, and proceeded to her room.

Pha entered her room, she worked fast with stiff arms and shoulders.

Katrina sat down before her dressing mirror.

Even as Pha walked over with the nightgown, her eyes sought anything in the room besides her. Katrina turned around and stood facing her.

"Are you still angry about what my mother said? You know how she is."

Pha nodded, her lips pressed in a thin line. She took a deep breath before she spoke. "I've got this feeling. Maybe it's just me, but I don't like this prince from Gryph being involved. We should be taking you home by boat, the way we originally planned."

Pha's hands took hold of Katrina's waist to turn her around and proceeded to release the ties to her garments.

"Your form is the most highly prized in all of Madar," Pha said. "Men from all over will travel to attend your rally and win you."

"You make fighting to the death sound like some grand game." Katrina said.

"It's not a game," Pha said. She stood still — her dark eyes fixed on Katrina through the mirror. She spoke in a whisper, but the force of her voice was like a shout. "Don't encourage this human prince."

"I'm not," Katrina said. "I don't think there're many options beside his offer of help, but no one's ever consulted me about the best ways to return home."

"I know," Pha said as her shoulders dropped. She stooped down and helped lift the orange Ladies dress from Katrina.

"I wish I never let her grab you."

"You were a little busy saving everyone," Katrina said, turning and taking hold of Pha's hand. Pha looked at their hands and then up at her.

"Not everyone."

Katrina squeezed Pha's hand, it echoed the pang of loss she felt at the old memory of Regina Delany and Lady Tellydia.

"Even if you were human, my Princess, this Parade business, it disgusts me."

Katrina grinned as Pha's hand cupped her chin and turned her face to meet hers.

"I don't care what the Skrieni did, or how long you've lived as a human. You're not a human, darling. Even if you never get your wings back, you're still Airetti, and you'll always belong to Madar. The only man who deserves you is Mahigan. A man who'll lay down his life for you, not just his coin."

"I really don't want anyone to lay down their life or money for me." Katrina said. "But you don't need to worry about Prince Willmont. I'm not going to make the same mistake twice. I'm doing what Valgu has instructed me to do, and we should be happy. This is good news, we finally get to go home."

8

Parties and Departures

Jance leaned on the windowsill and smiled at Katrina who lazed in the high backed chair. He had not acknowledged her presence all day, but here they were in the fifth floor of the university library in neutral. Jance continued his pretense of being a witless suitor as an excuse to spend time with her. Pitying his boredom, she met him here. Incurring sleep deprived days, in exchange for his pleasant company and conversation at night.

Jance liked to pepper her with questions about other Ladies, and each question he posed about them, he wanted her to answer. She did, and then demanded he provide an answer as well. He learned how she liked to study histories of famous battles. She learned about his research into the memories Thulane shared with him. He learned how the athletic stress of cadet life challenged her more than she expected. She learned how he excelled as a runner but hated running.

Jance shared details of his appointments with the other Ladies. His tea with Lady Paige, the evening spent playing cards with Lady Mahogany, and the afternoon he picnicked with Lady Elana.

"You need to start giving me better information," he said. He eased off the windowsill and began a slow pace back and forth across the room.

"I'm so sorry Captain," she said. His playful grin made her laugh. "I've told you everything I know about the Ladies you've called on."

"Well, it's not been enough, obviously," he said, throwing his arms up in mock exasperation before falling to his knees and settling into a sitting position on the floor beside her chair.

"Don't you want some of it left open to your own discovery?" she said.

"Is there more to the life of Lady Paige Wendt she hasn't told me?" he said.

She giggled and he looked over his shoulder, leaning into the side of her chair. She could see the way his black hair curled into a wave at the crown of his head. She folded her hands in her lap and diverted her eyes.

"I like her stories," Katrina said, "They can get a bit long, but I... talk to her."

"They go on forever," Jance said. He closed his eyes laughing and let his head fall back to rest against the arm of the chair.

Many Ladies would kill for hair like his. Did he inherit the natural curl from his mother or father?

"Poor Paige won't be a future Willmont," she said.

"No she won't," he said. He opened his eyes and stared at the ceiling. Katrina watched as his navy eyes found her. Keeping her in focus, Jance turned around. Placing his forearm along the length of the chair, he rested his head on it.

"Do you think you can give me some better information about tonight?" he said.

"It's a reception for the suitors to meet the Ladies," she said. "Nothing special, I'm sure nothing like what you've attended in Gryph."

"You seem so sure of that," he said.

"This is formal, but it's modest," she said. "Don't pretend — we both know Gryph could surpass it without trying."

He gave her a lopsided grin and shrugged.

"Can I talk to you at this thing?" he said.

"You can, but I probably won't have much to say." He gave her a small hurt look and she laughed. "No, Jance, that's a bad idea. You stay focused on the other ladies, while I stay focused on blending with the furniture. Do you want another suitor to summon me to Parade?"

"I'm the only suitor who's doing that," he said poking her playfully in the knee.

"Stop that," she said pushing his hands away.

"I hate things like this," he said. "One time, promise me I can come over and talk with you one time."

She shook her head at him and he crossed his arms and looked away.

"No, it's for your own good, Captain."

"Can I wander to you? Mention how Massie lied when he said you were nothing special to look at?"

She grinned at him and sighed. "See, you're so good at that. Such a flirt, how many women do you really have waiting back in Gryph for you?"

His smile broadened as he arched an eyebrow.

"I won't be special tonight either," she said. "I'm not trying to gain attention at these things."

"I look forward to seeing you try and look unappealing," he said.

"This is not my first Parade season. I'm pretty good at it," she said, and answered his quizzical look with a, "You'll see."

It took detailed planning to become unappealing while conforming to the standards of the House. The odds were against her, surrounded by the instructors who trained her to be alluring. Her suitor avoidance methods needed to be effective without provoking the House instructors, or her mother.

If she knew a suitor's language, she conversed with overbearing enthusiasm. She butchered words with mispronunciations, used odd verb conjugations, and strange word usage. If the suitor's native language was unfamiliar, she mispronounced names, and mixed up important historical events from where the suitor hailed.

She injected nervous laughter at inappropriate moments. Talked glowingly about other suitors attending Parade. She liked playing games off their height. For a short suitor, she invaded his space and loomed over him. If the suitor were tall, she pointed out every other Lady taller than herself and exclaimed how a woman of her height suited a man of his stature better.

Yawning while a suitor spoke only worked if his interest in her reaction outweighed his interest in hearing himself talk. To repel a self-interested man, she talked over him, and switched subjects at random to topics outside his interest. During the last Parade season, she pretended to talk in the strange high voice of Lady Paige Wendt. Rambling in her Lady Paige voice, she even devoted an entire tea service to a conversation about the room's draperies. It worked very well.

The construction of her most recent formal gown, for events such as tonight's, occurred during the construction of her Parade gown. Distracted by the details of her Parade gown, her mother overlooked the other. Katrina flustered the dressmaker's apprentice. Convincing her to switch the silk dress fabric from maroon to a dour shade of brown. The fabric's deep shade contrasted with her skin and gave her a sick pallor. Elegant beading and fine trim adorned the completed dress, but it looked nothing like what her mother requested. Paid for in full, the brown gown made it home before Lady Lena discovered the fabric error. In secret Katrina and Pha altered the dress further, changing the bust line and undergarments to give her as boyish a figure as possible.

Pha created an elegant hairstyle of spun curls that Lady Lena watched Katrina leave the house with. On her walk to the Etrasa Mansion Katrina lessened the symmetry of the style by removing a hairpin and ribbon as Pha instructed. By the end of tonight, her hair would fall from its style and a house worker would rush her away to fix it, or better yet send her home.

She made one small stop on her walk to the House mansion, picking a flowering weed at the edge of the forest. One whiff of the bright yellow sodden hip, and her nose and eyes began to water. Tucking several of the detestable flowers into her hair, she sneezed and smiled. She took pride in her novice gardening achievement. The entire patch of sodden hip she planted months earlier. She arrived at the House of Etrasa mansion drab, flat chested, and looking ill.

On a direct course to a lone divan in the corner, Instructor Able stopped her. Able's eyebrows arched and with one hand she motioned for Katrina to follow her.

Able brought her down a hallway and into a vacant classroom. Alone in the room she closed the door and turned on Katrina with a cool glare.

"Lady Katrina, you look…terrible."

As much as Katrina wanted to celebrate, she contorted her smile into dismay.

"I've not been well, Ma'am. I think I have a head cold."

"I can see that, but I think you would suffer less if you removed those weeds from your hair."

"These, they're for good luck, the locals swear by them," Katrina said as she dabbed a handkerchief under swollen eyes that itched so much they watered.

Able crossed her arms and a smile cracked her domineering glare.

"I know the games you play Lady, I just think next go round, you should stick with over eating garlic and not stoop to injuring yourself with noxious plants."

Katrina stared, glad her sniffles and tears covered her sudden panic.

"Relax, Lady Katrina, if I was going to reveal your games I would have turned you in four seasons ago," Able said.

"Games, Ma'am, I-I-Iiee-" Katrina said before unleashing a loud sneeze.

"When I saw your red eyes, well for a very brief second, I thought it was due to Lady Lena's departure. Then I saw the nasty yellow flowers in your hair. Take them out this instant before you risk death. Don't worry, your exposure to them should keep you ill the rest of the evening."

"Ma'am-"

"Remove them, and then you will return to the ballroom," Able said.

Katrina straightened, pulled the flowers from her hair, and placed them into Able's outstretched hand.

"Lady Lena's departure?" Katrina said.

"I was sorry to hear it," Able said. "I know how close you two are."

Katrina rolled her lips and forced a grin. The assumptions people made about her relationship with her mother bothered her. People thought Lady Lena lived with her out of some inseparable doting fondness.

With a thrust of her chin Able dismissed her. The instructor was chuckling by the time Katrina reached the door.

"Lady Katrina," Able said.

Letting go of the door handle Katrina turned and faced Able.

"I'm in pain looking at you," Able said. "How can you possibly breathe in that dress?"

Katrina tilted her head and shrugged one shoulder.

"It's amazing, but tonight I think you've outdone the spiking of Lord Harper's tea," Able said.

Katrina shook her head. "I had nothing to do with that man's bowel ailments."

"Don't deny it; I thought it was very well played," Able said.

It had been well played, by whomever was responsible, but Katrina had nothing to do with it.

"I swear to you, I didn't. I've never poisoned anyone," she said.

"No, just yourself," Able said holding up the flowers in her hand.

Katrina made a small groan and resisted the urge to scratch her eyes as she opened the door and proceeded back to the ballroom. Her evening was a success; the only suitor in the room who gave her more than one glance was Jance. She should have forbidden him from looking at her too.

She sat on a corner divan watching the evening's procession. The other Ladies vied for a place to hover near Jance or cast him longing looks from other parts of the room. Like the trained royal he was, Jance was polite. Gracious to everyone, he handed out his smile like it was candy.

Always eager to leave any Parade event, she waited through the long hours. Tonight made her more restless. She needed to get home and learn what Instructor Able meant when she used her mother's name and the word departure in the same sentence.

"Lady Katrina," Instructor Able said.

Katrina's head shot up to see Jance beside Instructor Able, and followed the protocol of standing to make a new introduction.

"I apologize, I've been under the weather," she said.

Lady Katrina Larksbur, may I introduce Captain Jance Willmont."

"It's very nice to meet you," Katrina said.

"You as well," he said. Jance gave her the lopsided grin, and despite her ailments, it was easy to smile back and linger in their hidden familiarity.

"I believe we'll have a chance to become better acquainted two days from now," Jance said. He turned to Instructor Able in confirmation as Katrina eyed him in confusion.

"Is that right? Two days?" he said.

"Yes, Captain," Able said. "Hopefully the weather will be nice."

I told you, no visiting outside of neutral, Katrina wandered to Jance.

And I've already requested a visit with every Lady in the house, he wandered back. *That includes you.*

"Exciting," Katrina said. "I look forward to it."

"I do as well," he said before following Able who had already moved on searching for the next Lady.

The rest of the event was miserable, and unlike its start, went according to her plan.

Returning home she debated who to interrogate first, Pha or her mother. Entering the house she went straight to the kitchen for one reason, and one reason only; the wine was kept there. She was mid-pour when Pha walked in and almost dropped the armload of wood she hauled.

"Dear God! What happened to your face?"

"A very effective gardening experiment. Instructor Able didn't like my sodden hip hair adornments. She told me so, right after giving me her condolences for Lady Lena's departure."

Pha hefted the wood and turned to the fireplace.

"Do they itch bad?"

"Where is she going?" Katrina said.

"Let me get you a wet rag," Pha said, stacking the wood. She dusted off her hands and turned to the kitchen pantry.

Katrina took a swig of wine and then a deep breath. She willed the wine to ease the ache in her chest.

"Toss the rag, Pha! I've wanted to scratch my eyes out all night. Tell me, where she's going?"

"Darling, I-no, I can't." Pha's voice was strained and quiet. "You need to hear it from her."

"But she is, she's leaving here. How long have you known?"

Tears gathered in Pha's eyes. Katrina took another large gulp of wine and set her glass down so hard the remaining contents splashed the counter.

Grabbing the bottle of wine Katrina marched out the back door.

She walked, and the wine began to set in. Her tears eased the itching in her eyes.

"Damn her," Katrina said muttering into the darkness.

Her mother was leaving the island without her. Would she have left without telling her? Sure, why not? Her mother did it before. Her mother should have left her then. Left her in Mozgas and never come back. How dare her mother leave, while she stayed trapped in a contract with the House. She brought them here. She deserved to suffer every second of their confinement. Never gaining one moment free of the House before Katrina.

Katrina wanted to run but the constrictive brown dress prevented it. She walked fast. Aimlessly she marched into the forest crying tears she made no effort to hide. She would cry out the frustration and be done. Why did she bother getting so upset? She herself was leaving. Logic failed to curb her anger as it continued to bloom. An awful pain, boring into her and holding on.

When Jance found her she lay sprawled on the ground with her head propped up against a tree trunk, the wine bottle cradled in her arms.

"Captain Willmont," she said. "Why are you out here?"

"I spotted a Minotaur leaving the barracks, decided to follow him."

Her vision swam as she scanned the forest for Thedmir. She saw no sign of him, but knew without wandering that he sat somewhere nearby.

"My Lady, may I join you?" he said sitting down beside her.

"No," she said. "Go back to the party and seduce a human."

"I think my friend needs me more right now," he said. "Your eyes look better."

"Yes, my crying tantrum helped," she said. "I was just laying here, sulking. Blaming myself, hating myself, for not taking the one chance I had to never be in this mess."

"Say that again," he said.

Katrina looked up to where Jance sat beside her, his back resting against a tree they now shared.

"When I was in the tunnel, I should have run back. That was my chance, to go back, and go home. If I had taken the tunnel, none of this would have happened. I might have gotten lost, been scared out of my mind, but they would have found me eventually. Sol would never have been attacked. I'd be home. I'd still have my wings."

"A tunnel?" Jance said.

"Yeah, a big dark tunnel that leads in and out of the plateau. I could have run back but I didn't. I was a girl who didn't want to let my mother go." Katrina took a sip of wine and closed her eyes. "But she can leave me, without saying a word. I've hated her, and loved her, cursed her and protected her; and now she's going."

"I'm sorry," he said.

"The last time I saw any of my family in person, I was ten," she said. "My father's taken two more wives since then." Katrina held up two fingers and watched her hand swim in her vision.

She brought the wine bottle to her lips and took another swig of wine.

"I wanted to protect her," she said, hugging her wine bottle.

"And you did, you have," he said. "When she leaves, she'll still be safe, right?"

"Right," Katrina said. Sniffling she pushed herself up and shifted back sitting up higher on the tree.

"You'll miss her, but if it were me, I wouldn't be too upset. I'd enjoy the freedom," he said.

Katrina sighed and let her head fall back against the tree.

"Right," she said.

"You should give me that bottle, I think you've had enough," Jance said. He reached for it and Katrina yanked it back slapping at his hands.

"Paws off Captain. I'm drinking this until all the trees are spinning."

Drips of wine fell onto the front of her skirt and she fussed with the fabric trying to remove them.

"Look what you made me do."

"Oh no, not the ugly brown dress," Jance mocked. "Feel free to leave that thing here when we leave. I never want to see you in that again."

"You say the sweetest things," she said.

"I'm the one who had to spend the whole night staring at you, in that," he said.

"I noticed," she said.

"I kept wondering what you did with your breasts," he said, his brow furrowed with exaggerated concern.

"Captain Willmont," she said, glaring at him as he crawled closer to her. She gave him a light shove when he dared to crawl into her lap. He smiled grabbing the hand she shoved him with as he kneeled across her, sandwiching her legs between his.

"How dare you abuse them this way," he said.

Katrina laughed and shoved at him as he eyed the bodice of her dress.

"I demand you release them," he said.

"Stop it," she said.

"I need to ensure their safety," he said.

"They would love to oblige, but I reminded them how crazy you are."

"You're my Lady," he said. "You must never do this to them again."

"No, I'm not," she said.

"I hope you are not too drunk to remember this," he said.

"I'm very drunk," she said letting her head roll to the side as she avoided his eyes.

"I'm going to summon you to Parade," he said.

"As I've been warned," she said.

"And I'm looking forward to taking you home," he said.

"Oh will this night never end!"

She pulled her hand free of his and shoved him back while pulling her legs free from under him.

"What? I look forward to showing you Gryph. I enjoy spending time with you," he said.

"You should never say anything like that to me again," she said. "I hate you."

"And that makes you a liar," he said, and laughed.

"And don't touch me," she said. "This is a favor to my brother, not something to get yourself killed over."

Jance stood up and reached his hand out to her.

"Come on, I'll walk you back to the road."

"No," Katrina said crossing her arms over her bottle of wine.

"Aren't you tired?" he said.

"Yes, but I'm staying right here."

"You're spending the night out here?"

"I'm a cadet, I've slept out here plenty."

"Alright," he said with a sigh. "I guess I'll go get you a blanket or something."

"No," Katrina said. "I'm not sleeping tonight. I'm drinking."

Jance laughed and settled against the tree again.

Her eyes grew heavy and she curled onto her side, facing away from Jance.

"Want me to loosen your dress?" Jance said.

She frowned over her shoulder at him and turned away again. The brown dress and his advances caused discomfort. She preferred to tolerate it, over caving to her instincts that cried out for what he offered.

"I won't touch you," he said. "But you do look really uncomfortable."

After a few more minutes of strangling in the dress, she let out a long sigh.

"Yes, would you? Just loosen it a little."

Jance untied the laces at the back of her dress. He pulled the lacing loose enough to ease the bodice pressure on her torso. She took in her first deep breath of the evening. When Jance pulled at the lacing of her undergarments she stiffened. The ties relaxed. She remained tense until she heard him move away to sit back against the tree.

Her head spun from the wine, Jance Willmont, and all the change. The change that pulled and pushed her life so hard it was sure to tumble from her grasp and shatter when she stopped.

She awoke the next morning wrapped in two wool blankets. Jance sat beside her, on his own blanket, eating bites he tore from a roll of bread. She squinted at the early light filtering through the trees and tried to swallow away the horrid taste in her mouth.

"Good morning," he said. "Here, I brought you some water."

She rolled up onto an elbow and took the jug of water offered. His hair was slightly messed. How did he manage to look good first thing in the morning? She swallowed a large gulp of water.

"How's your head?" he said.

She rubbed one hand across her forehead and blinked. "Fine. I'm a little light headed."

"I'm impressed," he said, "I think I'd still be passed out if I had as much as you did."

"It wasn't a full bottle when I started," she said.

"Ah, well, of course not."

He held out a roll of bread to her. She mumbled a thanks as she took it. He watched her eat and she tried not to stare at how the long rays of sunlight reflected in his eyes, and made them a brighter blue.

"I can't get over something you told me," Jance said.

"What's that?" she said.

"Your father's Veilede, in charge of a province in Madar."

"Mozgas," she said.

"But your mother, she's human. Born to a Bisma Lord."

Katrina nodded her head and took another drink of water.

"So your father married a human royal," he said. Katrina paused and met his gaze. "Why can't you?"

"You know this Parade for you and I— it's pretend," she said.

"Will you calm down?" he said with a scowl. "I'm asking because I'm curious."

She shook her head in agitation while rolling to her stomach and shifting onto both elbows.

"My mother was offered as a gift to my father," she said. "He accepted her as his wife out of courtesy. Their marriage, in Madar, it's not typical. In Madar, because of what I am, I'm only allowed to marry the man who wins my rally."

"What's a rally?" he said.

"It's a fight. The winner wins the bride," she said.

"What happens when you're not in Madar? Do the same rules apply?"

"Yes," she said.

"Really? Because you know humans and Veilede marry all the time in Bisma."

"Yes, but humans never marry my form," she said.

"That you know of," he said,

"It's never happened," she said.

"Right, it's so different for you because why?" He said, "Because of what you shift into?"

Turning onto her side she pushed up to where she was sitting and facing him.

"I, well, I'm Airetti," she said. "My form is referred to as the first. The Veilede believe when God descended to bless our people, the first ones to be gifted were given wings like His angel escorts."

"So God prohibits it?" He said.

"No," she said stifling a laugh. "Jance, honestly. Look, any other Veilede form, sure marriage to a human is possible, but not mine."

She shifted forward moving off her blanket, and searched for the best way to explain the difference. She turned her back to him and began folding her bedroll.

"Airetti are the traditional mate for Mahigan. It's this sacred ancient thing, and there're so few Airetti, rallying for one is a big deal. It's a tradition rooted in something primal."

"And you're this Airetti," he said. "You have angel wings?"

She stopped moving and stared at her bedroll.

"No," she said. "Mine were taken."

"Taken?"

She nodded.

"How?"

With bunched shoulders she shook her head. She flinched as a finger traced the skin at the base of her neck. He brushed aside the loose garment ties to expose more of her back. She knew what he saw, long thick scars, smooth with a lighter skin than what was left unmarred by the Skrieni.

"What did this?"

She said nothing, afraid to revisit the worst pain of her life.

"This is awful," he said.

"Yes," she said trying to cut him off. She pulled away, and reaching behind her to try and retie her garments. Fumbling to hide what was exposed. She closed her eyes as her throat constricted. Garment strings brought her dress to close around her again.

"The pain went on for weeks," she said, clearing her throat to help force tears back. "A pain that makes you wish for death."

"Are your wings gone for good?" he said.

"There's a team of healers in Mozgas who claim they can restore them."

"You can get them back then," he said. "That's good."

"I hope it's possible," she said nodding in agreement. "All I used to think about was going home and getting my wings back." She finished tying her dress and turned back to him. "I think I gave up on my wings or going home a while ago. I mean, I want to return, but the desire doesn't crush me like it used to."

"How old were you when they were taken?"

"Ten," she said.

The cold look on his face surprised her. An up-close glimpse of the fighter he was lauded as. His usual casual demeanor made it hard to imagine him in battle, but now she saw the familiar warrior's glare.

"Jance?" she said. His navy eyes met hers, but his face remained tense.

"You were a child," he said.

"Yes."

"Do you know who did it?"

"Yes."

"We'll hunt them down."

"That's a really sweet gesture," she said, giving him a weak smile to try and mollify him. "But no we can't."

"I'm not joking."

"I can see that, but no, you can't," she said.

"I can."

"No, my father's already done it."

His look softened, and his eyebrows lifted in interest. They sat eyeing one another in silence. She looked down and saw her hand clutched in his. Astonished she met his gaze and searched his eyes as she spoke.

"I'm very flattered the gallant Jance Willmont thinks well enough of me to want to destroy my enemies."

He gave her a brief head nod and stared down at their hands. Cradling her hand, he lifted it to him. With slow movements, his free hand stroked the back of her hand. The gentle touch sent a warm sensation up her arm and across her body. Her protest sat trapped in her chest as he lifted her hand to his lips. He kissed her hand and another wave of warmth passed through her. The kiss lingered on her skin. She continued to feel the press of his lips there, and expected to see her hand branded with a mark. With another caress of her hand he lowered their hands to her lap. Her stunned posture broke when he released her hand, and his eyes looked up to meet hers.

"Think well of you," he said, smiling in an open boyish way. "Yes, I do," he said. "Far more than I expected to. I admire you, and it'd be a lie if I said my only motivation here was Massie or a potential alliance with Madar."

"You don't need to flatter me."

"No, it's the truth. Is that so strange, friend?" he said. "Besides it would be irresponsible for me to leave you here to torment other witless human men."

"You're a credit to mankind."

They shared a quiet moment. He settled into a more serious demeanor, and played with a signet ring on his right hand.

"I've never made friends easily," he said. "For a variety of reasons. It makes my loyalty to the friends I do have … a bit fanatical."

"And you include me as one of your friends?" she said.

"Of course I do," he said, his brow lowered in indignation.

"We've only known each other how long?" she said.

"There're people I've known for years but care less about. Then there're people I connected with the moment we met. You I connect with, we're friends, and if you lost something important I'll help you get it back."

"Thank you," she said, "But, I think you've already done more than enough to help me. There's really nothing you can do about my wings."

"Except return you home," he said.

"Yes, well except that."

Lena sat at the tapestry rack when Katrina walked in the back door. Her mother frowned as she looked her up and down.

"What happened to you?" Her mother asked.

"Good morning," Katrina said, walking to the staircase. She made it to first step before her mother sprang from her chair, grabbed her arm, and pulled her to a stop.

"You're risking our future when you disobey the House."

"Do I?" she said, jerking her arm from her mother's hold. "Last night Instructor Able informed me of your pending departure."

"Where have you been all night?"

"And you don't even try to deny it. When were you going to tell me you were leaving?"

"It's fortunate the House Guard didn't come around."

"Spare me your outrage," Katrina said as she proceeded up the stairs. "Why do you care if I bend or break the House rules? The only future I'm risking is my own."

Her mother followed on her heels.

"What were you doing out all night?"

Pivoting at the top of the stairs Katrina put both hand on her hips and stared down at her mother.

"Drinking, I went into the forest and drank a bottle of red wine."

She turned around and walked into her room as her mother shouted.

"With who?"

Katrina marched to her doorway and smiled. "My suitor, Captain Jance Willmont."

She returned to her room with the sound of her mother's steps pounding across the landing behind her.

"You let him defile you in the forest?"

Katrina sat on the edge of her bed with her arms crossed.

"I don't think anything I let him do qualifies as defilement."

"You can't bed a man and expect he'll pay your bidding price."

"I didn't bed him," Katrina said. With narrowed eyes her mother studied her. "If I wanted to, I could have. He proved he has a definite preference for women."

"Captain Willmont really said he's your suitor, that he plans to pay your bidding price?"

"Yes."

Her mother twined her fingers together and tapped her index fingers on her chin. She paced to the window and looked out lost in thought. She shook her head and turned around to face her again.

"My darling," she said. Her hands dropped to her side as she broke into a joyful smile. "That's marvelous!"

"Is it?"

"Of course."

"I'm glad it makes you happy. It's too bad you won't be here to see us walk the finale together."

"Yes, well."

"Where are you going?"

"Nowhere as fine as Gryph."

"Who's taking you?"

"Who do you think?" her mother said, walking to the door.

"Devon Quraishi."

Her mother nodded and lingered in the threshold. "He offered a little money to Rudolph for me. I'll tell Pha you're back. She can help get you cleaned up. We can't risk having your suitor come by and see you like this."

One of the House of Etrasa carriages arrived after lunch. Pha was assisting Katrina to the carriage when Jance rushed to her side and took her arm.

"I can walk just fine," Katrina said.

"Yes, but I actually get to do this today," he said.

Katrina nodded hello to Guard Bonner who waited in the carriage slumped down in his seat. He lifted one hand in greeting and rubbed his eyes with the other. Bleary-eyed and wearing the most rumpled uniform Katrina had ever seen, she wondered if Guard Bonner was drunk.

"Where are we going?"

"That's part of the surprise," Jance said.

The carriage took them away from town and into the surrounding countryside. She decided the only place worthy of a long carriage ride was the ocean. They stopped at a small fishing village on the eastern coast named Norbreg. It boasted a market, a ship outfitter, an outdoor cafe, and a small bar and boarding house. Guard Bonner sent them on with a wave.

"I'll be sitting at the cafe if you need me, Captain."

"Astounding work ethic I've seen by you House Guardsmen," Jance said.

"Right so," Bonner said. He scratched the thick stubble at his chin and pointed at her. "I've known that one since before she had tits. Scooped her up off the docks the first day she was here. You remember that day, don't you, Lady Katrina?"

"I do."

"Go ahead," Bonner said. "Ask Lady Katrina what I'm willing to do to protect the girls dressed in blue and orange on this island."

"Please, Jance, let's go."

"I'll tell you this Captain, she has a fine face but this one's also smart. Don't touch her, cause I won't blink if she feels the need to cut away your balls and take them home as a keepsake." Bonner shifted his focus to her and gave her a real smile. "Have a nice time, Lady Katrina."

"Thank you," Katrina said pulling Jance away by the arm.

She and Jance walked through the town and onto a path leading to the beach. Crossing the sand dunes to the beach, they heard voices and laughter. A large gathering of people played games in the sand or sat on blankets nearby. Katrina recognized everyone. Astonished, she halted and stood studying Jance.

"My class gathering, how did you know?"

Jance laughed and urged her to keep walking.

"You told me the House barred you from coming," he said. "I wasn't a Cadet that long ago. You can't miss this. Most of your squad leaves in a few days."

"You made arrangements just so I could see my friends?"

"You deserve this time with them," he said.

"Hey Larksbur!" Cadet Vacek's voice yelled from the crowd. Katrina smiled over at the cadets from her squad lounging on the beach. They waved and beckoned her over.

"Come on, Larksbur, we've been waiting for you," Cadet Mickle said.

"I'll be back after dinner," Jance said, walking her over and encouraging her to sit down among her squad. "I won't be far if you need me."

"Promise me, you won't go back and tangle with Guard Bonner," she said.

Jance scoffed and smiled. "Have fun."

She regretted him leaving, and as she watched him stand, her thoughts pleaded for him to stay. With a smile he dusted sand from his hands and made his way up the beach.

"I always thought you'd be with one of us, Larksbur, but look at you — running around with a Captain," Cadet Flint said. He laughed at his own remark as new chatter erupted around her.

"I know how much you have all been lusting after him, but that one's mine," Katrina said. "Make a move for him and I'll take you out."

Cadet Mickle lay sprawled on the beach beside her with his eyes closed.

"You can try Larksbur," Mickle said, "but I can take you. Besides I know how much you still love me."

He opened one eye to her and Katrina tilted her head and smiled at him.

"Aw, Mickle you know I'll always love you. You're one of the only people in our squad who doesn't snore."

"If it wasn't frogs keeping us awake, it was all the damn snoring," Vacek said.

"It's good you never fell for one of these idiots," Mickle said.

"The idiotic charm did grow on me, but I managed to keep my wits," she said. "Besides none of you were ever really interested."

"That's because of Thedmir," Nellmon said. His words were slow and Katrina imagined it had something to do with his pain medicines. "No one's that stupid."

Her squad laughed in agreement and her gaze met Thedmir's. At the edge of the gathering he sat on the base of a sand dune. She smiled when he gave her the hand gesture for "sit with me."

She got up and joined him as she had done so many times before, falling into a routine entirely theirs. They sat back to back and watched the banter of their friends. It was a comfortable position for her because she could rest against the rock of his massive form.

"You knew Jance's plan for today," she said.

I did, Thedmir wandered. *He's a generous friend.*

She felt the steady breathing of Thedmir and held onto the calming sensation it infused in her. Sadness edged her thoughts when she realized this might be the very last time they were able to sit like this.

I've been looking forward to going home, he wandered, *but sitting here I'm grieving this place.*

"Me too," she said.

I had very low expectations. I feared loneliness being far from home and my kin. It worried me, being sent without a wanderer.

"You didn't seem too afraid when I met you."

He huffed a breath in protest. *Our friendship, my time here, it's changed my perspective on a lot of things. My impression of humans, my people's misgivings about the Veilede, and my own capacity to deal with change. I've had a hard time envisioning where I'll be when I go home, because my mind hasn't caught up with our parting.*

"I don't even let myself think about that," she said.

I have something to leave with you.

He pulled a wooden box from a bag nearby. It looked tiny in his massive hand. Painted black, it had an engraved Minotaur holding a stone. Nestled inside the box was an intricate owl necklace, set with neutral colored stones of amber, diamond, and dark shades of garnet. A gold band circled the owl and held an inscription of Minotaur glyphs.

"What does it say?" she asked. Lifting it from the box, she dangled it before her. Undoing the clasp, she fastened it around her neck.

I call you friend, for all things that I am, I have made known unto you.

"This is really unfair, I don't have anything to give you," she said still admiring his gift.

And I didn't expect anything. You wear that and know I'm never further than a wander away.

"No need for goodbyes then," she said.

No, not for us.

The cadets shared funny stories both recent and old. They protested every unfair assignment given, and hashed out the worst exam of the last four years. They feasted on cheese, crackers, and fruit. Consumed more wine than food, and the afternoon became a floating high of friends relishing their last moments together. Wine dulled the pain of loss. Katrina sat back watching the sun's descent over the inbound tide. Giant waves rolled in as the water line inched closer.

Cadet Nellmon slept heavy beside her. The rest of their class busied with the construction of a bonfire down the beach, and played games in the sand dunes.

Something bobbed into view, coming towards her in the water. At first it looked like debris floating in on the tide. She made out a larger more defined shape cresting the water. Confirming their presence with a wander, she sat up with a start. Delphi were swimming towards her, with Puternic among them. Dolphins crested between waves as they coasted to the beach. They disappeared, dissolving under a wave near the waterline. The wave crashed onto the beach and when it receded the dolphins were gone, replaced by the bodies of men.

She found it strange to see Puternic. A man her body knew intimately, but her mind no longer rejoiced to see. Puternic stood at the water's edge with seven men. His long black hair clung to his neck and back. He walked out of the waves while the other men stayed back.

Unsure of what she should do, she stayed on the blanket. If they planned to take her away, her window to flee seemed nonexistent.

"Hello, Puternic," she said.

A light smile played at the corner of his lips when he knelt down in the sand next to her. He looked handsome as always.

"Hello, Katrina."

He held out his hand, offering her something. A hair barrette, fashioned out of gold and silver with a carved iridescent brown and white seashell. It featured the profile of an outstretched wing.

"What's this for?" she said, and took it.

"A token offering to go with my apology," he said. "I've been carrying it around, a long time."

Katrina looked down at it and ran her thumb along the perfect feather details. She searched his face and examined her feelings for him now. A fondness maybe, but a listless shadow of the joy she once felt with him.

"I made you doubt me," he said, "I'm sorry."

"I haven't graduated yet."

"I'm a few day's early," he said. "I saw you sitting here, and I couldn't help it. My feelings have never changed. My offer to take you home remains."

"You took advantage of me," she said.

"From what I recall, you came to me."

"Thank you," she said, cutting him off with a hard look.

He stared at her, waiting for her to say more. As the quiet lengthened, his lips became drawn and his hands slowly curled into fists.

"Is that all there is to say?" he said.

"I have nothing to say to you," she said.

"You're not going to be the wife of a human," he said.

"Nor will I ever be the wife of a Delphi," she said.

"You're mine," he said. "An inquiry about us has already been sent to the Madar Council."

"You forfeited any claim to me," she said, "My father will never turn me over to the Delphi. You're a fool if one word of us gets back to him."

Puternic stood up and while she expected him to glare at her, his face was pained. He turned away and walked back to the water. He looked back at her once before diving into an unfurling wave. She scanned the beach wondering if anyone else witnessed it. She glanced down at the hair barrette in her hand, and looked up when she heard Jance shouting her name. He skidded to a stop in the sand next to her. Jance looked to where the Delphi had stood in the water, and then back at her. Falling to his knees, he grabbed her by the shoulders and inspected her person.

"Are you all right? What did they do?" He was breathing fast from his sprint.

"You saw them?" she said.

"Yes, I saw them. I ran down here as fast as I could. Come on, get up."

"Everything's fine," she said. She looked at the barrette as she rested a reassuring hand on his shoulder.

"No it isn't, we need to go," he said.

She scoffed and shook her head.

"Come on, I'm not telling Massie I watched you get dragged into the ocean," he said. He stood up and pulled her up by the hand to a stand.

"That's not happening," she said. "They're gone."

Jance pulled her along behind him in a fast paced walk towards town.

"Why were you alone? Where's Thedmir? I knew I should have stayed. I agreed to come here to stop that kind of thing from happening. But you, you didn't even scream when they walked up the beach."

"Why would I scream?" she asked, fastening the barrette in her braid. "He's the only one who came onto the beach. That was his attempt to get me to willingly go with him."

"Well we're not going to sit next to the ocean and wait for his next, more persuasive, attempt," he said.

It was late when Katrina returned home. Pha smiled and was humming to herself as she entered Katrina's bedroom. From the hall came a stomping echo and Lady Lena's happy voice.

"How was your afternoon?" Her mother asked, entering her room. "Where did Captain Willmont take you?"

Before Katrina answered, her head was jerked back as the barrette was torn from her hair. Yelping, Katrina turned to her mother and yelled.

"What was that for?"

Lady Lena held the winged barrette in her hand and her face looked drawn. "Who gave this to you?"

Katrina yelled in wide eyed-defiance. "Captain Willmont!"

"Tell me who gave you this!"

"No," she said.

"You will say where you got this."

"I can't decide. Should I do as you do—say nothing? Maybe tell a tale. Something so full of lies you won't know the truth when you hear it."

"How dare you speak to me that way!"

"I have nothing to tell you."

Lady Lena threw the barrette on the floor with a scream and stomped her foot on it repeatedly doing her best to crush it. Her scream a near howl.

"I came back for you!"

"No, you came back to kill my father!"

Her mother's scream trailed off in a wail unlike any she heard before. Gripping her chest and sobbing, Lady Lena retrieved what was left of the barrette, and smothered it in her fist.

"Mother, please—" Katrina reached out, afraid of the way the broken barrette cut into her mother's hand.

Her mother slapped her hand away and attempted to flee the room.

Katrina stepped in her way. "Apologize," she said. "For taking me from Mozgas."

Lady Lena tried to duck around her.

Katrina blocked her again. "Apologize, for not telling me you were leaving."

Her mother stepped close, trying to bull her way by.

Katrina held her ground. "Apologize, for what the Skrieni did to me. You dragged me to that village and let them hold me down and tear open my back."

Her mother pivoted away as she scrubbed tears from her face.

"I've been waiting, and waiting, and waiting for apologies or explanations. But you're never going to give them."

"You had better—" Lady Lena said, her voice becoming eerie and distant. She looked up at the ceiling with tears on her face. "I wanted to protect you—"

"And that's all you're ever going to say, isn't it?"

"Why would you ever let a Delphi this close to you?" Lady Lena snapped, her demeanor changing as her head leveled a furious glare. She raised her hand and revealed the mangled and blood stained barrette on her palm. She extended it toward Katrina in accusation. "As if I never taught you anything, you went and whored yourself out to one of them. You did, didn't you? Where's your apology to me for that?"

Katrina stilled with shock. She allowed her mother by. Lena dove past her, fleeing the room, and stomping down the stairs.

Pha walked to Katrina's side and took her trembling hand. Defeated, Katrina pushed her frustration away with well-practiced ease. Pha's hands were warm and smooth as they patted hers. Pha moved behind her to unlace her dress.

"Were you frightened when you saw Puternic?"

"No, I knew he'd do one of two things and there was nothing I could do about either one."

Pha's eyebrow arched and she motioned for her to step out of her dress. Pha shuffled the dress across the room to the wardrobe, and returned with a clean nightgown.

"He still loves you."

Katrina's head fell to the side and she inspected her nails.

"He's never made that claim."

"I see," Pha said.

Katrina scoffed, "He's only mad I didn't fall into his arms when he apologized."

"That barrette he gave you, it's a traditional Delphi gift. One a man presents to the wife he's claimed."

Katrina pulled her sleeping gown on and sat down at her dressing table. Pha untied her braid.

"It was a beautiful barrette," Katrina said.

Pha passed a loving hand along her hair. "Yes, but you never could have worn it."

Katrina lay in bed willing sleep to come. Thoughts of her mother plagued her mind. She stared up at the smooth white stucco in-between the large wooden beams above her bed. The stucco was a perfect shade of white, but not once had Pha or she ever cleaned it. It never needed their attention.

Shutting her eyes, Katrina wished she were a little girl again. Back at the age where she looked at her mother and considered her perfect. Time would never bend and Katrina felt the handful of hours left with her mother slipping by. Their separation always a breath closer than their long past inception. She tried to let go, think of how she could stand alone, enter a dark tunnel of the unknown, and press into the fight.

It's lonely to love a liar. Having a close bond with a habitual liar was a sham, a myth, an unattainable goal. Secrets and lies created a separation her mother preferred. Katrina's access to her mother's life was rudimentary and superficial. The things Katrina knew about her mother were only gleaned because they shared a dwelling. Their bond was a bittersweet contrast to Katrina's relationship with Thedmir, where nothing was hidden. The good and bad were all there, take it or leave it.

I call you friend, for all things that I am, I have made known unto you.

A large gust of wind whispered outside. Another gust followed, and traveling over the forest and into Etrasa's streets. They swept through town, banging outdoor furniture, and shimmying against shutters. Katrina rolled onto her side and stared into the darkened bedroom. In Mozgas such noise would carry the lingering smell of pine. She found herself straining to inhale more, desperate to catch a whiff of pine, of home. The wind only carried the smell of rain, which made her cringe and gather her blankets around her.

The next morning, the door to her mother's bedroom stood ajar and without setting foot in the room she knew. Her mother never left her bedroom door open. Katrina inspected the odd sight of light filling the floor, and illuminating the hallway. Pushing her mother's door open wide, she stood in the threshold. The bed was made, the wardrobe closed, but the room rang with emptiness. The lack of her mother's few belongings a shouting proclamation of finality. Her mother was gone and the likelihood of seeing her again was never. A familiar sadness fluttered in her consciousness but failed to breach her wall of tolerance. She turned and left the room unshaken. She refused to suffer loss or mourn   someone   she   had   never   truly   known.

9

The Parade

The first time Katrina allowed her mother more than a passing thought since her departure was at the Parade season finale. Her Parade gown brought forth all kinds of memories of her mother. With the unlimited wardrobe budget Rudolph rewarded, her mother put together the most extravagant gown possible. She spent days fussing over the color alone, and declared a celebration when she selected the right shade of light blue to best match Katrina's eyes.

Wearing the Parade gown, Katrina waited to walk in the finale. A surreal experience. She cared little about the A-line skirt or how the seamstress constructed the bodice in a pairing of blue chiffon and silk. She never intended to wear it, and for years considered her Parade gown a tragic waste of money.

"Congratulations, Ladies!" one of the House instructors called into the dressing room. "It's time. Everyone line up, line up, get into your positions please."

They did as instructed. Getting into position, with light footsteps and a whisper of shuffling fabric. A flood of heat and noise hit them as they stepped onto the glossy stage floor. Clapping and cheers thundered from the people filling every audience seat. One by one the Ladies walked forward to meet their suitors.

Katrina stepped forward and emerged onto the stage she rehearsed on since she was a girl. The stage area felt different, more humid, and stage lights seemed brighter. The many years of practice proved to be of some use since she retained her composure despite knowing this was no rehearsal.

Jance stepped away from the line of suitors and met her in the middle of the stage. He took her hand and locked eyes with her as he led her downstage. They stopped and faced each other on a designated spot close to the audience. Held up between his thumb and forefinger, Jance presented what looked like a miniature gold sculpture, but it was a ring. His voice was quiet, as if they somehow had escaped the crowded theatre and talked alone.

"My Lady, I present this gift to you, and I ask you to honor me by wearing it as a reminder of my desire to spend the rest of my life as your husband."

He slipped the wide gold ring onto her finger. It was heavy with an intricate depiction of two Gryphons facing each other with their beaks and one claw touching. Every crack and crevice held small blue diamonds and the slightest movement of her hand made the ring sparkle and shine. He bent towards her ear and whispered.

"I couldn't let Thedmir outdo me."

If he tried to say more Katrina missed it. Applause echoed around them in a deafening volume. Pulling her attention away from the ring, noise and protocol trapped her. Jance played to the audience, waving and making a grand show. He lifted the hand he placed the ring on and kissed it. Shouts of excitement from the audience matched the shiver that shot up her spine. Jance glanced at her with a look of mischievous pride at his fluent execution of the showy gesture. He really was too good at this.

They were exiting the stage when screams and a thunder of running footsteps came from behind them. Stopping short, they exchanged a confused look and glanced behind them. The glare of lights masked the darkened audience chamber. Jance squeezed Katrina's arm and pulled her towards the exit.

"This dress is incredible," he said. "Can you run in it?"

"Yes," she said. Panic rose with his question and the increased amount of screaming coming from the audience. Hand in hand they ran off stage, down a long dark corridor, and past several confused House workers.

"This is a maze," he said. "How do we get out of here?"

"This way," she said pulling him into a different hallway.

They startled a House worker in a dressing room doorway as they hustled by. Reaching the backstage entrance, they stopped and looked at one another.

"Do you think they've reached this exit?" she asked.

"I estimate they have this place surrounded," he said.

"And we're unarmed," she said throwing up her hands up in agitation. "I told you we should have left. Why did we stay for this?"

"I tried," Jance said. "These people really like their show. I wasn't getting labeled a thief by stealing you if I didn't have to. I'm not a thief."

"Well, what do we do now? Where's Thulane?"

"Thulane," he said and his eyes seemed to gloss over as his whole body tensed.

"What?"

He turned stony eyes to her and she grew more concerned as his words flowed in a quiet mumble.

"They did something, because she's not asleep. Is she unconscious? She was with me a second ago."

Thulane was their means of immediate escape; if she was injured or worse, they were stranded.

"Is she hurt?" Katrina asked.

"No, I don't know," he said. "I can feel her, but she's not responding to me."

The noise from the theatre entered the backstage hallways, and Katrina's name was heard over other panicked screams.

"Katrina! Katrina!"

She recognized the swift gait of the short figure rushing towards them.

"Katrina, wait!" Pha shouted.

Katrina's fear subsided as Pha joined them at the exit.

"Thulane, something's happened to her," Katrina said.

"I'll go out first," Pha said. "I do all the talking, and you two are going to do whatever I say."

"Wait, what?" Jance looked startled and then annoyed as he eyed Pha who was busy pushing her hand wraps free, shoving them up each arm.

"Where's Thulane?" Katrina asked.

"Up the hill."

Pha nodded her head once before stepping towards the door.

"Are we ready?" Pha said.

Jance stared at Pha as Katrina took his arm and nodded to Pha.

"She's my guardian," Katrina said pushing Jance behind Pha who opened the door to the outside. "She can handle this."

Following Pha they stepped free of the noise filled theatre and into the hush of night. The alley appeared vacant, but a flash of light sailed from Pha's hands, spiraling up to surround a row of figures perched on top of the building across the alley. They slumped back and Pha took off in a jog down the alley. Katrina gripped Jance's arm and pushed him after her.

"Come on," Katrina said.

"Did you see that?" Jance asked.

"I'll tell you all about it later," Katrina said.

They ran by the shops in the fountain courtyard and onto the sex market thoroughfare. Crowds of people slowed their pace, but hid their movement. Hectic, the sex market surged with the added business the festivities the Parade finale brought to the island. A man regaled the crowd in front of a statue. He raffled off Parade kisses from a row of people dressed in small glittering undergarments.

"I'll be your fine Lady," a woman called from a balcony. She stood with two other women and each wore what looked like genuine Parade gowns, except altered cutouts exposed their breasts. Men shouted jeers of approval and waved coins at them.

Exiting the sex market they ran along side streets to the row houses of the Ladies.

"This way," Pha said to Katrina's confused look. She ran up the alley towards the back of their row house.

"Where is she going?" Jance asked.

"We agreed to do whatever she said, come on."

They followed Pha into the back door of the row house.

"Captain, close the door," Pha said. "We'll work in the dark, and we do this fast."

"Why are we here?" Katrina asked.

"You can't fly over an ocean in that, darling, you'll freeze to death," Pha said gesturing to her Parade gown. "We'll get you changed. Then we'll find Thulane." Pha rested a reassuring hand on Jance's arm. "Captain, they're not going to hurt your Gryphon. I promise you, she's fine."

Pha pointed Katrina to the stairs.

"Up those stairs now."

Katrina looked out her bedroom window. Everything appeared calm outside, as if it were the start of another normal evening in Etrasa. Shedding her Parade gown, Katrina stumbled into travel trunks and got dressed. The trunks served as another reminder that tonight was not normal. These contained almost everything she owned and would be loaded onto ships in the morning. Tonight she changed clothes in preparation for leaving Etrasa.

Flying over an ocean, Katrina was stepping into her future life. The Delphi threat tonight seemed minor compared to the challenge of her life in Etrasa. Where she learned to be a woman, a soldier, and a friend. Etrasa, the place God had sent her to wait. She would leave the island that trapped her and taught her the value of freedom.

Pha's movements lacked their usual grace as she assisted Katrina into her travel attire. Pha's lip quivered and she pressed them together tight. The emotions she attempted to stifle became plainer.

"I don't like this," Pha said.

"I know," Katrina said.

"I don't like you being taken so far from me. The last time..." Pha swallowed and looked like she would speak but stood silent.

"The last time, you saved my life," Katrina said. "And the next time I see you, we'll be home, in Madar."

Pha gave her a weak smile and nodded, "We will."

Tears welled in Pha's eyes and Katrina bent down embracing her. Her throat tightened as Pha's body shivered and softly cried. Pha pulled away and put her hands on both sides of Katrina's face.

"I know you have a mother, but to me, you're the girl I never gave birth to, but love like I did."

Katrina nodded her head frantically in agreement as a heavy tear fell down her cheek.

"I know," Katrina said. "I love you too." Katrina closed her eyes and Pha's hand bent her head towards hers. They sat for a moment with foreheads pressed together, each gathering the strength to let go.

"I'll see you, my Princess," Pha said.

"I'll see you," Katrina said.

Letting go of Pha, Katrina wiped her face and cleared her throat. Pha handed her a pre packed bag.

"Now, it's time to get going," Pha said.

Katrina secured the bag and descended the stairs after Pha. Jance waited for them in the dining room, and fell in beside Katrina as they exited the row house. The three ran all the way up the hill to the university campus. It stood quiet, with walkway lights illuminating the familiar buildings. Passing the equestrian stables Jance motioned to a road that went off to nearby orchards.

"Thulane's housed down this road in a barn," he said.

Running down the road Pha stopped short and threw out her arms in a silent order to halt. Pha's skin began to shimmer and emit light. She extended her arms in front of her with her palms facing up. The scars on Pha's palms looked like they were drawn in light. Swirls of white light danced from her hands; they lit up the ground and surrounding forest as they shot down the road ahead of them. For several minutes Katrina and Jance stood in amazement watching Pha work. The light receded and when it was gone Pha's scars were made of flesh again.

They followed Pha up a short rise and into a clearing with a barn. The number of sleeping Delphi they passed was astounding. Puternic spoke the truth when he said he would take her home using a large force. A unit from the Delphi regiment lay sprawled on the ground asleep.

The Delphi had fallen where they stood in a tight formation around the barn.

Next to the barn they saw the prone figure of Thulane. The Delphi encased her in a Mahigan net. Thulane's big golden eyes lazed open, and peered at Jance. With a thin call Thulane cried out to him.

"She's okay," Katrina said, grabbing his arm to hold him back. "The net weakens whoever it contains, but she's not injured."

A soft whistling sounded. A hollowed thud followed it. Pha stumbled and fell back against her. Pha grabbed at the arrows fletching and where the shaft lodged into the right side of her chest. Katrina screeched as another arrow struck Pha in the thigh. Pha grit her teeth and stifled a moan. Katrina laid her on the ground and inspected her wounds.

"Free your Gryphon, Captain," Pha said.

Without hesitation, Jance ran to Thulane. There was more whistling as arrows aimed at Jance fell past their mark. Katrina looked to the roof of the barn where the arrows were being discharged. Adrenaline heightened her conflicting desires, to grab Pha and flee to safety, or find the archers and kill them.

"I'll be fine," Pha said. "Go, there's not much time."

Katrina stayed frozen in place, stricken by the sight of Pha's injuries. Pha swatted and pushed her with weak hands.

"Now, go now."

Swallowing hard Katrina shook her head. She would never leave Pha like this. She could recognize defeat without her cadet training. They should have left for Gryph after Puternic came to the beach. They lost this fight with the decision to stay on through Parade. Their window of escape closed when the Delphi netted Thulane. Even if Jance succeeded in pulling Thulane free, there were enough Delphi able and ready to end his struggle, and if necessary destroy a Gryphon.

Aimed arrows pinned Jance behind Thulane. His left bicep bled from where an arrow grazed him. As the net loosed, Thulane stood up. Her gold eyes trained on the Delphi archers on the barn roof.

"Katrina," Puternic said from behind her.

Puternic walked side by side with a man who looked like an aged version of himself, his father, Raynes Jenke, Regent of the Delphi. Another two men walked at their flank. Their hair and clothes were wet. Thin braids mixed with Raynes black waist length hair. Different colored binti stone beads were strung intermittently at the end of each braid and glowed soft in the darkness. As the Delphi Regent approached, sleeping Delphi began to rouse. Some sat up and others were quick to regain their feet.

Holding Pha, a helpless despair gripped Katrina. Pha took shallow breaths. Blood seeped around the arrow penetrating her chest. Desperate to help Pha, Katrina yearned for a way to ease her pain. None of this was worth losing Pha over, and her death achieved nothing if the Delphi succeeded in taking her. A million ideas of what to do next ran through her head, but each was wrong, flawed in some way.

Her hands trembled as Raynes stepped in front of her and Pha. Thoughts of murder filled her mind when she looked from Pha's fight for air to Raynes who knelt down in front of her. Observing Raynes, the other Delphi followed his lead, and a wave of men fell to their knees with bowed heads towards Katrina.

"I bow before one of the first to be blessed by God, may the Airetti forever help us."

Pha lay dying. Her guardian would die without help. How could they honor the ancient ritual, when her guardian fought for life?

Katrina wanted to scream as she looked over the bowed Delphi. She would snub them all, and say nothing, but Pha's gaze was expectant. Fighting to breath, Pha watched her, waiting to see if she taught her well. Anger flipped to bewilderment and Katrina grappled with what to say. Her insides churned as she looked over the many Delphi honoring her with a sacred respect. One thought emerged as she searched for words to acknowledge their honor, and her connection to God. She met Pha's gaze when she spoke,

"May we be wise enough to recognize His call."

Pha's eyes flickered with a smile as she squeezed her hand.

Raynes lifted his head, his deep amber eyes met hers. He considered her with a look of reverence she in no way felt she deserved.

"Please, My Regent," Katrina said tilting her head to Pha.

Raynes motioned with one hand and several Delphi stepped forward with a stretcher. Racked with guilt, Katrina relinquished Pha. The men lifted Pha from her hold and eased her onto the stretcher. Katrina suppressed the urge to run after them as they carried Pha into the nearby barn.

"We'll be sure she's well tended," Raynes said. "Your Alvara guardian?"

"Yes. Thank you for sparing her."

"She will be restored and returned to you," Raynes said. "I promise."

What looked like a shadow passed by overhead. Something large enough to block out the stars. Searching the sky, she tried to pinpoint the shadow when it swept through her field of vision, much larger this time. She almost threw herself to the ground when the shadow emerged over the trees and hit them with a gust of air.

The image of a Gryphon emerged from the shadow. It dropped from flight and settled beside Thulane. Oversized metallic black feathers shimmered in the moonlight, and appeared larger as the Gryphon extended its wings in a partial arch.

A rider unsaddled from the Gryphon's back. Massie tore off his helmet, his blond hair sat matted to his scalp. His eyes blazed behind a face of formal courtesy as he marched over. The black Gryphon leapt at the nearest rank of Delphi with a chattering beak. They fell back, swarming away from giant talon swipes and a bellowing scream. Everyone winced from the black Gryphon's piercing cries. It continued to scream, and the sound reverberated over and over again as it herded more Delphi back.

Raynes got to his feet. The black Gryphon's screams muted his attempts to speak.

"Don't you have any control over that animal?" Raynes bellowed.

Massie stood next to Katrina and made a small shrug as he watched the Gryphon intimidating the ranks of Delphi.

You're bonded to a Gryphon? Katrina asked Massie in a wander.

You're bonded to a Minotaur. Massie replied as he offered her a hand up. She took it and stood up. "Why does that surprise you?"

"Make him stop," Raynes said.

"My Regent," Massie said with a bow of his head. He spoke in an awkward staccato, saying a few words at a time between Gryphon screams. "I'm sorry, but Helos is over three hundred years old, and a Gryphon. He doesn't take orders from me. His mate being netted and all really put him in a foul mood. He wanted to kill everyone here, and I begged him not to. So screaming's good."

Thulane screamed then, and stepped clear of the net. Stretching she beat her wings, which sent bits of dirt and sand flying at them.

"My Regent," Massie said, "as Princess Katrina Aranysarga's brother, I provide her with the binding protection of our family."

"Yes, I should hope so." Raynes said in a condescending tone. "But how is passing her into the hands of a human any kind of protection?"

"He's her betrothed," Massie said. He offered Katrina his arm and she slid her hand into the crook of it. His confidence helped restore her bearing. To everyone's relief, Helos ceased screaming and took up an anxious pace in front of the Delphi ranks.

"I'm charged with seeing her safely to Gryph," Massie said.

"Pavaldon, give up a daughter to betrothal? Human betrothal?" Raynes said, a wide grin spread across his face and he began to laugh.

"Yes, well, people do like to call him the Mad Regent." Massie said. "He's been building a human alliance for decades."

"We are here to collect her," Raynes said.

Katrina cringed on the inside and she met Puternic's gaze. He stared back and wandered her a memory. Him holding her naked in the lake inside the cave. "No one's coming between you and me," he said. In an instant she remembered the warmth, the smooth strength of his body, the joy she felt in his arms, how he was everything.

Katrina heard herself in the memory saying, "Do you promise?"

She risked everything for him back then. The intimate memory incited her and she lashed back at him in a wander.

You promised me, then you kissed me, and that was the same week you left.

I made you a promise, I never intended to break it. I'm here for you now. I came back.

He intended to enforce his old promise, his claim. Did he really believe all this could restore what he abandoned? Even if they took her, he was too late. She stopped caring for him a long time ago. Now he was a catalyst for her rage. She vowed if Pha died from her injuries, she would gouge Puternic's eyes out with her bare hands.

"I have pursued Puternic's claim of Princess Katrina Aranysarga with the Madar Council," Raynes said.

"Apologies to you, Regent Raynes, because I can't let her leave with you," Massie said. "The Madar Council already backs my father. I witnessed Regent Sepihne Luex's approval of the betrothal myself."

The youngest of the Madar Regents, Sepihne Luex of Milios, presided as head of the Madar Council. This made him arguably the most powerful man in Madar. If Sepihne approved anything, there was little Raynes could do to refute it.

"Sepihne agreed to this?" Raynes said. "I've received no word of the sort."

"This creates an alliance. It helps garner support for the displaced Veilede in Bisma," Massie said. "Something that helps the collective interest of Madar."

"My son's claim supersedes any betrothal," Raynes said.

"While Sepihne might see that as a reason to reconsider," Massie said, "I doubt my father will. He's sure to take insult at the amount of time Puternic's waited before asserting this claim to Katrina. The daughter stolen from him when she was a child. I bet the first thing My Regent will ask is, how long you've known where she was."

"Regent Raynes," Katrina said inserting herself between them. "May I have a moment to speak privately with my brother?"

Raynes held Massie's glare a moment longer before giving an answer.

"Of course, My Princess."

Raynes made a quick head bow to her and motioned for Puternic to follow him. When they were a safe distance away Katrina turned to Massie and wandered.

I only marginally followed most of what you said, but I don't think he believes you.

Massie nodded his head in agreement.

They're not planning to leave here without me.

The Delphi need to acquire an Airetti bride in as legal a means possible. Massie wandered. *There's really only one way for that to occur, by a new Regents first rites.*

I know, he's already told me he intends to hide me, until Raynes dies. They're pressing Puternic's claim, as a way to justify taking me.

"Yes, his claim," Massie said in a hiss. "If Father ever hears of it." Massie closed his eyes and grimaced in disgust before reverting back to a wander. *They do have a petition before the Madar council.*

Backed with what?

Massie swallowed and averted his gaze. *Puternic's memories, of you.*

He'll wander memories? His memories-of us, to every Regent in Madar?

"Yeah," Massie said with a sniff. "It's essentially a formal request for war. Even mad. Father's traditional; marriage by rally, that's it."

"But you just told him-"

A version of the truth.

"Do I get to know the truth?"

You're going home with me. I'm retrieving you from Gryph, and no matter what Father asks about who knew where you were all these years, you tell him I was the one who found you. We can't ever let him learn that Valgu had any part in hiding you. That's a secret that has the power to destabilize Mozgas.

And now you're talking ahead, like we have a chance at getting out of here. Your Gryphon put on a good show, but they have Mahigan nets. There's a regiment of Delphi here, and how many more off shore? The Delphi can mass, get in a few more well placed arrows, and they'll have what they came for.

Massie laughed and Katrina looked at him confused.

"What are we going to do?"

"Buy time," he said.

"With what?"

Massie ignored her question, tucked her hand back into his arm, and gave it a loving pat as he walked them to where Raynes and Puternic stood waiting.

"My Regent, are you open to negotiations?" Massie asked.

"Negotiate?" Raynes said, frowning in skepticism. "What's being offered?"

"A chance at avoiding my father's wrath," Massie said, "and a better means of securing an Airetti bride."

"Sounds too good to be true," Raynes said, "but please do continue."

"In exchange for an Airetti betrothal," Massie said, "you cease the pursuit of any claims to Princess Katrina Aranysarga."

"And who do you have the authority to betroth?" Puternic said.

"My children," Massie said, piercing Puternic with a look of triumph. "I'm willing to betroth the Princess Delany Aranysarga to the Jenke family."

"You have a daughter?" Raynes said.

"Yes, her wings appeared only a little more than a month ago." Massie said.

"Massie?" Katrina said, grabbing his arm and digging in her nails. Massie looked at her as he spoke, and she saw past his polished confidence. His eyes exposed to her just how much the offer cost him. He wandered images of a girl who was no more than three, with green eyes like his, and a tumble of dark brown hair.

"She's my darling," Massie said. "I can't put into words how much I adore her."

Katrina's heart sank and she shook her head. Massie was offering his child? The offer was too much.

"No, Massie," she said. "Please, let Father and the council sort this out."

Raynes had a serious look of consideration on his face.

"Father," Puternic said in protest.

"And you readily pledge her?" Raynes said ignoring Puternic. "Your daughter in lieu of honoring my son's claim?"

"Yes," Massie said.

"Why are you so willing?" Raynes said.

"I want what's best for Delany," Massie said. "She will be a Guide, it's an opportunity, an honor which affords her many advantages."

"Advantages your father doesn't appreciate," Raynes said.

"My father and I have differing opinions on many things. I can't speak to what he would have for Katrina."

Raynes inspected Massie's face for a long moment, and diverted his eyes, staring off for a time before he spoke.

"I accept the betrothal of Princess Delany Aranysarga and agree to end any pursuit of Puternic's claim to Princess Katrina Aranysarga. Princess Delany will be given the Jenke Gideem, and promised to my descendants. Your daughter will be the future Guide to the Delphi." Massie swallowed hard and bobbed his head in a swift nod.

Massie bought her freedom, by sacrificing his daughter's future. Guilt swirled in her stomach as she looked at Puternic. She turned away. She deserved to bear the weight of her mistake, not the innocent niece she had never met. It was hard to see straight thinking about the debt she had incurred, something she was entirely unable repay.

10

Royals and Snakes

Massie formalized his agreement with Regent Raynes Jenke. In parting, they shook hands. Massie remained the most composed of their group, his gait confident as he stepped over to Helos. Jance said nothing. His intense stare avoided Katrina as he secured their gear. Thulane shifted as she ground her claws into the packed dirt. Overwhelmed by what just transpired, the activity around Katrina seemed distant.

Puternic charged his father with arms raised and animated eyes. They were in the midst of a wandering exchange, a very tense wandering exchange. Their private conversation ended with both men glancing at her. Puternic's gaze remained as Raynes waived off his son and walked away. She scolded herself for enjoying his predicament. It was wrong to take this much satisfaction in his misery.

Jance came to stand beside her. He looked at Puternic like he wanted to gut him. Pulling at her elbow, he beckoned her to Thulane. Instead of coaching Katrina up into the saddle, Jance picked her up and tossed her. He fastened her in before climbing up to sit behind her. She understood his anger, but disliked bearing so much of it. When Jance reached around her to grab hold of the saddle's pommel she shrunk away.

"Katrina," he said.

"I didn't deserve that."

He pulled her against him with a gentle hand.

"I'm sorry, you're right," he said then eased back from her before shouting over his shoulder to Massie, "Where do you want me to hold on?"

Katrina craned her head to see Massie giving Jance a stern stare. Thulane paced away extending her wings. With a skipping hop she jumped in the air. In a few hard strokes she lifted them airborne.

When the earth dropped away she gripped Jance's forearms. A small smile crossed her lips and she forgot his foul temper. She missed flying and wished she could fall in beside Thulane, flying under her own power. They climbed to a height where half the island was visible. House lights and the street lamps of Etrasa glowed like tiny orbs. The island shore was dotted with the many small binti lights of the Delphi retreating.

Then the island was gone. Thulane turned north, gliding out over the open ocean. Her graceful wings swept them forward over an unobstructed view of ocean water stretching in every direction. Large waves were barely glimpsed from their height. The ever-moving black water shimmered, reflecting every swell as a canvas of moonlit dots below them. The moon traced everything in stark contrasts of black and white, with highlights of silver, and deep shades of blue.

Wind pushed against them. It trailed cold fingers across every inch of exposed skin, and snuck between clothing seams. Feeling chilled, she hunched into her jacket. Katrina felt ever grateful Pha made her change clothes for this leg of the journey.

No one wandered or spoke, and she struggled to stay awake. Exhaustion overrode her mind's fragmented sorting of what transpired, and she fell asleep. A few hours later she awoke huddled against Jance. She apologized through a yawn and Jance glanced down at her with a small smile.

"What?" she said. Finding him in the dim light.

"It's good you were able to rest," he said.

"What's that look?" she said.

He looked away and shook his head still smiling as she pressed for an answer.

"Are you laughing at me? What's so funny?"

"Nothing, it's just really dark tonight. It's hard to see."

"Hard to see what?"

"Hard to see you," he said. "I wish I would've gotten a better look at you earlier, back in the theatre. So much detail and work went into all that."

"You have no idea," she said. "It's nice to know you appreciated it."

Jance touched one of her blue crystalized hair pins, inspecting the curl it held in place. She had forgotten about her hair. It was still in the elaborate style she wore for the finale. Embarrassed by his study, she tried ignoring him. She lifted her hand to see the heavy ring he gave her.

"Do you like it?" he asked.

"You were talking about my parade gown," she said.

"What about it? I told you earlier I liked it," he said.

"No, you didn't," She said peeking up at him. She was prodding him, trying to coax out the lighthearted side of him.

The playful Jance emerged and not backing away, he inched his face close to hers saying, "Yes, I did."

"Well, tell me again," she said. "What did you think about all that work?"

She expected a flippant response. Instead he went silent, and she grew concerned.

"I have never seen you more beautiful than how you looked tonight."

Even in the darkness she could make out his intense study of her. The way he cradled her brought his face close to hers. A boyish smile crossed his face.

"The suitor behind me, as we were going on stage, cursed. He said, 'There's no possible way I overlooked that.' Every man in that theatre envied me. All of them staring at you and wondering if they'd ever met you before."

Jance laughed at the memory, as Katrina held a tight smile, doing her best to not look away. She wanted to hide, or maybe squirm into a giggling fit. Or he could just let the space between their lips disappear. She held his gaze, doing her best to stay in the moment without falling apart.

"The ring," she said. "It's over the top and way too much."

"It's my gift to you," he said, in an exaggerated tease, "And there's nothing you can do about it."

He edged back from her then and looked out at the night sky. She wanted to take hold of his shirt and pull him back to where he was a second ago. She stared at his eyes, wishing for more light so she could see their full blue hue.

"I can give it back," she said, and his mouth turned in an annoyed line.

"You could," he said, turning abruptly to face her again. His nose almost touched hers and she could feel his breath on her cheek. "But it was made for you, you should keep it."

His response was to neutral. His words cut as accurate as a rejection. A confirmation she needed. She forced herself to replay his response with the same distant inflection. The ring meant nothing. She wore a prop in the charade they staged to exit Etrasa. Disappointment weighed on her and she blamed herself. Such romantic impulses were easier to prevent outside of this current forced closeness. She knew how to handle a fleeting infatuation. An easier thing to smother when she could avoid the distracting person. When his hands were less familiar with the curve in her waist, and the separation between their lips exceeded a few mere inches.

The wise thing to do was keep her head. What was she thinking flirting with him like she was his actual Etrasa bride? She needed to be responsible and behave in a sensible manner. The appeal of him would fade, it always did. They would remain, as they were, friends. The encounter with Puternic a solid reminder of the mistake she refused to repeat.

The first sight of Gryph came in the early hours of morning, a sliver of something unchanged by the rhythm of the water below. It gradually increased in size, a solid line on the horizon to intersect and halt the ocean. As the sun announced morning, the cloudless sky became a saturated cerulean blue. The land they approached grew immense and soon grey and milky white sand was beneath them. Large chunky rock of what looked like mirrored glass scattered the shore. Jance began to point out and name the different land formations of the mountain foothills.

The Glass Mountains were a visual surprise, a formation of rock unlike anything she had seen.

"The only way to travel the Glass Mountains is to fly them," Jance said. "Or you could take a really long journey and walk around."

She laughed at his understatement. These were mountains no person could walk through or explore. There was no slope to them, as each peak shot straight from the ground to an elevation so high, on an overcast day clouds would surround them. On this clear morning, they appeared connected to the sky. The peaks resembled blunt raw crystals. They jutted out of the ground and massed together as a natural wall that surrounded the whole valley.

The face of the mountains stood firm. Impenetrable, the rock structure was inhospitable for life. Slim blue veins ran through smoky grey rock. The rock surface was where the mountains got their name. Each one cast a reflection like glass. Blazing streaks of sunlight winked off the rocks, scattering beams of light in random directions.

The valley below stretched off to a distant edge. Fields and deciduous forest grew here with larger trees growing along the steep grades at the base of the mountains. The valley floor stretched flat and wide with a gradual incline towards the capital, which rested against the highest of the Glass Mountains - the Heights - the mountain home to all Gryphons. The capital was constructed with rock from the Glass Mountains. The great grey stone palace rose above a vast city of tall buildings. Every building reflected light, and shone just like the Glass Mountains surrounding them.

The vastness of the Gryph capital magnified as they descended. Thulane seemed too large a creature to even perch where her body aimed to land. With a reflexive cringe, Katrina ducked. Holding her breath, she reminded herself to trust Thulane's three hundred years of flying experience. They closed in on a sheer wall of the Gryph Palace. Thulane eased down onto an expansive terrace. Helos and Massie landed beside them.

Jance removed her harness and helped her down. Stretching stiff legs, she walked to where she could gaze up at Thulane's face. Round gold eyes watched her approach.

"Thank you," she said.

Thulane lowered her beak and made a low melodic trill. Jance drew close to Thulane's chest, stroking and fluffing feathers at the crest of her throat. The look on his face indicated a wandering conversation between them. Here and there Jance chuckled or mumbled a response.

"Tired?" Massie said stepping next to her.

"Yes," she said.

Jance walked over to them, and Massie lunged at him, wrestling him to the ground. They rolled into a good natured scuffle. The kind her squad reserved for deciding small disputes.

"What did I tell you?" Massie said.

"My arm, stop! I haven't had time to bandage it," Jance said. He pulled his injured arm away from Massie's assault. "Nothing happened, get off. I did you the favor remember."

Their horseplay continued until a small army of servants filtered through a set of double doors. With the incoming audience Massie and Jance stopped fighting and rose to their feet. Jance regained his composure and relayed orders with practiced ease.

Three servants descended on Katrina, making introductions, taking her bag, and asking an endless array of questions. Some were trivial, others so unexpected, she hesitated responding. What was her tea preference? Did she have a reading or shopping list to hand off? What time did she prefer her curtains drawn? Did she like lavender, citrus, or rosemary? Jance squeezed her shoulder and smiled an apology.

"I have about six people asking me to do a dozen different things," he said, "All to be done immediately. I'll do my best to find you this afternoon."

Katrina nodded and watched Jance walk into the palace with a trail of people talking around him.

The Gryph Palace was exquisite. Every corridor, room, and hall assaulted her with visual masterpieces. She passed paintings that took up entire walls. Grand columns supported sweeping arches along hallways where the ceiling held more painted artwork than what hung from the walls. Gryphon and feather motifs adorned every fixture and finishing. Gryphons were the primary statue subjects. Each rendered with a beautiful life-like precision. The doorways were massive. Fitted with double doors so large they needed hinges as long as her forearm. A clear indication the Gryph palace accommodated more than a human monarchy, it hosted Gryphons as well.

The endless hallway to her room served as a preview to her oversized quarters. What the servants called a room, was actually an apartment of several rooms. A space twice the size of her row house in Etrasa, it far exceeded her needs. While some saw this as lavish pampering, she saw the time wasted walking between bedroom, parlor, and private bath.

Within a few hours the novelty of Gryph's abundant splendor wore off. She missed Etrasa. Smiling, she remembered the blue glazed bricks of Etrasa's narrow streets. The kitchen garden she adored. The way morning sunlight glowed on white stucco walls. How a late afternoon sun seeped warmth into the plain wood furnishings. Gryph was magnificent, but held none of Etrasa's easy grace.

The next day Massie took her on a tour of his palace room. Stacks of books and newspapers lay about his apartment's parlor. She wondered if he spent more time in Gryph than at home. Massie brought her out on a massive outdoor terrace, which looked identical to the one outside her rooms. He called it a Gryphon Keep, and said, "This just makes it easier for a fishy smelling Gryphon to drop out of the sky and tell you how smart they are."

Helos gracefully landed a few feet away from them, smelling nothing like fish.

Without turning to Helos, Massie said, "Nice to see you."

Helos sprawled his massive body along the length of the Gryphon Keep, and fell asleep. Massie directed Katrina to a table and chairs where they sat down to tea.

"Do you spend more time in Gryph than at home?" she said.

"Why do you ask?" he said, adding nothing to his tea and dragging his cup over to him.

"There's a lot of reading material in there for a casual tenant."

Massie huffed, "Part of the job. When we get a real ambassador here, that mess will be someone else's."

"You're an unwilling ambassador here?"

"Of sorts," he said.

"Was that your area of study, in Milios?"

"No," Massie said. "Valgu mentioned where I went to school?"

"Years ago, when he went looking for Puternic. He said Puternic was your classmate in Milios."

"He was."

"That's all he said. With the strain of neutral we were always pressed for time. He never offered much about family. Eventually I stopped asking."

"After Lady Miandes' death, I was done with life at home. I went to a university located as far away as I could get. I went to Milios. Father didn't care. What else was he going to do with his Fayette son?"

The Fayette form of Veilede possessed the ability to shift into a different human appearance than their own. Some were rigorous in mastering their shifting ability, learning upwards of ten various forms and holding onto the shift for several hours at a time. Other Fayette might attempt to shift once or twice, but saw no benefit to regular shifting. The Fayette form was common. However, a Fayette son born to Airetti and Mahigan parents were rare. A Mahigan's sons were usually Mahigan.

"What did you study?"

"What they usually teach a royal born Fayette — entire courses on how retrieve useful information from places like this."

"I didn't realize Lady Miandes passed," Katrina said. "I'm sorry. She's Dermot's mother, that's the most I knew of her."

"She mothered all of us," Massie said. "Valgu brought in a staff of Alvara guards after we lost her. They've helped, and they're the best protection we've got against him. But I still don't like home. There's nothing I can say to help you understand what you're going home to."

"I didn't expect it to be the same," she said. "I used to dream things would magically go back to the way they were, but I know better. Seeing you is proof. I'm not sure I would've recognized you if we weren't in neutral together first."

Massie smiled. "Too true. You know one thing that is the same?"

Katrina sipped her tea and shook her head.

"Your bedroom, it's just like it was the day you left. Very creepy."

"As long as it gets a dusting now and then."

He balked like he smelled something foul. "Just do us all a favor and change the wall color, it's faded and sad."

"That should be easy, I'm a pretty good wall dresser."

"Your serious?" he said frowning as he waited for her to recant.

She laughed and sipped her tea. "That was too easy. What did you go to school for again?"

"Don't start with me," he said. "Keep it up and I'll see you painting that room yourself."

She grinned and nodded. "So, unofficial Gryph Ambassador, you should fill me in more on your work here."

"Well," he said and cleared his throat. "What you need to understand first is the very tight situation Bisma is in." He swiped one of the larger cookies from the tray. He ate it in small bites, and gestured with it as he emphasized various points. "Their monarchy is in an unstable position. King Armond Dhanda's been losing the popular support of his people as Gryph exerts more control and influence on their affairs."

"Like their Crown Prince marrying the Bisma Princess Armina Dhanda?"

"Yes, that's just one," Massie said. "Each winter, Bisma needs access to ports when their northern coast freezes up. There's been many treaties between Bisma and Madar, specifically Mozgas, where we allow access to ours. The last treaty was one of Father's best works before he went mad."

"I'm assuming that treaty was dissolved?" she said.

Massie nodded his head, "Gryph persuaded Bisma to abandon their treaty with Mozgas and enter into a monopoly. Gryph has all of Bisma's winter shipping, and have leveraged this to create Bisma's dependence on them. Initially, this was nothing more than a disappointing financial loss for us. But it grew and turned hostile. The monopoly fostered the change in Bisma's opinions towards the Veilede. Now the Veilede living in Bisma do so in secret, adopt Skrieni ways, or they leave to immigrate into Madar."

"And this is a reflection of Gryph's opinion?" Katrina asked.

"Yes, you won't find many Veilede besides, well just me, openly living anywhere in Gryph. The humans fear us here. Religious leaders claim exposure to us will deform a good man or woman into a Veilede."

"We're deformities now?"

"Apparently," Massie said. "I would have been forced home if it wasn't for Helos. Being selected by a Gryphon became my official pardon. It granted me full citizenship to Gryph, human or not."

"You like it here that much?" she asked.

Massie shrugged, "It's nice."

"They must resent you," she said.

Massie nodded his head and said, "They'll resent you too, arriving here betrothed to one of their own."

"That's not true," she said. The muscles in her neck tightened and her fingers closed around the heavy Gryphon ring on her hand. She really wished this leg of the journey home were over.

"It's a version of it," Massie said, closely observing her. "Jance is my friend. He wanted to help because he's a man looking to make change. He knows the practical gain Gryph would receive if relations with Madar were restored. He's already researched and presented the historical precedence based on Gryphon knowledge. He's convinced the Queen, pushed for an alliance, and now he just needs to prove his theory to the rest of Gryph."

There was a knock and they turned as the Gryphon Keep door opened. Sol entered with a small group trailing behind him. He grinned, wandering greetings to them. Katrina shot up from her seat and rushed to him. Leaping into his embrace, she wound her arms about his neck, as he lifted her up and crushed her to him. So focused on Sol, she forgot about the other people assembled around them. They smiled in understanding as Sol set her back down.

She made a double take when she saw Professor Tegija Wythe. His washed out gold eyes searched hers, holding her fixed, as a jolt of awe swept through her. What was this? She hoped this affliction ran both ways. Anything otherwise was unfair. No man should be able to steal all the air in the room simply by being in it. His eyes moved on, and she took a deep breath. Rattled by his effect on her, she rebelled against it. Smiling, she dawned the veil of proper courtesy. She would ignore Professor Wythe's appeal, at least until they shared one conversation.

Anticipating introductions in a human fashion, Katrina tensed as Sol and his companions took a knee. With bowed heads towards Katrina, the lone female of the group spoke. She had light brown hair, which framed her round face and flowed around her ample shoulders.

"I bow before one of the first to be blessed by God, may the Airetti forever help us."

Receiving and responding to the Airetti greeting remained new for her. Pausing, Katrina recalled the hope on Pha's face, and found the words she spoke to Regent Raynes and the Delphi.

"May we be wise enough to recognize His call."

The contingent rose, and Sol conducted introductions in a wander, gesturing to the woman who spoke first.

"Assistant Trade Minster, Raldine Cantor."

A tall wispy man with dark eyes, slight features, and a mop of untamed dark hair stepped forward.

"Inspector Le Ironwood, he's from the trade office."

Another man stepped forward. His youthful face contrasted against cropped silver hair.

We're claiming he's an assistant to Tegija, he goes by Brentin, Sol wandered.

Katrina returned Brentin's smile before giving Sol a questioning look.

Sol raised his eyebrows back at her. *They won't tell me anymore about him either.*

Sol stood ready to step away, when Professor Wythe stepped forward. Standing with his hands held behind his back, he gave Sol a serious look. Realizing his error, Sol's eyes went wide with surprise before making a meek expression of apology.

Professor Tegija Wythe, Sol wandered. *Please forgive my mistake for assuming you've been introduced.*

Katrina gave Sol a merciful look. "It's not your fault," she said, tilting her head to glower at Massie who now stood beside her. "Valgu or even Massie should have introduced us."

Massie ignored her rebuff, stepping to the side to speak with Brentin.

"Prince Valgu sent our assembly to work in dual roles as needed," Minister Cantor said. "We intend to take full advantage of the access you and Prince Massie have provided us here, but our primary directive is to see you home safely."

"I imagine you've all had a long journey," Katrina said and gestured to the table and chairs. "Please, let's sit and you can tell me more."

Minister Cantor smiled in gratitude and everyone found a seat. Katrina learned Madar's trade ministry had not met with the guild of Gryph traders in decades. Minister Cantor was saddled with the burden of meeting with the guild and cobbling together future meetings with its members.

Inspector Ironwood planned to travel around the largest port. He had a matrix of questions he intended to answer. Some of the information he collected would be useful for Minister Cantor, while the rest of the matrix would update trade records Madar kept on foreign ports.

Professor Wythe arranged to meet with other healers in Gryph.

"What I have to do here is uncomplicated." Professor Wythe said. "Politics tend to make exceptions for information exchanged that can combat diseases everyone's affected by. I'll be meeting a few peers I've had previous written correspondence with."

"And we hope his meetings are a success," Minister Cantor chided. "Don't let Professor Wythe's modesty undermine the importance of his work, my Princess," Minister Cantor said, shaking a friendly finger at him.

The contingent excused themselves before the afternoon meal. A servant arrived with a sealed message from the Crown Prince, Chane Willmont. The servant left as she opened the message and found a formal invitation. Chane wished to greet Sol, Massie, and Katrina the following day.

"He's invited us to join him on a tour of an exhibit hall where my tapestry is set on display."

"Tapestry," Massie said, and plucked the invitation from her hands.

"There's an explanation for our father's madness," Massie said, as he scanned the invitation card. He tossed it aside. "I'd like to know what his is. I'm not going. If I want to tangle with a mad man, I'll go home and visit Father."

"Do you really consider Chane Willmont insane?" Katrina asked.

A servant entered Massie's apartment with an armload of fresh linens. Massie shook his head at her and said, "Another time."

Massie's reaction to the invitation intrigued her. Sol said nothing, but hearing Massie's assertions, he cast her a doubtful look.

Sol and Katrina met Chane outside the exhibit hall entrance the next day. After introductions, Chane motioned to a pair of servants, and beckoned them to open the gallery doors.

"Has your family seen this tapestry?" Chane said to Katrina.

Katrina looked up at Sol and said, "No, actually they haven't."

"I think you will be impressed," Chane said to Sol, as he led them into the Gallery. "I insisted it be flown here when I saw it. I wasn't going to risk, what was it, two and half years of work?"

"Yes," Katrina said surprised to hear the detail Chane knew about her work. The mention of seeing her tapestry before its arrival in Gryph snagged her attention. Jance mentioned his bond with his twin brother, but now she suspected their bond was even more unique.

"They did a decent job of displaying your work," Chane said as they passed a row of Gryphon statues. Large exotic paintings were hung in a neatly spaced line, and small painted containers and jars sat on narrow shelves. She blinked hard when they entered a round gallery where her tapestry hung in the center of the room. Accustomed to viewing it on a white washed hallway, its new grand display humbled her and left her speechless. Another tapestry set on the gallery periphery caught her eye.

Chane followed her gaze. "What do you think? The workmanship reminded me of yours. I knew it had to be set as a companion piece."

"Where did you get it?" She asked.

It's from us, one of our gifts, Sol wandered.

"A gesture of goodwill from your family," Chane said.

"It's like mine because this was made by my mother," Katrina said stepping towards the tapestry. "She taught me."

She recognized her mother's craftsmanship and design trademarks. Her mother's eye for symmetry was easy to find in her backgrounds. The whimsical touch she added to the realism of her trees stood out, a feature too unique to be replicated by chance.

She stared at the tapestry her mother loved and then wanted to cut apart and destroy. She saw where her mother used too much green, and the series of stitches that ran uneven on the right side. The work featured a blond haired man and brown haired woman astride horses. The couple, her parents, rode close enough to hold hands.

Does Father know this is here? Katrina wandered to Sol.

We found it in a long forgotten storage crate, Sol wandered. *I'm surprised you remember it.*

"It's in excellent condition," Chane said. "We're grateful for the generous gift." Directing his gaze at Katrina, he said, "You were taken to Etrasa against your Father's will."

"Yes," she said.

"And my brother was kind enough to accept reward money in exchange for bringing you home," Chane said.

"Yes. I'm very grateful for his assistance," she said.

"Your father sent a very large sum of money for finding you and keeping you from harm. He was very generous. He even offered more if we could provide the whereabouts of your mother."

"My mother?" Katrina crossed her arms and looked up at the likeness of her mother in the tapestry. "I couldn't say, I don't know where she is."

"That's too bad. Maybe we'll get lucky and stumble upon her someday." Chane adjusted the cuffs of his jacket, straightening them with a sharp shrug.

"Maybe," she said.

"I'm afraid you and I can never be friends," Chane said, with a flat intensity in his voice. "I don't like any woman who has the audacity to refuse my brother."

She shared a conspiratorial look with Sol and wandered, Massie was right. Standing rigid, she considered the most logical response to his illogical comments.

"That's a shame," she said. "In my defense, I think it's only fair to say, I didn't refuse Jance. He's never offered me anything I haven't accepted."

Chane's eyes gleamed with excitement and a small smile arched the corners of his mouth.

"In Gryph, returning a gift is the same as a refusal."

Katrina tried to figure out what Chane was talking about. Clenching one hand she felt the weight of the Gryphon ring on her finger. A flush of anxiety crept down her body.

"And I must politically object, to all of your kind," Chane said. "We sit on the cusp of a war."

"Some alliances are formed to avoid war," she said.

"There's no alliance. While you have the Queen's consent to remain in Gryph, you in turn pose a threat to her."

"We're not here to threaten anyone," she said.

"Your being here undermines my family," Chane said. "It subverts our house, placing the Queen and my entire family in danger."

"We intend to leave at the Queen's convenience," she said. With careful steps she walked over and faced Chane. He stilled, and avoided her gaze, like a soldier who waited to pass a formal inspection.

"I should despise you, and Massie, for inserting yourselves into my brother's life the way you have," Chane said.

"But you don't?"

"No," Chane said meeting her eyes. "I'm the victim of my brother's good opinions."

"But, you still object," she said. "I'm curious, about your bond with Jance."

"Yes?" Chane said with renewed eagerness.

"What will Jance think when he learns all of this in your thoughts?"

Chane grinned and relaxed into laughter. "No. My brother avoids the truth at all costs." In one swift move Chane stood close, and spoke quietly in her ear. "I don't expect him to invade my mind, until he is unsettled by your absence."

Her skin prickled with his harsh pronunciation of the word "absence."

"I think the odds are better my brother will learn of our conversation from you before he discovers it in me," Chane said.

"That's possible," she said, lifting her chin in defiance. "But I think your prediction of his reaction is an exaggeration."

"You don't know my brother. For his sake, as well as mine, it would be better if you were right."

She waited for more, but he stepped back. Donning a formal posture, Chane turned and motioned for them to follow. Sol stepped beside her, offering his hand in escort. She took it, inhaled slowly, and anticipated the end to their formal introduction to Chane.

At the gallery doors Chane stopped and turned to them. "We anticipate the pleasure of your company at court tomorrow night." He looked from Katrina to Sol. "Queen LaBell is eager to make your acquaintance."

"We look forward to the privilege," Katrina said, bowing her head in farewell as Chane turned and exited the hall.

That was unpleasant. Sol wandered as they walked back.

"I was really hoping Massie had exaggerated," she said.

The sound of something impossible made her halt. Focusing, she searched for the sound again. The echo of a stomping footfall she knew as well as her own.

"Do you hear that?" she asked.

Sol faced her with a dubious look. Letting his arm go, she turned and followed the sound to an open set of doors. She had to investigate. There was no logical reason to hear her mother's footsteps.

Her mother paced back and forth before a bank of five large windows. She wore a green dress, and someone had spun her hair into the Gryph fashion of layered ribbon and curls.

A warm heat rose to Katrina's face as her hands became cold. Sol reached to hold her back but she evaded him rushing into the room. She rounded a couch and stopped short at the sight of Devon sprawled out on its length.

"I wondered when I would see you," her mother said.

Pulling her gaze away from Devon, she stared at her mother.

"What are you doing here?"

"I'm here to see you, darling. I wasn't going to miss my own daughter's wedding."

Katrina swallowed and tried to hide her astonishment.

"My sweet," her mother said to the man on the couch. She walked over and stood beside him. "Stand up and greet her properly, please."

Devon dropped his boots to the floor and rose from the couch with a tired sigh. He stood beside her mother, and made an exaggerated bow of his head.

"My husband," her mother said. "Devon Quraishi, owner of Suge Trading."

Katrina felt Sol walk up behind her. Her mother gaped in recognition.

"This is my second eldest brother, Solyom Aranysarga, Prince of the Mozgas Province."

Devon's eyebrow lifted as he gazed up at Sol, and nodded.

"You're here, as wedding guests?" Katrina said, watching them both for signs of silent communication between them.

"Devon's always welcome in Gryph," her mother said. "I asked him to bring me here. It's only right for a mother to be with her daughter before she's married. My husband's so obliging, I made one mention of it and I swear the next day we were here."

Katrina smiled at the absurdity of her mother having maternal instincts. She heard a thread of sincerity in her mother's words, but suspected other reasons brought Devon to Gryph.

"It's a shame you didn't write first." Katrina glanced at the doorway where a servant escort now stood.

Lady Lena's smile fell at the hidden warning in her tone.

"My father has rewarded the Willmonts' for their help in finding me,"

Katrina said. "They've graciously assisted in affording me safe passage home. They've also promised to keep a look out for my mother." She inched closer to her mother, lowering her voice. "It's not safe here."

Lady Lena waved her away in a fluster. "Don't be silly."

"There's no reason for you to stay."

"What?" Her mother's voice rang with outrage. "Unbelievable. I raised you a Larksbur, a Lady of the House of Estrasa. You're here to marry Prince Jance Willmont."

"No, I'm being restored to my father's household." Katrina said.

"What a waste," her mother said. "Ungrateful."

"There's no wedding. If there's business waiting for you elsewhere, I recommend you tend to it," Katrina said.

"The princess is right," Devon said.

Her mother whipped her head around and glared at Devon. He held her silent with a look. Frowning, her mother turned away.

"It was a pleasure to meet you Prince Solyom, good to see you Katrina." Devon said. "Thank you, for notifying us on the change. Have a safe journey home."

Her mother glared at Devon again.

"I wish safe travels for you both," Katrina said. She and Sol bowed their heads in farewell.

A sharp whispering argument ensued as Katrina and Sol left the room.

I love you dear sister, but will you please lighten your grip on my arm? Sol wandered.

Obliging him, she glanced up in apology.

Sol patted her hand and smiled. "Lady Lena hasn't changed much, has she?"

"No, I can't say she has."

Entering her rooms, Katrina startled at the rush of her attendant, Trui.

"Ma'am, I've readied the traditional gown your brother brought. They keep coming round to tell me to hurry. Seems you're running short on time."

Katrina glanced over at Sol. "I trust you can tell Massie what he missed by declining the Crown Prince's invitation."

Sol grinned and released her to follow Trui into another room to change.

"Better hurry up," Massie shouted after her from where he lounged in her sitting area. "All of Gryph awaits us. What'd I miss?" The conversation between her brothers faded away behind doors Trui closed.

The sight of the traditional Airetti gown Sol brought from Madar stopped her mid stride. A barrage of emotions flooded her and it took effort to breath. Trui held the garment aloft and presented it with genuine reverence. Katrina gazed at the delicate drape of white silk with amber and evergreen accents. The collar and trim were fully embroidered and beaded. A draping shawl of evergreen silk lay against it with matching embroidery.

"This is so lovely," Trui said. "I've never seen anything like it."

Katrina stared as Trui laid it out in front of her. Trui made quick work of unlacing the gown Katrina wore. Katrina clutched at her loose undergarments. Before she could protest, Trui hoisted the backless Airetti gown over her head. In a heartbeat her undergarments dropped and the gown smoothed against her body. It left her bare back. She readied herself for Trui's reaction.

"Oh God," Trui stammered.

Composed, Katrina watched Trui through the full length-dressing mirror.

Trui clasped both hands over her mouth. "Forgive me," Trui cried. "I'm so sorry, I wasn't, I didn't know."

Katrina turned and tried grabbing after Trui's hand to reassure her. "It's all right."

"Excuse me, Ma'am, I'm so sorry, I need to go." Trui ducked out from behind the dressing screen.

Katrina peered over her shoulder at her reflection in the mirror. She saw the sweeping plunge of the open backed dress. An important design detail meant to accommodate a pair of wings. On her the dress set her scars on display. A latticework of marred skin to document her wings removal.

"Is everything all right?" Sol wandered.

Katrina gave no reply. She stared at the image of her scared back.

Katrina, Sol wandered as he knocked at her door. She heard him enter the room. There were tears in her eyes when he peeked around her dressing screen.

"I can't wear this," she said. "I'm sorry."

Sol gazed at the reflection of her back before stepping over and coaching her into his arms. Sol held her as she cried.

She hated herself for being raised human and feeling strange in the traditional gown. For allowing the pain of her past to gain a formidable foothold in her present; for being so utterly weak. The strength of their connection steadied her. Thank God she had Sol. Even if it meant he witnessed her falling apart like this.

Will you consider wearing this? Sol wandered. *For me, sometime after we get home? Owl designed it at my request.*

The Veilede would find it strange for her to wear anything else besides an Airetti gown like this during formal occasions. The thought of bearing her scars, and shocked strangers reacting as Trui did, made her ill.

"I'll think about it," she said.

The evening was warm and Katrina relaxed into the contingent's easy camaraderie. Their table laughed through dinner as Inspector Ironwood spun his day's tales with vocal inflections and comedic timing. Katrina hung on Professor Tegija Wythe's every word, the very few he said. She liked when he talked, it gave her the freedom to watch him.

"How are all of our friends from Mozgas this evening?" Jance said, approaching their table and coming to stop behind her chair.

"Very well," Massie said motioning for him to sit in a vacant seat.

Tegija tilted his head as he considered Jance. His gaze trailed down Jance to land on her. Meeting Katrina's eyes Tegija's grin widened, and she openly smiled back.

"I would, but I promised a drink with Chane and some traders," Jance said, before wandering to Katrina, *I'm jealous of your Professor.*

Katrina turned in her seat and gave him a questioning frown. Jance leaned down with a smile and spoke quietly into her ear.

"I've never seen you look at me the same way you look at him."

Katrina made a sour look and batted him away with one hand.

"Enjoy your drinks," she said, picking up her own glass of wine and taking a sip.

Jance walked over and joined the table where Chane and Armina sat. A beautiful, dark-haired woman walked in a slow pace around them. The woman's silver gown highlighted her pregnant form, and contrasted well with her long dark hair. Armina went still when she saw her. The dark-haired woman looked from Armina to Chane. Jance caught sight of the dark haired woman and his jovial expression dissolved into an odd frown. There was history among them.

Maybe the dark-haired woman belonged to the rumor her mother told. The woman who caused a rift between the twin Princes of Gryph. Thoughts of the dark-haired pregnant woman's connection to Jance lingered, a puzzle she toyed with.

Sol and Massie escorted her when she retired to her room for the night. Sol reinforced his hold on her left hand, as Massie walked in step with them on her right.

"I have a question," she said. "Do you think my presence is a burden to Professor Wythe? He's Mahigan. Pha told me I needed to be mindful of the stress I might place on Mahigans."

He would excuse himself if he needed to, Sol wandered. *Valgu would never have sent him if he thought there'd be a problem.*

"He's a healer." Massie said. "I bet he's mastered all kinds of reflexes. But don't torture the man, smiling at him the way you did at dinner. It's very unkind if he doesn't interest you."

"What?" Katrina asked.

Sol chuckled.

"Please don't make Valgu have to kill off his best friend," Massie said. "They've been friends since he went into the compound. It would be tragic."

"I should have just wandered my question to Sol."

"And left me out?" Massie said. "What a stupid idea."

They stopped at her door. First Sol, then Massie kissed her on the cheek and wished her goodnight. Trui stood ready as she entered her room. She worked with quiet efficiency, transitioning her from evening to sleeping attire. Trui lowered the lamps in the room.

"Is there anything else I can do for you Princess?"

"No," Katrina said as she stretched onto her bed. "Thank you Trui, have a good night."

Katrina lay awake waiting for the aches in her feet to subside. A loud bump and shuffle sounded from the Gryphon Keep. Startled, her body went rigid as she strained to hear more. Taking shallow breathes, she debated what to do. In a rush she sat up and slid from the bed. She took up an ornamental sword she had borrowed from a nearby hall. Pulling it out of its heavy sheath, she tossed the elaborate scabbard to her bed. With soft footsteps she approached the patio doors, and peeked out the etched glass. A heavily distorted window pane revealed nothing in the faint moonlight.

With a yank, she opened the door and stood ready. A large shadowed figure moved in the corner of the portico. Seeing just the outline, she had a clear enough target to attack in the dim light.

"Don't take another step," she said.

"My Princess, please. It's me," Tegija held his arms up in submission as he stepped into the light from the door. She breathed in relief, but kept her sword trained on him.

"Professor, why are you out here?"

"This is the most vulnerable entrance to your room."

"Guarding me isn't your responsibility. Sol or Massie would be here if it was."

"Prince Sol would be sitting guard here, but he can't."

"What? What do you mean he can't?"

There was a long pause before Tegija answered. "He lost more than his ability to speak clearly when he was injured. It causes him pain to fully shift into his Mahigan form. It's another reason why Valgu selected me to come here."

"Sol can't fly?" she said. "He doesn't shift?"

Tegija said nothing, and Katrina lowered her sword. Her thoughts drifted from the bolt of sorrow that hit her and loitered as she considered everything Sol had lost.

"He never said."

"It's not well known," he said.

"Yes, but I'm his sister," she said. She stared at the silent figure of Tegija and made a frustrated sigh.

There it was, even annoyed, she felt something pulling her to him. She wondered if this came from his physical Mahigan form. Perhaps some force pushing and pulling at them from their base makeup.

"You can't be out here all night," she said. "Any human who sees you here will not think you're here to guard me."

He grinned and said, "I don't care what they think. I made a promise to your brother to protect you."

"Protect me? Which of my brothers ordered that?"

"Valgu."

Shaking her head, Katrina walked back into her room as Tegija loomed into her doorway.

"I'm perfectly capable of protecting myself."

Tegija had an amused smile, but said nothing as he inspected the doorway and the surrounding area in her room.

"I am," she said.

"I didn't disagree with you," he said.

"You didn't agree with me either, and you still haven't left."

"I made a promise," he said shrugging his shoulders.

"Ugh, my brothers and all their loyal friends."

"He did mention you were training as a soldier."

"I was a cadet at a University."

"A cadet, is that different than a soldier?"

"Most of a cadet's training is like soldier's, but it's not really the same. Soldiers tend to think cadets have it easy. A few of my classmates were prior soldiers. They claimed the training was more advanced, but I couldn't say."

"But you know how to use that?" he said, pointing to the sword still in her hand.

"This," she said looking down to the sword. "Yes, I suppose I do."

She walked to her bed, retrieved the sword's sheath, and slid it back into the elaborate scabbard.

"If I had to use this particular sword it would be for emergencies only."

"Really?" He crossed his arms as she approached holding up the pommel of the sword for him to see.

"To me this blade was made for decoration, I doubt its craftsman ever intended for it to be used for anything outside of resting against a wall. Based on how the blades added to the pommel, I don't think it would last more than three strong hits."

"That would be no good after three hits?"

"I'd expect it to break, many do. It's the ugly truth of fighting with a sword. Be prepared to grab a weapon from the fallen, and flexible enough to kill with something else, or so I was taught."

"Is that your argument, to convince me to leave your patio door unguarded?"

"I didn't realize I had a chance at swaying you to leave."

"You didn't. You just confirmed my spending each night on this patio while we're here."

"Do what you will, but don't make my life harder by getting spotted out there." She shooed him back with her hand as she motioned to close the door. He stepped back and she tried not to frown at the amused smile on his face.

"Goodnight, Professor Wythe."

"Goodnight, My Princess."

11

Gryph Tour

Katrina awoke before sunrise, and with more curiosity than concern checked the patio. The bulk of Professor Wythe's shadow was visible through the door. She moved on to her dressing room and went about getting ready for the day. Once dressed, she returned to the Gryphon keep and pulled the door open.

Professor Wythe sat with his back against the portico, his legs spread out and crossed at the ankles. He awoke with a start and looked up at her with dazed eyes.

"I'm going down to eat," she said. "That frees you from your night's watch if you want to go sleep in a bed for an hour or two."

Rubbing the palm of his hand over one eye, he moved to a stand.

"I'll join you."

"Are you sure?"

"I wouldn't have said as much if I wasn't," he said with a husky voice still coated in sleep.

"Well, good morning to you too, Professor Wythe," she said, smirking at his harmless frown.

His eyes trailed down her, and when his study of her intensified, a heat rose to her face. A nervous energy pushed up from her stomach fast, like her insides turned on themselves. Trying to contain the sensation she moved through the Gryphon keep door and gestured for him to follow. Grabbing a shawl, she threw it around her, crossed the room, and exited through the main door.

The outdoor dining area was vacant of patrons. They sat sipping tea before he spoke again.

"Good morning My Princess," he said in a tone that offered an apology.

"We'll have to find you something better than stone to sleep on if you insist on pulling guard duty every night."

"I hope we travel home this week," he said.

She nodded, and poked at the fish and fruit on her plate. She liked fish, but not cold, and not for breakfast.

She considered how very close home was, and a sick nervous energy grew in her stomach. In a few days she would be home. What would it really be like? She knew her youthful ideals of home were inaccurate. What she enjoyed as a child was now quaint, and unimportant.

Memories of her family had retained the most significance. All of them were older, altered, and there were additions. New siblings, her father's new wife, Massie's wife, and a niece she had yet to meet.

Confident in her ability to accept change, fear always tried to edge its way in. Fear's most recent stake was a tough one to shake. It stuck to something she cared about, but had little control over: her ability to meet her family's expectations. The dress Sol brought, and her reaction to it, seemed to validate this fear.

"Have you always lived in Mozgas?" she said, trying to pull herself out of her anxious thoughts with polite conversation.

"I was raised in Dinhac and came to Mozgas when I was fifteen," he said.

"Why did your family move to Mozgas?"

"I was sent alone," he said.

"For school?"

His brow furrowed in confusion at her question and then relaxed.

"No, I was sent to Mozgas on behalf of my family, at the request of Regent Pavaldon. He requested my mother. She works for the Dinhac Regent. He didn't want to lose her abilities to another province. They should have sent my sister — her talent's stronger than mine, but they sent me."

"What's your family's talent?"

"A form of healing, we can see into the body. If something's broken, or not working as it should, we can identify it."

"That's an amazing gift. My father requested your mother after his poisoning?"

"No," he said. There was a mix of pity and astonishment in his eyes. "She was requested to come help you."

Gripping her teacup with both hands she shrunk in her chair.

"And they sent you, at fifteen. Before you'd even graduated the compound?"

"I wasn't the only one brought to Mozgas. Regent Pavaldon summoned healers from all over. Our charge is restoring your shifting ability."

It was strange to know she was the reason his life, and how many others, had been dramatically altered.

"Why didn't they send all of you home when I wasn't found?" she said. "That's such a long time, I'm sorry."

"Sorry? No, why would you apologize?"

An unexpected gust of wind ran through the dining room, toppling over table ornaments and rumbling dishes against the table. She caught a loose lock of hair and tucked it behind her ear as she pulled her shawl around her shoulders.

"You had to leave your family at fifteen to help someone who wasn't even there."

"I did just fine," he said with a smile. "My Regent knew he'd find you at some point. The work we've done, what we've learned in the meantime, its helped others."

Sipping her tea, she found it too strong. She set the cup down and sat back in her seat, gripping the chair's armrests. Thinking about the group of healers waiting for her in Mozgas caused a new nervous expectation to descend on her. They spent over a decade working on a method to restore her shifting ability, and what if it failed?

"I was given opportunities for school and training in Mozgas. Things I would have missed if I'd stayed in Dinhac," he said, and then gained the attention of a nearby servant. "We would like some more tea please."

The servant acknowledged his request with a quick nod, darted off. Nearby two servants struggled to tie back a massive set of curtains the wind had tossed and made a mess of.

"Valgu always gave me hope," she said. "He said there were healers who could restore my wings."

"A whole team, and we will restore them. Like My Regent, we've been waiting a long time for you to come home."

A servant brought a new cup and poured Katrina fresh tea. She smiled to see the steam rising from the cup. The confidence in Professor Wythe's eyes reassured her. It made the swirling nervousness fade and build into excited anticipation.

"Eating alone with my sister," Massie said in a cheerful bark as he approached their table. "Are you attempting to smudge her reputation Professor?" Massie yanked out the chair beside Katrina and flopped himself down in it.

"I don't think my reputation among humans concerns him," Katrina said.

"Of course it does," Massie said, his sarcasm heavy.

Professor Wythe's amusement creased the corners of his eyes. The rest of the contingent found a seat at the table.

"The woman you encountered yesterday," Massie said to Katrina.

"Which one?" He meant her mother, but part of her hoped he meant the dark haired pregnant woman.

"The one without the wedding invitation." Massie said.

"Yes?" she said.

"Her companion — I'm eager to see if you can recall the trading company he's with. Sol failed to remember for me."

"Suge trading," she said, looking to Sol to see if he really had failed Massie. Sol ignored Massie's early morning torment and nodded at her mention of Suge.

"Suge?" Inspector Ironwood said leaning forward in interest. "Are they in port right now?"

"I doubt they left yesterday," she said.

"I'll be altering my schedule then, I need to search them out," Inspector Ironwood said.

"Is it something I could help with, Inspector?" Brentin said, as he heaped a spoonful of honey into his tea.

"Perhaps," Inspector Ironwood said. "But I'd really like to see their operation for myself."

"Why is Suge so interesting?" Katrina asked.

"There's been an appeal made to the Encartha court, requesting a ban be levied against Suge vessels. Encartha's been investigating a series of rare contagious disease outbreaks in their more remote territories. Initially it was a few occurrences that seemed like a run of bad luck. Then one of Suge's sailors arrived, sick and disgruntled, to report to the trader guild in Encartha. He claims Suge deliberately infects various cities with illnesses in order to increase the demand for their commodities."

Another gust of wind ran through the outdoor eating area. The interruption startled new guests. Minister Cantor let out a sharp whoop of surprise, and some unoccupied chairs toppled over as the room braced against the wave of cold air.

"Did Encartha's court issue a ban on Suge Trading?" Katrina said.

"Not yet," Minister Cantor said, taking up a utensil to scrape away the onion garnish from her fish. "But they have sent out requests for any evidence that could support such a claim."

"Seems difficult to prove," Katrina said.

"Difficult, but not impossible," Inspector Ironwood said.

"Suge Trading is known for dealing in medicine, and poison," Professor Wythe said.

"You'll never meet a medicinal trader who won't immediately turn that accusation around and tell you all medicine is poison when taken in the right amount," Inspector Ironwood said, smiling as if he had told a funny joke. Seeing the lack of levity around him the inspector cleared his throat and grew serious. "Of course this is more than poison."

"Yes, Inspector," Massie said. "I think what the Professor's hinting at is Suge Trading's connection to the South Trident Province."

Professor Wythe nodded his head and met Katrina's gaze saying, "Where they operate from, it's one of the only places where White Fire grows as a native plant. It doesn't grow well indoors, and it's illegal for most non-native growers to cultivate. It's a very rare species of plant."

"How many trading companies come from the South Trident Province?" Katrina said.

"A few," Massie said. "But yesterday you and Sol met the owner of one, and as you recall, his companion is responsible for giving that particular rare poison to our father."

The shattering of something outside the dining area announced another interruption of wind. Katrina wrapped her shawl about her and ducked her head to lean into the invisible force blowing through the dining room. The wind rattled and chimed dishes. It stirred and rocked the wooden scaffold overhead until it creaked. The dining room sat quiet, poised and searching for signs of more wind chasing the last torrent. Katrina made use of the silence and let the connection Massie insinuated sink in.

She's a smart woman, Massie wandered to Katrina, *But someone placed the poison in her hands, and that person had something more to gain than Lord Dacamera. What was Dacamera to gain by killing the local Regent? Father gave those Skrieni the freedom to live as they wanted.*

"I don't know, I never understood what happened," she said. Her mind pulled at random memories from her time spent among the Skrieni. "She refused to tell me anything about it."

"She used Dacamara," Massie wandered. "Dacamera and that whole village of idiots died to hide the real people responsible. She did it for someone else. Someone with ties to something bigger. If you see her again you should ask how long she's really been Devon's mistress."

Katrina recognized her mother's intimate attachment to Devon the day they arrived in Etrasa. Yesterday her mother introduced him as her husband. She ignored it at the time, assuming she lied. Her mother had called Devon all sorts of things, benefactor, friend, associate, patron, lover, but what she called him yesterday was new. That was the first time Katrina heard her mother refer to Devon as her husband.

"You know what, I just might," she said.

The first drops of rain began to fall. Guests scrambled to their feet and hurried indoors. She lowered her eyes when Massie stood and offered her a hand up. Taking his hand she sighed.

"I knew I could convince you; we'll go with Inspector Ironwood this morning," Massie said.

"No, what? Why would I want to go looking for vessels potentially contaminated with disease?"

"In Gryph? They wouldn't dare," Massie said.

"Do we have to go out today?" Katrina asked. "After my years at the university I promised myself I would never voluntarily subject myself to rain."

"Not such a soldier after all. How dare you tamper with my inflated opinions of you," Massie said. "Tegija, did Katrina tell you about the beast snake she killed?"

"Massie," Katrina said.

"I would have loved to see that, my sister killing a snake capable of eating a man, but then here she is complaining about a little rain."

"Why do you keep bringing up the monster snakes?" Katrina said.

"Because that's a great story," Massie said. "Wait, snakes? There was more than one?"

"I will go with you and the inspector, but I'm not telling you that story again."

"I understand you don't want to tell your war stories this early in the morning, but I know you'll be happy to entertain our contingent with it later."

"It shocks me sometimes that a woman agreed to marry you," Katrina said.

"She didn't agree," Massie said. "She begged me."

Already exasperated by Massie, she was astonished by how sincere he sounded. They began walking towards the palace, when a loud crash shook the rafters and support beams around them. Movement in the dining room stopped as everyone looked towards the noise. A small Gryphon, about the size of a grown horse, was screaming and flopping just outside the eating area. With wings extended the Gryphon stumbled a few feet and stood panting, its eyes half closed. It squawked a series of painful cries.

Without hesitation Professor Wythe ran across the dining room and leapt over the dining room partition. Katrina and Massie trailed behind him and stood under a canvas cover. The wind snapped it repeatedly over their heads. The rain soaked Professor Wythe as he approached the injured Gryphon. More Gryphons landed near the injured one, their feathers dripping with rain. Professor Wythe spoke to them, but the wind and noise from the rain made it impossible to hear what he said.

"A healing team is on the way," Massie said.

Professor Wythe approached the injured Gryphon who took a defensive stance, before bowing its head and aiming its beak towards an outstretched wing. Professor Wythe had hold of the wing, and was manipulating it some, when a Gryph healing team arrived. Wind tossed errant bits of rain past the canvas cover. Katrina shivered in her shawl. Professor Wythe guided the medical team through the splinting of the small Gryphon's wing.

"All the Heights is going to be twittering about this tomorrow," Massie said. "Helos will want a detailed account from me. That bird is a gossip hound."

Her snickering grew into laughter, and Massie frowned.

"Why are you laughing?"

She paused to catch her breath and said, "Of all the people to complain about enjoying gossip."

"It's part of my job, there's a reason for it," Massie said.

"You mean there's a good reason you're suitable for the job," she said, and began laughing again.

"No one's ever complained about my work," Massie said. "Now keep it down, I'm trying to pay attention. There's a famous Mahigan healer out there showing those humans a thing or two."

The Gryph healers shook Professor Wythe's hand before leading the small Gryphon away. The larger Gryphons made chirping squawks of appreciation as Professor Wythe waved and walked back towards the outdoor dining room. Katrina removed her shawl and handed it to him as he scaled the partition and came out of the rain.

He looked from the shawl, to her, and then again back at the shawl as he took it, saying, "Thank you." He inspected it as if he was uncertain about what he held in his hands. He hesitated and gingerly used it to wipe the rain from his face.

"What did he break?" Massie said.

"His ulna. He won't be flying for a while, but it should heal all right," Professor Wythe said.

"You're a brave man getting that close to an injured Gryphon," Massie said.

Tegija shrugged, "I'm glad I was able to help. It'd be a crime to lose the ability to fly that young."

They found Inspector Ironwood waiting for them at the dining room entrance.

"Were you still interested in accompanying me?" Inspector Ironwood asked.

Massie pulled Katrina onto his arm and barked, "Follow me, Inspector." Massie waved and greeted his acquaintances as they walked through the common areas of the palace and proceeded to a large carriage yard. They stepped from the covered perimeter and entered one of the carriages that waited for patrons. Cold, she realized Professor Wythe still held her shawl. She hefted a wool travel blanket around her shoulders as the carriage rolled underway. Inspector Ironwood took a large ledger from his shoulder bag and sat engrossed in its contents. Massie looked lost in thought watching the rain wet streets pass by.

The morning's conversation loomed in her mind. What Massie said about her mother was a revelation, but it felt like old news. While no proof existed to substantiate it, somehow she knew it was true. Massie's allegations made all the small inconsistencies of the past line up, fall into place, and for the first time make sense.

Most importantly, it satisfied the question without a suitable answer: Why did her mother really come back for her?

Her mother's patent answer was to protect her, but that was a lie. A lie Katrina despised because it rang with a sharp falseness every time her mother said it. No, her mother brought Katrina to Lord Dacamera's village knowing the palace would search for her. Her mother needed Lord Dacamera and his village destroyed to conceal those really responsible for the attempt on her father's life.

"Are you mad about what I said this morning?" Massie said pulling Katrina from her thoughts.

"No. Yours is the best explanation for things I've been wondering about for years."

"Despite what I'm accusing her of? I mean, she is your mother," Massie said.

"Yes, she's my mother, but that's not my fault." She crossed her arms and played with the edge of her travel blanket. "You owe me an explanation. About why you insisted on bowing out of our meeting with the Crown Prince."

Massie's face soured and he shifted in his seat.

"You met the man, what did you think?"

"I got a sense of it, but you compared him to Father," she said.

Rubbing his palms together, Massie considered his answer.

"Did you see the striking pregnant woman with dark hair yesterday evening?"

Katrina nodded and Inspector Ironwood glanced up from his ledger.

"I recall her," Inspector Ironwood said. "A lovely looking woman. She had that glow pregnant women often get."

"Yes," Massie said. "Well, for a long time that woman was associated with the Crown Prince. Their relationship ended when he traveled to Bisma to wed Princess Armina."

"You question his sanity because he has a jilted lover?" Katrina asked.

"I question his sanity because he would have had Jance wed his jilted lover," Massie said.

Katrina felt her face twist in confusion as her hands twined into the edge of her blanket.

"To legitimize the child?" Katrina asked.

Massie nodded his head and looked away saying, "Chane and Jance share an unusual bond."

"Jance mentioned something like that to me once," Katrina said.

"Our friend struggles to find ways of coping with it. Meanwhile his brother Chane revels in it, enjoying the involuntary transfer of emotions, memories, and thoughts flowing back and forth between them. If Jance is with Chane's mistress, then it's like Chane is with her as well."

"That's, oh…that's enough to give me a headache," she said with a sour look.

"Do you now see my comparison?" Massie said.

"Yes, and now I wish I hadn't asked."

"That level of voyeurism is beyond…well it's very distasteful," Inspector Ironwood said as he fumbled with his ledger. His eyes wide and darting about.

For a moment they sat in quiet agreement before the carriage pulled to jarring stop at the top of a pier. Inspector Ironwood stepped down from the coach with ease, embracing his freedom from the coach and looking untroubled by the rain.

"I'll venture down," Inspector Ironwood said. "I won't object if you decide not to join me in this mess. I promise to work swiftly." He adjusted his jacket collar and stepped away, his long bird-legged stride taking him to the pier where a cluster of four ships docked.

"I feel like our trip here is a waste," Katrina said.

"When there's a break in this rain, we'll go down," Massie said.

"What for? What do you plan on learning down there?"

"We'll learn exactly how long Lady Lena's been mistress to that trading company's owner."

He had a reckless bent she was getting familiar with, but his idea to answer that question seemed strange, foolish, and necessary all at once. He watched her with a dogged look. She answered with a grin and a nod. He leaned forward and outlined his plan.

A lapse in the rain soon came. They exited the carriage and walked down the pier. The imminent threat of rain gave her an urgent desire to get this over with. They searched along the dock for a man unoccupied with hauling crates and pulling lines. They found a short man who walked and issued orders with the attitude of someone triple his size. With a hand on each hip he looked them up and down, turned his head and launched a brown wad of spit to the nearby decking.

"Are you the dock master for Suge Trading?" Massie asked.

"That's me," the man said. "If you've come down here looking for transport, Sir, I'm sorry. We haul cargo, nothing else. You'll need to travel up to Pier Five for businesses taking passengers."

"Right," Massie said. "If you'd spare us another moment, my sister was hoping to see the Mistress of your company. She and my sister became good friends in Etrasa."

"My Mistress left this morning, and she didn't say when she'd be back."

Katrina sighed, "We'll have to stop down again. I must congratulate her in person on her recent marriage."

The dock master gave her a strange look, "Then the friend you're looking for isn't my Mistress."

"I thought she said this was the pier. What's your Mistress's name?" Katrina said.

"Mistress Lena Quraishi, she's been the Master's wife since before I was hired."

"How long has that been?" Massie said.

"Oh well, I've been with Suge going on sixteen years. They'd been married long before that."

Katrina clung to the dock master's words, surprised how easy it was to get the confirmation they set out to find. The dock master had turned his full attention to them then and Katrina kept tight control over the heady excitement she felt from their success. Loitering much longer might leave an impression they preferred to avoid.

"You're right," Katrina said. "She can't be the friend I hoped to see. I apologize for the mix up in piers."

A rumble of thunder rolled above them and the sky released a new shower of rain. Katrina ducked her head to hide a small smile. She never expected to feel happy at being caught out in the rain. The dock master's attention shifted to an awkwardly tipping crate nearby, and Massie took the diversion to seize Katrina's arm and steer them away.

Massie and she fell into a jog, moving back up the pier. His smile was exuberant as they climbed into the carriage. Inspector Ironwood gaped at them dripping wet and falling into their seats panting.

"I didn't know where you two had gone." Inspector Ironwood said.

"That was fantastic, absolutely fantastic!" Massie said.

"Oh, Inspector," Katrina said, sighing as she regained her breath. "Did you have to wait long?"

"No," Inspector Ironwood said.

"We'll have the driver bring us back to the palace," Massie said. He opened the door to lean out of the carriage, but ducked back inside.

"Katrina, look," Massie said, pointing to a carriage across the road.

Devon Quraishi assisted her mother out of a carriage. Katrina held her breath as she watched her mother and Devon. The pair huddled under a lap blanket and scurried across the road and onto the pier.

"A man and his wife of more than sixteen years," Katrina said.

Massie leaned out to speak to the driver again, and Inspector Ironwood's mouth twitched as he gave her a queering look.

"Do you know Master Quraishi?" Inspector Ironwood said.

"Not really," Katrina said. "I've just heard different things about him."

They sat in the carriage and watched as the dock master hailed Devon and her mother. The fear of being caught made Katrina's heart begin to pound, as she watched the dock master gesture up the pier to their carriage. Katrina took a deep breath before stepping out of the carriage. What did she need to be afraid of? Her mother was the murdering liar.

The rain fell harder as she walked to the edge of the pier and stood looking down to the docks. Her mother shielded her eyes with one hand to block the rain as she looked at her. Katrina wanted to march down there where she could shake and scream at her mother. She stayed in place. Standing at the top of the pier, she glared down at her mother, and let her get a good look at her.

Her mother's hand fell, but they continued to stand on either end of the pier staring at one another. The small attachment she held for her mother splintered and fell away, joining the tainted mosaic shards of their history. Katrina shivered but this cold rain was nothing like the endless rain she remembered suffering in Etrasa. This rain was just a temporary inconvenience, and had no chance of inflicting the same misery it did in the past.

Massie was at her shoulder then and he gently took her arm. She moved to turn back to the carriage and saw the searching look of worry on his face. She gave him a small reassuring smile and then climbed back into the carriage.

"I'm sorry we made you wait," Katrina said to Inspector Ironwood. "I promise not to let my brother cause anymore delays to your schedule."

"My fault?" Massie said brushing water from his hair with one hand as he sat down in his seat.

"Of course it's your fault, it wasn't my idea to go down there and delay us," she said, patting rainwater from her face with the travel blanket.

"It was my idea," Massie said. "And it worked."

His plan had worked, and she grappled with the new information. Why did confirming her mother's involvement trouble her? She knew her mother was a master of deception.

This morning she uncovered another one of her mother's lies, but this one surpassed all others and changed so much. The length of time her mother maintained this deception was over fifteen years, over half of Katrina's life. Everything her mother had ever said or done, good or bad, was now questionable. It cast new light on old truths, and the wall of lies separating them felt like the Mirror Mountains, unsurpassable. The years of deception, being shut out by the wall, the endless doubts, it left her smothered in old pain.

"I'm sorry," Massie said.

"You can feel sorry for me if you want," she said. "I don't mind pity, if it means you might try to cheer me up with a treat. But please, don't apologize for things you didn't do."

"What kind of treat?"

"I have a weakness for chocolate," she said.

"Chocolate it is then," Massie said. "Thanks for going down there with me."

She gave him a small smile, and felt her smothering tension begin to ease.

She spent the afternoon in her quarters, getting dry, warming up, and regaining control over her unease. After surveying the assortment of furniture in her rooms she decided a settee bench was the best comfort she could offer the Professor turned Gryphon Keep door guard.

The settee nestled under the shelter the door's portico offered. She dragged another chair out to the portico and positioned it opposite the settee. She sat in the chair and imagined Professor Wythe opposite her, reclined on the settee while they enjoyed an evening talking.

Professor Tegija Wythe. The amount of effort she needed to keep her composure around him was exhausting. Why was she doing this? After Jance's chiding, she started to worry about her behavior around him. The chair should be taken back inside, but no. She brought it out here because she wanted to sit out here. She wanted the opportunity to talk with him.

There was more to him than physical strength, and a face she caught herself gaping at more than once. Both of these were nice, yes, but his appeal was deeper. Tegija had surpassed the phase in life where a person planned to become something. He was something. A unique strength and assuredness marked a person who no longer struggled to find their identity, and she admired him for it.

The rain created extra work for the servants of Gryph. Many had spent the day opening the winter dining hall and preparing it for dinner service. Katrina liked the more intimate space of a continuous series of small adjoining rooms. She enjoyed a meal with fewer sly looks and occasional open gawkers.

After dinner she fell into a fit of laughter as Massie moved to tell her goodnight and handed over a small ribbon-wrapped dish of chocolates. Taking it in one hand she threw the other arm around him in a hug.

"I was just joking with you," she said.

"I wasn't," he said.

"Thank you so much," she said.

"You're welcome, I'll see you in the morning."

Katrina sat in the portico with a book in her lap and the unwrapped dish of chocolate beside her. A light haze of rain continued to fall but the clouds in the sky had gained some form and the sky glowed a dim yellow in the fading light. After reading the same paragraph three times she sighed and sat back. Tegija could be there any moment and it made her too excited to concentrate on pages of words. She needed to regain her senses or she would be a twittering mess when he arrived. With a resigned sigh she clapped her book shut and moved to stand when she caught sight of movement.

She swallowed to see Tegija land at the edge of her Patio. The last time she had seen a Mahigan in shifted form, even a partial shift, was her childhood.

She sat in awe of him. Like observing the magnificence of a Gryphon, there was power and grace in his form. His silhouette looked similar to an Airetti's, with wings, except his were the taut skin and bone wings of a Mahigan. He stood with them outstretched wide, before collapsing them against his back where they melted into his body. He approached her with a calm expression carrying a sheathed sword in one hand, and a flowering plant in the other.

Katrina eyed the plant as Tegija stepped under the portico.

"Are the flowers for me?"

Tegija furrowed his brow and looked from his hand holding the sword to his other hand holding the flowers. He shook his head and held out the sword to her, tucking the plant behind his back. "This is for you."

"What's this?"

"I'm told — a weapon that can suffer more than three hits."

"Really?" She stood and set her book and chocolates on the chair. "I saw the flowers and hoped you were following the human courtship ritual of bringing me flowers."

His baffled expression made her smile. She reached for the weapon. It looked diminished in his grasp, but when he passed it to her it became an appropriate size. Fitted with a simple hilt, the sword had a plain design. It reminded her of the Etrasan training blades and she liked it.

"Does this mean you trust me to defend myself if an intruder decides to invade my room through the Gryphon Keep door?"

He grinned but said nothing.

"I see," she said. "Well then, thank you for the weapon." She set it beside the chair. Moving the book and chocolates, she sat down again. Tegija turned to the settee and stood appraising it. He sat down on it and set the potted plant beside him. Katrina held back a chuckle. Only a third of him was ever going to fit on the settee if he reclined. The way Tegija dwarfed the furniture reminded her of Thedmir, and made her smile.

"I picked that because it didn't jet out beyond the portico," she said.

"It's fine, you didn't have to, but thank you," he said.

"Where did you get the weapon?"

"I bought it."

"You picked it out?" she said, her voice betraying her astonished appreciation.

"I did, why does that surprise you?"

"I remember being taught that no self-respecting Mahigan carries a weapon."

"I'm not going to carry it." He leaned forward, resting his elbows on his knees, he smoothed his palms together.

"I wasn't trying to offend you, I'm just curious," she said. "I mean, how did you know what to buy? Did someone help you?"

Tegija shook his head. He sat up and shifted as he leaned his back against the wall. "My Regent always said to study the weapons that can be used against you; it's easier to destroy or defend against something you have knowledge of."

"My Regent, you mean my father said that?"

"Yes."

"When?"

Tegija's cheer fell away to a thoughtful stare as he looked off into the growing darkness. "Early on, when I first entered the Mahigan compound. I didn't have a mentor when I went in. They told me one would be assigned to me since all my family was back in Dinhac. That was the first time I realized how much I missed them. I went into the compound without my own father. Valgu and I met, we'd become friends. When Regent Pavaldon came to mentor Valgu, he decided to take me on too."

"I knew that's where you and Valgu met, but I didn't know my father mentored you."

"It was an honor. Regent Pavaldon elevated me to a rank no one in my family ever expected me to achieve."

"He elevated your rank? I don't know what that means."

"Regent Pavaldon was made Regent for a reason. Your father, he's one of the best Mahigan fighters there is. But I think it says a lot about him as Regent that the people of Mozgas have supported him ruling in his condition for this long. Even at half his normal ability, he's still done better work than a good percentage of his peers."

"I've always heard so little about his condition," she said.

"He's always been in a decline, but early on he had more good days than bad."

"It's interesting; I didn't know you advanced because he was your mentor."

He nodded. "Before you gain rank from things like rallying, battles, or specialized training, you get it from the Mahigan who mentors you."

"So the more acclaimed the mentor, the higher the assigned rank is?"

"Yes."

"That's a pretty big assumption — that a mentor's skills will be passed onto the Mahigan they train."

"It is, but from my informal observations, in most cases I'd say the ranking is correct," he said.

"What about Sol? Was my father well enough to mentor him?"

Tegija sat stunned, searching for the right words.

She closed her eyes, understanding the error she made before Tegija confirmed it. "If it causes him pain to shift, then he never entered the compound."

"Sol's done exceptionally well for himself, he shouldn't be judged on that."

Her eyes went wide as she let out a strangled laugh, "Of all people, do you think I would judge Sol poorly for that?"

"You're right," he raised a hand in apology. "I didn't mean for it to sound like I was accusing you."

She retrieved a chocolate from the dish Massie gave her and bit into it as she slid back in her chair. She liked the mix of bitter and rich sweetness. It melted smooth and lingered in her mouth.

"I think it's better if I'm told these kinds of things before I go home," she said. "I'd rather have some advanced warning of bad news. Otherwise, it's like I'm standing on a trap door. One wrong question and poof! I fall through the floor."

"I promise, I'll do what I can to help you. Try and steer you away from any holes in the floor."

"And what do I owe you for such a favor?" she said, popping the remaining half of chocolate in her mouth. Chewing it slow, she savored it.

"Not much," he said. "In exchange for my honesty, it's fair I ask for your honesty, and given the value of what I provide you with, perhaps your first-born child."

While he quietly laughed at his jest, her mind took an unexpected turn, considering the latter part of his request. She swallowed what was left of the chocolate, and fought a sudden nervous cough as it tried to interrupt her answer.

"It sounds like a bargain."

Her mind spun a happy and very graphic vision of how she would like to go about giving him a child. She mentally berated herself for transforming his jest into such lust filled thoughts. A more intimate part of her already warmed to the idea. Her body's rapid response proved what kind of temptation he had become.

"Seems fair, don't you agree?" he said.

"Yes," she said, her mouth dry as her face grew heated. Embarrassed, she cleared her throat and made a small laugh. "Of course."

She stood fast and moved to the door. She needed to forgo eating any more chocolate with him around. The sooner she found a servant to fetch a glass of wine the better.

"Are you going in already?" he asked.

Delighted by the question, she turned to face him. The elation running through her coursed so fiercely, she swore if she looked down she would see herself lifted off the ground. The warm sensation she hoped to deaden with wine became a storm wall of heat running up her body and into her extremities.

"Would the flowers convince you to stay?" he said, pulling the flowering plant into his lap. There was a slight pleading in his voice. It matched her own pleading desire for him. Her palms were sweating now and her guard melted from the question in his eyes. She wanted to push the stupid plant aside and crawl into his lap. Did he know his presence was enough to lure her to stay? He could lure her to do a lot of things. She was vulnerable near him, and it would be stupid to make him aware of it. Taking a deep breath she smiled.

"I know those aren't for me," she said, pointing at the flowering plant. "I'm going to go in, to get something for you and I to drink. When I get back, you're going to tell me who those are really for."

He smiled and sank back against the wall saying, "Good."

She returned bearing two glasses of red wine. As promised, Tegija explained how the Gryph Kasalli plant was for Minister Cantor. "She's an avid gardener. She mentioned wanting one, but wouldn't have time to buy one. I told her if I found one I'd get it, as long as she promised to give me a few of the seeds she can harvest from it later."

"You want the seeds?" Katrina said.

"Yes, the few patches of Kasalli in the Mozgas gardens died a few years back. We had no idea it would be as difficult as it's been to replace."

"The little blue bell shaped flowers are sweet, but why were you offering me the Minister's plant?"

Tegija held his wine cup in both hands, and considered it before looking at her with an unapologetic smile. "We're in Gryph. I can always get the Minister a plant tomorrow. Tonight might be the only night I can get you to risk your delicate human reputation, and stay out here with me."

The air felt like it was becoming thin again. She overcame a bashful urge to look away, and let herself admire his washed out gold eyes.

"I brought this chair out here especially, so I could sit and risk my delicate human reputation talking to you."

"Then I hope it remains out here, and you're willing to keep me company on the nights I swore to protect you."

She took a sip of wine, but gave no answer.

"What about this human flower tradition?" he said. "If I bring a gift of flowers tomorrow night, would they persuade you to join me?"

With a small laugh Katrina beamed and said, "It might."

"Being from a family of healers, I was raised in the garden. I can see the appeal of this human courting ritual," he said.

For the first time Katrina saw the appeal of the ritual too, so long as the man gifting her flowers was Professor Tegija Wythe.

12

Danger and Mistakes

Getting to the hall where Gryph's Queen held court was a small journey. Massie led Sol and Katrina to what he liked to call, "The big party," in the Great Hall. Katrina wore a brown gown, but one free of any figure-marring contraptions. An attendant curled her hair up in a coiled Gryph style, but no noxious plants were woven in. For the second time since the Parade finale, she leveraged her House of Etrasa training with real pride. For the first time, since she was a child, she presented herself to a monarch in true name and title.

Three evenly spaced sets of double doors served as the entrance to the Great Hall. A giant staircase dominated one end of the room, leading to a second floor gallery that ran the upper perimeter of the space. The expansive room was a vision of dark blue and gold décor, but the floor stood out most. A solid slab of rock from the Glass Mountains. She fought the distraction of staring at the dim reflections it cast of everyone in the room.

"Here, Katrina," Armina called. "My Kit Kat, come sit by me." Armina motioned her to one of the room's many sitting areas. Armina's friendliness appeared genuine, but she had already earned Katrina's mistrust. When they were introduced Armina declared, "Just because your grandfather was killed for treason, doesn't mean we can't be friends." If Armina intended to throw her off with words, it worked. She knew nothing about the death of her grandfather, Lord Jasper Larkspur.

"I can't handle all the standing anymore," Armina said, resting both hands on the swell in her belly.

Chane and Armina were expecting their first child, and guests showered her with compliments on the first maternity gown she wore to court. Katrina joined Armina and the swarm of people around her. Introductions came one after another as if she stood in a receiving line.

An ensemble played music, and the buzz of conversation grew. Servants strutted by in attire so well-cut she almost mistook them for foreign military in dress uniform.

A man's loud voice echoed over the crowd, but his words were drowned in the conversation of the room. The Great Hall fell silent.

The man's voice spoke again, "Her Royal Highness, Queen of Gryph, LaBell Willmont."

Doors in the middle doorway opened and Queen LaBell appeared. She wore blue robes and a raw silk gown the color of aged copper. A gold crown in the shape of a Gryphon's claw glinted as she walked forward. The puncturing grasp of talons held the crown in place. A symbolic reminder of the installation of Gryph's monarchy through the Gryphons they cohabited with. The people could support their ruler, but only the Gryphons ordained the human who occupied the throne of Gryph. Helping Armina to her feet,

Katrina joined the room in its collective bow to the Queen.

Music played again and conversations resumed. Chane stepped forward and escorted Queen LaBell into the room. They walked to Armina and Katrina, and Queen LaBell took Armina's hands. She lifted them and admired Armina's pregnant figure.

"Oh my, it is such a delight for me to see you like this. My grandchild just gets bigger every time I see you."

Queen LaBell released Armina, who smiled and ran a hand over her belly.

Princess Lilly Willmont embraced Queen LaBell who said, "My dear, your hair is amazing. How are you?"

Lilly smiled and exchanged private words with her mother. Her hair was amazing, a mass of black curls intertwined with silver ribbon, flowing in a coiled Gryph style about her head. Lilly shared the same navy eyes and curly black hair as her brothers, but her face held a close resemblance to Queen LaBell. Lilly spoke to Katrina once, during their formal introduction. Since then, Lilly ignored her.

Katrina's stomach twisted when Queen LaBell's navy blue eyes locked on her.

"Princess Katrina Aranysarga, the woman who has captured my younger son's attention. Your father graced us with a letter. His words were very...kind."

"Your Majesty." Katrina said.

Chane introduced Sol and Queen LaBell turned to Massie, addressing him with a familiar fondness.

"Good evening Prince Massie. How is our friend Helos?"

"Very well, Your Majesty," Massie said, smiling as he bowed his head. Queen LaBell's focus returned to Katrina.

"I am happy you're here. I hoped my son would be keeping you company this evening. I'm disappointed he's not."

Disinterested in a reply, Queen LaBell turned away and moved on to greet more guests.

Relaxing stiff shoulders, Katrina took a deep breath. She wanted to fall back on the nearest couch and put her feet up. Armina stepped close to her and spoke in Bisma.

"We should hunt for the trays of treats."

Katrina looked at Armina with a sly grin. Armina took her hand with a quiet laugh.

"I'm starving," Armina said in Bisma, "but all I want is something sweet."

Armina's Bisma flowed in elegant unconstrained waves. Speaking in Bisma with Armina reminded Katrina of her private Bisma exchanges with her mother. A rare enjoyment attached to good memories.

"Well then, in your condition we must do what we can to find the right tray," Katrina said in Bisma.

A servant lowered a wine tray in front of them, and Katrina took one. Taking a sip, she stood and moved to go. The sight of the unknown dark-haired pregnant woman stopped her. Armina moved fast to stand in front of Katrina. Armina stared down the woman with a stiff formal posture. The dark-haired woman approached Armina.

"Good evening, Princess Armina."

"Good evening. Lieutenant Salani Ansar."

The hostility in the exchange sounded sharper than any verbal fight Katrina witnessed at the House of Etrasa.

"May I introduce you to our guests," Armina said. "Prince Solyom Aranysarga, and Princess Katrina Aranysarga of the Mozgas Province in Madar."

The formality in Lieutenant Ansar's posture dropped. She frowned and stepped back. Her green eyes darted over them.

"It's nice to meet you Lieutenant Ansar," Katrina said.

With a brief nod Lieutenant Ansar moved back into the crowd. Katrina took a sip of wine, watching her go.

"It's no coincidence she introduced herself." Armina said. "I hear she's been asking everyone about you."

"Really? Someone else eager to gawk at the Veilede guests? Am I that odd she'd choose to cross swords with you?" Katrina asked.

Armina studied her for a moment and said, "Chane's right, he'd never tell you." She waved her hand in dismissive disgust, and reverted to Bisma again. "She's pathetic. Pathetic and stupid to think her charm could win a husband with the pedigree of anything outside the merchant or traders guild. I don't know why she's interested in you. The Prince who fancies you is not the one she wants."

"Jance never mentioned her," Katrina said.

"He was probably embarrassed," Armina said.

"What for?" Katrina said.

Armina touched Katrina's arm and tilted her head in a question. She lowered her voice and leaned forward speaking in Bisma, "He adores you."

Katrina looked away and scoffed, "No, we're friends." She shook her head and took a sip of wine.

"Well, if you ask him about the Lieutenant, Jance will tell you," Armina said. "He's honest this way."

Katrina felt a heat rising to her face. She took another sip of wine. Blanching at the wine's musty aftertaste, she set it aside.

"I'm going to go find Massie, and those treat trays," Katrina said.

Armina smiled as she nodded and Katrina gave her a weak smile.

Sol touched her arm and wandered, "Are we leaving?"

"I'm going to find Massie," she said. "If I find the treat tray on the way do you want one?"

Sol's eyebrows lifted and he nodded. She turned and found Jance standing behind her.

"Katrina," he said, making a long inspection of her attire. "Now this is a suitable brown dress. Don't you agree?"

"I wondered how involved you were in the attire the attendants brought," she said.

"I may have mentioned brown," Jance said. "Other than that, I knew it would be better than that thing you called a dress in Etrasa."

He stepped closer and quietly asked.

"What were you and Armina talking about?"

"Many things," she said. "Why do you ask?"

"Because you were frowning," he said.

She avoided his eyes and said nothing. The ballroom erupted in polite applause for the completion of the latest dance. Jance sighed and looked around as he took her by the hand. He walked her from the Great Hall, up a flight of stairs, and through a small door that led to the outside. Stepping off a narrow stone staircase, she tried to recognize where they were. Elevated rows of staggered seating stretched up in each direction with more rows stepping down to an arena floor. Judging by the number of Gryphon statues, Katrina guessed where they were.

"The Arena of Ages," she said.

Jance grinned and nodded his head.

She had been here before, in this exact arena. This was her first time here, but a strange chill passed over her. She remembered her cadet reading assignments on Gryph. According to those, this ancient arena was the site of most Gryphon selections. She struggled to understand why she had a vivid memory of this place.

"Chane and I played here when we were little," Jance said, leading her along a terraced aisle. He pointed to the arena floor. "Gryphons present their eggs on the arena floor before they hatch, and any unpaired wanderer can be presented to the new hatchlings. Sometimes hatchlings select their wanderer right away, but there's been whole clutches where no one was selected." Jance pointed to the upper edge of the Arena. "I was sixteen and standing over there with Chane when I was selected. Thulane flew down from the heights and wandered to me for the first time."

"What happens after someone's selected?"

"We throw a big party."

Katrina laughed as he brought them to stop by one of the Gryphon statues.

"You've been selected and given a friendship you'll have the rest of your life. It can only happen to a wanderer, and a wanderer can wait half their lives for selection. When it does happen, we celebrate."

"Do wanderers in Gryph ever get left unselected?" she said.

Jance thought for a moment. "Not that I know of, but I could be wrong."

She walked over to the base of a Gryphon statue.

"Will you talk to me now?" he said.

She turned to face him and leaned back against the statue. "I met Lieutenant Ansar."

"You met my mistake then," he said, sliding beside her and closing the distance between them. "It's good to see you fared better than I did meeting yours."

"Excuse me, what?" she said.

"Salani didn't try to kill you."

"No," Katrina said, looking away as she waved him off. "Why would she?"

"Because the baby she's carrying is mine. I'm the father."

"What?"

"She loves my brother, he loves her, and I can't tell you if I'm in love with her or if those emotions are his."

"Jance," she said, shaking her head. She crossed her arms, backed a few steps away, and walked into a nearby aisle.

"Chane and Salani were together a long time," he said.

Stopping she looked back at him. Still leaning against the statue, he kicked a heel at the stone pavers, crossing and uncrossing one ankle over the other. "Chane did as he was told, went on an extended trip to Bisma to court Armina. Salani was sick over it, and I stepped in...offered comfort."

"And Queen LaBell doesn't approve of Lieutenant Ansar."

"No," Jance said shaking his head as he ceased his kicking. "Chane's at odds with her for it. He demands I marry Salani and legitimize my child, but it's posturing. It's his way of keeping his mistress close."

His situation sounded like a trap. While the circumstances revolted her, they also riled a protective instinct for her friend. Comprehending the way his life intertwined with his twin brother's was hard. The depth of their connection mystified her as she tried to understand a bond that disabled their capacity to define their own feelings.

"Etrasa was a good escape for me," he said. "A very good break. I had time to try sort out what feelings are his and what belong to me."

"Is it possible to figure that out?"

He studied her for a long moment and made his lopsided grin.

Standing up from the statue, he said, "Yeah, I think so. Chane wasn't around when I met you."

She caught her breath and glanced away. He walked over to stand with her. She held up the hand wearing the Gryphon ring.

"This was just a favor," she said.

"Was it?" he said.

"Yes," she said.

"Are you sure? Because I'm not," he said.

"I've seen the way you look at Salani," she said.

"That's Chane," he said.

"I'm not mad about it, Jance, so don't lie to me. Seeing you look at her, it's clear how much you love her. She's carrying your child, I'd think less of you as a man if you didn't have strong feelings for her."

"Salani and I will never be together," he said.

"I know, neither will we. Just because you saw me before Chane did, doesn't magically make me the one you want."

He huffed and grasped her hand with the ring on it, raising it up between them again. "Why is it we can't be together?"

"It's a Veilede cultural rule remember? The one where a bunch of Mahigans will kill you." She bunched her hand and looked at the ring. "Then there's what Chane said."

His eyes were hard when she met them again.

"According to him, your time with the Veilede will cause all of Gryph to revolt against your mother. Queen LaBell will be dethroned, and the Willmont succession destroyed."

Scowling he shook his head and let go of her hand. "My mother runs Gryph, not my brother. No one's being dethroned."

She considered what he said. When she made no reply, he sighed and offered her his arm.

"I'm expected to introduce you. We should go back."

They descended the stone staircase, and Jance took them back a different way than they had come. They walked over a small bridge and through a set of doors into the second level gallery where Massie and Sol stood waiting for them. Jance lead them all to stand at the top of the staircase inside the Great hall. The music playing mysteriously quieted.

"Your Majesty, may I have the floor?" Jance said.

The crowd below them separated and Queen LaBell appeared. She walked towards them and stopped at the bottom of the staircase.

"Yes, my son."

"I have the privilege of introducing new friends, Prince Solyom and Princess Katrina Aranysarga, of the Mozgas Province. Brother and sister of our Gryphon-installed resident, Prince Massie Aranysarga."

A light applause erupted and Katrina watched Armina and Chane move through the crowd to stand near Queen LaBell. The applause died down as a humming sound began. It started out low, but soon a symphony of different pitched warbled humming was echoing into the hall from outside.

"What is that?" Katrina said.

Jance answered with a grin and took her hand to lead their small group down to the dance floor.

"You're not going to tell me?" she said.

"Patience, My Lady," he said.

Queen LaBell took Katrina's hand when she exited the stairs. "I am pleased we could assist you." She kissed her and Jance on the cheek. Lilly Willmont approached, extending a glass of wine to each of them.

"Jance, this. You must try this," she said, pressing one glass of wine into Katrina's hand.

"Thank you," Jance said, declining the glass. "I was hoping to show everyone here how well a Veilede woman can perform our human dances. Will you join me in this dance My Lady?"

Katrina considered him with a small grin, and had to withhold a laugh when he edged closer. His look a playful plea as he held one hand in the air waiting for her consent. Sol lifted the glass of wine from her hand and tilted his head in a gesture that told her to go.

"It would be a pleasure," she said placing her hand in his.

The ensemble began to play and in a flourish, Jance spun her around, swirling them onto the floor. Leaning in, Jance spoke quietly into her ear. "The Gryphons in the Heights are celebrating, they endorse an alliance between Gryph and Madar. But the truth is, Thulane started it. Being near you makes me happy, which also makes Thulane happy. It's the kind of happiness that makes them sing."

Hearing his words and the humming echoing his affection, twisted a knot of guilt in her.

They were surrounded by revelry, but it was forced. While the Gryphons celebrated, the court audience seethed with fake smiles and glares.

"Are you leaving tomorrow?" Jance said.

"I'd say we should just leave now," she said. Avoiding his eyes, she searched the room for a friendly face.

Sol sat hunched over in the sitting area near Armina. Massie knelt beside him with a worried look. Stopping short, Katrina left the dance, and began to work her way across the crowded room to them.

Sol? she said in a wander. Her call to Sol went unanswered. Panicked, Katrina rushed to Sol, her alarm increasing with every step. Sol attempted to stand and fell to the floor.

"Sol!" she screamed, and ran forward, pushing people aside. Massie looked at her with eyes reflecting her panic. She fell on her knees beside Sol and took his hands. They were cold and Sol's skin went grey as he strained for breath. She touched his face and moved his head to look at her.

"Katrina," he said, looking at her with mortal fear.

"What happened!" she said, looking from Sol to the crowd of strangers that stood around them.

Sol breathed in shallow gasps and he reached a trembling hand up to touch the side of her face.

Tegija lifted Sol, and she stumbled to her feet wondering where he had come from. His armored Mahigan scales covered most of his body. His eyes held a focused intensity when he glanced at her and then Massie.

"Make a path," Tegija said.

The crowd followed his order and Massie lead them from the Great Hall to their quarters. Even carrying Sol, Tegija could move fast, and she jogged to keep pace.

"It's a fast-acting poison," Tegija said.

"How do you know that?" Jance asked.

She started, realizing Jance walked beside them.

"What can we do?" Katrina asked.

"There are at least four things this could be. I think there's nothing we can do in the time we have. Do you have any idea what they put the poison in?"

Thinking of all the things she witnessed Sol eat or drink, the memory of Lilly Willmont carrying two glasses of wine flashed in her mind. Locking eyes with Jance, she passed the image of his sister in a wander, and followed it with the image of Sol draining the glass during their dance. Jance blinked with wide eyed understanding.

"Wine, it was the wine," Katrina said to Tegija. She turned to Jance. "It wasn't meant for Sol. She put that in my hand, but she also tried to give it to you. Sol took mine so we could dance."

"Lilly?" Jance said.

"Would she try and kill you this brazenly?"

"Chane, maybe. We haven't spoken in months, but he couldn't do it directly or I'd know."

"What if he hired someone?" she asked.

"It's possible," Jance said.

"That's a fine mess of speculation," Massie said.

"It's probably someone for hire," Jance said.

"If it was a hired man, he missed his mark, caused a scene, and most likely isn't going to get paid," Massie said.

"Or he's a professional with more than one way to finish a job," she said, searching each servant they passed.

"Massie, stop," she said.

Massie and Tegija stopped, and each looked over their shoulder at her.

"We should leave, right now. We need to get out of the Palace."

"Katrina," Massie said in frustration as he looked to Sol in panic.

"You said you keep a place outside the Palace," she said.

"It's for emergencies," Massie said.

"This is an emergency," she said hearing her voice become shrill.

"We're taking him to his room to lie down," Tegija said, his voice brokering no argument.

They continued on to Sol's room. Tegija placed Sol on the bed. She approached Sol, her mouth dry, and her legs trembling with each step. Sol's body arched and a rising tightness gripped her throat. She tried to deny the certainty of what was happening to Sol. Massie stood guard, his arms crossed and shoulders hunched. Tegija pressed his hands to each side of Sol's neck and looked like he was in some kind of trance. Letting go of Sol, Tegija rested the palm of his hand on his chest.

"I'm so sorry, my friend," he said.

Sol's eyes drifted open and then shut in a tight scowl of pain.

"Katrina," Sol gasped.

Her throat constricted as she realized Sol spoke with his voice and not his accustomed wander.

Tegija stepped aside and Katrina edged next to Sol and took his hand. Sol's eyes fluttered open and his gold eyes darted about searching for her face as he gripped her hand. His eyes dilated, a sheen of sweat layered his skin and dampened his clothes.

"Katrina," Sol gasped again, his voice hoarse from lack of use.

"I'm here, I'm right here," she said.

"G—g—go… home," Sol said, "My—m—my promise."

"Yes, we're leaving," she said.

"No," Sol said, struggling to form more words. "N—n—now—now, you g—g—go now." He grimaced and panted for breath before turning his face to something unseen above him. He spoke softly in strained but stunning clarity. "You must go now."

Sol's head rolled and a choked cry of pain caught in his throat as another convulsion rocked his body. Tears burned in her eyes, as she held onto a tightening and contorted hand. The convulsion ended and his body went still. Sol sagged and his head rolled limp against his shoulder. His eyes were fixed; their perfect gold color stared at nothing. Sol, her childhood companion, treasured brother, first real friend, lay dead.

Katrina screamed, as reason and all rational thought left her. An emotional pain tore at her chest while rendering the images around her into a disjointed mess. The acute onset of pain left her deaf to her surroundings, trapped in a void of impenetrable silence, leaving her unable to hear her own wailing. She barely recognized the sensation of Massie lifting her away from Sol, where she clung in desperation and cried.

13

Honorable Intentions

Several hours or five minutes may have passed, but Katrina sat unaware in a shroud of grief. Katrina's body ached, while her insides were a carved out hollow. Sol's death took away direction, and misplaced the priorities which used to govern her life. It was like facing a tossed over game, with pieces rolling in all directions. A perfect strategy lost to the floor. She sat in the moment where frustration and anger overwhelmed the need to pick it all up and play again.

A cup of tea set in her hands brought her back to the room. Tegija crouched in front of her, waiting to make sure she had hold of the cup. He watched her with a look of deep concern. She gripped the cup and the noose of sorrow eased its hold. Tegija stood and joined Massie and Minister Cantor near the center of the room.

Sol told her, "Go home now." Katrina owed it to Sol to do what he asked. Setting the tea aside Katrina rose and walked to the door. Jance was at her elbow with a look of panic.

"Katrina, where are you going?"

Yanking her elbow out of his hold she glared at him. "Home. You need to get ready to leave too. Can someone else get Thulane ready for the flight without attracting attention?"

"Leave, now?" Jance asked.

"I think you should join us. Your assassin failed, but I doubt he'll wait long before striking again. I suggest you stay near Tegija until we leave. I'll be back, it won't take long to get what I need."

Both doors to Sol's room opened and Queen LaBell entered with two guards trailing behind her. Queen LaBell looked concerned as she glided towards them. Massie came to stand by Katrina as the Queen spoke.

"I've come to apologize and offer my deepest condolences. Someone has made a mockery of my court, and the elder Gryphons are extremely displeased. They saw the heart of your brother, and while he was marked Mahigan, he never came to Gryph with malicious intent. The Gryphons intend to return him home with a funeral flight. It's his due, as a Prince of Mozgas, and a person in Gryph with honorable intentions."

"Your Majesty, we gratefully accept," Katrina said. "Please, I would like them to begin assembling now. We'll leave before sunrise."

"Wait, we're not leaving tonight," Massie said.

"Yes, we are," she said. "And Jance, please, I really think you need to come with us."

"We don't know that's what happened," Massie said.

"Have the traditions changed?" Queen LaBell said to Massie. "Do your people no longer listen when one of the first gives advice? I'm not even one of you, but I see the value in Princess Katrina's words. If I were in your place, I'd follow her lead." Queen LaBell's eyes met Jance's as she spoke to him. "I have no evidence, but I suspect she's right; you're in danger. You're seeking to bridge Gryph's future by connecting us with an old history. You pursue a way to keep us back from the precipice of war, but it's made you a threat. Gryph has become a haven for many who worship at the altars of power, money, and religious dogma. Go with your friends, and finish the task I've given you."

"It's the Gryphon's will," Jance said, with a formal bow of his head.

"It is," Queen LaBell said. Inching closer to Jance, she made a weak smile taking one of his hands. "It's what I've always taught you, and it's the one thing that's never failed me all these years. When opinions differ between humans and Gryphons, its wise to side with the Gryphons. The Gryphons say you should go, and I agree."

Jance went to his knees before Queen LaBell and bowed his head, "Yes, Your Majesty."

"When you arrive in Mozgas, deliver my apology to Regent Pavaldon. In light of what has happened to his son, Gryph respectfully declines any reward for Princess Katrina's safe return."

Queen LaBell ran a hand through Jance's hair. Fear crept into the her eyes as she gazed at her son. Sorrow filling her face despite her composed posture.

"I'll work to uncover the truth of what transpired tonight."

Queen LaBell left a short time later, issuing orders to prepare the funeral transport lift.

Katrina tensed as she stepped into it. Facing the long wooden box where Sol's body lay, her mind teetered at the edge of comprehension. No, she thought. *No, no, no.* She closed her eyes and fought the rush of sorrow making her legs quake. She needed to remain composed, do the task of sitting in the lift, and get the contingent home. Taking a deep breath, she reached for the hard discipline learned as a Cadet and used it to clear her mind. She side stepped around the wooden box and sat on a low built-in bench.

The other contingent members filed in behind her and sat on the benches. Swallowing hard, she rested one hand on the top of the box. The door to the lift swung shut and a bustle of activity was heard from people outside.

Someone shouted, "Lift's secure."

A voice further away shouted, "Gryphon harness one through four secure."

Katrina could see the dim outline of the front two Gryphons. In perfect synchronization they stretched their wings and flapped, the motion propelled them straight up from the ground. The lift gently rocked and swung, hoisted up following the rapid ascent of the four Gryphon team. The sky was a violet hue with a white cast of the approaching morning light. They pressed the limit of their goal, but achieved it. The Mozgas contingent succeeded in leaving Gryph before first light.

14

Welcome Home

The air became cold fast as they gained altitude. Tegija passed around blankets from a pile set beside him. She wrapped herself in the blanket and drifted to sleep.

The smell of pine and a bright mid afternoon sun awoke her. Tegija sat awake, but the other contingent members huddled around them slept.

"We're close," Tegija said. "We left the ocean about an hour ago, we should see the plateau soon."

The top boughs of Iron Pines sat just a few feet from the bottom of the lift. The smell of pine potent enough to work its way inside of the enclosed lift.

The Gryphons pumped their enormous wings and the lift bobbed and rocked as they rose higher. The Mozgas Plateau came into view, a mass of landfall amid a sea of trees. Sun lit up the plateau's sides. The exposed stone glowed a bright yellow beige and contrasted with the recessed shadows of blue.

The Palace, surrounding buildings, and gardens magnified until everything settled into a normal field of vision. The lift made contact with the ground in a jostling bump that awoke anyone still asleep in the transport. A crowd gathered at the edge of the field. Katrina scanned the tiny figures, searching for any familiar faces. Helos and Thulane landed nearby with Massie and Jance.

Tegija opened the door to the lift and stepped out to assist the contingent members exiting. He ducked his head back in. She still sat on the bench staring at the box that contained Sol.

"We're here My Princess."

Katrina took a deep breath, her gaze traveled down the length of the box before meeting his eyes. Gripping her necklace from Thedmir she closed her eyes and turned her face back to the box.

Tegija gave a small nod and shifted his gaze outside the lift. They remained silent for a short time before he looked at her again.

"Sometimes, the hardest step is the first one."

She turned and stared at the hand he extended out to her. Side stepping to the door, she took his hand, and exited the lift.

"May I escort you?" he asked, retaining her hand when she moved to let go of him. She nodded and he guided her hand to his arm. His friendship grounding her as she readied herself to navigate the unpredictable stress of returning home.

Fifteen years had passed since she stood on the plateau and looked at her home. Squinting into the light she saw Valgu walking from the edge of the field with three women, a young man, and little dark haired girl. The little girl broke away running towards Massie shouting, "Daddy-daddy-daddy!" Massie walked ahead of the contingent, and moved fast to scoop up the girl in a hug.

Katrina looked at the contingent members outside the lift. One of them needed to tell the awful news of Sol's death. Human customs dictated this responsibility went to the most senior ranking, which would be her.

"I should tell them?" she asked.

Tegija nodded, his expression acknowledging the importance of her task. They approached Valgu, and the others she assumed were her siblings.

When they were close enough to see the other's expressions, Valgu's excitement shifted to concern.

Katrina released Tegija and stepped over to stand face to face with Valgu.

The formal words she formed in her mind seconds ago vanished. She thought of dear Sol. How he should be the one escorting her to greet her family, not lying dead in the transport behind them. Tears constricted her throat, and dimpled her chin. She swallowed and Valgu took one of her hands.

"Tell me what's happened."

She swallowed again, but her first few words came out choked. "Sol died, he was murdered."

Valgu took a deep breath. His gaze left hers with a sudden need to search the promenade and then the sky.

"An assassin tried to kill Jance and I. The poison, it was meant for me."

"Dear God," Valgu said.

Katrina scrubbed a tear from her cheek and nodded.

"We regain our sister and lose our brother," Valgu said.

She let go of his hand and tried stepping back. Valgu captured her hand and jerked her into his arms where he held her in a tight embrace. His voice cracked as he spoke.

"We finally have you back."

She fought back tears through an intense wave of grief as Valgu held her. His breath shook and acknowledged his own suffering. Eventually he did loosen his grip. Turning her around under one arm, she caught her first real look at her siblings.

Two young women stood close, each with red hair and their father's gold Aranysarga eyes. They had mirroring expressions of bewilderment. Off to her left stood a young woman with caramel colored hair. She leaned against the towering young man beside her. He looked to be fighting tears and she ran a soothing hand across his back.

Valgu gestured to the taller red haired woman. Her long red hair was pulled back in a simple ponytail.

"Princess Nuala Aranysarga."

"Welcome home," Nuala said, extending her hand. Katrina took it and marveled at her unmistakable Bisma accent. Aside from the Aranysarga diadem on her forehead, she wore no jewelry. Her simple cut green dress was constructed in elegant fabric, but its lack of embellishments made it plain.

"It's nice to finally meet you," Katrina said.

The other young woman stepped forward.

"Princess Ilona Aranysarga," Valgu said.

Katrina tried to hide her shock as she took Ilona's hand.

"I know," Ilona said. "I'm a surprise. Don't feel bad. I surprised almost everyone here."

Ilona too had a Bisma accent. She wore her red hair in a short layered style that played off the wave in her hair. It looked untamed but somehow matched the boldness of the blue dress she wore. Large pressed silver earrings dangled from each ear, and her necklace of several uneven bands went well with her Aranysarga diadem.

"It's good to meet you," Katrina said.

She turned to the woman still comforting the boy. Chin length curls of caramel colored hair framed a face similar to Katrina's, but her body was more petite and slender. Katrina recognized the woman by her Aranysarga eyes, that were the same shade of green as Massie's.

"Owl," she said, and searched for some indication her sister remembered the same treasured childhood moments she did.

"Hello," Owl said, looking at her with the same guileless curiosity Nuala and Ilona had when they were introduced.

Logic told Katrina to expect this reaction from Owl, but she had hoped for more.

"That means you must be my youngest brother," Katrina said, looking at the tall young man whose eyes were hidden by hair.

He cleared his throat and pushed his mass of brown hair back off his forehead as he nodded.

"Prince Dermot Aranysarga," Valgu said.

Owl lay a reassuring hand on Dermot's forearm and gave an encouraging squeeze.

"It's nice to meet you," Dermot said.

"You too," Katrina said.

Massie brought Jance forward and Valgu proceeded with another round of introductions.

"Come," Valgu said, when they had finished. "Let's go inside."

Their steps rustled the dead winter grass underfoot. The only sound made through the aching silence as they walked to the palace's main entrance.

Massie came beside her bouncing Delany in his arms.

"Who did Daddy leave to go find?" Massie asked.

"My aunt Katrina," Delany said, her cheerful grin a warming sight.

"Yes, and do you know who she is?"

Delany looked over at Katrina with a smile. "She's right there."

"Are you sure that's her?"

Delany straightened her body and lifted her chin, assuming a formal posture, which was adorable to see on such a small girl. Massie must have spent hours drilling her. Delany extended her hand out to Katrina.

"I'm Princess Delany Aranysarga of Mozgas. It's an honor to make your acquaintance."

"You as well," Katrina said, taking her small hand.

"Why is your hair up?" Delany asked.

"It's how I'm accustomed to wearing it," Katrina said.

"No, you need to wear it down. Airetti wear their hair down. Daddy says so."

"Thank you for the advice," Katrina said. "But how do you know that's my form?"

Delany touched her hand over her heart and said, "God told me."

"Are you sure you don't have the eyes of a Delphi?" she said.

"I know what you are," Delany said. "You're Airetti like me."

"I am?"

Delany pointed a small finger at Owl. "So is Aunt Owl, and Uncle Aaron," Delany furrowed her brow as she thought and then sighed. "That's it. I don't know anymore."

"Uncle Aaron?" Katrina said, hoping her curiosity over rode another wave of shock, as she considered the prospect of yet another unknown sibling.

"My brother," Dermot said. "Aaron's my mother's son, from her first husband."

Katrina considered how their father met and married Dermot's mother, Miandes. She was one of the people brought back to the plateau after he burned Lord Dacamera's Skrieni village. She remembered the two Airetti boys who tried to help ease her pain after her wings were taken. The probability of her encountering two male Airetti, both from a Skrieni village, and each named Aaron seemed impossible.

"Your brother Aaron, is he the same Aaron I met in a Skrieni village as a child?"

"Probably," Dermot said.

"And the other Airetti boy I met with him, Cye?"

"Cye left several years ago," Owl said. "Cye and Aaron grew up here with us. Aaron recently moved away, but he comes to visit us occasionally."

"Aunt Katrina will live here with us," Delany said. "She won't leave."

Katrina grinned over at her niece, "Yes, that's the plan."

A sizable crowd lingered around the front of the palace. They applauded and shouted cheers of welcome to her as the Regent's family made its way up the stairs to the entrance doors. Assessing Valgu's expression, she mimicked his formal smile with one practiced at the House of Etrasa. She joined Valgu, as he turned and waved to the crown from the top steps. Mahigan guards dressed in formal tan uniforms stepped forward and opened the doors.

Valgu ushered her into the foyer where a man adorned in traditional Alvara robes approached. A thin patch of dark hair sat centered at the top of a clean shaved head. His light brown eyes complimented his deep bronze completion.

"Atton," Valgu said, "This is Princess Katrina. He's the supervisor of our Alvara Guardians here." Atton made a formal bow of his head and extended his wrapped hands.

"It's good to meet you," Katrina said taking Atton's hands in greeting.

"Your father is resting," Atton said. "His body does not obey daylight's call like it used to. I assure you as soon as he is able, we will bring him to see you."

The group moved further into the front hall. Her eyes traveled the room. Taking in elegant tapestries, the large staircase, and the binti stone chandelier. The warm wooden pieces of the parquet floor swirled in an endless floral pattern she had missed. She remembered it all. Home, she was really home. The anxiety of her return eased with the swelling contentment of standing in the home her heart longed for.

Valgu touched her arm. "It hasn't changed has it?"

"No," she said, "It's like I remember, but somehow better."

"Do we need someone to show you to your room?"

She smiled up at her brother and shook her head. "Not unless you've moved me from my old room?"

"No, but there'll be no objections when you bring me a list of improvements you'd like."

"Massie mentioned it needing a new wall coverings."

"At minimum," Valgu said. "We planned for a small reception to celebrate your return, but you arrived earlier than we expected."

She shook her head, "No, please, no reception. It wouldn't be appropriate given the circumstances. Our efforts need to focus on Sol."

"I agree," Valgu said. He pulled her into an embrace again and kissed her forehead. "I'll leave you to get settled, and see you this evening."

Valgu set off, transitioning into his normal duties with an ease that reminded her of their father. Her siblings and the contingent scattered in his wake, and she found herself standing among the bustle of the Palace's normal activity.

She turned in the direction of her room when Tegija called out to her.

"My Princess," he said.

His formality was expected, but she missed the easy manner they had developed in Gryph.

"Professor Wythe."

"I request a time to introduce you to the medical team assembled to restore your wings."

"Yes," she said. "You said we should begin right away."

"From what we've learned, the sooner the better."

"How about tomorrow morning? I doubt anyone's claimed my breakfast yet."

"Weather permitting, the Regency usually takes breakfast on the promenade. We could join you?"

"Yes," she said. "And thank you, for earlier."

"Of course," he said. His eyes were soft and expressed genuine sympathy. "I'm always available to serve you my Princess."

She wanted him to take her hand, to embrace her, touch her in a way that reinforced this connection she felt to him. Instead, he nodded a formal farewell and left in the same direction as Valgu.

She navigated her way to her bedroom without any trouble. Little in the room had changed in her absence. The bedside lamp still added its glow to the sunlight filled room. She walked over to it and lowered the inner shade, halting the glow through the flying bird cutouts. Full replicas of the flying birds danced among pastel shades of pink and gold on the walls. The decor was faded but retained its childish charm. A knock sounded from the open door. Owl stood there with an eager look.

"May I join you?"

"Absolutely," Katrina said, "I was just admiring the room. It looks just the way I remember. Minus the storybook paintings that hung over there."

Owl looked to the wall she pointed to. Three faint rectangle outlines marked out where the paintings once hung.

"Delany liked them, and Father had them taken to her room. Only Delany, anyone else he'd have throttled for asking."

"We used to spend a lot of time in here together," Katrina said.

"I wish I could remember it," Owl said. "Valgu, Sol, and Massie used to make me jealous with their stories about you. I could remember your face, and this one memory of us flying to see a bird's nest."

"A swallow's nest. You used to sing to the babies."

"Yes," Owl said, and smiled. "I remember that."

"You were tiny when everything happened."

"I was. My memories of then are mostly of my mother and Lady Tellydia's funeral."

"I don't envy you that," Katrina said.

"It's also when my empathy talent came to full fruition. I can't really remember what my life was like before it set in."

"Empathy talent," Katrina said. "You can feel what others feel?"

"Can feel?" Owl said with a laugh, "No, I do feel what others feel. Like it or not, I feel it. It's exhausting. I can only block the emotions of others for so long. Massie calls me a recluse. Maybe I am. If I could control it I'd be a better asset to the family."

"What do you mean?" Katrina said.

"I can't be the public figure Valgu wants me to be. I don't have the stamina for it. I even passed up attending University because I can't handle large crowds. If I were normal, I'd already be the Acting Regina for Mozgas."

"Are there no other Airetti in Mozgas?"

Owl shook her head, apologizing with her eyes. Katrina turned away. Home less than a few hours, and she faced the real-life prospect of taking on the role of Acting Regina. Crossing her arms she walked to her bed and inspected the state of the linens.

"I'm sorry, it's not my place to mention it," Owl said.

"No, you're allowed, we're sisters."

"I expect Valgu will eventually broach the subject of Acting Regina with you."

"Is that why Cye and Aaron left?"

Owl adjusted a gold bracelet on her wrist as she considered her answer. "I think so, yes. I've tried to help Valgu as much as I can. I go and observe meetings now and then. I've never had guided moments during any of them, but I do feel out when someone's hiding something or telling lies. Valgu says it's useful. Massie took me to Bisma to do the same sort of thing once or twice. I'm happy to help, but I can't manage it everyday. It's too much."

"That's understandable," Katrina said. She pulled back the top coverlet and smiled at the sight of fresh linens. She sat on the edge of the bed, as Owl settled in the ornate chair beside the bed. "Well, do you want to help me figure out what to do with this room?"

Owl grinned and gave a light chuckle. "I'd love to. I enjoy a big design project."

"Sol mentioned your design work."

"Sol," Owl said. "My greatest advocate."

"He was one of the best parts of returning home."

"It feels like he'll still return home. That he's off traveling and will be back soon. Sol encouraged my design work. It's what I spend most of my time doing. Usually I create dresses and garments. But, I'll gladly help redesign this room with you."

"Maybe you can help me with some dresses and garments too," Katrina said.

"Yes, of course," Owl said, sitting forward in excited interest. "Nuala and Ilona won't let me do a thing for them. They grew up with a master seamstress in Bisma. The one time I offered to teach them about Veilede fashion, they both took offense."

"Really? Well, you won't offend me. All my experience with fashion is human. I think the only clothes I own that match Veilede taste is the dress Sol had you make for me, a few undergarments, and one pair of shoes."

Owl laughed and Katrina smiled, admiring the way Owl's laugh remained the same. Loud, free, and wonderful.

"We'll fix that," Owl said.

They spent the morning discussing clothes, what colors to use in her bedroom, and where they should acquire some Veilede garments for her to wear as custom items were made. Owl introduced her to the servants assigned to the family quarters and they were soon notified about lunch on the Promenade. They sat down at a large table centered in a wide expanse of grass that ran between the family quarters and the gardens. Nuala and Ilona were already seated and adding honey to fresh cups of tea.

"May I pour for you?" Nuala offered.

"Thank you," Katrina said.

"Yes, please," Owl said. "How was your morning?"

"Boring," Ilona said.

"It wasn't, it was fine," Nuala said.

"Reading—all we did was read this morning," Ilona said. "It was boring."

Nuala groaned and Ilona gave her a look that dared her to deny it. Katrina grinned at their banter.

"Massie said you trained to be an officer," Ilona said.

"Yes," Katrina said. "I attended the University of Etrasa."

Nuala's eyebrows rose with recognition, and Ilona gave a low chuckle as she sipped her tea.

"You've heard of it?"

Ilona set her tea down and laughed harder as she lightly hit Nuala in the shoulder. "Nuala was in love with a Bisma Officer who graduated from that University."

"Illie," Nuala said in a chastising tone.

"Lieutenant Collins was very handsome, light hair, dark eyes. Nuala insisted on doing all of his alterations herself."

"He was a very nice man," Nuala said. "I never said I was in love with him."

"You didn't have to."

"Illie, stop."

"Do you prefer to be called Illie or Ilona?" Katrina asked.

Ilona shrugged, "Either one."

"Where were you living in Bisma?" Katrina asked.

"Osnovo, right near the opera house," Nuala said. "We lived and worked with the head seamstress for the Bisma Opera."

"It's where Massie hid us after our mother was located," Ilona said.

Nuala frowned at Ilona who ignored her.

"Lady Juniper?" Katrina asked.

"Yes," Nuala said.

"Is she here?" Katrina asked.

Her sisters looked at each other and then stared back at her with an awkward frown. They exchanged another round of looks as they decided who would be the one to answer her question. Nuala almost spoke when Ilona cut her off with a huff of frustration. Lifting her tea, Ilona answered.

"Dead."

The worst answer Katrina could imagine, and in her mind she had succeeded in falling right through the floor. Sitting stunned for a moment, she tried to find a response. This exact situation was the kind she worried about when she thought about coming home. Her surroundings were as familiar as breathing, but life here felt sharp and foreign. Every interaction forced her to take social risks. So far she botched most of them.

"I'm so sorry," Katrina said in wide eyed shock. "Truly, I had no idea."

"It's not her fault she didn't know," Owl said.

"I didn't know you grew up in Bisma," Katrina said. "I knew nothing about Nuala or your mother until a few years ago. And this morning, Ilona, you were right. I didn't know about you until we were introduced."

Ilona shrugged it off and sipped her tea. "That's all right, neither did our Regent."

Nuala gave a solemn nod.

Dermot approached the table and flung himself down in a chair beside Ilona. Turning to him, Ilona reached up and ran a hand through his bangs in a futile attempt to tame them back as she greeted him in Bisma. "Hey, *mozni bracisz.*"

"Mighty Brother," Katrina translated.

Dermot extracted Ilona's hands from his hair and did his best to hide a smile.

"He's our little brother, but he's mighty," Ilona said.

Dermot blinked at her in annoyance. "I'm a full year older than you."

"I've seen him practicing for the compound," Ilona said. "He's very *mozni.*"

Dermot leaned forward, grabbed a roll from the basket, and tore it in half. He stuffed one half of the roll in his mouth and chewed.

"We should have Katrina watch him practice," Owl said. "She's the only one seated here capable of judging if someone's truly *mozni.*"

Dermot's gaze met Katrina's. She saw the question in them as he assessed her before they darted back to his plate.

"Perhaps," Katrina said, before sipping her tea. "But as a Mahigan, Dermot's innate abilities are superior to many with years of practice. I'd wager *mozni* is a suitable nickname."

Dermot quirked a smile as he chewed and peeked at her from under his bangs.

"Where's Massie?" Ilona said, with heavy irritation in her tone.

"We haven't seen him since this morning," Owl said.

Dermot shook his head and took a bite of cold chicken.

Nuala studied Ilona's somber expression and said, "I think he would have said something to us if he knew anything."

"We're talking about Massie," Ilona said. "Not Sol."

Owl set her utensil down and covered her mouth as she laughed. Dermot leaned back in his chair smiling as he pushed his bangs back with both hands. Nuala smiled over at Ilona who sat rigid with frustration. An ache ran through Katrina as she thought of Sol. Then she too smiled at Ilona's humorous stab at Massie's nature.

"I'm not even asking," Katrina said. "I've created enough awkward lunch conversation for one day."

"Don't either one of you say one word about it in front of Delany," Owl said, pointing at Ilona and Nuala. She turned to Katrina and explained. "Massie's wife, Bedelia, is missing. Father's men brought Nuala, Ilona, and Delany here without her."

"She's been missing for months," Ilona said.

"And we'll have a distraught little Lany the rest of the day if you don't watch what you say," Nuala said.

"I know that," Ilona said. "Thank you very much."

Owl straightened in her chair, her eyes fixed on something across the promenade behind Nuala and Ilona. Seeing the change in Owl, Nuala and Ilona glanced over their shoulder. Dermot got to his feet, then Owl stood. Trusting they needed to do the same, Katrina, Nuala, and Ilona joined them. Peeking around Nuala, Katrina caught sight of three people moving in their direction. Her breathing stopped. It was her father. He approached flanked by two Alvara guardians, Atton on his left, and a grey haired woman on his right. He had a pleasant grin, and confident posture.

A deluge of thoughts descended on her as she tried to determine her best response. Edging away from the table, her legs trembled. She sucked in a breath and tried to breathe away the nervous energy creeping up her legs. Her hands and arms started to tremble. Self-doubt roared in her mind. She needed to stop second-guessing her instincts. It was making the transition home harder. Finding courage, she took a few steps forward.

Noticing her, he faltered. The look in his eye hardened. Unable to read his expression, Katrina stopped. Her father kicked into a run. In less than a full breath, his Mahigan speed brought him to a halt before her. Edging back in surprise, she stared up into wild wide eyes.

"Father," Owl said.

Something was off. She heard fear in Owl's voice, and saw her father's bizarre look. Her heart raced as all her base instincts told her to run. The thump of her own heartbeat drowned out raised voices and panicked shouts.

Her father lifted his right arm. Flicking his wrist, a long black Mahigan weapon emerged. It flowed from the skin beneath his palm and landed in his grip.

"Lena," he said.

"No!" Owl screamed.

The ingrained defensive habits of her University training kicked in. Her best option was to avoid his blow. His close proximity and speed made that impossible. She would take a hit. She readied her stance. She needed to accept a blow she could recover from. She moved, jumping in the direction his weapon traveled. It bit into her left side as she skidded sideways along the grass. Seized with terror, she watched as her father lifted his weapon to strike.

A burst of light blinded her. Disoriented she blinked, and saw nothing but white. Like seeing through a dense fog, her vision returned. She craned her head up. Her father lay sprawled on his back. A wet warmth dampened her left side. Looking down she found the clean cut through the side of her dress. A gash beneath it stained the opening and surrounding fabric with bright red blood. More time lapsed than she expected before the burning pain hit her. By then a swarm of people and activity surrounded them.

Hoisted from the ground, she cried out from the pain.

"I've got you, hold on," Dermot said.

Her younger brother, the one she met just this morning, carried her at a run. He took her off the promenade and into a side palace entrance. He ran at an alarming speed. She leaned into him. Holding his jacket front with one hand, and grasping part of his sleeve with the other. Digging her fingers into the fabric, she shut her eyes against the pain. She heard the alarmed voices. Doors opened and others slammed shut. Then came the steady authority of a voice she recognized.

"Take her in there and set her down," Tegija said. "Someone fetch my son, hurry up."

Her eyes flew open. Tegija's words served as a fitting distraction from the pain. He had a son?

Dermot laid her on a bed. He backed away as Tegija and two others crowded in. She inhaled sharply as Tegija cut her dress away to expose the wound. He moved up and met her eyes. Leaning over her he wrapped his hands around her neck. His hold could be the intimate touch of a lover or the strangling grip of an enemy. She knew it was neither, and tried to relax under the light weight of his fingers. They pressed where her heart beat the strongest. His eyes left hers and took on some far away look. Someone pressed against her wound and she stiffened, biting back a groan of protest.

"Keep breathing," Tegija said. "You're going to be fine. We can mend this."

She swallowed and grimaced as she tried to do what he ordered. A younger version of Tegija appeared beside him. He had his father's hair and eye coloring. She stared at him in disbelief. What else was going to go wrong today?

"Where's Bastion?" Tegija asked someone behind him.

"Here," came a male voice from another room. "I've got it ready," said a man with dark hair who entered the room bearing a tray.

"My Princess," Tegija said, "We need to roll you onto your good side."

She nodded and gentle hands assisted her onto her side. The man with dark hair knelt at her bedside. He placed a steaming pot near her face. She recalled the last time she saw one like it. The healer who helped her before she was taken to Etrasa.

"Take deep breaths," he said.

Steam wafted against her face and filled her lungs. Her eyelids became heavy and with her next breath sleep descended.

"Katrina?" Massie called, tapping on her bedroom door as he entered. She rolled and grimaced at the tender twinge of pain in her side. Blinking, she opened her eyes to the bright sunlight filling her childhood bedroom.

"Yes?" she said, her voice a dry rasp.

"The healers were asking if you were awake yet," Massie said. "I promised to come in and wake you."

"Massie," she said, groaning in protest as he stopped beside her bed.

Another set of footsteps came from behind Massie. Tegija's son edged around Massie and smiled down at her.

"Good morning, My Princess," he said. "I'm here to check on you. This won't hurt." His hands encircled her neck in the same way his father's had.

"You look like him," she said.

"Eleric Whythe, My Princess. It's nice to meet you. You're much more dehydrated than we expected."

"I could use a drink of water," she said.

Eleric walked over to a pitcher and poured her a cup of water. He handed it to her as Tegija entered the room.

"Good morning," Tegija said. "Looks like Eleric beat me here."

Eleric smirked at his father and turned his attention back to her. "Try and take your time, no big gulps. Small sips."

"Small sips," she parroted, and drank the way he directed. She watched Tegija cross the room and stand near the foot of her bed. His gaze met hers and his features softened with a small reassuring grin.

"He's very protective My Princess," Tegija said motioning with his head towards Eleric, who subordinated his posture and moved to stand alongside his father. "Eleric recently came on board with your restoration team. You're one of his first important patients."

"Thank you, Eleric, for your expertise," Katrina said.

"The worst of the pain should be gone," Tegija said. "If I'm wrong, you'll need to let us know. You're free to get up and move around. No riding, heavy lifting, or strenuous exercise for at least a week. Otherwise, you should be feeling more like yourself again."

Taking another sip of water, Katrina took in the sight of Eleric and Tegija standing side by side. The mature filled out form of Tegija contrasted against the youth of Eleric. Valgu and Tegija were close in age, which made Tegija around thirty years old. This meant Tegija fathered Eleric near the age of seventeen or eighteen. The probability of a Mahigan that age winning a rally seemed impossible. Most Mahigan's would have just left the compound. There were other possible explanations, but the news of his son troubled her.

He never mentioned a wife or a son. Who was Eleric's mother? Who could she aim this new despicable jealousy towards?

"It's time we left," Tegija said.

She took another sip of water and watched Tegija and Eleric go. She wished the water were wine, and she could take huge gulps to deaden this new tumult of ugly emotions. She wanted to lay back and fall into an instant sleep, or wake up and learn Eleric and his unknown mother were all part of a dream. She looked over at Massie who lounged in her ornate chair. She motioned for him to come closer. When Massie leaned over the edge of her bed, she beckoned him closer. Massie leaned in more, eyeing her with a questioning look.

"How many days did I sleep?"

"Several," Massie said.

"How many?"

"I want to say three?"

"And no one's bathed me during that time."

Massie grinned holding back a laugh. Katrina shut her eyes with a grimace. Reaching up, she grabbed the front of his vest and pulled, forcing him up off the chair and directly over her. She spoke in a low voice.

"If you ever let that man in my presence with me smelling like this again, I will kill you."

Massie narrowed his eyes and smiled.

"I'm happy to see you're back to your usual self," he said.

"Oh dear God, I stink," she said pushing Massie away. "I smell-not good," her voice rose in agitation.

"I don't think he cares," Massie said.

"I care."

Massie chuckled and shook his head at her saying, "He's a healer, he deals with smelly sick people all the time."

"Find someone to help me take a bath before that brilliant man or his perfect son come back."

Massie's eyebrows lifted in interest. He sighed as her squinting glare persisted. "I'll see what I can do."

A small army of servants arrived to help her bathe and dress. There had to be five of them, and she wondered if this much attention was typical. Amazed, she gaped at the wound in her side. She expected to find stitches and a scabbed over wound. Instead, a neat line of bright pink scar tissue marked where her father's blow landed. The muscles underneath ached if she twisted her torso or leaned over, but it was nothing to complain about. She had heard about healers with the talent to bind wounds together. They possessed one of the rarer gifts among the various healing talents.

An attendant fastened the back of a modest deep blue Veilede dress Owl had picked out for her. It covered her back, but the boatneck collar held the dress up by two narrow margins at her shoulders. She stood before a mirror in her bathroom watching another attendant comb out her hair. There was little style in the Veilede fashion of wearing hair down. Her hair flowed over her shoulders. She considered the look unsophisticated, and more suitable for a child.

There was a knock at the door and she heard the attendant's formal greeting.

"Prince Valgu, good afternoon. Yes, she's dressed."

Katrina stepped into the bathroom doorway and waved off the attendant still fussing with her hair.

"Am I interrupting?" He asked.

"No, I was going to find something to eat. I'm feeling a little weak on my feet."

"May I join you?"

"Of course."

Valgu offered his arm, and she took it as they walked together out onto the promenade.

"None of us anticipated what happened with Father," Valgu said.

"I know," she said.

"I'm grateful you're okay," he said.

She stopped and faced Valgu before they reached the table.

"You should have told me about what he did in my absence."

Valgu held a calm face of authority as he answered. "I told you returning home was dangerous."

"You did, but you left out a lot of important details."

"I did what I thought was best," he said.

"Leaving me to find out about Nuala and Dermot from Puternic. Why are you so set against giving me information?"

"There's really no way to adequately warn anyone about Father."

She sighed and urged him to continue walking to the table.

"I'm sorry. I didn't know Puternic told you," he said. "That should have been me."

Tea and a covered food tray sat ready for her at the table. Katrina lifted the cover and set it aside before sitting down. She poured the tea. Valgu added nothing to his tea and smiled when he noticed she did the same.

"You were a fan of honey, what changed?"

"Cadet training, I grew accustomed to plain." She pressed her lips together. He might think the topic neatly finished, but no. "Why didn't you ever tell me about them?"

Valgu sighed and sat back. His posture still perfect in the way it commanded authority. "Nuala and Ilona were in hiding, like you. They, too, knew nothing about you. If either of you were compromised, the other could remain safe in hiding."

"Dermot was never in hiding."

"It wasn't from a lack of trying," Valgu said. "It's good you're wearing your hair down."

"I look like I'm twelve," she said.

"Twelve," Valgu said furrowing his brow. He scoffed, "Hardly. No, dressed like this you shouldn't be mistaken for your mother."

Katrina sipped at a spoonful of soup. The broth was thick.

"Have you considered what you'd like to do now that you're here?" he said.

She dipped her spoon again.

"I've thought about it, and I don't know. Most of my plans were focused on getting home. I'm here, and much of Mozgas feels new to me. It's a whole different place as an adult."

Valgu nodded his head and grinned with quiet understanding. "You're happy to be home?"

"Yes," she said. "And I'll be happy being wherever you think I can be of service."

"You spent some time with Owl. Did she mention how she helps me from time to time?"

"Yes."

Valgu cleared his throat and said, "We wanted her to step into the role of Airetti Guide."

"And she can't manage it," Katrina said.

"No, it's really too much for her," he said. "But with you home, we need you to consider it."

Tension rolled her stomach. Realizing she held her breath, she refilled her lungs with a sharp inhale.

"You want me to work as the Airetti Guide? I don't know how to do that."

"Everybody has to be a novice at one point in their occupation. That's just how it works," he said.

"Isn't that the role of your future wife?" she said.

"There're no guarantees for me or my future wife. Yes, husband and wife teams make things simpler, but you and I will not be the first brother and sister Regent and Regina. Sepihne is the Regent of Milios and his sister Rosalba is the Acting Airetti Guide." When Katrina said nothing he pressed, "I'm only the Acting Regent."

"Valgu," she said with a scowl. His statement was ridiculous. All of Madar considered him the Regent of Mozgas. "No one's going to contest you."

Valgu's lips pressed in a hard line and he sucked a breath through his teeth. "Listen, we need you to consider the role."

"Is that why you decided to bring me home?"

Valgu shook his head. "No, you know why we needed to do that. Look, the timing's what it is. Father wants to install you as the Airetti Guide, the Regina of Mozgas."

"I don't know. What happens when you become Regent? When you decide to rally and marry?"

"You would lawfully remain the Guide," he said.

"What about me? Will you forestall my rally until after Father's death?"

"No."

"But wouldn't my installment before yours mean my husband could make a claim for the Regency?"

"That doesn't concern me."

"It should; why would you want that potential conflict?"

"The odds are in my favor," he said.

"Are you boasting?" she asked, holding back a smile.

"Is it bragging to state a fact?"

She sat back and sunk in her chair. Gripping at her necklace from Thedmir she shifted in her seat. Anxiety wormed its way into her demeanor, and her control cracked. Straightening, she let go of her necklace, and lingered over her answer.

"I didn't expect you'd want me to be in such a visible role, right away."

"Is there a reason we should wait?"

"Me, making a fool of myself, and in the process embarrassing our family."

"I'll be with you."

"It's awful, I feel awful. I don't know half my family. I know more about human customs and politics than I do about my own people."

"So you'll learn. Your experience is an asset."

"Even when we're at war?" she said.

"Especially then, and we won't always be at war," he said. "We need to think beyond the conflict."

She tried to imagine what about her human experience would serve as an advantage in the Veilede world.

"I did say I wanted to be of service."

"Yes, you did," he said.

"I guess, if it's really that important, and you're willing to accept the risk. It can't hurt to try."

"Good, you can start accompanying me the day after tomorrow."

Her eyebrows raised and she made a tight smile. Valgu came around the table, bent over, and kissed the top of her head.

"I must go, but I'll see you later today," he said.

He had what he wanted and was leaving before she had the opportunity to reconsider. He stepped back into the palace, and she wanted to chase him down and retract her consent. While his confidence in her was reassuring, she felt paralyzed by the enormous responsibility.

Rolling onto her back, a pang in her side roused her awake. The small bedside lamp cast long warped shadows. She guessed it was middle of the night by the gloom outside. A dry paste coated her mouth. It taste awful. Lying awake, her eyes adjusted to the dim light. She studied the place she used to wish to wake up in. How wonderful and odd to be home and laying in her bedroom.

A shadow moved at the corner of her eye. Someone leaned forward in the ornamental chair. A scream caught in her throat. Lamplight revealed the intruder, her father. She froze like a cornered animal.

He had the same straight shoulder length blonde hair, only his hairline had receded at the temples. Even with laugh lines marking the edges of his eyes, they were the same shape with the perfect shade of gold she remembered.

"I hope I didn't wake you?" Pavaldon said.

Katrina lay in shock. Nothing about him seemed off.

"I couldn't help myself," he said. "My Katrina, home, finally. I had to see you, and prove to myself you're really here." Pavaldon gave her a small grin and rubbed his hands together before lacing his fingers and resting his chin on his hands. "It's amazing to watch any of my children sleeping. Your faces, they relax, and I marvel at how in sleep you each take on this look like you had as sleeping babies. I hadn't seen yours in years."

Pavaldon's well-dressed figure looked odd seated in such a feminine chair. Apprehension held her still.

"Do you remember me?" Pavaldon said, a worried frown deepening on his brow.

An uncontrollable tidal wave of emotion hit her, as she nodded a frantic yes. Her reunion with her father held none of the one-sided affection she experienced with Owl. Her love for him erupted as her heart began an impassioned song of adoration. She missed him more than she ever realized.

"Yes, Father." She said.

"I abhor what I did."

She reached out her hand to him, and he leaned forward to take it in both of his.

"I hope you can forgive me," he said.

"Yes," she said.

He stared at her, searching her face.

"I've never forgiven Lena for stealing you. I can see Lena in you, but I sit in wonder at what I see. My perfect blue-eyed baby girl. My Katrina, look at you, a strong woman resting in a nursery so old it's turned into a mausoleum. It is such a joy." Still holding her hand in one of his, he sat back and leaned on one of the chair's armrests. "I was told you trained to be an officer."

She restrained a nervous cough, as she tried to find her voice.

"Yes. It's how I was able to attend university. I hope that's not a disappointment. I, well I-" She tripped over her words.

"Disappointment?"

"My human upbringing," she said. All of her recent worries seemed to rush forward. Concerned her former human life might cast a shadow over her future life in Madar.

"None of that's a reflection on you," he said.

"But attending the University, it was my idea."

"I'm happy you're alive," he said. "To have you back, I hardly care how you spent each day."

"There is so much I don't know," she said.

"You were always a clever girl. I'm not worried," he said.

"Is my upbringing, will it...will I?"

Pavaldon laughed and a smile stayed on his face. "It's nothing. We'll say its given you a broad outlook and leave it at that. No, I was curious, Valgustatuile mentioned it to me. It made me laugh because I remembered how much I secretly reveled watching you hold your own with your brothers. My Katrina, a girl ever able to give back what Solyom and Valgustatuile tried to give you. I would have enjoyed seeing your training."

His words and this moment were such a relief. To talk and see him well. She was blessed with one of his genuine lucid moments. She willed it to continue. In one blink he could change and fall away into the sickness that dominated him. Grateful for this reunion, she wished she never had to see him sick.

"There's nothing of our people you can't discover or rediscover and make your own," he said. "As for me, you're my daughter. It's impossible for you to do anything that will stop me from loving you. All of you, it's imperative you all remember that. Change is coming, you being here is proof of it. I don't want any of you to forget that when I'm gone."

"I won't," Katrina said.

She gloried in this rare precious moment with her father, and grieved knowing at any moment he might be gone. He stood up and bent down and she embraced him.

"Stay in Madar, Katrina. Let me watch over you with what time we have left. No matter what happens I want you to be who you are, strong, and don't be afraid when it comes time to take on your future. Will you do that for me?"

"I will," she said, as he released her.

He kissed her forehead.

"I love you. Welcome home."

She dawdled the next evening, finding a hundred small tasks more important than dinner. After reminding her several times of her need to go, one of the servants had the gumption to stand over her with a shawl.

"My Princess, they might postpone until you arrive."

Katrina took the shawl the servant, Tilly, handed her. A timid woman with blonde hair, she had small hands and a quiet manner. The best sort of woman to be prodded by.

"Thank you, Tilly," she said.

Approaching the dining room, her hands began to sweat. She tried drying them on her shawl. How odd, she walked Parade in front of hundreds of people, but entering a dining room full of her family gave her sweaty palms. The strange sensation of her hair hanging about her shoulders and back added to her distress. The only time she wore her hair down was to go to bed, and without her hair braided she felt like her diadem was slipping out of place. For the third time since leaving her room, she pressed her fingers along the front of it to ensure it had stayed in position.

Standing outside the dining room, she reached to open the door when she heard a familiar voice call to her.

"My Lady."

Jance walked up behind her as she turned around. He wore a formal custom fit jacket. Its blue trim complimented his eyes. Seeing him, she brightened. Her mood lifted knowing she would enter the dining room with a friend.

"I heard," he said.

"I expect everyone in Madar has," she said.

"I'm glad to see you recovered. You left me with only Massie around to talk to. That was highly unfair."

Katrina scoffed, "And for a moment I was happy to see you."

Jance bowed his head in a friendly greeting. "My Lady, I know you're as thrilled to see me as I am you."

"Walk in with me?" she said.

He smiled and offered his arm, and she took it as they entered the dining room. Everyone in the room stilled and turned to gawk at them.

Cast metal statues paraded down the center of the table depicting people doing activities in winter. A man pulling a child on a small sleigh. A horse drawn carriage fitted with skids. Boughs of Iron Pine and open pine cones completed the decor and filled the room with its refreshing fragrance. The table dressings marked the seasons and Katrina remembered how they changed at the start of each season. These would soon transition.

"This way, My Princess," a servant said motioning for her to follow.

Katrina and Jance walked along the long side of the dining room table past Ilona, Nuala, then Valgu. Katrina's step almost faltered at the sight of her father seated at the head of the table. His eyes were fixed on another part of the room. He wore an odd blank expression, like he was lost in a prolonged day dream. They passed where he sat at the head of the table, and then the short Alvara guard seated to his left. The servant motioned to the empty chair, on the opposite side of the table from Valgu. She sat and watched as Jance went down to a seat past Massie, Delany, and Dermot.

She looked at her father and the uncomfortable way he held one shoulder raised. She wondered how aware he was of his surroundings. His demeanor remained unchanged through the first course. They were eating the second course when the entire table jolted and her father stood up.

The servants halted their activity and left the room. Their precision made her wonder how often this sort of thing happened. Pavaldon moved from his seat and chased the last servant from the room. He slammed the door behind them hollering a stream of gibberish. Returning to the table, he moved to sit, then keeled over, throwing himself on the floor. His Alvara guard stood by watching with calm vigilance. Shaking and thrashing, Pavaldon mumbled an undecipherable rant.

Nuala appeared the most shaken by their father's outburst, sinking into her chair with wide eyes and trembling hands that gripped the edge of the table. Jance sat stiff with his back braced against his chair. Owl's lips moved in a silent prayer. Massie and Dermot reached to comfort Delany who hid her face in Massie's side. Katrina looked across the table to Valgu who ate his food unfazed by the situation. Trying to follow Valgu's example, she picked up her utensils and focused on her plate. A few minutes passed before the rest of the table joined them and ate. No one spoke and the occasional thump or bang sounded as Pavaldon rolled back and forth on the floor shouting unintelligible words.

The silence at the table broke as Ilona shrieked. Toppling her chair back, she scrambled to a stand, and backed away from the table. Her raised finger gave a silent warning, but who she aimed it at was unknown.

"Out, now!" Ilona shouted at the empty space in front of her. "Get out of here! I know what you are, and I command you to leave."

A chill ran up Katrina's back and down her arms. She dropped her utensils and sat back balling her hands into fists as she scanned the table trying to find who or what Ilona spoke to.

Ilona heaved a deep breath. She tucked hair behind both ears and relaxed her shoulders. She collected her chair. Delany stood on her chair bouncing up and down in glee. Massie tried to settle her but Delany laughed.

"You did it!" Delany said, as she bounced and clapped.

Ilona grimaced as she flopped back in her chair before leaning forward to grasp her water glass and drink its contents with a few long swallows.

Delany wormed out of her chair. She ran to the front of the table where Pavaldon sat on the floor. Crawling into his lap, she held his face between both of her little hands.

"Hello Grandpa," Delany said.

"Hello little Princess," Pavaldon said before swooping her up in a cradle hold and rising to his feet. Carrying Delany, Pavaldon returned to his seat where he slowly took inventory of everyone seated at the table. When his eyes landed on Ilona, they halted. Ilona withered under his examination.

"It's good to meet you, Prince Willmont," Pavaldon said, drawing Delany close to where she rested her head against his chest. "Or do you prefer Captain Willmont?"

Everyone seated at the table watched Pavaldon, astonished at the dramatic change to this lucid state.

Jance cleared his throat. "My Regent, Jance or Prince Willmont, whichever you prefer."

"You're no longer an officer?" Pavaldon said.

"I had to give up my command when I started my journey here. The title doesn't fit when I'm no longer assigned to do the work."

Pavaldon had a small closed mouth grin but his eyes were animated as they inspected Jance. He gestured to Valgu and his Alvara guard.

"These two tell me I've been having a stretch of good days." Pavaldon looked down at Delany and asked, "What do you think, Princess?" Delany nodded and Pavaldon smiled. "Yes, I think they're right. Being happy has some influence." Pavaldon's smile broadened as his gaze once again traveled over his children.

"I'm so happy to have my daughter's home. It's been many years I've waited, to stare from my ugly chair in the conservatory, and see all of my children looking back. As you can see Prince Willmont, my wait's over. But, I'll never get to see all of my children standing on the dais together. There will always be a gap where my son Solyom once stood."

"Yes, My Regent," Jance said. "My family and I regret and offer our deep condolences for the unexpected loss of Prince Solyom."

"It's wretched to be me, with the power to control much, but have no means to go back and fix an old mistake." Pavaldon lowered his eyes and sniffed, adjusting his embrace on Delany. "Sol's death was not your doing. I know that," Pavaldon said in a low dismissive tone. "You didn't come here to participate in war as an officer of Gryph. You're here to build an alliance, or so your mother's correspondence tells me. Due to the circumstances of Prince Solyom's death, Queen LaBell wishes to return the reward for Princess Katrina."

"Yes, My Regent," Jance said.

"Then I turn the reward money over to you," Pavaldon said.

"My Regent, that's not necessary," Jance said.

"It is," Pavaldon said in an easy contradiction. "You'll need my good favor, and the money, if you plan to continue this journey of yours into Madar."

"I gratefully accept your generosity, thank you My Regent," Jance said.

"You want to marry my Katrina to build an alliance," Pavaldon said.

Stalled, Jance's mouth hung open in a fluster before he regained his voice and said, "I'm very fond of Katrina, My Regent, and if Veilede culture allowed me to, I would."

"But it doesn't, and you won't," Pavaldon said. "Airetti and Mahigan, are two beings God created so they could be brought together as a unified whole." His eyes trained on Katrina and he smiled. "You can't have Katrina." Then he pointed to Owl. "And you can't have Owl either, and don't go roaming Madar with the ambition of marrying any woman with wings. The only female with a pair of wings who'll be returning to Gryph with you is your Gryphon."

Jance made a quiet good-natured laugh as Pavaldon grinned at Nuala and Ilona.

"You can take a look at my other daughters if you like. This one," Pavaldon said pointing to Ilona, "You'll need to come back in about three years if you want her. She's got a talent that's in serious need of some training."

Pavaldon shifted his gaze to Nuala. "My Nuala is a very good option. You could take her back to Gryph, form your alliance and be done." Pavaldon looked back to Jance and gave him a stern glare. "However, I suggest you go. Explore Madar, find the reasons this alliance is right for Gryph. Then find the wife you need. When you do, bring her back to Mozgas and we'll host a celebratory banquet before you make the trip home. How does that sound?"

"Very well," Jance said.

"Good, at the end of the week I don't expect to see you loitering about," Pavaldon said.

"My Regent," Valgu said, "You've already welcomed Prince Willmont and Thulane to stay for as long as they wish."

"You can see the way he looks at her," Pavaldon said. "He's confessed he wants to marry her."

Owl scowled at their father, reproaching him with an irritated, "Father."

Delany tugged at Pavaldon's jacket and motioned for him to lower his head so she could whisper in his ear. The room waited in charmed amusement as Delany and Pavaldon carried on a hushed conversation.

"Are you sure," Pavaldon said to Delany who gave a big nod of adamant affirmation. Pavaldon straightened and addressed the table once again.

"Princess Delany has reminded me that I did welcome Prince Willmont and Thulane to stay for as long as they liked. She also wanted me to make sure Prince Willmont is aware he can't marry her either."

There was a quiet chuckle from everyone at the table before Jance sat forward to give a good-humored reply.

"Thank you My Regent, and someday I hope to recover from the blow your other clarification has laid on me. It is my wish that the Princess Delany will endeavor to offer me the kindness of her friendship, even though I have been denied her hand in marriage."

Delany again whispered in Pavaldon's ear and he restrained a laugh as he said, "She'll think about it."

Most of the formal tension in the room vanished as everyone laughed. Pavaldon grinned and smoothed Delany's hair before placing an affectionate kiss on the top of her head.

"Smart girl," Pavaldon said. "Very smart girl."

Massie leaned over to Katrina and said, "See how perfect she is; she was born for this."

Shaking her head was the only response Katrina managed as she furrowed her brow at Massie and laughed even harder.

The rest of dinner went fast, and Katrina enjoyed it. They all enjoyed it, and realized it in unison as the levity fell away with the return of Pavaldon's blank face. Helpless, she watched her father's eyes lose focus. She wanted to press Delany back into his lap or make Ilona do whatever she did during dinner that seemed to bring their father back.

Valgu reached over and placed a hand over Pavaldon's as he quietly said, "It was really good to talk with you tonight."

Her father retired with the assistance of his Alvara guards. One by one her siblings bid everyone goodnight and drifted out of the room. Content to sit, Katrina found herself watching the servants clear the table away around her. With his head propped in his hand Jance looked down the three seats separating them.

"I've had a few days to adjust to your father's illness. Tonight wasn't really a surprise. What happened with your sister Ilona, I've never seen anything like that in my life."

She nodded.

"So what was that?"

"I don't know."

"Is it something to do with her form?"

"Maybe, I don't know. She's Alvara, like Pha."

"Like Pha," Jance said with his eyebrows raised. "She can do the light thing, with her hands."

Katrina laughed, "It's a little more involved than that, but yes. She'll need some training first."

"I'm not sure I can describe what I felt after I watched her yell at what, I don't know. But I felt like something was there, and then it was gone."

"Me too," she said. Rising from the table, Jance mirrored her movements. He gave her one of his crooked smiles, and his eyes gleamed in a way she recognized. That look used to pull at her.

"I'm glad my proposal of marriage tonight didn't put you off of me."

"What marriage proposal?" she said walking to stand with him.

"The rejection still hurts."

"I've never rejected you," she said, smiling as she stopped beside him and leaned against the table edge.

"As you told Chane."

Her eyebrows lifted with interest, and she waited for him to say more. She sighed when he said nothing.

"You know better," she said. "I'll never have the luxury of accepting or rejecting any marriage proposal."

"Right, that's right. Now I remember," he said taking one of her hands. "Can I see you to your room?"

Massie entered the room fast, and halted before them where he leveled a stern look at Jance.

"I knew I'd find," he said, then pointed at their joined hands. "Doing this. No, no, you really, you shouldn't even touch her." Massie pulled her hand from Jance's. "Unless you have some kind of death wish, you can't escort an Airetti female."

"That's ridiculous, I've escorted her plenty," Jance said.

"I know, but you need to listen to me quick. It's important while you're in Madar, that you only escort a female you can defend."

"You're saying I can't?"

"I'm saying you're not a Mahigan, and you're not a member of her family."

"Fine," Jance said. "That's fine, good evening." Jance turned and left the room.

Massie wrapped her hand around his arm and pulled her away from the table.

"Was all that really necessary?" she asked.

Massie's face broke out into a broad smile. "Absolutely." He motioned with his head for them to leave, and she let him walk her back to her room.

"Why are you glaring at me like you want to kill me?" he said.

"I'm not," she said.

"What it is? Are you pouting, over Jance?"

"I think what you did was unnecessary."

"And?" He prompted.

"And I want you to be honest with me," she said.

Massie's brow furrowed, but he lifted his chin and stared down at her like he dared her to hit him.

"What happened with Ilona tonight?"

"No," Massie said looking away and gaining a sudden interest in the direction they traveled.

"Massie," she said.

"It's better if you ask her about that yourself."

"I'm asking you. Is it something to do with her being an Alvara?"

"Not that I'm aware," he said.

"But you do know."

"She doesn't deserve people defining her by something she can't control."

"Can you give me some idea, so I don't make a fool of myself when I do talk to her?"

"As long as you promise you'll discuss it with her," he said. She nodded as he stopped them, looking up and down the hall checking for other people. Meeting her eyes, he spoke in a hushed voice. "Ilona communicates with the dead."

"She what?"

Massie shook his head and held up his free hand in surrender. "I'm not making it up. I know how it sounds, but trust me, the longer you live with her, the more you're going to see it. She can tell a total stranger incredible details about their relatives, so long as they're dead. I don't know how she does it, or what they communicate with her, but I've witnessed it enough times to know it's real."

"Is that what happened tonight? Was that normal?"

Massie shook his head, "Actually, I've never seen her like that."

He pulled them back into a walk and they entered the family quarters corridor, and stopped at her door.

"You're not going to believe what Delany can do now. She's memorized a poem that has over four verses in it."

Irritated by Massie's change of subject, she felt unsure about redirecting him back. Her thoughts lingered over questions about Ilona's gift. How could she reconcile the carefree lightness of Ilona with what many considered a very dark gift? Passive about learning more, she planned to avoid the subject. Her time with Ilona would be better spent learning the less terrifying qualities about her.

"Katrina."

"I'm sorry," she said turning her focus back to Massie. "I'm still rattled by what you said."

"About Ilona. Yeah, well I've never gotten used to it, and it was my wife and I, well mostly my wife who raised her."

"Your wife," she said. The usual animated charm of Massie fell. The silence brought on by her question lengthened. She waited and felt a rising anguish to see a shadow fall over Massie's eyes as his stare became distant.

"My wife Bedelia," he said, and paused with his mouth open. The words he was about to say hung up or forgotten.

"The morning I met Nuala and Ilona, they told me about how she's missing. They were eager to see you, hoping you had news about her."

His green eyes met hers, he closed his mouth, and shook his head. That was enough of an answer, and Katrina refused to push him into voicing, what the pain on his face revealed. She grabbed hold of him, wrapping him in a tight embrace. Stiff muscles dissolved in her arms as he griped her and fell forward with a shuttering breath.

"Oh God, Massie, I'm sorry. I'm so-so sorry."

They stood undisturbed in the hallway for a long time. Massie thanked her as he regained his composure. They said their goodnights and Katrina watched until he disappeared behind a door further down the hall.

The following morning Katrina sat picking at her food when Tegija approached with the four others members of her healing team. Rising to her feet, she greeted them.

"Good morning, My Princess," Tegija said.

"Good morning, Professor," Katrina said.

"You've met my son, Eleric. These are my colleagues, Professors Kyloria Rath and Bastion Stantivo, and Apothecary Proserpere Duomoro."

"It's a pleasure to meet all of you. I understand this work has exceeded ten years. With that much of a time investment, I hope this procedure is as much a success for you as it would be for me."

"We've had success with it," Professor Rath said. "Tegija told us you're a very good candidate for a successful outcome."

"Is it true the spires were not left in your back to form properly?" Proserpere said. Katrina turned her attention on the female Tegija had introduced as an Apothecary. Adding Proserpere's accent and style of dress, her Skrieni heritage was clear. A heat crept up Katrina's neck and she swallowed hard trying to halt the look of disgust twitching its way to the surface of her face. Fighting to restrain her reaction, she forced herself to remember Proserpere was on the team of healers meant to help her. A bite remained in her voice when she answered.

"What they did I'm not familiar with; all I remember is the pain."

Proserpere said nothing in response, but lowered her eyes. An awkward silence descended over the group. Professor Rath leveled a hard look at Proserpere as Professor Stantivo shifted on his feet. His movement made it easier to discern he was Delphi, as his binti light hair beads clicked with his sway.

With clenched teeth she considered the odds of having both a Skrieni and Delphi healer on the team assigned to help her. Irritated, she tried to be reasonable. They deserved professional courtesy, and after waiting more than a decade for her homecoming, they deserved the opportunity to make their own impressions. Concessions she found difficult to make.

"We should sit," Katrina said turning and walking back to the table laid out for them. "Then you can tell me more about your specialties and how this procedure will work."

Proserpere explained the Skrieni practice of using poisonous nodules to prevent an Airetti's shifting ability. The "spires" as she called them, were inserted into back muscles and emitted poison over a long period of time. They interrupted the shifting process inside the infected muscles' tissue. When the poison in the nodules stopped working, the damage was permanent.

The team planned to excise Katrina's scars and remove the spires from her back. Without hesitation she consented to their removal, which the team intended on doing after the burial of Sol. In preparation, Tegija needed to make a detailed study of her back, and remained after the conclusion of breakfast.

In her bathroom, Tilly assisted her in stripping naked to the waist. She wrapped a blanket around her, and emerged. She crossed the room and sat on her bed with her back to Tegija. His expression serious, they started the study in silence. Sweat on her hands began to soak into the cool fabric of the blanket, making it crease and bunch in her grip.

Exposing her back to Tegija was more difficult than she expected. Her stomach fluttered and clenched. Logic reminded her the man was a professional and his inspection routine, but revealing her scars was a rare event. Displaying her scars to him meant she exposed them to someone capable of identifying their origin and their consequence. Her disfigured back was proof of her imperfection. Evidence of a change so severe, some Veilede might question her suitability as a wife, a guide, or a Regina in training. Her scars were a warning sign of damage, an alteration, and a body incapable of more than a human existence.

Why did it matter? Tegija knew her situation and inability to shift. A flurry of unease gained momentum in her stomach. She worried the exposure of her back to him would ruin what regard he did have for her. The fear made her realize how much his opinion meant to her. Tegija's opinion mattered.

"We can do this another time if you like," he said.

Resigned to what needed to be done, she released the blanket from her aching grip. It slid down her back and she took a breath adjusting to the air gracing the skin and scars of her naked back.

"I'm going to touch your scars, one by one," he said. "This shouldn't hurt, but if you feel any pain let me know."

Katrina nodded her head. His fingertips were smooth as they pressed at the scar on the lower left of her back. With a light press, he worked his fingertips across the entire length of the scar. Letting her head fall forward, she closed her eyes, grateful she was unable to see his face.

"Usually I'm good at ignoring student gossip," Tegija said. "Most of it's trivial. Things they pass around about one another. But, this morning I heard something about you. It's stuck with me."

"You can ask me," she said. "I won't be offended."

How could she? It seemed likely the gossip could be true.

"They said you still plan to be Puternic Jenke's wife," he said.

Or the gossip was far, far, far from the truth. She huffed and shook her head. "No, not true." In silence he continued to work as she debated telling him more. "It's true he claimed me. Then we were discovered, and he left. The way I see it, he gave me up a long time ago, and I don't want him back. I wish I could make excuses about our history, but the truth is I made a mistake. I knew better. I cared for him. I knew being with him, I was willfully disobeying my brother."

"He must still care about you."

"No, he'd just prefer me to the child he's betrothed to," she sighed and picked at the edge of her blanket. "Is that the only rumor you've heard about me?"

He chuckled. "I've heard talk about how you were in a contract on Etrasa, and Prince Willmont paid money to make you his wife."

"See, now even you know that one's not entirely accurate," she said. "He did it as a favor, and his family expected payment. Not so he could actually make me his wife."

"I've seen you two together," he said with an accusing lift of amusement in his voice.

"We're friends, that's all."

There was a pause and she heard a faint huff of protest, before he went on.

"The talk was more focused on the way women are being sold under a contract. It's a strange way of acquiring a wife. Distasteful."

"Hmm, yes, well that's minor compared to what most humans would label rallying. Not all the Ladies were under contract. Many paid to be there, seeking the prestige associated with the House of Etrasa. Those who can't pay to attend become eligible under a contract."

"And what happens if they break this contract?" he said.

"The House expects payment," she said. "If I had violated mine, tried to leave, they would have forced me into the sex trade."

"Buying a wife isn't considered part of the sex trade?"

She took a deep breath measuring the irritation in his voice. His disgust heartened her.

"No one would ever say such a thing to the Ladies of the House who were not under contract."

"Did they know you were Veilede?"

"They didn't care. Even with my scarred back, I had potential to make them money, that's what mattered."

"And you accepted it?"

His tracing press halted, but his hands remained on a scar near her left shoulder blade.

"No," she said. "I tried to make the most of the situation while I waited for my brothers to allow me to come home."

Tegija's fingers took up the tracing press again.

"Eavesdropping on gossip about you, it surprised me. I hate to admit it, but I was curious."

"That's very revealing, Professor," she said, in a playful mock. "Admitting to being a gossip."

"I know," he said, his voice rising with good humor. "I should be ashamed."

"Are you usually this candid?" she asked.

"I think I am."

"No wonder I like you, you're honest," she said. "In recent years, I've grown a bias against perpetual liars. Life's better when you don't have to spend time sifting for the truth in the words of those around you."

"And what if I lied to others, but never to you? Would you still visit with me?" he asked.

"You wouldn't," she said, stifling a chuckle.

"But what if I did?"

"What if?" she said, "I'm guessing that if I caught you lying to anyone, I'd also discover you were being imitated by an imposter."

"Fair enough," he said.

She stifled another laugh and Tegija held his fingers lightly in place as she settled. Silence lingered in the air. He pressed under her shoulder blade and she felt something move under his manipulation. She shrank away from the touch.

"That's one of those things, isn't it?" she asked.

"Yes, did it hurt?"

"No, it felt really odd."

He paused before reaching back to continue his inspection. The momentary silence spread again as his hands paused in place at the edge of the next scar.

"Did Eleric receive his healing talent from you or his mother?"

"Both," he said. "He has Bethanne's binding talent, and mine."

"You married young."

"We were practically children. She and I met after I left the compound and started work on the team."

"You two must be so proud."

"I am, and I know she would be. Bethanne's pregnancy was perfect, but she died of an infection shortly after childbirth."

"I can't believe I did it again. I went straight through the floor. I'm so sorry."

"No, you can't fall through the floor. That goes against our bargain. Remember?"

"Yes."

"Trust me, there's no harm done. I should have mentioned Eleric to you in Gryph."

He gently pressed along the scar near the base of her spine on her right side. Then his hands and the silken touch of his fingertips were gone.

He lifted her blanket around her shoulders to cover her back. She grabbed hold of it and pulled it snug around her. Glad to have her scars hidden again, her body relaxed into the reassuring comfort of the blanket's soft fabric.

"Can you wander me an image?" he asked.

She peeked over her shoulder and met his gaze, waiting for him to continue.

"Will you show me what you remember of your wings?"

Her head snapped forward and her eyes closed in protest to his request. Her mind already filling with images of her brown and cream wings. Tucking her head into her shoulder, her voice failed under a knot gathering in her throat. The resolve to deny his request slipped from her grasp as memories of what she yearned for erupted with a sob.

She nodded her head yes, and passed the images in her mind, everything she could remember. How her light brown primary feathers were striped with a deep brown. The graceful arc each wing made when they were extended, and how sturdy the shafts of her pinfeathers were.

The memories of racing in the garden with Sol were her undoing. Her breath let out in an uncontrollable shutter as a heavy tear fell down her face. Her crying came on so fiercely she missed Tegija bringing her into his arms. She cried against his chest, and in mortification tried to cover her face with the blanket.

What did it matter? He witnessed her loose control after Sol's death. He'd inspected her when she lay as a bedridden mess in recovery. He just finished an up close inspection of her back, and she confessed to her mistake with Puternic. She had exposed her flaws to him, each one big and awful. His embrace came from pity, but she lacked the strength to reject his kindness.

"I'll do everything I can to get them back, My Princess," he said.

His promise eased her rattled emotions. She relaxed into the safety and reassurance in his voice. Self-conscious by how she infringed on him, she obeyed the urge to release him. It astonished her when the movement was not immediately reciprocated. She peeked up at him in surprise and he startled before loosening his hold. He remained close with his hands in a loose hold below her shoulders.

"I didn't mean to trespass," he said. "I'm sorry."

"No," she said. "Thank you."

He continued to study her face as he released her. Dodging his gaze, she tried to pat her face dry with the blanket.

"I-well, thinking about them, and then Sol." She stopped talking, as her throat constricted with tears again.

"I understand," he said, hesitating as he moved away. Turning in a circle, he looked lost. Scratching the back of his hair, he grabbed his shoulder bag up from the floor, and focused on putting it in order.

"The day after Sol's burial, we'll remove the nodules," he said. "Nothing else should delay it."

He slung his bag over one shoulder and turned to her. With a weak apologetic smile he nodded his goodbye and left the room.

Swallowing the ache in her throat, she hung her head. Loath to lying, especially to herself, she accepted how much she liked him. She considered how he held her while she cried. He would have held her longer, and she wanted that. She wanted him, she craved him. With a frustrated groan she flopped down on her bed. Tegija and the unexpected stress of the examination left her worn out. Burying herself beneath blankets, she wanted to fall asleep.

She lay beneath her blankets, but sleep eluded her. Restless and tired of tormenting thoughts of Tegija, she threw off her blankets and marched back to her bathroom. Wrestling with the bodice of her dress, she wondered where her vast team of attendants went.

"My Princess, here," Tilly said appearing behind her. She set aside a stack of towels and reached over to fasten the side of her dress.

"Oh good, thank you," Katrina said. "I worried I might violate my medical restrictions trying to get this back on."

"Hmm, I don't see why Princess Owl didn't send even one Airetti dress."

Katrina frowned at Tilly. The woman had bathed and changed her after her recent injury. She knew the condition of her back. How could she ask such a question?

"Tilly, will you please find the Alvara Guardian assigned to me today? I want to go walk the garden."

Her favorite attendant left and returned with the short grey haired guardian, Bou. Advanced age and a slight build made it difficult to determine Bou's masculinity on first glance. His hand wraps were clean and his robes flowed beneath a matching wool cloak.

"Is it chilly out?" Katrina asked.

Bou smiled and gestured to his cloak. "I wear this frequently, My Princess. I'm cold most of the time."

Tilly handed her a shawl saying, "Just in case."

Bou kept pace with her as they crossed the promenade and entered the formal gardens. Meticulous paths wound through beds of dormant plants and shrubbery. Some lay covered in coarse cloth, coated in a winter's worth of grime from barring snow and ice. They made her think of Tegija's plant research and how he taught students about the medicinal applications of plants.

"Do you know where Princess Ilona is?" Katrina asked.

"I believe she's in the glen with Master Atton," he said.

"Are you considered a Master?" Katrina asked, stepping to the path leading into the glen.

Bou laughed quietly and shook his head. "I chose not to be. Some people are made for leadership. I'm not one of them."

"But you educate others,"she said.

"I spent most of my life teaching in the colony. But that doesn't qualify me for the title of Alvara Master."

"Have you instructed my sister?"

"Princess Ilona, no. Master Atton's taken charge of her. She's got a lot to catch up on. For Alvara, training our talent can't start early enough."

They passed through a natural gateway of large boulders to the glen. Ilona sat at the table with a book in front of her. Atton stood a ways off by the pond.

Ilona smiled when she saw them. Flopping the book shut she stood from her chair. Atton turned to her with a frown.

"I know you're not finished," he said, crossing the glen from where he stood over by the pond.

"My sister needs to speak with me," Ilona said. "There'll be time for that later." Ilona hurried to greet Katrina. With mussed red hair, she tucked wild bright curls behind her ears. Her coloring was set off well by her dress of deep amber.

"Thank God you're here," Ilona said in a wander. "I've never been forced to sit and read so much. It's making me crazy."

Bou drifted away to sit with Atton. They were close enough to watch over them, but far enough away to afford some privacy.

"You want to know what happened last night," Ilona said pulling Katrina over to sit beside her at the table. Katrina gaped, and Ilona laughed. "Well, you do, right?"

"Yes, but," her words faltered.

"Do we need pretenses between us? We're sisters."

"Yes, but, well you surprised me," Katrina said.

"Why make things harder when we don't need to?"

Katrina felt a swell of affection for her.

"We really are related."

"Don't expect the same from Nuala," Ilona said. "She'd die before talking openly about anything."

"I wasn't sure if I should bring up last night."

"You can, and you should. I can see things most people can't. Usually, I'll see and hear them. Occasionally I'll only hear them."

"What are they?"

"Spirits. Usually it's spirits of the dead, sometimes benevolent spirit creatures."

"What did you see last night?"

Ilona sobered and shifted in her chair. Tucking an errant curl behind her ear she answered, "That was a demon."

"You've encountered demons before?"

"A handful of times. The one yesterday, its been here awhile. I saw it the day the Regent attacked you."

Ilona talked with seasoned authority, dismissing doubt about her truthfulness.

"What does it want?"

"Death and sorrow would be my first guess."

"Did it say anything to you?"

"It's a demon."

Katrina frowned at the way Ilona's tone implied she should know something about the nature of demons.

"You don't talk to them," Ilona said, her tone incredulous. Her gestures grew more animated as she began to rant. "They're liars. If you encounter one, you send it away. You don't ask for its name, or a bunch of questions. That's just stupid. A demon's not going to give you its real name. Don't ever waste your time with them."

"Well then," Katrina said sitting back with a relieved shrug. "That's good to know." Her bewilderment broke Ilona's tension and made her laugh.

"I've never encountered such a thing," Katrina said "I don't know anything about them."

"What? You should," Ilona said. "You know the nature of Angels."

"Do I?" Katrina asked.

Ilona quieted as she studied her. "You mean I'm not the only one here needing remedial training?"

Katrina held her look with a grin, but remained silent.

"It's nice to not be alone," Ilona said.

"It is," Katrina said. "What do you think we can do about this demon?"

"I've been asking myself that question for months. I think it feeds off his torment. Your return has made the Regent happy. All of Mozgas is excited. Being restored home, after most considered you dead, it gives people hope. This demon, you're taking what it lives on."

"Is it possible to get rid of the thing?"

"That's a question without a complete answer. I can send it away when it presents itself to me. You could send it away if it came after you. The Regent, he's vulnerable. Half the time he can't speak. When he's normal, I don't think he sees it or can recognize it."

A queasy ache turned her stomach as she considered just how long this malevolent creature existed in her household. Did it focus its attention only on her father, or had it influenced her mother as well?

"I tried to meet with a spiritual leader at Amber Glass. My age put them off. I tried to use my title, but that didn't mean anything to them. They told me I'm too young to discuss such things."

"Did you try to get Valgu to vouch for you?"

Ilona hesitated as she considered the question. "I don't want to disappoint him. He knows about me, but he doesn't really approve. So I've kept this quiet. I've been trying to get information without doing anything that would cause a fuss."

"Sounds tricky."

"I'm trying. Sol's funeral could help me get in contact with some of the less conceited religious leaders."

"If there's some way I can help, let me know," Katrina said. She considered her youngest sister who looked lost in thought. While young, she possessed an unexpected sophistication. Her unusual ability making her wise beyond her years.

"So," Katrina said. "How long do you think it took you to adjust to Veilede customs?"

Ilona's head dropped to the side and she frowned. "You're joking?"

"No, it seems like you've adapted."

"No, no, no," Ilona said shaking her head. "It's all a bluff. I have no idea what I'm doing most of the time. Nuala and I, we knew this would happen someday, but we had no idea what to expect. Do you know how weird it is, to go from being one of the girls who lives over the seamstress's shop, to the life of Princess Ilona Aranysarga? No, I'm sorry, I'll stop. I can't complain. Poor me, living in a Palace with everything I could ever want."

"You're homesick."

"Am I even allowed to admit that?" Ilona paused and lowered her voice. "That I consider Bisma my home? I'm not supposed to, right?"

"Maybe when the war ends, you can go back and visit."

Ilona shook her head. "I doubt it. Valgu says I need to go to the Alvara colony in Idania soon. And there's nothing to go back and visit. The shop burned down with half the city. My life's changed. I've accepted it."

Her last words sounded like a lie, but even the untrained Alvara were incapable of speaking falsehoods. Blessed with the ability to shift another's state of consciousness, the Alvara were bound in such a way they were prohibited from speaking false. They could lie through omission or remain silent, but never put words to a lie. 'Words have power,' was the only explanation Pha offered on the subject.

Katrina knew about longing for home. She also knew nothing she said could alleviate the heartache.

"I have another question for you," Katrina said. "This one's been bothering me." Ilona's interest perked up and she turned to her, waiting for the question.

"Do I look like a twelve year old girl with my hair like this?"

Ilona burst out laughing.

"I do ,don't I? Tell me the truth, if I were in Bisma they'd mock me for hair like this."

"They would,"Ilona said as she continued laughing. "Why do you think I keep mine short? But don't change it. That's what they like here."

Laughter came in short supply during the following week. Sadness became the staple. Heaping portions of it, offered to Katrina's family over and over. The days flowed into a blur of formal gatherings, all leading up to the very ceremonial and public burial of Sol. The activities extended the time and stress level well beyond the actual ceremony. A limitless show she found tiring and impersonal. While she would be the first to demand every respect paid to Sol, none of it helped her in dealing with her own grief.

Sol's burial procession was the last and most attended of the formal funeral activities. Walking beside Valgu, she passed the scores of crowds lining the streets. A surging fan of arms extended with hands reaching to touch Sol's casket leading the processional. Pavaldon and his Alvara escort walked behind the casket, with the Aranysarga family trailing behind him in pairs.

The walk to Amber Glass temple was far. The streets from the palace grew narrow, uneven, and congested with people as they approached the ancient site. The Veilede revered Amber Glass as the location where God descended to bestow their shifting abilities.

An ancient building was erected around the site, decorated with seven massive carved panel reliefs. Each stone panel held images of a different form of shifting ability. Reliefs of Airetti and Mahigan figures filled the borders between each panel and stared down from the over door when they passed the gated entrance. The light beige stone used in the buildings construction was rounded and worn smooth with age. Discoloration highlighted the features of the carvings and accented the seams and cracks in the stone.

The procession walked through the underpass. A vibrating energy flowed through Katrina as they stepped into the massive arena. It reminded her of the vibrations experienced when she entered neutral, but felt softer. Rings of benches rose from the floor perimeter around the large focal point in the center of the arena. A solid surface of light amber tinted glass. Although the glass was translucent, it appeared bottomless. As they walked out to the middle of the floor, she peered down amazed. Nothing of the ground beneath the glass could be seen. The glass held its transparency with light failing to reveal the bottom.

A group of spiritual leaders stepped out onto the floor and met them at the center. A younger man in what looked like apprentice robes strode around Sol's casket and bowed his head to Regent Pavaldon.

She caught Valgu's eye and wandered, *I thought Marcus Ulithi was presiding over this?*

That's him, Valgu wandered.

She gaped at the young Marcus Ulithi, a man people claimed to be over one hundred years old. The other leaders wore robes of higher quality with sashes and pins distinguishing them and their years of profession. They sat in bright contrast to the modest attire of the famous seer Marcus Ulithi.

"My Regent, we grieve your loss and celebrate Prince Solyom's life," Marcus said.

Pavaldon's head swiveled in a sharp jerky motion before he raised a hand to swat at the air by his head. With an overextended arch of his back, he straightened and in a slow effort mumbled the words, "Thank you."

The crowds seated around them chanted a song unfamiliar to her. The priests formed a shoulder-to-shoulder circle around Sol's casket before they stooped down and lifted it up. They carried it to the doorway they entered, and as they passed the threshold a gate lowered behind them.

That evening Valgu requested she and her siblings gather in the glen for a private farewell to Sol. The real glen appeared identical to the familiar one in neutral. Small yellow glasses were set out on the table for them. Each half filled with a dark black liquor. Picking one up, she balked at the astringent smell. Nestling the delicate glass in her hands, she stood as one of Sol's seven remaining siblings.

Wind rustled in the Iron Pines overhead, and Valgu cleared his throat.

"One of my first memories of Sol is from before he was born. I told Father I needed a brother, and asked when he planned to get me one. Father said he was happy to fulfill my demand, and asked if I had any other requests. I told him I wanted a sister too."

Valgu paused while the group chuckled. "I got exactly what I wanted, Solyom then Katrina. They were supposed to be my playmates, but no-I was the odd one out." Valgu huffed a silent chuckle and gave Katrina a knowing look, "You two made me look forward to more brothers and sisters. Sol could always find the good in all, even when things seem completely bad. He chose happiness when the world gave him every reason to be discontent."

Valgu's head tipped forward with his last word, pausing he took a deep breath. Raising his head, Valgu also lifted his glass. Everyone there did the same.

"To Sol, my first brother, may we have the courage to face the bad and see the good. We miss you."

In one smooth movement Valgu brought his glass to his lips and emptied its contents. Katrina fought the twisting in her chest from Valgu's words. Holding her breath she downed the liquor. The sharp taste mixed well with the bitterness that tightened her breathing whenever she reflected on losing Sol. She had endured all the burial activities for Sol. The violence of her grief edged near the surface again. It rose with a force so powerful, she feared she made a mistake. A tear fell and she forced herself to sit down in a chair. Her concern fell away as the liquor's calming pull curbed the sharp pain of her sentiments.

Taking in the faces of her brothers and sisters, she recognized her loss as one they all shared. Her acquaintance with her youngest siblings still fresh, she sensed the power of their grief uniting them. They now shared a unique bond created by the tragic loss of a brother they each loved.

"Finish eating, or I won't walk you over to the University to see your brilliant man," Owl said.

Katrina's eyes widened with horror as she peered at Owl over her cup of tea.

"Massie told me that's what you called Tegija. You have good taste, he's one of the most wanted Mahigans in Mozgas, and he's been very attentive to you."

"Most wanted? What?"

Katrina set her cup down slow, doing her best to hide her shock from Owl's words.

"No one really knows why he swears off rallying," Owl said. "Tegija never told me this, but Valgu said-"

"Owl," Katrina said, trying to interject.

Owl continued, "Tegija has no plans to rally for another wife."

"Owl," Katrina said.

Oblivious to her annoyance, Owl grabbed her hand and squeezed it in excitement.

"It's Valgu, why would he say that if it wasn't true?" Owl said.

"What are you talking about?"

"Lots of people are speculating," Owl said, bending forward as she lowered her voice. "They think you've gotten to him."

Exasperated, Katrina's shoulders slumped and her eyes rolled away in disgust.

"He's been sleeping in the Mahigan compound," Owl said.

"So?"

Owl threw her hands up and shook them. There was liveliness in her voice and it rose in pitch. "I think it's true, I think it's because of you. He never slept there before you arrived."

"No, Owl, no, let's think a little more logically about this," Katrina said. Leaning forward she gestured for Owl to do the same. Owl leaned forward and extended her hands to hers. Katrina piled Owl's hands one on top of the other and held them between hers as she spoke. "There's been all kinds of people coming and going since Sol's burial. If he's really sleeping there, he's probably just taking a reasonable precaution a lot of other Mahigans make with this much activity going on."

"Oh, I just love it, you really like him," Owl said.

Katrina dropped her head and closed her eyes with a sigh as she tried to curb her annoyance. "Of course I like him, he's a nice man who is very well respected." Her words a gross understatement. By far one of the most despicable lies she had ever told.

Owl huffed a laugh.

Peeking up, Owl's green eyes leveled with hers in disbelief. Owl had sniffed out all of her emotions without any effort. Glowering she stared back and tried to fight a smile. With anyone else there was a chance she could fake ambivalence, but it was impossible to deny the truth with Owl.

"Why did you have to be born an empath?" she said releasing Owl's hands. "Please don't say anything."

"I wouldn't," Owl said, "but you shouldn't tell Massie."

"Because you want to tell him first?"

"No, you tell Massie everything," Owl said.

"I do not."

"You told him before you told me," Owl countered.

"I had just woke from a medically induced sleep when that slipped out," she said, but Owl's hurt expression remained. "That's not fair, you two were the ones talking about me."

"You know he's impossible when he wants to know something," Owl said.

"Yes, exactly."

"This will be our secret," Owl said.

"Fine, yes, our secret," Katrina said, with a thin smile of annoyance. She wished none of her siblings knew about her attraction to Tegija.

"Good," Owl said setting her tea aside.

Katrina touched the edge of her teacup with the tips of her fingers and tried to keep the eagerness she felt from coloring her voice. "Has he really sworn off rallying?"

Owl shrugged, "That's what Valgu said." Her face bloomed into a bright smile, "But I think the gossip's true, I think you've gotten to him."

Katrina wanted to ask if Owl based her opinion on more than gossip, but decided her encouragement was enough.

Owl walked her to the healer hall at the Mozgas University. The place

Dermot ran her to after the terrifying event with her father. They were shown into a private room designated for the removal of the poisonous spires.

Owl attempted lending her comfort, but her anxious pacing made the chore of stripping naked and sitting huddled beneath a blanket worse.

"I don't think you should stay for this," Katrina said.

Owl gave her a look of denial.

"You're the most perfect sister, but I don't want you to stay and watch them do this."

"I'm staying," Owl said.

"Please," Katrina said.

"I should stay," Owl said.

"No, you should go, and come back as soon as it's over."

Owl paced another lap of the room before coming to a stop and crossing her arms. Her head bowed, her caramel curls fell forward and obscured her look of discontent.

"Please," Katrina said.

Owl conceded with a nod.

Eleric entered the room fallowed by Tegija. A flutter of joy lifted Katrina's spirit. Diverting her gaze, she balled her hands against the excited floating sensation.

Tegija and Eleric moved about the room retrieving instruments and bottles from cabinets and drawers.

Owl approached Tegija saying, "Wander at me to let me know when it's over?"

"Yes, as soon as she's awake we will," Tegija said.

Owl walked over, took her hand, and wandered. I hope this works.

"Me too," Katrina said.

Owl kissed her cheek left the room. Tegija's hand settled on her shoulder. Hope and pleasure swept across her body from where his hand rested. Her back stiffened as she tried to stop the sensation. This was just kindness, a part of his job.

Tegija wandered her an image of herself. She wore a backless traditional Airetti gown, and looked over her shoulder with a smile. On prominent display were a full-grown pair of cream and brown wings. Tegija used the childhood memories of her wings to craft a vision of how she would look with her wings now.

With the image rooted in her mind, she looked up at him. His hand still rested on her shoulder when their eyes met. She saw what she kept letting herself doubt. His gaze held no pity, sympathy, or the formal composure of someone going about their job. He looked at her with the affirming gaze of a friend. Incredulous, she swallowed the truth. He was more than a healer, and she was more than a patient. Their friendship existed beyond this room.

"Are you ready for this, My Princess?"

"Yes," she said.

"All right, let's get started."

The other members of her healing team stood by. Proserpere stood behind a narrow table with several glass containers set on it. Professor Rath looked over a logbook of some kind while consulting with Professor Stantivo on something he mixed in a shallow bowl.

She lay face down on a table, and the blanket was pulled down to reveal her back. Eleric cleaned her back with a foul smelling ointment. Resting her head on her hands, Professor Stantivo had her inhale fumes from a bowl.

"How many children does Regent Pavaldon have?" Professor Stantivo asked.

"There's eight of us," Katrina said.

"Good, I like big families. I came from one myself. Are you feeling light headed yet?"

"Yes."

"Go ahead and name each of your brothers and sisters, in the order you were born."

"Valgu, Sol, me, Massie, Owl, Nuala, Dermot, Il-" her word broke off as she lost consciousness.

She awoke with heavy limbs, laying relaxed in a cocoon of warm blankets.

"Well done, my Princess." Eleric said in a quiet voice. He crouched down to meet her eyes. He smiled, but she saw shadows of fatigue in his eyes.

"Thank you," she said, her voice cracking from sleep.

"Come on now," Professor Rath called to Eleric, pulling him under one arm and steering him towards the door. "Our patient needs rest and so does our young healer."

Proserpere examined a jar and dictated a list of unfamiliar terms to Professor Stantivo who wrote in a book beside her.

Tegija cleaned a row of small knives and clamps set on a table nearby.

"Is he okay?" Katrina asked as she watched the door close behind Eleric and Professor Rath.

"He'll be fine," Tegija said. "Binding can be draining. Rest will bring him back. How do you feel?"

"Tired...heavy."

"When the heavy feeling wears off you'll regain sensation in your back. It's going to be sore for a while."

"I don't feel anything right now," she said.

"That's normal," he said.

"We're going to take the spires down to work area storage," Professor Stantivo said. "From what we see here, it looks like the procedure went very well."

"Thank you," she said.

Proserpere gave Katrina a weak smile but said nothing as she followed Professor Stantivo from the room carrying a tray of jars.

"You did very well," Tegija said.

"Hmmm, you say that, but what did I do? I was asleep the entire time. How could I have done poorly?"

Tegija's chuckle was quiet.

"It's possible. It's why we have restraint devices in here."

Katrina's eyes went wide and she scanned the closed cabinets lining the room.

"I'm sorry, I shouldn't have said that," he said.

He pulled a chair over and sat down beside her.

"You look tired too," she said.

He narrowed his eyes at her and scratched the back of his head as a grin played at the corner of his mouth.

"I speak too freely around you," he said.

"Is that bad?"

"You remind me of Valgu."

"He is my brother," she said. "Don't worry, I'll keep quiet about the devices."

He eased back in his chair and tilted his head. Her expression bloomed with affection, easy and strong. She wanted to pull it back but medication left her her mind unburdened. Her walls were down and the fire he lit in her shined in a bright display.

He paused and questioned her with his eyes. Too levitated to obsess about what she revealed, she waited for the fall out. For him to break away with a polite excuse, leave, and pretend he saw nothing.

Her heart pitched when his gaze steadied and intensified. She had to force herself to breathe when his eyes revealed his own fire.

"I like how you speak freely to me," she said. "I don't always feel like just a patient."

"You are a patient," he said, but the unguarded fire in his eyes told her she was more, and remained steady.

"Yes, but I like thinking you interact differently with me." The intensity of their joined gaze persisted.

"Please don't say my title made you do it," she said recoiling at the idea, and cutting off their uninhibited moment. She closed her eyes and scrunched up her face in disgust.

"Made me do what?" he asked.

She opened her eyes to see him shaking his head and smiling at her.

"Talk so freely to me."

"Generally titles have the opposite effect," he said, as he slid down the back of his chair stretching his arms up and over his head before dropping them into his lap with a sigh. "I promised Owl I would get her when we were done."

She wanted to protest, to know if their intense moment really happened. She wanted to find some clever thing to tell him to keep him here with her longer. Tegija stood up. Her mind groped for something as he walked over to the collection of items he had been cleaning. There was a soft knock at the door and Proserpere peeked her head in looking at Tegija.

The admiring look on Proserpere's face sent a jolt of nervous energy through her. Tegija turned and met Proserpere at the door. Katrina gripped the edge of the table as her stomach tensed. Tegija and Proserpere stood in the doorway speaking in hushed voices. How had she missed their connection? The way Proserpere's face softened when she looked at Tegija. The light and open tone in Tegija's voice when he spoke to Proserpere. Their body language announced a current or past attachment. Closing her eyes, she tormented herself by straining to hear their words.

"You said that last time, and I was thinking…" Proserpere said, her voice fading.

"No, and this is neither the time nor place to talk about that," Tegija said.

"Tomorrow…see the…and I'll forward the full report in the afternoon," Proserpere said.

Katrina lifted her head, watching as Tegija closed the door. He returned to cleaning his instruments with an acid look. She closed her eyes and listened to his boots pace in even footfalls on the wooden floor, the clack of items against each other, and the squeaks of cabinet hinges opening and closing. Her blankets rustled as she shifted onto her side. Curling her body caused a tingling sting. Sensation began returning to her back.

Tegija flopped down in the chair beside her and her breath hitched. She swallowed hard when his gaze met hers and they were lifted into the unspoken intensity from before Proserpere's interruption. Breaking formality, Tegija folded his arms and placed them on the edge of the table where she lay. His comfort made her stomach flutter like she was in a free fall. With a look of concern he studied her face, before leaning forward to rest his chin on his arms. He was with her again, and she wanted to reach out, hold him, and keep him here in the ease of this moment.

"You let me know if the pain becomes more than discomfort, or if something doesn't feel right."

"Okay," she said.

"The good news, the poisonous nodules appear intact," he said. "The bad news, we'll have to wait and see if this restores your ability to shift. I don't want you to attempt any shifting without my say."

"Alright," she said.

"We'll talk more about it in a month. Until then…" Tegija sat back and unfolded his arms. "Get some rest and heal well."

A month, he planned to check on her in a month. He got up to leave. It might be the last time she saw him for a month.

"Thank you," she said, hiding behind a polite smile.

At least they were parting as friends. That thought the only thing helping to alleviate the ache in her chest. He responded with a smile, and walked to the door. In the doorway he turned, nodded his goodbye, and closed the door behind him.

A month, her insides were numb from the shock of it. The painful sting in her back grew stronger. He returned to his normal life, while she had to wait as hers began to take shape.

The rest of her day was marked in pain. Massie offered the comfort of his company, sitting with her during the first sleepless night. The pain of losing her wings made her current discomfort seem petty. However, her back hurt enough to keep her awake. Massie sat with one leg propped on the other in the ornate chair, which he claimed exceeded in comfort. She reclined against a small mountain of pillows and did her best to remain still.

"Its been bothering me since it happened," Katrina said.

"What did I do now?" he said.

"What do you mean?"

"I know that look. I'm here to support you, but not if you're going to mentally dismember me all night."

"Why did you really offer Delany to the Delphi?"

A smile of satisfaction quirked the side of his mouth. "That, I see. It's like I said, it was the only option that bought us some time."

"But she's just a baby."

He shrugged, "I know, and a lot can happen between now and when she's a woman full grown."

"That's not why you did it."

"Maybe," he said with the smile of a mischievous child. "Maybe I like knowing my daughter is destined for a position worthy of her."

"She's three years old."

"You've met my daughter," Massie said. "Her age has nothing to do with it, it's obvious."

She gawked at his seriousness, and closed her eyes with a sigh. "Why do you think that's obvious, because she's your child?"

"Of course."

"Oh, that's sweet, and ridiculous."

"Maybe," he said, and scratched the edge of his right hand with his left. "I also think the best way we can deal with Suge Trading is by leveraging the Veilede province with an ocean reach no navy in existence can rival."

She sobered, tucking a strand of hair behind her ear.

"Think about it," he said. "If we're partnered with them. It's the Delphi, they're organized, financially stable, and respected in the Madar council. We need their goodwill."

"You say that like its been compromised." she said.

"Yes, the business between you and Puternic, a bit of a setback."

"I see," Katrina said, shifting against the pillows, causing an uncomfortable strain on her back.

"Now, if you're done lighting me on fire with your eyes, there's something else we need to talk about. I have an idea I think would work, but I don't think Valgu or Father will approve." He paused, his face eager as he said, "I think we should go to Lavieth, or what's left of it, and find our uncle Jerard."

An image entered her mind, it was her grandparent's castle in Lavieth, but not as she remembered it. Turrets were missing, and several walls demolished. The transparent nature of her vision turned solid with each breath until she stood in front of the ruins of the castle, and not in a bed in Mozgas.

The ground opened up, and a force dragged her underground into a series of underground tunnels. With increasing momentum something pushed her forward. She blinked and cringed trying to dodge the walls her body looked ready to collide with. She passed through walls, room after room, with increasing speed. She sensed traveling a great distance. Passing more rooms and tunnels in a blur of blinding images.

She slowed to a stop, where her body lifted from the tunnels. She rose out of the ground, and high above the iron pines. She stared at the ground far below and saw the tunnels she traveled through, etched in light on the ground's surface. An immense network of tunnels and rooms spreading out in all directions beneath her.

With a startled jolt, she returned to her bedroom. Blinking fast, she looked over to see Massie watching her.

"You alright?" he said.

"I'm sorry," she said. "I...what were you saying?"

"Nothing, I could see you were...well," he made an airy gesture with his hand. "You were communicating with...well, you know."

"Really, no, I don't know," she said, scanning the room as she fumbled for an explanation. "I wasn't even here."

Massie appeared unsurprised, waiting to hear more.

"I was—I don't know, in Lavieth or on the border? I saw the castle, but it was in ruin. Then it was like I was sucked underground and flown through all these tunnels. Endless tunnels, like a giant city, but all underground."

They sat in silence. Katrina rolled to her side and caught her breath, wincing from the pain in her back. With the tips of her fingers she clutched her necklace from Thedmir. Her thumb rubbed the etched Minotaur script. With a deep breath she relaxed back on the pillows again.

"Are the people of Lavieth living underground?"

Massie shrugged, "I don't know. It seems possible."

"Was the castle destroyed?"

"Yes, years ago. The castle is in ruin. There's just a few farmers using it to store livestock now."

"My mother took me to Lavieth after the Skrieni took my wings. The fever set in, and the Skrieni wouldn't help me. As we left the castle, I saw it under attack. There were boulders and walls collapsing. My mother said it was all part of a fever dream. What do you think? If I saw the destruction of Lavieth's castle, even sick, would that be considered a guided vision?"

"I don't know specifics, but in my opinion yes. Anytime an Airetti witnesses something before it takes place, it's considered a guided vision."

"Do you know what happened to our grandparents and the rest of our family there? Armina said Grandfather was killed for treason."

"Lady Lena never said?" he asked.

She shook her head.

"Why doesn't that surprise me? Our uncle Jerard destroyed the castle in Lavieth."

"Wait, what? Why?"

Massie scowled as he spread his fingers wide, repeatedly tapping the tips of his fingers together. "I know your mother knew," he said in a statement directed more at himself than at her.

"She probably did, but is it necessary to examine why she didn't tell me?" Massie continued his musing. Groaning, she fought the frustrated urge to roll onto her back. "I hurt, Massie. I just experienced something really strange, and now you tell me my uncle destroyed his family home. Please, for the rest of tonight, will you do me the kindness of speaking plainly?"

His, "Yes," came out in a grunt as he sunk back in the ornate chair.

"I learned all this well after the fact," he said, folding his hands on his chest. "Our uncle destroyed the castle after King Armond Dhanda of Bisma said it wasn't his anymore. I guess it goes back to when my mother was betrothed to Prince Allon Dhanda. When Grandfather sent her to Mozgas instead of Bisma, King Dhanda wasn't very understanding. King Dhanda claimed it an act of defiance and treason."

"When was your mother betrothed?" Katrina's face scrunched in confusion. "Why would she be betrothed before my mother? My mother was the eldest."

"Right, she was. Lady Lena was betrothed to Prince Allon, but then our father demanded her as a gift."

"She was offered as a gift."

"No, that's not what happened," Massie said. "Father hand picked your mother, and Grandfather made amends to King Dhanda by promising my mother."

"That explains a lot. That must be why my mother never went to the House of Etrasa like she wanted," Katrina said.

"When they discovered my mother was Airetti, there was no way she could wed Prince Allon. Grandfather broke the betrothal a second time. My mother had Owl around the time King Dhanda accused Grandfather of treason, claiming he collaborated with the Veilede to overturn the Bisma crown. After Father was poisoned, King Dhanda sent a force to lay siege on Lavieth, but eventually Grandfather turned himself over to the King who promptly had him hung. The remaining Larksbur family was stripped of all titles and lands, and some merchant turned lord was sent to take his place."

"I had no idea," she said.

"The people of Lavieth didn't like the lord King Dhanda sent. They revolted, hung him, and declared our uncle Jerard the Lord of Lavieth. Uncle Jerard took down what remained of the castle as a sign of defiance, to prove he can rule and protect the people without it. He challenged the King, saying, 'The people decide who rules, and if Dhanda's going to strip our sovereignty, he has to come take it himself.' King Dhanda's sent a handful of Lords to try and assert rule in Lavieth. Each one dies the same way. Their battalions are scattered, worn down with raids and skirmishes. They never reach the castle ruin and never find the elusive Lord Jerard Larksbur. The Madar Council considers Lavieth an unguarded territory, known for having no law and order of any kind."

"Is that true? Is no one in control there?"

He shrugged, "It's pretty quiet. Our soldiers are never troubled going through there."

"Why do you want to find uncle Jerard?"

"If he's going to live as a forsaken Lord, who snubbed the Bisma crown because of an alleged Veilede alliance, then why not make a real one?"

"Why do I need to go with you?"

"Because you're going to be the Regina of Mozgas, and treaties like these are no small matter."

She ducked her head and cleared her throat. "It still seems like you're perfectly suited to do that on your own."

"You just had a vision about it."

She set her jaw and leveled her gaze at him. Massie leaned forward and lowered his voice.

"I think he knows who's responsible for what happened to Father."

Sighing, she closed her eyes. "We already know that. We agreed it was my mother, on behalf of Suge."

"No, we didn't." He said, and remained quiet until she opened her eyes and met his gaze. "We agreed it was Lady Lena working for someone who had a lot more to gain."

She understood Massie's need for an answer. It was her need too. Why target their father? Why did her mother poison him, change him? Why leave him altered as an unpredictable accelerant capable of flashing up and destroying their family bit by bit.

Massie's plan tempted her, the same way the plot to visit the docks in Gryph had. However, she was the Regina in training. If she were to go, the mission must benefit more than her own curious desire. The mission needed to benefit Mozgas, and it did if they achieved an alliance with Lavieth.

"I was gone over fifteen years," she said, "I doubt Father will approve of your request to take me with you."

Massie's eyes lowered as his lips pressed into a hard line. He chewed at the edge of his thumb and studied a place on the floor.

"But," she said. "I think he'll agree if it's my idea."

Massie dropped his hand to his lap and grinned. "You'll do it?"

"I say we seek out our uncle and see if he'll talk to us. I think he will. He is our uncle. It seems like the hardest part might be finding him."

"But you'll do it, you'll ask Valgu and Father?"

"Yes," she said, "but you have to promise to go, even if I can't."

"Done," he said.

15

War, Politics, and Courtship

She spent the next two days in bed. By the morning of the third, aching back or not, she wanted to do something, even if it meant preparing to assume the title Acting Regina. It felt good to get dressed and walk out onto the promenade for breakfast with her family. Valgu did a poor job of concealing his excitement when he saw her. In the blink of an eye he stood and moved to pull her chair out for her. She considered teasing him, but smiled and thanked him.

"Do you need another day to rest?" Valgu asked. He watched her with eager interest as he returned to his seat.

Without prompting, Owl poured her tea.

"You're the best, thank you," she said and lifted the warm cup. Cradling her tea, she glanced around the breakfast table. All eyes were on her, waiting for her reply to Valgu.

"No, I don't think so," she said.

"I don't mean to pressure you," Valgu said, "But the meeting with trade commission is this afternoon. It's infrequent, I hoped you'd be well enough to attend."

"I'll attend," she said.

"That was too easy," Valgu said.

"What do you mean?"

Valgu grinned and forked a bite of food. Owl looked down at her plate and tried to hide her smile behind a sip of tea. When he continued to eat, Katrina pressed.

"Valgu."

"I thought maybe I'd need to bribe you out of your sickbed."

"Bribe me?"

"Massie's always needed extra convincing after he's fallen ill."

Dermot laughed and Massie scratched under his chin considering Valgu.

"It's true," Massie said. "I won't even try and deny that."

The rest of the table laughed and Massie flashed a good natured smile.

"What were you going to ply me with?" she asked.

"I'll show you after breakfast," Valgu said.

She followed Valgu after breakfast. They ascended the several flights of stairs to his office. She wondered if he forgot about the bribe. There was no mention of it as he talked through today's itinerary. Entering the office, she stopped short. His office had changed, dramatically. There were two desks sitting side by side where before sat only one.

"What's this?" She said.

"Your bribe," he said. "Do you like it? I think we'll get more accomplished with this arrangement."

"This is so, well it looks so permanent."

"It is. Far too big a hassle getting yours here. I'd hate to make the staff turn around and take it away again."

"You really don't mind?"

"No," he said beaming with pride. "Do you like it?"

"Yes," she said, approaching the new desk and running a hand along the carved edge. The necessity of working alongside Valgu would only increase during her apprenticeship as the acting Regina. Since accepting the responsibility, many hours of her days were spent seated in a guest chair drawn up beside his desk. She sat down behind the new desk. Easing back, her still tender back muscles rested against the chair. Somehow seated here, it made the work, the weight of the position, more hers.

"Thank you," she said.

"You're welcome."

Valgu doted on her the rest of the week. Slowing his pace to match her walk. Sending querying looks or quiet questions about her comfort level. If this was how he wooed and warded off thoughts of her forfeiting her new position, it worked.

When she first started shadowing Valgu, he expected her to learn through observation. In private she answered questions he posed. Over and over he asked her to articulate the various plans and initiatives within Mozgas. Peppering her with questions until she could discuss the finer points without hesitation. Recognizing their ministers and advisors took the most time. All the new information combined became a mountain she got up and climbed everyday. Fumbling her way behind Valgu, who spent more than half his life scaling it. Valgu made everything look easy. He worked with a fast efficiency. She strived to emulate him and hated falling short of his expectations on anything.

As she gained more confidence, more occasional arguments occurred. The mission to Lavieth would cause one, and Massie agreed. "Valgu will never authorize it. You need to request it the next time Father's lucid."

When their father hit a string of good days, Massie hounded her for an answer. When lucid, their father took all his appointments in the conservatory. The dampness of the humid room helped hide her nervous sweat as she anticipated the moment to make her request. They were waiting for the next appointment to arrive when Valgu leaned over his armrest and spoke in the quiet tone he used when tutoring her.

"The day after tomorrow you'll be attending the Regents brief with us."

"Have the Mahigans been notified?" Pavaldon said.

"Yes, My Regent," Valgu said.

"Two days notice, for what purpose?" she asked.

"You," Valgu said. "Every Mahigan attendee gets a choice. If they're too affected by you, they're allowed to prepare and send substitutes."

"I've never heard of such a thing. Allowing a work disruption by someone whose presence isn't required? I think it's wrong for me to go."

"You will go," her father said. "Your presence is essential. If they're too weak to sit in a room with you, we don't need them."

If Valgu said it, she would have pressed the issue. However, even unwell, her father was an unquestioned authority in her life. She studied Valgu who watched her with a mild look of guilt. He notified her of this within their lucid father's earshot, knowing she would obey their father without question.

She posed her own question then. It could have come from spite. Maybe she did the usual and followed Valgu's lead, taking advantage of Pavaldon's lucidity while she could. Either way, she spoke before putting more thought into it.

"My Regent, I request your permission to travel to Lavieth. I would like to seek out Lord Jerard, and attempt to create a formal treaty between Mozgas and Lavieth."

Valgu did nothing to hide his shock. Her father's eyes roamed in a contemplative way as his brow knit in thought. A fast decision maker, she anticipated a prompt, "No." Instead he sat considering it.

"The Bisma court refuses to recognize Lord Jerard Larksbur as their sovereign in Lavieth, a disinheritance based on accusations of his father's collusion with Mozgas. Those still in Lavieth say he's their Lord. While we've had no disruptions moving our soldiers and supplies through Lavieth, a formalized treaty could help us with the war in Bisma."

"The Acting Regina of Mozgas shouldn't be anywhere off the Mozgas plateau, let alone outside our borders," Valgu said. "You're too valuable."

"My ability to travel projects the strength of our province. Prince Massie can escort me."

Her father squinted his eyes, closing them as he took a deep breath. He said nothing.

"Your leaving is unnecessary," Valgu said. "We have many trained to go out on our behalf."

"Well..." she hesitated, disliking the need to say what would most likely persuade their father.

Why bring it up here without mentioning one word of it to me first? Valgu wandered.

"I had a vision about it."

Her father's eyes flew open and settled on her in approval.

"Yes," her father said. "Then you must go."

Just like that, her father approved. Without any details about her vision.

"I'd like to hear more about the vision," Valgu said.

"Fine, fine," her father said. "But she goes. We don't hinder these things. Don't ever try."

"Yes, My Regent," Valgu said, and bowed his head.

Fixing his gaze on her, Pavaldon qualified his decision.

"When you get back, your training's over. You will become the Regina of Mozgas."

Katrina bowed her head in acceptance of his command. It was inevitable;

the chance of being relieved of the Regina of Mozgas duties had long passed. Her father's declaration still made her shoulders tense with apprehension.

Later that evening, she and Valgu walked alone to the family quarters. Valgu peppered her with questions about the vision. He not only believed her, he seemed joyous about it. The plan to go to Lavieth bothered him, but he conceded to her going. She and Massie would travel north when spring arrived and the threat of frost lifted.

Stopping in front of her bedroom door Valgu faced her and placed his hands on her shoulders. She stiffened even though his grip was soft and his expression kind.

"Promise me you won't withhold a vision from me again?"

She saw the smallest outline of grief in his eyes. He used their father's authority to prevent a lengthy argument, while she used it to trump his concern for her safety. She used the occurrence of a vision as leverage. Something he considered sacred. Her omission hurt him more than she realized.

Her throat grew too tight to speak and she answered with a bobbing head nod.

"I can see the way you doubt them when you speak of them," he said.

"I do," she said.

"Your visions are important, and I will never doubt them. You'll always tell me about them in the future?"

"Yes."

On the morning of the day for the Regents brief, Valgu left her alone to administer a meeting. She should have expected it. Valgu had begun encouraging her to participate in meeting discussions. She tried, however the authority she now possessed meant her comments carried an unaccustomed weight. She had managed the responsibility of her words, and as much gossip as she could, by avoiding meeting commentary whenever possible.

As Commerce Minister Hamar stole Valgu away from the room, she made a silent curse. She flexed her fingers and sat back in her chair. Masking her internal roil of nervous discomfort behind a confident look ingrained by the House of Etrasa.

Of all the meetings with inspectors and magistrates, her first dealings alone were with the insipid Inspector Killeen Stepfeld, liaison to the contract for the port refurbishment in Amber Sound. Valgu nodded and even laughed when she remarked in private, "I wonder if we'd see more progress in Amber Sound if Inspector Stepfeld had the same enthusiasm for her work as she does for her position's elaborate attire."

At least Minister Cantor remained in the meeting. She liked her in Gryph, but had grown to appreciate her even more since their return home. Minister Cantor blessed meetings she attended with logic and common sense.

As the door closed behind Valgu, Minister Cantor glanced from Inspector Stepfeld to her with a brief expression of irritation. Katrina grinned and tilted her head in silent agreement. Inspector Stepfeld shifted her shoulders fidgeting. A bad sign. At Valgu's departure, Inspector Stepfeld's expression soured and distorted the normal symmetry of her face. Someone considered herself too important for Prince Valgu's prompt dismissal.

"You may proceed with your update, Inspector Stepfeld," Katrina said.

Inspector Stepfeld opened and closed her mouth like a fish, and glanced to the door. "Prince Valgu," she said, and gestured at his empty chair.

"Yes, I'm sure he'll return shortly. Please, proceed."

"Very well," Inspector Stepfeld said. She rifled through a handful of documents in front of her. "Here, I'll read directly from what the Master Stonemason sent. There's been a delay in rock shipments from Milios." Inspector Stepfeld cleared her throat and proceeded to read the letter. It detailed the holdup in port footing repairs caused by an overdue shipment of rock from Milios. She listened to Inspector Stepfeld, in awe once again by her incompetence. Holding back her impatience, she considered the merits of cutting the letter short against continuing. At the end of the letter, Inspector Stepfeld looked up, pride radiating in her smile. Katrina took a deep breath and spoke in a calm voice.

"Is that letter dated?"

"Dated?" Inspector Stepfeld said, already answering the question with an unconscious shake of her head.

"Yes, what's the date of the letter?"

Inspector Stepfeld's smile dropped and she peered down at the letter. She looked up once to try and read her expression. Katrina held her gaze until it bent to search the letter in greater detail.

"Two weeks ago you briefed the rock shipment delays."

"What?" Inspector Stepfeld said.

"You read that letter to us two weeks ago."

Inspector Stepfeld frowned still staring at the letter. "Perhaps I did, my apologies. Let me find the most recent correspondence."

Katrina watched and waited. Inspector Stepfeld grew animated, sifting through her small pile, one after another, she searched.

The door opened and Valgu entered the room. Taking his seat beside her, he watched Inspector Stepfeld.

"Can you tell us the information that's in the document you're searching for?" Katrina asked.

"I know I brought it with me," Inspector Stepfeld said.

Katrina allowed the delay. They waited, the length of every minute growing, making the dramatic rifling more difficult to watch.

"You must have forgotten it," Katrina said.

"No," Inspector Stepfeld said.

"Without this recent letter, you'll have to summarize the information."

"I would," Inspector Stepfeld said. "I, well, see, recalling all the details. It's just not that simple."

"Exactly," Katrina said. "It's why we have inspectors and magistrates, because it's not simple. It's your responsibility to illustrate our more detailed correspondence."

"We'll adjourn for today," Valgu said. His voice light, without any hint of annoyance.

"My apologies," Inspector Stepfeld said. "Do forgive me, I'll have everything in order at our next meeting."

Inspector Stepfeld had gathered her documents and fled the room before Katrina noticed the hard gaze Vaglu held on her. She lifted an eyebrow in question. Valgu ignored her with a small head shake and directed his attention to Minister Cantor.

A flood of irritation and fluster coursed through her. It pressed against the tight hold she maintained on her demeanor. It was terrible, the worst. To know he critiqued her, but have no idea why, or when he might talk to her about it.

Valgu called for an early lunch. Sending runners to fetch the inspectors scheduled next.

"You're inviting them to lunch?" she said. "How can you be hungry already?"

"I'm not," he said. "We have the Regents brief this afternoon. Father's attending; we should arrive early."

She picked at her food, unable to stomach a bite. Thoughts of the Regents brief killed her hunger.

Are you unwell? Valgu asked.

His wandering question jolted her from her thoughts. She nodded to him. Valgu set his jaw in a way that expressed his disbelief. She sipped her water. She would be better by dinner. After the Regent's brief ended.

"The best things you can do in a hostile room is listen more and talk less," Instructor Able said, in a lecture once at the House of Etrasa. More often she found herself reflecting on things taught at the House. She remembered paying attention to Able's lecture on dealing with hostile people.

"Don't hold the room hostage by talking. Sharing uninvited opinions provides those who seek your faults, with more reasons to hold you in contempt. Remember the three r's: remain quiet, resign yourself to your duty, and remove yourself from the room as soon as propriety allows."

Instructor Able's "three r's" were at the front of her mind as she entered the large hall used by the Mozgas Commander of the Amber Division. Curiosity would make following the "three r's" difficult here. Strategy and warfare planning interested her. If the room welcomed her, she might enjoy this.

Crossing the room's threshold with Valgu, she felt every pair of eyes in the room on her. Their welcome was like walking through a thin sheet of ice. Her insides cringed against the cold shards sliding across her with every glance.

She expected this welcome. Most of Mozgas learned of her years in Etrasa. The University she attended caused the strongest reactions among the Veilede. Mahigans held strong prejudices about soldiering. For them, only Mahigans worked as soldiers. A belief rooted in an ancient tenant from God's descent to the Mozgas plateau. God bestowed the art of war to the Mahigans, and every aspect of their shifted form supported this. It caused each province in Madar to segregate its military units. Keeping Mahigan and non-Mahigan soldiers in different units. Non-Mahigan units were few, and their soldiers lacked opportunities to advance in rank.

Massie laughed at Katrina's shock when he told her this.

"If you ask a Mahigan what he thinks about female soldiers, at best you'll hear unique. At worst they'll give you some Dinhac slang equivalent for quaint."

As Katrina's disgust grew, Massie expanded his details of the Mahigan cultural view on female soldiers.

"The average Mahigan considers every female soldier a foreigner, and refer to them as battle wives. They refuse to engage women in battle. If a female attacks, they'll respond with enough force to subdue them. Leaving them immobile, but alive. When the battle's over, the women still alive are rallied for. What a way to meet your mate, huh?"

Katrina glared at Massie but refused to respond.

"It's a long standing historical practice with origins dating back to the Airetti genocide."

"It's nearly as appealing as rape," she said.

Massie gave her a wry smile. "But most rapists don't marry their victims after a battle. Makes it meaningful right?"

She narrowed her eyes at him. "That's why it's nearly as appealing. To be raped and then forced into a relationship, that's revolting. I'd be one of the dead women in that scenario, because anyone who tries to force themselves on me I'll do my best to kill first."

"Well then," Massie said before chuckling. "Let's hope your rally winner gains your favor first, huh?"

She waved his amusement off. His comments were meant to bait her, but some of their base honesty remained.

Pushing aside nuisance thoughts of battle wives and rallying, she turned her focus back to the brief.

The room rose to their feet when her father stepped into the entrance. Everyone bowed their heads in respect to Regent Pavaldon. He appeared lucid and walked upright to his seat beside Vygrath Luca, the General of the Amber Division.

She admired the elaborate stitching in the upper right portion of General Luca's uniform vest. The formal insignia served as little more than an embellishment since his countenance declared who he was. An average looking man, General Luca stood as neither the tallest nor bulkiest man in the room. Close in age to her father, General Luca smiled with an open grin that displayed crooked teeth. His eyes held sincere respect as he looked at her father.

"Vy," Pavaldon said as he settled into his seat.

"My Regent, Prince Valgu, Princess Katrina, welcome," General Luca said.

Valgu took his seat and glanced back at her with a look of accord. Her perfect brother, an ally in all things. His look reassured her, passing a surge of calm. With practiced grace she took her seat. The soldiers set to work. Their cold regard for her thawing into short glances of avoidance.

General Luca's executive officer, Colonel Olyn Roiger, administered the brief. A wide heavyset man, Colonel Roiger embraced baldness by shaving what hair he had off. His gruff way of talking to his staff officers reminded her of Instructor Wells, and made her instantly fond of the Colonel.

"Major Kaldyr Ehnis will brief the current offensive plan in Bisma," Colonel Roiger said.

A lean man with short black hair and keen eyes stepped up to the scale model topographic map table. He scanned down the row from General Luca, her father, Valgu, and lingered for a moment on her. His look both scrutinizing and curious. She held her necklace from Thedmir with two fingers, staring back with formal indifference. With a small look of approval, Major Ehnis began his brief. His words flowed automatic. Beyond rehearsed, his easy confidence proved he studied the material until it became second nature.

She followed along as he pointed to each unit on the map table and provided a summary of their activity and expected progress over the next two days. The conflict in Bisma was more wide spread than she imagined. Skirmishes riddled the countryside south of the Bisma capitol Osnovo.

All Mahigan units remained along the border of Bisma. Veilede units of Fayette, the Veilede form able to shift into other human forms, were the main effort fighting in Bisma. The logic behind using Fayette instead of Mahigan units had to do with winning the trust of the population. Religious pressures in Bisma drove the Veilede there to live in secret or flee. Using the Mahigan forces was a double edged sword. Using them would end the conflict, but create martyrs of the opposition, who decreed them monsters. The battle moved slowly, but Madar's forces dominated the opposition. She sat relaxed when the brief came to a close. General Luca addressed her father, and then Valgu before looking down the table to her.

"My Princess, do you have any questions?"

She took a moment to collect her thoughts, grappling for a harmless question. Her eyes fell on the icons representing the Mahigan units on the map table. A series of vivid images flashed in her mind. A frozen forested landscape with Mahigan soldiers living in a rugged makeshift camp. She knew too well their stoic misery. Remembering the weeks spent living in cold rain. How much more dreadful was the ice and snow.

"Yes, General," she said. "The Mahigan units on the border, how long have they been arrayed in reserve there?"

General Luca looked to Colonel Roiger who in turn looked at Major Ehnis.

"About three months," Major Ehnis said.

"They're living in a traveling camp?"

"I'm not sure," Major Ehnis said. "I can get you a full report by this evening."

"It's winter," Katrina said, and heard the biting reprimand in her tone. She took a breath to quiet her voice. "Three months, most of winter, and they've never crossed over to support the main effort?"

"No, My Princess," Major Ehnis said.

Sitting in reserve must gall God's chosen war champions. She still saw them, as clear as she could see Valgu sitting beside her. Did they stay silent about the living conditions because a call to the field was imminent? But three months, that's not imminent.

"Is it mission essential to hold them in a remote border position?"

"It's not," Pavaldon said. "Move them back to garrison."

Her father's clear voice grabbed the attention of everyone in the room.

General Luca was nodding and without hesitation said, "Yes, My Regent."

A major change based on her. Surprised and a little shaken, she inhaled and met Valgu's look of approval.

Pavaldon rose from his chair and the entire room rose with him.

"Good work," he said, settling his gaze on her with a grin. He reached out his hand, beckoning her to him. She moved to his side and placed her hand in his.

"You saw the Mahigan units," Pavaldon said, tucking her hand into his arm.

"I did," she said, walking in step with her father as he lead her from the room.

"Good."

The public praise and walking on her father's arm were rare occurrences. She left the Regents brief feeling like she won an award or received a perfect test score. They passed into the family quarters, and the bustling noise of the other palace areas fell away. Pavaldon turned to her and leaned down kissing her cheek. Releasing her, he exited through a door to an area secured for his use.

"Have you ever been behind those doors?" she asked Valgu.

"Yes."

"What's back there?"

"There's a room where he sleeps, and there's an entrance down to the tunnels."

She remembered the dark tunnels inside the Mozgas plateau. What did her father need a private tunnel entrance for?

As if Valgu heard her thoughts he replied, "He carves on the walls. He used to only go down there when he was having one of his bad days. Now good or bad, he's down there all the time."

Carving on stonewalls, it was the last thing she imagined her father doing.

"Should we take our ride early today?" he said.

She nodded.

"Good, I'll meet you at the stables."

She waited for her horse and any sign of Valgu in the cold damp air outside the stables. She huddled in her jacket and adjusted her scarf. A low hanging fog covered the ground, matching the sky's solid white. Kicking frozen gravel, her brown suede boots only scratched away pebbles. The later edge of winter held on, even while daylight stretched across more hours. They were inching into spring despite winter's bitter cold dominance at night. Groomsman Mobias led her trim bay mare Simple Rain over and offered the reins.

"My Princess."

"Thank you, Mobias."

He watched her, but refused to bring his gaze above her waist.

"Did you decide on the University yet?" she asked.

Mobias swallowed and said, "I did, I start this spring. If I do fail out, I can come back here. It's not bad."

"You're not supposed to talk failure before you've even started," she said, hoisting herself into the saddle. "A dear friend of mine once told me, think about a successful end and assume that's where you're going."

Mobias gave her a weak grin. "I like that, Princess."

Perched atop his roan Raucous, Valgu emerged from the stable. Raucous had a temperament the opposite of what his name implied. Well built with a clean stride, Raucous blinked dark languid eyes.

"The glen?" Valgu said.

"Yes, but let's take the long way by the University when we circle back," she said.

Valgu kicked Raucous off in a trot and she and Simple Rain followed. When they reached the carriage road leading out to the glen, they rode side by side.

"Can you see grey? Do you ever?" he asked.

His words killed her smile as she remembered his hard look after the meeting with Inspector Stepfeld.

"What's so bad about me seeing black or white?" she said. "It's right or it's not."

"There are lots of situations where right and wrong are mashed together."

"Sure there is, but there's always a baseline right or wrong," she said.

"I think you got that from all your time as a Cadet."

"It helps me make decisions. I don't struggle over answers. A task is done correctly or it's not. Someone is doing their best work or they're not."

He sighed.

"What, what would you have me do?" she said.

"Calm down, and give people more room to learn and improve."

She gawked at Valgu in disbelief. "Of all people to say that to me. You think I'm too rigid."

"And some of your questions are a bit too direct," he said.

"Too direct?"

"You could soften the way you say things. You sound accusatory when I don't think you mean to be."

"If I sound accusatory, then I am," she said.

"Okay, well you need to stop that," he said.

"Do I need to worry about hurting people's feelings when I ask questions? When I sound irritated because an overpaid inspector isn't doing her job?"

"I'm not telling you to not ask questions. You can be justifiably irritated, but I'm asking you to soften the blow next time," he said. "You have a tendency to hit every problem hard when not every situation requires force. Most of the time all you really need to do is nudge people in the right direction. Save the power of your tone for when it's really needed."

"I'll work on it," she said, and let her head list to the side. She released a long breath that rolled away in a long puff of fog.

"You don't know your own strength, that's why I told you," he said.

"Well," she said. "I'm glad you did."

"Good," he said, in a clipped way that sounded just like their father. "It's something you should fix."

"I'll work on it," she said, frowning at him. "Once the sting of your lecture wears off."

"I know," Valgu said giving her a pacifying grin. "Because that same impossible expectation you use on everyone is also what you like to torture yourself with."

"Was that a compliment?" she asked. Valgu grinned and avoided answering by urging Raucous out in front. "Oh, I see, was my question too direct?"

"See, you're learning already."

Confounding older brother, she never asked to be elevated to this position. Did she really have some special connection to God, making her essential to the continued success of the province? Everyone around her thought she did. They abided by this tenet with a confidence that left her feeling like someone just told a funny joke and she was the only one in a room full of people not laughing.

In her opinion, her best qualification for the position was her regular reading habit. The day-to-day workload would be pure misery for anyone opposed to mass quantities of reading material. As for the writing involved, she knew her time of being spared the task would end soon. Her hand ached as she considered the amount of writing Valgu composed each day. The writing part of the job scared her the most, since things written down were crafted with the intent of someone reading it. Valgu's years of experience as the acting Regent shone in the documents and letters he crafted. His skill made her few attempts look like elementary composition.

"What did you think of Major Ehnis' assessment?" Valgu asked.

"His assessment? It seemed fine."

"That's all you thought?"

She shrugged and adjusted the grip on her reigns, "No, but I can't offer an informed opinion when I really don't know the situation well."

He grinned and looked at her from the corner of his eyes. "So what did you think of Major Ehnis?"

She furrowed her brow at him. "What did I think of him? I don't know. I was more focused on what he was saying than on him. Why are you asking?"

"He's interested in you."

"He is, and you're telling me."

"It's how Airetti women are courted in Madar. Father's delegated our families rallying responsibilities to me. I made the announcement today that you're ready to entertain potential suitors."

A cold dread swirled in her stomach. She knew too little about the customs for courting and rallying in Madar.

"Some of your potential suitors will speak to me first. I'll tell you of their interest, and you'll tell me if you're willing to meet them. Others might send you a written request."

"Why do they approach you first, and not come directly to me?"

"Same reason Mahigans are given two days notice before the Regent's brief. It can take a lot of strength to be near an Airetti. Maintaining control can be exhausting. It's considered unfair for a Mahigan to exert that much energy if the female is not interested in them."

She considered the way she imposed herself on Tegija in Gryph, and felt a flush of guilt.

"Am I expected to meet every Mahigan who attends my rally?"

"No, you don't have to meet any of them. But it's considered wise if you do."

"Are you planning for my rally to happen soon?"

"No, not yet," he said. "It's much better to give you some time to meet the Mahigans who express an interest in you."

"Does meeting them narrow down who will attend?"

"You think they'll meet you and decide not to rally?" He huffed a laugh. "These aren't human men you can run off with costumes and backhanded remarks."

"That's too bad," she said.

"You're the next Regina of Mozgas."

"I see. They'll be rallying for rank and title."

"Yes. In general, Airetti women meet their suitors to help a potential marriage become a success. If an attachment forms or feelings arise, it might strengthen their suitor's resolve to win."

"You don't say," she said raising one eyebrow.

"I'm trying to honestly advise you on our customs," he said.

She dropped her sardonic expression with a sigh. "Sorry." With a shrug she said, "All right, I'm willing to meet Major Ehnis."

Valgu nodded and looked ahead.

"What do you think of him?" she asked.

He tilted his head to the side as he considered her question. "We were in the compound together."

When he said nothing else, she chided him, "That's not an opinion."

"Kaldyr doesn't need my endorsement; his biggest fan is himself."

"Oh my," she said. She had never witnessed Valgu make a snide remark about anyone. "Well, I think confidence is a good trait for an officer to have."

Valgu furrowed his brow and glared at her in disbelief.

"Why can't you just say you don't like him?"

"I do my best to appreciate people for their skill and not necessarily their personalities."

"Major Ehnis must really annoy you," she said.

"Not all the time," Valgu said. "I like him just fine when he's doing his job."

They reined their horses to a slow walk as they approached the stables. Two stable hands met them where they brought the horses to a stop. Tegija was waiting for them next to the stable. Katrina wanted to feign ambivalence at seeing him, but he caught her quick glance and held her eyes. She returned his smile as her heart lurched into a faster rhythm.

"What's got you waiting out here for us?" Valgu said. "You could have rode out to join us."

"Maybe next time," Tegija said.

Katrina turned away as she dismounted her horse. The foolish girl in her wanted to rush over and insert herself in their conversation.

"I heard you talking about Kaldyr when you rode in," Tegija said, his gaze drifting over to meet Katrina's again.

Removing her riding gloves, she approached them.

"We were," Valgu said. "I was filling Katrina in on one of our cultural courtesies. She's a quick study, even when she balks at half the material."

"I do not," she said. "He told me how he knew Major Ehnis in the compound."

"Did he tell you how Kaldyr repeatedly tried to increase his rank by sparring with him?" Tegija said.

"No, he didn't." She looked at Valgu and felt a surge of protective anger. In Gryph, Tegija explained how a young Mahigan's rank was allocated based on family lineage, and their mentor in the compound. Mahigans were able to increase their rank by challenging and beating someone of higher rank. Valgu would have out ranked all of his compound peers, which must have made him a constant target.

Valgu sniffed, "He wasn't the only one."

"The most persistent one," Tegija said grinning at Valgu. "All they ever did was make you better."

Valgu said nothing and looked away as if Tegija mentioned the weather.

"Was Major Ehnis able to best you at spars in the compound?" Katrina asked Tegija in a playful jest.

A sly smile played on Tegija's lips as he gave her a knowing look with narrowed eyes and a lowered brow. "What do you think?"

Tegija's mischievous retort thrilled her, and she wanted to hear him boast.

She wanted to hear every detail of how he hurt anyone who had targeted her brother to gain a boost in rank. Hiding her curiosity with the kind of flair only her mother could rival, she feigned indifference and shrugged.

"It's understandable if you don't want to share your defeats. I've never liked hearing my friends retelling their humiliations."

"Humiliation!" Tegija said, restraining a laugh. "You think you're funny."

Tegija's playful humor sent her insides on a tumbling wave of joy. With a broad smile she took a deep breath and scrambled for a response.

"Massie likes my humor," she said, before stepping away from them in as casual a manner she could, and walked to the palace entrance.

"I never would have guessed you and Massie shared the same sense of humor," Valgu said walking behind her, with Tegija in step beside him.

"Well, it's like you said, we must appreciate people for their skill and not necessarily their personalities."

Valgu and Tegija's laughter echoed off the stone doorway as Katrina entered the Palace.

"You reminded me of Thedmir when you told me that," she said and smiled.

"Speaking of Thedmir," Valgu said, "I was going to ask you if you would pursue discussions with Tvarchus."

"Thedmir's a new officer," she said. "He has little power or sway in Tvarchus' ruler's affairs."

"Their ministry seat here in Mozgas is unoccupied. If they're willing, we would reciprocate and send a Veilede foreign minster."

The narrow hallway opened up into a broad two-story hall with a staircase leading to the second floor. It was a back staircase, but Katrina thought it rivaled the main staircase in the Etrasa Mansion. She touched the carved floral motif banister and began to ascend the stairs. Gone were the whitewashed modest walls of the Etrasa row house, and Katrina wondered how long it would take to overlook the stunning beauty of the parquet floors and wood carved paneling in the Mozgas Palace.

"Do you think Thedmir could pass a message to the correct someone?" Valgu asked.

"Yes, of course," she said.

"Are you willing to try?" Valgu asked, taking the stairs in quick succession behind her.

"I'm uncomfortable," she said, and paused to look back in irritation at Valgu and Tegija following her.

"Because he's your friend?" Valgu said.

"No, because it's another important, new thing, that I've never done," she said, turning and continuing her climb up the stairs. "The outcome's important. Don't you think it's a little early to let me fail something that important?"

"And you were just chastising a groomsmen for thinking about failure this morning," Valgu said.

Katrina glanced back, this time scowling at Valgu as she moved faster up the stairs.

"I don't think you'll fail," Valgu said. "But this is worth the risk of failure; it's important."

"You haven't had me handle anything on my own that's of any real importance, but now you want me to do that?" she said.

"Communication with Tvarchus was lost before we lost ties with Gryph. Your friendship, it's the most contact we've had with the Minotaur in ages. The requests we send to Tvarchus usually get no response. If yours generates a no, well, that's an improvement."

At the top of the stairs Katrina rounded on Valgu. "Oh good, I'm so happy my imminent failure will still be a success."

"Katrina," Valgu stopped on the stairs and sighed in frustration. "I didn't mean for it to sound like that. I think you're entirely capable of opening discussions with them."

"I'll do it, okay. I'll do it."

"Good," he said.

"Now can I go change for dinner, without the two of you in tow?"

Valgu glanced back to see Tegija looking at Valgu with a quirked eyebrow and an impatient expression. Valgu's head dipped briefly in mollification, and Katrina wondered what they were wandering about. Valgu took a breath before he looked back at Katrina. "We'll talk more after dinner," he said.

"Thank you," she said, and watched Valgu and Tegija turn and walk back down the staircase.

"Kaldyr? Kaldyr Ehnis." Tegija grumbled at Valgu.

"I know —I know," Valgu breathed in resigned agreement.

Katrina's mind swam back and forth between learning the courting rituals of her kind and the need to discuss politics with her closest friend. Her mind flopped from one to the other as each topic made her balk with equal amounts of frustration.

Discovering Valgu's dislike for Major Ehnis, made it unlikely he learned of his acceptance as her suitor before dinner. Major Ehnis used both options for expressing his interest in her. He penned one of the many letters she found piled on her desk before dinner. Each letter came from a different Mahigan suitor, all of them requesting the opportunity to meet with her. The letters weighed on her and seemed to follow her into dinner as word of Valgu's announcement became dinner conversation.

Massie sipped his wine and had an amused grin as he teased, "How many letters arrived today? Do I know any of your declared suitors?"

She frowned at him and said, "Kaldyr Ehnis."

Pavaldon made a chuckle that ended with a small scoff as he said, "Ehnis."

"Hmm, he would be the first," Massie said exchanging a look with Valgu.

Katrina glanced up at Owl, who gave her a sympathetic smile. Owl did not need her empath ability to sense her indifference.

"He requested we meet tomorrow afternoon," Katrina said, and waited to see Valgu's reaction to this new demand on her time.

"Seems reasonable," Valgu said.

"I'd have to skip our ride," she said. The pile of letters flashed in her mind. How in the world was she going to work and oblige all those requests? It could take weeks, and the letters today were just the start. Who knew how many to expect tomorrow?

"Make him take you," Valgu said. She lifted her eyebrows in consideration as she lifted her glass to take a sip of wine.

"If he gets annoying, wander to me, and I'll remember a more pressing matter that needs your attention," Valgu said.

"I should be fine," Katrina said.

"That's not true," Jance said, drawing confused glares from everyone seated at the table. With a small laugh, Jance took up his glass and gulped his last bit of wine. "She will be fine," he said setting the glass aside with a small rattle before directing his gaze at her. "Katrina could teach a University class in how to dodge unwanted attention."

She felt the bite in Jance's words, and his tacit commentary on their relationship.

Pavaldon stood up fast and everyone at the table sat in alarm. The Alvara guard beside him stood with an air of calm but began to trace a finger at the wraps on his hands. Katrina tried to read her father's expression, but it was hard to gauge what his intense stare meant. In a few long strides Pavaldon towered over Jance who looked up in astonishment. Pavaldon slapped a hand to Jance's shoulder as his face cracked a smile. He gave Jance a pat and snickered. Without a word Pavaldon released Jance and sauntered from the dining room, his Alvara guard a few steps behind him. The door closed and Jance sunk down in his chair.

"Dear Elder Gryphon," Jance said to the collective astonishment of the room. "I thought he was about to kill me."

"Yes, I thought we were going to get some good use out of his guard today," Massie said. "But the look on your face makes up for my disappointment. It's a miracle Father tolerates you at all."

"Do you think he's starting to like me?" Jance said.

Owl erupted in laughter, and soon the entire room was laughing. Katrina's laughter sounded hollow. The sting of Jance's earlier remark pulled all levity from her. What Jance said held some truth, but it applied to human men. The men requesting to be her suitor wanted more than her as a wife. Valgu already admitted how these suitors were motivated by her title, and the rank gained by winning the future Regina of Mozgas. She doubted insults and frumpy attire would sway their pursuit.

Pha was the only person she trusted to give advice on this subject, but Valgu said her safety was at risk while their father lived. Pavaldon would have endless questions about where Pha had been these many years. Given Pha's inability to lie, her truth would mean her death. Katrina felt a nagging inequity for being reunited with her family and home, while Pha continued to live in exile with the Delphi.

You're not making that face because of what I said, are you? Jance wandered.

She shot him a glare and replied with a curt, *No.*

Pushing away from the table, she stood and left the room. When she passed into the next hall she heard Jance calling to her, and then his more demanding wander.

Will you please stop?

Stopping, she turned and waited for him to appear.

He approached her with a determined look. "Things—they've been different since Gryph."

"Yes."

"Why, why were we more in Etrasa?" Jance stared at her but she paused, letting the silence grow between them before answering.

"I told you, we've talked about this. If you're putting off your trip to Milios because of me, then you're wasting time."

"What happened in Gryph?" Jance said stepping closer to her.

Why was he pursuing this? She stared at his navy eyes that demanded a response.

"When I was a girl, Pha said my father was poisoned because of my mother's jealousy."

Jance's eyes danced in frustration at her dodging his question.

"I've learned more about her motives since then, but I still think jealousy was her main reason. She needed to be my father's world, and she wasn't."

"If you're jealous of Salani, I told you-"

"No," she said. "They weren't exaggerating at dinner. You should see the stack of letters on my desk, and those are from just a few of the suitors considering my rally. All of them potentially forfeiting their lives for me. It's awful, and most of them are only motivated by my rank. But that's how it's done. My rally winner might not be my first choice in men, for some stupid reason, I am comforted knowing I'll be his."

"It was Salani."

She furrowed her brow and grit her teeth behind tight lips. "Go to Milios, Jance. Stop stalling, go do your duty, and leave me here to do mine."

"I don't know if I can."

She gripped her necklace from Thedmir, and the thought of her friend collided with thoughts of Jance and Thulane.

"What does Thulane say?"

Jance's eyes flared and his hands clenched into fists. She outmaneuvered him, there was little wiggle room when it came to the opinion of his Gryphon.

"I can ask her myself, but it looks like I don't need to."

She stepped back from the stand off and looked away. She had no words capable of taking away the hurt in his eyes. What could alter their circumstance at this point? Nothing, their course was set and impossible to change.

"Good evening, Captain Willmont."

"Good evening, My Lady."

Jance remained where he stood when she turned to walk back to her quarters. It was awful to see his pain, and know she had a hand in causing it.

"Katrina," he called when she reached the end of the hall. She turned at the door and looked back at him. While his navy eyes projected sadness, he looked just like he had the first time she saw him, standing confident with the enigmatic grin of well trained royal.

"I really hope you get your wings back."

Katrina gave him the best smile she could muster. His pending departure set a new burden of remorse on her. The better part of her wanted him to find the kind of love he deserved. He needed to go. If she really cared for him, he had to be sent away. Nodding her head once, she bid him what she knew would be their last goodbye for a long while. Turning away, she walked into the hall and back to her room.

The following morning Katrina followed Valgu back to their office. She had tried to keep up with the talk about the spring's agricultural forecasting during their first meeting of the day.

"How long did it take before you began to understand the variables discussed by agriculture's ministers?"

"You're assuming I understand them now?" Valgu said.

She scoffed, "If you truly don't, then you fake it well. Can you recommend a book on the subject?"

"There are books, but they might contain more than you need. I recommend patience. Give learning about agricultural matters some time."

"I'll take the books."

Valgu gave a quiet laugh as he exited the stairs and rounded the corner to their office. Exiting the stairs she saw Tegija standing outside the office door. She caught her breath at the sight of his warm expression. He greeted Valgu, and she remembered he was there to see Valgu. She was an interloper on their exchange. With an awkward smile, she ducked behind Valgu and entered the office.

Avoiding their conversation, her body remained keenly aware of Tegija standing a few feet away. All the things she intended to do before their next appointment vanished from her mind. Trying to reign in her reaction to Tegija, she hesitated beside her desk. Starring at the array of documents and book, she tried to remember, to find something, anything besides Tegija to occupy her focus. Catching sight of the stack of suitor letters, she wanted to groan. Her next appointment was the ride she promised Major Ehnis. Why had she agreed to see him?

"My Princess," Tegija said.

Her spine went rigid at his use of her formal title. He never came in here and referred to Valgu as My Prince. Her arms were crossed before she turned around to face him.

"Professor Whythe," she said.

"I came to arrange a time to evaluate the success of your procedure."

Valgu turned to her, eager excitement animating the normal blank formality of his expression. "Nothing we have this afternoon supersedes the importance of that. Name your time."

While she agreed with Valgu, she hated the way he continued to speak for her. She shot him a frustrated look and waited for him to register her annoyance before turning her focus back to Tegija.

"Can we meet at the stables? I have time after my ride."

"We can skip riding for this," Valgu said.

"That would be rude," she said, hitting him with another annoyed look. "Per your suggestion, I arranged to ride with Major Ehnis today."

A small furrow twisted Valgu's brow. Tegija eyed Valgu and then met her gaze.

"I'll wait for you at the stables," Tegija said.

She returned his nod of farewell. He had exited and walked down the hall before she spoke again.

"You should have told me more about my ability to refuse suitor requests."

Valgu stood with her in the middle of the room. He diverted his eyes to the nearby windows.

"Or you should have been more willing to share your opinions of Major Ehnis."

"No, I can't influence your suitor interactions in good conscience. I don't want to interfere with your personal decisions."

"How can you say that? You influence my daily life. I welcome it. I trust your opinions."

Valgu maintained his bland expression and commanding posture. A guise used to reinforce his authority. It also kept others from invading his personal space. She grinned and stepped close to him. His expression eased into a grin. She enjoyed being one of the few people he allowed this close.

"Up until this, you've shared your opinions freely with me," she said.

"I shouldn't get involved. Not in matters of the heart."

"Matters of the heart?" She huffed and shook her head. "With the math I've run, the heart will have little to do with the outcome of my rally. Do you know the probability of my having a love connection with the Mahigan who wins?"

She waited for him to make a guess. He gave her a confused look and she laughed. "The odds aren't good. So small they're fractional."

He considered her, but remained silent.

"You aren't convinced," she said. "My birth rank to the Regency and position as the future Guide, it dominates the equation. Those factors bring Mahigans to my rally who otherwise wouldn't bother, which inflates the number of participants. Even using a modest participant number, it overwhelms the equation, and diminishes the probability of a favorable outcome."

"You've never seen a rally. How can you put together a math model for something when you're naive to all its factors?"

"What factors do you think I'm missing? I'll put them in, but it won't matter."

"I don't like your math," he said. "I didn't realize you were such a pragmatist."

"Yes, well, I didn't realize you were such a romantic." She poked his arm. "Don't worry, I won't tell anyone your secret."

"I have work to do, and you have that appointment."

"Are you worried for me, meeting with your old rival?"

"No. I agree with Jance Willmont. You're fully capable of diverting unwanted male attention."

"My perfect brother," she said. "You know I'd rather keep to our afternoon ride."

"Yes. Dress warmly, it's colder out there than it looks."

She followed his advice and donned a heavy riding jacket, thick scarf, and lined riding gloves before going to the stables. The chilled late morning air made her gasp. Cold bit her throat and she coughed. Adjusting the scarf, she tucked it tighter around her head. The deceptive sunlight warmed the grass still tinted by winter the color of dead straw. Cold seeped into her boots and she wondered if the exertion from riding would be enough to fight it off.

"Good morning, My Princess," Kaldyr said. He wore his tan military uniform, and looked unaffected by the cold. He held out the reigns to Simple Rain.

"Good Morning, Major," she said, and took the reins.

"Thank you for meeting with me," he said.

"Yours was the first verbal request. Immediately followed by a written request. It was hard to ignore."

"I had a very narrow window of time before my request would become just another in an ever growing pile of correspondence."

Mobias exited the stable leading a dark brown mare. They mounted their horses and Kaldyr lead them off at an easy pace. His bearing, short hair, and lean stature reminded her of Mickle, and a press of fond memories relayed through her mind.

"I was told you come from a family of soldiers," she said.

"Yes, that's true," he said over his shoulder. He halted his horse long enough for her to come around and ride beside him. "I might have one cousin who's a trader. Even my mother was a soldier."

"Really?"

"That surprises you?"

"No, the pride in your voice does. I'm familiar with Mahigan biases toward the unordained forms taking up a soldier's occupation."

"Ah, yes, well let's just say I respect all who have the fortitude to become a soldier."

"Interesting. I don't know if I'm convinced. Are you claiming that sentiment because of my background? Maybe you say that because of your mother. Are you a mother's boy?"

Kaldyr laughed. "I won't deny it. We're close. I was small when my father died in a rally. My uncle took charge of my education, but otherwise it's been just her and me. I'm her only family here."

"Your father chose to rally, when he had a wife and young son?"

"He had a battle wife, and the half human she bore him."

The raw honesty of his words struck her. A brief flash of pain clouded his eyes and she realized they were grey. A human eye color. A stark mark of his half human heritage. Grey eyes, as pronounced among the Veilede as her blue ones.

"Not a love match then," she said.

"They got along."

"Why did your mother choose to stay in Madar after he died?"

"There're many places she could have gone, but not with a Mahigan son. She had to stay here if she wanted to provide a stable future for me."

They rode in silence for a time. Katrina found her thoughts lost in the story of his mother and unable to pick up a thread of normal conversation.

"Are you warm enough?" he asked.

She lifted her chin over her scarf and smiled. "Yes, thank you."

"My mother said graduates from the University of Etrasa were some of the best officers she worked with."

"Where's she from?"

Kaldyr slipped into Bisma and said, "Osnovo, Bisma, of course. She trained at the University in Gryph, but accepted a commission in Bisma."

Katrina replied in Bisma, "I'm surprised she left Gryph. Most of my class would have given their left arm for a commission there."

"I think she regrets leaving," he said. "But she'd never admit it. Did you know you speak Bisma with a Lavieth accent?"

She shook her head and switched back to the common language. "How does she feel about the war?"

"Like most, she wants it ended. Preferably before her son is called to the battlefield."

"Even if the time spent there would further your career?"

He shrugged and said, "She's a mother. She likes my current assignment."

"You're well versed in the war plans. Have you been working on them for a long time?"

"Yes."

His short answer and the subtle face he made hinted at disinterest in the topic.

"Are you displeased with it?"

"Yes and no. You can't be married to the initial plan. I know this, but adjusting it to fit the current situation is a never ending puzzle."

"Did many things happen that you hadn't anticipated?"

"We haven't used the Mahigan reinforcement. We've had too much success, if that makes any sense. I don't trust it. That's why I never suggested pulling our reinforcement back."

"I didn't expect my father would make that choice," she said. "I thought we might build barracks or better fortifications for the Mahigan units."

"Your observation based on a guided moment trumps my mistrust of our success. As for pulling them back, I'm in no position to question your father's judgment."

"You must have an opinion."

"I do."

"You won't share it with me?"

"Advising the Regency on war matters is my job. I'm happy to do it, however this might be my one opportunity to speak with you as a suitor. Can you fault me for wanting to steer the conversation in a direction that has less to do with my job?"

She grinned at him. "What if I told you I enjoy talking about war plans and battles?"

His eyebrows lifted. "I could make arrangements. Sit down privately with you to talk about the current situation. So long as you promise not to put me on the spot during future briefs."

"I might do that even if you don't brief me."

"If I reveal my opinions, even privately, I risk being seen as someone jumping the chain of command."

"I'm asking you to do it, requesting it specifically."

He made no answer, and the way he avoided her eye angered her, even when her voice came out jovial and sweet. "You have the choice. Risk trusting me, or risk this being our last conversation."

"I'll make the arrangements, and send for a formal appointment. Will you do this with me again, sometime in the future?"

There was an eagerness in his eyes he failed to hide from the rest of his expression.

"I received more suitor letters this morning," she said. "This is all very new to me."

"I imagine you'll never be lacking in suitor requests."

"I didn't ask for any of them."

"Because you're disinterested in the prospect of marriage, or because someone already claimed prominence among those vying for your affection?"

She masked her unease from his bold question and said, "What I need are friends and reliable acquaintances. Not a never ending appointment list with suitors who will attend my rally regardless of their true feelings about me."

His eager look changed to understanding, or maybe acceptance.

"Then I offer you my sincere friendship."

"Thank you," she said. "And since you won't discuss war matters with me now, I look forward to our next appointment."

"It's fortunate Mozgas has a Regina with more than a rudimentary understanding of battle planning."

"I'm fortunate to have a Mahigan officer willing to accommodate my war interests without fuss."

He laughed as she kicked Simple Rain into a trot and moved ahead of him. They descended a rise and made their way to the front of the stables.

She came here expecting to find fault with Kaldyr Ehnis. Now if pressed for her true opinion of him, she would admit to enjoying his company. While the pull that drove her to distraction around Tegija was absent with Major Ehnis, she did recognize an easy sort of kinship.

When they returned to the stable yard she spied a familiar figure sitting on a bench by the horse entrance. Tegija sat cradling something in his hands. He stood and approached her as Mobias took hold of her horse's bridle. She dismounted, eager to get a better look at what he carried. She smiled when she recognized the small Kasalli plant with one modest vine extending a row of petite bluebells in bloom. The look in his eyes confirmed the plant was for her.

"Professor Tegija Whythe," Kaldyr said. "Am I reading things wrong, or do you have an appointment?"

"I have an appointment."

A dark look passed over Kaldyr's eyes even as he smiled. "It seems your rally will acquire you many suitors, My Princess. It's even tempting Mahigans known for swearing off rallying."

"I'm infringing," Tegija said, in a tone that was more a statement that an apology.

"Thank you for your company, Major Ehnis. I look forward to our next meeting."

Kaldyr's gaze softened as it met hers and he nodded a bow of farewell. "Thank you my Princess." He turned and followed Mobias, who lead his horse into the stable.

"Did you enjoy that?" Katrina asked.

Tegija only answered with a smile. A smile she returned as he extended the plant to her.

"This is for you. While I couldn't get a new one, I was able to coax this from a cutting Master Cantor let me take."

Katrina took it from him. An excited thrill ran through her, heating her body from the inside out.

"I've never cared for such a fragile plant before. I helped weed and water our kitchen garden in Etrasa, but I think most of those plants would've thrived without my help."

Together they turned and walked towards the palace.

"You should have enough sunlight near the windows in your room for it."

"Maybe I should turn it back over to your care? Poor innocent plant, being entrusted to me with so little experience."

"You're meeting with Kaldyr again?"

She glanced up at him, amused by his shift back to Kaldyr.

"To discuss war planning."

"You've accepted him as one of your suitors."

"You say that like it bothers you."

"You think there's a difference between a meeting to talk about war and time spent with him as your suitor. To him there's no difference."

"I see," she said. "What about my perspective? I have questions about the war, and he's the one who can answer them."

He frowned and shook his head. "The main difference between human and Veilede courtship is humans don't have to bury dead suitors after their wedding night."

"So I've been told."

"You should spare your suitors the small kindness of only acknowledging those you would cherish as your husband."

"How can I know I'd cherish any of them if I've never spoken to them? Valgu told me I should get to know some of them before my rally."

"He's never even attended a rally." Tegija stepped to the road that went around the palace and onto the University grounds.

She slowed to a stop. "Where are we going?"

"To the medical unit at the University."

Her hand grabbed for her necklace from Thedmir and fumbled into the folds of her scarf. Her fingers played along its thick border.

"You expected somewhere different," he said.

"Yes, I thought I'd be in my room."

He licked his lips and ran a hand through the back of his hair. "Your room."

She lowered her head. "That's improper isn't it? A bad idea."

Tegija dropped his arm shaking his head. "Your comfort's important. We can go there. This shouldn't take long."

They entered a side entrance. Using a back staircase, she unwound her scarf as they crossed the last landing. The quiet of the family quarters greeted them. She entered her room and turned back to find him hesitating in the hall.

"What is it?"

He took a deep breath, nodded to her, and followed her in. She closed the door behind him. "You've been in here with me before."

"Different circumstances."

Focusing on their task, she walked to her wardrobe, leaving him standing alone in the middle of her bedroom.

"You'll have to explain the different circumstances to me after I change," she said opening her wardrobe. She sifted through the hanging garments, paused at a blue Airetti dress, then continued her search.

"Wait, what's wrong with that one?" Tegija said.

She startled, he stood just behind her shoulder. His proximity sent a wave of excitement through her.

"The blue one? It's one of Owl's old dresses. It's a little short."

"Is it? Let me see." Tegija reached into her wardrobe, pulled the blue dress down, and offered it to her.

The ease of his gesture thrilled her. Taking the dress, she gave him a sideways glance. Stepping into her bathroom, she shut the door.

Drinking in a deep breath, she tried to calm her racing heart. What possessed her to think bringing him here was a good idea? She recognized her old reckless drive. For some reason, Tegija's fear of something improper taking place, only urged her on.

She changed clothes. Appreciating the simple side fasteners of the traditional Airetti dresses. They were easy to close without assistance, and she managed to still hook them despite trembling fingers.

Emerging from the bathroom, she found Tegija lounging in the ornate chair beside her bed. In recent weeks, Owl had transformed her nursery mausoleum. Creating an adult space filled with light yellows, gold tones, sandy beiges, and dark green accents. But for some reason, Owl forgot the ornate chair. Tegija looked as ridiculous sitting in it as her father. His sophisticated masculine form a stark contrast to the chair's gaudy feminine style.

His eyes traced her with slow scrutiny. If she could bottle up his appreciative look, and save it for later, she would.

"I told you it was too short," she said.

He rose from the chair shaking his head. "I disagree." He approached her, motioning for her to turn around, and she obliged.

"I need to inspect your scars."

She inhaled and braced against her growing excitement. His fingers brushed the length of her back. A ripple of pleasure shot through her and she shuddered an exhale. Heat crept up her neck and into her cheeks. She tried separating his professional inspection from her body's growing delight, but her desire saw little difference. The press of his fingers triggered something deep and beyond her control.

"What's your perspective on our interaction?" he said.

Her posture stiffened. "What?"

Hands gripped her shoulders and prodded her to face him. She turned around and met his gaze. Her eyes widened in surprise as his hands wound under her arms and splayed across the latticework of scars on her back.

"You need to reach for your wings here," he said pressing gently where his hands rested.

Sarcasm colored her voice. "It's been a long time, but yes, I remember that."

"Good," he said. "Do it."

She glared up at him. "I'm too distracted by your other question."

"Your wings," he said pulling her closer to him. "Please reach for them."

She closed her eyes and lowered her head trying to do as he commanded.

"I'm reaching, but I can't feel them."

"Try one more time."

She ignored the tumbling flips of her stomach that began when he pulled her in close. She reached for her wings, fumbling for the sensation she accessed daily as a child. Concentrating on the memory of what it felt like to shift, she tried to force it. Muscles cramped in her back. Crying out, the pain made her knees give way. She fell against him. He caught her and held her steady, speaking in a soothing tone.

"It's early. If there's pain, of any kind, then you have to stop."

He propped her back on her feet, his hands gripping her waist as she regained her stance. Disappointed, she avoided his gaze and concentrated on the fading pain and staying upright.

"We can try again in a week," he said.

She nodded. "We can meet at the University. I feel bad forcing you to do this in my bedroom."

"If you make it a habit, people will talk. They'll say I'm favored."

"Hmm, well," she said with a sigh. "That's not inaccurate."

His arms tensed. "It's not?"

She peeked up at him, mortified by her casual admission and his unreadable reaction. Her pride demanded she avoid his question.

"You've long been in favor. Your Valgu's closest friend."

"But am I in your favor?"

"You need to ask me that?" She dropped his gaze and stared at her fingers as they traced along the front seam of his tunic. "You still have hold of me. I haven't protested or moved away."

He tightened his hold on her waist. "Why won't you say it?"

She met his gaze and held it even as the whole world seemed to shift beneath her feet.

"Because my answer's only relevant if you've declared yourself my suitor."

He pulled her body flush against his. His eyes were angry even as he lowered his mouth to hers in a tentative kiss. A shock of pleasure radiated through her, and joy made her head swim.

"I brought you flowers," he said in a tight voice.

"I know, they're perfect," she said.

He brushed another light kiss to her lips and said, "I've sworn off rallying."

"I know," she said running a hand behind his neck and pulling him back.

He kissed her, deeper this time, longer. A lover's kiss that flared heat all over her body.

"I want this," he said, even as his hold on her eased. He let go of her and stepped away. Bowing his head he gripped the back of his neck and looked ready to double over in pain.

"I can't," he said.

Stunned, she crossed her arms and moved back. Her whole body trembled in confusion. She lost track of her emotions between the intensity of his kiss, and a rising swell of embarrassment as she processed his rejection.

"You should go," she said.

"I owe you an explanation."

"No," she said, putting a hand out in defense as she walked to her wardrobe. "I don't want one." She opened it and yanked out a wrap dress.

"Katrina, please."

She hurried to the bathroom. "We're done here," she said. "If you don't mind, please, see yourself out."

She slammed the door before tears flooded her eyes. The sharp thud of her bedroom door closing echoed from the other room. She sunk to the floor, swiping tears away as anger and adoration ripped at her insides.

She still sat slumped against the bathroom door when a knock sounded and startled her from her misery.

"Katrina?" Valgu called.

"I'm getting dressed."

"No, you're not."

She stood and opened the door just enough to see out. Valgu stood with his arms folded, and a frown of concern.

"Give me a moment," she said, and shut the door. She dropped the wrap dress to the floor and worked the fasteners loose on the blue Airetti dress. Yanking it over her head she cast it aside and scooped up the wrap dress. Sliding her arms in, she cinched the front ties and secured it. Smoothing the top of her hair, she exited the bathroom.

"Why are you here?"

"Tegija wandered to me, said you needed me."

"Did he?"

"It didn't go well," Valgu said dropping his arms as he approached her.

Looking down she shook her head.

"You've been crying."

Katrina touched a hand to the swollen tightness in her cheeks. "It hurt more than I expected."

Valgu narrowed his eyes at her, invading her space the same way she had invaded his earlier that morning. He rested a comforting hand on her shoulder.

"What really happened?" he said.

She scowled at him and sighed. "It's complicated."

"Yes, I'm sure it is."

Her sour expression faded as she considered him. She expected to confide what happened to Owl. Seeing the genuine compassion in Valgu's eyes, she realized she preferred confiding in him. That made her want to curse Tegija even more. How dare he break her heart and then send the right sibling to her aide.

"Is it obvious?" she asked.

"Maybe, for those that know you."

"How can he be angry about the suitors I choose to interact with, when he's made it clear he won't be my suitor?"

"Because that's what he wants to be."

"Did he tell you that?"

"Formally, no."

"But you believe he does."

"He's my oldest friend." He gestured with his chin to the Kasalli plant sitting on the stool by the window. "And him fussing over that plant for you—made it pretty obvious. He needs time. His life's been his son and his work. Meeting you blind sided him."

"Oh God, Valgu," she said pressing the palms of her hands against her eyes. "Don't say anything else, I don't need false hope."

"It's not false hope."

Dropping her hands she looked up at him. "You really are a romantic, aren't you?"

Valgu chuffed a laugh and wrapped one arm around her shoulder. "You swore you'd keep my secret." He pulled her into a slow walk to the door leading out to the promenade. "It will pain me to see you two make fools of yourselves trying to avoid one another."

"I barely see him, I won't look foolish."

Valgu looked unconvinced.

"The times I do see him, I can use one of your aloof expressions that I've been practicing."

"Good idea, he'll never see through that."

"I'm not going to cry openly, or sit around pining for him. I'll pretend it doesn't hurt, until it really doesn't. I know how to do that."

"Or you might play off his possessiveness. Have several public appointments with various suitors. Get lots of gossip circulating, look happy, until he can't bear it."

"Valgu."

"Look at his reaction to your appointment today. One ride with Ehnis and he's at the stables hauling you off your horse to get you away from him."

"Where did you hear that? He didn't haul me off anything."

"Tell me I'm wrong," he said.

She sighed in annoyance. "No. You're never wrong."

She woke drowsy and waiting for the sound of Pha saying, "My Katrina. Darling girl, it's time to rise." A pang of loss flowed through her, and grew painful as she thought of how Pha hummed and went about her routine. The silence in the room magnified the large emptiness of the space. She rolled out of bed with a sigh. Pha's absence left a hole as deep as the one Sol's death created. While her grief for them was different, her desire to have them near was equal.

Pha's absence from daily life was like walking around in a pair of shoes with a thrown heel, every step stunted and awkward. With Pha gone, she saw the reason and balance she lent to her life. She wanted her back, to tell her everything that had happened. To solicit her advice. See her beam when she learned a Mahigan had won her heart, and comfort her when she heard how he broke it. She missed their private laughs, and telling Pha everything in just a few words.

The desire for Pha's advice increased as the days passed and more letters arrived from Mahigan suitors. Some lived locally, while a few were from parts of Madar she needed a map to locate. The initial exchange of correspondence with a new suitor was easy. They sent a formal request and she sent cordial reply. The later letters became difficult. She struggled remembering each one without confusing them with someone else. Writing letters became more time-consuming. A new and unwelcome part of her routine with Valgu. Together in the office they shared, each at their desk, quiet as they drafted correspondence for a few hours in the late afternoon.

"If this is cutting into my other duties, you must tell me," she said.

"Have I accused you of anything?" Valgu asked.

"No, but I haven't been reading as much as I was before," she said.

"You're doing exactly what you need to be doing, if you weren't I'd say something. Here-" he lifted a letter from a stack of documents he was sifting through. "A letter for you, I forgot about it. It came with our dispatches from Milios."

"Milios," she said, standing to retrieve the letter he offered. The script was neat with elongated letters. She noticed the same hand that penned her letter also addressed the letter in Valgu's other hand.

"I think you'll like this one," he said, with sincere affection as he looked at the letter in her hand. She fingered the orange wax and regarded the sharp symmetry of the ancient text that comprised the seal. Opening the letter she scanned down to find the author.

"Rosalba Luex?" she relaxed, the letter from a non-suitor came as a nice surprise.

"She's the sister of Sepihne Luex," he said.

Katrina gave him a contemptuous look. The significance of being graced with a letter from the Regent of Milios' sister was not lost on her. She wondered if Rosalba was a woman she should fear or reach out to? Once again her missing shoe heel smacked the ground as she wished for Pha's guidance. She did have Owl. She would provide a fair opinion about Rosalba.

Katrina pursed her lips and finished Rosalba's letter. It outlined her desire for them to become better acquainted, and offered to answer questions Katrina might have about her new role as the Mozgas Guide.

"She says you speak highly of me?"

"I speak highly of all my family," Valgu said.

"Of course you do," she said with a quiet laugh as Valgu tried to divert his interest in her letter. He sat rigid in his seat, unsure of his next move. A very odd posture for him. Valgu stood up, his letter from Rosalba clutched in one hand as he walked to the door.

"I'll be right back," he said over his shoulder. He exited before she had the chance to ask where he was going.

Setting the letter aside, she walked to the door. Standing in the threshold she wondered about his return. She crossed her arms and leaned on the doorframe looking back at the stack of suitor letters on her desk. She wanted one letter, but it sat nowhere in that stack. Letters came everyday. None of them from the Mahigan who held her interest.

Every time she thought of Tegija, a voice inside her begged him to change his mind. She managed to avoid him. Going on two weeks and a day, but who was counting. Memories of kissing him ambushed her. They arrived out of nowhere and tumbled her backwards into heartsick misery. Recovering from Puternic seemed easy in comparison, and that took months. Puternic had vanished. Tegija was here. Stupid infatuation, it refused to fade even an inch. Disappointment loomed, forever clouding her future. What if the cloud never cleared? What if this gloom never went away?

The more she considered it, the more meeting the Mahigans who planned to attend her rally seemed pointless. Whenever she imagined one of them winning, she experienced the same pang of disappointment. Since Tegija swore off rallying, disappointment was a guarantee. No amount of letter writing, or meeting with Mahigan suitors offset her predicament.

She pushed off the doorframe and walked into the hall. No more letter writing today, and none tomorrow. She would stop this madness. Face her interest, or lack of it, with integrity. Who benefited from her faking an interest in them? They would all attend her rally regardless of their interactions with her. She extended the fingers of her writing hand, stretching them. It felt good. She massaged her hand and considered all the time she'd save. The hours she could spend on other things. Her decision buoyed her spirits, lifting her heavy heart off the floor in a small reprieve.

"That's good enough for today," she said and sighed. With Valgu's unexpected absence, and a distaste for every letter cluttering her desk, she left the office. When she arrived in the family quarters she decided to find Owl.

Owl's room would shock anyone with regimented opinions on room decor or preferred order and tidiness. The room was more an art studio than bedroom. Owl spent a great deal of time sitting in a windowed alcove surrounded by an easel, a small desk of sketchbooks, and a board covered in a multicolor scale of fabric swatches. Owl remained seated in her alcove when Katrina entered. She acknowledged her with a warm smile before returning her focus to her work. Katrina crossed the room and pushed aside a stack of books in the widow seat across from Owl.

"I received a letter from Rosalba Luex today."

"She's brilliant," Owl said.

"She offered to answer any questions I had."

Owl bobbed her head in a nod, "You should take her offer, it's sincere."

"It looked like she sent Valgu a letter as well. He left with it and didn't come back. It had the same handwriting, same seal."

Owl stilled and avoided her gaze. She shifted in her seat before saying, "She's his peer in Milios, they exchange official correspondence all the time."

"She mentioned some of the things Valgu told her about me. He was out of sorts when I read my letter. Do they share more than an official friendship? Is Valgu her suitor?"

Owl made an unconvincing stiff shrug saying, "I know they're friends."

"Where's the fun in gossiping with a sister, who knows other people's feelings, but holds some personal obligation to keep some information private?"

Owl gave her a chastising 'you know my bounds' glance.

"Fine," Katrina said with sigh.

She had learned the more Owl knew about a person's private emotions, the more elusive she became when questioned. Owl's ambiguous answers were similar to the kind of response her mother gave under questioning. An unfortunate disadvantage for Owl, since Katrina had far more practice eliciting information than Owl did at hiding it. If she applied the questioning techniques she mastered with her mother, little bits of information could be extracted over time. In this particular case, Owl's noncommittal response did more to confirm Katina's suspicion than deny it.

"What about your suitors? You and Valgu are never done with correspondence this early."

"He left, and I'm done. I'm forever done with anything suitor related."

Owl's eyebrows lifted and she set down her stylus. "You're done writing to your suitors."

"Yes, indefinitely. If I were born to a normal life, where their interest was more in me than my rank, I'd continue. I'm the future Regina of Mozgas, my suitor correspondence is a waste of time."

"That'll cause gossip," Owl said.

"I don't care. The gossips can have all the fun they want with that. I'm done."

16

The Lord of Lavieth

Katrina's pack sat at her feet, propped against her desk in the office shared with Valgu. After a few days on the road she'd miss their office, with its tall windows, and abundant sunlight. She already missed the familiar routine of working in the easy quiet of Valgu's company. They said their goodbyes after breakfast. She made one last trip up to retrieve the treaty documents for Lavieth. Her usual mess of books and paperwork were tidied away. The desk sat clean and ready to greet her when she returned.

She sat down and rolled out the treaty documents to review one last time. A quiet knock at the door made her look up. Tegija stood in the threshold, quiet but ever confidant. Something in his look told her he saw more than her diadem and travel attire.

Her heart sang as she looked at him. Could she do this, talk to him and pretend she forgot his kiss? Morning light etched him in rich tones of apricot and gold and made the sight of him achingly perfect. A smile crept to the edges of her mouth, and she let the image of him sear itself into her memory.

"If you're here to try and talk me out of going, don't bother. I'm already packed."

"You make it sound like I had a chance at changing your mind," he said.

"No, you didn't."

Afraid of his effect on her, she tried to hide any blissful reaction by busying her hands. She rolled the documents in front of her and slid them into a sturdy leather courier's tube.

"I have something for you, it's for the trip," he said

She paused, doing her best to neutralize her excitement, feeling her heart beat faster. She arched her eyebrows in interest. "I've already packed the sword, the one that can take more than three hits."

Tegija smiled and stepped towards her, "That's good, but a sword's not going to do you any good against a Mahigan who decides not to control himself." He held up what looked like a tube of gold metal with some kind of fabric tucked inside.

"What's that?"

"A Mahigan net, it's the only defense that'll work, if you insist on traveling without another Mahigan."

He offered her the net and she took it.

"Now, so long as you don't run into more than one rogue Mahigan at a time, you should be fine."

"Are you going to show me how to use it?"

He shook his head, "Massie should; I've never used one."

"You've never needed one."

"No, and I hope you won't either."

"Thank you," she said, inspecting the smooth metal rod in her hand. The clean leather grip looked new and rested in her hand with ease. What she thought was fabric on the inside was actually the thin wire of the netting collapsed and bundled into the tube.

"I heard Major Ehnis' offered to escort you."

Her posture stiffened and she had to force the sour pucker on her lips into a smile.

"He did, and I tried not to let my pride feel insulted. Major Ehnis is needed more here."

"I wish you didn't feel the need to go," he said.

Her stupid infatuation began to plead with her to forget the entire mission because it was something he wanted. One glance from his washed out gold eyes, mixed with a few honest words, and she lost her desire to leave. The sudden need to please him was like a spell and served as only more proof she needed to go. Maybe with time and distance separating them, she could clear him from her head.

"I do," she said, stacking the Mahigan net on top of her courier's envelope and opening her pack. "I think there's something there I need to see, with my own eyes."

Tegija nodded, but his eyes continued their worried protest. "I hope my gift didn't offend you like Ehnis's offer?"

"No," she said. "You've always seemed to have some level of faith in my ability to take care of myself, while still keeping the promise you made Valgu."

"That's why you think I'm concerned?"

"No, I —" she was cut off from saying more by Massie. His voice an echo from somewhere distant and down the hall.

"Katrina, you're taking forever. It's like you're some kind of entitled Princess. Helos keeps chattering like he has somewhere special to be. Will you please spare my patience and hurry up?"

She sighed, securing the courier's tube and Mahigan net to her pack. She grinned at Tegija as she lifted her pack onto one shoulder. "I'll see you when we get back."

Tegija's eyes were still focused on the doorway. He stood poised, ready to say something. The longer he hesitated the more her heart pounded. Hope flared and she stood like a frightened rabbit, holding her breath and terrified any sudden movement might scare him off. What was he going to say? Her mind chanted an urgent plea, 'Please say you changed your mind.' What could she say or do to help encourage him?

Massie shouted down the hallway for her. His grumbling breaking the stillness.

"Acting Regina of Mozgas, are you coming or not?"

Katrina's head fell forward in defeat. She gave a silent laugh at the poor timing of Massie's antics. Her chest felt tight as she held her breath glancing back at Tegija. Clinging to a last bit of hope, she waited to hear more than goodbye.

"Have a safe trip."

Her heart dropped and all the air left her lungs. Sadness held her for a brief second, but her next intake of breath brought a burst of anger. She bit back a fierce protest. Gripping the pack, she wanted to throw it down and shout the old mantra of her Cadet Instructors, 'Try again, that's not it!'

Forcing another deep breath, the strength behind her anger faded. Self-loathing came on as she considered the utter fool she was for him. The way she dared assume he might declare himself to her. Thinking he might change his stance against rallying, just for her. This vanity needed to stop. So did the misery caused by getting her hopes up. A way to rid herself of this nonsense must exist.

Now, she needed to leave right now. The urgency to shake off her embarrassment grew. Leaving became a priority as her composure eroded with each passing second.

"Thank you," she said, and gave him a quick nod goodbye. Hitching the remaining pack strap over her other shoulder, she left.

Gutted, she hurried down the hall in search of Massie. She tried letting go of the desire for the impossible, and beat back thoughts of doubling back and telling Tegija she would miss him. She kept moving forward, away from him. Ignoring the pathetic hopeful desire nagging her to go back.

At first glance Massie looked happy to see her and eager to be away. As they walked to the garden, she spotted the dim melancholy in his eyes.

"Delany," she said.

"Yes." His smile furrowed into a pained expression. "I underestimated my ability to leave her, when I talked you into this."

Unsure what words could comfort him she offered a sympathetic smile.

Against flying with a rider, Helos refused hauling two at once. Massie said a shoulder injury sustained in an old conflict bothered Helos too much.

"He carries me out of some kind of bonded to a Gryphon obligation, but even one rider wears on him."

Helos agreed to fly them individually. Sparing them a two-hour journey down the Mozgas Plateau. They landed at the stables of a village near the main entrance to the Plateau's tunnels. A pair of bay mares stood saddled and waiting for them. Fastening packs and mounting the horses, they rode the main road towards Bisma.

"How much practice will it take for me to learn to use a Mahigan net?" Katrina asked.

"Did you bring one for me? That was a good idea," he said.

"You don't have one?"

"Don't be daft, what kind of simpleton do you take me for?"

Glowering, she pursed her lips at him. "Tegija gave me one before we left."

Massie's eyebrows rose and he grinned. "Did he? Well, what else did your brilliant Mahigan say before we left? It must have been important. You sure took your own sweet time."

"He said you could show me how to use it."

"It's a marvelously simple device, my Delany could use it. No need for practice. You just point the thing and hit the release. Then just stand as far back as you can while you hold onto it."

"Oh, well that's good."

"I'm sorry I trampled all over your doting suitor's goodbye."

She worked her lips in agitation. What would Tegija have said without Massie shouting for her?

"Now, what's the point in pretending the famous professor's not one of your suitors?"

"No, he's not," she said, wishing once again none of her siblings knew anything about her interest in Tegija. "And I don't want to talk about the Mahigans who are."

"Of course he is," Massie said. "That's a stupid thing to lie about." He frowned as she continued to shake her head no.

"That's you making an assumption," she said.

"Is it?" he said with a challenge in his voice.

"Yes," she said. "I wouldn't lie to you, and certainly never about a stupid thing like that. I know who my suitors are."

"Really, all of them? If I were you, I'd have lost track weeks ago."

"Yes, it's not easy. I look at my correspondence and envy the Airetti women born to merchants and farmers. Would any Mahigan be willing to risk their life if I wasn't an Aranysarga? Would the blue eyed human half blood turn them away on sight? Would some stop writing now if word got out about how damaged my shifting ability is?"

Massie studied her for a time before looking ahead. They rode in silence and her frustration from his teasing faded.

His voice was soft when he said, "Is that your way of telling me the procedure on your back didn't work?"

Stunned by his question, she met his eyes and nodded her head yes.

"You didn't tell me," he said.

"No, there's not much to tell." A wash of guilt swept over her for keeping from him what Valgu and Owl knew.

"There was one attempt to shift. I'm sorry I never mentioned it. It's hard enough dealing with my own disappointment. Adding everyone else's just makes it worse."

"Is that it then, is there nothing else they can do?"

"Tegija said it might have been too early. Valgu remains hopeful."

"But you're not?"

"It shouldn't be hard to shift."

"If Tegija thinks there's a chance, then there's still a chance."

"I've been without them this long. If I'm meant to remain this way, then I need to just accept it and move on."

"I don't believe you. Those are words you'd make yourself believe. Do you really see yourself as damaged?"

"How else do you categorize it, Massie?"

"You think what happened to you makes you somehow less worthy for all your suitors? Who's the one really making assumptions?" He shook his head and looked ahead. Narrowing his eyes, he looked at her from the corner of them. "I get it now, you think Tegija's interest is influenced by your wings too."

Massie turned to face her when she ignored him. She worked to feign ambivalence the way Valgu did.

"I'll admit," Massie said. "I don't get it, he's a determined man. If he couldn't tell you in person, why didn't he just write a letter?"

"Please don't tease me," she said closing her eyes and lifting her face to the sky with a pleading expression. The morning was bad enough. Thinking about Tegija now was like prodding an open wound.

"I'm not," he said in a sincere tone. "I'm really not, I never expected he wouldn't tell you."

"We've discussed lots of things," she said, dropping her head forward and adjusting her hold on her reigns. "Tegija has no plans to rally."

Massie scoffed, and she glared at him. His eyebrows rose in challenge to her wide-eyed offense.

"His intentions are obvious," he said and lifted a closed hand between them, releasing one finger at a time as he listed each point to his argument. "I know about the plant, and I know for a fact he started eyeing you back in Gryph."

Back in Gryph, she recalled it with beautiful clarity, the long night spent talking to Tegija. The pleading in his eyes when he offered her the Gryph Kasalli plant meant for Minister Cantor. The memory and Massie's observations made hope stir. She considered Massie and the kind of nonsense he liked to start. Her mouth went dry, and she worked to form the question she dreaded hearing the answer to.

"What did you say to him?"

Massie shrugged, "It's not my place, but you should ask Valgu about it when we get back."

"You did say something." Her eyebrows lowered.

"Perhaps."

"Some people respond to your brand of boldness and sarcasm with more sarcasm or lies because you annoy them."

"Because Professor Wythe is so full of sarcasm and witty humor? Be serious. I can't name anytime when I've witnessed that man tell a lie," Massie said.

"I bet he doesn't see me the way you think," she said.

Laughing, Massie made several attempts to catch his breath to speak. "He's obviously had a hard time making his intentions known, but if I were taking bets, I'd wager your brilliant Mahigan will be at your rally."

She nudged her mare closer to Massie's and shoved him hard in the shoulder. "I really can't stand you sometimes."

"Stop it, woman! I'm not above shoving back, even when the offender is the future Regina of Mozgas."

Katrina's face brightened with a smile as she reached over to swipe at him again. Laughing at their game, Massie grabbed her wrist and dodged her hand.

"I should warn him about you. My older sister's violent, she tends to lash out at random and without cause."

"Promise to never tease me about him," she said, wrenching her wrist free of him.

"She tried to put me off my horse and have me trampled."

"Please, Massie, promise me."

Laughing, he nodded, "Nah, I won't say anything. You should know me better than that."

"I know you say crazy things all the time, and I'm sick thinking about what you must have said to him."

"I promise. I won't say anything," he said.

They each relaxed and Katrina eased her horse back to a normal riding distance.

"We should all be blessed with someone who cares as much for us as we do for them," Massie said. "I pray that over my daughter and sisters every day. I want that, for each of you."

Typical Massie, infuriating her one second, and the most endearing brother the next. Maybe her hope had merit. Maybe Tegija planned to state his intent to be her suitor. A thin thread of hope dangled and she clung to it, refusing to let her logic cast it aside. She twisted it around her aching desire. Letting it levitate her with the euphoria of possibility.

Their safety risks were the normal hazards every traveler faced. The benefits of masking their identities was outweighed by the difficulty in concealing them. Hiding a diadem is easy, but attempting covert travel with Massie was effort wasted. Once locals spotted their Gryphon security escort, they began looking for Prince Massie. They traveled undisguised and prepared for the excited fuss they caused. Accepting the over-attentiveness of hosts with grace, and enjoying long interactions with the locals they encountered in their native province.

They spent the first two nights in small roadside towns, with economies established by travelers. The journey became challenging as they entered Lavieth. Off the main road the pace slowed, and their meals came from rations. The woods provided better sleeping accommodations over the empty towns in Lavieth, which stood vacant and vandalized. Absent of people and animals, the abandoned towns disturbed Katrina.

"It's so strange, we leave a thriving town in Mozgas this morning, but by the afternoon everything we encounter is abandoned."

"Towns in the heart of Bisma would look on the old occupants here with envy. These people have it easy," Massie said

"Easy," she said, riding through what remained of a humble street. Easy seemed an inappropriate term for the many lives disrupted here. What kind of sadness and loss would she see in the areas marked by battles? "No, what's easy is to ignore war. Especially when the only thing witnessed is a few written facts."

"That's how I prefer to experience war," he said.

"As anyone should, but you and I have a better sense of what's written."

"I do, and I know I'll never have the gift to go to war over and over again," he said. "I admire those who do, just like I admire those who work with other people's children day after day. I can do those things, but I'll never try doing them on a regular basis."

She spoke in a cadence used to recite something from memory. "To explore wars hardships with all the senses, leaves fresh carved memories, hardened by a purer form of life's darkness."

"I like that, who said it?"

"Thedmir."

"No kidding? Sounds like a smart fellow. Much more poetic than the things my ancient friend up there likes to ruminate at me."

"He has his moments," Katrina said, smiling at the memory of him. She followed Massie's gaze up to the shadow of Helos flying above. His dark wings outstretched in what looked like an effortless soar. Those were the same wings she now treasured sleeping under each night.

Sleeping outdoors in early spring still felt like a night outdoors in winter. The cold produced mornings of numb fingers and heavy frost. She showered Helos with gratitude for allowing them to bed down with him in Lavieth. Asleep, Helos sometimes breathed in a rhythmic trill that sounded similar to a cat's purr. Massie said the sound bothered him, but she found it soothing as she snuggled into the silk of Helos' warm black feathers.

It was anti-climactic to reach the destination of Lavieth's castle ruins. Massie described its condition well, calling it "wretched." The upper floors and ceilings were demolished. The largest tower stood alone, its windows gaping black holes. Glass panes were shattered bits among the debris. The buildings used by farmers were the only ones repaired, including the stable and a larger out building.

Katrina stood in the entrance hall, a husk of scorched walls and open sky. Rubble hid the old checkered floor of maroon and cream marble. A narrow path exposed patches of floor and the charred tiles. On the surrounding fields outside, hulls of old war machines lay like bone carcasses, their timbers gradually chopped away and consumed as firewood. The castle ruin stood barren, without even the resident shepherds or their livestock nearby.

"What now?" she asked. "We haven't seen anyone since we entered Lavieth. How are we to find our uncle?"

Massie stepped over a pile of bricks. "We find the entrance to the tunnels you saw."

Taken aback, she stared at him.

"You had a vision of tunnels here. I think those are connected to our uncle.

You must have some idea," he said. "It was your vision."

"I saw tunnels, but I never said I knew how to get into them."

"Oh, well, that's a problem isn't it?" he said, crossing his arms.

"I was drug underground," she said, frowning as she tried to recall details from the vision. "It was so fast, I was high above the ruin and then just plunged straight down into it."

"Great, I guess we get to poke around until we find them, or run into someone who can tell us where the Lord of Lavieth is."

She pressed her lips into a tight frown, and stepped past him onto another rubble pile.

The ruins possessed a looming eeriness. Their presence seemed like a kind of desecration. At every turn she expected to find someone ready to step out and strike her. The unsettling feeling clung to them as they searched the ruins. The continuous unease raised her suspicions. A dread too pure. Far more steady than a normal feeling, and she knew better than to be frightened of a vacant ruin.

She grabbed Massie's hand.

"What?" He asked turning around.

Looking in his eyes she wandered. *That feeling, like there's something more here.*

Yeah?

I have an idea, but first tell me, where in the ruin do you feel it the most?

He considered her question and pointed to the courtyard, *Over there.*

She pulled him by the hand and they walked into the courtyard.

"Where's Helos?" she asked.

"Not far," he said,

Helos peeked over the edge of a crumbling wall near the courtyard.

"Don't go leaning on those bricks," Massie said, swinging his arm, motioning for Helos to move back. "Those, are full of dust. We've talked about how to best avoid getting dirty."

Helos lowered his face further onto the bricks.

"My three year old minds better than you do."

"Massie," Katrina said.

"What? I'm the one he'll fuss at later, grumbling about his dirty feathers." Massie dropped his voice into a low mocking tone with a Gryph accent, "Oh, Massie can you fetch some barrels of water from the well? Please, my sheen has disappeared. Six dozen barrels or so will do."

Helos had a wry look in his eye as he crawled over the wall, holding his body low, and pulling rock and rubble loose.

"And the whole world reveres your kind for being smart," Massie said. "You saw that, he did that on purpose."

Helos turned to Katrina and she smiled. "It's nice to know I'm not the only loved one you like to tease." She walked to Helos and asked, "Do you sense it?"

Helos's bright gold eyes peered around the courtyard before wandering,

Yes.

"Have you experienced anything like it before?"

Helos settled onto his haunches as he considered her question. Massie picked his way towards them with renewed interest.

Yes, Helos wandered, and narrowed his eyes as he inhaled. He exhaled with a low moan-like growl. It was long ago, during the age of Paggio.

Katrina looked to Massie for clarification.

"They associate time to their elder Gryphon; the elder Paggio died over a hundred and fifty years ago."

It's a trick, there's a door here and someone's trying to keep it hidden with a repelling spell.

She nodded and asked, "Can you see the door?"

"What do you mean, 'can he see the door'?" Massie asked.

"He's a Gryphon, they can see all kinds of things we can't."

"You can see the door?" Massie said as more an accusation than question.

I can, Helos wandered.

"You let us stumble around here for hours, while you could see a door."

"That's not really fair," Katrina said.

It's behind you, Helos wandered, pointing his beak to the far wall. *Follow your hand along the length of that wall and you'll find it.*

"Hours, we've been here hours," Massie said.

With an annoyed glare at Massie, Helos rose up and walked over a pile of stone. Block scattered as he scaled the wall and exited the courtyard.

"I swear, sometimes," Massie said watching Helos leave.

She moved to the far wall and walked its length. Following Helos's instructions, she ran her hand along the wall. Her hand disappeared into part of the wall's surface. She pulled her hand back and turned to Massie.

"Let's get our gear."

She gripped at the straps of her pack, taking a deep breath as a familiar tension moved through her. She encountered it a hundred times in Cadet training. Coming whenever her squad did a search for an unknown mission. These often morphed into a kill whatever you find mess, which she hated. Those missions were awful, traveling with the least amount of information, trying to remember contingencies, and things always got changed up at the worst possible time.

Her tension grew stronger with her awareness of the real situation. If weapons were drawn, an opponent's kill blow would deliver more than angry bruises.

They found the hidden door, and she held her breath stepping through. As her face neared the wall, she winced expecting an impact. Passing through the illusion of stone, she emerged in a round, dimly lit, chamber. Massie followed, walking right into her.

"Are you going to step forward?" he asked, edging aside to stand next to her. "Or not."

They stared at six archers, each one holding an arrow at the ready.

Her hands lifted in surrender as she spoke in Bisma. "We're here to meet with our Uncle, Lord Jerard Larksbur. We've brought treaty documents from the Regent of Mozgas."

The archers held their position. As the stand off lingered on, Massie sighed with impatience. "Are any of you capable of notifying someone that we're here?" His Bisma flowed fast, demonstrating his frequent use of the language.

"We've been aware of your presence," a feminine voice said. A woman emerged from a darkened tunnel behind the archers. She had an ageless quality, a Delphi look, with straight dark hair and deep amber eyes. "You say our Lord Larksbur's your uncle?"

"My mother was born Lady Lena Larksbur, and his mother Lady Delany Larksbur."

The woman stepped past the archers and inspected them. "You look a great deal like Lady Lena, very beautiful."

"Thank you," Katrina said.

"Come, let us see if my Lord has any interest in speaking with you."

Two archers stepped beside Katrina and one ordered, "Your pack, Lady."

They gave a similar command to Massie and Katrina met his gaze. *Should we?*

Massie made an irritated face and gave her a short nod as he removed his gear.

"It's for your own safety, the stairs down are treacherous," the woman said.

The only light in the dark staircase the woman and archers held. Steps were missing in the staircase, at times two or more. Others shifted up or down making the pace uneven and jarring. Fastening the front of her jacket, Katrina dug her gloves from her pockets to fight the frigid air. The descent was long, but they arrived at the bottom and exited into a chamber.

Their breath misted into the room lit only with four red binti lights set in wall sconces. The archers returned their packs, and the woman ordered them back to their guard duties.

Time passed in awkward silence. Katrina shifted on her feet and Massie dropped his pack and took a seat on top of it. Katrina glared at him.

"What, am I being rude? They haven't even introduced themselves."

She shook her head, looking away, hoping whoever came would take no offense from Massie's impropriety. The door furthest away opened and a young woman with shoulder length brown hair and bright blue eyes stepped through.

"Lady Dina, I didn't expect you." the woman who escorted them said, her brow knit in dissent.

"If they're my cousins, it's more appropriate for me to greet them," Dina said, extending her hands in welcome as she approached. "I'm Lady Dina Larksbur, daughter of Lord Larksbur."

Katrina returned her open smile and introduced Massie and herself.

"Lord Larksbur's invited you to dine with us this evening, and until then

I'd be happy to provide you with a tour before showing you the guest quarters."

"Excellent," Massie said. They followed Dina and he wandered to Katrina, *It will be very excellent, as long as the guest quarters aren't part of the dungeon. If we're alive at nightfall, then I think this has the potential for a very lovely visit. Don't you think?*

Why do I let you talk me into doing anything? she wandered.

Because listening to me is the right thing to do, of course.

She expected more of the cold gloom, but instead they entered a hallway made of a light grey stone, all visible by daylight. Large crossing swaths of sunlight lay on the floor, cascading through windows placed in the same even fashion as above ground buildings. She stopped at the first window peering out at a clear view of the Iron Pine forest.

"How is this possible?" she asked.

"Using the same magic that hides the door that brought you here," Dina said, continuing down the sun-drenched hallway. Massie met Katrina's puzzled gaze with a look of suspicion. Every window held the bright visage of spring grass, and the budding trees of the outside world above them. They entered a round courtyard, above the ceiling shined with blue sky filtered through Iron Pines boughs. A sight she would claim impossible without looking at it with her own eyes.

Have you ever seen illusions like this? Katrina wandered. *Or even heard about them?*

Never, Massie replied.

They followed Dina on to what looked like a castle rampart. They gazed out over an expansive orchard of grapes. The afternoon sun shone from a ceiling illusion so seamless she expected to feel the breeze moving the clouds.

"We have several different orchards, and three large grain fields. Please, if you do encounter any bees down here, don't harm them. It's hard to maintain the bee colonies here. The underground sunlight works well to grow food and ease our spirits, but the bees are tough to fool," Dina said.

"Can you do everything down here that you do above ground?" Katrina asked.

"Most everything, we don't like cooking here. The smoke," Dina shook her head, turning her mouth disgust. "We cook in hidden rooms above ground unless there's some emergency."

"Is it daylight down here when it is night above ground?" Massie asked.

"No, whatever the sky is above ground is what we see down here. At night we have starlight and an ample supply of binti lights."

Dina took them to an apartment with two bedrooms, a small washroom, and a common room outfitted with parlor seating and a desk. They washed and dressed for dinner. Waiting in their common room, they stared out a wall of windows at the perfect illusion of sunset in the forest.

"I can't stop thinking about it," Massie said. "It's so impossible."

"Me too," she said.

"Do you remember the old childhood stories about the Fifth?" he asked.

"Yes, I wanted to meet a Regiek so badly when I was small. Didn't you?"

Massie grinned and nodded, "The people who begged God to take them, and he almost did. They stepped so close to God time for them stretched."

"And they could do incredible things," she said completing his thought. She thought about the famous relief at Amber Glass depicting the Regiek. Figures with arms raised to bright light, their image altered by the light's proximity. The Regiek were known for living twice the lifetime of an average Veilede, and having abilities so unusual they were hunted, captured, and brought to extinction long before the Airetti genocide.

"This place—it's the kind of thing I use to imagine when I heard the legends about the Regiek," Massie said.

"And that might be why we shouldn't press for too much information about it," she said.

Massie nodded. "I'm thinking if they were going to tell us, they'd have bragged a little more during our tour."

Dina escorted them to a modest room inside another apartment dwelling. A man of middle ages with a full head of brown hair and blue eyes sat at a round wooden table.

"My father, Lord Jerard Larksbur of Lavieth," Dina said.

Jerard stood in formal greeting. "It's a nice surprise to welcome my niece and nephew. The last time I saw you," he said gesturing to Massie, "you were very small. And you, well it's a miracle to see you alive."

She felt her lips tighten at his words. She remembered their encounter, laying in a wagon with fever and a scattered consciousness.

She let the genuine affection in his words warm her. For the first time since their arrival, her tense back muscles eased and relaxed.

"Please join me at our table."

They ate dinner as Jerard questioned them about their family, educations, and the conditions of the road as they traveled to the castle ruin. Restless with the formalities of polite conversation, Katrina worried about how to broach the never appropriate subject of her father's poisoning. But after dinner Massie's impatience bested hers.

"What do you know about the motives behind our father's poisoning?"

Lord Jerard looked unsurprised by the question, and seemed somewhat pleased to answer. "Before it happened, Regent Pavaldon's influence in Bisma was unsurpassed by his peers. His treaty work for the winter shoreline trading was significant here. Its approval meant a great deal of traffic through Lavieth."

"More travelers and more money," Massie said.

Jerard sat back in his chair and balanced a wine cup between both hands. "Father had no trouble appeasing King Dhanda after Pavaldon demanded Lena. Dhanda met her the summer prior, and found fault with her wit."

"My mother wasn't smart enough for him?" Katrina asked. Many labels were appropriate for her mother, but stupid would never be one of them.

Jerard made a quiet laugh. "That's a silly question coming from her daughter. Lena scared him; she was half his age and bolder than his son. She liked picking at his arguments and opinions. Lena can veil her tongue and say things right on the edge of what's tolerable to say to a monarch."

"So he preferred my mother Delany for betrothal ?" Massie said.

Jerard smiled and shook his head, "No, not really."

"If King Dhanda was fine with the broken betrothals, and our father's treaty was a success, then why did he want him dead?" Katrina said.

"He didn't, King Dhanda didn't care about your father or mine. The only man I've ever known with a long standing desire to kill your father was mine."

Katrina and Massie stilled, sharing a quick glance before waiting in wide-eyed astonishment for Jerard to continue.

"Father didn't want the traffic and trade the winter shipping treaty brought. He lobbied against it with King Dhanda, he bribed merchants, he solicited allies from Gryph, and he expected the treaty to fail. When it didn't, he wanted them all brought down. His rage got worse with Pavaldon taking Lena, and then Delany. His credibility was undermined. He'd worked years for the marital union to the Bisma crown."

"I don't understand," Massie said. "The traffic guaranteed new profits, an increase in finances for Lavieth. Why was Grandfather upset about the winter shipping treaty?"

"My dear nephew, look around you, you're in it. It's hard keeping large secrets like this. The more people you have walking back and forth, the quicker one of them will turn up with the talent to sense it." Jerard's gaze settled on Katrina as he paused to sip his wine. "Our family's hidden this place for centuries, and my father preferred death over being the heir the world would remember for exposing it. He also only liked to hear himself using words like new or change. When Lena came home crying of a broken heart, Father already had a plan to fix the winter trading treaty, he just wove her into it. Channeled her jealousy into the right weapon."

"But if grandfather set to destroy our father, then why did King Dhanda hang him for treason to the crown?" Katrina said.

"Like I said, he picked death over dishonor. He died a martyr, just the way he wanted. Leaving a legacy as the good Lord who was persecuted by a mad King. No one dares speak of King Dhanda's madness, but if you ever meet him, I bet you'll see him do things you've witnessed your father do."

"Did Grandfather poison any other monarchs?" Katrina asked.

Jerard grinned and shook his head, "Pick the right poison, spread the right misinformation, and you'll get the right chaos to end a treaty, and maybe start a war." Jerard made a quiet laugh, looking at them amused. "Father can't take credit for the wings prophecy though. That one Dhanda hates enough, he's made it an offense against the crown to mention it."

"Wings prophecy?" Katrina asked. "Is it something made up, to stir his madness?"

"He's an unwell, superstitious man," Jerard said, sighing as he jerked his head in a slow side-to-side motion, issuing a grinding series of pops as he cracked his neck. "It was a Veilede prophet who visited the capitol. Dhanda asked the clever question of who would be the King of Bisma when he died. The prophet told him it was the Regent of Mozgas." Jerard's eyebrows lifted and he grinned wide in amusement at Katrina and Massie's astonishment.

"What?" Katrina blurted out. "Our father was named in a Bisma prophecy?"

"No, no-no, he was never named," Jerard said, furrowing his brow in thought. He slowly rubbed his thumb across the pads of his index and forefinger. "The Veilede prophet made the prediction, and he never used Pavaldon's name. He just said it was the Regent of Mozgas, you get the idea."

"What else did he say?" Massie asked.

"It's really cheerful stuff. There'd be a devastating war, a big fire, and a sickness that's going to kill everyone. Then the Regent of Mozgas will become the King of Bisma and God will ordain him with some giant windstorm caused by a thousand wings. You two never heard about that huh? I'm surprised. I know your father has."

"Our father's heard a great many things, but some things he doesn't find fit for repeating," Massie said.

"I've never heard of it," Katrina said. "And I like to consider my habit of reading worth something."

"It's a crazy prophecy, and all it's ever done is fuel Dhanda's paranoia. He thinks the Regent of Mozgas is out to get him. It's rewarded the religious nuts as well, a boon for the fear mongers from Gryph. All of them using paranoia to bend people's minds to their version of God. I say it's all nonsense, there's not a stitch of proof any of its true."

"From the Veilede perspective, Marcus Ulithi is considered one of the more accurate prophets," Massie said.

"So you have heard his wings prophecy?" Jerard said.

"No," Massie said, "But Marcus Ulithi's as famous as Veilede prophets get. He'd be the only prophet out of Madar prominent enough to meet foreign kings. Do you think the war in Bisma, and the fire that's consumed its capital are part of his prophecy?"

"Well, if the great sickness comes behind it, be sure and let me know," Jerard said with a laugh. "You won't see me wringing my hands and pleading to gods like a mindless dog. Brooding about death is a waste of time. Anybody with that habit is someone I avoid. Death comes when it comes, and there's not a damn thing anybody can do about it, except speed it up."

Gripping her necklace from Thedmir, Katrina pressed her lips together and met her uncle's gaze. She took a shallow breath and steeled herself for her question, "Do you share Grandfather's need? Is your honor tied like his to guarding this place and keeping it secret?"

"If you mean, are you in danger being here? The answer's no. Do you remember the Larksbur crest?" Jerard said, gesturing to a decorative tapestry on the wall behind them. Katrina and Massie turned in their seats to look at the tapestry more closely. There was a dragon prominently laid across the foreground with fields and a castle behind it. Formal Bisma script ran in a banner beneath the dragon that read, This we will defend.

"The monarchy in Bisma has always assumed our family motto was some kind of declaration of loyalty to their defense," Jerard chuckled. "Idiots. We've never corrected them."

"Do you see Mozgas as a threat to Lavieth's defense?" Katrina asked.

"I've never shared in my father's obsessions, or his honorable legacy. He guaranteed us a life of privacy, for many years to come. My people are content to remain here while the wars above roll on. No, if we didn't want you here," Jerard paused and made a small grin suppressing a laugh. "Well, we'd have killed you in our threshold." Jerard leaned forward and set down his wine, waving an apologetic hand. "Ugh, that didn't sound right. You're family, you're safe, and you're welcome to stay here. I'm sorry, even I've had enough of my rambling tonight." Jerard rose from his seat and collected the packet of treaty documents she delivered. "I'll take what you've offered us off to bed with me, and consider it all in the morning."

Katrina and Massie rose from the table as well, and bid their uncle and cousin goodnight before returning to their apartment. They passed through the underground interior in silence. The surroundings stood as a magnificent imposter of an above ground palace. The ceaseless moan of wind working through ventilation shafts reminded her of where they were. As well as natural cave formations incorporated into various hallway and room designs. Like the wall of auburn rock, slick with water and ridged with glossy shells of mineral deposits, it ran the full length of their apartments sitting room.

"We should try to sleep," Massie said from the doorway to his room.

"I know," she said with a yawn.

"You're fighting it?"

"I am. There's a pocket of damp air in my room, and every time I walk through it I remember how far underground we are," she said, and shivered. "And, I don't know, it bothers me."

Massie walked over and offered her a hand up from where she sat, "It's one night. We can leave tomorrow, even if he doesn't give us an answer on the treaty. Those documents can always be returned on a later date."

Taking his hand, she pulled up to stand. "No, we'll stay until he's made a decision on the treaty."

He tilted his head, looking at her with concern, "You sure you're okay?"

She studied the glossy look of the auburn wall in the dim light, and nodded her head. "Uncle Jerard seemed very candid with everything he told us. He confirmed my mother's involvement."

"He did."

"They must have been plotting for a while."

Massie placed his hands on Katrina's shoulders in gentle reassurance. "He also revealed things we never knew. Like how ruthless a man our grandfather was." He squeezed her shoulders. "We need sleep."

"Goodnight," Katrina said, as she leaned forward, resting her forehead on his shoulder, and falling into a hug. A tired but soothing hug.

"We're both going to feel better in the morning," Massie said, releasing her. He turned her around, and steered her towards her room. "Sleep and a clear head will make this place and everything we've learned easier to stomach."

Overtired, she yawned as sleep pulled her to bed. She stirred half awake and restless, dozing in and out of strange dreams. Tossing against a damp pillow, she huddled deeper under blankets trying to fight the humid chill in the air. Massie's soft knock on her door the next morning brought relief. She peeked around her door wiping sleep from her eyes, and met his curt greeting.

"We're not spending another night down here."

A tired grin crossed Katrina's face, "No?"

"I'm happy to sleep on ice, beneath the dusty feathers of my snoring Gryphon, if it means I never again have to listen to the evil vent howling over my bed all night."

Katrina chuckled and slowly shut her door saying, "I'm going to get dressed."

She emerged and Dina arrived to walk them to breakfast. True to his word, Jerard read through the treaty documents the night before. He sat prepared to discuss them with her after breakfast. His diligence eased her fear of a lengthy negotiation. Massie joined Dina on an extended tour of the tunnel city, while she stayed to consider the treaty with Jerard.

Dishes were cleared away and a fresh tray of tea was brought for their discussion. Jerard laid the treaty documents on the table, each one crafted with the intent of making this negotiation a success. Written without flourish, in the Bisma language, with simple goals, and generous terms.

"These don't read like your father's work," Jerard said.

"I drafted them," she said.

Jerard's face was a stony mask. A tide of self-doubt swirled around Katrina's knees as thoughts began to suck her down. She was too young for this. What made her think she could do this? He must see flaws in the documents she missed. Would her work ever be as strong as her father's or Valgu's? Her mind raced, dismantling the credibility of her effort, with a speed that mocked the time she used to construct them.

Jerard tipped his head in a slight nod. "He's unwell then."

She paused to search for the best answer. "He monitors us, but authors very little now."

Jerard gestured to the documents laid out on the table in front of them. "Do you intend to use this as leverage in your war?"

She was shaking her head no before she answered. "It's part of our preparations, for what will need to be done after the war. We'll have several challenges when we assist rebuilding."

"Do the Veilede hold Lena's crimes against you?"

She caught her breath and met his blue eyes, shaking her head once before looking down at the cup of tea in front of her. The draft of cold air she disliked in her room seemed to find her again. She shifted in her seat, in an attempt to avoid the weight of it. "No, no one's ever said anything openly to me."

"But you do, you expect it. You feel responsible, for how your brothers and sisters lost their mothers."

"I—" she said, and swallowed. He had run her through with the truth, using such speed and power she sat stunned in shock. When she managed to catch her breath, she closed her eyes. Covering her mouth with one hand she tried to regain control of her mind, which shrieked in panic. How did the negotiation dissolve to this?

"The blue eyes, you look a lot like her, you even sound like her when you speak Bisma."

Katrina blinked her eyes open and stared at her uncle, biting back a retort. Yes, she looked like her, and what could she do about it? What could she do about anything her mother had done? Notorious criminals left more than legacies; they cast curses over their family, like the curse of misdirected hurt or hate. The measuring looks as victims considered the part you must have played in unknown crimes. A sting of tears rose behind her eyes.

"You're not Lena, and the weight of guilt is hers, even when she won't carry it. I know what it's like to live under that."

The familiar blue in his gaze reached for her with the same understanding as an outstretched hand. He too walked in the wake of someone he loved and regretted. Dropping her hand into her lap she accepted the solace offered in his eyes. Her voice was tight when she said, "She and I are a lot alike."

He smiled, tilted his head as he considered her words. "I think you inherited a fair share of her cleverness, but not her selfishness."

She shrugged, "I can be selfish." She sniffed and her eyes searched for something beside her hand to dab her nose with.

"Not like Lena," Jerard said, his face hardening with a look that brokered no argument. He pointed to the treaty documents, "This here's proof that your Pavaldon's daughter. If you ever see my sister again, you should go ahead and tell her I said that."

She choked a small laugh, and the threatening tears were gone. "If ever I do, I will."

Jerard held no objections to a treaty between Lavieth and Mozgas. Their brief and informal negotiation provided a start, a formal acknowledgement of an alliance, with the intent of building future ties through regular communication. The biggest thing Mozgas requested was for Lavieth to consider offering assistance to the ever increasing population of Bisma refugees seeking asylum.

Jerard's terms for Lavieth were unexpected, but something the Madar council would likely accommodate. He requested a Veilede academic team to study the oldest areas of the tunnel city.

"By keeping this place a secret, we've kept it safe, but now we're losing parts of it," Jerard said, rising from his chair and bidding her to follow him. "Please, come with me, I need to show it to you."

He led her through many tunnels, corridors, and staircases. If her uncle decided then to abandon her, she would be lost in an underground maze. The tunnels began to change. At first the ceiling seemed lower. Then the pattern of the paved floor changed from wide square stones to bricks the size of her hand. The small bricks formed a swirling pattern from the center of the floor outward. More natural underground cavern features were incorporated into wall construction.

They stepped into an enormous round room with carved panels spanning its three hundred and sixty degree perimeter. The construction paralleled the Amber Glass Temple. The ceiling here a smooth reflection of sky, free of any tree cover.

Massie stood in the center of the room with Lady Dina. His face guarded, listening to her talk.

"It outdates everything we know. It's from a time when all the borders were blurred in Madar and Bisma." Lady Dina's sweet voice echoed with untamed awe.

The panel opposite the door looked identical to a panel in the arena façade at Amber Glass. It was the panel representing the fifth, the Regiek. What spread out from this panel was a series of new images. Clear images, immortalized in stone, and each rimmed with a script so ancient, it would take specialized scholars to translate their meaning.

The first look Massie gave her read as the question, "Are you as amazed by this as I am?" Katrina tilted her head and made a slight nod of agreement.

The room gripped her with the desire to linger. These were ancient art works, who beckoned with clear images, but to the untrained observer they were mysteries. Their messages lost to posterity, as the forms captured no longer announced the artist's purpose with ease. You could marvel at their beauty, but spend a lifetime translating their meaning into any form of understanding.

"This is what you want the scholars for," Katrina said to Jerard.

"Yes, as you look closer, you'll see this is part of Veilede history, as much as it is a part of ours," Jerard's eyes did a fast tour of their surroundings and a nervous smile edged his lips.

"Father and I have had many discussions about it," Dina said.

Jerard grunted and met Dina's eye. "My father and forefathers would beat me if they heard what I said; kill me if he knew they were down here."

"But dead ancestors can't help fix ancient drainage pipes, or explain why the windows in some areas are starting to go out," Lady Dina said.

Jerard's face grew somber as he nodded his head in agreement.

"If my family's legacy is tied to maintaining this place, then I'll decide what's best for it," Jerard said as he gestured to his daughter. "Dina and I agree, too much has already been lost because our family's old compulsive need to possess this heritage as ours and ours alone." Jerard looked up at the perfect sky moving on the ceiling above them. "Any idiot can look at this and see its history's entwined with more than just us."

Katrina agreed with him, and followed his gaze to marvel at the ceiling. "Have either one of you ever been to Amber Glass?"

Jerard and Dina shook their heads.

"We just have old drawings of the reliefs at Amber Glass and the ones from the Mozgas Plateau," Dina said.

"You have drawings of Amber Glass and the Mozgas Plateau," Massie said. "Could you show us those?"

"Actually Father had our curators compile some of our better copies to take with you. We hope they aid in luring some of your better scholars here," Dina said.

"I'm certain they will," Massie said.

Katrina stepped towards the first of the panels and began a walk around the circumference of the room, considering what was shown in each one. The very first one displayed people building the underground fortress. A giant dragon wound its way behind them through the tunnels. One appeared to be a map of some kind. The next a Minotaur and a man held keys before a door with a sleeping dragon behind it. More panels showed rows of Airetti impaled on spikes, battle scenes, and Mahigans with Gryphons overhead. Another depicted an ocean battle between Delphi and massive serpents. On the next was a serpent coiled around a hill, with a city at the top, engulfed in fire.

The rows of dead on a beach made Katrina avert her eye and look away again when faced with the one beside it showing people collapsed ill over everyday tasks. It was easier to wonder about the young couple with intertwined hands, standing before a door, with the sleeping dragon behind it. Or the couple with a young woman holding a key in one hand, while an Airetti man held her other hand intertwined with his, using his wings to shelter her from a mass of shadows and monster-like creatures.

Katrina stopped in front of another couple with a man and Airetti woman. The couple's hands were intertwined and birds lowered crowns to their heads. The panel was edged with a motif of flying birds, and all around the royal couple, people knelt with bowed heads.

"That man..." Katrina said, feeling a pulse of energy ripple through her body as the hair on her arms stood up. She crossed her forearms and tried to rub away the sensation.

"He looks like your father," Jerard said.

Katrina furrowed her brow and glanced at Jerard before looking back at the panel.

"There's a resemblance," she said, focusing on the eyes of the man in the panel as she shook her head. "But, I actually think he looks more like Valgu."

"Dammit if it doesn't," Massie said putting his hands on his hips as he stepped beside Katrina. "It looks like Valgu posed for that."

"But it could just as easily be an Aranysarga ancestor," Katrina said.

"Perhaps," Dina said. "But the curators insist these were carved with visions given to the ancients of a distant future."

"Let me be the first to guess," Massie said. "This panel here depicts the Wings Prophecy." Dina arched her eyebrow as Massie turned to Jerard, "Last night, you made all that up, didn't you? You knew about the prophecy, but not because you heard about it from King Dhanda, you learned about it from these walls."

"Massie," Katrina said. She knew he heard her scolding, but kept his focus on Jerard.

"I know these walls better than some of our curators," Jerard said. "But I don't put stock in prophets anymore than my father did. He was furious when he heard about the Wings Prophecy. He thought someone sold our secrets here to the King of Bisma."

"Is that what happened?" Massie said.

"From what we know, this remains a secret from him. We learned everything we could about the day King Dhanda met the Veilede prophet. His ideas might run with some of the images on these walls, but that prophet's never been down here. I don't know if what he's said is true. One might be related to the other, or not at all. It could be, everything you see in this room's already happened. Prophecies amount to one of two things, an odd coincidence or a bedtime story. Neither one affects a common man's life."

Katrina considered Jerard's words as she gazed at the panel with the carving that looked like Valgu. Her uncle might be right, but it was an eerie coincidence to see Valgu's face here. As the first-born son of a Regent, Valgu would never be considered a common man.

17

Hide and Seek

Dina and two guards brought them back to the world above ground. Helos sat in the castle ruins when Katrina and Massie emerged from the tunnel city. Brisk wind and an overcast sky greeted them. Taking a deep breath, Katrina savored the freshness of the air.

Helos sat upright as they approached. His current steady gaze meant he had something urgent to relay. Alert to this, she turned to Massie. His features had a slight stoniness, and she knew he and Helos wandered privately.

Massie gave Katrina a brief bleak expression before turning to Dina and saying, "I guess we're not going to need the horses, cousin."

"What?" Katrina asked.

"There's Delphi teams scattered in a line of observation posts along our route back. There's too many of them to assume their presence is random. The first one is about an hour from here. They've surrounded us here with a staggered line to catch us if we divert south on foot. They intend to find us."

"Who's out looking for us?"

"I don't know," he said.

"That many Delphi?"

"Who's to say it's not Puternic's last attempt at securing you for the Delphi?"

Katrina sucked a breath through her teeth and then groaned in frustration. "That is so absurd."

Massie shrugged and said, "But I wouldn't put it past him to do something like that. It's more likely a crew for hire."

"It really doesn't matter who waits for us, and I doubt they went to this much trouble for a friendly chat," she said.

"Right. So do we ride past and let them spot us, or avoid them on foot and see what we run into in the next town?"

"We should avoid them," she said.

Massie nodded.

"Pardon my intrusion, but may I offer a suggestion?" Dina asked. Katrina nodded and Dina continued. "We could send a team to ride your horses back. They'd be a small diversion, but it might help. They could meet up with you in one of the towns along the way, or even ride all the way down to Folmander."

"It's a good idea," Massie said.

"I agree," Katrina said.

"We should have them go ahead of us, take the lead," Massie said. "They can stay in the first village and wait for us."

"We'll walk cross country," Katrina said. "Avoid the main road and concentration of observation posts."

"It's a setback, but it's feasible," Massie said. "Helos will travel with the diversion. Tonight you and I will need to scout out the best observation post to sneak by."

"Why deal with them at all?" Katrina asked. "I say we go back down into the city. Tonight I'll wander with Valgu in neutral and request a Mahigan escort come for us."

"Oh great," Massie said, his face tight with agitation. "Then we'll get to listen to Valgu say he told us so."

Katrina frowned and shook her head. "It's the safest option. We don't know why they're out here, or what they have planned. I think it's best if we just avoid any and all risks."

"Brentin, I need to talk to Brentin," Massie said.

"Brentin, what?"

"He'll know what's going on," Massie said, and put one hand on his hip. With a single head nod he smiled as if everything was decided. "I meet him in neutral. Whatever's going on, if Brentin doesn't have information about it, then nobody does."

"He's that good?"

"Yes, he's that good."

"I have a better idea, you go see Brentin in neutral, and I'll find Valgu."

"We don't need a battalion of Mahigans to get us home safely."

"Why should we deal with this extra trouble alone? Why take a risk? Do you really want to do that, just to avoid Valgu gloating?"

"Yes, don't you?"

She sighed and shook her head. He was serious. Despite his plan, she intended on finding Valgu in neutral tonight. Then something strange came over her. As Massie spoke, she felt an unusual softening of her resolve.

"Can you even imagine us on this trip with the likes of Major Ehnis and friends in tow? No, we're fully capable of dealing with whoever's out there. I have a sword, you have a sword, and we're traveling with a Gryphon."

Katrina tried to hold onto her determination to find Valgu, but the stronger she held onto the thought, the weaker her conviction to follow through became. How bizarre yet interesting; she never suspected Massie of possessing any unique talents outside of his shifting ability. This immediate tempering of her resolve raised her suspicions. How many things had Massie talked her into doing? He was known for his charm, and people praised his natural way of eliciting information. Was his power of persuasion more than a personality trait? Knowing the intensity of Owl's empath ability, the potential for Massie to be gifted as well was very probable. She wondered why she had never considered it before.

"Looks like we'll be treading on your hospitality for another night," Massie said to Dina. "We need to inform Lord Jerard of our plans, and get his approval for a diversion team."

Reconnaissance, the kind of mission Katrina was good at as a Cadet. Having mediocre weapons skills, she liked any mission without a need for combat altercations to be successful. Scouting out enemy positions was generally a combat free mission. Sometimes a change of mission order came, but normally engaging the enemy during a reconnaissance meant mission failure.

Putting into practice her reconnaissance lessons, here among the Iron Pines, was a unique challenge. Each tree served as an obstacle and had to be navigated with care. Staying close to the base of each tree trunk, moving at an agonizing speed slow. Every step made had no sound, a practiced ability she took pride in. Her ears trained in on the noise in the forest and its remarkable quiet. The only sounds heard were the occasional knocking of branches far overhead. She peered among the shadows, searching for targets she knew would be settled overhead in the trees.

The slow pace rewarded them when they found the first outpost. Three men sat on low branches with backs propped against two different tree trunks. Her heart raced with the excitement of finding them. They sat nestled in cloaks woven and dyed with patterns that resembled the bark of an Iron Pine. One of the three Delphi men sat awake.

These Delphi men struck her as odd. They were odd because these Delphi cut their hair close to the scalp. Every Delphi she had ever met wore their hair long.

She and Massie continued on past the first observation post. The second observation post they found looked identical to the first. Three men perched in a tree, wearing camouflage cloaks. The one alert man in the trio, leaned forward in his perch, peering towards them. Her pulse quickened.

Does he see us? she wandered.

I'm not sure.

The longer the man stared into the shadows hiding them, the harder she cringed. She swore he looked her in the eye. Blood running cold, she tensed as the chill extended through her entire body. A wave of sickness rose in her throat, and she wanted to run. The man's eyes sat deep in their sockets, yet bulged enough to make his eyelids stretch tight as they blinked closed.

He's looking right at me, she wandered.

He can't see this far into the shadows.

I think he can, I think he can see us. Her mind raced in a frantic search for the best possible solution to this dilemma.

The man was thin, with dark hair receding at his temples. The sharp creases in his cheeks marked him as someone the same age as her father. His gaze ran to the ground as he scrubbed his temple. Shifting on his perch, the man reclined back against the tree.

Katrina stepped back, moving away in small increments. Massie followed her lead, and they worked their way through the forest back to the castle ruins. At the ruins, they sat down together along a crumbling inner wall, and drank water in silence. She studied the way Massie's fair hair and skin reflected different shades of blue and lavender in the darkness. She debated, trying to decide if they should continue on with their intended plan, or if she should contact Valgu in neutral tonight and wait for a unit of Mahigans to arrive and escort them home.

"Jlande didn't see us," Massie said.

"Jlande? You recognized one of them?" She remembered how the alert man gazed into the shadows and met her eyes. She wandered Massie the memory.

Massie took a tentative breath and nodded. "He's the one in charge of them. Father employed him for years to help search for you and Nuala. He found Lady Juniper."

"But he no longer works for Father," she said.

"No, I don't know who his employer is." Massie took a long sip of water.

"I don't want to play games with these people," she said, feeling a rise in frustration from Massie's continued calm. "I want to get home. When I go to sleep I'm going to find Valgu. Then I'm going to wait here for however long it takes until a unit of Mahigans arrives."

Massie fixed the stopper on his water container. Bunching his eyes closed he sighed and let his head fall back against the wall. "No, Katrina, no. That's extreme, nobody out there saw us."

"You don't know that. He was looking me in the eye. I think I know when someone is looking me in the eye."

"He didn't see you, and these observations posts don't need to be a big deal. We can avoid them and continue on home just the way we planned."

Once again her resolve softened. "I don't see why we even bothered planning for them at all. I wish we were home already."

"Don't bother Valgu tonight," he said. "Please, will you trust me?" His head jerked up and he stared at her.

Valgu had never risked her safety, and Tegija had taken every precaution to ensure her protection. She trusted them, but as she considered Massie and the risks taken with him, her trust wavered.

"Why am I always the one trusting you? I need to trust you, but that same kind of trust never seems to flow towards me."

"That's not true," he said.

"Well that's how it feels right now," she said.

"I do this, it's my job. They trained me to do this, to deal with these kinds of morons all the time." His face alive with emotion, anger and frustration waiting for his patience to fold. "I'm trying not to be angry, and not take offense by you thinking I would risk the safety of us both. This kind of work has been my life for years. When I say he didn't see us, then I guarantee you, he didn't see us. I'm going to meet up with Brentin in neutral, and in the morning we're going to continue on just like we planned. "

The question of Massie's potential power was answered, she was convinced. The safe thing to do was find Valgu tonight. But Massie filled his words with strange magic, and her better instincts faltered. Her opposition neutralized, and she felt patient. He swayed her into being patient. Ridiculous, her first instinct was never patience. She fumed, angry at how her brother manipulated her with some kind of magic.

"I'm going to bed," she said, standing and walking to the entrance where Dina waited for them.

Without a word or goodnight, Katrina went into her room and closed the door. She removed her boots and lay down in bed with her clothes on. It would only be a few short hours before they returned to the surface to try and sneak by the Delphi.

She awoke to Massie nudging her. Startled out of her sleep, she blinked at the dim outline of his face. He looked drowsy.

"Hey," she said.

"Hey," he said. "We need to avoid those checkpoints while it's still dark."

She cleared her throat, "Yeah?"

"Yeah."

She held his gaze and rolled onto her stomach, propping herself up on her elbows. "I know what you were doing to me last night."

He blinked at her, and there was a mild apology in his eyes.

"You and Owl received your gifts from your mother?" she asked.

Massie gave her a half smile and squinted his eyes studying her for a moment. "No, we got them from Father. I thought you knew."

Katrina's head reeled back in surprise. "No, I didn't. Owl's gift came from Father?"

"It's faint in Father."

"Can he do what you did to me last night?" she asked.

"Think about all his wives. Do you really think he's naturally that charming? He's half mad, the whole world knows it, but he's managed to stay in power and wed two more women."

Katrina sat up and slung her feet over the edge. Grabbing her boots, she began lacing them on. "I'm amazed."

Massie got up and stood for a moment with his arms crossed. "Let's talk about it later, we need to go."

"Alright, but one more question. Does your ability work on everyone?"

Massie chuckled quietly. "Everybody but Helos. I tried to stop him from selecting me. I kept telling him he was mistaken, but it didn't do any good."

Massie held open her door and looked back. "I'm sorry you didn't know."

She yawned and made a dismissive wave as she stood and followed him to the door.

"What did Brentin have to say?" she asked.

Massie shook his head and picked up his bag, slinging it over one shoulder. "He knew nothing."

"The man who would know, knew nothing?"

"He got pulled into the group escorting Rosalba to Mozgas for your ceremony. He said nobody expected us to make Folmander before the end of the week."

"Did you try to find out from anybody else?"

"I did. Nobody can explain why Jlande's crew is out here. The only information they had was who he's working for."

When he hesitated, her lack of patience got the best of her. "And who's that?"

Massie stood tall and cinched a strap on his bag before meeting her eye.

"The King of Bisma."

"They're certain?"

"Our people nabbed a recent defector from his crew. He said he left because the King of Bisma had them working a job, and it was going to get everybody in the crew caught and killed."

"Caught doing what?"

"Not sure," he said crossing his arms.

"If Jlande's crew is working for our wartime enemy, then this is a danger greater than we expected."

"It is," Massie said bowing his head. "I told them to send a unit to meet us in the next town."

"You did?"

"I did," he said nodding. "Is that a fair compromise? We get past the outposts this morning, and make it to the next town. We can wait there until our escort arrives."

She still preferred avoiding Jlande and his Delphi all together, but Massie's concession for better security was an unexpected surprise.

"The sooner we get past Jlande's crew, the better," she said.

Everything above ground became vivid and real. Being spotted by unknown Delphi men, that was real. The potential of drawing her weapon to defend herself, that was real. The need to focus and move through the forest as taught, that was real. They faced a dangerous situation, and the realness of it could break her nerves if she let it.

She could do this-she was doing this. As she settled into their pace, she felt an amusing irony remembering she was kind of good at this. Time seemed to move faster, yet their movements continued on achingly slow. Reaching the first observation post, they paused. The trio of hired men sat nestled in the tree they occupied the night before. The man seated furthest from her sat awake now. Her every breath was controlled. Time seemed to move slow and come to a halt. She felt every blink of her eyes, and each second spent gauging the men long and intense. She remembered Jlande's strange bulging eyes peering into the shadows and the overwhelming need to move, to flee, to get out of there - now. Relief coursed through her as she took a step, and then the next. Each pace beyond the observation post brought a sense of relief, and the small confidence they completed an obstacle.

They walked on, picking up the pace. Images of treetops flashed in her mind and she halted. Massie took her arm with gentle care and urged her to keep moving as he wandered to her.

"It's just Helos. He's confirming the terrain ahead is clear. They didn't station observation posts in depth in this direction. The other ones are still along the main road to the west."

She nodded and moved forward, glad they had the blessing of a Gryphon providing security.

Two hours past the observation post, the dim sky of an approaching sunrise bathed the forest in blue and grey hues. In less dense areas, ice fog settled and frost crusted the ground. Spent pine needles as long as her forearm wore coats of iridescent white. They shimmered in the early glow of morning. Her breath rolled away, misting into the first rays of sunlight that dotted the ground in large patches.

She and Massie had fallen into an easy rhythm walking side by side. Katrina stopped and took out her water. Massie stopped a few paces ahead before turning back to join her. He unslung his pack and pulled out his water container.

"I never suspected the gift you share with Father," she said.

Massie considered her with a brief glance before unstopping his water container. He took a long swig, wiping the edge of his mouth when he finished.

"Owl and I each have one of Father's two gifts. But our single gifts are much more concentrated. Owl has his empathy, and I was blessed with his charming persuasion. It's why he and I have always butted heads. We tend to cancel each other out. Neither one of us can succeed at swaying the other."

"How often have you used it to sway me?" she asked, placing the stopper to her water container and putting it back in her pack.

"Deliberately? Never, but when my mind is fixed on something, when I'm in an argument...let's just say I rarely lose. It's not intentional. I've learned to use caution, but I don't know how to stop or shut it off in an emotional situation. I have as much control over it as Owl does, which is to say very little."

"How many people know you can do this?"

"It's a family secret, with a few exceptions of people on the Madar Council, and a few people in Gryph. Otherwise I'm not around other people long enough to give them a chance at figuring it out."

Massie put his water away and adjusted his pack.

"I feel a little bit better knowing you weren't trying to manipulate me," she said.

"No, of course not," he said, smiling as he shook his head. "It wouldn't be right to manipulate the future Regina of Mozgas, even if she's my sister."

They set off again, and by the afternoon her feet ached with fatigue. She spent more time exercising from a saddle recently than on her own two feet. Pressing on, she did her best to think of other things, ignoring the aches and pains of her body after a long day's journey. They were still hours from the border when the long shadows of sunset began.

"If I could, I'd try and make myself keep going," she said.

"I'm ready to make camp," he said.

"I'm not," she said. "The nights have still been bitter cold. It's going to be a long night without Helos."

Massie gave a small grunt of agreement. "No Helos, and no fire. Maybe we turn in early and when the cold wakes us we just get up and press on."

"I like that idea," she said.

They forced down food neither one of them felt hungry for and went to bed in a grove of young pines. She fell asleep and Valgu summoned her in neutral. Sick with remorse, she approached him as he paced the length of the glen patio.

"You're okay," he said gripping her arms and inspecting her with a frantic concern.

She smiled and pulled him into a hug saying, "Yes, yes, we're fine. We made it past the perimeter."

"Nothing else has happened then?"

"No, we're just tired and cold."

"If it wasn't for that, I'd tell you stay where you are until Major Ehnis arrives."

She sighed, "Somehow I knew it would be him."

"Yes, he was quite adamant. I'd be accused of favoritism if I picked anyone else."

"Aren't you allowed to play favorites as the acting Regent?"

Valgu smiled at her sarcasm. "Not when I'm trying to keep you out of harm's way." He pulled a chair out for her and offered her a seat. She took it as Valgu sat beside her.

"Major Ehnis and a unit of Mahigans are on their way to find you. We're doing what we can to determine why one of Father's old hires is out hunting for you. It's likely the King of Bisma. Most of what we have points to him."

"Most of what we have."

"I'm convinced it's him."

"Who else could it be?"

"Among the reports concerning Regina Rosalba's safety, there's a threat that listed both you and her. It's a touchy accusation made against one of the Tiarnas Princes in Dinhac. Milios has evidence he's looking to kidnap you or Rosalba. He'd be happy with either of you. He intends to wed by force over winning an Airetti rally."

"That's ambitious," she said sitting back in her seat as she traced one finger along the grain of wood in the table. "When you say force, you mean…"

"I mean force. He'd forcibly claim one of you. Regent Selig adamantly denies the rumor, but it's hard to say what one of his sons might do."

"I hate this," he said. "We should have planned for more security."

"You pushed for it, and I didn't listen. It's my fault," she said.

"I wanted you to be right. It's fortunate you can deal with this, even if you're not an Alvara."

"I thought you were going to say Mahigan," she said, smiling as she leaned over and embraced him. He circled his arms firmly around her shoulders. She rested her head against him and sighed as their surroundings began to vibrate and she felt the strong pull of neutral ending.

"Get home," he said releasing her from their embrace. "We have more and more people showing up for your Regina ceremony. Everyone's excited about it, but we need you here to make that happen."

"I'm coming home," she said, gripping his hand even as their time together in neutral was yanked away.

She blamed the cold for waking her. Lying huddled next to Massie, the heat of his body was some of the only warmth she felt. The ground seemed to have frozen beneath her and invited chilly gusts to worm under her blankets, across her back, and down her legs. Her feet ached and she wriggled her toes in a vain attempt to warm them.

"Massie," she whispered.

He grunted and his eyes half opened to peer at her, exhaustion showing in his tired frown.

"I'm freezing," she said.

"Me too," he said.

"Let's go."

Massie groaned as he sat up, but managed to stand and start packing his bedroll before she had fully sat up.

"You know what I hate?" he asked.

"What's that?"

"When everyone is all excited for spring to come." His words were spoken in a hoarse grumble. "I don't know why people like spring, unless you live where it's warm year round. Spring here; it's just a dark, cold, muddy prelude to actual nice weather. No, see, summertime is the only season worthy of notoriety. It's warm during the daytime and at night. Food is ripe, fishing's good, and you get to enjoy life under more blessed hours of sunlight. Spring. I hate spring. I hate everything about it. It's diabolical the way the weather never decides if it's going to be hot or cold."

If she needed to pick her favorite part of Massie's antics, his crabby ranting would win. Thedmir used to listen to her carry on in a similar manner about inconsequential things. She understood Massie's frustration, but was too cold and tired to turn his outburst into a joint tirade.

With slow progress they walked through what was left of the night. At midmorning they reviewed their maps, and determined they had crossed the border back into Mozgas. Tired, they both agreed it was a good idea to lie down and get some rest. The ground was still chilly, but the air was warm and the sunlight felt fantastic. It was late in the afternoon when they walked up a rise that overlooked the small town of Nactulli. The town and surrounding farms sat in a dormant flood plain for the Tulli River. Nactulli was the last town in Mozgas if you were traveling the main road north, and the first town in Mozgas if you crossed the border from Lavieth, Bisma heading south.

"I say we don't risk getting spotted until we decide to find an inn for the night," she said.

"Next town then?" he asked.

"Next town," she said.

They succeeded in avoiding Nactulli, keeping to the Iron Pines and passing Nactulli's orchards and farm fields.

"How far ahead is Helos with our diversion?" she asked.

"You mean how far ahead are our horses?" he said, giving her his teasing smile.

"Yes, our horses," she said. "Where are they?"

"They're still a day ahead of us. They haven't been approached or asked any questions about us, but Helos is suspicious."

"What does Helos recommend?"

"I hate his recommendation," he said.

There could only be one recommendation from Helos that could make Massie scowl like he was. He wanted them to spend the night in the forest again.

"Oh, please tell me you're kidding," she said.

Massie shook his head.

"I never thought I'd say this," she said, kicking a loose rock. "But I'm starting to prefer the option that might include killing a man, if I can sleep in a warm bed."

Massie chuckled, "It's tempting. We did it last night. If we've got to do that again tonight, then that's what we do," he said.

"I can't wait to get home," she said.

The long shadows of evening dimmed as night broached the horizon. Massie halted in place and looked about in a frantic search. His look sent a shiver of dread through her.

"What is it?"

Massie took off at a jog and she followed. A sick panic settling in her stomach by Massie's sudden action.

It's Helos. This way, stay behind me.

They ran across a glade and then through another copse of trees. There was another break in the forest and Massie slowed his run to a jog as he approached the prone figure of Helos, stretched between the trunks of two giant Iron Pines.

"What's happened?" Massie said, throwing his pack off and running towards Helos.

The diversion team was ambushed, Helos wandered. Helos wandered images of the team. The team lay side by side in a line along the main road, all dead.

"When I flew low enough, they launched Mahigan nets at me. One succeeded."

Helos rose up and stepped forward dragging something near his left rear claw forward. Massie gripped and worked at releasing the netting caught up around Helos' hind leg. Katrina gasped when she noticed more than the Gryphon's leg tangled in the netting. The limp form of a man was caught up in it.

Katrina looked from the fury in Helos's eyes to the man sprawled out behind him.

That one tried to net me, Helos wandered. *Let him die from his own misdeeds.*

By the looks of the man, he probably was dead. She edged closer to him. Swollen bruises obscured over half of his face. He had one leg bent at an unnatural angle. His clothes were torn and the legs of his pants were shredded and stained dark with dried blood. Every time the man exhaled, she heard a wet gurgling sound. Without the immediate help of healers, the man would die.

She joined Massie in prying Helos free. The feathers at Helos' neck rose in agitation. An odd numbness affected her fingers as she manipulated the smooth metallic strands of net. The memory of being enfolded inside a net like this hit her, and she wanted to fling it away. She paused, took a deep breath, and increased her grip on the strands she had pulled free.

Massie succeeded in disentangling the largest section, which was snared around Helos' hip. It fell away, and the rest of the netting became easier to pull free. Helos lifted his leg as she and Massie looped the last of the netting off his foot. When Helos stepped away, he walked with a noticeable limp.

"Are you all right?" she asked.

"He'll be okay," Massie said.

"Where are you going?" she called after the retreating form of Helos.

"He's going to rest somewhere long enough for me to question him," Massie said, walking over to the man. Massie stood with his arms crossed, looking him over.

He yelled over his shoulder in the direction of Helos. "Nice work, did you drag him against every tree on the way here?"

With a silent chuckle Massie grinned and looked back down at the man. He pulled a dagger from his belt and knelt down over the man.

"There's a reason the people in Gryph like to do battle alongside Gryphons." With the tip of his dagger, Massie poked the bruised side of the man's face. The man's one good eye blinked open and stared at the blade poking him. Slowly the man shifted his focus to Massie.

"Gryphons kill with impunity," Massie said. "Make a bird angry, it'll fly off. Make a Gryphon angry, it'll find a way to kill you."

The man made a high pitched groan.

"Who hired your crew?"

The man wheezed in a deep breath and his mouth worked to try and form words. Closing his eyes tight, he took another breath and said, "Jlande wants an exchange."

"No, he doesn't," Massie said. He tapped the tip of his dagger up the man's bruised face until he reached the base of his swollen eye. "Try again."

The man was wheezing harder and his voice was a strange mix of a high-pitched whine and a hoarse cough. "No-no-no, it's true! He can, he can give you," the man started coughing and Massie lifted his dagger away, and waited until the man settled back into several hard breaths. When he regained his ability to speak, he managed to say only one word with each breath. "It's. Your. Wife."

"My wife?" Massie asked, disbelief thick in his voice.

Katrina caught her breath. Massie looked unimpressed.

"Her for your sister," the man said.

"Delia," Massie said.

"Her. For the one...being made. Regina."

"That sounds a little more like the truth. Who wants my sister?"

"Jlande," the man said.

"Yes, I got that part. Who's she for? Who's paying Jlande for her?" Massie asked.

"King Dhanda." the man said, his eye scrunching tight as he gasped for air.

"Why?" Massie asked.

"I-I don't know," the man said.

Helos returned, limping over to where he stood over Massie and the man. The man looked up at Helos, his one good eye wide with terror. His breath became a rapid wheezing pant and his voice was a whining mess of air and a high-pitched pleading.

"I just do what he says. It's just a job. I didn't know."

Massie stood up and stepped away as Helos seized the man with his front claws.

"I'm sorry, I didn't know. I didn't-I'm sorry-please."

Helos lifted the panting man to his chest. The man cried out in pain and made a muffled protest. Even with his injured hind leg, Helos leapt half of the forest height. Extending his wings, and angling his torso, Helos gained the space needed to stretch his wings. In a few strong flaps he broached the forest canopy and was gone.

Part of her was curious about how Helos intended to kill the man, but fewer details made some things easier to forget.

Massie picked up his pack and opened it. "Let's eat something while we wait for him to get back."

They sat down together and ate a few bites of food. Massie walked over to the Mahigan net and began laying it out.

"Is that salvageable?"

Massie nodded. "It is, I can show you how to fold it."

"I was wondering why you didn't cut it," she said, dusting off her pants and taking the end he gestured for her to grab.

"You can cut it, but it will wreck a knife and destroy the net's value."

She paid attention to the steps Massie showed her to reload the Mahigan net. Reloading it alone would require more practice.

A misting rain began as night set in. With Helos still gone, they packed up their gear and left. Rain dampened their clothes and brought the chill of night faster. With numb fingers she pulled at the straps to her bag. In this rain and deep cold, sleep was impossible.

She bumped into something. It hit her thigh flew away from her and coasted back. A wooden seat suspended from a rope spun by. A chair lift, one of several stationed in a line in the clearing they crossed.

Katrina stood and waited for it to swing back. She grabbed hold of it and inspected the branches and alignment of trees overhead. Massie, who was a few steps ahead of her, stopped and came back beside her.

"What's this?" he asked.

"Looks Skrieni. I think there's a village, or at least the buildings for one."

"We've formed a decent relationship with the village closest to the plateau," he said. "I have no idea how Skrieni living this far out would welcome you or me though."

"Worst-case, they send us back down," she said. "Best-case, we have somewhere warm to sleep."

"You okay, seeing a bunch of Skrieni?"

"I'm okay with a warm place to sleep," she said.

"For sure, my favorite part too," he said.

"Have you ever used one of these?" she asked.

Massie shook his head, "Can't say I have."

She walked him through getting on, and riding the lift. Massie followed her instructions and bent his knees to lower his body weight.

"Ho-ho!" he said as the lift quickly began to rise towards the top of the trees.

"I'll meet you up there."

Getting onto the nearest lift, she followed Massie into the treetops.

This time of night she expected to smell cook fires, and the glow of lamps from family homes. Instead the elevated pathways were in disrepair and the doors to the nearby buildings stood open to vacant rooms. The small village appeared abandoned.

"Well, no one's telling us to go back down," Massie said.

Traveling higher into the trees exposed them to more rain. Their boots skid on slick platforms as wind pelted rain and bits of ice at them. They entered a room and closed the door. The enclosed space muffled the sound of falling rain. Being out of the wind provided them with instant comfort. Katrina removed her binti light from her bag and held it out so they could get a better look at the room. The space looked like it had once been used for storage, with rows of empty baskets stacked against the far wall.

"Do you know what those are for?" Massie said, sweeping rain and ice from his hair.

"I think they're for collecting pine nuts?"

"Maybe this place only gets used for harvesting," he said.

Katrina nodded and rubbed her hands together, "Should we try to find a room with a fireplace?"

He nodded and followed her along the main platform running between buildings. They came to the end where the largest buildings sat. Inside was a large square hearth with several benches and tables lined up neatly on two sides of the room.

"This will work," he said.

The far wall had cords of firewood neatly stacked against it. Large cooking pots and utensils hung on the wall with wooden pegs. Katrina grabbed several pots down.

"Where are you going with those?" Massie asked.

"I'm going to set them outside for rainwater. We both need a refill."

Massie built a fire. They took off their boots and set them as close to the fire as they dared. They draped wet cloaks over benches to dry and laid out their bedrolls near the hearth. Katrina sat on her bedroll warming her feet and flexing her fingers. Her fingers ached like they had forgotten how to warm.

They stacked the fire and settled in for sleep.

"What do you think, about that man offering an exchange for Bedelia?"

"I thought he was a liar," Massie said.

"You don't think there's a chance she's still alive?"

Massie was quiet for a long time. Still waiting for him to answer, Katrina sat up to get a better look at him. His brow was furrowed with angry frustration, but his eyes were glossy with tears. He poked the fire with another log before adding it to the flames. Thumbing the corner of his eyes, Massie sniffed and lay down. Rolling onto his side, he faced his back to her.

"Goodnight," he said.

A scraping noise outside the door woke Katrina. It was the pots she set outside the door to collect water. The noise was followed by a louder one of pots clamoring against one another. She sat up and whacked Massie on leg, speaking as loud as she dared.

"Massie. Massie get up!"

She was out of her bedroll with her boots on when Massie sat up and looked to the door. Footsteps sounded on the planks outside. Massie quickly followed her lead, by pulling his boots on. The room was dark as Katrina approached the window closest to the door. Her sword held in one hand, and stuffing a Mahigan net into her belt. Flush against the wall she peeked out the window.

It looks like Jlande's crew, she wandered.

It must have been the fire. He crouched beside her and peeked out the window. I see six.

Do we try to talk to them?

After all the conversation they had with our friends on horseback, he wandered.

Just checking, she wandered. You take the first one through.

You don't want the advantage of surprise?

She took a position on the opposite side of the door.

Thank you, but I always have the advantage of surprise. There's not a man alive who isn't surprised when a woman's gutting him.

The door opened and moonlight cast a shadow of a man with a sword at the ready. He stepped through the door and another man walked in close behind him. They squinted into the darkness beyond the pool of light at their feet.

Massie's arms came out of the darkness, encircling the first man's neck. With one sword stroke, she lunged forward to open the second man's stomach. He slumped forward and turned to her. The man's neck was long and completely unprotected. She sliced the side of it, and grimaced at the amount of blood it unleashed as he fell to his side. The still legs of both men were the only things visible in the light from the open door.

The noise of running steps pounded closer and another man stepped into the door. He held a sword outstretched in a confident stance, but his face was terror-stricken. Katrina made a hard blow and knocked his blade sideways. The man cried out in shock as he slipped and stumbled back, failing to regain a fighting stance. He looked ready to run and this frustrated her. He wasn't going anywhere.

She went for his leg, hacking into his groin area, and completing a blow to drain him from the thigh. He let out a loud wail, and fell to the platform screaming. He writhed on the ground making incomprehensible cries. She had seen men die, but this was new.

"Where's the rest of them?" she asked.

Massie joined her in the doorway looking down the long row of platforms. He shrugged and stepped over the dead men as he went to collect his pack. "Maybe they heard that last one and took off."

"I don't fight well when I'm carrying all my gear," she said walking over to retrieve her bag.

"If the other ones are anything like those three, I think you'll manage."

The way her glance collided with Massie's meant he smelled it too, smoke.

"Smoke us out. They're going to smoke us out," she said.

She slung her bag over her shoulder and wormed the other strap on as she ran. Massie was at her heels again as she made it to the first lift. It was in motion. Without hesitation she whacked at the lift line with her sword, severing it with a hard two handed blow. The scream told her all she needed to know about the rider on the lift.

She moved on to the next lift. The flag indicating its vacancy at the bottom was triggered. She pushed down on the pedal, which shifted a series of weights and brought the lift up. There was shouting from someone further down the platforms.

"I'm trying!" Said one man seated on the lift.

She ran towards them with Massie in step, beside her on the right.

"Mine's left!" she barked, as she and Massie approached the two men at the next lift. With one hand she grabbed the man on the left by the collar. Throwing him backwards, he landed on his back and reached his arms up in a vain attempt to block her sword. She ran her blade through the base of his neck. Jerking her weapon free, she spent no time observing his death. She stood ready scanning for her next target.

Turning to the lift she froze. Massie and the man he attacked were gone.

The lift's rope spun, turning over its nearby counter weights at an abnormally fast-pace.

She looked into the lift entrance but could see nothing but the rope and the vast dark space below. The sudden split from Massie made her panic. She had never given their separation any real consideration. Seeing a dark hole where her brother had stood a moment ago filled her with mind-numbing shock.

She turned around and ran back to the lift she summoned earlier. A man stood before it like he waited for her. She slowed to a walk. Continuing forward, she brought her sword to the ready.

The man stood in a trained stance, but unlike the man who died screaming, this man faced her with a look of total calm. Tall and lean, this was one of the Delphi who butchered his hair with a close shave.

"I've orders not to hurt you," he said.

She struggled against an anger that flared up at his statement. If she could suppress her emotions, she could play off his arrogance. Manipulate the situation with more than her sword.

She swung at him. The flicker of surprise in his eyes pleased her. Her anger shifted into an odd pleasure. It felt good to lash out. Have him feel what she thought about his orders. He parried the blow, and she wanted more. Sparring had always been a challenge, but it was a challenge she missed.

The urge to antagonize the man nagged at her. She wanted to cuss at him, bait him, shock him with the obscenities members of her squad used during practice drills. With careful pacing she stalked him, and he moved to avoid her reach. They walked in a circling dance around the lift.

"We need to go down," he said. "It's not safe up here with the fire."

A fire, he probably set. With a fast bound she leapt across the lift seat and aimed to hit the man's right torso. He parried the blow, and she tried a counter strike but he danced away. She moved in closer, leveling a drill she always hated in practice, but now moved through with unexpected speed. Each hit he managed to deflect, except the very last one. She grazed his thigh. He made a short cry as he stumbled out of range. He recovered fast, masking the pain from his face.

A thick wall of smoke passed over them. The fire in the closest building had grown. She realized it was the light from this fire that made the man so visible in the darkness. The fire continued to push out more and more smoke and flame. The darkness around them mixed with a thick haze of ash. This fire would soon collapse the building and make the platform around the lift where they stood unstable. If she was going to use this lift to get down, she had to use it now.

Katrina lowered her weapon and tilted her head, giving the man an exaggerated look of concern.

"You're right," she said, coughing and making a series of panting breaths. She worked her expression into flustered disorientation. "We should go down."

She stepped towards the lift. It was like baiting a fish. It took all of her concentration to mask the excitement she felt as the man considered her.

"You won't hurt me, right?" she asked.

He nodded, looked puzzled for a brief moment, then lowered his weapon and took a few steps towards her. Sheathing her weapon, she stepped onto the lift, and grabbed hold of the rope with both hands. The man hesitated, and kept hold of his sword in one hand. Taking hold of the lift rope with his free hand, he stepped onto the lift.

She felt heady satisfaction from her success, and smiled. Leaning back, she sent the lift plummeting down. The sudden movement took the man by surprise. Katrina seized the opportunity and swung the lift into a violent spin. The man lost his footing and clung to the rope with one hand. Katrina leaned in and bit his hand. Screaming, the man lost hold of the rope. He was flung away, too far for him to try and regain his hold of the lift.

The turning of the lift slowed as the man fell, and Katrina sat down. She circled her legs around the seat of the lift and held on. The weight adjustment slowed the lift's descent, and she glanced over the edge into the darkness. Seconds later the crash of the man colliding with the ground sounded from somewhere far below.

When she reached the bottom she got off the lift, and stood looking around. Massie sat in the middle of the clearing. He was bound and surrounded by men from Jlande's crew. Jlande walked towards her.

"I was worried that crash was you. I'm glad it wasn't."

The dim light in the clearing made the lines in Jlande's face deeper. She stared into his odd bulging eyes and gripped the pommel of her sword.

"Now, now. I think it's best if you just keep that put away. You see, we're just running out of time. We can't afford to be doing anymore of that tonight." Jlande gestured around at the men gathered in the clearing. She tried counting them but stopped around twenty. She shifted her stance and loosened the grip on her sword.

"My princess, as you can see, the numbers are just not on your side tonight. I don't know what my friend Prince Massie told you about me, but see, I'm the kind of man who does nothing in moderation. If one's good, then a couple more's even better."

"Smart," Katrina said.

"Why thank you," Jlande said. "I have a reputation to keep." He came closer to her and frowned as he inspected her appearance. "Have you been injured?" Jlande glanced over his shoulder scowling at the crowd of men behind him.

"I'm fine," she said.

Jlande's eyebrows bunched in a look of either fascination or disgust. "We'll need to see you get a bath and some fresh clothes," Jlande said. "Most normal people don't like the sight of that much blood on a person. I know I don't."

Jlande stopped short at the sound of a distant scream. Everyone in the clearing stiffened as they looked in the direction of the scream. There was another scream, this time louder, and it lingered as a frightening echo. A Mahigan, screaming a warning of his approach. Jlande's men grabbed gear and started moving about with panicked speed.

Massie stayed seated and laughed as the men guarding him ran into the forest. Jlande beckoned his men, raising his arms as he tried to stop them.

"Everyone-everyone! Calm down, listen!"

None of the men heeded him. Jlande grabbed a hold of one by the arm.

The man turned and yanked his arm free saying, "I didn't agree to tangle with Mahigans."

"You told us there was no chance of them," another man said hauling on his pack and pointing a finger in Jlande's face. "You lied. I could be doing much easier things, for much better pay."

Another Mahigan scream came. Katrina covered her ears, bowing over under the intensity of the scream.

"You staying to say hi to Major Ehnis?" Massie asked. "He's in charge of the Mahigan unit sent to escort my sister home."

Jlande scowled at Massie from where he stood with his ears covered. He reached down and lifted a pack from the bushes. Slinging it over his shoulder he stalked off into the forest.

Katrina walked over and untied Massie. He stood up and flexed his arms as he looked around the clearing.

"Where did they put my pack? One of them must have taken it," he said, and began searching the edges of the clearing.

"How did Major Ehnis make such good time?" she said.

"That's not him," he said. "Where's my pack?"

"It's not?" she said.

Terror gripped her and she threw off her bag. Fumbling through its contents she said, "Were you carrying the net we pulled off of Helos, or did you give it to me?"

"I don't remember," he said. "Mine's in my pack."

The Mahigan scream made them both stop and cover their ears. Massie shook his head and began fumbling with the satchel at Katrina's belt.

"Get yours out," Massie said. "I'm sorry, if I had one I wouldn't leave, but I've got to go hide."

"Take this with you," she picked up her bag and pressed it into his arms. "I think that other net's in here."

He hugged the bag, gave her a concerned look, and headed in the opposite direction of the scream.

She held the Mahigan net Tegija had given to her. Looking at it, she felt completely lost.

"What do I do?" she shouted.

He had already disappeared into the forest, but answered her in a wander. *The moment you see him, point the net and hit the release. Don't hesitate.*

"Don't hesitate," she repeated. Taking a deep breath she tried to calm herself. With just the net in her hand she felt none of the calm focus she had when she held a sword. Her hands were cold but her body was flushed with heat. Her legs felt light and her muscles trembled.

Katrina, Massie wandered. The way he spoke needled the fear she was trying to suppress. The tone of his voice projected calm but it failed to mask the undercurrent of worry in his voice.

You're calm, you feel very calm and alert.

He was using his magic on her, persuading her, and she clung to the calm washing over her. She took several breaths, accepting the calm relief he forced with his words.

If the net fails, which it's not going to, but if it does you're not going to panic. If he gets ahold of you, you will not fight. Okay? Do you understand? You're not going to fight or provoke him. You're not going to fight him, but you are going to net him.

"I'm going to net him," she said. "I'm not going to fight him."

You're going to net this one.

She waited, listening to the surrounding forest, scanning to catch sight of any movement. A tall dark figure broke free of the forest near the other end of the clearing. She stood aiming the net, but the person was too far away to capture. With only one shot, she was going to make sure it was used on the proper target.

Mahigans possessed a speed that made them capable of crossing the clearing in a matter of seconds. The figure came towards her at a walk. The wait for this person to get closer felt slow. Anxious, she shifted her stance and balled her free hand into a fist.

She recognized his shaved head first, and growled in frustration to see the man she had thrown from the lift. How was he still alive?

There was an ear splitting scream. Her whole body winced forward in pain as a blur came out of the forest. The man she threw from the lift was tackled to the ground. His attacker was still a blur, but she could see the man being pummeled. She recognized the Mahigan's weapon before it was heaved into the man.

The blurring movement of the Mahigan stopped. Katrina got one good look at him. Still in his human form, he had a wide young looking face, and dark hair. The only part of him shifted into his Mahigan form was the weapon in his left hand. He jerked around, focused on her, and his whole body froze. She lifted the Mahigan net and aimed it at him. She felt for the trigger with her thumb, and in the instant he began running, she pressed down and released the net.

It worked; she blinked and the net collapsed around the Mahigan. He tossed about in the net and she held the net's grip with both hands. The Mahigan settled, lowering to his knees. He lay down and the net collapsed more, binding him in a strange automatic way.

The Mahigan was more boy than young man. He breathed in an endless pant, and the color in his eyes was hidden behind large pools of black. Massie emerged from his hiding spot in the forest. He inspected the young Mahigan lying still on the ground.

"Did you cut him?" Massie asked. "He has blood all over him."

"He did just kill a man," she said.

The young Mahigan spoke, and while Katrina could not understand his words, she recognized the language he used as Skrieni.

"Do you know what I'm saying?" Katrina asked in the common tongue.

The boy looked at her, there was a pleading hunger in his eyes and he rolled onto his side with a groan. Curling his legs into him, he whimpered as his face contorted in pain.

"I don't think he understands," Massie said.

Katrina tried repeating the words again in Bisma, but the boy gave no indication he understood, letting the net collapse against his hair as he rested his face against his knees. Massie knelt down by the Mahigan and inspected his back.

"His entire back is bleeding."

Katrina swallowed and took a breath before looking at his back. The back of his shirt was darkened with the stains of dried blood and some areas seeped brighter fresh blood. An open wound at the base of his neck had a long shape that made Katrina's heart morn with recognition. She knew exactly what had happened to the boy.

Her voice cracked as she spoke, "They made him human."

"They made a mess," Massie said. "But I wouldn't say he's human, not with the way he came at you. He looks like he's at an age where he should be in a Mahigan compound."

Any fear she felt vanished under the familiar horrors of what the boy had endured. The urgent desire to help him kept the acute agony of her memories at bay. "I didn't know Skrieni did this to their Mahigans too?"

Massie's face was a snarl of disgust and pity. "This is...ugh. We can't even see it all. It's brutal."

Katrina's heart clenched as memories of how her wings were taken played fresh in her mind. "If he fled his village, he had good reason."

"If we're going to help him, then we're going to need help," Massie said. "The safest way to contain a Mahigan is with another Mahigan."

"And Major Ehnis is still a day away." She sighed.

Massie's brow furrowed as he looked at the boy's injuries. "By the look of these injuries, this boy needs somebody fixing him right now."

"What about Helos, would he help carry him back?"

Massie shrugged, "He might, if I show him the boy's injuries. I think there's a chance he'll consider being generous about flying with a rider. Either that or he'll tell us to put him out of his misery."

"No," she said.

"The law disagrees. He attacked you with the intent to claim you, that's a life-taking offense. It's my legal right as your brother to kill him. You can do it too, I really don't care."

"That's not funny," she said.

"I know," Massie said. "Look at him, he's just a confused, highly dangerous, out-of-control Mahigan boy. The only thing he'll do if he gets free of this net is kill me and claim you."

She gave Massie a stern look.

Massie gave her a placating shrug.

Katrina knelt down while keeping a firm grip on the Mahigan net.

"I'll help you."

The boy lifted his head; his dark eyes trembled as he looked at her. Marked with need and pain, they begged her to make good on her promise. The loud crack of tree limbs and feet demolishing underbrush announced the approach of Helos. Concern glowed in the Gryphon's gold eyes as he emerged from the dense forest.

I apologize for my lack of vigilance, please forgive me, Helos wandered.

"I'm relieved to see you," she said.

"Forgive you? You almost lost me, you know," Massie said crossing his arms.

Helos ignored Massie and leaned over to inspect the young Mahigan.

My priority is your safety, he wandered. I'll fly you to the plateau, and then return for the boy.

"We can't leave Katrina here," Massie said.

Helos swung his head and clapped his large beak at Massie.

"I know, I know," Massie said laughing as he ducked away. "That was a bad joke. Leave me here all alone to defend myself. Won't be the first time."

Helos stretched forward and gently nudged Massie with his beak. Massie smiled and ran his hand along it. Katrina grinned and diverted her eyes from their affection and private unspoken apologies.

Massie added Katrina's bag to Helos' cargo. She and Massie tied the Mahigan in the net to a tree. Massie strapped her into Helos' saddle.

"We almost made it back on our own," he said.

"Almost," she said.

"I'll probably see you in the morning," he said stepping away and waving as Helos rose to his feet.

She waved back to Massie as Helos leapt and began his ascent out of the forest.

18

The Regina of Mozgas

The slender torso of Helos expanded and contracted beneath her. He flew without effort, and she admired his expertise. Capturing air currents and soaring for lengths of time. The late afternoon sun cast moving shadows of clouds across the pine and rock landscape below. They ran alongside clouds, the thin blue sky chilled and stingy with air. She strained to fill her lungs as she looked down at the Mozgas plateau. She had never flown this high before. While she stretched for more air with each breath, she grinned at the amazing panoramic view.

Helos shifted his wings and they were falling. She leaned down and held on, enjoying the rushing sensation in her stomach from the speed of their dive. Being home was wonderful.

Helos lowered his body to the ground and Katrina fumbled with the harness around her waist. There was a larger crowd gathered along the promenade than she expected to see. Dermot and Nuala hurried towards her surrounded by a small army of servants. When her harness was free, servants took hold of her and pulled her from the saddle. Peppered with questions, flustered by the attention, and dizzy from the thin air, her happiness of a moment ago sunk.

"No, no, please, I can stand," she said, and gave a pleading look to Nuala.

"Everyone's been so worried," Nuala said, her eyebrows lifting in amazement as she inspected Katrina's appearance. "I'm not even sure what to say, except maybe, well, you've definitely given everyone here something new to talk about."

"Good, that's great," Katrina said. "Let them talk. What I need right now is a bath and a full night's rest."

Helos stood and extended his wings and Katrina pushed her way back through the gathering to him.

"You're flying back now?" she said.

Yes, have a team ready to take the boy when I return. He wandered.

"I will," she said. "Thank you again."

Helos made a giant leap forward, and his wings flapped twice. Ascending with ease he turned and she watched until he dove off the north end of the plateau.

Katrina walked beside Nuala and Dermot, surrounded by the gathering of servants. When she stepped into the side entrance towards the family quarters, she saw Valgu descending the back staircase. His pace never slowed until he was standing in front of her smiling. His eyes gradually grew concerned as he looked her over.

"Are you all right?" he asked.

Katrina signed and nodded, "Yes, I swear, I'm fine. Just very tired."

"You aren't cut?" he asked. "I could have Tegija and Eleric sent up."

The mention of Tegija did make her pause.

"No, no, there's no cuts," she said. "I do need to speak with Tegija, and my medical team needs to be assembled."

"Find Professor Wythe," Valgu said to one of the servants gathered about them. He turned to a different one and gave the order, "Have Princess Katrina's medical team summoned to my office." With swift bows both servants moved fast to complete their tasks. Valgu offered Katrina his arm and she took it, letting him walk her up the staircase.

Valgu left her at the door to her bedroom saying, "We'll catch up tomorrow. I'd hug you, but I like what I'm wearing. After you clean all that mess off, just go ahead and burn everything you're wearing."

"I love you, brother," she said in tone that was equally sincere as it was sarcastic.

"I love you too. Welcome home."

Her quiet room seemed odd after all the bustling excitement. A few servants trailed in after her. One proceeded to draw her bath while the other gathered linens and a fresh nightshirt.

She sat down near the tub and yanked off her boots. They were in decent shape, minus the blood and mud. There was a knock on the door in the other room, and she heard a servant answer it.

She played with a button on her tunic and looked down at her clothes. They were torn in a few places and heavily stained with blood. Valgu was right, salvaging these would be a waste of time. The condition of her clothes, paired with the smeared blood stains, made it easy to understand why everyone had looked at her with concern.

"My Princess, you summoned me."

"Yes, I'm in here," she said, and moved to stand.

Tegija wore a serious expression when he entered the bathroom. She liked to think of it as his medical face. Like a soldier's look before battle, healers had a look to them when they faced off against medical problems.

"What happened? Are you in a lot of pain?" he asked, moving to kneel on the floor beside her. His hands were on her face as he assessed it for bruises.

"No-no," she said pulling his hands away. It was Tegija. His touch, holding his hand in those brief seconds, made her insides bubble with joy. The sight of him, the feel his hand in hers, made her yearn to hold it longer.

"I'm fine. I'm uninjured," she said.

Tegija furrowed his brow in confusion. He reached for one of the linens nearby and wet it. Unsure for a moment, she hesitated as he brought the wet cloth to her face. He held it near her face and gave her an insistent look. She sighed in acceptance, and let him wash the blood from her face. She would do whatever he wanted. She was too tired and unguarded to be this close to him. She needed to tell him about the young Mahigan, and get him to leave.

"The message I received said you urgently needed my help."

"I do, but it's not for myself," she said.

She explained the situation as Tegija continued to rinse the cloth and wipe her face, neck, and hands free of blood.

"You netted a Mahigan?" he asked.

"I did," she said.

"You weren't supposed to use that net," he said, with a teasing lightness in his voice.

"Then why did you give it to me?" she asked.

"Because if you had it, then you wouldn't need it."

"But I did. Will you and the team help him?"

"Of course," he said. "I'll gather everyone and wait for Helos to return. We'll do what we can, and I'll send you a report about it tomorrow." He set the wet cloth aside and scrubbed water from his hands.

"Thank you," she said.

"I'm glad you're okay," he said, tucking a dirt-streaked lock of hair behind her ear. The small touch, it happened so fast, but her mind began replaying it over and over.

She remembered the conversation with Massie as they left for Lavieth. Could her hope for him really be viable?

He gave her a reassuring grin, stood up, and with a respectful nod, left.

She tried to set her questions of him aside. Staff filled the tub with warm water. She stripped off her clothes and entered the bath. Thoughts of Tegija persisted, and she caved to the happiness she experienced with him. His friendship and easy confidence were as inviting as the hot bath surrounding her. Clean, warm, and relaxed, the fatigue in her body nagged her to crawl into bed before she fell asleep in the tub.

Her relaxation and the comfort of returning home faded the next day. The routine of her life pulled her into a sprint of activities.

Valgu stood from his desk and greeted her with a hug. "There now, that's the sister I remember."

She grinned and waved him off to take a seat at her desk. Stacks of suitor letters sat in rows of neatly tied bundles. She grimaced and wondered what people would think if she just burned them all. Would anyone notice?

"You've amassed a nice collection."

"Hm, yes." She tried to set them aside by stacking them on a corner of her desk.

"I think most of them were hand delivered."

The stack fell over in a disorganized mass on her desk. She sat back in her chair scowling at them. Sinking down in her chair she made a frustrated sigh as she gave Valgu a helpless look. He laughed and fanned the ink on the letter he had just finished.

"Why is this funny?" she said gesturing to the letters.

"I was laughing at you," he said. "I don't know why they bother you as much as they do."

"What else did I miss?"

"Let me see, where should I start?" He set his letter aside and turned towards her in his seat. "Ilona was with Father and a group of prophets at Amber Glass. She had one of her odd outbursts, and the next day she left with one of Father's best Alvara guards. They went to Idania, without giving any notice. The influx of guests for your ceremony keeps our dinner table full every night. Regent Selig brought the entire Tiarnas family here, all of them. Someday, I hope our entire family can return the favor." She laughed and he grinned with a knowing look. "Owl's in hiding from all the additional people. The day Regent Raynes arrived, he asked to present Delany with the Jenke Gidccm during your ceremony."

"Wait, he what?" She sat up gripping the arms of her chair.

"It gets better." He leaned on the arm of his chair. "Regent Sepihne refuses to allow Rosalba to leave Milios and come here for your ceremony without an increase in her security escort. Dermot's tutors tell me it's time to send him to the Mahigan compound, but he wants to put it off until after your ceremony. Little Delany keeps talking about her mother. A heartbreaking thing to witness over dinner, that's also eerie and disturbing. Did I forget anyone?"

Katrina grinned, "Just Nuala and Father."

The cheer in Valgu's face fell away as he ran the tips of his finger along the edge of his desk. "She's perfect so she must be hiding something."

"Doubtful," she said.

"He's not been well."

"What happened?"

"The incident with Ilona, no one can give me details of what happened, but when they came back he went to his quarters. Father's been living, down in the tunnels ever since. His guards say he's been eating and sleeping fine, but he won't leave the tunnels."

"Looks like you and I will need to lure him out if we're going to make this Regina ceremony happen."

"Yes. The ceremony will happen. The sooner, the better. I can't wait for this business to be done. All these people here, it's pleasant to attend a thing like this, but hosting? I've had more than enough of it. I want things back to normal."

"You mean back to war planning, merchant treaties, and foreign politics."

"Yes please, back to more of that."

Katrina laughed and stood up. "Speaking of treaties, I forgot our most recent one, back in my room."

Her bag and the few belongings she stowed in Helos' cargo bags were set out beside her bed. She retrieved the leather document case with the Lavieth treaty documents and proceeded back to the office. She approached the office door as Proserpere walked towards her from the opposite end of the hallway.

Proserpere spoke in a formal manner to her, but omitted the use of her title. Katrina never corrected her, and ignored her intended slights. Others noticed Proserpere's behavior, and it satisfied Katrina to watch Proserpere's pettiness damage her own reputation.

Proserpere offered a sealed envelope to her and she took it.

"Was Professor Wythe able to help the young Mahigan?"

"I was able to help him."

She surveyed Proserpere, while masking her distaste. "Professor Wythe mentioned how his studies with the Skrieni gained him the greatest insight into developing a way to restore my wings."

"I did help Tegija with that, yes."

"So credit for the cure is yours?" Katrina smiled in false admiration.

Proserpere glowered and quickly amended, "It was an accident. I couldn't help myself when I stepped in. I was tired of watching Tegija fumble."

Katrina bristled at Proserpere's familiar candidness with Tegija.

"You stepped in, because you care about Professor Wythe's, reputation?"

"More than his reputation," Proserpere said. "We have a mutual affection."

Proserpere lied, or maybe she spoke a half truth. She had revealed her own desire, not his. But a new doubt took root. What if Proserpere was the reason for Tegija's reluctance with her?

"Oh, I see," Katrina said, nodding her head and smiling as if one of the Ladies from the House of Etrasa had just confided in her a genuine secret. "I must say, you two hide it so well."

"We're professionals." Proserpere squinted in agitation.

"And you don't mind all the hiding and secrecy?"

"No." Proserpere winced her denial. She crossed her arms and her shoulder jerked.

"I admire your strength," Katrina said.

"Thank you." Proserpere thrust her chin up.

"I once tolerated someone I cared about hiding our relationship. I hated it, and well, he and I didn't end well. Based on what you said, Professor Wythe really has a remarkable trait. I mean, what Mahigan doesn't feel compelled to claim the woman he loves? They're known to kill for their women, not hide them."

"Skrieni don't abide by such compulsions." Proserpere's voice was low and her gaze fierce. "Tegija respects that."

"Of course, but somehow I get the impression you wouldn't mind if he didn't."

"He and I are different."

"Hm, yes," Katrina said, placing the envelope from Proserpere on top of her document case.

She smiled and it was genuine.

"You and he are different," she said. "I completely agree." Without another glance, Katrina entered the office and let the staff close the door behind her.

The afternoon transitioned into a private discussion with Nuala who expressed an interest in the ancient discoveries in Lavieth. Katrina explained to Valgu and Nuala what she understood about them as they reviewed the documents Lavieth's curators sent back with her. Nuala revealed how during their last visit to Amber Glass, she and Ilona viewed similar documents for tunnels in the Mozgas Plateau. Katrina and Valgu planned to meet Nuala in the University Library after the formal welcome of Regent Anteus Gaddison of the Pandion Province.

Katrina used an unfrequented passage on the second level to sneak into the library. Halfway across the upper gallery walk she was stopped.

"Katrina," Puternic stepped out in front of her. He wore a glib smile, but his eyes shone with purpose.

Puternic, the prince who had stalked her on an island, now tracked her inside her own home. Irritated, but unwilling to make a rude display in public, she resigned herself to a conversation she would rather avoid.

"Puternic."

She just told Valgu she preferred to make the few minutes walk back alone. The bitter irony stung as she stared at Puternic and wished for an escort.

"You're hard to track down," he said.

"There's much to do."

"Can I join you?"

Katrina hesitated, her mouth opened to speak, but everything she felt the urge to say was either improper or rude.

"What's the matter? You and I are old friends, we should talk."

"What is there to say?"

"A lot, there's a lot I'd like to talk about, but you've refused to see me." His usual charm dissolved. "Your niece, would you really have this betrothal for her?" Puternic's eyes were wide and bore into her as much as the question did.

"It's not my decision."

"You have the power to influence things, to change this."

"No, I don't."

Puternic shook his head, "You know Massie—he takes things too far."

"It isn't fair to my niece," she said, "But her father swore an oath to yours. It's done."

"You and I should not be punished for their mistake."

"Punished? The only one being unfairly punished is Delany."

"You feel nothing for me then?" he said.

Anger crept into her posture, tightening the muscles in her back. Part of her wanted to break down and laugh at his ridiculousness, while another part wanted to strike him for asking such a question.

"I'm fond of you," she said, "but I'm fond of many things, none of which add any specific meaning to my everyday life."

"Fond of me," he said.

"Your place is in my past," she said. "You're in my infatuated girl memories of my first kiss."

Puternic shifted his weight and clenched his jaw. He closed his eyes and scratched his forehead.

We did more than kiss.

Feeling a heat rise to her face, she crossed her arms and glanced around.

"We did, and it earned me a nickname as the Delphi's whore. What we did never held you to me."

"What?" The shout in Puternic's voice turned the heads of people seated nearby.

She gave him a condemning look and lowered her voice. "I don't want to discuss this here."

His voice lowered to match hers, but the staccato clipping of his words retained anger. "If you didn't make me hunt you down, we wouldn't have to."

She glared at him as her fingers dug into her arm.

"I didn't know how to handle it," he said. "I wanted to keep my promises, but I didn't know how." His shoulders slumped, his glare subsiding as he bowed his head.

"You mean you didn't know how to be brave," she said. "You succeeded in gaining my trust, but you were too big a coward to fight for what you'd won. You left me. Then you dared to try and assert a claim for something you forfeited years ago. What's left to explain? I already know everything. I was the Airetti guide the Delphi needed to secure, and your father sent you to claim me."

"That's not the full truth."

Katrina restrained an exasperated chuckle and shook her head. "You just admitted it, did you hear yourself?"

"They're rushing to make you the Regina of Mozgas to block my claim. I've gained a majority with the Madar council. Did you know that? They're throwing a title on you because it's the only way to prevent me from putting things right. Making you the Regina has nothing to do with your abilities. Everyone knows you're not ready. They're doing it with the vain expectation that Mozgas will be as understanding of your inadequacies as they are of your father's."

Puternic's verbal assault hit her weakness of self-doubt, but she refused to let him see his affect on her. Stepping away, she turned to look over the library. On the first level below, the still form of Tegija caught her eye. His rigid posture stood out and contrasted against the normal flow of library patrons. Their gaze met, and even in Tegija's stiff stance, his presence was a balm to her tension. If she needed his help, she knew he would lend it.

As if he had been following her thoughts, Tegija wandered to her, *Are you all right? What did he say?*

Katrina gave him a small nod, and forced a smile. *Puternic's sharing how unfit he feels I am to become the next Regina of Mozgas.*

The protective anger in Tegija's look caused joy to stir in her stomach. His opinion meant so much more, and his opposition to what Puternic said, helped her shake off the doubts clouding her thoughts. With reinstated confidence, she turned back to Puternic.

Valgu brushed past Puternic then, looking at him with ambivalence. Startled, Puternic stepped back and looked up at Valgu.

Valgu appeared calm, but concern flashed in his eyes when he stopped next to her. His look became an ambivalent mask as he inspected Puternic.

"I know I promised Nuala the afternoon," Valgu said to her, "but there's something that couldn't wait."

Nodding to Puternic, she took Valgu's arm. He walked them to the main stairwell. Piecing together Valgu's timely appearance, she met Tegija's eyes again.

Smiling she wandered to him. *Valgu?*

Tegija lowered his gaze but she saw him fighting a smile as he wandered back. *Valgu has good timing.*

Especially when prompted by his closest friend. She wandered.

You seemed uncomfortable; if I erred I'm sorry. Tegija met her gaze again.

Why summon Valgu? Why didn't you intervene? She asked.

It's not my place, and Valgu's much better at faking ambivalence.

Tegija's words excited her and made her shy away. She turned her full attention to Valgu as they crossed the landing. Catching her look, Valgu made a small knowing smile.

"What?" he asked.

"I think Tegija's right, you have mastered ambivalence."

Valgu coughed lightly in his throat and his gold eyes took on a hard edge.

"Puternic knows I'm not ambivalent about his aspirations for you," Valgu said. "Tegija didn't even speak to me when he wandered; it was just an image of Puternic near you. If it wasn't for the promise I made you years ago, that gutless waste of a man would be dead."

She crossed paths with Puternic only a few times after that. Each occurrence part of a formal reception, where his access to her was limited to expected formalities. Beyond that she treated him as she had for years; she ignored him.

More people arrived in Mozgas every day. The influx of visitors became a burden on the palace and local boarding establishments. Formal complaints came in daily with reports of overcrowding and increased nuisance behavior. The rehearsals for her ceremony were completed, and Regina Rosalba had arrived safely from Milios. Only one thing stalled her Regina ceremony from going forward. Pavaldon remained in the seclusion of his chambers. He failed to attend the rehearsals his guards promised he would. Every conceivable reason to delay the ceremony had vanished, and time had run out.

"We have to go down there," Valgu said. "If we can't talk him out, then I don't think the ceremony will happen."

"We could put him to sleep and carry him out," she said.

"And see if he's able to do the ceremony when he wakes up? It's times like this when I really wish Massie had some effect on him."

"That would be nice."

She looked into the dark corridor beyond the tunnel entrance from their father's bedroom. They needed to wheedle their father out of this hole. At least get him to surface long enough to perform the ceremony he set into motion.

The Alvara guard Valgu introduced as Fianna lifted a bright white binti stone lamp and beckoned them.

"My Regent did not eat much from his noon meal," Fianna said. "But he ate every item they sent at breakfast."

"When was the last time he slept?" Valgu asked.

"He fell asleep where he was working yesterday afternoon, and then was up in the middle of the night. He's lost all of his normal life rhythms down here. I hope you coax him out. He needs fresh air."

A small rhythmic tinkering tap echoed up the corridor. The sound increased as they approached the area their father had dwelled in for several weeks. The smooth floor underfoot became cluttered with rubble and loose stones. They approached an intersection where a pile of stones lay heaped in what looked like a scree pile.

Fianna gestured to a narrow path to the right of the pile, and offered Valgu a lamp. Valgu took it, leading the way in on a path around more piles of stones. Their father stood balanced on a precarious perch of loose rock. He cut fist-sized rocks from the wall using a mallet and chisel. With measured steps, she crossed the rubble-strewn floor to stand near her father.

Pavaldon worked by the small light emitted from a binti stone strung on a lanyard around his neck. As she came closer to the wall she gained a better view of what he was doing. Valgu followed her, and in the light of the large lamp they gazed up in awe.

"Valgu, I thought you said he was doing all the carving," Katrina said. "He's not carving these, he's uncovering them."

Valgu lifted the lamp higher, and they saw clear images in ancient stone panels. Pavaldon stopped his chiseling and turned around to face them. He held one hand up to shield his eyes from the light. Squinting, he peered at them. A heavy layer of dust made his long blonde hair murky. Debris and sweat turned his clothes grimy and they clung to him.

"Katrina," he said and smiled as he half stepped and half slid down from his rock perch.

She hoped his recognition was a good sign and smiled as she moved closer to him.

"I'm back, my Regent," she said. "I have good news from my trip. Could you set aside this work so I can tell you about it?"

"Yes." Pavaldon smiled and nodded. "Yes, yes. Come, this way," he said, motioning for them to follow him down the tunnel. They filed in behind him and occasionally he stopped to point up at the reliefs.

The conservationists in Lavieth mentioned ancient carved reliefs existed inside the Mozgas plateau. Nuala agreed with them, and believed the drawings and documents at Amber Glass supported the claim. General knowledge said the opposite was true. The tunnel walls in the Mozgas Plateau were known as solid spans of beige sedimentary rock.

A carved Minotaur stared down from one of the panels. Katrina frowned and grabbed hold of her necklace from Thedmir. The carving had an eerie likeness to Thedmir. The carved Minotaur held a plant in an outstretched hand. Pavaldon stepped in front of her nodding his head. He tapped a finger on the hand she gripped her necklace with and then pointed up at the likeness of Thedmir.

"Yes," Pavaldon said.

He led them further down the tunnel, and Katrina slowed as she tried to take in the reliefs they passed. There were images of snakes moving onto land from the sea. One image was carved across three panels and it depicted a sea battle between large snakes and Delphi. She noticed another Minotaur carving. This one had the Minotaur presenting a plant to a regent who stood holding the same plant in one and a key in the other.

Further down the wall she noticed the distinct eyes on several Regents depicted. Aranysarga eyes, they stood out in the image her father stopped in front of. How had the ancients captured the moment that came to define her father's legacy? Who had seen this and committed it to stone in the eons before it occurred?

Pavaldon rested his hand on the base of the relief and looked up at the carving of his own image. In the relief he stood posed with a woman, who had a close resemblance to her mother, Lady Lena. Her mother knelt before him, offering a cup with one hand. The delicate flower of the white fire grew as steam rose from the cup.

Katrina looked at the carved relief with remorse. What might have happened if someone uncovered and exposed this relief years ago? Had the ancients carved these as guided warnings for future generations?

Pavaldon pointed to the carving of him and said, "Me."

Turning, he motioned for them to follow him again. He led them to the next panel. It featured a Regent with his hand intertwined with an Airetti woman's. The pair stood on top of a giant snake. The Regent held a scroll in his free hand. The Airetti's wings were extended and in her free hand she held a sword. Katrina searched the Regent's face, but saw none of the features common to the Aranysarga family.

Pavaldon pointed to Katrina, he then turned to the relief and pointed at the Airetti woman. His mouth worked as he fought to pronounce each word. "That's you."

She stared at the image of the Airetti woman. Was that really supposed to be her? Anxiety coiled in her stomach as she considered the extended wings. How could that be her? It contradicted what she already reasoned impossible. She shifted her focus to the goal of convincing her father to come out of the tunnel. Forcing a smile, she took his hand.

Pavaldon placed a dusty hand on her shoulder and grinned. As he held her she saw his body relax and watched his gaze settle and meet hers. He was completely back, and his words flowed in perfect succession.

"You must see them in you, in your mind. That's you up there."

She swallowed hard and looked up at the relief again. The Airetti woman did have the distinct eyes of an Aranysarga. They were her eyes, and when she ignored the apparent impossibility of her wings being restored, it really was her own face staring down at her.

"The guests are all assembled for the Regina ceremony," Valgu said.

"Let's go up," Pavaldon said. "Shall we?"

Owl hovered behind Katrina, grinning at her through the dressing mirror.

"I was sent to come pull you out of hiding," she said. "You look beautiful."

Katrina gave a weak smile viewing the way she looked in her Airetti gown from Sol.

"I don't feel beautiful." She turned around to face Owl and gave a weak grin before shutting her eyes. Owl looked beautiful. Her light green Airetti gown flowed around her, a good color accent to her display of brown wings.

"You look beautiful," Katrina said. "I don't feel right, I don't know if I can do this."

"You're imagining this into something it's not," Owl said, taking her hand.

Katrina was grateful for something to hold onto. Owl's hand was delicate, but she was one of the sturdiest things in the room, the essence of calm strength.

"I feel like a damaged curiosity."

"It's never as bad as you imagine it," Owl said.

Owl pulled her hand around her arm and smiled as she led Katrina to the conservatory. They joined the gathering collection of Airetti guests in an antechamber off the conservatory.

Katrina sensed something resonating within each winged person in the room. Was this what other Veilede felt and honored in her form? The Airetti gathering stared back at her in open curiosity, and she adjusted to the discomfort of having her scars on open display. While the Airetti gowns around her showcased their winged beauty, hers held a hideous void.

White wings speckled with black surrounded the slender dark woman who approached her. Katrina knew Rosalba Luex the minute she saw her. A plain white gold diadem with etched ancient black script was half hidden by Rosalba's long dark hair. Black beaded roses on Rosalba's gold Airetti gown winked in the sunlight. Her intricate black crystal earrings danced as she walked. Rosalba outstretched her hands in greeting.

"I'm so happy to meet the woman I feel like I already know," Rosalba said with genuine warmth.

Taking her small outstretched hands, Katrina smiled in agreement. She enjoyed their regular correspondence. Meeting Rosalba in person was one of the few things she looked forward to during the recent ceremony planning.

"I'm so glad you could attend."

"Sepihne would be here too, if it were not for the health of our mother. I'm staying on a few more days. I must indulge in the opportunity to spend time with you and Valgu while I can."

"I'm glad," Katrina said. "Today will be so busy, I'd feel cheated if you returned to Milios right away."

Delany pushed her way between them, a weaving flash of brown curls. Her niece bounced with excitement as she took Owl's hand.

"Look — look what Grandpa gave me," Delany said gesturing to the child sized Aranysarga diadem on her forehead.

There was an echo of amused laughter from the gathering as they observed Delany. Owl bent down and adjusted a sash on the lavender Airetti gown she had made for Delany. With her dark brown wings on display, Delany looked perfect. Katrina admired her niece with open pride.

"It's a perfect fit, Lany," Owl said. "He spoils you."

"He said he must, because he loves me." Delany said.

Owl stifled a laugh and said, "Do you remember what we practiced?"

Delany nodded.

"We're walking behind all the Airetti into the conservatory." Owl said, and gestured to the other people in the room. "Then we're going to stand very quietly while the Regent talks. It won't take long, but what do we have to do while he's talking?"

"Be quiet."

"Good," Owl said, smiling as she steered Delany with one hand. "Let's get in line."

Rosalba gave Katrina a broad smile and squeezed her hands. She let go and walked into the lineup before the conservatory doors. The doors opened and one at a time the Airetti disappeared into the bright sunlight in the conservatory. At the end of the line stood Owl and Delany. They stepped through the door and a fast swell of nervous energy filled Katrina.

Her breath quaked as she moved to the threshold. Ahead, pairs of wings flowed in a glorious procession. Reconciling her place in line with them was difficult. Stepping into the doorway, she fought the urge to run, and her mind whimpered as her last chance to flee slipped away. She doubted her own suitability as the Regina of Mozgas, but today she would honor her father's decision. Pulling on the composure she had donned during a thousand Parade rehearsals, she moved forward with a soldier's discipline.

The room's furnishings were cleared away to make space for many guests, leaving only the permanent border of plant beds as adornments. The side galleries were filled with people. The crowds stood as a congested mass and hid most of the mosaic tile floor. Standing in a circle, the Airetti surrounded her father who stood with an Alvara guard at his side.

Pavaldon's stance told Katrina he was shrouded in illness. His gaze danced around the Airetti circle. His mouth worked and one shoulder twitched in an odd sharp manner. His illness filled her with a mix of pride and devastation. She felt connected to him and his plight. They both knew the anguish of living with a broken body. Their physical appearance inadequate in representing what lay hidden inside.

Katrina knelt before her father and met his gold eyes. He saw the hidden things in her that she tried to recognize in herself. Her father draped an amulet around her neck, made of an oval piece of amber as big as the palm of her hand. A winged Airetti figure was carved from the center of the amber and a long gold chain suspended the stone. The amulet was light, and hung low into the draping folds of her dress.

Valgu stood beside their father and spoke.

"Regina Katrina Aranysarga, the Airetti Guide of Mozgas."

Katrina took hold of one of her father's hands before rising to her feet. The room erupted in applause. It was the shortest ceremony she ever witnessed, but she liked the simplicity of it.

Guests began to mill about and music played from one end of the conservatory. Flanked by her father and siblings, she stood in a receiving line with guests pressing forward to congratulate her or make an introduction. Her father ran an arm around her shoulders in a sideways hug. She looked up and his easy lucid smile greeted her. He kissed her forehead before releasing her. He parted the crowd as he walked back into the palace.

Massie leaned across Valgu and said, "It's moments like this when I envy him. While Father's napping, the rest of us will be shaking hands for hours."

She gave Massie a sardonic glance before engaging with the next person in line.

The celebrating lasted the entire day. Guests ate food from tables set in the garden and mingled. She approached a table and inhaled the cool air outside. It felt good to escape the humid heat of the conservatory. Passing the incredible food display, she walked on until she stood alone. She relaxed her shoulders. Swiveling her head, she stretched her neck. Her feet ached from standing. There had to be a good place for her to sit. She entered a patch of shade when footsteps sounded behind her. Slowing to a stop, she resigned herself to returning to the task of entertaining. She turned and saw Tegija. Surprised, she smiled, glad to see no one else trailed behind him.

"The ceremony went well," he said.

"I thought so, I enjoyed the absence of any long speeches."

Tegija nodded and stood smiling.

"Are you going to wear your hair that way from now on?" He asked.

Katrina narrowed her eyes at him. "I was considering it."

"Good," he said.

Baffled by his comment she asked, "You like it?"

"Yes, I'm glad you didn't start a trend. If you'd worn it up in one of your human style braids, tomorrow every woman in Madar would be twisting and hiding their hair."

She puckered her lips in disapproval. She still preferred her hair up.

"It must be less time consuming this way," he said.

"No, it's not, but I won't bore you with the details."

"I'm sorry, what I meant as a compliment came out wrong."

"Yes, well, hair maintenance is a universal inequity between the lot of women and men. An average man can be bald and still considered handsome, but I've never known the same to be true for a woman."

"You're right," he said and gave her a broader smile than she expected.

"Did you really come over here to pay compliments on my hair?"

He smiled and shook his head.

"Then are you going to tell me why you look so happy? Are you one of the few who supports my father's elevation of me?"

"I think I'm in the majority of those who support your father's decision. The opinions of the Delphi don't quite match what's best for Mozgas. I'm happy for you, even while I shouldn't be."

Katrina crossed her arms and asked, "You shouldn't be?"

"I've been in mourning since the day I found out the woman I admire was being elevated to a rank so far above mine."

"I see, then you fake happiness well."

"No, I am happy. As the Regina of Mozgas, I know no decent man will dare touch you against your will."

She cleared her throat and to tried to keep her voice steady.

"Did that concern you before?"

"Not really, Massie would have fended off your admirers," he said.

"Even the Mahigans?"

"He's got that Gryphon," Tegija said with a knowing smile that made her laugh. "Massie has his ways. I've been the victim of his scowls once or twice. His were never half as serious as the ones from your admiring friend, Jance."

"Jance Willmont scowled at you." She smiled in amusement.

The good humor left Tegija's face. His lips pressed together as his gaze traveled down to inspect her hand. She followed his gaze and realized he was looking at the Gryphon ring she wore.

"He never declared I was more than a friend to him."

"You really don't think he's declared himself to you?"

Anger heated her chest, as a flush crept up her neck and down both arms. The only thing mitigating her sudden irritation with him was a compelling need to reassure him. When she responded, her own level of calm amazed her.

"What was it you witnessed or think you witnessed?"

Tegija's eyebrows lifted and his gaze lowered in thought. Her patience thinned as she watched him consider his answer.

"You promised me honesty," she said.

His gaze met hers again and without hesitation he said, "I was in the arena with you."

She remembered the night Jance brought her into the Arena of Ages to talk. The same night Sol died.

"That's how you got to Sol so quickly."

"My promise," he said, and Katrina waved off any further explanation.

"Right, the promise you made to Valgu." She paused, considering what she and Jance talked about in the Arena of Ages. "Jance didn't make any declarations when we were in the Arena of Ages."

Shaking his head, Tegija made a light chuckle and looked away.

"Even if he had, Jance left weeks ago, why mention it? Did I do something wrong? Did I behave inappropriately?"

"No," he said fast.

"Whatever Jance does or doesn't feel, it doesn't matter," she said.

Tegija lowered his brow into a look that argued with her. While he said nothing, she read the contradiction on his face.

"Why does it matter? I never acted on his advances."

"But you wanted to," he said.

"Really, you know my mind so well?"

"You're home now, but you don't write to any of your Mahigan suitors. His favor is done, but you still wear his ring."

Katrina looked at the ring and considered it.

"The ring? It's pretty," she said in a concession of the truth. "It was a nice gift."

"Do you wear it because it's pretty, or because you like the gift's meaning?"

Katrina felt the urge to take the ring off and hurl it at him. She would aim right for his forehead if it might actually make him realize where her real affections lay.

"I told you why I wear it," she said dropping her hand and scowling up at him.

"How can you wear that and not claim to want more than a friendship with him? How do you not think of him every time you look at it?"

"I don't," she said. "All I see is a beautiful object. I'm not a woman who needs an object to remind me of the man who holds my affection."

"And who's that?" he said. His eyes gleamed with anger, demanding an answer. When she hesitated he pressed her again. "Tell me."

"So you can tell my brothers, no."

"It's easy to figure out."

"Oh really? Are you a magician as well as a healer now?"

Tegija walked around to where he stood close behind her. The intimacy of his close proximity made her body respond, and despite her frustration a rippling wave of excitement coursed through her.

He leaned over and spoke into her ear. "All I have to do is review the crowd and catch the man eyeing me as I stand this close to you."

He was close, so close. It took effort to stay focused. She felt his breath caress the side of her neck, the sweet cadence of his deep voice in her ear. The heat from his body warmed her back and she wanted to lean back and pull his arms around her. She took a deep breath and looked at the few people she could see standing in the distance.

"I don't see anyone, no one's even looking over here."

She turned around and forced herself to maintain their aching close proximity. This was dangerous, she enjoyed it too much. Her whole body hummed and goaded her to take every risk to pursue what she wanted.

"Maybe you're not enough of a threat," she said. "My brothers trust you alone with me, and for a Mahigan, you're too relaxed. Why would your proximity to me concern anyone? You look completely unaffected by me."

"Are you so unaware of the affect you have on me?" he said.

The force of his words were an unexpected shock, like a kick to the ground in a sparring match, he knocked the wind out of her. Her senses felt tousled, but her eyes held steady as he spoke.

"Massie senses my intentions for you. Valgu confronted me with them. I worried they'd cost me my closest friend, but they didn't. He blasted me with them, and then turned around and endorsed them. He demanded I tell you, and said he trusted me. That he knew I'd never make any kind of advance unless it was proper to do so."

Her mind soared with happiness, while the more rational part of her needed more.

"I did encourage your advance."

Holding his gaze she watched his face go blank and his body still. If she were taller, she would end this back-and-forth and kiss him. His voice was barely above a whisper and she longingly focused on his mouth.

"Why did you stop writing letters to your suitors?"

"Did Valgu order you to do this?"

Tegija shifted his gaze away from her and stepped back. She sensed his answer; even without him speaking it. Her soaring happiness faded.

"Why do you care about my interactions with my suitors?" When he remained silent she sighed and shook her head. "You've sworn off rallying. I accept it. Why bring it up again? Why force me to endure more of your rejection? The most your admiration amounts to is flattery. It'll mean nothing when my rally starts."

Katrina waited for his response with an anxiety that made her toes tingle. She wanted him to deny it, to get angry at her accusation. He should be here to declare his intentions with no uncertain terms. Instead he stared at her and said nothing. His lack of response became a concession. Tegija might be daring enough to voice his regard, but he was still unwilling to act on it. The silence went on too long. Unable to take the crushing quiet any longer, she walked away.

Where was the audacious Tegija she first admired? Each one of her footsteps seemed to echo into some awful hollowness he managed to open in her chest. What more did she expect from the Mahigan known to swear off rallying? Why did he need to tell her anything about how he felt?

She regretted her own honesty and clenched her hands into fists until they hurt. Her thoughts were rattled, and a knot of pain grew in her chest and threatened tears. She wanted to fog out the growing ache. A glass of wine would nurse the hurt. Moving along the shaded path she ducked into a servant's antechamber. A moment later strong hands grabbed hold of her. They swung her around and steered her back against the chamber wall. She gasped and pushed back, fighting against the hands on her hips. She relaxed when she saw Tegija's face above hers, her gaze locked with his as he held her in place with his body.

"What are you doing?"

"You don't write letters, so I need to know. Who holds your affection?"

A thrill ran through her, and before she could take her next breath, the truth tumbled out.

"You."

With each hand she took hold of his jacket trying to counter her disbelief. It was Tegija, he was touching her, and this was real. His washed out gold eyes pleaded with her to say more.

"I'm an idiot," she said. "Even after you rejected me, I still carry thoughts of you around, just you. I hate being in the same room with you, because I can't concentrate. All I want to do is find a way to be near you. I stopped writing to suitors, because knowing them has never changed my feelings for you."

"I'm supposed to kill myself for you. I have a son. You want me to die and leave him without his father, before he goes into the compound?" Tegija's voice was a strained mix of anger and resignation.

"No," she said, her hands clutched at his jacket. Thoughts of the men who would die at her rally, to imagine him dead, made her cringe with disgust.

"I can live with your rejection, but not your death."

She touched the edges of his face, wanting to comfort and sooth away the lines of concern there. Tegija's face lowered to her hand. Their lips met in a rush, a heated collision, fueled by rising emotion, and paced with the panic of being found. Tegija's lips were hard and then soft as his tongue found hers and demanded what she was desperate to yield. She felt drunk with elation and only wanted more when he broke away.

"You'd have me die at your rally?"

"No," she said, "I need you. If you can live while I'm claimed by another, then stay alive."

Tegija looked at her in fierce reproach. His face bunched into a scowl as he groaned.

"Ugh! God, no."

He ducked his head into her hair and his arms were around her in a vice. She waited, enjoying the pleasure of his embrace. His body pressed against hers, dissolving every ounce of embarrassment and hurt she had felt.

He pulled back and met her gaze. "I'm your suitor."

Words she waited so long to hear. Letting her head fall back, she closed her eyes and smiled. He leaned down and kissed his way from the base of her neck to her mouth.

"You can write me suitor letters, but no one else."

"No one else," she said.

"I'll go mad. No other suitor touches you, unless I'm dead." His lips brushed hers as he spoke, "Please promise me."

"No one else but you," she said, "I promise."

He leaned in and kissed her again.

He released her fast from his embrace. She opened her eyes and he was gone. She glanced around, but he left as fast as he arrived. Once more she stood alone in the darkened antechamber. Bracing herself against the wall, she tried to collect her dazzled thoughts. Her heart raced and her body craved him with a ferocity that left her trembling. Did that really just happen? Closing her eyes, she rolled her lips into her mouth and found the sweet sting left by his kiss. With a sigh she let her head fall back against the cool stonewall. Her mind replayed his kiss and declaration over and over. She loitered there, happy to be alone and lost in a euphoric emotional symphony.

19

Visions of Death

Katrina stood beside Valgu in the antechamber, and peeked at the guests milling about in the Conservatory. They were waiting to witness Regent Raynes presentation of the Jenke Gideem to Delany.

"I feel like we're playing with fire," she said. "It's not how I would want to find out."

Regent Raynes wanted the presentation to take place in as grand and public display as they could muster. Valgu offered to hold the Gideem ceremony this morning, while the desired audience of visiting Regents and dignitaries were still on hand to witness the event.

"He'll have the same objections publicly that he would have privately," Valgu said.

"We're blindsiding him," she said.

"It's not like we've had any recent opportunities to tell him," he said.

They withheld Delany's betrothal from Pavaldon due to his regular diminished state. Massie had the authority, as Delany's father, to betroth her. However, the circumstances surrounding Massie when he entered the betrothal could provide Pavaldon with the necessary grounds to contest it.

"It'll be fine," Valgu said. "Everyone here is familiar with Father's condition. There's nothing he can say or do that will damage his reputation more."

"He's going to argue this, in front of everyone."

"I think so, yes."

"What do we do?"

"Nothing. I suspect Father's challenge is exactly what Massie planned for. If Father challenges it, he challenges it. Delany's three, there's plenty of time for them to sit around and debate it. Father could fight this at the Madar council for eternity, or approve it this morning. The legitimacy of the betrothal will only really matter on the day Regent Raynes dies."

An awful vision had dominated her thoughts all morning, but she hesitated confiding it in Valgu. Something inexplicable was about to happen, and her instincts told her there was no viable way to stop it.

Remembering her promise, she pulled Valgu to a stop outside the conservatory doors. "I don't know what it means, but I keep seeing the same thing, over and over. The conservatory, it's overrun with a battle, a Mahigan battle. It makes no sense to me. I can't tell why they're fighting or sense if Delany receiving the Jenke *Gideem* is tied to it."

Valgu sighed and licked his lips. Placing one hand on top of hers he said, "You need to be certain there's a connection if we're to convince the Delphi to postpone again."

"I'm not," she said. She wanted him to reassure her and dispel this urgent anxiety. Her hands trembled. She flexed her fingers, but it did no good.

"Okay," he said. "We'll proceed, but if something changes, or you see more, tell me?"

She nodded and followed Valgu in the conservatory. Pavaldon sat on an elevated dais near the double door exit to the garden. His guard Fianna stood beside him along with Nuala and Dermot. His gaze roamed about the gathered crowd in the erratic way that marked his sickness. He shifted like he was unable to get comfortable as his hands gripped and released his armrest.

Massie approached them, walking hand in hand with Delany. In a stranglehold she carried a stuffed dolphin toy, given to her by Regent Raynes.

"Massie," Katrina said frowning at the toy and looking back at him with an imploring look.

"I know," Massie said. "But she's in love with it. It's just a toy."

It was just a toy, but a toy that might incite their father. Was it wise to add fuel to the flare up? Something set to occur the moment Pavaldon learned what Regent Raynes intended to give Delany this morning.

"Are we ready?" Valgu asked, offering his arm to Katrina. Still eyeing the dolphin toy, she took his arm. Massie and Delany followed as they crossed the mosaic floor to the foot of the dais where Pavaldon sat. Delany let go of Massie's hand and ascended the dais stairs. She crawled into Pavaldon's lap, and a small grin lit his rigid expression with joy. Delany's easy familiarity with Pavaldon captured the attention of everyone in the room.

Regent Raynes smiled with an eager look of anticipation as he crossed the mosaic floor carrying a thin wooden box. His approach poorly timed, she had no way to delay him. Regent Raynes stopped beside her, bowing his head in respect first to Pavaldon and then to her.

"Regent Pavaldon, Regina Katrina, my family and I are honored to be guests during this historic and celebratory time for the people of Mozgas. As Regent of the Delphi, it is an even greater honor to seal the promise made between our families."

Regent Raynes did an about-face, and hoisted the lid on the box in his hands. Lifting up the box, Regent Raynes displayed its contents to everyone gathered in the conservatory.

"I, Regent Raynes Janke, herby present the *Gideem* of my family to Princess Delany Aranysarga. As the future wife to my heir, I pledge my family will watch over and protect her until the day I die."

Raynes turned back to where Delany sat on Pavaldon's lap. He raised the *Gideem* necklace from the box and unfastened it, and took a step towards Delany.

Pavaldon's expression was pinched tight as he banged a forearm against the side of his chair in wild repetition.

Pavaldon's eyes stilled with composed focus. His body relaxed and he gained the formal dignity of his full cognizance.

"Stop," Pavaldon said. He leveled an icy glare at Regent Raynes before shifting his gaze to Massie.

"Massie, my son, you did this?"

Massie cleared his throat and stood up straighter, taking one step closer to the dais. "My Regent, I did."

Pavaldon looked at the *Gideem* in Raynes' hand with annoyance. "The Princess Delany is far to small to be wearing the likes of that wherever she goes. Do hand that over to my son Massie, will you Raynes?"

Massie extended his hand to receive the *Gideem*. Raynes held still, his eyes locked with Pavaldon's.

"Her father made a promise, and now I am here to honor it," Raynes said.

"Coercion," Pavaldon said.

"You seek to assault my integrity," Raynes said.

Massie gestured to Delany, and she shimmied down from Pavaldon's lap as he spoke.

"When did this transpire? I need to hear every detail, because Aranysargas don't make betrothals."

Massie reached forward as Delany came down from the dais, and lifted her into his arms. He carried her over to Regent Raynes and stopped. With a motion of his head, Massie beckoned Regent Raynes to continue with giving Delany the *Gideem*.

"Our family is honored to be aligned with yours," Massie said.

Regent Raynes strung the *Gideem* around Delany's neck and fastened it in place. Smiling at Delany, Regent Raynes smoothed her hair before patting her gently on the back. Delany smiled and rested her head on Massie's chest. Massie carried Delany over to Nuala and handed her over. Massie kissed Delany on the forehead before Nuala took Delany and left the conservatory.

Pavaldon had sunk back in his chair during the exchange. His body rigid and still as his eyes tracked Massie. Katrina touched the side of her temple, the irritating pound of a headache starting. A chill of nervous dread prickled her senses and made the fine hair on her arms stand on end.

Regent Raynes bid her farewell, and through the fog of her fresh headache she watched the Delphi contingent leave the conservatory. Others loitered, like the Tiarnas family from Dinhac, Regent Gaddison from Pandion, and several of the dignitaries from Idania. Pavaldon stewed, biding his time while they bid formal farewells and bit by bit disappeared.

"Regina Katrina, when you were first reunited with Massie, did you recognize him?" Pavaldon said.

Confused by the question, she bit out a hesitant, "Sort of."

"Did he aid your mother's escape?"

"Lady Lena escaped Etrasa several days before I did," she said. "She left with a man named Devon Quraishi."

"And when she escaped Mozgas?" Pavaldon asked.

Faltering, she looked at her father in open confusion.

Massie stepped beside her and said, "Yes, Father, that was me. I confess. I was a very bright and conniving five-year-old. We lost track of Lady Lena's whereabouts the day before we left Gryph."

"You betrayed me," Pavaldon said. "You hid them."

Massie took a long breath, but seemed to follow their father's accusation without pause. "Yes, that was me," Massie said, nodding his head. "It's why Jlande found Delany with my sisters."

"You bartered with the Delphi," Pavaldon said.

"Jlande brought them here, but he left my wife. What did he do with Bedelia?"

"I'm not famous for my generous treatment to the women who bore my children. Why do you think I would know anything about the woman who bore yours?"

"You loved my mother," Massie said. "You loved all of them before the poison took you from us."

Pavaldon stood up and slowly stalked down the dais and stood over Massie. "You betrayed me, you stole from me, my own son. I don't know where your wife is. Do you believe me?"

Massie's brow lowered in frustration as he glared up at Pavaldon, his eyes searching for an answer.

"I know the pain of having your wife taken from you," Pavaldon said. "Now you have to decide, is my love for my children...my grandchildren, stronger than my need for revenge? What's fair is fair; you stole from me, I returned the favor. You took my wife, I took yours."

"You got them back," Massie said.

"Did I?" Pavaldon asked. "Nuala could barely walk when she was taken. Did I get back the years of her childhood? My granddaughters, Ilona, Delany, they should have been born here."

Pavaldon pointed his finger to the floor in a hard gesture. His head jerked to the side as his face stiffened. For a moment Katrina thought he might slip away from them again. Her heart was pounding, and the sick feeling in her stomach told her this was more than a fight with words. She sensed it with a trained eye, and felt the awful naked sensation of being unarmed. She remembered her father's articulate calm before he violently killed Lord Dacamera and his men. Her instincts screamed at her to take Massie by the arm and pull him to safety.

"Reckless," Pavaldon said. "You risked one of the first being snatched away, the same way they took my Katrina. Ilona's gifts, she's drowning in them, and you'd rather hide her from me, from her family, than help her."

"You killed her mother," Massie said.

"Massie!" Dermot shouted. He leapt from where he sat on the dais and ran towards them down the stairs.

Katrina reached for Massie but was too late. Pavaldon yanked him forward by the collar. Fianna had her hands exposed, but in one violent swipe, Pavaldon reached out with his weapon to sever Fianna's head from her shoulders. Her body slumped backwards to the floor.

"No one gets to touch my children!" Pavaldon screamed, face to face with Massie. Pavaldon dragged Massie forward and impaled him with his Mahigan weapon. As he withdrew, a Mahigan in shifted form pried Massie out of Pavaldon's grip and threw him sideways. Katrina caught Massie as he was hurled away. She lowered him to the floor and knelt beside him. Massie gripped one of her hands as he struggled to take each breath.

When she looked back, the Mahigan who intervened was on his knees, impaled by one of Pavaldon's weapons. A Mahigan howled. The scream so intense Katrina hunched over Massie, her headache pounding harder with sound. Another Mahigan tackled Pavaldon from behind. The speed of their struggle made it hard to track their movements. The attacking Mahigan clung to her father as he struggled to throw him off. Then the blur of movement ended. Her father stood with the Mahigan's weapon impaled through his lower jaw, penetrating out from the top of Pavaldon's skull.

The silence became thick, the only sound coming from Massie as he gasped for breath. Her father's body tensed and fell against the Mahigan who attacked him. The Mahigan lowered him to the mosaic floor. The bright blue, yellow, and green tiles were smeared and disappeared under growing pools of crimson blood.

Shaking, the Mahigan who killed her father shifted to human form. Dermot, sunk further against the floor under the weight of their father. Blood covered half his face, and he smeared it into his hair as he pushed his bangs back and looked over at the Mahigan curled on the floor.

"Valgu!" Dermot cried, squirming and reaching for him from under Pavaldon. Pulling free, Dermot moved to Valgu's side. He lay huddled around the Mahigan weapon he was impaled on, not moving.

Katrina needed to keep her wits, but her head pounded and the memory of Sol's death ripped at her consciousness. Her father lay dead, and the potential of losing Valgu and Massie made it hurt to swallow.

Valgu shifted to his human form.

"Valgu," Katrina said over the strain in her throat.

She looked from Valgu to Massie, who lay his head in her lap. Massie grit his teeth and closed his eyes. Would she lose them today? Massie's color was fading. With her one free hand, she brushed away the tears blurring her eyes.

Valgu made a weak gesture to her. "The vision."

Tegija stood over her father. Eleric moved in beside her and Massie. Servants were gathering all around them, and under Eleric's orders picked up Massie. He flinched, hissing his breath. He groaned through gritted teeth. She hated releasing Massie to them. At a run, Eleric led the servants who carried Massie. Their urgency increasing her fear for him more.

Tegija lifted Pavaldon's body and called over a group of servants standing in a doorway. They obeyed, scurrying over to claim the dead Regent and his guard Fianna.

Eleric returned with more servants to assist Valgu. Tegija dropped to his knees in front of Valgu and manipulated the wound around the weapon.

"Brace him," Tegija ordered motioning Katrina and Dermot to Valgu's feet and shoulders. With a sharp cry from Valgu, Tegija removed the weapon. He tossed the weapon aside and aided her in bracing Valgu's shoulders as Eleric moved down and placed his hands over Valgu's wounds. Blood seeped through Eleric's fingers. Valgu grit his teeth and strained against their hold.

"That's all I can do here," Eleric said. "We need to sedate him before I can work on the internal damage."

Dermot helped Eleric lift Valgu to his feet as Katrina braced him from the other side. Valgu stared at Katrina wide-eyed.

"The vision," he said.

"I saw a battle, not this," she said.

"A rally," Valgu said. "An unsanctioned rally."

Too much, no, that was too much. While her emotions screamed, some practical part of her brain latched onto Vaglu's revelation. Many of her Mahigan suitors remained in Mozgas after the Regina ceremony. All it took was one. One Mahigan with enough audacity to seize opportunity in the wake of the Mozgas Regency's vulnerability. Her gut rolled and she swallowed hard, and then swallowed again as she fought back the rancid taste of bile.

"I can't defend you," Valgu said, his voice strained with apology.

"No," she said.

Tegija came in front of Valgu and looked at her, "I need to get him out of here."

Katrina relinquished Valgu to Tegija.

"Don't fight," Valgu said as he walked away supported by Tegija and Dermot. "Don't fight."

Valgu shuddered and stumbled to a stop.

"Valgu," she said.

"Please," Valgu said, then fell against Tegija.

"I won't fight," she said, as frightened tears stung the back of her eyes and constricted her voice.

Tegija lifted Valgu and more servants rushed forward to assist in carrying his limp form from the conservatory.

The door to the palace slammed behind them. She stood alone.

Shaking, she sunk down to the floor. It only took one of her suitors. Her thoughts scattered. Was her rally minutes or days away? Nothing she forced her mind to dispelled the perpetual loop of her vision. Bright and clear she saw the Mahigans battling around her. The collision with that future inched closer.

Time passed and she sat with a vague awareness of a barrier being constructed on the other side of the palace door. The sunlight took on the warm glow of evening's approach. She watched dust float between rays of light and the dramatic shadows cast by the conservatory plants. She examined the blood where it dried. The blood stained mortar matching the blood caked at the edges of her fingernails.

A bellowing scream made her jump. Instinctive mortal fear unfolded in her chest, threatening to paralyze her. Another scream answered the first. Through doors leading to the garden, she saw dark silhouettes moving in a blur of speed towards the conservatory.

With Mahigans charging the garden door, she decided to move. The balcony seemed the best place to wait out the fight. Hitching up her dress, she jogged to the stairs. She ascended the stairs and reached the balcony right as the garden door shattered.

A Mahigan screamed, the volume so loud it vibrated the conservatory windows. The ear-piercing screams behind it made her cover her ears and double over. She scrambled to the door leading into the palace. On the main floor a swarming mass of Mahigans streamed through the shattered garden door. Mahigan's covered the mosaic floor in a running blur. She reached the door and tried the handle. The handle held tight, locked. She peeked through the web of iron and glass to see a barricade of furniture piled on the other side of the door. More screams erupted and the noise in the room became deafening. She shrunk down, leaning against the door.

The screaming abruptly ceased. After a few breaths she crawled to the railing and peeked around the iron latticework to see the floor below. A crowded mass of Mahigans stood below the balcony. Sunlight glinted off their armored plates, and shone in the hundred or so face shields turned up to gaze at her. The quiet unnerved her as much as the screaming. Unsure if they saw her or merely sensed her, she rose to her feet and looked out over the gathering below. She stood tense; afraid of the horrors their instincts were poised to create.

They came fast, blurring streaks of black and grey racing towards her. She yelped as one seized her by the waist and hauled her skyward. Bellowing screams came from those on the crowded floor. Their movements were hard to follow, a mangle of Mahigans clamoring to fly, mixed with those hit by Mahigan opponents with killing blows before falling away to be trampled. A few Mahigans reached the air and gave chase. Tables and garden containers were volleyed and smashed. The conservatory fell into a mess of gore set to screaming barks, and shattered glass. Her rally was underway, and as vivid a nightmare as her vision.

The Mahigan who held her flew clear of the conservatory door. He inhaled before unleashing an earsplitting bark. Another Mahigan came flying at them from the side. He ran his weapon under the torso plate of the Mahigan who carried her. Their course of flight faltered. The Mahigan arched in pain and let her go.

Tossed into a free fall, the attacking Mahigan grabbed hold of her in one smooth movement. He flew fast and the press of wind blinded her. They vaulted into a spinning descent, and judging by the twisting of her insides, they were flying off the Mozgas plateau. Her mind roiled in panic. The Mahigan's precarious hold was the only thing keeping her from falling to her death.

Another Mahigan flew over them and dropped down, scraping a weapon across the shoulder plates of the Mahigan who carried her. Unharmed, the

Mahigan flew faster, dropping their flight course to the tops of the Iron Pine canopy. He dodged between trees and evaded a side attack.

She adjusted to his weaving flight pattern. Relaxing her body, she grabbed hold and tried to ease his burden. The screaming faded. Faint emanations echoed somewhere far behind them.

Judging by the amount of time they spent flying, she guessed they were in route to somewhere specific. A place selected as part of a predetermined plan. Their flight slowed, and she blinked her vision clear to see. They descended to what appeared to be a Skrieni village. The Mahigan extended his body to lower her to a platform. They were hit from behind, and she slipped from the Mahigan's grasp. She landed hard on her left side. Her shoulder hit first with an audible crack. Her hip came down next, then her head struck with a thud. Her breath knocked out of her, she worked to refill her lungs.

The Mahigan who carried her landed, falling against her in a bumping roll. Jostled, she gasped in pain. He regained his feet and lunged back at the attacker.

She steeled herself against the enduring discomfort. Strange warmth spread through her whole left shoulder. Something in her shoulder had broke. She rolled into a crouch and crawled away on her knees, retreating from the blurring speed of the fighting. Thuds echoed off the planks as more and more Mahigans landed on the surrounding platforms.

Cradling her left arm, she tried to take in her surroundings. There were no buildings visible from where she sat, just a series of stepped platforms. Howling shrieks and screams were intermixed with the pounding strikes of weapons. The platform where she kneeled vibrated from the commotion, and the number of fallen grew.

She wrestled with her body, struggling to stand through waves of pain in her shoulder and hip. She made it to her feet and shuffled onto a platform now occupied by dead Mahigans. She searched for any sign of shelter.

A new sound began to emerge from the battle noise. The Mahigans yielding defeat began to make growls and a repetitive sighing huff noise. A chorus of growling and huffs soon replaced the Mahigan screams, as those forfeiting the rally abandoned the ongoing battle. The number of Mahigans who continued to fight dwindled. The few left fought among the bodies of the dead and dying.

Finding her way around the fallen was difficult. She stepped in the narrow pockets of space between the jumbled shapes covering the platforms. She tripped and fell forward. A corpse stared at her with blank eyes as pain rang through her in a shockwave. With a yelp she moved and pulled herself up to her knees. Crawling over more dead, she made her way to the edge of the platform. A better path lay ahead on the next one.

A hand grabbed at her left arm. Startled by the touch, she cried out. The offender held on and pulled her towards him. His sternum lay open. Internal organs peeped out of a long wound that cracked apart the plates covering his chest. She pushed against the hand that held her. He let go and she stared at the exposed part of his face. He was close to death, and his eyes were strange. Each of his pupils dilated so much they eclipsed each iris. His death was brutal, and it was because of her.

Could he be a suitor she knew through letters, or a total stranger she met at his death? There was no way to tell. They had come here, risked their future, all in pursuit of her. Forfeit their lives in the hope of gaining her rank. Was Tegija somewhere among them? Did he come here to die too?

For a moment she reached for him with her wander sense. When she felt Tegija's presence, her stomach heaved with dread. Her heart was praying for him before she could put words to the feeling. She squeezed her eyes shut and joined her heart. Breathing aloud what was more a plea than a prayer, "Don't let him die."

She crawled to the next platform. There was no way to know which way was best, but she wanted to find shelter. Logic screamed at her to sit down and wait, chastising her for imagining there was safety anywhere while the fight continued. This was her rally, the biology of her kind was at work. When this was over, the winning Mahigan would have an overwhelming need to procreate. If she failed to comply with him, she could die too.

Silence settled over the platforms. She stopped and listened for the fighting. A breeze cut through the quiet, passing through the treetops in a soothing whisper. Her shoes scuffled as she walked again. Her mind remained alert, but her body responded dully. She pushed forward in large, lax, and unsteady movements. She slipped on a plank slick with blood and fell forward. She landed on one of the dead. Bunching her eyes shut she sucked in a pained cry. After a few deep breaths she opened her eyes to the face of another dead Mahigan with strange dilated eyes. Scrambling back to her feet, she held her breath through the pain and forced out another series of deep breaths.

Someone snatched her up from behind, and she instinctively kicked back. The movement caused her too much pain, and her body buckled. She cried out as she landed chest first on the platform. The Mahigan, the one who must have won, kneeled and pinned her beneath him. She turned her head to try and see him as he claimed her.

His face shield hid his face. Helpless, she stilled as he sliced her gown with his weapon. The blade ghosted over her skin as it split her dress fabric. Her exposed back felt the press of Mahigan armor plates that eased as he shifted to his human form. He lowered more of his body weight on her. She protested in a weak choke. Catching her breath, she bellowed a stronger scream of agony.

His weight shifted as he gripped her hips.

"Hurry up," she said, and groaned from the spike of sharp pain in her shoulder. The command in her voice fell into a pained sob. "Hurry, please hurry. Please, please hurry."

He eased his weight off of her, and the flat of his palm pressed into the small of her back.

Desperation twisted into incensed anger. Why must he drag this out? A gust of wind chilled her exposed skin. Struggling against the pain, she managed to tuck her arms in beside her.

"What are you waiting for?" she said.

She braced herself and shut her eyes.

"No," Tegija said.

20

Remembering What You Love

Tegija's voice, Tegija.

Gentle hands turned her over and wrapped the remains of her dress around her body. Emotional shock hit her as she stared at Tegija's face. Relief struck her with a force so strong she sobbed. He lifted her into his arms and cradled her. Standing up, he held her against him.

Tegija won her rally, and her mind fumbled with the thought, waiting for it to set in and feel real. A safe calm came over her as she clung to him. He was alive, he lived through all that. He looked at her with somber consideration. His face was strained with weariness, and his eyes held the same strange and darkened cast as the dying Mahigans she encountered. What had he endured to win? A thick guilt rose in her and she closed her eyes, burying her head against his chest.

He carried her some distance before maneuvering a door open. Kicking the door shut, he brought her across the room and lay her on a bed. Only when she felt him gently touch her hair, moving it off of her face, did she open her eyes.

"I'm sorry," she choked out, "I'm so sorry."

He shushed her. With a gentle hand he wiped the tears from her face. Removing her shoes, he lifted blankets over her.

"I need to stabilize your shoulder," he said.

She swallowed and nodded. He grabbed pillows and more blankets from a storage trunk. She closed her eyes and held her breath as he positioned them under and around her shoulder and arm. Her injury ached in protest, but when he finished the pain returned to a constant thrum. Her upper body felt confined, which she assumed was the purpose.

"Rest, and try not to move," he said.

"I'll try."

She wanted him closer to her, but he stood rigid and guarded beside the bed.

"I have to go," he said blinking fast. He turned and walked to the door, his hands shaking. At the door he stopped. His hands clenched into fists, as if the effort of opening the door were painful. Of course it was, he was fighting off his base need for her. He wrenched the door open and hurried to close it behind him.

She regretted seeing him leave and reality set in. The intensity of her joy made tears return. She pushed them away with her good arm. Tegija survived, he was alive. He won her rally. Tegija was her husband. It's what she prayed for. Their lives, forever intertwined.

Guilt crept into the fringes of her thoughts, reminding her of how much her joy cost. How could she be happy? What kind of selfish person accepted this cost for their own personal gain. She fought against the guilt with gratitude.

Tegija was alive.

"Thank you, God. He's alive," she said.

The rally, with its instinctive purpose to fight, mate, or die, was over. Accepting it and all its associated tragedy, let peace descend over her. She lazed in exhaustion, with a headache, and all her energy spent. The piercing sharpness in her shoulder kept her on the fringe of sleep. A knock sounded on the door.

Clearing her throat she said, "Come in."

The door latch released and Eleric was the first to enter the room followed by Professors Rath and Stantivo, and Apothecary Proserpere. Without any hesitation Eleric placed his hands on the sides of her neck.

Professor Rath frowned at Eleric's informality and said, "Good evening Regina, we're here to set the break in your shoulder."

"It's her clavicle," Eleric said. "We can set it and I can start the mending process. I can coax the bones to hold to one another again. It'll help your pain. The worst of it will be gone when you wake up. Where they're mended will be brittle. You'll need to be careful for several weeks."

Katrina nodded and asked, "How are my brothers?"

"They're both recovering, my Regina," Professor Rath said. "We had all of our best healers working on them. When we left this evening, they were asleep." She moved beside Eleric and began smoothing back blankets from the bed.

"And Tegija?"

Eleric smiled, "Worried sick about you."

"He'll be good, once we tell him you're all taken care of." Professor Stantivo said. He stood by the only table in the room swirling liquid in a shallow bowl with steam rising from it.

Proserpere stood next to him with her arms crossed, giving Katrina an open glare. Every member of her healing team busied themselves with prep work, except her. Katrina considered pointing this out and having her sent back, but the gesture seemed cruel.

The team's fast response meant they must have witnessed some of the rally's more gruesome results. She imagined Proserpere's shock, being dragged here late at night. Forced to witness the fallout from an unsanctioned rally. Brought out of bed to attend the medical needs of the woman Tegija rallied for.

Proserpere stood before her, a proven fool and liar. Katrina pitied her and hoped tonight ended their rivalry. Tegija fought to be her husband. That had to be enough to compel Proserpere to return to whatever Skrieni village she came from.

"Take several deep breaths," Professor Stantivo said, holding the shallow bowl with a steaming concoction near her face. She took two deep breaths of the steam and her vision swam. One more breath made her eyes close. Her thoughts and cares drifted off into a pain free-oblivion.

She roused at the sound of a soft humming. Or this was some kind of a dream. Pha was humming.

Blinking hard, Katrina opened her eyes. Squinting she looked around. Bracing herself for pain, she rolled to her side. Her shoulder was sore, but the sharp throbbing pain was gone. Relieved by the miracle in her shoulder, she looked up questioning if she truly lay awake. Across the room stood Pha busy folding linens at the table.

"Pha?"

The short woman finished folding the towel in her hand and set it aside. With a big smile she walked over and sat beside her on the bed. She placed one cool hand on her arm and smoothed her hair with the other.

"Good morning, how's my Katrina?"

Katrina's eyes filled with tears. She blinked and sniffed as she tried to hold them back. "Are you really here?"

"I wouldn't have missed my girl's Regina ceremony. Regent Raynes did me a kindness and snuck me into Mozgas with his entourage," Pha said, and shushed her. "No crying love, none of that."

"But I've missed you so much."

"And I you, not a day goes by without a prayer for you. When I learned about what happened, I made my presence known. A good word of me must have traveled to your husband, for he ordered I be brought here himself."

"As my guardian," Katrina said.

"Always," Pha said.

Owl crept through the door with a tray of food, and Katrina's stomach grumbled in response.

"I knew you'd wake hungry," Owl said, the short caramel curls in her hair bobbing as she closed the door with the swing of her hip.

"I am, thank you," Katrina said scooting back to sit up.

Pha moved aside as Owl set the tray of food next her on the bed. The tray held a bowl of hot cereal with honey, another bowl filled with berries, and a mug of tea.

"Has my healing team returned to the Palace?"

"Some of them," Owl said. "A few of them stayed to help with the work details doing the post-rally recovery."

Katrina blew to cool her first spoonful of breakfast and considered the morbid work assignment. Owl nodded as if she had read Katrina's thoughts before crossing the room to a bag set in the corner. She pulled out and inspected a clean floor-length dress. While Katrina slept, someone removed her soiled and torn dress, bathed, and redressed her in a lightweight robe. It was nice to look down and see a clean garment and the dried blood scrubbed clean from her hands and fingernails.

Owl yawned and blinked at the gown.

Spying their tired expressions, Katrina asked, "Have either of you slept?"

Pha shrugged and Owl replied, "We've been busy." Owl stifled a second yawn and muttered, "I'm sorry, I'm really tired."

"It was a terrible afternoon," Pha said.

"And it went on late into the night," Owl said, laying the dress over a chair by the table sitting in the chair opposite. "I was there when Father was brought out of the conservatory. Then Valgu and Massie were rushed off to healers at the University. Word about Valgu," she snapped her fingers, "it traveled instantly. Just like that, chaos." Closing her eyes Owl leaned her elbows against the table and pressed fingers to her forehead. "I hope I never have to experience anything like it again."

"Yes," Katrina said.

"When you got hauled off, nobody knew anything for hours," Pha said.

"We waited for word," Owl said. "Then Tegija wandered to Eleric." Owl's tired expression took on a wistful grin. "I was so happy then, I couldn't have fallen asleep if I tried."

Pha chuckled. "Tegija requested us after the healing team."

Owl attempted to stifle another yawn.

"You two should go get some rest. Is there a place for you to sleep here?"

Owl stood up stretching both arms above her head. "Yes," she said with a nod.

Katrina motioned Owl away. "Please go to bed."

Owl made a small bow and with a grateful smile said, "Yes, my Regina."

Katrina grabbed Pha's hand in a subtle gesture, beckoning her to stay.

Owl waved good bye from the door, "I'll see you in couple of hours."

"Goodnight," Katrina said watching to see the door close before turning back to Pha.

"What is it?" Pha said.

"Nothing pressing."

"Is it about the rally?"

Katrina nodded her head. "The Mahigans I encountered, their eyes were strange, entirely black."

"You'll see it when a Mahigan's lost control of his instincts. They blacken when their restraint's gone. It's expected at a rally."

Katrina thought of the way Tegija looked before he left last night. His tight expression, and black eyes.

"Is he really all right?"

"No."

Hearing the truth cut her even as she expected the answer.

"He suffers for you. He's remarkably strong. To stay in control after a rally, fighting his instincts." Pha made a wistful smile. "He must already love you. Owl says you have strong feelings for each another. That your soul sings for him."

"Yes," Katrina said, smiling at Owl's description. "It's true."

"Ha-ha!" Pha said squeezing her hand in excitement. "Praise God. May your union be blessed. I'm so happy for you."

"It's the marriage you always wanted for me."

"Yes, it's what you deserve," Pha said. Smiling, she pat Katrina's hand once and stood up. "Would you like my help getting dressed?"

"No, thank you, not yet. I'm going to stay in bed awhile."

"Good idea, I'm going to go to bed myself." Pha walked to the door and after opening it looked back and waved.

"Enjoy your rest," Katrina said as Pha left.

Listening to Pha's footsteps fade, her heart beat faster. Pushing back blankets, her bare feet found the wooden floor. The soothing warmth on her bare feet surprised her. Her body felt chilled but her palms were sweating.

She had to find Tegija. Was she ready for what would happen when she did? She stood and the bruise at her hip gave a small ache of protest. Picking up her food tray, she carried it propped on her good arm. She set the tray on the table. Her fingers fidgeted and smoothed away non existent crumbs as she drained the remains of her tea. Why stall the inevitable? With a deep breath she set the cup on the tray and closed her eyes. She reached for Tegija with her wander sense. She felt the constant vibration of him and called.

Tegija?

He wandered a fast reply. *What's wrong? Should I send someone?*

I'm fine, the only person I need to see is you.

There was a long pause before he answered. *It's not a good idea...your injury.*

That's been well looked after. Please, come here.

Katrina.

Don't make me come find you. I'm not familiar with this place, but that won't stop me from searching you out.

No, don't do that. After another a long pause he relented, *I'll be right there.*

Heavy footfalls sounded on the planks outside. She stood beside the bed when Tegija opened the door. He entered the room and backed the door closed with his weight. Remaining flush with the door, he stood stiff. His eyes were as black and strange as the day before.

"Katrina," he said with a cautionary tone.

She stepped forward and released one of the ties securing her robe. One by one she pulled at the strings. They started at her shoulder, ran staggered on an angle across her bodice, and ended at the waist. She untied them as she approached him. Her small steps melted his tight expression into some kind of panicked shock. By the time she stopped in front of him her robe hung open.

He took a strained breath as his eyes took in the sight of her naked beneath the robe. She reached forward, took his hand and said, "Tell me what you want me to do."

"Your pain," he said.

Katrina shook her head. Lifting his hand she pressed his palm to the side of her face. "You're touching me right now. I know you can see into every inch of me. The worst of the pain is gone."

"I don't want to hurt you," he said in a low mumble.

"I know you won't." She guided his hand down her face and neck, and beneath the edge of her robe to touch her bare skin. "I'm yours, I'm your wife, and I know you need me."

His hand skimmed over her collar bone, and moved down to cup her breast. He swallowed as he nodded and reached for her with his other hand. It slid under her robe and around her waist. He moved in a slow guarded way. His head dipped down and he placed a light kiss on her mouth as he pulled her closer to him.

With careful hands he lifted her robe from her shoulders and let it fall away into a pile on the floor. She reciprocated, undressing him, and pushing at the fabric of his shirt until he relented. He pulled both shirt and tunic over his head and tossed them aside.

When they were both nude, he floated gentle fingers over the bruising on her hip. She wondered if this was another examination of her injury with his talent. She watched his eyes with interest, expecting to see them fixed on her body. Instead they searched her face.

He kissed her mouth, lingering with unexpected reverence. Taking her hands in his, he led her to the bed and pulled her on top of him as he lay back.

She settled against his chest and tried to relax. To enjoy the feeling of being nestled against him naked. Her anticipation and excitement were too great. Growing stronger as she indulged in the feel of his body beneath hers. Their naked skin warming where it made contact. Being this close to him primed her, and the desire for more increased with each passing second.

His hands roamed her body in a slow caress. She raised her head, and with parted lips leaned forward to kiss him. He was quick to capture her mouth with his and the delight became overpowering. She wanted to pace herself, to savor this, but her body demanded more. Their kiss deepened.

Hands kneaded and roaming fingers brought a look of pain to his face as he exerted restraint. She adored him too much to see him this way. The more she stared into darkened eyes, the more riled her protective instincts became. He needed her. She refused to see him suffer under such hard won control when she could free him.

Despite her long abstinence, practiced insight gave her confidence. Something she needed as the sharp newness of the moment grabbed her. She swayed her hips, positioning his erection in a motion half remembered and half instinctual. Leaning back, she eased the full length of him inside her. She gasped in pleasure from his deep penetration. Taking a few short breaths, she adjusted to the welcome sensation of him. How many times had she fantasized about this? Desired him, left rooms he occupied to avoid the way her body responded to him. Reality burned away old ideas. The here and now surpassed all her old lustful thoughts of him. She reveled in the way he touched her, kissed her, filled her. Her body quaked with unimagined intensity as she moved, setting a slow pace.

His eyebrows sat etched with resolve, a determination to keep her free from any additional injury. She smiled in reassurance. Brushing a fingertip along his brow, she wanted to erase his concern. She held his gaze, letting each of her cries of pleasure free. This was anything but painful.

His leg muscles tightened beneath her as their pace quickened. He urged her on. Moving, he matched her in a rhythm that ushered in her release.

She whimpered, melting into his kiss as he sat up. He gripped her thighs and continued to rock her in their set pace. She dove her hands into his hair and held on, opening wide to the tension coiling between them. He kissed his way down her neck, pressing her even closer to the brink.

They both breathed hard with exertion. He watched her in anticipation. Her release approached and she moaned a plea, wrapping her arms about his neck. He grabbed her hips and pulled her down. Absorbing his deep thrusts, she climaxed. Her panting shouts matched the fast swells of ecstasy that overtook her. They shuddered in harmony, enrapt in the sweetest kind of synchronization. He wound his arms around her, his chest heaving breaths as he held her tight against him.

When he lay back, she followed, falling forward to rest against his chest. She enjoyed the play of his fingers as they stroked up and down her back in a lazy rhythm. In blissful contentment, she listened to the sound of his heartbeat soften.

"You all right?" he asked.

"Yes," she said, angling her head to see his face. "But do you always have to make everything so intense?"

He smiled and propped his arm behind his head. "That was all your doing."

He lightly touched the back of her injured shoulder. She liked the way his sandy blond hair hung muddled across his forehead. The washed out gold eyes had returned. They seemed even lovelier than before. With relieved joy, she silently celebrated the absence of their earlier blackness.

"How are you?" she asked.

"Grateful," he said, and sighed. "Happy. Still a little stunned."

"Me too," she said, reaching with her hand to tame his hair. "Does this mean Owl and Pha have to go away?"

"It's not what you want."

She shook her head.

His small smile grew. "My answer should be yes. Having company right now, it's not customary. But you picked the right time to ask."

"I did?"

Tegija's eyes widened as his caress of her back halted. He faltered in his response, "I mean, I made them a promise, well they promised to stay, until you were healed. Owl and Pha stay."

"Wait no," she narrowed her eyes and pointed her finger at him. "You were talking about timing?"

"Ugh." Tegija moved an arm over his face, concealing his eyes. "I misspoke."

"Don't do that, tell me what you really meant." Smiling, she and pushed at his arm. He lifted it enough to peek at her with one eye.

"I never meant to say it." He pulled his arm back down.

She leaned her face closer to his. "Now you have to tell me."

He sighed and tucked his arm behind his head again. He met her gaze and his voice lowered. He enunciated each word like he savored the moment he spoke of.

"Right now, having just claimed you, holding you naked like this…I'm beguiled by you. I'm pretty sure I would give you whatever you asked for."

"I see." she said, resting her chin on her hands by his neck.

"Yeah, I shouldn't have told you that." He closed his eyes before scrubbing a hand over his face.

"Your response makes me think other requests might be granted under similar circumstances." She did not need to hear his answer. His smile and the look in his eyes confirmed it as he leaned forward and kissed her.

"I'm sorry you got hurt," he said, rolling onto his side and tucking her neatly beside him.

"I'm the one who's sorry," she said. "I pushed you into a situation that could have gotten you killed."

He propped his head up in one hand. "No, I'd still be here. Even if you'd said nothing, and I'd declared nothing."

"And now you're part of the Regency."

"By marriage." His tone neutral, and his face displaying no opinion.

"Is that something you wanted?"

"I wanted you," he said. "The Regency doesn't bother me. Why should it? That's why over half your suitors rallied."

She frowned, "I thought it was because they all adored me."

His laugh was dry. "Of course they did, but not as much as me. You made me crazy."

Katrina took his hand and threaded her fingers through his. "I'm grateful you're alive."

He smiled and leaned back so his eyes could travel the full length of her body. "Me too."

"Why didn't you claim me yesterday?"

"That's a silly question."

"I knew it was necessary," she said.

"Not injured. The way you cried out, and screamed. It brought me back fast, gave me grip to gain control."

"I think I could've handled it. "

"You mean suffered through it." He narrowed his eyes at her. "I know you've endured your share of horrors, but I'm glad that I wasn't one of them."

"I could've, to have it done and over with."

"Well, my lovely wife," he brushed a kiss to her forehead. "There's no being done with it." He arched one eyebrow at her. "It, is something we'll do, I imagine with some regularity. God willing, the rest of our natural lives."

Embarrassed by her own delight at his words, she hid her face against him restraining what would only emerge as a childish giggle.

"In the meantime, whatever you want, if it's within reason, it's yours."

"Really?"

"As a rally winner, I'm expected to woo and spoil my wife. It's my honor and privilege to serve the Regina of Mozgas."

"And I'm not expected to do anything in return?"

"No."

"Why's that? That seems out of balance."

"Traditions can be. I can't demand more from you anyway. You still owe me."

"I'm indebted to you?"

"Oh, yes. You still need to make good on our original bargain." She frowned in confusion as Tegija leaned over and placed a light kiss on her lips. He pulled back and held his face above hers, mischief sparkling in his eyes. "You owe me your first born. Until you make good on that, the only thing you can possibly give me that will make me happy is your time."

She laughed until her cheeks hurt. When she caught her breath she said, "Of course. How could I ever forget that?"

A loud banging emanated from outside the door. Noise created by one of the work crews outside. Recovering the wounded, transporting the dead, and restoring Tegija's home would take days.

"Why did you have to fly me to your home during my rally?" she asked.

They sat at the small table, talking over a shared pot of tea. He smiled hovering his cup near his lips. "I enjoy my home," he said, and took a sip from his cup. "If I was going to die, I thought it should happen here."

With a skeptical look she said, "Not because you intended to wear out or lose opponents by leading them to fight on ground where you held the advantage?"

He grinned and cleared his throat saying, "Maybe that too."

"When do I get to see the rest of it?"

He ran a hand through his hair and he squared his shoulders. She sat back and braced herself for unpleasant news.

"I'm asking you to restrict yourself here for the first few days of the recovery process. The mess outside is unsuitable."

"Unsuitable, for who? I'm not above hard work. I know what a dead person looks like. I think these dead are especially deserving of my aid, don't you?"

"It's considered unsuitable for a new wife to be out there, especially the new Regina."

"That's nonsense," she said, pressing one finger against the handle of her cup, moving it back and forth in its saucer.

"Your presence during the recovery will cause a distraction for the work crews. Seeing you out there will distress them."

She sighed and let her head fall to the side. "How many days will I be confined here?"

"Two, maybe three, they're working from this area out. When this area's cleared, we can take our meals outside if you want, and you can see the nearby outbuildings."

She sunk in her seat as she scanned the small dwelling. "I think the office I share with Valgu is bigger than this. Why did you make the place you live in so small?"

He shrugged, "I'm not here full-time. This room's bigger than my room in the Palace."

"Not anymore."

Realizing his new quarters in the Palace, Tegija balked and she laughed.

She agreed to stay indoors during the recovery process and tolerate her confinement to the small room. This became harder to endure when Tegija left to assist a work crew, fetch a meal, or leave on some small errand. His absence allowed her concerns of home to move to the front of her mind. Her thoughts ran to where she wanted to be: beside her injured brothers, comforting Delany and Dermot, tending to her father's funeral, overseeing the recovery of the palace, and digging into all the work waiting for her. She paced the small room when Owl came to visit her that evening. Katrina struggled to smile, but failed at containing her discomfort.

Owl closed the door and eyed her with concern. "I could feel your frustration from the forest floor," Owl said.

"I'm distracted, there's too much at home I should be dealing with."

"It's all being tended to," Owl said as she walked to the small table and settled into a chair.

"Yes, but my place is back there."

"Back there, in the thick of it," Owl said.

"Yes. I'm needed."

"No, you're not," Owl said. "There's always going to be chaos to manage. It existed before you returned home. It's there right now, and it'll be there when you get back."

"It's my job, my duty, my responsibility."

"Right now your responsibility is to be here. You're just frustrated because you don't like being left out."

Katrina stopped pacing and glared at Owl. She possessed a remarkable way of summarizing the truth. It surprised Katrina, how Owl spoke the truth like that, without making her angry.

"Maybe."

Owl huffed a laugh and motioned for Katrina to join her at the table.

"Your duty right now, to our family and Mozgas, is to be comfortable and happy here with Tegija." With her pointer finger aimed at the table, she leaned forward and tapped the table once to emphasize her statement. "The success of your marriage is more important than anything waiting back home."

"Right, but it doesn't feel right," Katrina said sinking down into the empty chair. "How can I indulge in my blissful happiness, when my entire family needs me?"

"Because you're the Regina, and your rally just ended. In your position, you can't go against tradition, not in this circumstance."

"I want to follow tradition, but it doesn't feel right." She rested an elbow on the table and leaned her head into her hand.

"That's guilt talking," Owl said as she mimicked Katrina's posture.

"Right, I feel guilty."

Owl replied with a chipper, "And guilt doesn't come from God. Ignore it."

How easy for Owl to talk like that.

"Maybe it doesn't, but knowing it doesn't make it go away."

Owl gave her a consoling smile as she said, "You've been blessed." She reached both of her hands across the table and clasped Katrina's. "Let the guilt go, at least for a week or two, and enjoy this. All your duties will still be there when you get home. I promise."

In the days that followed, the sounds of the recovery crews outside dwindled. Tegija's company made them all disappear. Beside him, she found it easy to ignore or let go of anything. She took Owl's advice, and allowed herself to experience this immense new happiness.

She discovered how wondrous it was to be part of a couple. As his wife, the social rules that governed their kind lifted. If she felt the urge to reach out and touch her husband, she could. What a gift, to wake next to him and watch the first rays of morning light play across his features. To take every meal with him, have small conversations perched in his lap, and learn all the intimate trivia of his life. She would memorize it all. Her husband had become her secret study, the subject of an unrestrained infatuation.

Inescapable, he held her affection with a new kind of strength. Maybe without his interest, her fixation might be less consuming, but Owl was right. They had a mutual affection for each other. Katrina binged on her husband's company, waiting to see how much time needed to lapse before they craved solitude. The days passed, and she marveled at her continued contentment by his side.

When the day came to leave their small room, to venture out and tour the buildings nearby, she experienced a small pang of disappointment. She never expected to miss being holed away in their small room. Laughing in surprise at herself, she took Tegija's hand and followed him outside.

She marveled at the impressive platform village he built in the Skrieni style. The village was large for its few regular inhabitants of Eleric, a handful of staff, and him. The platform village sat among a segment of Iron Pine forest he petitioned Pavaldon for and received later as a gift. A large grid of platform trails wove about the Iron Pine canopy. These connected the various buildings, greenhouses, and access points to areas of the forest frequently used. Tegija used his many greenhouses to grow the different plant species he used in long term medicinal experiments, and his own private studies.

They started taking breakfast outside. Owl joined them, always a little irritable before breakfast. Her lapse in alertness presented Katrina with more opportunities to gather information about the relationship between Valgu and Rosalba. With Owl she had to remain calm, work a convincing aloof performance, and ensure any statement made held some measure of truth. She continued to work the method of deducing an answer by defining what Owl avoided under questioning or openly denied.

"I heard Valgu was unconcerned about Rosalba's departure from Mozgas," Katrina said. No one had told her anything about Valgu's reaction. She made a likely guess based on her knowledge of his manners. The public guise Valgu used would display only an appropriate level of concern for Rosalba's safety when she left.

"Are you kidding?" Owl snapped, "He's been a complete mess about it." Catching her mistake right away, Owl glanced around the outdoor eating area with wide green eyes. Leveling a stern glare at her, she pointed a cautionary finger and said, "No one—you will tell no one what I just said."

Katrina smiled, "Of course not."

Owl took a deep breath and sighed as she hunched back in her chair and cradled a cup of tea.

"With my new-found freedom to roam around here, I think you should go back and be with Valgu and Massie."

"You want me to leave?" Owl said.

"I'm happy with you here," Katrina said. Her eyes searched the massive trellis above them as she fumbled for the right words. Vines wove their way to the top of the trellis supports and reached for each other across the expansive overhead beams. Reedy and brown, the vines had a flush of spring green running along them this morning. She looked forward to seeing them in summer heavy with flowers.

"I think Massie and Valgu would make better use of your company," Katrina said. She paused and Owl's eyebrows lifted waiting to hear more. "And I know my husband would prefer to spend this time alone, with just me."

"He told me to stay," Owl said.

"I know, but I also know he'd rather follow tradition."

"I'm staying," Owl said.

"You're the one that convinced me to follow tradition, but now you're staying?"

"There's something up here," Owl said. She leaned forward and set her tea on the table. "I don't like it."

Katrina pressed her lips together as she held her tongue. What was it like for Owl up here? The strain of feeling all the emotions from the restoration crews must be exhausting.

"The restoration, it's another reason you should go home. It's brave of you to endure it this long."

"It has nothing to do with that. I've been sensing an anger. It's thick, and directed at you. I have to stay here and look out for you."

The thought of sweet, introverted Owl protecting her seemed ludicrous. Katrina dipped her head and hid her smile behind one hand. She failed in her attempt to restrain a laugh.

Owl frowned at her.

"I'm so sorry," Katrina said. "Don't be angry with me." She reached for

Owl.

Owl leaned away and crossed her arms. With pursed lips, Owl glared at her in agitation.

"Forgive me," Katrina said. "It's just, and don't hate me for saying this, but dear, have you ever held anything larger than a table knife?"

"It's not something I can fight. I just need to keep you away from it," Owl said.

"I'm capable of defending myself. Pha's here, and let's not forget about my husband. He's Mahigan, and his over-protective habits towards me started long before my rally. I think I'm safe."

"I'm staying, and if you won't take me serious then I'll tell him. We'll see what he thinks."

"All that'll do is set him on edge."

"I swear I'll give you your privacy."

Katrina studied Owl's set jaw. She took a moment, considering Owl's usual accommodating and generous manner. It was rare for her to insist on having her way about anything.

"Have you encountered this before?" Katrina asked.

Owl nodded and her green eyes drifted to the side, her focus shifting inward to a memory. Whatever troubled Owl was real.

"If you need to stay, stay." She leaned across the table and took Owl's hand as she tried to draw her focus back to her. "Will you tell me what you know?"

"Yes," Owl said, as her face went blank, but her green eyes widened with fear. When Owl looked at her, Katrina felt a chill run up her arm. Owl's look mirrored her look at three, when she begged, "Promise to come back."

"It's jealous rage," Owl said. "The kind I felt before Father was poisoned."

Katrina's stomach clenched and she swallowed against a churning sick feeling."When did it start?"

"It woke me up the first day I was here," Owl said. "I'd had such little sleep I wasn't sure at first. I'm so used to it remaining in nightmares. It terrified me, to wake up and still feel it."

"And you feel it right now?"

"It's distant, but it's here," Owl said.

"It's good you told us," Tegija said stepping under the trellis. Katrina felt a flush of sheepishness, and recalled how well he could hear things from a distance. He stood behind her and rested a hand on her shoulder, giving her a reassuring squeeze. "Please alert either of us when you feel it again."

Owl nodded her head and stood. She looked disoriented for a moment. There was a weariness on her face that concerned Katrina. Did this anger keep her from sleep? Owl left, and Katrina stood up and steeled herself for Tegija's irritation. She turned and saw him giving her a small smirk.

"I should have known you were listening."

"I try to ignore your private conversations, but when I heard the tone in

Owl's voice I listened," he said.

"I should have listened better," she said. "I was so intent on us, I failed to remember how rare it is for her to have concerns about anything."

"And you weren't going to tell me?"

She knew he was going to say that. If he were Lady Lena, the tongue lashing would have already started. She readied herself for his lecture, but saw he waited for her response.

"No, I wasn't," she said. "Owl wasn't making any sense. Only when she made the connection to Father did I start to take her warning seriously."

Tegija coaxed her with a mild voice as his expression softened to a plea. "I need you to promise that you'll tell me about these things. Not the private things you keep between you, Owl, and Pha. All that's fine, until it deals with your safety. Promise you'll never try to hide knowledge of a threat against you."

"I'm sorry," she said taking his hand and stepping closer to him.

"You're right," he said. "It does set me on edge. Any threat to my family sets me on edge. It doesn't mean you should keep it a secret from me. Am I that hard to deal with?"

"No."

He wrapped his other arm about her shoulders and pulled her into a gentle hug. "Then promise me."

"I promise," she said. Tilting her head to look at him. "And what do you mean private things between Owl, Pha, and I?"

"I assume there are things you find easier to discuss with them versus me," he said.

"Some, but you shouldn't think there're things I would tell them and not you," she said.

He quietly studied her, grinning in a way that brought a smile to his eyes.

"Nothing about me is too sacred for you," she said.

A true statement, she had proven it daily, even if it was only with her body. She obliged his need, which arrived like a storm. His eyes dark and strange, he altered his path to grab her up, fierce and potent, he pulled her into his frenzied passion. She liked being his catalyst, and adored being his. She wondered how his desire would shift when a child began to grow inside her.

"What kind of vines are these?" she asked, gesturing with a look at the vines above them.

"Clematis," he said. "I labored to get this one right." He wandered to her then, sending an image of them in summer. The surrounding trellis vines transformed into a lush green with variegated blooms of pink and yellow.

"Impressive," she said.

"Thank you."

"I'm starting to understand why your greenhouses exceed your lodgings."

"I told you," he said giving her side a playful nudge. "Until you arrived, it's only ever been a place to sleep."

She smiled and before she took time to consider it blurted out, "Really?"

His smile fell from his eyes. He blinked several times as his eyes narrowed, before answering, "Yes."

"Hm, good," she said trying to retain the warmth of their conversation. Smiling, she raised up on her toes, reaching her face towards his. She pulled at his tunic until he bent down to kiss her. He gave her the briefest peck on the lips before he continued to inspect her. His frown making her cower with regret for broaching the subject.

"You imagine I've had lovers here?"

She dropped his gaze and smoothed where she grabbed his tunic. Her stomach hitched and tightened as she rolled her lips into her mouth and pressed them out into a purse. Already sitting in an awkward moment, she decided to press ahead, and use the opportunity to ask about Proserpere. A topic her logic had always cautioned her to avoid.

"I saw it, the history between you and Proserpere."

"You did."

It was her turn to study his reaction, to see if his expression said something more. He had a mixed look of surprise and interest.

"It was obvious," she said. "I could see you two had something bigger than just a friendship between peers."

"Uh huh," he said.

"And she told me."

"She told you?" His brow lifted in puzzled shock as she nodded. "What did she tell you?"

"She said you were different. That you adopted Skrieni practices and that was why you never made her your wife."

He rubbed his forehead, and the sound he made to clear his throat was more growl than cough. Taking a deep breath he sighed.

She waited, trying her best to avoid looking eager for his explanation.

"It's complicated," he said. "And not something I'm especially proud of." He pulled away from her and walked to the trellis entrance where he stood with his back to her.

Hating the sudden separation between them she fidgeted, but made herself stay in place. She sensed a gap in their stories, and relaxed some. While desperate to hear his tale, she considered his pride, and her own avoidance of anything related to her romantic history.

"If you don't want to talk about it, you don't have to," she said.

"No, I do," he said, looking back over his shoulder at her. "You and I, we still speak the truth to each other, right?"

Katrina nodded and he extended his hand to her. She stepped beside him and took it.

"I'm a little thirsty," he said. "Want to help me dig out my hidden wine stash? Then we can find a better place to talk about this."

"Lead the way," she said, and he pulled her in step beside him as he walked towards their room.

"You've had a stash of wine up here this whole time?"

"I'm not responsible for the wine shortage here. The students drain my supply faster than I can replenish it. Where I keep the good stuff is a closely guarded secret."

They skirted the outside of the room and entered a passage between the back of the building and a neighboring storage shed. He approached a large covered bin. Bending down, he pulled at the trimmed edge at the bottom of the bin. A piece of the trim came free and revealed a small compartment. The heads of three wine bottles were just visible. Tegija selected one and handed it up to her before reaching his arm into the compartment and pulling out two round hand fired cups. They reminded her of a goblet without a stem.

"Here," he said handing her one. He replaced the trim piece over the compartment and stood up. He glanced inside his cup. "We should rinse these, and hide that if we run across anyone," he said gesturing to the wine bottle.

"I'll try," she said, lowering it into the folds of her skirt. She followed him to the building which housed the kitchen. He rinsed their goblets before setting to work opening the wine. Using a small knife, he trimmed off the seal and then pried at the stopper.

"Students," he grumbled. "A barrel's so much easier to open."

The stopper pulled free and he sniffed the contents. "I enjoy red wine now. It was all your doing. I developed a taste for it after our time in Gryph."

"You didn't like it before?"

He shrugged, "Not like I do now. I came home from Gryph liking red wine, and crazy for my best friend's sister."

"Your charm and secret wine stash are making me nervous. Is what you're going to tell me that bad?"

He shook his head and grinned. "No, I was just stating the facts of what you did to me when we were in Gryph."

"Flatterer," she said.

"It's the truth," he said, and motioned with his head for her to follow him from the kitchen.

They returned to the small room and she sat at the table as he poured the wine. He offered her a cup, and taking a sip she nodded. He filled his cup and began to reveal his story.

"Proserpere and I met when I was studying with the senior apothecary in her village. The only reason any of the Skrieni put up with me was because of Pavaldon." He took a small sip of wine and for a moment eyed his cup before sitting down. "They refused to use any common speech, so I was forced to learn their language. Then when I could manage to talk to them, it was impossible to coax an answer from them." He took a drink of wine and sat forward, leaning on his elbow. "I slowly developed a friendship with Proserpere. Finally, I had at least one person willing to tell me things." He shook his head in irritation and took another drink of wine. "She came to me one afternoon and told me she wanted more. She said the more I gave her, the more she'd teach me. Didn't seem too bad. She was pretty, smart, and she wanted me. I didn't spend much time thinking about it." Tegija watched his own fingers play at the sides of his cup. "I mean I knew what I was in for, I'd had a wife. So being with her, according to our practice, she'd be considered my wife." He met her eyes and shaking his head he shrugged. "I didn't mind because at the time I thought loved her."

Katrina tensed against a wave of jealous anger. She held his eyes and asked, "Did you?"

"Not according to her, she insisted nothing had formed between us. She was adamant, I had no claim on her. For the Skrieni, sex is routine outside of marriage. She liked me bedding her, but she didn't want me as her husband."

"She didn't?" Katrina asked, her eyes wide in disbelief.

"No, she didn't. So I gave her what she wanted, learned what I needed to, and returned to the University."

"And that hurt, she hurt you."

"Yeah," he said with a nod. "She did." He drained his cup dry and set it back down. Lifting the wine he refilled it.

"But then she followed you here?"

"No, I don't think so. She never said that," he said and reached the bottle across the table to top off her cup. "Professor Rath had requested the village send an Apothecary to the University. A sort of educational exchange, they'd get to study at the University, and we'd get to ask questions about the methods being developed."

"When she came to live at the University, were you...with her?"

He grimaced and shook his head saying a quick, "No, no."

"But she wanted that?"

"She did, and I said no. We hadn't seen each other in years. I thought seeing her I might have some tie to her or a desire to be with her, but I don't." Tegija frowned into his cup before taking a sip. "I shouldn't be surprised she said I adopted Skrieni beliefs."

"From what you've said, you tried to follow your beliefs with her."

"Did I? Can I claim I'm trying now? If she's supposed to be my wife, then according to my customs, I'm obligated to reconcile with her."

"No you're not," she said, her words sharp with unchecked anger. The idea of him relenting to Proserpere's manipulations, that he'd make her his wife, it was enough to make her scream. She took a large sip of wine and worked to calm herself as she set her cup back on the table. Lowering her voice into a more mellow tone she said, "She can't reject you and your beliefs, but then expect you to abide by them when it suits her. She's the one who made the mistake of making you conform to her practices."

"It's what she wanted," he said.

"Exactly, she has to live with her mistakes just like everybody else."

"I don't feel anything for her. Does that mean she's right? Is my ambivalence to her now proof that I took on some backwards Skrieni belief?"

"No. I think some bonds can't be mended once they've been cut."

"I'm relieved she's not my wife."

With a small grin she stood and walked around the table. Lifting her skirt with one hand, she braced against his shoulder with the other as she crawled onto his lap. He grinned as his eyes roamed over her with appreciation. Looping her arms around his neck, she straddled him and let her legs dangle at his sides.

Looking him in the eye she said, "I'm your only wife." She ran her fingers into his hair and kissed him. He groaned in approval.

"I'm relieved she means nothing to you," she said. "I'd be miserable if you still had feelings for her. If you made me share you with her. Don't ever make me share you with another woman."

"You'll suffer no misery over that," he said skimming his hands along the curve in her waist and pressing a small kiss to her lips.

"As your wife I'm allowed to dislike her for the way she treated you."

He chuckled and said, "You never liked her before I told you any of that."

"It's true, I didn't, but in my defense it takes effort to be civil when someone has no respect for you." He was nuzzling her neck the way he knew tickled her. She laughed and pulled away.

"Come back here," he said, pursuing her neck.

"There was something else I was going to say," she said.

"I don't want to talk anymore about her," he said, running his hands up her back and leaning in to kiss her neck. "We have better things to do."

She let her head fall to the side, exposing her neck to oblige his kisses. Each one making it more difficult for her to remember what she wanted to say.

"She's a bigger fool than I thought. I don't know if I'll be able to see her...without looking annoyed."

He grabbed her by the thighs and stood up. With her legs around his waist and her arms about his neck, he carried her to the bed saying, "I'm sure you'll manage."

On the night Valgu was able to summon her in neutral, Katrina barely maintained her composure. She wanted to rush over and hug him, but the sight of his reclined figure snuffed out the instinct. He lay on a day bed in the violet binti light glow of his mother's old parlor. The stillness in his posture and the melancholy in his eyes spoke of hidden pain. With a tired wave, he gestured for her to sit across from him at a colorful Palai gaming table.

"I'm still learning this," she said. "I'm not very good at it."

"You also have a habit of claiming mediocrity at something when you possess above average skill for it."

She shrugged and smiled, "If you say so, then I won't disagree. I've missed you. I've been worried sick about you and Massie."

Valgu gave her a scoffing grin, "Have not, Owl said you've been holed away with Tegija for days, happy as can be."

"She reveals the true nature of my feelings to you, but clams up the minute I ask her anything about you."

"Questions about me? Did you ever think to just ask me? What is it you want to know?"

"It's your turn," Katrina said moving a clear glass pyramid into a space. A move she made without any planning or long term strategy.

Valgu glowered as he considered the board.

Katrina smiled at the memory of her small achievement prying Valgu's interest in Rosalba out of Owl. Valgu's focus shifted from the board back to her.

"That was a wasted move," he grumbled.

"It took you that long to see that?"

"Well, are you going to ask me your question or not?"

"You and I have never talked about your prospects for marriage," she said.

Valgu kept his eyes on the game board. "I think the question you're searching for is, do I ever plan to rally?"

"Do you?" she said.

Valgu shrugged and shifted against his pillows. "For a long time I wasn't allowed. I've wanted a wife, but when Father told me I was free to rally, it seemed like a bad idea. What would happen to our family if something happened to me? Who would hold Mozgas together if I were gone for even a few months? Was it right to bring a wife into the chaos of living with Father?"

"So your reservations have never been about rallying for the right woman?"

"No," he said, his expression turning somber. "Not really."

"Will you rally now that Father's gone?"

"Maybe," he said, looking at her from a lowered brow as a small grin surfaced. "Why do I get the sense there's a more direct question you wish to ask?"

"I'd like to see you happily married, that's all. You've dedicated your life to taking care of our family, across great distances, and at great personal expense to yourself. You make tending to the needs of others look easy. Your wife would be a blessed woman."

His look eased into a relaxed smile as he said, "Thank you."

"You're welcome. It's still your turn," she said eyeing the board with impatience.

"Did you read through the correspondence from Milios?"

"No, why? Is there another delay on the Amber Sound rock shipments?"

"There is, but I was hoping you'd read the big surprise yourself."

"What surprise?"

"Tvarchus replied to your request, they're sending a Minotaur contingent to work here and in Milios."

"They sent a reply? They're really coming here?" Katrina laughed, "I don't believe it!"

"It was all your doing, they just routed the reply through Milios out of courtesy." Valgu slid a clear sapphire blue piece resembling the arch of a giant wave. It stopped in a move she failed to recognize.

"Hm," she said shaking her head. "I thought you said starting with blue wasn't recommended?"

"It's not," he said. "That doesn't mean you can't do it."

"I hate this game," she said sinking into her chair.

"So your strengths lie in real life strategies," he said. "Someday you'll learn to embrace the important things in life, and take this game more seriously."

She met Valgu's smirk with a frown. Her scowl cracked as he stifled a chuckle, and eventually they both caved, sharing in a much needed and long overdue laugh.

The next morning she still lay in bed when Tegija left to fetch them breakfast. Once dressed, she sifted through a stack of correspondence, and grew impatient. What was taking Tegija so long? She set her letters aside, wrapped a shawl around her, and opened the door to a morning of thick cool air. A spring wind skimmed along the platforms, stirring a haze of warm humidity as the sun baked dew from the wood surface underfoot.

A torn piece of parchment tumbled to a stop in front of her. Reaching down to retrieve it, she noticed others fluttering about the platforms. She picked up the parchment and turned it over. It was part of a clothing sketch Owl recently made.

She knew this particular sketch. It had shocked her, and they argued over Owl designing maternity attire for her. Owl dismissed her annoyance, along with any facts, like how she wasn't pregnant, and had married less than a month ago. Her sister insisted such a wardrobe took far too long to construct, and their assembly needed to begin immediately. Having zero experience with pregnancy or specialty garment construction, she let the topic drop. While many mysteries about Owl remained, she knew her sister would not tear apart her work this way. Katrina walked towards the eating area, grabbing up the bits of torn sketches she could catch.

Coming under the trellis she found Owl laying, sprawled face down in an awkward position. She dropped the sketches as she inhaled a gasp. She stepped back, turning to scan the area for any immediate signs of danger. Realizing she had reached for an absent sword, she smoothed her hands on skirts and moved to Owl's side. Turning Owl over, she found no signs of injury. Owl's breaths were shallow and her complexion was drained of its normal color. Katrina took off her shawl and lay it under Owl's head. She smoothed Owl's hair back and gripped her limp and cold hand.

She squeezed and rubbed Owl's hand. "Owl, what happened? Wake up dear, please. Wake up."

Owl's eyes fluttered open then rolled as her body remained limp.

"Owl honey, please. Ah, sweet, come on." She patted and jostled Owl before collecting her in an embrace. "Don't do this, Owl. Wake up. You need to wake up." She looked around again and screamed, "Tegija!"

A gust of wind tossed the scraps of Owl's sketches about as she held Owl's limp body. She reached for Tegija in a wander, and felt nothing.

Rattled, she took a deep breath and tried again. Nothing—gone, she felt nothing when she wandered for him. Cold beads of sweat formed on her back as fear rushed in. A familiar and overwhelming fear. The paralyzing kind that could send her into shock if she caved to it. It started scattering her thoughts. Her mind ran in one direction as she tried to formulate a plan. Simultaneously her mind ran in three other directions as she tried piecing together what happened. What was wrong with Owl? Where was Tegija? What should she do first?

Slow footsteps approached from behind her. They stopped, and the sound of tearing paper sent a chill through her body. Katrina took a deep breath, reigning in her thoughts.

She lay Owl down and stood up. Turning around she saw Proserpere rip another page from Owl's sketchbook. Proserpere stared at her as she ripped another page from Owl's sketchbook. Holding the torn page aloft she dropped it into the wind. Katrina bit back a curse. She mentally dismembered her, and ached for a decent weapon to do it with.

"What did you do to Owl?"

Proserpere tossed the sketch book aside, and hunched her shoulders. The feral grin on her face made Katrina strengthen her defensive stance.

"You play games with him," Proserpere said. "Pretending you're feeble. Pretending your wings are missing. Pretending you still can't shift. All part of a game to trap him."

Proserpere charged her. Standing ready, Katrina landed a punch to her jaw. Grabbing Proserpere by the shoulders, Katrina kneed her in the gut, and tossed her to the platform.

"I'm his wife," Proserpere groaned from the floor. She rolled and crawled to her knees. "He can't deny me, and neither can you."

"You've gone mad," Katrina said.

"I'm mad. Yes, he's mine and I won't share." Proserpere lunged forward, grabbed Katrina around the waist and tackled her to the ground. Katrina restrained a hand Proserpere tried to rake across her face.

"I'll kill you," Katrina said.

She yanked Proserpere's arm across her body and twisted her wrist. Using her other hand, she struck Proserpere under her chin with the base of her palm. Proserpere yelped, clawing at Katrina's clothes as she fell sideways. With a kick she threw Proserpere off her, and stood up. Proserpere came at her again, a flailing mess of arms and legs that clung to wherever she grabbed. Snagging the sleeve of her dress, Proserpere yanked with enough force to make the seams of her bodice rip apart. The top of Katrina's dress splayed open as she spun free. Katrina grabbed Proserpere's scalp and rammed her face against her knee. The contact produced an audible crack. Blood poured from Proserpere's nose as Katrina tossed her against the platform again.

Katrina expected a small reprieve. Instead, Proserpere rolled towards her, grabbed her by the ankle, and tried to pull her off balance. Katrina stumbled, trying to stay on her feet. Little by little their fight had brought them towards the edge of the platform. Proserpere got on all fours and sprung at her, grabbing her by the shoulders, and landing a head butt near the bridge of her nose. The blow sent a shock of thrumming pain through Katrina's head and made her eyes water. She blinked fast to clear her vision. She stomped kicks into Proserpere's shins as she tried to free her arms from Proserpere's claw like grip. Long nails gouged her, leaving behind long bleeding scratches as Katrina yanked free. Proserpere shrieked, extending one leg to curl around hers, she wrenched them off balance. They fell, landing sideways, and tumbled across the platform. Katrina lurched away as they stopped, but the move sent her torso arching off the platform edge.

A jolt of terror ran through her. She tried to sit up. Proserpere pushed her back. Her whole body inched closer to the edge.

"Let's see how you fly," Proserpere said.

"Not before I see you die," Katrina said. Gritting her teeth, she took hold of Proserpere's wrists and pulled. Katrina kicked and launched Proserpere into the air. Gripping her shoulders, Katrina leaned back and entered a free fall. The momentum pulled Proserpere over the edge with her.

Proserpere kicked and screamed. She scrambled to hold Katrina as she released her. Proserpere's panic stricken face dropped faster to the forest floor.

Katrina continued to fall, but her heart no longer raced. Her pulse slowed. She saw every second as it passed. Why did she need to panic? If her entire life, or only a few parts of it, were pre-determined, ordained, on some course so specific a seer thousands of years ago glimpsed it and carved it in stone, then she had nothing to fear. She knew how to rise. She knew how to fall. Both were an integral part of flying, and she loved to fly.

Yanking at her ripped dress, her bodice came free and exposed the upper half of her torso. Her body would remember how to shift or she would die. Dropping closer to a tangle of Iron Pine limbs, an old instinct took hold. The shift moved beyond her control, rolling through her body in one immense burst of energy. She cringed in anticipation of the pain from failing to shift. She relaxed into the surge of energy as her body reached for her wings.

Wings unfurled from her back. She took a breath and another as shock quickened her pulse. Still dropping, she pushed them out, spreading them wide. Another breath and then another as she held to her wings in the right position to stabilize her descent. She wanted to gape at them, but there was no time. The fatigue in her back muscles enough proof and reassurance of her shift. She controlled her descent, clearing obstacles of branches, and the mangled and dead body of Proserpere.

When her feet touched the ground, her whole body sagged. She dropped to her hands and knees. Her breath came in aching heaves. It worked, she could shift. Her wings were back.

She looked up to the trees above as tears of frustration surfaced. Fisting her hands, she beat the ground as her body shook. She needed to get back up there. Tegija and Owl, they had to be okay. She needed Tegija to be okay. She stood up, worry pulling her down as she considered the worst. She swayed between fear's weight and the levity of what she just regained. Guilt wanted her to cry for the cold part of her that killed without remorse. Guilt wasn't from God. She needed to start walking before the realization she accepted her connection to God sent her back to her knees. She walked and peace rushed over her.

Tucking strands of hair behind each ear, she glanced over her shoulder. The ache from spent muscles indicated their presence, but she had to see them. The restoration procedure worked. Her wings were amazing. Larger than she remembered and beautiful. Tegija needed to see them. A ringing happiness spurred her to move faster.

She gathered up her torn dress, tugging it around her, she held it with crossed arms to keep herself from tripping on it. The scratches on her arms burned, and the healing injury in her shoulder ached. She walked the circumference of the nearest tree, looking to orient herself by finding the river. Hearing it, she followed the river north until she reached the bath house. She knew the lift access here and wasted no time throwing the lever to bring the lift down. The time it took for the lift to work its way down and then haul her back up was agonizing. The lift was still in motion when she jumped off, running to the kitchen and food storage building. The last place Tegija had gone.

The door to the kitchen stood open, but there was no sign of him. She checked the food storage rooms, and grew panicked as she ran towards their room. A small gathering of workers stood outside their room. The crowd turned to her with looks of surprise.

"Where's Tegija?" she demanded.

"In here," Pha said, standing in the doorway to their room.

The crowd stepped aside as she moved to the doorway and stepped past Pha. Tegija lay in their bed fully dressed. His eyes were closed, but he was breathing and his face was warm to the touch.

"What happened to him?"

Pha shook her head, her face rigid with concern. "We don't know, we found him this way just outside the kitchen."

"And Owl?"

"We took her to her room," Pha said. "She says she'll be fine."

Katrina used her fingers to comb back Tegija's hair. She sat down, leaning in close beside him.

"What did she do to you, love?"

"My Katrina," Pha said in hushed voice.

The tears in Pha's eyes glistened, and she held one hand over a trembling smile as the other gestured to her.

"Your wings, you got your wings back."

Katrina nodded and turned back to Tegija saying, "I did."

Her vigil started then, a long and difficult wait. She relented to Pha's insistence, and put on fresh clothing. She paced back and forth between the table and his side. She ate little. Forcing a few bites from each tray of food Pha brought her. She lay in bed curled against him. The sound of his heartbeat the only thing able to console her anxiety.

Eleric arrived the next day. He hid his own fear for his father well. Wrapping his hands around his father's neck Eleric's gaze glazed over as he examined his father with his healing talent.

"He's fine," Eleric said. "He'll be just fine. He's had a heavy dose of sleeping medicine, but eventually he'll wake."

"Thank God," she said.

The second night passed into morning when sleep finally claimed her. His movement brought her back to their room, still and dark. Only the dim light from a small binti light on the table glowed. He shifted beneath her and she lifted her head with a start. He moved again, turning his head to one side and then the other as his eyes blinked open.

"Tegija, I'm here," she said lifting up so he could see her better. "Are you all right?"

"I'm tired. I have a headache."

"What happened to you?"

Tegija frowned, blinked heavy eyelids, and coughed. Clearing his throat he took a deep breath and held it as he looked at her.

"Katrina," he said. His eyebrows bunched as he inspected her. He gaped, his mouth open to speak, then shut. He swallowed and asked, "Is this real?"

"Yes," she said.

His forehead relaxed as his eyes widened in amazement, "When did it happen? How long have I...when did you get your wings?"

Forgetting herself, she grinned and breathed a short laugh of humor and relief. "Right before I found you unconscious."

"You can use them? You shifted without pain?"

"Yes," she said. "My back muscles ache but there was no pain."

"Amazing," he said.

She pressed one hand against his cheek. "Are you really okay? What exactly did she do to you?"

"Proserpere?" he said, and she nodded waiting for him to continue. "I was going to the kitchen, and she was there waiting. Seeing her up here, I got mad. I told her she had to go. She refused and we started to argue. She said she wasn't going anywhere. That she was my wife and had every right to be here. I told her I've only had two wives in my life, and she wasn't one of them. Then she threw a powder at me. It must have been raw codlata root. It's normally seeped in boiling water. It's used to put patients into a deep sleep."

"You slept over two days," she said.

"Then it's good I ducked when I did," he said. "It could have been longer. Too much of the raw stuff is lethal."

"You're going to be okay?" she asked.

"Yes," he said. "I'm okay."

"I love you," she said. "I have for a long time. Sitting in here with you waiting, I kept wondering why I never told you."

He smiled but then gave her a confused look. "Why are you upset about that?"

"When I couldn't feel you, and I thought you may have died, I couldn't even reason why I wasted so many opportunities. I hated myself for potentially losing you, and you never knowing."

He grinned and smoothed a lock of her hair between his fingers. "I assumed it, like I assumed you knew how I love you."

She considered him with a tilt of her head and shrugged, "I did assume, but I should have said it."

He scoffed, "You said it to me all the time, you just never put it in words." He pulled her against him and held her."Don't think any more about it. Stay right here and rest with me. I want to stare at you with these wings of yours for a while. It's not every day I wake up and get to see something so perfect."

She closed her eyes, and made a silent prayer, thanking God for protecting him.

EPILOGUE

On the morning Katrina and Tegija left behind the privacy of their room to return to the palace, the sky appeared flat. It looked like a giant blanket of white lay draped above the trees, muffling the sun, and hiding any trace of blue. Its bleakness fit the long oral updates they received during the journey home. They traveled the forest on horseback, surrounded by a palace entourage the size of a small army. The conversation depressed her with details of her father's funeral, and the pending ceremony to honor the Mahigans who died at her rally. The predominant peace and solitude enjoyed in Tegija's home slipped away as the full weight from the mantle of the Mozgas Regency returned. Tegija took it on without complaint, while she conceded to its return with resigned reluctance, already missing their idle days spent alone.

Her mood lightened when they reached the entrance to the Mozgas tunnels. The locals entered the streets shouting greetings and blessings over their marriage. They dismounted in the city and when Katrina moved to follow their entourage towards the tunnels, Tegija held her back.

"What is it?" she asked.

"I think we should make some kind of grand entrance."

"Grander than all of this?" She glanced around at all the palace staff swarming around them.

"Yes, you and I. What do you say we fly up?"

"Fly up?" Her eyebrows rose in disbelief. "I thought you said I shouldn't fly long distances or near any large obstacles until I was stronger."

"You shouldn't. I'll carry you up, and then we can glide down."

"I didn't know you were such a show off."

"I've never had much to show off. I could use a break. Flying up the plateau is exhausting, but if we do, we'll escape the next two hours traveling the tunnels being briefed."

Katrina nodded and said without hesitation, "You're right, we should fly up."

The staff appeared concerned when Tegija announced his plan, but no one voiced an objection. A few of the eager young Mahigan soldiers stepped forward to join the more seasoned ones who committed to guarding them during the challenging flight to the top of the plateau. Katrina removed her riding cloak and handed it off to Pha.

"I'll see you up there, my Regina," Pha said.

Katrina gave her a tight grin as she hugged her. Hearing Pha use her formal title never felt right. 'My Regina' never rang with the same love and connection as 'my Katrina'.

"We'll see you up there," she said, releasing Pha and walking over to Tegija.

He smiled with pleasure as he wrapped his arms about her, embracing her tight against him.

"Do you want me to shift now or when we get up there?" she asked.

"Now," he said, as he shifted into his own rugged wings of thick skin and gnarled bone.

She reached for her wings and with the ease of opening her hand, she shifted into her wings. They extended wide before she tucked them against her back.

Tegija's wings reached back and within one beat they were off the ground, propelled up at a speed she would have considered impossible before she experienced it. She clung to his shoulders. Tucking her head to his chest, she heard his pulse as it beat faster. He maintained a steady pace and they soon emerged over the edge of the plateau, and flew on towards the palace. When they reached the promenade he halted midair, holding a steady position as he loosened his grip.

"Are you ready?" he asked.

She extended her wings and nodded as she leaned away from him and held herself aloft under her own power.

"You lead the way," he said. "I'll be behind you."

She turned and held her wings in a simple gliding posture, then descended to ground. Fluttering her wings, they lifted her in a few gliding hops before she stopped with both feet on the ground. People gathered at the edge of the palace, but Delany was the first to come bursting from the doors at a run. She was less than five paces when she shifted into her wings and launched herself in their direction. Katrina extended her arms and laughed as Delany floated into her embrace.

"I missed you," she cried touching both hands to the sides of Katrina's face. "We all missed you. Daddy said of course you'd take forever, that you always do."

"How is your Daddy?" Katrina asked as she carried Delany towards the palace.

"Walking, but he doesn't like it."

"You must make him."

"That's what Uncle Valgu says. He says I'm the only one who can make Daddy do anything."

"I think Valgu's right," Katrina said with a chuckle.

"Your big friend is here. He's sitting in the pretty room with Uncle Valgu."

"My big friend?" Katrina asked.

"With the horns," Delany said pointing a finger at the side of her head. "He can't talk, but he knows what I say."

"Thedmir?" Katrina asked.

"Yep," Delany said.

Katrina looked at Tegija in surprise as he fell into step beside her.

"I'm guessing he's one of the Minotaur waiting on the veranda," Tegija said pointing to a group of five Minotaur who had stepped from the palace.

Delany looked over her shoulder and nodded, "That's him." She turned back and smiled at Katrina."He's funny."

It astonished her to see Thedmir. She wanted to run over and greet him, and might have without Delany in her arms. She met Thedmir's gaze and smiled as he made his hand gesture for hello.

Thedmir stepped forward from his peers as they approached and wandered to her, *My dear friend, you look terrible. Did you forget how to tie up your hair?*

She smirked at him as she wandered back, *You're an officer now but you still forget how to bathe.*

Thedmir laughed into her mind. *Thank God, I've missed you.*

"You too," she said. "They sent five of you, this is quite the surprise."

Sent on behalf of Tvarchus to formally greet the new Regency in Mozgas. It was going to be just them, but I was made to come along.

Katrina set down Delany and smiled over at Tegija who stared at their Minotaur guests with a look of apprehension and awe.

"Tegija Wythe, Consort to the Regina of Mozgas, may I introduce my dear friend Thedmir of Tvarchus. He's part of the contingent sent here to formally greet us."

Tegija stepped forward and began a series of greetings with Thedmir and the other Minotaur.

Thedmir wandered to Katrina, "The Minotaur with the white head, that's Bijel, he's in charge."

Bijel and Tegija grasped hands, greeting one another before Tegija motioned for them to return to the Palace. Bijel's fur lacked the same color and curl as Thedmir's, it lay more coarse and flat. He had a leaner face with horns set wider apart and higher in length.

It's really too bad you didn't shift back at the University, Thedmir wandered, adjusting his stride beside her as they followed Tegija and Bijel into the palace.

"Why do you say that?" she asked.

Because the Freshman would have spent more time staring at you than me.

"Oh shut up," she said with a hushed smile.

You could have flown to formation, and been on time.

"Now you're just trying to make me mad."

One more, come on, I've got one more.

Katrina laughed.

You really wanted to gain a commission in Gryph so you could blend in with other flying creatures.

"Anytime you want to leave, feel free," she said with mock conviction.

No, I'm not going anywhere, friend. I'm too excited that my new assignment has brought us together again. With your consent, Bijel will be our ambassador to your people.

"And we are very excited to have a new ambassador for Tvarchus here. Whatever part you played in making this happen, thank you."

I provided an opinion on the matter, when it was requested of me. Otherwise I think it's the ancient carved images on the walls of the this plateau that swayed their decision.

"Your people are as intrigued as mine."

Yes, but my people were also impressed with how well I adapted to life at the University. I tried to tell them different, but they think I have the ability to thrive in the new.

Katrina laughed quietly. "Do you plan to thrive in the new in Madar? This must be like starting out at the University all over again."

In a way, yes, he said. But here I'm with my kind, and I have the comfort of knowing I'll be in good company.

The evening proved interesting as the reception for their homecoming changed into a formal welcoming reception for the new ambassador. Notifying guests of the change caused a flurry among the servants and staff for most of the afternoon. By the start of the welcome reception it looked like it had been planned as such from the start. For Katrina, hailing Thedmir and the new Tvarchus ambassador was the best thing to occur that day.

Learning of Valgu's upcoming departure was the worst. He brought her to their office where he broke the news in private.

"You're still recovering," she protested. "And what about Dermot? He's counting on you to be his sponsor when he goes in."

"Tegija promised me he'd sponsor him. Everything I learned from Father, Tegija knows. He's your consort. Nothing will affect Dermot's rank. He'll be well looked after."

"No, you should at least stay until you've fully recovered. There's no need for you to go anywhere until you can at least ride a horse."

"I can ride a horse if I need to, but there aren't many equestrian pursuits where I'm going. I'll have more time than I need for recovery during the voyage over. Who we send to Tvarchus is important. I'm the most qualified of those available."

"I agree with you, who we send on this is important, but why must it be you? You need to stay and be Regent. Your expertise is needed here."

"Tegija can have the Regency."

"He'd never do that to you."

"I need to do this."

Katrina dropped her gaze. "I feel like you're abandoning us."

"You know I'm not," Valgu said. "And I'll be back. I need some time."

"How will I get to see you married when you're living in Tvarchus?"

"I'm sorry to disappoint you about that," he said with quiet laugh. "I had a feeling you envisioned grand marriage plans for me."

"Maybe I did," she said.

"Well, those will have to wait. There aren't many women of our kind living where I'm going." He offered her his hand and she sighed as she took it.

"I'm going to miss you, too much. Promise you'll make frequent trips home."

"I promise," he said. "But you must promise me to improve your Palai game. You and I will play in neutral, at least once a week, agreed?"

"Agreed," she said.

He grinned, "Then it's settled."

Valgu and Katrina returned to the reception. She squeezed Valgu's arm when she spotted Massie in a conversation with Thedmir.

"Uh-oh," Valgu said. "The look on your face tells me you're worried about those two. Are you worried for our brother or your old friend?"

"A little bit of both," she said and moved across the conservatory to where they stood.

"So there were two Monster Snakes," Massie said.

Thedmir tilted his head in a nod as Katrina cried, "Massie, I've told you that exact story at least half a dozen times."

"My Regina, I'm so honored by you gracing me with your presence. Or did you only come to speak with your dear friend? If that's the case, I'll step away."

Katrina grabbed Massie by the arm and turned to Thedmir.

"I warned you about him," she said to Thedmir.

"His version of the story's better by the way," Massie said. "You know I was a bit concerned today. You being home, making the rounds, saying hello, acknowledging every one of your siblings in the palace. Except for the one who's actually risked his life for you on occasion. It didn't make sense. I was wondering if you were angry with me?"

Thedmir grinned and shifted his ears with a huff of amusement.

"I missed you," she said to Massie.

"Of course you did. So tell me, yes or no, are you pregnant yet?"

"Massie. I swear, not in front of our guests," she said, and moved to let go of him, but Massie placed a hand over hers, reinforcing the hold.

"This guest happens to be one you're bonded too, which means he likely already knows the answer to my question. Owl showed me her sketches, it's a completely fair question since she's apparently already heard the news."

"No, Massie, it's not," she said.

"So, is that a no, as in no, you're not?"

"I don't know," she said, shaking her head.

"How is that even possible?" Massie asked, gripping her hand tighter as he turned in to her with a confused look. "When you're married to a man with a healing talent like his?"

"I don't know, and when I do know I'll tell you."

"Hm, yeah, okay. You're going to tell me first, or will I be an afterthought like I was today?"

Exasperated, Katrina shook her head at him, but placed a swift kiss on his cheek. "I'll tell you first."

"Before Owl. When I say first, I don't mean the first out of all your brothers that you tell. I get to find out first."

"Yes, that's what I meant. You will be the first, out of all our siblings, that

I tell," Katrina said and then looked up at Thedmir saying, "See, what I mean? This is why I warned you about him."

What Massie brought up stuck with her. She wondered why she never considered it before. Tegija could see inside her body. Of course he could tell her if she were pregnant. He could also tell her if there was something wrong with her that prevented her from having a child. The thought lingered in the back of her mind for the rest of the night. By the time she returned to their new Regents quarters, she had to know what he saw. He could look at her using his talent, and then she would know one way or the other. It was too simple. No more of this waiting for days and days only to have her monthly bleeding start, and make the whole awful wait start again.

"How are you?" Tegija asked as he embraced her from behind. His hands circled her waist and one rested firmly on her belly as he nuzzled the side of her face.

She leaned into him enjoying his embrace.

"I'm fine," she said.

"Are you?" he asked.

She turned in his arms and met his concerned gaze.

"You look troubled by something," he said.

"You can see into my body, whenever you touch me."

"When I'm trying, yes."

"So if there was something wrong with me, you'd know, and you'd tell me."

"Are you worried about something?"

"I'm not a patient person," she said. "I don't think I can handle months on end of hope and despair, hope and despair. I will lose my mind if I have to suffer years of that. I don't have that kind of endurance. I've been praying that God will have mercy on my faulty patience, just this once."

"What are you talking about?"

"What if I can't get pregnant?"

Tegija cleared his throat, "Ugh, I don't believe that's a problem."

"You could tell then, if there was something wrong with me?"

"My mother or my sister could say for sure," he said. "But I think everything's just fine."

"Well, look now," she said pulling his hands up to where they touched her exposed neck.

"Where did this concern come from?" He asked as he obliged and adjusted the placement of his hands. His eyes took on a far off look as he trained the focus of his healing talent. "It all looks completely normal."

She frowned as she studied his tunic, playing with one of the buttons.

He slid a finger along her jaw and tipped her chin, prompting her to look at him.

"Where is this coming from?" He asked again in a quieter tone.

"The only thing you've ever asked from me is our child."

"No, I've asked for other things."

"You want a baby, and because it's what you want, now it's what I want. And I want it, really bad."

"But you're worried there's something wrong with you?"

She nodded looking down at his tunic again. She pulled away from him and busied herself getting undressed. Opening a nearby wardrobe she sighed seeing it held men's clothing. She left it open as she stepped to the one beside it where she found her attire. Tegija walked to the wardrobe she left open, eyeing the contents with curiosity. He closed the wardrobe, removed his clothes, and piled them in a random heap beside it. By his intent passing glances, she knew he waited for her to say something.

"Why do you think something's wrong with you?" he asked.

Her back was to him as she pulled on a nightgown. She cringed as she gathered the courage to articulate where this fear came from. She moved to the bed, and for a moment stood amazed as she considered the large scale of it. Yanking back the fresh and unfamiliar blankets she crawled in. He lowered the room's binti lamps, turning the room into a thick darkness. He opened the shades to their terrace windows, brightening the room with moonlight. The covers lifted as he climbed into bed, and she relaxed as the warmth of his body settled beside her. He watched her, his head propped against one arm. The honest way his gaze met hers, held a look of patient understanding even without her answering his question.

"After Puternic claimed me, I kept waiting for signs I was pregnant. I'd have taken any of them," She held up one hand, raising shadowed fingers in the darkness as she listed them off. "Stomach sickness, no monthly bleeding, odd appetites, a tenderness in the breast. He promised to take me home when there was at least one sign I was pregnant. Waiting all those months, it was awful. Here I am waiting again, but it's worse because I really want a baby. Between the months I waited then, and the months I've waited now, I'm worried there's something wrong with me. What if I can't conceive a child?"

"I'm telling you right now, there's nothing wrong with you, and waiting is normal. My mother would tell you worrying won't help." He kissed her forehead and pulled her closer to him. "And love, you do know, there're a lot more signs that can come about when a woman's pregnant?"

"I know," she said, irritated by his carefree demeanor and how it clashed with her darkening mood.

"Mood swings," he said holding back a laugh as she scowled up at him. "Fatigue, sometimes a heightened sense of smell."

"Promise me," she said.

"Promise you what?"

"Promise me you'll tell me as soon as you know."

He gave her a sideways grin.

"Don't do that," she said pressing a finger to his chest.

"Don't you want to be the first one to figure it out?"

"No, promise you'll tell me when you know."

"All right then," he said, smiling in satisfaction as he relished his words.

"You're pregnant."

"I am...what?"

He nodded and said, "Again, I'm not an expert like my mother, but my first lessons using my talent were all spent looking at babies in pregnant women. I know what a baby growing in a woman looks like."

"How long have you known?"

"A week," he said giving her a sheepish smile. "Maybe, a little longer. I'm sorry, I couldn't help myself. I had to know."

"You're terrible," she said.

"You would have done the same thing."

"I know, but why didn't you tell me when you knew?"

"I already told you, I thought you'd want to know first. I didn't want to wreck it for you."

"I've been getting tortured, while you knew the entire time. No, never do that again."

"I didn't want to spoil it."

"Please spoil it, spoil away. I can't stand waiting," she said. Her gaze traveled the strange new shadows of the room before she looked at him again.

"Am I really pregnant?"

He chuckled and said, "Yes, are you doubting me? Why would I joke about that?" With a playful smile he made a trail of light kisses down the side of her face until he reached that place on her neck that tickled. She squirmed and shouted a laugh, ducking her head as she rolled to her side trying and fend him off. His hands gipped her hips and pulled her back to him. She rested her back against him as he slid a hand under her gown and held it against her belly. She knew he was using his talent to spy on the baby inside her. Tucking his head over her shoulder he said, "That's my baby in there. Now we have a different wait. We'll see how well you bear the torture of waiting to hold your first child."

The idea of holding their baby thrilled her. She placed her hand over the one he spread wide against her belly, and steadied her breath against a rush of excitement.

"You're right. I can hardly wait."

The accustomed dim cast from the moonlight added some of the cozy aesthetic she enjoyed back at his home. Among everything here, the warmth of him beside her felt the most familiar. Their day had been marked with all sorts of changes. Some of them wonderful, while others she would learn to accept. She would adapt. Let their surroundings change, the people, their occupations, even her own physical body. She could manage it. She could manage all sorts of things, including an entire Province. There was only one exception to her flexibility and that was Tegija. Her rally marked their union with permanence. He owned a fixed position in her heart. The one constant she needed in life, and God willing, she would never spend a day without him.

Acknowledgements

Thank you for finishing my first novel Missing Wings, I hope you enjoyed it. Please share your opinions and leave a review.

I began crafting Missing Wings in January, 2013. It's been a long journey working on my first novel, which means I have a lot of people who've helped me out along the way. My biggest thank you goes to my husband who has stood by my efforts and provided me with an unwavering amount of support. To my best friends, Lori Bethke and Kerri Lorig, thank you for enduring drafts, especially from my horrible days of draft one. Your encouragement and honesty helped me move forward when I felt overwhelmed.

To my larger crew of beta readers: Mark Walsma, Larry Laswell, Anne Johnson, Shelly Nemitz, Aaron Hubble, Terri Carlson, and Andrea Kostiuk - thank you all for providing me with your perspective, honesty, and heartfelt feedback. To Adam Lorig, you helped keep the fight scenes real, and I wish you were still here with us to celebrate Missing Wings publication.

To the wonderful professionals at the Editorial Department in Tucson, AZ, including: Ross Browne, Shannon Barefield, and most especially Shannon Roberts. Thank you all for pushing me, helping me hone my craft, and providing me with a wealth of expert advice. Hiring you guys was one of the best decisions I ever made.

Robert Kroese, thank you for being candid, taking time to answer questions, and providing feedback when you really didn't have to.

Special thanks to my cover art artistic team: illustrator and cover artist, Ryan Alexander Lee. Working with you is a dream come true. To my title artist, Artie Cabrera, you have a gift.

www.ingramcontent.com/pod-product-compliance
Lightning Source LLC
Chambersburg PA
CBHW060341260626
47160CB00006B/2164